"As entertainment goes, this is exp   rp and often funny dialogue, tight pacing, and light moments . . . to balance the darker scenes—the work of a pro who hasn't forgotten any of his old tricks."   —*Los Angeles Times Book Review*

"Action's been a reliable staple in the Scully series, but here Cannell gets the people right, too. The best yet for the *Rockford* man."

—*Kirkus Reviews* (starred review)

"Once I reached a certain point in this fast-paced police story, I just did not want to put it down. . . . Hats off to Cannell. He knows his crime stuff and he can write a novel even better than the many successful TV shows he created."

—*San Jose Mercury News*

"Readers will enjoy watching [Scully] puzzle out the twists and turns of the plot and watch breathlessly as he undertakes a climactic high-speed chase."   —*Publishers Weekly*

"*Vertical Coffin* nails it dead-on. . . . A fast-paced, intriguing ride."
—*The Bakersfield Californian*

"Cannell certainly knows how to tell a story. . . . You'll probably read the entire book with a smile on your face."

—*Cleveland Plain Dealer*

Praise for *Hollywood Tough*

"Cannell, creator of such TV shows as *The A-Team*, clearly knows the ins and outs of the entertainment industry, and the detective story, with its wry, subtle humor, doubles as Hollywood satire . . . the cops-and-robbers sequences hit the mark as well. Well-drawn characters and keen observations on the similarities between

Hollywood and the mafia make this a winner."

"Scully has ample opportunity to prove how 'Hollywood tough' he is . . . veteran writer/TV producer Cannell has concocted his special brand of reader candy." —*Kirkus Reviews*

Praise for *Runaway Heart*

"A cop thriller with a futuristic, sci-fi twist . . . Cannell has a genius for creating memorable characters and quirky, gripping plots . . . this is a fun read." —*Publishers Weekly*

"This rip-snorting novel is part political thriller, part sci-fi and all galvanizing, nonstop action . . . the story races." —*Tulsa World*

"Cannell, one of the most successful television producers of all time as well as the best-selling author of the Shane Scully thrillers, creates memorably endearing characters and places them in harrowing situations with clearly defined moral choices." —*Booklist*

Praise for *The Viking Funeral*

"Stephen J. Cannell is an accomplished novelist." —*New York Daily News*

"Stephen J. Cannell's *The Viking Funeral* is the sort of fast and furious read you might expect from one of television's most successful and inventive writer-producers." —*Los Angeles Times*

"Solid plotting with nail-biting suspense and multiple surprises keep the reader guessing and sweating right up to the cinematic ending. . . . Cannell has a knack for characterization and a bent for drama that will satisfy even the most jaded thrill lover." —*Publishers Weekly*

Praise for *The Tin Collectors*

"I've been a Stephen Cannell fan since his remarkable *King Con,* and he keeps getting better. *The Tin Collectors* is an LAPD story that possesses both heart and soul, a fresh and different look at the men and women who, even more than the NYPD, are the most media-covered police force in the world. Stephen Cannell has the screenwriter's fine ear for dialogue, and great sense of timing and pacing, as well as the novelist's gift of substance and subtlety. Cannell likes to write, and it shows." —Nelson DeMille

"Cannell is a first-rate storyteller and *The Tin Collectors* never stops: it's compelling, frightening—and, in the end, very moving. Don't miss it." —Janet Evanovich

"Exhibiting a new sensitivity to his characters' emotional depth, Cannell continues to improve as a novelist." —*Publishers Weekly*

Praise for previous titles

"The Emmy award–winning TV writer/producer of *The Rockford Files* and *The Commish* strikes again . . . with this quirky new action-driven nail-biter." —*Publishers Weekly* on *The Devil's Workshop*

"[A] fast-paced adventure." —*Booklist* on *The Devil's Workshop*

"The dialogue and action scenes are unsurpassed . . . and the heroine is an engaging lead. . . . Be prepared for an all-nighter on this one." —*The Internet Writing Journal* on *The Devil's Workshop*

"Cannell is at the top of his game. A terrific plot and a great read. I highly recommend it." —Larry King on *Riding the Snake*

THE TIN
COLLECTORS

THE VIKING
FUNERAL

THE
TIN
COLLECTORS

THE
VIKING
FUNERAL

STEPHEN J. CANNELL

St. Martin's Griffin ≈ New York

www.stmartins.com

ISBN 0-312-35384-7
EAN 978-0-312-35384-1

The Tin Collectors was originally published by
St. Martin's Press in January 2001

The Viking Funeral was originally published by
St. Martin's Press in January 2002

First St. Martin's Griffin Edition: October 2005

10 9 8 7 6 5 4 3 2 1

THE
TIN
COLLECTORS

Principles serve to govern conduct when there are no rules.

—LAPD MANAGEMENT GUIDE
TO DISCIPLINE

THE
"CHOOCH"
LETTER

Dear Dad:

Charles Sandoval, who everybody calls Chooch, arrived this afternoon as planned (actually, I picked him up). This is already shaping up as one of my biggest boners. I pulled up at the fancy private school Sandy's got him enrolled in and I had to go to the principal's office to sign the pickup permission slip. The principal, John St. John, is a wheezing, hollow-chested geek who seems to honestly hate Chooch. The way he put it was: "That child is from the ninth circle." I had to ask, too. It's from Dante's Inferno. Apparently, the ninth circle is the circle closest to hell. Now that I've met Chooch, not an entirely inappropriate analogy. Then, this pale erection with ears hands me a packet of teacher evaluation slips. For a fifteen-year-old, his rap sheet is impressive . . . pulled fire alarms, and fights in the school cafeteria (food as well as fists). Mr. St. John informs me that they have notified Sandy that Chooch is not to return to the Harvard Westlake School next semester and that I need to get him enrolled elsewhere (like this is all of a sudden supposed to be my problem). But it's not as if this boy doesn't have a good reason to be angry. I think I wrote you, he's a love child with one of Sandy's old clients. Making matters worse, Sandy doesn't want him to know how she makes her living, so she's been shipping him off to boarding schools since third grade.

Needless to say, I had no idea what I was getting into here.

3

Maybe I can last the month until Sandy takes him back or sends him to the next sucker on her list. One way or another, I'll work it out.

I'm planning to get out to Florida again sometime next year. I was thinking you and I could rent one of those fishing boats like we did last time, drink some beer and cook what we catch over a beach fire. Those memories are treasures in my life.

I know, I know, cut the mush, blah . . . blah . . . blah. I miss you, Dad. That's all for now.

> *Love,*
> *Your son,*
> *Shane*

USE OF 1 FORCE

SHANE WAS IN deep REM black. Way down there, but still he heard the telephone's electronic urgency. The sound hung over him, a vague shimmer, way above, up on the surface. Slowly he made his way to it, breaking consciousness, washed in confusion and anger. His bedroom was dark. The digital clock stung his eyeballs with a neon greeting: 2:16 A.M. He found the receiver and pressed it against his ear.

"Yeah," he said, his voice a croak and a whisper.

"Shane, he's trying to kill me," a woman hissed urgently.

"What . . . who is this?"

"It's Barbara." She was whispering, but he could also hear a loud banging coming over the receiver on her end, as if somebody was trying to break down a door.

"He's trying to kill you?" he repeated, buying time so his mind could focus.

Barbara Molar. He hadn't seen her in over two months, and

then just for a moment at a police department ceremony, last year's Medal of Valor Awards. Her husband, Ray, had been one of three recipients.

A crash, then: "Jesus, get over here, Shane. Please. He'll listen to you. He's nuts, worse than ever."

Shane heard another crash. Barbara started screaming. He couldn't make out her next words, then: "Don't, please . . ." She was whimpering, the phone was dropped on a hard floor, clattering, bouncing, getting kicked in some desperate struggle.

"Barbara? Barbara?" She didn't answer. He heard a distant, guttural grunting like a man sometimes makes during sex, or a fight.

Shane got out of bed and started gathering up clothes. He slipped into his pants and grabbed his faded LAPD sweatshirt. He snapped up his ankle gun, hesitated for a moment, then pulled it out, chambered it, and strapped it on. He ran out of his bedroom toward the garage without even looking for his shoes. He was already behind the wheel when he realized he had forgotten that Chooch Sandoval was asleep in the other bedroom. He wasn't used to having fifteen-year-old houseguests. He knew he shouldn't leave Chooch alone. The garage door was going up as he backed out his black Acura. Grabbing for his cell phone, he dialed a number from memory. He streaked down the back alley away from his Venice, California, canal house, as cold beach air slipstreamed past the side window onto his face.

Brian "Longboard" Kelly, his boned-out next-door neighbor, picked up the phone. "Whoever this is, fuck you" was the way he came on the line.

"Sorry, Brian, it's Shane. I got called out, and Chooch is still asleep in the guest bedroom."

"Chooch? Who the hell . . ."

"The kid I told you I was taking for the month. Sandy's kid. He came yesterday."

"Ohhh, man . . ."

"Look, Brian, just go over and sleep on my couch. The key is in the pot by the back door."

"Good place, dickbrain. Who would ever think to look there?"

"Just do it, will ya? I'll owe ya."

"Fuckin' A." Longboard slammed the phone down in Shane's ear.

Shane was now at Washington Boulevard. He hung a left and headed the short distance to the Molar house. When they'd still been partners, he'd made this trip at least once a day to pick up Ray, heading across Washington to South Venice Boulevard, through Gangbang Circle, where, once it got dark, the V-Thirteens and Shoreside Crips staged their useless, life-ending street actions, occasionally killing or wounding a tourist from Minnesota by mistake.

He shot across Abbot Kinney Boulevard and turned right onto California, finally coming to Shell Avenue. All the way there, he wondered why Barbara would call him. Why not dial 911? Of course, the answer was sort of obvious after he thought about it. Even though she was scared spitless, she still didn't want another domestic-violence beef in Ray's LAPD Internal Affairs jacket. He was a thirty-year veteran with a big pension, which another DV complaint would jeopardize. That pension was an asset that was half hers.

Still, Shane Scully was the last guy Ray Molar would want to see coming through his door, quoting departmental spousal-abuse regulations at two A.M. *So why Shane? Why not Ray's current partner?* He guessed he knew that answer, too. She called him because she thought she could control him, use him for protection, then keep him from talking. Also he was handy, only five miles away. . . . Just like before, he had turned up as the double zero on her slow-turning roulette wheel.

When he got to Ray's small, wood-sided house, he pulled into the driveway behind Ray's car and jumped out. The hood was warm on the dark blue Cadillac Brougham; the lights were on in the house. Then he heard muffled screaming.

"Shit, I hate this," he mumbled softly, feeling the cold grass on his bare feet. He moved toward the house, tried the front door and, to his surprise, found it was open. Reluctantly, he stepped into his ex-partner's living room.

Ray's house always seemed delicate and overdecorated. Too much French fleur-de-lis upholstery, too many knickknacks and hanging lamps. It was Barbara's doing and definitely didn't seem like the lair of a street monster like Ray Molar. Ray should live in a cave, cooking over an open fire, throwing the gnawed bones over his shoulder.

Shane could hear Barbara's screams coming from the back of the house, so he moved in that direction. He came through the bedroom door just in time to see Ray Molar hit his slender, blond wife in the solar plexus with the butt end of his black metal street baton. Then, as she doubled over, he expertly swung the night-stick sideways, catching her in the side of the head with a "two from the ring" combat move . . . a baton-fighting tactic taught to every recruit at the Police Academy. Shane stood frozen, as Barbara, her head bleeding badly, slumped to the floor, almost unconscious.

"Ray . . . " Shane's voice, a raspy whisper, cut the temporary silence like a sickle slashing dry wheat. "What's the story here, buddy?"

Ray Molar swung around. He was at least six-four and weighed over two-forty, with huge shoulders and long arms. He had bristly blond hair and a corded, muscled neck. Adding to these Blutoesque dimensions was a huge jutting jaw and almost total lack of a forehead. "Get the fuck outta here, Scully. We don't need the Boy Scouts," Molar growled, his pupils round points of focused hatred.

Shane had seen that look in the street many times before and had come to fear it. "Let's just back off, slow down, and give it a rest, Ray." Shane was moving slowly toward him, not wanting any part of the fury and craziness he saw on his ex-partner, but feeling compelled to get close enough to protect Barbara if he swung on her again. When Ray lost control, he could turn instantly murderous. He spewed white rage without thought, violence without reason.

"You got anything to eat?" Shane said, trying to refocus the energy in the room. "I'm starved. Missed dinner. How 'bout I get us a beer and a sandwich, something. . . . We chill out a little . . . Cool out . . . Talk it down . . . Get solid . . ."

"You wanna eat somethin'? Eat shit, Scully!" He was halfway between Shane and Barbara, still brandishing the black metal police baton.

"Ray, I don't want trouble, but you can't go hitting Barbara with the nightstick, man. You're gonna fuck her up bad."

Then Ray started toward Shane, swinging the metal stick in a lose arc in front of him. "Yeah? Who's gonna stop me, dickwad?"

"Come on, let's stay frosty here, Ray. Let's . . . let's—" And he stopped talking because he had to duck.

Ray swung the nightstick. It zipped through the air an inch from Shane's ear. As he was coming back up, Ray swung a fist, hitting him with a left hook that landed on Shane's right temple, exploding like a pipe bomb, sending him to the floor, ears ringing. Then Ray yanked a small-caliber snubby out of his waistband. It looked to Shane like an off-brand piece, a European handgun of some kind, maybe a Titan Tiger or an Arminus .38, definitely not standard police issue. Ray always kept a "throw-down gun" on him to drop by a body if some street character got funky and had to take a seat on the sky bus.

"Put it away, Ray."

"You fucking this bitch, too? You fucking her? 'Cause if you ain't, you should get in line—everybody else is."

"Come on, Ray, that's crazy. I never touched your wife; nobody's messin' with Barb, and you know it. Why're you doin' this?"

"She's been getting snaked by half the fuckin' department."

He turned back and glowered at her. "Am I right, baby? Tell him 'bout all the wall jobs you been doin' in the division garage."

Barbara groaned. Ray, turning now, aimed the gun at Shane, pulling the hammer back. Shane watched the cylinder begin to rotate on the center post as Ray applied pressure on the trigger. He was strangely mesmerized by the hole in the barrel; a dark eye of damnation, freezing his stomach, dulling his reactions. He was seconds from death. . . . Almost without realizing it, his right hand slipped down to his ankle, fingers encircling the wood-checked grip of his 9mm automatic. He slid the weapon free.

Shane dove sideways just as Ray fired. The bullet thunked into the wooden doorframe behind him. Shane was operating on instinct now, with no control over what happened next, going with it, not questioning, rolling, coming up prone, his Beretta Mini-Cougar gripped in both hands.

As Ray turned to fire again, Shane squeezed the trigger. The bullet hit Ray Molar in the middle of his simian brow.

Huge head jerking back violently.

Brainpan exploding, catching the 9mm slug.

Then Ray looked directly at Shane as the gun slipped from his meaty paw and thumped onto the carpet. Ray's pig eyes, bright in that instant, registered hatred and surprise, or maybe Shane was just looking for something human in all that animal ferocity.

Ray Molar took one uncertain step backward and sat on the edge of the bed. Even though his heart was probably still beating, Shane knew that his ex-partner was already dead. But the street monster sat down anyway, almost as if he needed a moment to consider what he should do next or where he should go, momentum and gravity making the decision for him, toppling him forward, thudding him hard, face first, onto the carpet.

Shane looked over at Barbara, who was staring at her dead husband, her mouth agape, her puffed lip split and bleeding.

"Whatta we do now, Shane?" she finally asked.

M-417-00

I**N THE SECONDS** after the shots were fired, the bedroom seemed so quiet that he could almost hear dust settle. Then the sharp smell of cordite, mixed with the coppery smell of blood, began to fill his nostrils. Barbara was still on the floor not ten feet from Ray's body. Shane moved first. He stood slowly, feeling his knees shake as he rose. He stumbled to the dresser and leaned on it heavily, propping himself up for support. They were both trying to digest it, understand what had just happened and comprehend how it would alter, in a ghastly way, events stretching before them. Then, from the floor, Ray Molar farted. Shit ran into his pants as his bowels let loose. The perfect punctuation mark for the past few minutes.

"We need to get a story, Barbara," Shane said. "This isn't going to go down smooth. You know how they all feel about Ray."

"I don't know . . . I don't know . . . He just . . ."

"Barbara . . ."

Her eyes were darting around the room in a desperate escape dance. Her face was also beginning to swell where Ray had hit her on the right side, distorting her natural beauty.

"Tell me," he prodded softly, "what set him off?"

Somewhere in the distance they could hear the faint wail of a police car.

"Already?" she said, referring to the sirens.

"You were screaming, shots were fired, you've got neighbors. Nine-one-one response time is supposed to be less than five minutes. If something more is going on here, I need to know, Babs. You and I, we're not completely clean, if you know what I mean."

"I know." She pulled herself up on the bed and sat. He could see that her hands were shaking as she brought the back of her wrist up to wipe the blood oozing from the corner of her mouth. Her hand came away with an ugly red streak on the back. "He . . . he just . . . I don't know."

"He just what? Let's go, there isn't much time. What set him off?"

"I got a call yesterday from a woman. She asked me if I'd seen the videotape yet."

"What videotape?"

"I don't know. That's the whole point. I haven't got any tape, and I told her. She sounded like she was crying. Then she said it was coming in the mail, and it will show me what a cheating bastard Ray was."

"Who was she?"

"Didn't say. I didn't recognize the voice. She just hung up."

The sirens were now less than a block away as Barbara Molar looked at Shane in desperation. "What're they gonna do?"

"They're gonna separate us. Take statements. This is our only chance to coordinate. We need the same story. Stay with me here, Babs. Keep goin'. What happened next?"

"Ray hasn't been home much since he got his new assignment.

He's been away days at a time, so when he got home tonight, I asked him where he was all the time. I told him what the woman said and he . . . he just . . . went nuts. You know his temper, how he gets. You worked patrol with him. He accused me of sleeping with his friends. He called me a whore. He started beating me. I can't take any more beatings. I can't. I told him I was going to leave him, and then he chased me into the bathroom. I locked the door and called you. Then he just—"

The sirens growled to the curb outside, and Shane quickly looked around the bedroom, taking mental pictures of the crime scene, filing them in his memory for later. Oddly enough, it was Ray who had schooled him in this technique, quizzing him at "end of watch" on what he remembered. They'd sit in some bar at EOW, betting drinks on the answers. Ray would ask questions: What was on the dresser? How many windows in the kitchen? Were there screens? Ray was violent and unpredictable, but he sure knew how to police a crime scene.

"They're gonna take me downtown," Shane said. "They'll take your statement here, then probably transport you to the ER. Just say exactly what happened. He would have killed you, Barbara. He fired first. This was self-defense. Just leave out you and me. Whatever you do, stay tight on that."

They could hear cops coming into the house through the open front door.

"We're back here, LAPD!" Shane yelled. Then, as an afterthought, he whispered to Barbara, "Call the phone company and see if you can get an AT&T printout of calls to your phone so we can try and find out who that woman is."

Barbara nodded just as a uniformed South Bureau "dog and cat" team came through the door, guns drawn. Shane had his hands in the air and his Beretta Mini-Cougar hanging down, dangling uselessly from his right thumb. "LAPD," he said again.

The cops didn't know him, and not seeing a badge, the male officer rushed him, disarmed him, and threw him down onto the floor right next to a puddle of Ray's blood. The female kept her Smith & Wesson trained on him until her partner had Shane cuffed. Then they both roughly yanked him up.

"Where's your shield?" the lady cop said. Her nameplate read S. RILEY.

"On my dresser, at home. I was asleep. She called for help. I live four miles from here. I'm Sergeant Shane Scully, Southwest RHD. My serial number is 50867."

They looked down at Shane's now-bloody bare feet, then at Ray. The male cop was a policeman III; his nameplate read P. APPLEGATE. He knelt down and looked closely at the body. "Shit. This is Steeltooth. You shot Lieutenant Molar."

Shane stood quietly as Applegate fingered his shoulder mike. "This is X-ray Twelve. We're Code Six at 2387 Shell Avenue. We have a police officer down. We need a sergeant on the scene and the coroner. Notify South Bureau Detectives we have the shooter in custody. He claims to be Southwest Robbery/Homicide Sergeant Shane Scully." Then he turned to Shane. "Gimme that serial number again."

"It's 50867," Shane said into the officer's open shoulder mike.

"You get that?" Applegate asked. The female radio-transmission officer answered quickly.

"Roger, X-ray Twelve. That's 50867. You're Code Six Adam at Shell Avenue, requesting a supervisor and a Homicide unit. Stand by." There was static, and in less than thirty seconds, the RTO came back on. "X-ray Twelve, on your suspect ident: that badge number is confirmed to Southwest RHD Sergeant Shane Scully, 143 East Channel Road, Venice, California."

"Roger. We're locking down this crime scene for Homicide and moving outside." The officer then turned to Shane. "Who's your direct supervisor?"

"Captain Bud Halley, Southwest Division Robbery/Homicide."

"You got his call-out number?"

"Just call the squad. I can do it myself if you take these cuffs off."

"Hey, Scully, you done enough already. You just croaked the best fucking cop on the force." Then he unlocked the handcuffs. "Shannon, take Mrs. Molar into the kitchen. I'll hold Sergeant Scully in the living room." They left Raymond Molar in an expanding pool of his own blood to wait for the Homicide team and lab techs.

. . .

On every unnatural death in L.A., the RHD assigns a fresh homicide number and the next team up on the division rotation gets the squeal. The numbers start on January 1 and continue sequentially until the last day of December. If the body is a male, the number is proceeded by an *M*; if female, by an *F*. On that chilly April morning, Lieutenant Raymond George Molar became M-417-00.

The RHD team got there a little after three-thirty A.M. as the crime lab was just finishing photographing the scene. The two lab techs had already done their preliminary workup. They'd bagged the lieutenant's hands, outlined the DB in tape, and were standing around, waiting for the detectives to show before rolling the body.

Both Homicide dicks were veterans and had been notified before they got there that the officer down was the legendary LAPD Lt. Ray "Steeltooth" Molar. They had both signed Patrolman Applegate's crime-scene attendance sheet and now stood in the bedroom looking down at the body with stone-cut expressions as the lab techs flopped Ray over. His face had already begun to fill with blood, causing a darkening of the skin, known as lividity. More postmortem renal jettisoning had occurred, and the smell of feces in the room was getting strong as the two detectives from Robbery/Homicide silently policed the area, making their preliminary notes and observations. They graphed the location of the body and marked the bullet in the doorjamb that Ray had fired, then instructed the lab techs to dig the slug out and get it to the Investigative Analysis Section for a ballistics comparison. They bagged Shane's 9mm Beretta; it would be booked as evidence.

Shane was waiting in the living room with Patrolman Applegate. After half an hour the lead Homicide dick, an old, wheezing department warhorse with a basset-hound jawline, came out and sat on the sofa opposite Shane. His name was Garson Welch; he and Shane had shared a few easy grounders back when Shane was still working uniform in Southwest. One case had been so simple, they solved it in less than ten minutes when Shane arrested the perp half a block away as he was trying to stuff the murder weapon down into a Dumpster. The man had confessed on the spot. Shane and Welch had gone EOW at the jail and had had a few beers in a cop bar on Central known as the Billy Club. They didn't have what you'd call a friendship, but they were at least friendly—better than nothing.

"This ain't gonna go down too good at Parker Center, Shane," the old detective said, rubbing his ample forehead with a big, liver-spotted hand.

"Yeah, Gar, you're right. I should've just stood there and let him kill her with his nightstick."

"Calm down and listen," Welch went on. "What we got here is a brown shit waffle. Lieutenant Molar had big juice with the Super Chief. People you and I only read about in the *L.A. Times* are getting phone calls right now over this piece of work. I just got a call and found out he's been Mayor Clark Crispin's police driver for the past two months. So there's gonna be big interest at the city level. We're gonna go slow and get it right."

"The mayor's driver? Shit," Shane said. He hadn't known that was Ray's new assignment.

"I'm gonna take your preliminary here, then send you to the Glass House and let your captain do the DFAR," Welch said, referring to the Division Field Activity Report that had to be filed after any incident involving violence or death at the hands of a police officer.

"I got my car. I can meet you there," Shane volunteered.

"I'll have one of the blues drive it in and park it for you in the underground garage, but you're gonna go downtown in the back of a detective car. By the book. That way, nobody gets days off for bullshit nitpicks."

"Yeah, sure, if that's the way you want it." Shane was beginning to get a premonition of disaster. Then he followed Detective Welch out of the house for the long drive to Parker Center.

3

DFAR

THE TRIP DOWNTOWN at four A.M. on deserted freeways took only twenty-two minutes. The black-and-white slickback that the RHD dicks were forced to drive now finally made a wide turn off Broadway, its headlights sweeping the south side of the Glass House. It pulled up to the security station. Sergeant Welch showed his badge, signed them all in, and drove into the huge underground parking garage that adjoined Parker Center.

The building was known as "the Glass House" to everybody on the job because of the excessive amount of plate glass that draped its huge boxy shape. The otherwise nondescript building had been designed in the fifties, which had proved to be a decade of architectural blight. The parking garage next door went down nine stories underground. The detectives found a spot on U-3, and both led Shane out of the parking complex, through a security door, and into the third basement of police headquarters. They took the elevator to six and got off at the Robbery/Homicide Division, which took up half the floor and was fronted by a thick glass partition.

Garson Welch buzzed them through and found the OOD, a thin-faced sergeant in uniform, sitting at a computer just inside the squad room. "Is Captain Halley around? He was supposed to get a call out on this activity report."

The sergeant nodded and pointed down the hall. "Interview room Three," he said.

They moved single file down the linoleum-floored corridor and turned into a small, windowless interrogation room that contained a scarred desk, two wooden chairs, and Robbery/Homicide Captain Bud Halley. Halley had his jacket off and was showing the beginnings of a twelve-hour beard, having missed his shave at four A.M. He had also missed two belt loops. Other than that, he was a remarkably handsome, fit, prematurely gray man in his mid-forties. He was Shane's Southwest Homicide Bureau commander. They had a good professional relationship. In the two years Shane had been assigned to Southwest Detectives, Halley had given him two excellent evaluation reports. As Shane came through the door, Captain Halley motioned him to a chair. "You guys don't have to stick around unless you need him. I'm gonna send him home after the activity report," he said to the two detectives.

"Thanks, Cap, check you later," Welch said as they left the room and closed the door behind them.

"We only have a few minutes and then God knows what happens," Halley said.

"A few minutes? What're you talking about? You're doing the DFAR. What's the rush?"

" 'Cept I'm not doing it. Deputy Chief Thomas Mayweather is on his way in. He's doing it."

"The head of Special Investigations Division is doing my activity report? You can't be serious. Why him?"

"Chief Brewer ordered it," Halley said.

"Same question, then."

"Don't you know what Ray Molar's assignment was?"

"Yeah . . . he was Mayor Clark Crispin's bodyguard and driver. He was also killing his wife with a nightstick. He fired a shot at me. Barbara Molar is my wit. This should be a slam dunk. So what's the deal?"

"Lemme give you the secret to survival around here." Shane waited for the punch line. "Everything that's not department history is department politics. Chief Brewer was awakened by Mayor Crispin, who called the Big Kahuna from the Dark Side, who got rousted off his sailboat at the marina. He was planning to sail across the channel for a long weekend in Avalon. Now, instead of salt air and sea chanteys, Deputy Chief Mayweather is coming here, in his fucking yacht attire, looking to tear you a new asshole."

"Cap, let me say this again, so none of us miss it. Steeltooth was killing his wife. He shot first. If I hadn't returned fire, we'd both be in the county icebox bleeding from the ears. I know for a fact Ray has two spousal-abuse beefs in his IAD package. He's a regular at rage-management counseling. Aside from that, we both know he was a head thumper from way back. You don't get the nickname Steeltooth just because your last name's Molar."

"Don't convince me. Make Mayweather believe it," Halley said softly.

Shane's hands started to shake. He was coming down from a two-hour adrenaline rush. He had killed Ray Molar, his ex-partner, a man he had once respected, then came to fear, and then finally to hate. His emotions hovered just below consciousness. He knew he couldn't afford a mistake, so he pushed personal feelings aside and concentrated on his plight, his survival instincts taking precedence.

- - -

Deputy Chief Mayweather was six three and ebony black. He had a shaved head and always carried himself with the athletic grace he had shown as a first-string point guard on the UCLA basketball team in the seventies.

He moved through the predawn stillness of the Robbery/Homicide Division and looked at the tired collection of swing-shift detectives who were manning their desks, sneaking glances at the clock, waiting for the day-watch to show up and relieve them. Mayweather stuck his gleaming black head into the interrogation room containing Scully and Halley.

"Let's do this upstairs." Mayweather's voice was cold and smooth, Vaseline on ice. "We'll use the conference room on nine. Bud, see if they got some coffee down here and bring it up." Then, without even looking at Shane, he moved out of the room, leaving them there.

"Good luck," Halley said as Shane got up off his hardwood chair and followed Mayweather, who was already halfway down the hall, striding toward the elevators with a Yul·Brynner elegance, his arms swinging freely, his hips slightly forward. He was not in yachting attire. He'd dressed for this gig. The suit he wore was charcoal gray, creaseless, and fit him like a second skin. Tom Mayweather could easily have made a nice living on the pages of GQ.

Shane moved along behind him like a barefoot, dark-haired, brown-eyed shadow, his own gait more the shuffling stride of a street fighter. Although Shane had always been able to attract women, he found his own looks pugnacious and off-putting. In his mirror, he saw a face marred by cynicism and loneliness. He was always surprised when he heard someone describe him as attractive.

He caught Mayweather at the elevator. Both men remained silent as they waited for the stainless-steel doors to open and take them to the ninth floor, where Tom Mayweather and the other deputy chiefs had their offices down the hall from Chief Burleigh Brewer.

"Sorry about the Avalon trip, sir," Shane said, going for a little pre-interview suck.

"Let's save everything for when we get the tape running, okay?"

"Sure," Shane said.

The door opened and they stepped in and rode the humming metal box to the light-paneled, green-carpeted executive floor. All the way up, Deputy Chief Mayweather said nothing, but he was staring at Shane's bloodstained bare feet.

Shane had been on nine only once before. He had been in Chief Brewer's office three years ago when he received a Meritorious Service Medal. He had risked his life, the citation said, freeing two children from a burning car wreck on the San Pedro Freeway.

They moved down the hall. Shane glanced out the plate-glass windows and could see the morning sun beginning to light the corners of the buildings across Sixth Street, throwing a fiery glow on the stone roofs and concrete balconies of the old brown buildings that surrounded the huge police monstrosity like tattered memories.

Mayweather opened the door to the conference room, turned on the lights, and left him there.

The room was paneled in the same light-colored wood. It was huge and windowless, being part of the interior structure of the building. On the walls were portraits of all of L.A.'s past police chiefs. The father of the new department, Chief William H. Parker, was hanging in a place of honor on the wall at the head of the table.

They had all learned about Bill Parker in the Academy. In 1934 then-Lieutenant Parker, a law school graduate, was assistant to L.A. police chief James E. Davis. From that post, Parker saw the workings of L.A. city government close-up. The Shaw brothers presided over a corrupt city, and Chief Davis was beholden to the Shaws. Mayor Shaw's brother controlled the Vice Squad and was selling sergeant's tests for five hundred dollars apiece. Working with Lieutenant Earl Cook, Bill Parker campaigned for the passage of the city charter amendment that contained Section 202, which provided for a Police Bill of Rights and administrative reviews to protect police officers from inappropriate charges of wrongdoing. That section of the city charter set the model of police disciplinary review that the LAPD still uses today. Portraits of Chiefs Davis, Reddin, Gates, Williams, Parks, and Brewer hung on the walls of the conference room and seemed to glower down at him, silently reproaching him for killing one of L.A.'s finest.

"Guy was murdering his wife," Shane muttered to himself and to the stone-faced gallery of disapproving ex–police chiefs.

Mayweather returned with a tape recorder and plugged it in. He chose the seat at the far end of the table, under the recently hung painting of Burl Brewer.

Mayweather glanced at Sergeant Scully. "You're a sergeant one, is that right?"

"Yes, sir."

"Okay, Shane, you and I don't know each other. I guess we've probably met once or twice, but we're not really acquainted. It's important you know that I'm just here to take your statement. I'm going to try and determine what happened and then make a recommendation to the department as to what our next step should be. A police officer died at your hands. His death may have been completely unavoidable, but either way, we're into a mandatory use-of-force review. I'm not here to hurt you, take advantage of you, or trap you in any way. Okay?"

"I appreciate that, sir."

The door opened and Bud Halley entered with a pot of coffee and three mugs. He poured. They each took one, blew across the steaming surface, then sipped gratefully.

"What goes on here is subject to the Police Bill of Rights under Title One," Mayweather continued, "so this pre-interview will not preempt any of your Skelly rights or privileges guaranteed by Section 202 of the city charter." The Skelly hearing was his chance to answer the charges against him before his case went to a Board of Rights, if it got that far.

"This is an administrative review and is subject to the provisions laid down in Section 202. I'm going to record the interview." Mayweather turned the tape on. "Raise your right hand." Shane did as he was instructed. "Do you, Sergeant Shane Scully, swear that all information given by you during this interview is the truth, the whole truth, and nothing but the truth, so help you God?"

"I do."

"This tape-recorded interview is for use in an Internal Affairs investigation only. For purposes of department statute-of-limitations requirements, today, April sixteenth, will be the due date of this inquiry. If no action is taken within a year of this date, the investigation will officially be determined to be closed. Is this interview being conducted at a convenient time and under circumstances you find acceptable?"

"Yes, sir."

"Are you aware that the nature of this interview is to determine if the escalated force that resulted in Lieutenant Molar's death was within departmental use-of-force guidelines?"

"Yes, sir."

"It is April sixteenth, at five-seventeen A.M. We are in the main conference room, on the ninth floor of Parker Center. Present is the interviewer, Deputy Chief Thomas Clark Mayweather. Also present is the officer being interviewed, Sergeant One Shane Scully. Witnessing the interview is Captain Bud Halley. In accordance with departmental guidelines, it is noted that no more than two interrogators are present. Okay"—Mayweather paused and glanced at a crib card in front of him—"Section 202 governs this part of the administrative process and establishes procedures for the completion of a chronological log. If you could take care of that, Captain Halley? And then if you could get us a fresh DR number to file the case under." A DR number was a Division of Records number, issued in all nonarrest reports.

Bud Halley nodded then took out a pad and pen to begin a chronology.

"Shane, if you could just start at the beginning and tell us what happened this morning . . . Don't leave anything out. Give us approximate times if you can. I want to get it all down on tape because the preliminary interview will be an important part of the record, if anything more comes of this later."

"Okay." Shane cleared his throat and began to tell exactly what had happened, starting with the wake-up call from Barbara at 2:16 A.M., followed by his call to Longboard Kelly. He told how he drove to Shell Avenue, found the front door open, saw Molar beating his wife. He related the conversation that ensued, telling how he tried to settle it down. Then how Molar, moving toward him, swung the baton at his head, hit him with his fist, pulled his gun, and fired. Shane explained how he returned fire, killing the huge LAPD lieutenant with his 9mm Beretta Mini-Cougar, just moments before Unit X-ray Twelve arrived.

When he finished, he looked up at Mayweather, who was making notes on a pad, a puzzled expression on his face.

"That's everything," Shane finished.

"Tell me about your relationship with Raymond Molar."

"Uh . . . well, he was sort of a mentor, I guess you'd call it. I met him when I went through the Academy. He was conducting a self-defense lecture. He and I were at the same table for lunch. We sort of hit it off, gravitated to each other. He did three street-combat classes while I was there, and we became friends. After I graduated, I ended up in Southwest, in the Seventy-seventh Division. He was a sergeant there. I was still just a probationer, and since we were friends, he got himself assigned as my training officer. He was my partner for the first six months of my tour. After I finished probation, we rode together for six more months."

"Sergeants don't usually ride with partners."

"Well, in the Seventy-seventh, a lot of the sergeants took a shotgun rider. It's pretty hairy down there. Anyway, we rode together for that last six months, and then I got reassigned. I went to the West Valley Division for four years, then spent six in Metro. I've been back at Southwest for the past six years and in RHD down there for twenty-eight months. Ray was in Central, then Newton, so we didn't see much of each other after that."

"I see." Mayweather made some more notes on his pad. "You see him socially during that first tour in Southwest when you were partnered?"

"Yes, sir, we were friends."

"Right about then you had an Internal Affairs complaint that wasn't sustained, isn't that correct?"

"Excuse me, sir, but I thought I had immunity from background on unsustained IAD complaints." Shane knew that since Mayweather was head of the Special Investigations Division, which supervised IAD, he had access to those old Internal Affairs records. Obviously, the deputy chief had done more than change clothes before coming in for this interview.

Mayweather looked up and lay down his pen. "I'm just trying to determine if, when you were before that Board of Rights in March of '84, you were still partnered with Ray Molar."

"Yes. That was just before we stopped working together."

"Okay." Mayweather picked up his pen. "You say Lieutenant Molar pulled a gun. Did you see it clearly?"

"I was only a few feet away."

"What kind of gun was it?"

"I think it was a European handgun, a Titan Tiger snub-nose thirty-eight is what it looked like."

"That's not a department-approved handgun."

"Well, he was at home. I suppose he can have any kind of weapon he wants at home."

"And then, after you shot him with your Beretta, what happened to his gun?"

"I guess he dropped it. I don't know, I was kind of jacked up after the shooting."

"Sergeant Scully, do you mind taking a urine test? As you know, you can refuse under the Police Bill of Rights, but I should warn you that in an administrative hearing, unlike a criminal case, your refusal can be viewed by the department as insubordination. You could be brought up on charges. If you *do* refuse, I'll have to send for a DRE to examine you anyway, and his opinion will go in the record and carry the same weight." A DRE was a drug recognition expert who would make a judgment on sobriety by observation, checking vision and reflexes.

"That won't be necessary. I'll take the test, sir," Shane said.

"I'll get the paperwork ready." He leaned over and picked up the phone. "This is Mayweather. Send somebody up from the lab for a urine sample and have whoever's on the duty desk out there dig around and get me an authorization form." He hung up the phone, having never shifted his gaze from Shane. Then he leaned back in his chair and templed his fingers under his chin.

"Barbara Molar is quite an attractive woman."

"Yes, sir, she is. The lieutenant was very lucky."

"Until tonight."

"Well, yes, that's what I meant, sir.

"Right."

They sat in silence for a few moments.

"Did you and Lieutenant Molar retain a friendly relationship after you were reassigned to the Valley Division?"

"Well, sir . . . no. Like I said, we sort of drifted our separate ways."

"I heard you and he got into some kind of scuffle one night, back in '84, just before you were separated as partners."

Shane looked over at Captain Halley for help, but the captain only nodded slightly, encouraging him to keep answering. It was now painfully obvious that Mayweather had someone in the IA Administration Section open his sealed jacket in violation of his rights under Section 202. The fight with Steeltooth had been logged because Shane had needed medical attention for his injuries. However, neither he nor Molar had pressed for a hearing, so it went into his sealed record as an unsustained incident. He couldn't prove that Mayweather had opened his file. The deputy chief could claim he had heard about the fight secondhand. Now Shane had to answer the question or face insubordination charges. He felt used and double-crossed.

"I need an answer," Mayweather said. "Was there an altercation?"

"I guess you could say that. We had a kinda problem once."

"What was that all about?"

"Shit, it was nothing. . . . I mean, shoot . . . we . . . we'd been working long hours and I was nervous, facing that Internal Affairs board. I was stressed. Molar was fucking around. We were in the detective squad room in Southwest. He threw ice water on me, so I pushed him and he went down over a chair. If you knew Ray at all, you wouldn't have to ask what happened next."

"What happened next?"

"We went down into the parking garage, and while six or seven guys from the squad stood around and watched, Ray punched out two of my teeth, broke my nose, and pretty much destroyed me."

"And you're not mad about that?"

"Well, for a while I guess, but that was Ray. He and I had just about ended our tour by then, so we unhooked. I was rotating out. He was on the lieutenant's list back then. Pretty high up. The sixth band, I think, so he was going to get his bar in a month or two anyway. We both just moved on."

"And you didn't harbor any resentment? I find that hard to believe."

"Chief, if I could ask . . . has anybody looked at the damage on Barbara Molar's face? Has anybody seen what he did to her? 'Cause if all these questions strike to some other possible motive, that's why I went over there. I tried to break it up. He fired first, and I was forced to return fire. He was seconds from killing both of us. I hope you photograph those injuries because all I was trying to do was keep us off Forest Lawn Drive."

"We'll get photographs, don't worry about that."

There was another charged silence in the room that lasted for almost a minute.

"Anything else you want to say for this record?" Mayweather said.

"No, sir. That's what happened. I'm sorry he's dead, but he gave me no choice."

"Okay, then." Mayweather looked at his watch. "This interview is concluded. It is five thirty-five A.M. This tape recording has been continuous, with no shutoffs, and it has been witnessed throughout by Captain Bud Halley." Then he snapped the machine off and rubbed his eyes. "That's it, Sergeant. I'm going to forward this transcript to the Officer Involved Shooting Section of the Robbery/Homicide Division, and they will schedule your Shooting Review Board. Don't sweat it. That board is mandatory with any incident involving firearms."

"I know, sir."

"Then get outta here. Go give the lab tech his sample and go home."

"Yes, sir."

Shane got up and moved past Captain Halley, into the hall. He waited for his CO to come out, thinking they would ride down together and Shane could get a performance critique, but Captain Halley didn't come out. The door was slightly ajar, and he could hear Mayweather and Halley talking. Then suddenly the door was kicked shut, cutting off the conversation and leaving him alone in the hall.

STREET 4 DIVORCE

SHANE WAS FORCED to wander in the Parker Center garage, looking for his car. It was six A.M. He had started on the top level, which was aboveground, and had moved slowly through the garage, heading down, deeper into the bowels of the parking structure. He had his keys in his right hand. They had been left for him at the OOD's desk in Robbery/Homicide, but the uniform who had driven his car in didn't tell the duty sergeant where in the garage it was parked. The structure was huge, and his bare feet were cold on the concrete floor. As he walked, he could occasionally see flashes of red on his feet—Ray's blood. He had stood in it, and it had seeped up, between his toes, staining his skin. After giving his urine sample, he'd been in such a hurry to get out of there and get home, he hadn't remained in the rest room to wash it off.

"Sergeant Scully. Over here," a voice yelled at him; he turned around and looked back. He could see two uniformed officers standing by the elevator. He was six stories down, and the garage was dimly lit by the neon overheads. The two policemen moved out of the darkness toward him. The overhead lighting threw long shadows under their visors, and he could not make out who they were. As they got closer, he realized he had not seen either of them before. It was not unusual for members of the LAPD not to know one another. There were over nine thousand sworn members of the department sprawled over a huge geographic area. From the markings on their uniforms, he could tell that they were both first-year officers—policemen I's.

"What is it?" he asked.

They were close enough now for him to see that they were both in their early twenties. Their silver nameplates indicated that the shorter one was Officer K. Kono, the other, Officer D. Drucker. Kono had a wide, flat face and the complexion of a native Hawaiian. Drucker was a bodybuilder. His arms bulged the short sleeves of his Class C uniform shirt. They stood in front of Shane, studying him as if he were roadkill that one of them would eventually be forced to scrape up.

"Whatta you want, Officer?" Shane asked Drucker. "I've had a long night. I wanna get home."

"That Ray's blood on yer feet?" Kono asked. He had no Hawaiian accent. He was pure West Valley, but his voice was shaking with emotion.

"Whatta you guys want?" Shane repeated.

"Why'd you have t'butt in?" Drucker asked. "Who asked you?"

Shane could now see that they were both extremely emotional. They had obviously heard about Ray's death, which was spreading through the department like a raging virus. He speculated that Drucker and Kono must have come in and waited for him in the garage.

"He was killing his wife. He was taking batting practice on her with a baton."

"So you butt in and give him a fucking street divorce," Drucker hissed. A "street divorce" was police slang for any domestic argument that turned into a murder.

"Get outta my way." Shane tried to push past the two cops, but they held their ground and he found himself bumping shoulders with them violently. They weren't about to let him through, so Shane backed up and reevaluated the situation. He didn't have his gun. It had been booked by Homicide as evidence. He was alone in an empty garage. He was barefoot and tired, and his head still ached from where Ray had hit him. The two cops in front of him were jacked up on anger and out of control emotionally. In that moment, he had a flash of how it must feel to run up against enraged, violent cops in a desolate part of the city with no witnesses and no way to prove what really happened. Here he was, a sworn officer, standing in the police garage, yet he was beginning to pump adrenaline and fear for his safety.

"Is this about to turn into something?" he asked softly, glaring at both of them.

"Ray was the real deal, asswipe," Drucker hissed. "You're department afterbirth. Ray knew we had to take this fucking town back a street at a time. Since Rodney King, we've been eating shit and smiling about it. Ray knew that had to change. He knew the war was on, knew what we had to do out there. He understood you can't just stand around while a buncha freeway-dancers put it to ya."

"If you believe that, both you guys need to take a swing through the Academy retraining program."

"Swing on my dick, Tarzan," Kono hissed.

Shane shook his head and smiled. "Okay," he said, "I guess that ends this discussion. Your move."

"This is police headquarters," Drucker said. "This is the Glass House, man. Nothing happens here. But stick around, Scully. There's gonna be some payback."

"Now you're threatening me, Drucker?"

"You killed the best cop to ever ride in this department," Kono said. "Shot him just 'cause he was straightening out his old lady? Okay, it's done. Ray's gone. But we loved him, man, we—" He stopped, and Shane thought he saw moisture in the young Hawaiian cop's eyes.

"You two guys need to go home and think this out," Scully said.

"We don't need to think nothin' out," Drucker snapped. "You think it out. We've got someone pulling your card right now. From now on, nobody's gonna take your side. Nobody's got your back, Scully. You're a walk-alone."

"I'm putting you both in for this."

"Have fun," Drucker said, touching the brim of his visor. "Your word against ours. Have a nice morning, asshole." They both turned and walked away. He could hear their footsteps echoing in the concrete darkness. Then a car started, headlights went on, and they pulled past him, going fast. The wind from their black-and-white flapped his sweatshirt as they sped away.

Shane stood alone in the garage; he suddenly felt a shiver of dread come over him. Then he turned and again started looking for his car. He found it way down on U-9, at the back of the garage, on the bottom level. When he looked at the car, something seemed wrong, it seemed lower. He knelt down in the dim light and saw that all four of his tires had been slashed. The black Acura was squatting sadly on its rims.

"Shit," he said, looking at the car. Then he suddenly remembered Chooch. He wondered how he would ever get home in time to get the boy to school.

CHOOCH

5

SHANE ARRIVED HOME at a little past seven, driving a slick-back he'd checked out of the motor pool. He parked the black-and-white detective's car in the driveway and entered the back door. As he walked into the kitchen, Chooch was bent over with his head deep in the refrigerator. Startled, he jerked around and glowered.

"It's fucking bleak in there, Chuck. Don't you got nothin' to eat?" Chooch was dressed in baggy jeans pulled down low, gang-style, exposing two inches of his red plaid boxer shorts. His white T-shirt read EAT ME.

"There's some strawberry Pop-Tarts in that cupboard," Shane said as he quickly headed through the kitchen, hoping Chooch wouldn't see his bloodstained feet and put him through a description of the early-morning shooting. Shane moved into the master bedroom, which was furnished in "relationship-eclectic." Nothing matched. All the furniture in his house was salvaged from broken love affairs. It had gotten to the point where every time he and a new female roommate went furniture shopping, there was some cynical side of him that would wonder which of the new bedroom or living-room ensemble pieces would become his in the post-relationship settlement. The result was a depressing mixture of colors and styles.

He stripped off his blood-spattered sweatshirt and pants, then got into a hot shower, scrubbing Ray's blood off his feet with his shower nailbrush, rubbing so hard that he was afraid his toes would bleed.

Shoot it; frame it; hang it in his gallery of defining moments. The Lady Macbeth Exhibit. He finished with his feet and then stood under the hot spray, trying with less result to cleanse his spirit. Finally he got out of the shower, wrapped himself in a towel, and looked in the foggy bathroom mirror. The face was angular and rugged. Dark eyes wore a raccoon's mask of sleep-lessness. His hair hung black and limp on his forehead. He stared at himself for a long time, trying to see if he looked as different as he felt. In his thirty-seven years Shane had never killed anyone before; on the drive home from the department, that change in his life experience had started to weigh on him. Now, as he stood in his bathroom, it was plunging him into a fit of depression, which, according to the self-help psych books he had started read-ing recently, was self-hatred turned inward, driving his spirit down. He turned away from the mirror and dressed in slacks, white shirt, maroon tie, and a blue blazer. He slipped on socks and loafers, clipped his backup gun onto his belt, grabbed his pager, badge, and handcuffs, then went into the living room, where Longboard Kelly was snoring on the sofa.

Shane shook the twenty-eight-year-old blond-haired surfboard shaper's shoulder to wake him. Brian had turned out to be a surprisingly good friend. In the two years since Kelly had moved in next door and had started running his surfboard business out of his garage, the resinhead and the cop had surprised themselves with their unlikely friendship.

"I'm back, Brian. Thanks, man."

"Mmmmsaaakjjjjaaaawww," Longboard said, and rolled over, turning his back on Shane.

Shane smiled and headed into the kitchen, where Chooch was now seated at the small wooden table. Chooch had one of the strawberry Pop-Tarts in his hand, nibbling at the edges. He had struck an insolent go-fuck-yourself pose with one hand jammed deep down in his pants pocket. His bare feet were up on the table.

"So, how much is the upslice bitch paying you?" Chooch started, unexpectedly.

Shane knew, from years on the street busting gangbangers and pavement princesses, that *upslice* meant a cheap woman and referred to the vagina. It pissed him off that this kid would refer to his own mother that way.

"She's not paying me anything."

"So what's the deal, then? She carving you some beef?" Another gangbang sexual reference.

"I'm not sleeping with your mother, Chooch. I've got other reasons. Now get your feet off the table, we've gotta eat off a' there." He slapped Chooch's feet hard, knocking them off the wooden tabletop. Chooch exploded out of the chair, anger and violence seething.

"Don't fuckin' hit me," Chooch said, breathing through his mouth, his right hand balled into a fist at his side.

"Go on . . . take your best shot," Shane said softly, "but you better tell me where you want your body sent first."

"Oh, you're gonna swing on a fifteen-year-old?"

"Hey, son, I've seen fifteen-year-olds roll pipe bombs under taxis and peel a clip-a'-nines at a passing squad car. Being fifteen gets you nothing."

Chooch unclenched his fist and stood there for a long moment.

"Gee, look't this. I think we're really beginning to communicate," Shane said sarcastically, then moved over and grabbed a second strawberry Pop-Tart out of the box on the counter. He dropped it in the toaster and pushed the lever down. "You do your homework last night?" Shane asked, not really knowing what to say to the hostile Hispanic youth across the kitchen, glowering at him with smoldering eyes. At six feet, he was almost Shane's height, and already Shane could see he'd been hitting the weights. He had Sandy's dark good looks.

"I don't do homework. I got fly bitches do it for me."

Shane could see why Sandy had begged him to take Chooch. *"Do whatever it takes,"* she had said. *"He needs a male authority figure. He's got to see where this path he's on is headed."*

"Chooch, you and I have to get along for a month. Let's try and keep from peeling the skin off each other. Now get your stuff together, we gotta get you to school."

"I ain't goin' to school. I quit. Where's the TV? I can't find it. What kinda jerkoff ain't got a TV?"

Shane didn't answer. He moved out of the kitchen and into the guest bedroom. The house was on one of the Venice, California, grand canals, and through the side window he could see the morning sun glinting off the still water. It was 7:10; he figured if he hurried and there wasn't much traffic, he could still get Chooch across town to the Harvard Westlake School by 8:15. The school was located on Coldwater, in the Valley.

As he started to grab Chooch's book bag, he saw that there was a stash of tobacco tucked into the side pocket. He took the Baggie out and held it up. Two ounces of marijuana. He carried the book bag into the kitchen, where Chooch was standing, looking out the back door, his arms folded across his chest. He pretended not to be watching as Shane emptied the Baggie of Mexican chronic down the kitchen sink and turned on the disposal. It finally dawned on Chooch what was happening. He exploded away from the wall and made a grab for the Baggie.

"Hey, what you be doing with my bale, man?"

Shane grabbed Chooch by the collar, spun him, and backed him up, slamming him hard against the refrigerator, pinning him there.

"Hey, asshole, take this to the bank. Rule one: You're not gonna smoke grass in my house. Not today, not ever!"

"That shit was hydro, man."

"And you can stow the rap dictionary, okay? We're talking English in this house."

"Fuck you."

They were nose to nose, breathing hard. Shane was close to the edge, focusing his frayed nerves and growing depression on this angry fifteen-year-old. He took a deep breath to calm down. Then he let go and took a step back. "I don't know whether you get away with stuff like this at school, but it won't work here," he said in a calmer voice.

"I don't wanna stay here. I'm leaving," Chooch said softly.

"Okay, here's the deal. . . . One: Use any dope in this house, you're gonna get a chin-check from me. Two: You do what I tell you, when I tell you. Three: Knock off the Hoover Street attitude. Four: You're gonna do your own homework and not farm it out to girlfriends. If you live up to those four rules, here's what you get from me in return. You get room and board. You get my friendship and respect. You get a fair deal; I'll lay it out straight. I won't ever lie."

"Like I give a shit."

"And clean up your mouth."

"You think I wanna stick around and go to your bullshit white-slice Gumby boot camp?"

"You take off, I'll put the LAPD Runaway Squad on you. You'll go to juvie detention and then to a CYA camp, where you won't have to worry about some private-school geek in a bow tie who teaches chemistry. You'll be slappin' skin with the heavy lifters from south of Hawthorn."

The two of them held gazes. Even though Shane was tired and mad, he had to admit that Chooch Sandoval had been dealt a bad hand. Sandy had made a bunch of horrible choices when it came to her son. Now Chooch was full of anger and resentment. His hormones were raging, and he was looking for a place to park all that frustrated hostility. On the plus side, Chooch had not whimpered. He didn't feel sorry for himself, and he was no cupcake. Somewhere deep down inside, Shane had already begun to respect him.

"I'm through going to that school," Chooch said. "I got no friends there. It's not what I'm about."

"That's one of the best private schools in California. You're throwing away the chance of a lifetime, and for what? So you can hang with a bunch a' street characters?"

"They're my brown brothers. My home slice."

"They don't care about you, Chooch."

"And you do? Or Sandy? I ain't for sale, asshole. You can't buy me with clothes or a school or this crummy deal you got here. You ain't got what I need, Mr. Policeman."

"Get your shoes on. Where are they?" Shane asked. "And change out of that shirt." Chooch snorted but didn't move, so Shane went into the guest room, found another T-shirt and Chooch's tennis shoes. He reentered the kitchen and handed them over. "Let's go. . . . Put 'em on, or face the consequences." Chooch changed shirts, then slipped his shoes on without bothering to tie them. Then he exited the back door, insolently brushing Shane with his shoulder as he went past.

Shane followed him out into the alley behind the house, where the department Plymouth was parked. It was a detective car but looked exactly like a regular black-and-white minus the Mars-bar light on the roof.

Back in 1997, Chief Willy Williams had started making sergeants drive them instead of the preferred plainwraps. In the old days, before Chief Gates, one of the perks of being a detective had always been driving an unmarked car, but now nobody bothered to check out a department car off duty except in extreme circumstances. Trying to work a stakeout or surveillance in a slickback was absurd, so detectives ended up using their POVs—personally owned vehicles.

"I ain't gonna show up at school in this," Chooch said, looking at the car, appalled.

Shane opened the passenger door, then spun Chooch around, took out his cuffs, and slapped them on, cuffing his hands in front of him.

"What you doin', man? What's this for?"

"Comin' to school handcuffed in a squad car oughta harden your rep. You'll be chasing the fly bitches away for a week." He pushed Chooch into the front seat of the car, and he could see the boy smile slightly as he walked around and got behind the wheel.

■ ■ ■

It was 7:45 A.M. before Shane finally caught his first minor break of the day. Traffic on the 405 was unusually light. It took him only forty-five minutes to get over the hill, into the Valley. Harvard Westlake was half a mile up Coldwater Canyon, on the left side. All the way there, Chooch had remained silent. He had pulled his CD player out of his book bag and plugged himself in.

Even with the break on the traffic, Shane arrived at Harvard Westlake fifteen minutes late. He pulled past the Zanuck Swimming Stadium and the Amelia and Mark Taper Athletic Pavilion. He let Chooch off at the Feldman Horn Fine Arts Building, where his first-period class had already convened. The intended image-enhancing uncuffing ceremony passed without audience.

"I'll pick you up at three-thirty," Shane said, putting his handcuffs away.

"Whatever," Chooch growled. Then with his book bag over his shoulder, he did a gangsta lean into the building.

Shane watched him go, feeling a sense of frustration and use-lessness. What on earth was he ever going to be able to give this boy? It had seemed like a good idea two weeks ago when he'd told Sandy yes. . . . A chance to contribute to Chooch Sandoval's life in an important way. Shane had been fighting recent bouts of intense loneliness and had seen himself helping Chooch sort out his adolescent problems. Shane hadn't expected him to be such a hard case. Now that he had him, he doubted he would be able to make any deposits in Chooch Sandoval's adult experience ac-count. This boy was already molded by the strange circumstances of his life. And now, in the harsh reality of Chooch's anger, it occurred to Shane that maybe he had just planned to use Chooch to find meaning in his own life. While Shane was pondering these thoughts, his cell phone rang and dropped him back onto an even more distressing playing field.

"Yeah."

"Shane, Captain Halley."

"What's up, Skipper?"

"I don't exactly know how to tell you this, but the Molar shooting is turning into a red ball." A red ball was any depart-ment case with such a high priority that failure to succeed threat-ened career advancement. "They're not going to take it to a Shooting Review Board."

"Whatta you mean, they're not gonna? They have to."

"Your case is jumping the Officer Involved Shooting Section and going directly to a full Internal Affairs Board of Rights."

"It's what?" Shane couldn't believe what he was hearing. "How can they send it to a Board of Rights without first giving me a shooting review?"

"The chief can send any case he wants to a full board on his sole discretion. He doesn't have to give any reason. Look, Shane, I don't know why this is happening, but you can't stop it. It's inside departmental guidelines."

"Sir, you gotta talk to them. I mean, I don't wanna go through another BOR. I'm gonna get time off without pay. It's career poison. It's gonna be in my jacket. This is nuts. Anybody would've done what I did. For God's sake, he fired on me. It was self-defense."

"It's what the chief wants."

"I don't even know Chief Brewer. I only met him once. He gave me a Citation of Merit."

"I've gotta go. You'd better get in touch with a defense rep. Who handled your case last time?"

"DeMarco Saint."

"You like him?"

"I guess. He got me off," Shane said dully.

"I think he's retired, but because of IAD crowding, there's a new provision for using retired officers. If you want, I can get you his address and give him a call."

"Sure, check and see if he's still living at the beach." Shane waited on the line for a few seconds. His head throbbed. His stomach churned. The captain came back on.

"He still lives in Santa Monica, on the Strand—3467 Coast Highway. I'll let him know you're coming."

Shane put his car in gear and pulled away from the shaded, tree-lined splendor of the private school, then made his way back toward the beach and the shrewd counsel of DeMarco Saint.

All the way there, he kept trying to figure it out. Ray Molar had been a black hole in his life from the day he first met him seventeen years ago. In the beginning, he'd been too green to see it. Eventually he recognized Ray for what he was and had gotten away from him. Last night, with Barbara's call, he'd been pulled back into Ray's sinister orbit. In one second he'd ended Ray's life and opened some kind of evil vortex that now threatened to destroy him as well.

DEFENSE REP

ANY POLICE OFFICER facing an administrative review gets
to choose a defense rep to defend him. According to Section 202 in the Police Bill of Rights, that representative can be
anyone in the department below the rank of captain. The charter
provides that the chosen officer *must* serve as the accused's defense representative unless such service would cause undue hard-
ship or unless the chosen officer has a current duty assignment of
such a sensitive nature as to prohibit the time commitment.

Over the years, several officers had become very adept at winning Internal Affairs cases and, as a result, got chosen as defense
reps time and time again. They became schooled in the legal va-
garies of the department disciplinary system, and most of them
viewed Internal Affairs as a black hole of intrigue that they referred to as "the Dark Side." In a way, these men and women
were mavericks inside the department, seeing themselves as an

important demarcation line between the accused officers and the meat-eating "politicians" who worked at Internal Affairs.

Such a man was retired Sergeant DeMarco Saint. He lived on the beach in Santa Monica. His house was run-down and desperately in need of a new roof and paint. He had made his place a hangout for a young, breezy beach crowd: everybody from surf bums and Rollerbladers to volleyball players and sidewalk musicians. They hung in clusters in front of his wood-shingled bungalow. DeMarco Saint presided over this collection of party animals like a wise, bearded guru. He had been a police officer for thirty years and had pulled the pin just last December. Then he had made an almost seamless transition from maverick cop to New Age swami.

Shane pulled his slickback into the public parking lot two doors down from DeMarco's house and showed his badge to the attendant, who greeted the free-parking move with a frown. Shane locked the car and walked to the beach bike path. He could hear loud rap music pounding before he even got on the pavement. As he got closer, he saw several young girls in string bikinis and some tanned surfers in boxer shorts sitting on DeMarco's low brick wall like prizes in a game of beach Jeopardy being played all day at high energy under a synthetic drumbeat.

Of course, Shane looked like a cop to them right off, and the conversation shriveled up like rose petals in a hot summer wind. By the time he got to DeMarco's wall, only the recorded rap of Snoop Doggy Dogg managed to ignore his presence.

"DeMarco around?" he asked the closest girl, a tall brunette in her mid-twenties.

"Inside," she said, arching a pierced eyebrow and clicking her silver tongue stud against her teeth to see if it would piss him off.

"That's nothing." He smiled. "I've got mine through my dick."

She laughed as he moved past her and through the front door of DeMarco's house.

He found the fifty-eight-year-old defense rep on his hands and knees, trying to adjust one of the blasting speakers while a teen-age boy watched.

"Fucking bass is vibrating. Sounds like shit," the young surfer with bleached blond hair and black roots said sullenly.

DeMarco kept fiddling and finally took some of the low end out. He leaned back on his knees to listen. "Whatta you think?" he asked. "Better?"

Snoop Doggy Dogg's staccato voice was bouncing ghetto ha-tred off the walls while DeMarco leaned forward again to screw with his woofers and tweeters.

"*Gotta fuck the pigs. Gotta make da man die, if he come passin' by da pork's gotta fry,*" the Snoopster rapped violently.

"You got a minute?" Shane yelled.

DeMarco turned and saw him, grinned, and stood up. He was over six feet tall, and since Shane had last seen him, he'd let his gray hair grow. It was now tied in a ponytail that hung a quarter of the way down his back. He was wearing a tank top and had added a few tattoos that Shane thought looked ridiculous on his spindly arms, but not anywhere near as ridiculous as the silver cross that dangled from a chain in his left ear.

"Halley called. Been expecting you." He turned to the fifteen-year-old surfer. "You tinker with it for a while."

As the rap banged against their ears, he led Shane through the kitchen, where he grabbed two cold Miller Lites out of the re-frigerator, and then out the back along the side of the house, onto Santa Monica's long, sandy beach. The waves were unusually high that morning because of a storm in Mexico. They broke energetically forty yards away, shaking the sand under the two men's feet.

"I must be getting really old," Shane said. "That shit pisses me off."

"I like having the kids around. So what're you gonna do?" He smiled, then reached into his ears and pulled out some cotton balls.

Shane couldn't help himself, he started laughing. "You're tuning your speakers with cotton in your ears. No wonder your low end is vibrating."

Shane and DeMarco sat in the warm sand and ripped the tabs off. The beer cans chirped and hissed foam. They clinked aluminum, and both took long swallows.

"I need help," Shane said.

"I know. Captain Halley already filled me in. He thinks you're being schmucked."

Shane looked at DeMarco. Sixteen years ago, a much younger DeMarco had saved him at a BOR. He was praying the newly ponytailed defense rep could do it again.

"Alexa Hamilton is back down there," DeMarco continued. "I figured she'd've transferred to some cushy job in administration by now."

"She's still there after sixteen years? I thought an average tour at Internal Affairs was only five years."

"She used to be their number one tin collector," DeMarco said. "They brought her back just to get you." A tin collector was an advocate who got convictions that resulted in an officer losing his badge. Sergeant Alexa Hamilton was the department prosecutor who tried him all those years ago, only she had failed to get his tin.

"They're all a bunch a' ladder-climbing suck-ups," DeMarco said, his hatred for the Dark Side spewing out of him unchecked. "Everybody in the fucking division is looking to get to the top floor of the Glass House. It sucks, the way it's set up."

Shane had heard DeMarco's complaints before and knew the old defense rep was talking about the fact that most of the captains and deputy chiefs on the ninth floor at Parker Center had also spent time as tin collectors in Internal Affairs. That made assignment as an IAD advocate a coveted post. It was a club. Lieutenants and below were selected by virtue of their test scores and oral boards, but to make captain, you had to be picked by the chief of police. The fact was, it was hard to be picked if you hadn't spent some time on the Dark Side. This phenomenon had the effect of making Internal Affairs a catcher's mitt for every hot dog and ladder-climbing politician in the department.

"Why did you mention Alexa Hamilton? What's she got to do with this?" Shane asked, thinking of the attractive but overly severe woman who sixteen years back had prosecuted him with such fanatical enthusiasm. She had quite a reputation, both personally and professionally, leaving a long trail of busted careers and broken hearts. More than one Parker Center Romeo had moved in with her, only to discover that her personal demands matched her professional compulsions. Shane wondered if her apartment was furnished in relationship failures as his was.

He had grown to despise her in the few months that his case was going through the division. One of his best moments on the job was seconds after his not-guilty verdict had come in. He looked over and saw such distress on Alexa's face that it gave him a moment of pure, soul-cleansing vengeance. When she caught him looking, he smiled and surreptitiously flipped her the bird.

"I thought you knew," DeMarco said, interrupting his thoughts. "She's got your case. She put in for it."

"You can't be serious," Shane groaned.

"Yeah. If at first you don't succeed, and all that good shit." DeMarco took another long pull on his beer and let out a deep belch. "Maybe you shouldn't've flipped her off."

"Wouldn't matter, she hates me anyway."

DeMarco went on. "It's not good that they hopped over your Shooting Review Board and went straight to a BOR. It shows the department is going to war."

"Why? Barbara Molar is my witness. She'll say what happened."

"I made a few calls down to my old crew at the Representation Section in Parker Center. The rumor down there is, this whole railroad train is coming right out of Mayor Crispin's office. He wants your balls in his trophy case."

"Why?"

"Lemme take a wild guess. . . ." He drained his beer. "How 'bout 'cause you lit up his bodyguard. Blew his arithmetic all over that bedroom wall."

"You gotta help me, Dee. You gotta get me off."

"I'd like to, Shane. I really would. But frankly, I can't get into that rat race again. Alexa Hamilton is one tough, nail-chewing piece of business. I faced her fifteen or twenty times. Lost more than I won. I don't like it one bit that she's volunteering for this case. That tells me there's a big political payoff somewhere. Maybe lieutenant's bars and a transfer to something sexy like Organized Crime or Special Investigations. Mayweather could set that up for her, no sweat."

"You're telling me I'm cooked before we even get a hearing?"

"Tell you what . . . you know Rags Whitman? He's a good defense rep, smarter than me. I used to ram my dick up their asses and piss on their hearts. Ragland, he's mellow, he plays the game—Mr. Wheel of Fortune. They like him at Parker Center. I was you, I'd get him to take your case. Ask him to plead you out, see what kinda deal he can get. My bet: maybe he gets you a six-month suspension without pay and no termination."

"For defending myself from that crazy bastard? What kinda deal is that?"

"You shot Ray Molar. Not a good move, but you got an eyewitness who, we hope, backs you up. You got Ray's bullet in the wall, proving he fired before you got him. You also got Molar's record of spousal abuse. All this is good. On the bad side, you got the fuckin' mayor of L.A. tail-gunning you. You got Chief Brewer with his ears back, and you got some tricky 'undue use of force' statutes that could go against you. Your best bet is to see if Rags can spin the big wheel and plead it down."

"You won't help me? Come on, Dee, you're off the department. They can't threaten you; they can't get to your pension. What's the problem?"

"I'd do it if I could, man. I just can't. I've got no stomach for it anymore. I go down there, and my guts start churning. I'd choke. I hate those pricks worse than the National Anthem. You wanna know why I pulled the pin? It wasn't 'cause I had my thirty in. It was ulcers. My stomach lining looks like a Mexican highway. I can't put myself back in that mess. Go talk to Rags. Get him to negotiate a kick-down."

Shane stood up and handed DeMarco his half-empty beer. "Okay," he finally said. "Sorry to take up your morning." Then he turned and walked away, his shoes filling with warm sand as he went.

"Hey, Scully," DeMarco called, and Shane turned around. "Whatever you do, don't volunteer to take a polygraph. I think the IA poly is rigged. They use it to get confessions. I've had more than one case where I think I got a bum test."

"Okay," Shane answered. "Thanks for the warning."

●●●

Shane pulled out of the parking lot and back onto the Coast Highway. As he started toward the Santa Monica Freeway, his stomach was churning and he could taste bile in his throat. Then he heard a siren growl and saw a black-and-white behind him with its red lights on. Since he was in a black-and-white slickback, it surprised him that he was being flashed to the curb like a civilian. He pulled over and got out.

A young uniformed cop with two stripes on his sleeve moved up to him.

"What's up, Officer?" Shane asked.

"You Sergeant Scully?" the man asked.

"Yeah."

"I'm Joe Church. I was ordered to accompany you to Parker Center forthwith. Apparently your mobile data terminal is turned off."

"They get the gallows up already?" Shane quipped.

"I'm sorry, what, sir?" Officer Church said, deadpan, maybe with a tinge of cold anger.

"Why?" Shane asked. "What do they want?"

"Chief Brewer wants to see you immediately." He sort of barked it at Shane.

"Did I do something to piss you off?" Shane asked.

"You wanna follow me?"

"I can make it. You afraid I'll get lost?"

"Why don't you wait till I pull around. Since you haven't got a bar light, I'll put on the flashers and siren. It gets us there faster."

"You got a siren, how cool. I can hardly wait."

Shane got back into his unit and waited until the squad car pulled around in front of him. Joe Church growled his siren once, then raced out into the fast lane with Shane behind him.

The two police cars shot up onto the Santa Monica Freeway, heading back to downtown L.A. and Parker Center, Code Three.

7
SUPER CHIEF

TRAFFIC WAS JAMMED UP because some jackass had issued a motion-picture permit to an Arnold Schwarzenegger movie that was now shooting on Wilshire at Spring Street. The film crew had moved in downtown, parking their honey wagons, dressing rooms, and sixteen-wheelers up and down the curb on Third, laying out barricades and blocking traffic for ten city blocks. Shane couldn't believe that some dummy in city government had signed a film-location permit that would tie up all of downtown L.A. Twice, Patrolman Church had to get out of his car and talk to an off-duty policeman working for the movie company so they could get through.

After struggling for over forty minutes, they finally drove into the parking structure next to Parker Center. They both found a spot on the top level. Shane got out of his car, and Joe Church immediately joined him.

"Damn movie has this town tied up worse than my colon,"

Church growled as they looked at a low-flying helicopter that was hovering half a block away. There was a cameraman hanging out of the side door in a harness. Suddenly the rotors changed pitch, and the silver-and-red Bell Jet Ranger took off after a car that was speeding down barricaded Main Street after a motorcycle, Arnold Schwarzenegger kicking ass on celluloid.

"Let's go," Church said, getting back to business, taking Shane by the arm.

"I can make it. Even go to the bathroom now without Mommy's help."

"Don't be an asshole, Scully. I've got orders."

Shane decided not to push it, but he pulled his arm free and followed Church into the building.

For the second time in four hours, he found himself back on the ninth floor. They moved off the elevator, onto the thick, sea-foam green carpet, past the blond paneling and executive furniture, until he was finally standing in front of a massive woman who sat behind an oak desk the approximate size and shape of a Nimitz class carrier. She was parked directly outside Chief Burleigh Brewer's office.

Joe Church had shifted gears. No longer the stern centurion, he was now wearing an ingratiating, apple-polisher's smile. "Patrolman Church," he effused. "I was called specifically by Chief Brewer for this assignment. I've brought Sergeant Scully in. It was a 'forthwith.' "

"Thank you, Officer," the linebacker-sized woman said. Her heavy body wasn't helped by the shoulder pads in her tan suit coat. The name on her desk plate read CARLA MILLER. "You can sit down over there, Sergeant," she said to Shane, pointing to a chair. Joe Church took a position of advantage, guarding the exit.

"Jeez, Church," Shane growled, "I'm not Clyde Barrow. I'm not gonna shoot my way outta here. Try giving it a rest."

Carla Miller nodded to Church. "We'll be okay."

Church shuffled his feet, flashed a gee-whiz smile, and a few seconds later backed out of the office and was gone.

Carla buzzed Chief Brewer and talked to him softly for a second, then hung up the phone.

Shane waited in the chair for almost thirty minutes, watching the efficiency with which Carla Miller fended off appointments and people. She was a tough, competent goalie, crouching in the net, deflecting problems. She never looked at him once. Outside, he could hear the distant drone of the movie helicopter as it whirled and turned, its rotors whining above the streets of L.A.

Suddenly the intercom buzzed. Carla picked up the phone, listened, then looked at Shane. "You can go in now."

He got up and moved into Chief Brewer's office. The first thing that struck him was that the movie helicopter seemed to be almost inside the office. The chief had a huge expanse of glass. You could see all the way down Main Street to the Financial Center. The Bell Jet Ranger was hovering loudly only fifty feet from the chief's plate-glass window. It was a startlingly eerie effect.

Chief Brewer's back was to him. He was looking out the window at the chopper and the movie company in the street below. The camera ship hovered, stirring air gusts against the window. The rotor sound inside the office was almost deafening. Shane could see the pilot's features clearly. The cameraman hanging from straps inside the open side door was still hunched over the eyepiece. It occurred to Shane that while he had been outside, waiting with his heart in his throat, his police commander had been watching them shoot this fucking movie.

Then Chief Brewer turned. Making it worse, he was holding a pair of field glasses. He set them down on his desk and motioned to Shane to come forward.

"You wanted to see me, sir." Shane's voice was lost in the noise from the helicopter. Somewhere in the pit of his stomach he knew that what he was about to be told was not going to be good. Sergeants get summoned to the COP's office for only two reasons, and Shane was pretty sure he wasn't about to get another Meritorious Service commendation.

Then the chopper turned and flew away abruptly, photographing some part of the movie in the street below. The silence that ensued was a blessing.

"Sergeant Scully, you've had a busy morning," the chief said. He was a stout forty-five-year-old red-haired man with cheeks that always seemed to have a ruby blush. He had his suits carefully tailored to hide a growing midsection. Recently he had added rimless glasses that blended a touch of severity into an otherwise unremarkable face.

"Yes, sir. Busy morning, sir," Shane said, trying to read where this was going.

"Movies," the chief said. "Boy, they use a fuck of a lot of equipment. They've got four whole blocks tied up down there. Three helicopters. That one there is the camera bird. God knows what the other two are for. We let 'em use one of the police choppers for a picture ship."

"That's very generous, sir. I'm sure they're grateful."

"It's a Schwarzenegger flick called *Silver and Lead*. He plays a cop who breaks up an armored-car robbery. It's a silver shipment, but it turns out the robbery is just a decoy to pull the cops away from a presidential assassination. Arnold signed a copy of the script for me," Chief Brewer bragged.

"Bet that'll be worth a few bucks." Shane felt like a moron, standing there with his asshole puckered, talking about the movie business.

"People would feel a lot better about you, Sergeant, if you were more of a team player."

No segue. One moment it's show biz, the next it's team ball.

"Oh?" Shane said. "I think I'm a good team player, sir. Check with my captain, my watch commanders."

"I'm not talking about your field performance, Scully. I'm sure you're a good detective. That's not what this is about. What I'm talking about is attitudinal."

"Attitudinal?" Shane was lost. He didn't have a clue.

"Sometimes a guy will find himself in a position where he thinks maybe he's got an advantage. He thinks maybe he got lucky, stumbled into a piece of good fortune, but the fact is, he's not lucky at all. Fact is, he's stepped in a vat of shit and doesn't even know it. Then he's isolated—a marked man. That's not a good thing. It's better if you're a part of the team."

"Exactly what is it we're talking about, sir? I'm kinda lost."

"Are you? How come I knew that's what you were going to say?" Chief Brewer stood there, looking at Shane as if he were a grease spot on one of his new silk suits. Then he let out some more line. "Sergeant, there are items missing from Lieutenant Molar's case files. According to his duty logs, they were in his house before you shot him. They are no longer there. We questioned his wife. We believe she knows nothing. That leaves you. You were in a position, after you killed him, to remove those items."

"And you think I have them?"

"These items might appear to you to be some kind of windfall or perhaps something an ambitious person might think he could use to his advantage. They aren't what they appear to be. Lieutenant Molar was involved in something very sensitive, and he had the full cooperation of this office. This material could easily be misinterpreted if it got into the wrong hands. It needs to be returned now!"

"Sir, I don't have anything of Ray's. *Nothing.*"

"I fully expected you to deny this because we both know it's against departmental regs to remove another officer's case material. You could be terminated if you admit you took it. However, Sergeant, there are things in this life that are worse than job termination. I expect that you're going to continue to deny it until the full gravity of the situation becomes clear to you, but by then it may be too late. There may be nothing I can do to help you."

"What items?" Shane's heart was pounding now. He was feeling as if he were trapped in a nightmare and couldn't find a way to wake up. "I didn't take anything," he repeated.

"In which case, you probably wouldn't object to taking a polygraph test."

"A polygraph? I . . . I don't even have a defense rep yet. I . . . I'm not sure I want to submit to a lie detector test without legal advice."

"Again, exactly what I thought you would say. Believe me, Scully, you're making a horrible mistake."

"Sir, I'm not saying I won't take a polygraph. It's just . . . I'm having a hard time figuring out what's going on. I shot a man who was trying to kill me. He'd been beating his wife with a nightstick. Since that happened, my shooting review was canceled. I understand my case is being directed to a full administrative hearing, and now you're telling me I'm supposed to have stolen something from Lieutenant Molar's house? I took nothing, sir. I'll swear an affidavit to that fact."

The chief made a waving motion, brushing all this aside. "Here's my deal, Scully—and if you know what's good for you, you better take it. You've got four hours to turn over what you took. Drop the material off here. If you think you can use it to extract either money or career advantage, then you're going to find out that the entire city of Los Angeles, from Police to Sanitation, will go to war against you. It won't end well. By way of example, the district attorney, right now, is seriously considering filing murder charges against you for killing Lieutenant Molar."

"What?" Shane couldn't believe what he was hearing.

"Sergeant, do yourself a big favor and turn the material over."

Shane stood across from Chief Brewer with his knees shaking. He tried to collect his thoughts, then he took a breath to calm down.

"Let's suppose I have what you want and I turn it over," he

said. "What happens to the charge of removing case materials and my Internal Affairs Board of Rights?"

"Maybe something gets worked out there. We look the other way on the case material. Your undue-use-of-force gets sent back to the Officer Involved Shooting Section, they look it over. Maybe it gets disposed of in a few hours, the district attorney decides there's no case."

"So you're using the BOR and this murder charge to try and scare me into doing what you want?"

There was an awkward silence, then the chief took a step toward him and changed the subject.

"Sergeant, there are only three places that material can be, and we've already looked in the other two. You've got four hours. Your career, and maybe the way you spend the rest of your life, depends on your decision. That's all I have to tell you." Then he turned his generous backside on Shane and looked out the window again, at the movie company.

Shane hesitated, wanting to continue to try convincing him, but it was obvious he had been firmly dismissed. Shane turned and walked out of Burl Brewer's office, closing the door behind him.

When he got into the waiting room, Alexa Hamilton was sitting in the same chair he had been warming a few minutes before. She stood when she saw him. Alexa Hamilton was in her mid-to late thirties and was beautiful in a severe, hard-charging way. Coal-black hair was pinned up on the back of her head. High cheekbones and slanted eyes gave her an exotic look that Shane didn't think fit her no-nonsense, ball-busting personality. She had a tight, gym-trained body. He thought her beauty was badly overpowered by a raw will to succeed that made her sexually unattractive to him. He saw her as one of the new breed of LAPD ladder-monkeys, moving fast through the department, eating her dead, leaving a high-octane vapor trail behind her.

"We meet again," she said, arching a tapered brow and smiling without humor.

"This isn't a meeting, it's an ambush."

"Call it what you like, I'm ready. I don't usually have to take two swings at such a slow pitch."

"I'll try and put a few more rpms in my routine." He looked down at the folder in her hand. "That my package?" he asked. "My sealed background records seem to be making the rounds. Will I be reading about my confidential history in next month's newsletter, or is it just going up on the division bulletin board?"

"I'm not reading secure files, Scully. I don't need to cheat to hammer you in. The infield fly rule's on. We have a play at any base."

"If you say so." He walked out of the office and was heading down the hall when she stuck her head out and called to him.

"Hey, Scully."

He turned and faced her.

"I didn't 'peel the nine' at Ray Molar, you did. You go around shooting your ex-partners, you're bound to pick up a little grief."

"Lemme file that under 'shit to remember.' "

He stabbed hard at the elevator button, missed, and stabbed again. Thankfully, it opened almost immediately and he got on, stepping out of her black-eyed stare. It whisked him mercifully away, down to the traffic-jammed reality of downtown Los Angeles and Arnold Schwarzenegger.

8

TOKING

AFTER PICKING UP his Acura at the Spring Street Tire Center, Shane got back to the Harvard Westlake School at three-thirty to retrieve Chooch. He waited in a long line of British and German cars driven by Beverly Hills soccer moms. When he finally pulled to the curb where the students waited to be picked up, there was no Chooch. Then he saw him, off to the side of the crowd, sitting on a curb by himself. His CD player was hooked in his ears; he was lost in the music. Shane tapped on the horn to get his attention. Chooch picked up his book bag and ambled over to the newly shod black Acura now sporting four Michelin radials that Shane couldn't afford at a hundred dollars a tire.

As Chooch was sliding into the front seat, a tall, reed-thin man with a lipless mouth, curly hair, and heavy, dark-rimmed glasses stuck his head into the car. "Mr. Sandoval, I'm Brad Thackery, head of the Latin department and high-school assistant dean of admissions."

"I'm not his father," Shane said.

"Oh . . . uh, well, I'm sorry. I just got the job two months ago, and I'm still trying to get all the names and faces straight. Will you be talking to Chooch's parents today?"

"Whatta you need, Mr. Thackery?"

"We need to schedule a teacher's conference immediately. Chooch has some severe problems that need to be addressed, *ad summum bonum.*"

Off Shane's puzzled expression, he translated, "For everyone's good."

Shane looked at Chooch, who seemed not to be hearing any of it as he bobbed his head to the beat of some alternative rock leaking at high decibels from his earphones.

"I'll call his mother. Thanks."

Parents behind him were beginning to tap their horns impatiently, so Shane put the car in gear and pulled out onto Coldwater.

Shane said nothing until they were on the Ventura Freeway. "Hey, Chooch," he said, looking over at the boy slumped down in the seat beside him. "Chooch, you wanna take off the headset for a minute!? We need to talk."

Chooch paid no attention. He was bobbing his head to the music, oblivious.

Shane suddenly reached over and ripped the jack out of the CD.

That got his attention. Chooch spun around and glared. "What!" he said angrily.

"They want a teacher's meeting."

"I heard him. Thackery's a dick. Who the fuck cares? I hope they kick me out."

"Whatta they wanna talk about?" Shane asked. "I've gotta call and tell your mother."

"Whatta they wanna talk about? They wanna accuse me of dealin' drugs at school."

"Of what!?"

"You heard me. They think I'm dealin' drugs."

"Are you?"

Chooch didn't say anything, he just shrugged.

"You're not gonna tell me?"

"You're a fuckin' cop. Don't I get a lawyer and my Miranda rights first?"

Shane pulled the car off the freeway, down the Sepulveda ramp, and parked on the busy cross street. Then he turned to face Chooch. "Listen, Chooch, I'm not a cop where you're concerned. I'm your . . ." Shane couldn't think of the right word. What was he?

"My what?" Chooch challenged. "My fuckin' guardian? My baby-sitter? My spiritual coach? What the fuck are you?"

"How 'bout your friend," Shane finally said.

"You're not my friend. I don't have any friends. Not one."

"Chooch, if you're selling drugs to kids at school, we've got a big problem. They could go to the LAPD. They could file criminal charges against you."

Chooch leaned back in the seat, not sure what to do.

"I'm not gonna bust you," Shane continued, "but I've gotta know what the deal is if I'm going to help."

"Not gonna bust me, huh? Where'd I hear that before?"

"Tell me. Were you selling drugs?"

"No. I didn't sell nothin'." He leaned back and closed his eyes. "Once or twice, maybe . . . I loaned some Rasta weed to somebody. And then maybe once or twice I found some cash in my locker that I don't know where it came from. . . ."

"Shit," Shane said, not sure how extreme his response to this should be. "You're in deep shit if they can prove it. Is anybody there gonna talk?"

"You mean, will my dickhead clients roll over and give me up?" Chooch asked. "In a fuckin' heartbeat. You want my opinion? They're not gonna go to the cops. That school doesn't want some newspaper story about drugs on campus. Since I'm Mexican, they're also probably scared shitless somebody will charge 'em with race discrimination. They're just gonna demand I go quietly, something I'm real prepared to do."

Shane looked hard at the teenager, still sitting with his head back on the seat, his eyes closed.

"It isn't your problem anyway," Chooch said. "You're just this month's paid jerkoff."

"Right. That's me." Shane put the car in gear and headed back up onto the freeway. They didn't speak all the way back to Venice.

Finally, Shane pulled into his house at 143 East Channel Road. He parked in the garage and got out. Chooch grabbed his book bag and slouched along after him as they opened the back door. The two of them walked into the kitchen, and Chooch slung his book bag angrily onto the counter.

"Take that into your room and start doing your homework."

"Homework? Ain't that a little off the point?"

"Do it anyway," Shane said. Then he moved out of the house into his small backyard, which looked out onto one of the narrow channels of Venice. What had been a cold April morning was now turning into a surprisingly pleasant California afternoon.

From Shane's small backyard on Venice's East Channel, he could see all the way down the intersecting Howland Canal.

Venice, California, had been the brainchild of Abbot Kinney in 1904. Kinney had wanted to create a luxury community in the style of Venice, Italy. He supervised the design of channels to carry water in from the ocean two blocks away. He designed his development around four long canals, intersected by a series of concrete, arched Venice-like driving bridges that spanned each canal. He added small walking bridges and brought some scaled-down gondolas over from Italy. It had been quite a place in the early 1900s but had seen hard times ever since. The canals still had a sort of rustic charm, but the once-grand houses of the thirties had been knocked down or subdivided and in their place were smaller, cheaper structures. The architectural style ranged from antebellum to trailer-park modern. The people who now lived on the canals were an even more interesting mix. Young doctors who smoked dope lived next door to disapproving retirees. New Age musicians and mimes competed for hat tips on the boardwalk, while four blocks inland, on Fifteenth Street, gangbangers and unaware tourists fought and died over wallets and watches. Jammed in with all of this confusion, next to a longhaired surfboard shaper, was LAPD Sergeant Shane Scully. There was something about the canal blocks of Venice, California, that suited him; something offbeat and sad. Venice seemed as misplaced as her residents.

Less than half a mile to the south were the yuppified environs of Marina del Rey, where young ad executives and airline flight attendants took sexual aim at one another in the crowded waterside bars and fish houses. A mile to the north was Santa Monica, with its population of trendy superagents, junk bond salesmen, and Hollywood power brokers. Halfway in between, sitting on its silly three-foot-deep canals, trying to be something it could never duplicate, was the other Venice, sinking into the mud of social indifference as surely as Venice, Italy, was sinking into the sea.

But Shane Scully was at home there, like no place else on earth. Venice, California, defined him.

As he watched a hummingbird hang energetically over the still East Channel, he opened his cell phone and dialed Sandy.

She answered after the tenth ring and seemed out of breath. "Yes," she said. "Hello." She also sounded angry and impatient.

"Catch you at a bad time?" he asked sarcastically.

"Shane, I can't talk now. I was already out the door. I'm late."

"Then let me make it quick. I think they're going to throw

Chooch out of Harvard Westlake for dealing grass. Some guy named Thackery wants a teacher's meeting with you. I told him I'd let you know. That's the whole message. Nice talking to you."

"Wait a minute. He's dealing what?"

"Grass . . . Mary Jane, Aunt Hazel, African bush, bambalacha. You pick the cool name. He's selling shit to his classmates, and Mr. Thackery ain't one little bit amused about it."

"Well, what am I supposed to do? I can't . . . I mean, can't we . . . ?"

"Unfortunately, I don't think there's much *we* can do. But *you've* gotta call and set something up. As Thackery says, 'It's for everybody's good.' *Ad mumble bubble gum.* And before you ask, lemme say that as this month's paid jerkoff, I'm not up for the teacher's conference."

"Come on, Shane, it can't be that bad."

"Sandy, I'm in some very big trouble myself right now. Big enough that I could end up getting fired or, worse still, even prosecuted by the DA."

"But—"

"No. Listen. I can't handle this problem. I didn't know what I was getting into with Chooch."

"He sounds worse than he is. He's not that bad. You just have to be patient with him."

"You're sure about that? 'Cause I think he's one very confused, very angry kid. I think he's in the diamond lane to Juvenile Hall, and not that you care, Sandy, but I think you need to pay more attention to him. This kid is being passed around like a hot rock. Nobody's giving him what he needs."

"Including you?" she said darkly. "I thought you told me you *were* up for it, that you wanted to make a one-on-one investment in something with lasting dividends."

"What the fuck were we drinking, anyway?"

"Shane, look, I hear you. Unfortunately, I'm working for the DEA right now. I'm up to my ass in a dangerous sting that is days from going down. You know from the jobs we've pulled together that my biggest jeopardy is right before I drop the dime. If I get made now, I could end up the captain of a fifty-gallon oil drum at the bottom of the Catalina Channel. I can't take Chooch. I can't take a chance he'll get hurt, and I can't divert my energies or my concentration at this point in the sting. You said you'd take him. You promised. Otherwise, I wouldn't have left him there."

"Okay, Sandy. I'll do the best I can. But you wanna know something . . . ?"

"Not if it's gonna be a lecture."

"It's an opinion, baby. This boy is hurting bad. He's on fire. He's so self-destructive, I'm heartsick for him. But I'm up to my ass in department bullshit. I shot my ex-partner."

"That was you? It was on the news." Shane didn't answer. "Well, good," Sandy finished. "Ray was a son of a bitch. He deserved to die."

"No, he didn't. But if this goes like it's been going, I'm not going to be available for Chooch, either. So start figuring what you're gonna do and call this prick Thackery and get him off my ass."

"Okay, okay, sugar. I'll call him. Gotta run. Bye." And she was gone.

He slumped down in his rusting metal lawn chair, and then someone cleared his throat. Shane turned and realized that Chooch had come out the side door and had been sitting in one of the other metal chairs at the side of the house.

"Well, she's probably got a lot more important shit on her mind," Chooch said. "Want me to roll you a number? It's pretty fine Jamaican ganja."

Chooch had some Zig-Zag papers and a small cloth drawstring bag in his hand. Shane hadn't had a hit of marijuana since the Marine Corps, but he was so tight, so frayed, that he was worried about his imploding psyche. "Yeah, sure, roll me up one."

"No shit?" Chooch said, "What about Rule One: No smoking grass in my house, not now, not ever?"

"I gotta do something to bend the energy in this day. Rule One is temporarily suspended."

Chooch rolled a bud, fat and short. Then he handed it over. Shane sat there, holding the jay, wondering what kind of example it was going to be for him to blast a joint in front of Chooch or, worse still, get high with him. But then he thought of the events of the day, starting with his shooting Ray Molar at 2:30 A.M., all the way through to his disastrous meeting with Chief Brewer. Somehow, in the light of all that, passing grass with an angry fifteen-year-old just didn't seem all that important.

"Fuck it," he said, then reached back and grabbed one of Chooch's matches, fired up, took a hit, and passed it to Chooch.

The two of them sat in metal chairs in the small, green-brown garden behind Shane's house, sharing the joint and trying to unwind their separate but equally devastating problems.

THE "FUNERAL" LETTER

Dear Dad,

Boy, do I wish you were here so we could sit down and talk this one out like the old days. I'm really in the shit this time, Pop, and no matter which way I turn, I'm faced with a new set of terrible options.

Where to begin?

I guess Ray's funeral is my biggest unanswerable right now. The department is going to give him a full-dress good-bye: honor guard, speeches, everybody wearing black ribbons across their badges. Today we got a department directive demanding that all officers not on day watch attend in dress blues. There's going to be a parade led by two hundred Mary units (motorcycle cops), followed by a hundred black-and-whites. The damn thing forms up at the Academy training field and will wend its way out of the foothills to Forest Lawn. Full TV and press coverage, of course.

Part of me wants to go. I feel like hell, and going to Ray's funeral might help me through it. Another part of me is scared to death. They're going to have this giant turnout of my brother officers: a twenty-gun send-off, with everybody mourning Ray Molar, "the Policeman's Policeman" and double Medal of Valor winner.

My problem, of course, is I'm the asshole who shot him.

I don't know if I can bear to stand there under all the hatred I know will be directed at me.

What would you do, Dad? I could really use the advice. I remember you told me once that, in matters of the soul, the thing that is the most difficult to do is generally the thing that you must *do. You said that in order to grow spiritually, one must not turn away from emotional hardships. But, still, I feel so isolated, so alone, so out of the loop.*

Having you so far away has made things difficult. I know you can't get around much and having emphysema makes flying difficult, but I need help, Dad.

I guess one of my problems is I always tried to make the department my second family. All that bullshit they preach up at the Academy . . . the long blue line, fraternity of police, brothers in blue . . . I wanted to believe all that. I think maybe it's why I decided to become a cop. And now, despite almost seventeen years on the job, I've found a way to fuck it up. I'm alone again.

If you have any thoughts, gimme a ring. I'm still undecided about Ray's funeral.

I wish I had your strength, willpower, and sense of honor. I'm trying to do what I think would make you proud but, damn it, I'm panicked to go to that funeral.

You're probably saying I should just bite the bullet and go. So, that's the answer. You always did know what was best.

I miss you and love you. I know, enough already, blah, blah, blah.

> *Your loving son,*
> *Shane*

WARRANT

SHANE DIDN'T GO to the funeral.

He put in for a sick day and, mercifully, it was approved. He hated himself for not having enough guts, but he just couldn't make himself attend. Chooch, showing more backbone, had not objected that morning when Shane loaded him into the car, took him across town to Harvard Westlake, and dropped him at school. They barely exchanged words as Chooch got out of the car.

Shane drove back to Venice, trying hard not to think about his emotional cowardice. He arrived home and busied himself cleaning the small house. He did some deferred maintenance, fixing a sprung hinge on the back screen door, then managed some idle conversation with Longboard Kelly, both of them talking over the back fence. But he couldn't keep his mind on what Kelly was saying . . . something about Hawaiian North Shore supersets and the merits of a stubby board compared with a nine-foot Hawaiian classic. As he walked back inside, his recollection of the conversation hovered over him like a dream barely remembered. Then he checked his answering machine, something he hadn't done for almost ten hours. There was only one message:

"Shane, it's Barbara. I know it might be dangerous, but we need to meet. I assume you'll be at the funeral, but obviously we can't talk there. How about 'our spot'? I could be there by one. The funeral is scheduled to be over by twelve-thirty. Don't contact me, I'm worried about my phone. I'm calling from a pay booth. Just be there. I have news. I love you." *Beep.*

Their "spot" was the outdoor restaurant at Shutters Hotel on the beach in Santa Monica. Once or twice, when they'd been dating, they'd taken a room there. The place was picturesque, and most of the units overlooked the water. Back then they'd both been in their early twenties and single. Having lunch together on an open patio before going up to a rented love nest was fine. Now, after shooting Ray, the last thing he needed was to be seen hunched over a table, in whispered conversation with his widow. Still, Shane was drawn to her in a way he couldn't describe. Maybe it was guilt, or maybe the feeling that she had been the one, and he had lost her through bullheaded pride, or maybe she had become just a fantasy in his memory. He had saved her from Ray, setting up, God help him, possibilities for some sort of future together. Or maybe it was just that he hadn't been laid in almost three weeks. Whatever the reason, he decided to take the chance and meet her there. After all, he rationalized, she said she had "news."

He dressed with more care than usual and even used the hair dryer on his dark, unruly mop. Then he got in the Acura and drove the short distance up the coast to Santa Monica.

He arrived at Shutters at about quarter to one and selected a table near the back of the patio. He ordered her favorite bottle of wine, a French Montrachet. While he waited, he tried to justify the meeting in his guilt-ridden conscience. Maybe her "news" would shed light on his problems. Maybe it would be something that would help dig him out of the mess he was in. Of course, lingering always, like a sour aftertaste, was his desire for her and the knowledge that he wanted to sleep with her again. It was another picture for his gallery: guilt-ridden lust . . . presenting a portrait of carnal self-hate. Hang it in the Virginia Woolf exhibit.

She arrived at 1:25 and stood in the doorway of the patio restaurant, wearing a black dress with a single strand of pearls. She wore large dark glasses to cover a black eye. The swelling from the nightstick was gone, and miraculously she no longer appeared to have any bruises. Her blond hair shimmered in the bright afternoon sunlight. She looked around the patio, spotted him, waved off the maître d', and walked toward him with her athletic dancer's step. She had once performed in the chorus of several musicals at the Dorothy Chandler Pavilion. She slipped gracefully into the vacant chair, puckered her lips, kissed the air, and smiled. Now that she was across the table from him, he could see that she had expertly covered the effects of the beating with Dermaplec, an over-the-counter makeup that is the best product available for hiding bruises. Every patrolman answering a spousal-abuse complaint quickly learned to check the medicine cabinet for Dermaplec. If it was there, it was almost as good as a confession by the husband that he had engaged in wife battering before.

"Hard day," she said sadly. "I thought you'd be at the funeral."

"Truth is, I chickened out."

"I can hardly blame you. It was a real Hollywood layout. Chief Brewer made a speech. Said Ray exemplified commitment to community and police honor. Mayor Crispin talked about his courage. Said he set a new standard for police excellence. They had a twenty-one-gun salute, gave me the flag off his coffin. There was a helicopter flyby, the whole police air unit."

"I'm surprised Schwarzenegger could spare the bird."

She cocked her head.

"Nothing," he said, not wanting to go into it.

"Anyway, Ray's in the ground. Lots of ceremony, lots of news crews and crocodile tears. Jeez, you wouldn't believe what a big deal it was."

Shane poured her a glass of Montrachet. She sipped the wine and looked out over the sandy beach and the ocean a hundred yards beyond. A light wind ruffled her perfectly streaked blond hair. She seemed to be working up to something. He waited and let her get at it in her own way. Finally she turned back to him, a small, sad smile on her face. "This is strange, sitting here again after all these years, isn't it?" He nodded his agreement. "God only knows why I chose to marry him, Shane. All day I've been trying to figure what was going through my mind. You were always the one."

"You don't have to explain it," he said, shifting awkwardly under the weight of the conversation and her penetrating stare.

"You were what I was looking for, but Ray told me *you* had beat that kid half to death in Southwest Division. He told me horrible things about you and I just . . . got mixed up. It wasn't until after we got married that he told me one night when he was drunk that he did it and that you had just taken the blame so IA wouldn't kick him off the job. He thought it was funny. 'Scully's just a dumb fuck,' he said."

"It's okay. It's done. Forget it." He felt his self-respect washing away like water rushing back to the sea, taking the sand beneath his feet, altering his stance, threatening his balance. It seemed wrong to be discussing this on the day that Ray went into the ground. Wrong to feel desire for his widow, wrong not to have found the courage to go to the funeral.

Barbara went on, in a hurry to rid herself of her own painful memories. "Back then, when I told you not to call me anymore, I cried for a whole night. I thought you had done what Ray said, you were on trial at Internal Affairs for it . . . and I . . ." She stopped and shook her head. "Ray started coming around a month later, and he seemed so strong. At first he could be so sweet, so tender. It was sort of touching, a huge brutish guy like that with an inner softness. I was looking for something, I don't know what. Then he kept at me . . . calling . . . gifts . . . it went on for years before I said yes. My dancing career was going nowhere, and I just thought . . ." She shook her head in exasperation. "Whatta mistake, huh?"

"Barbara, you don't have to explain it to me. Please. I understand."

"I want to, Shane. I need to. I know this is a shitty day for it, but frankly, in the twelve years we were married, I'd come to despise Ray, and I had come to despise myself for getting into such a mess with him. He drank, he cheated, he didn't come home sometimes for a week. Then a few years ago, he started hitting me. At the end, I was so frightened of him. I swear, it was a relief to see that casket go into the ground, almost like his grave was the doorway to my future." She took a deep breath. "If that seems coldhearted, I'm sorry. It's how I feel."

Shane looked at her for a long time. Under the dark glasses he knew she had beautiful aqua-blue eyes, the exact color of tropical reef water. She had a luscious body and chiseled features. More than once, in the old days, he had walked into rooms with her and felt the gaze of every man in the place undressing her. She was a physical trophy, but it went beyond that. He thought she had intense feelings and a depth of personality that this conversation betrayed. God help him, Shane still desperately wanted her, wanted to hold her and make love to her, but the feeling diminished him. Making it worse, he could tell that she was reaching out to him, asking him for forgiveness and inviting him to try again.

"Barbara, I think, no matter what eventually happens between us later, this needs to wait."

"I know. I know. It's just . . . I've been thinking about what it would have been like if things had been different. Sounds like a sad Barbra Streisand flick, doesn't it?"

He sat there looking at her, afraid to mention the number of times he had lain awake with the same thought. They'd really fucked it up. Ray had given it a nudge, but it had been the two of them, accelerated by Shane's pride and anger, who had pushed something special over the cliff. Now any future relationship was destined to be a reclamation project. Ray's memory would forever be between them.

"You said you had news," Shane said, changing the subject.

"I got the phone printout like you asked, from AT&T. I got the number that woman called in on."

"Great. Lemme see it."

She handed over a slip of paper and he frowned. "This is a Venice exchange."

"I know."

"Why would somebody send an important package through the mail, where it might get lost, when they could just drive by at midnight and stuff it into your mailbox?"

"I don't know. Doesn't make much sense."

He pulled out his cell phone and dialed the number. He got a recording. "Disconnected," he said as he snapped the phone closed. "When you gave your statement, did you tell the police about the woman who called and the videotape she said was coming?"

"Yeah. I told them everything." Then she added with a strange smile, "I told them Ray fired first, that it was self-defense."

Shane sat, thinking for a long moment. "We need to take a look through your house. I want to do a thorough search."

"There's nothing there. Robbery/Homicide looked already when they did the crime-scene investigation."

"I wanna look anyway. Maybe they missed it. I think that tape the woman was talking about may be what this is all about. Can we skip lunch and go there now?"

"What if they have someone watching the house? They'd see us together."

"With two-thirds of the department taking the day off for Ray's funeral, I doubt there's any spare manpower for a stakeout. Now is the best time. Let's go. If it's there, maybe we can find it."

He paid for the wine, and they walked out of the restaurant. On the way through the lobby, Shane had another thought. "Barbara, do you know Ray's cell phone number?"

"No. It was strictly a business phone. He told me never to use it, but I think he had it written down somewhere. Why?"

"When we get there, see if you can find it."

"Okay." She got into her red Ford Mustang convertible. The parking attendant stared openly as she pulled away, her blond hair streaming in the wind. Invisible in her wake, Shane got into his Acura and followed.

■ ■ ■

When they got to Barbara's house on Shell Avenue, the front door was ajar. Shane pulled up to the curb as Barbara pulled into her driveway. They both got out of their cars and looked at the half-open door with concern. Shane pulled his gun and handed Barbara his cell phone.

"Call nine-one-one if I'm not out in two minutes," he said. Then he moved up the steps and onto the front porch. He could see that the front-door lock had been drilled. Part of the tumbler mechanism was lying on the porch at his feet. With his toe, he edged the door open, staying to one side, out of sight. Then, when he had determined it was clear, he slipped into the house.

He could hear drawers being opened and closed in the back. He moved silently in that direction, finally looking into the bedroom where, seemingly a lifetime ago, he had killed Ray Molar.

There were two uniformed police officers going through dressers and closets. Shane decided to retreat. He didn't want to be caught in this house with Barbara standing outside. As he took a step back, the floor squeaked; both policemen spun and saw him standing there, gun in hand.

"What the fuck're you doing going through Ray's house?" Shane snarled, switching to offense and glaring at the two officers.

They were both first-year patrolmen. One of them he recognized as John Samansky, Ray's last probation partner. He was almost too short to be a cop, probably barely reaching the LAPD five-seven male height requirement. He had made up for his short stature by lifting weights. His wide trapezius muscles were straining his uniform shirt collar. The other police officer Shane had never seen before. He was also young but prematurely balding, with a narrow, pockmarked face. His nameplate read L. AYERS.

"Whatta you doing here, Scully?" Samansky asked. He had the blown voice of a pack-a-day saloon singer or a throat-punched club fighter.

"You got a warrant?" Shane asked, ignoring the question.

"Show him, Lee," Samansky said. Patrolman Ayers pulled a folded slip of paper out of his pocket and waved it under Shane's nose. "Not that you got any rights in this house, least not that we know about."

Shane ignored the comment, turned, and moved out of the bedroom, back to the front door. He waved to Barbara, who closed the cell phone and walked into her house. He didn't need more cops added to this party.

"Give her the warrant," Shane demanded as she entered the living room.

Lee Ayers handed it to Barbara.

"Why?" she asked. "Why are you searching my house?"

"That's none of your business, ma'am," Samansky said, his sandpaper voice gruff and irritating.

"You two are patrol officers," Shane said. "Long as I've been on the job, it's always detectives who administer warrants and paw through the dressers. Shouldn't you guys be parked on a corner somewhere, writing greenies?"

"You're the asshole who's headed for Traffic Division," Ayers said with a smirk. " 'Sides, we got this squeal direct from the top of the Glass House. You got a problem with that, take it up with the warrant control officer at Parker Center."

Shane took the warrant out of Barbara's hands and looked at it. It had been signed by Judge José Hernandez, known by police and trial attorneys around the municipal courthouse as "Papier-Mâché José" because he was willing to hang all the paper the cops wanted: subpoenas, arrest warrants, wiretaps. If they wrote it up, Hernandez signed it. Defendants had their own moniker: "The Time Machine," because the judge was infamous for passing out maximum sentences. He was a Mayor Crispin ally.

Shane handed the warrant back to Barbara. "You guys about through?" he asked.

"Yeah, we did the whole place," Ayers said. "You need to vacuum behind the furniture, lady. You got a fuckin' butterfly collection back there."

The two cops moved out the side door. Samansky had Barbara's garage-door clicker, and he opened her garage, exposing their black-and-white. They had parked it there to avoid calling attention to their presence.

While Lee Ayers got into the patrol car and backed it out of the garage, Samansky turned to Barbara. "You should be ashamed of yourself. Scully is the guy who shot your husband."

"That's none of your business," she said weakly.

" 'Cept it is my business. Ray was my friend, my partner. He was special. A guy like Ray comes along once in a lifetime. You had the best, lady. I'm fuckin' dyin' here . . . can't even believe he's really gone. You're his wife, and you're walking around with the shitwrap who dropped him. You should be ashamed." Then he turned, moved to the squad car, and got in. He glowered at them from the passenger seat. "I wonder what Robbery/

Homicide's gonna say about you two bein' together. Wonder how that's gonna play downtown." Samansky cleared his raspy throat, hawked up a spitball, and shot it in their direction. It landed two feet from the step they were on. Then he threw the garage-door opener at Shane, who snatched it out of the air.

They backed out of the driveway, around Barbara's Mustang convertible, and onto the grass. The squad car bounced over the curb, banging hard into Shane's black Acura, caving in the front fender with its pipe bumper, knocking Shane's car away from the curb. Then Lee Ayers cranked the patrol car's wheels and sped off up the street.

"It just keeps getting better," Shane said softly. "I can hardly wait till the tin collectors find out you and I were spending time together."

They turned and walked back into the house. Shane stood in the living room. It was probably a waste of time, but he decided to make his own search anyway. He checked the living-room furniture first. The carpet indentations were exposed, proving that the two cops had moved the sofa as promised. He pulled off some of the seat cushions and saw that they had all been stabbed with a kitchen knife that had been left on the floor under the sofa. That meant they had been looking for something that was small enough to be hidden inside a seat cushion. Something about the size of a videotape, he thought.

As he moved through the house, it was obvious that Samansky and Ayers had done a thorough job. It was also obvious that whatever was missing was still missing. The whole house had been searched. If they had found what they were looking for, they would have stopped when they recovered it.

Shane kept looking anyway, but he was getting dispirited. He ended up in the bedroom closet. He carefully went through the top shelf. Nothing. He checked the shoeboxes. Nothing. As he was getting set to close the closet doors, something caught his eye. He looked again and saw that there were half a dozen white shirts in plastic cleaner bags. What stopped him was that several of the shirts were on white hangers with printed plastic that read BAYSIDE CLEANERS, while two others were on plain hangers with light green cellophane over them. He took all the shirts off the rod and held them up.

"What is it?" Barbara asked.

"I don't know. Why do you use two different dry cleaners?"

"I don't. I just use Bayside, here in Venice."

Shane held up the Bayside Cleaners shirts. The covers indicated that Bayside was located at 201 South Venice Boulevard. He put them on the bed, then examined the other shirts with the plain hangers and greenish cellophane covers. There was no printing to indicate the name and address of this second cleaner. He pulled the laundry tag off one of the Bayside shirt collars. It was a small yellow strip with a number and bar code. Then he found the laundry strip for the unknown cleaner: a purple square stapled through the bottom buttonhole.

"You say Ray was away a lot. Maybe he had these cleaned somewhere else." Shane took the shirts with the purple square strips and folded them over his arm. "We have a database for laundry tags. Sometimes, when we get a John Doe with no ID, the laundry mark helps us identify the body. I'll drop this at the Scientific Investigations Section and see what they come up with. I better get out of here. Did you find that cell phone number?" he asked.

She snapped her fingers. "Forgot," she said, and went digging around in one of Ray's drawers. She found the box the phone had come in. Inside, with the warranty and sales slip, Ray had written the number. She handed it to Shane.

"Same number as on the AT&T printout," he said, holding up both sheets of paper. "Whoever she is, she was using Ray's cell phone."

"So we can't trace it."

"Guess not."

Shane moved toward the front door but stopped in the entry as Barbara put a hand on his arm. She looked at him softly with her beautiful blue-green eyes.

"Can we see each other?"

"Barbara . . . that's gonna get us nothing but grief."

"Tell me you don't want to see me. Just say it, and I won't bring it up again."

"I can't say it, 'cause I do. It's just . . ."

"If we're careful?" she said. "I feel so lonely, so frightened."

Why is this happening this way? he wondered. Finally he put a hand up to her face and held it there for a moment. "I'll think about it. I guess if those two cops notify RHD, the damage is already done," he heard himself say stupidly. Of course, he knew he could probably explain away one incident. He could say he'd come over to apologize or pay his respects. All he needed was to start seriously fooling around with Ray's widow in the wake of this shooting. A first-degree murder charge would probably be his reward for that behavior. *How could he even consider seeing her again?* His heart was beating fast, slamming in his chest like a broken cam shaft, his breath coming in rasping gasps. Loneliness swelled. He looked at her and wondered again how this had gotten so fucked up.

"Buy a cell phone," he said impulsively, "a new one. Leave the number on my home machine. You have mine. Since these cells aren't secure, don't use my name if you call me."

"Okay," she said. Then she reached up to kiss him, and he found his lips brushing against hers. He started to put an arm around her but then pulled away and quickly left her house without looking back.

Samansky was right. They should be ashamed, but a hard-on was stuffed sideways in his Jockey shorts. He reached down and adjusted it. Another work of art, *The Pagan Love God*; hang it with the others. The Shane Scully Gallery was filling fast.

He got to his car and knelt down to survey the bashed front

fender. It was hard to tell whether he or his poor black Acura had been taking more hits recently. He reached over and tugged the fender slightly off the new radial front tire. Then he got behind the wheel, and with the front fender rubbing badly, he turned the car around and drove back to his house on the East Canal in Venice.

Two hours after he got home, another uniformed patrolman showed up. He hand-delivered the PERSONAL AND CONFIDENTIAL envelope Shane had been dreading. Inside was an LAPD Letter of Transmittal.

THE
LETTER OF
TRANSMITTAL

POLICE DEPARTMENT

LETTER OF TRANSMITTAL
APRIL 21, 2000

ADJUDICATION
Complaint filed by Robbery/Homicide and IAD. Place of Complaint: 2387 Shell Avenue, Venice, CA. Complaint Investigation CF no. 20-4567-56. This complaint form contains allegations of misconduct against Department employee:

SERGEANT I. SHANE SCULLY   SOUTHWEST DIVISION
Serial No. 8934867   RHD

Allegations are listed below with recommendations for classification and supporting rationales.

ALLEGATION ONE: That on April 16, at approximately 2:30 A.M., Sergeant Scully inappropriately involved himself in an incident of domestic violence.

ALLEGATION TWO: Sergeant Scully drove to the house of his ex-partner, Lieutenant Raymond Molar. He did not use his police radio to call uniformed police, instead electing to inject himself into a potentially dangerous incident where uniformed personnel would have been in a better position to contain the situation.

ALLEGATION THREE: Sergeant Scully arrived on the scene and used inappropriate and out-of-policy escalating force. (Force may not be resorted to unless other reasonable alternatives have been thoroughly exhausted.)

ALLEGATION FOUR: After engaging in an inappropriate escalation of force, Sergeant Scully fired his police weapon, which resulted in the death of Lieutenant Raymond Molar.

ALLEGATION FIVE: Sergeant Scully removed from the Molar residence certain related case items that he believed would reflect badly on him in the subsequent investigation. (Note: The confidential nature of these materials prohibits notification and description of same in this letter of transmittal, but such notification will be made available to the accused upon discovery.)

CLASSIFICATION

It is recommended that all allegations be classified as *sustained*.

RATIONALE

It has been determined by investigating officers that Sergeant Scully had a prior relationship with the wife of the deceased. As a result, Sergeant Scully should have known that his involvement in this domestic dispute would not produce a favorable outcome. His reckless attempt to intervene in a family dispute where he had an emotional history, and his refusal to call for uniformed assistance, produced a situation that resulted in an undue escalation of force and the death of Lieutenant Molar. Further at issue is Sergeant Scully's prior relationships with both the deceased, Lieutenent Molar (ex-partner), and Molar's wife (former girlfriend). This throws doubt on his use of force and gives rise to questions of personal motive. It is also noted that on February 12, 1984, then-Patrolman Scully was involved in a physical altercation with the deceased in the underground parking structure at Southwest Division. This altercation resulted in the breakup of their partnership and Scully's transfer to West Valley Division.

COMPLAINT HISTORY ANALYSIS

Sergeant Scully's use-of-force history has been examined, and it has been determined that this officer has had six complaint investigations in ten years (none sustained). However, he has received one departmental admonishment due to a nonsustained Board of Rights involving the severe beating of a nineteen-year-old Hispanic gang member in Southwest Division. (It was determined by the board that some eyewitness accounts of the beating were perjurious, and this perjury resulted in the subsequent not-guilty verdict. However, in the estimation of Sergeant Scully's commander, some undue force had taken place.) In reviewing his complaint history, it has been decided that this officer has shown a pattern of failure to exercise good judgment. Additionally, he has received admonishments for two separate (preventable) traffic accidents. There are no negative-comment-card entries from his current commanding officer.

RELIEF FROM DUTY CONSIDERATION

It is recommended that this officer be relieved from his duty in Southwest Robbery/Homicide and that he be suspended without pay until further notice. Note: The complaint copy and Relief from Duty Suspension Form (1.61) issued by Internal Affairs Division and signed by Deputy Chief II Thomas Mayweather is being faxed to Sergeant Scully's CO, Captain Bud Halley, in accordance with departmental regulations. Upon receipt of same,

Sergeant Scully shall surrender his gun, badge, and identification card to Captain Halley for safekeeping.

RECOMMENDATIONS
The chief of police has directed this case to a full Board of Rights, said board to commence ten days from the date of this letter.

COMMANDING OFFICER'S RESPONSE
None.

Respectfully submitted,
Alexa Hamilton
Internal Affairs Division

PANEL

A LETTER OF TRANSMITTAL is always delivered to an accused officer and is, in essence, a summons and complaint. It gives the preliminary results of the IAD investigation and the determination by the department of the appropriate form of adjudication.

Shane had received the letter just before going out the door to pick up Chooch from school. He ripped open the brown envelope with trembling fingers. He had figured it would be bad, but this was even worse than he had expected. He shook with rage as he read the allegations. Then he stuffed the document into his side pocket and headed out the back door. *Fuck 'em,* he thought, *I'm not gonna plead this out. I'm gonna fight it.*

He pried the crushed front fender farther away from the tire, using the Acura's tire jack. Then as he took the 405 over the hill to Coldwater, he turned on his cell phone to call his new defense rep, Rags Whitman. He had talked with him once yesterday, but

Rags was in the middle of defending another BOR, so they had agreed to meet at six that evening.

He punched the number into his cell phone.

Rags Whitman was on a break outside hearing room three when he answered the phone. Internal Affairs had rented the top three floors of the Bradbury Building in downtown L.A. It was a beautiful turn-of-the-century structure with a glassed-in courtyard and black wrought-iron banisters. Because Parker Center had become so overcrowded, the entire Advocate Section of IAD, as well as its four main hearing rooms, had been moved to this architectural treasure at the corner of Broadway and Third.

"Yeah," Rags answered in his surprising soprano voice.

"It's Shane. I just got the Letter of Transmittal."

"Bad?" Rags asked.

"They suspended me without pay. They're alleging I shot Ray because I used to date Barbara. It's total bullshit!"

"You'll probably do much better with DeMarco, if that's the way they're going. He fights gladiator-style."

"DeMarco won't take the case."

"He changed his mind. Your machine was turned off. He's been trying to reach you all afternoon. He didn't have your mobile number, so I gave it to him. The way this is going, you better start leaving your cell phone on."

"Oh," Shane said. He'd turned his answering machine and cell phone off because he was afraid that Barbara would call. He'd been having second thoughts about seeing her and wanted to put some distance between them for the time being. "You got his number handy? I don't have it with me."

Rags Whitman gave it to him, and Shane dialed.

"Go," DeMarco said when he answered. Shane could hear a mellower brand of rap being played in the room behind the conversation. This time he thought it was L. L. Cool J.

"It's Shane."

"Where've you been? I changed my mind. I gotta get one more swing at that bitch advocate Alexa Hamilton. I've been trying to reach you all day."

"I had my cell off by mistake. I'm glad you reconsidered. I got this fucking Letter of Transmittal. It's a complete load a' shit. They're fuckin' me over, Dee."

"Meet me at the beach as soon as you can."

"I've gotta go pick up a friend's kid at school. I promised his mother. Okay if I bring him?"

"Sure, I'll meet you at the Silver Surfer. It's a bar-restaurant on the Strand, about six doors up from my place. How 'bout an hour?"

"How 'bout an hour and a half?"

"See ya then."

"Hey, Dee . . . thanks. I feel better with you on this. I wanna go to war. I don't wanna plead out this bullshit. I wanna fight it."

"We'll talk in an hour."

When he arrived at Harvard Westlake, Brad Thackery was waiting for him. Thackery followed Chooch to the car and immediately came around to the driver's side.

"We still haven't heard from Chooch's mother," he said angrily, shoving his thin, pinched features and wiry hair down into Shane's face.

Chooch got in the passenger side and pretended to pay no attention, looking out the side window at the football field.

"Whatta you want me to do about it?" Shane said sharply.

"I want you to have Mrs. Sandoval get in touch with my office."

"I told her to call you two days ago."

"Obviously, neither you nor she have any idea of the seriousness of Chooch's situation. This is about his future here at Harvard Westlake."

"I told Sandy. I can't do more than that."

"*Facta non verba*," Thackery said with a smirk, then added, "Actions speak louder than words."

"*Gobbelus feces*," Shane replied, and after a second to figure it out, Chooch burst into laughter.

Shane put the car in gear and pulled out onto Coldwater. He was smoking mad. Of course, he knew it wasn't Thackery, it was his whole damn life that was pissing him off.

"*Gobbelus feces*. Eat shit—pretty fuckin' good," Chooch crowed.

"Calm down, will ya . . . it wasn't that funny."

Chooch looked at him carefully, then turned off his headset and put the rig back into his book bag.

"Don't worry about Thackery, okay? It doesn't matter that Sandy didn't call. They're gonna throw me out anyway. It's a done deal. I'm not even in regular classes anymore. I'm in detention. They don't care if I do my homework or not. They're just sitting on me till they can tell her I'm dust."

"Shit," Shane said. "Good goin'."

"I don't care, so don't sweat it."

"Yeah, that's right, I forgot. I'm just this month's paid jerkoff."

"That was before. You're not a paid jerkoff anymore. You've been promoted."

"To what?" Shane was barely paying attention. His mind was spinning, a kaleidoscope of horrible, career-ending problems.

"You're my doobie brother," Chooch said with a grin, "my ganja gangtsa and Rasta weed warrior."

"Listen, Chooch, you gotta forget about that. Okay? I'm having a rough time right now, I'm not thinking straight. That was a huge mistake."

"Shit, it was the first thing you did that I liked. Showed me some stones, man. No other cop I know would sit around with some kid and bogart a fatty."

"Chooch, if you tell anybody about that, I'm gonna kill ya."

"No sweat. I can keep a secret." He smiled, then put his head-phones on again and cranked up the tunes. He stayed plugged in until Shane made the turn onto the Santa Monica Freeway. It was the wrong way home, so Chooch took off his headset and looked over. "Where we going?"

"I gotta go to a meeting down at the beach. It should only take an hour, maybe less. You can hang for a while, okay?"

Chooch cocked an eyebrow. "Something's going on, right? You're in the soup, just like me, aren't ya?" he said with sur-prising intuition.

"It's okay. I can handle it."

They shot off the end of the freeway, back onto the Coast Highway. Five minutes later Chooch and Shane were walking through the front door of an almost empty bar-restaurant with a sawdust floor and a neon sign that read SILVER SURFER.

It was 4:15 in the afternoon.

. . .

They found DeMarco seated at the bar. He was wearing cut-offs and a blue-jean vest with no shirt, working on his third beer. The other two empty brown glass longnecks were lined up on the bar beside him.

When Shane introduced DeMarco to Chooch, the teenager looked at the longhaired defense rep and smiled. "Cool fuckin' earring, dude."

"I like your friend, Scully. You're finally kicking." The defense rep smiled at Shane.

"Is it okay for him to be in here?" Shane asked, referring to the fact that they were in a bar that served hard liquor.

"Yeah, he can go play the video games over there. Technically, that's not in the bar area."

Shane dug into his pockets and gave Chooch some change.

The boy moved over to a small alcove in sight of the bar, sat on a stool, and began feeding coins into one of the machines.

Shane slid the Letter of Transmittal over to DeMarco, who read it carefully, then set it on the bar between them. "Mark, gimme another Lone Star," he yelled. "How 'bout you?" he asked Shane.

"Slow down on the brewskies, will ya? I'm on fire here."

"Then you're in luck. With this bladder, I can piss it out for you," DeMarco quipped. "In your telephonic absence, I went ahead and covered some pro forma ground. Tell ya this much, Alexa Hamilton doesn't let much grass grow under her magnificent gym-trained ass. She already got the rotation list for your judging panel and faxed it to me. Seven names: four sworn members of the department above the rank of captain and three civilians. If you remember how it works from before, you get to throw off two of the cops and two of the civilians, leaving you a panel of three judges: two sworn, one civilian." He reached into his blue-jean vest pocket and pulled out two slips of paper. "This ain't much of a beauty contest," he said, sliding both slips over to Shane. "In my opinion, all of these department guys are douche bags. Tell me who you like. I hate the whole bunch." DeMarco read the names aloud while Shane studied the list. "Captain Donovan McNeil, West Division; Commander Mitchell Van Sickle, Ad Vice; Deputy Chief Laurence Gadsworth—he's the chief's administrative staff officer, so forget him; and Captain Bernard Cookson."

"Jesus," Shane said, "except for Donovan McNeil, who I used to go fishing with occasionally, aren't these guys all in Chief Brewer's golf foursome?"

"Yep. But it gets worse. Look't the civilians: all lawyers from South Temple Street; one's a retired judge, a Crispin crony, of course. I checked the others—all work at the municipal courthouse and all have strong political ties to Mayor Crispin. This guy here, Knox Pooly, actually chaired his committee to reelect."

"What's going on here, Dee? This isn't right."

"No shit. You're getting screwed without the Vaseline. If Donovan's an old friend, I'm surprised he made this list of suckfish."

"He figures. A year ago he was the chief's community affairs officer. They probably picked him not knowing he was a friend of mine."

"Okay, so we keep him on the list and hope that he'll at least have divided loyalties. Who else?"

"Not Deputy Chief Gadsworth, of course. I'll take Commander Van Sickle." Shane looked at the list of three civilians and cocked an eyebrow at DeMarco for help.

"Beats me," DeMarco said. "Throw 'em out alphabetically or just drop 'em over your shoulder and the one closest to the door stays. Good a way as any."

"I'll take Clifford Finch. At least he's a defense attorney."

"Okay, then your panel is Captain Donovan McNeil, Commander Van Sickle—he'll be the chairman, based on rank—and Cliff Finch. Good fuckin' luck. This bunch would convict Santa Claus of home invasion, but I'll notify Alexa that these are our choices."

Shane sat and brooded as DeMarco was served his fourth beer, then started to gulp it down. "Go easy, will ya?" Shane murmured.

"When I'm being fucked, it feels better if I get a little loaded first," DeMarco said dourly. He picked up the Letter of Transmittal and reread the Rationale Section. "Two things here; let's take 'em in order. One: they think you took something from Ray's home."

"It's bullshit. I don't know anything about it."

"You wouldn't hold back on me again, would you, Shane? You did last time."

"I don't know what they're talking about."

"Okay, so what's with this old fistfight in the garage at Southwest Division?"

"Nothin', just frayed nerves. It was way back in '84, for God's sake. You and I were just going through the BOR. I was uptight. I boiled over, that's all."

"Shane, you gotta tell me the truth, the whole truth, and nothing but the truth; otherwise, we're gonna get blackjacked at that board. I'm gonna ask you again. What the fuck was going on between you and Ray and Barbara? Why did you get into that fight?"

"We never talked about it, but you knew who really beat that Hispanic kid half to death."

"My guess—it was Ray."

"Right."

"So, not that it matters all these years later, but why don't you do me a favor and finally spit it out. Tell me what happened."

"I was in a gas station, taking a leak. I came back to where our patrol car was parked, and Ray was beating this kid with his baton. I broke it up. If I hadn't stopped it, Ray would have killed him. Then, after the complaint got filed by the boy's family, Ray begged me to take the blame. The kid's head injuries had him blank on the incident. He couldn't remember who hit him. Since I was just a probationer and had no complaints on my record, Ray convinced me I would probably get only a few weeks' suspension. He said he'd make up my lost pay out of his own pocket. I was his partner—real young, impressionable. Back then I was just like some of these rookies today. I thought he was the best cop on the streets of L.A. He had a way of getting to you, making you believe in him. And he was brave. More than once he risked his life for a brother officer. His two Medals of Valor were not bullshit. So I said okay. I took the complaint for him. But later, while you and I were going through the hearing, I started having nightmares. In those dreams, Molar and I would both be beating that kid. We'd be taking turns. I'd wake up sweating, hating myself. I was under a lot of stress back then, and I guess it was the beginning of my seeing Ray for what he really was—a vicious, violent son of a bitch who wasn't a cop so he could protect and serve. He was a cop so he could kick ass and hold court in the street. . . .

"It boiled over that night in Southwest. Barbara had just broken up with me. I was under investigation at IAD, and I just snapped. I yelled at him. He went into the coffee room, got a pitcher of ice water out of the refrigerator, told me to cool off, and threw it on me. I pushed him; he fell; we ended up in the parking garage. It wasn't much of a fight."

"You were way out of your weight division," DeMarco said softly. "He had almost a hundred pounds on you."

"That's the whole story."

Again, DeMarco swigged on the beer. He put the bottle down and began making Olympic rings on the varnished bartop, stamping them out with the bottle's wet bottom. Finally he wiped his artwork away with his palm. " 'Nother longneck, Mark," he shouted.

"Listen, Dee . . . I hate seein'—"

"Give it a rest. Okay?" DeMarco said sharply. "Don't tell me how to lead my life. While you were running around with your cell phone turned off, I've been working this thing. I'm not through filling you in yet, so shut the fuck up." Shane nodded. "This morning I wrote up a standard petition to overturn the 1.61 and requested your return to duty. It's kinda pro forma when a police officer has been suspended without pay, like an automatic appeal, only I've never seen one get approved before. Guess what? You're the exception." He reached into his back pocket and shoved a fax over to Shane. "Signed by the Big Noise himself." Shane looked at the document. It was as DeMarco said, signed by Chief Burleigh Brewer. "The whole shebang, from application to acceptance, took two hours. Now go figure that."

"I can't," Shane said, staring at the fax in disbelief. The document put him right back on duty with full pay. It didn't make sense in the face of everything else.

"I called Bud Halley and asked him about it. He told me Tom Mayweather walked it through the system personally. However, Halley also told me where they've reassigned you. You're not in Southwest Detectives anymore."

"Where am I?"

"You ain't gonna believe it. . . ."

"Oh, shit. What is it this time, the grain and drain train at the city jail?"

"You've been assigned to the chief advocate's office at Internal Affairs."

"I've been what?!" he said, his voice so loud that Chooch momentarily turned away from the video game he was playing and looked in their direction.

"You report to the tin collectors at the Bradbury Building at eight-thirty A.M. tomorrow."

"That's nuts. I've never heard of an officer awaiting a Board of Rights being assigned to the very division that's trying to terminate him."

"Me neither. But after thinking it over . . ."

"They want to keep me where they can watch me," Shane said.

"A winnah. Give the man something from the top shelf. You is da new Dark Side kick-me. I guess Chief Brewer doesn't want you running around looking for whatever it is they think you took out of Ray's house. They want you on a tight leash."

The bartender brought DeMarco his new beer. He took three long swallows, then set it down with the others. "All in all, not a good start, Shane, but rigged boards are my specialty. These tin-collecting assholes can be had 'cause they all got target fixation. Just go down there and keep your nose clean. Let me do the grunting and groaning."

As he sat on the barstool, looking at the old defense rep, his heart sank, taking his hopes down with it. He had no choice. He had to go down to Internal Affairs. He'd been ordered, and failure to comply with a direct order was also a termination offense.

The only bright spot was that he was still on the payroll. He'd still collect his bimonthly base salary of $2,170.20, plus his ten-year longevity compensation of $60. In return, he'd be working down at IAD, forced to endure the biggest collection of milk-fed assholes on the planet. As he sat there, he decided that he would devote all of his nonworking hours to finding out what was missing from Ray's house.

"Yes! Kick ass!" Chooch yelled suddenly as his game buzzed victory and he was advanced to the next level.

"Don't worry, Shane. I'll unwind this for you. I'll get you off," DeMarco said, causing Shane to look back at him.

"*Factus non verba*," Scully said darkly.

THE PEOPLE RULE

As soon as Shane got home, he called Sandy. She said she was sorry she hadn't gotten in touch with Thackery, but promised she would. She said she'd had a tough two days.

"What'm I supposed to do with Chooch tomorrow?" Shane asked. "They've got him sitting in detention all day. He's not even going to classes."

"That guy Thackery is a complete ass," Sandy said. "He's on Chooch for smoking dope? What a hypocrite."

"Not smoking it, Sandy, selling it."

"I was there at the school two months ago when Chooch enrolled. Thackery was just driving out. He put down the window of his crummy, rusted-out van to talk to me, and the smell of old pot was so strong in that thing, I got a contact high."

"Sandy, lots of people smoke pot, okay? It's a sad social truth, but there it is. It doesn't matter what Thackery does in his off-hours. You've gotta call him and set up an appointment."

"Right. Okay, I promise, sugar."

"You promised yesterday."

"This time I pledge it. I *swear* it, okay?" She changed gears. "You go ahead and take him to school tomorrow. Forget Thackery. I'll have already called that snooty headmaster, Mr. St. John. I'll square him away. That guy is always leering at me. Wants to get in my pants."

"You always put things so delicately," Shane said, beginning to wish he'd never met the beautiful raven-haired informant.

"Don't be such a prude. When I get through with St. John, he'll be at Camp Fantasy, pitching a tent in his Jockey shorts. Don't worry about Chooch."

After she hung up, Shane went outside. Chooch was already out there in one of the metal chairs. Shane dropped his tired ass in the vacant seat beside him. They looked out at the still canal, both lost in separate thoughts. Finally Shane jerked his mind off his department problems and focused on the boy sitting sullenly beside him.

"If your mom and I could keep you in school," Shane started slowly, "would you go there and really give it a try?"

"Moot point, 'cause you can't. I already got the scarlet *E* for 'expel.' I'm gone, brother."

"Chooch, I've been thinking about it. You're really smart. You've got a great head on your shoulders. You could be something important in life. You have it in you to be anything you want."

"Like a cop?" he smirked.

"Better than a cop. You could go to college, pick any career. Your mom has money; she'll pay for anything. That's a big advantage for you. It's a chance most guys never get."

They sat in silence, looking at the still canal water, both of them rocking slowly in the old metal chairs.

"I know you're trying to help, man," Chooch finally said, "but it ain't about having a career. Y'know . . . it's just not what it's about. It goes much deeper than that."

More silence, then Shane turned in his chair to look at the teenager. "Wanna know something?" Chooch didn't answer. "I believe in you, Chooch," he went on softly. "I know that whatever you want, you've got the ability to get it. You've got what it takes. I think you're special."

"That's bullshit," Chooch shot back.

"No, it's not. I've been watching you . . . how you handle stuff. You've got guts. You stand up. You walk your own trail. That's very rare. It takes strength of character. Most people can't do that." More silence. "Listen. I told you I wouldn't lie to you— not ever. So this is the straight stuff. It's what I see in you, and it's impressive."

Chooch turned his face away from Shane. His breathing had changed. His right hand darted up and brushed his cheek under his eyes. Then he stood up, and anger flared. "Don't fuck around with me. Okay? I can't take any more bullshit. Just leave me alone." He moved quickly into the house.

Shane sat in his garden until the setting sun began turning the still canal bright yellow, then orange and purple, and finally black. After the sun surrendered its hold on the day, a cold evening wind came off the ocean, blowing marine air across the coastline. Shane was getting a chill, so he got out of his chair and walked back inside the house.

■ ■ ■

"It's fucking forty minutes too early!" Chooch glowered as Shane pulled up in front of the Harvard Westlake School the next morning. There were no waiting lines of foreign cars as Chooch opened the door and dragged his book bag from the front seat.

"I've got a new duty assignment downtown, so I need to get there early. Live with it," Shane said.

"Sure, no problem. Live with it. That's my fuckin' motto anyway." Chooch angrily moved away from the car and sat alone on a bench near the athletic pavilion.

Shane pulled out of the driveway and drove two miles to the Valley Division HQ. He figured if he hurried, he'd be able to get everything done before eight-thirty.

Fifteen minutes later Shane was back in the Harvard Westlake faculty parking lot waiting for Brad Thackery. After ten more minutes the assistant dean of admissions pulled his rusting Ford van into his parking stall and got out. Shane moved to him. "Good morning, sir," he said pleasantly.

"Maybe for you, but it's not a good morning for Chooch. I saw him sitting out front when I drove past. Since I still haven't heard from Mrs. Sandoval, you can just go right back around and pick him up and depart the premises, *ad quam primum*. He is no longer welcome at this school," Thackery said harshly, then added brusquely, "and remove your vehicle from faculty parking. This is a restricted area."

"How do you say that in Latin?"

"I'm through talking to you, whoever you are. Good-bye."

Shane pulled out his badge and held it up for Brad Thackery to read. Thackery looked at it, surprised, readjusted slightly, then with less anger said, "Big deal."

"You're right, it is a big deal, 'specially since your van there is crawling with vehicular irregularities. You wanna put that blinker on? Seems to me it wasn't working when you turned in here."

"I'm about to get it fixed."

" 'About to' doesn't cut it," Shane said. "Put it on, please. I want to check it out."

Thackery glared at Shane. "This is what really gets you guys off, isn't it?"

"Yep. Can't get enough of it."

As Brad Thackery opened the van, Shane moved to his Acura and opened the back door. A black Labrador jumped out and, with his tongue lolling, followed Shane back to the van. Thackery was leaning into the front seat, fiddling with the blinker and trying to get it to work, when the dog started barking and pacing back and forth along the side of Thackery's van.

"Whoa . . . whoa . . . whatta we got here?" Shane said with mock surprise. Thackery jerked his head out of the van.

"Get that dog away from me."

"This isn't a dog, Mr. Thackery, this is a drug enforcement officer. His name is Krupkee. It looks like Officer Krupkee's got a noseful. Where is it, boy? What ya got?"

The black Lab had moved to the rear of the van and now had both paws up on the spare tire, which was hooked by a locked bracket to the back of the van. Then the black Lab started barking and pawing at the tire.

"Oh boy, this ain't good, Mr. Thackery. You wanna give me the key that releases that back tire?"

"No. No, I don't."

"Lemme put it another way, sir. Gimme the key, or I'll pry the fucking thing off with my tire jack. Officer Krupkee just gave me probable cause for a search."

After a long moment, Thackery reluctantly dug into his pocket and produced the key that unlocked the tire bracket. Shane swung it away from the van and looked into the tire. There, attached by magnets to the inside of the tire drum, was a small metal box. Shane pulled it off and opened it. There were about four ounces of grass in a canvas bag and a bottle with a few pills. Shane opened the bag and poured some low-grade pot into his palm.

"This is not good, Mr. Thackery. As a matter of fact, you're under arrest, *regnat populus*." He poured the dope back into the bag. "So you won't get the wrong idea about me and think I'm some overeducated, Latin-quoting blowhard, that's just the state motto of Arkansas. I was stationed there in the Marines. It means 'the people rule,' and the people of Los Angeles don't like this one bit and are about to rule that you go to the city lockup."

Shane pulled out his handcuffs, spun Thackery around, and put them on.

"You can't do this," Thackery protested.

"Somebody should tell that to my watch commander. In the meantime, you're gonna sit this one out downtown. Don't worry, I'll call the principal for you and tell him his assistant dean of admissions is gonna be at County Jail riding the pine in the detox box."

"Is this about Chooch? Is that what this is all about?" Thackery's eyes were darting around, hoping no other member of the faculty would come driving in and witness this debacle.

"You bet it's about Chooch. But it's also about you, Brad. If you weren't such an insufferable asshole, I probably wouldn't have gone so far out of my way to knock your dick in the dirt."

"Look, Chooch has problems. Okay? He's got deep emotional difficulties. Besides, he's selling drugs."

"Bet he didn't sell you this crummy bag a' bird food," Shane said, holding up the bag of thin, seed-ridden grass.

"You think this is funny, is that it?"

"It's about as funny as prostate surgery. How do guys like you end up teaching school?"

"What do you want?"

"I want you to cut Chooch some slack. I want you to go to bat for him."

"I can't change the course of events. It's too late. They've already had a faculty meeting about him."

"I'd think the assistant dean of admissions would have a little pull around here," Shane said. "Of course, after this bust, you'll be lucky to be in charge of school bus schedules."

"Look, okay . . . maybe . . ."

"Maybe what?"

"If I . . . if I said to them I'd work with him separately, maybe do some drug counseling or something . . ."

"I don't think you're exactly the right guy for that, but go ahead, keep talkin'."

"Maybe if I really try, I could get him another chance. Just one . . ."

"Okay, that sounds more promising. You give him another chance, I give you another chance."

Just then, two other faculty cars pulled into the parking area and slowed as they passed Thackery's van. He was standing there with his hands cuffed behind him. A woman put down her window.

"Is everything okay, Brad?" she asked, looking at the handcuffs.

"We're fine." Shane said. "I'm the magician Mr. Thackery hired for next month's high-school assembly. Just showing Brad here how I do my handcuff escape." Shane smiled and she drove on, not looking too convinced.

"I want immediate results, Thackery. I'm looking for Chooch to get outta that detention hall this morning and back into regular class. If he gets goofy about anything in the future, don't bust him. Call me."

Shane shoved his business card into Thackery's shirt pocket and then unhooked the cuffs. He put the dope and pills in his jacket pocket, gave Brad Thackery back his car keys, then he led Officer Krupkee over to the Acura.

The Lab jumped into the backseat, Shane put the car in gear, pulled out of the faculty parking area, then drove back to Valley Division and returned the dog to the Valley Bureau Drug Enforcement Unit. He shot back onto the freeway and got to Internal Affairs downtown with ten minutes to spare.

THE DARK SIDE 12

THE BRADBURY BUILDING never failed to amaze Shane. He felt that it was the most magnificent building in Los Angeles. Only five stories high, it had been designed in the late 1800s by Gregory Wyman, a draftsman with no architectural degree. It sat bravely on the corner of Broadway and Third while slovenly men leaned forward to piss against her or curled up to sleep, rubbing the grime from their clothes on her magnificent yellow bricks.

Shane pulled into the modern concrete parking structure that had been built next door, took the ticket, then found a spot on the second tier. He rode the elevator down and came out onto a brick patio with umbrella tables that served as a lunch area. It was located directly behind the old building. Along the concrete wall adjoining the patio was the historic fresco depicting the life of an African-American woman named Biddy Mason. The wall chronicled her odyssey, from her birth as a slave in 1810, through her incredible life journey, all the way to her final heroic years of service as a nurse·delivering babies in Los Angeles hospitals in 1870.

The fresco had been placed there to show the early African-American commitment to the quality of life in L.A. Shane found it strange that in post–Rodney King L.A., this monument was behind the Internal Affairs building, in a patio where mostly cops accused of misconduct would ever see it.

He pushed through the back doors of the Bradbury, through a section under reconstruction on the first floor, into the building's magnificent covered courtyard. He looked up at the five floors stacked above him. Light brick contrasted with the intricate black wrought-iron railings. They wrapped around the interior hallways that surrounded the open atrium. Polished oak banisters snaked along the top of the ornate black-painted iron. On each side of the building's courtyard were beautiful, antique turn-of-the-century open elevators. They ran on exposed counterbalances that carried the filigreed boxes up and down. They moved slowly, stopping carefully at each floor as if time had not sped up in modern L.A. or had not fallen into desperate conflict with elegance. Over it all hung a glass roof five stories up, supported by black metal grates.

Shane stood there for a long time. He had been here for a week during his last BOR and had learned the rituals of the place. He knew about the waiting-room silence that followed the bustle of echoing voices in the atrium just before the nine o'clock commencement of the boards. He remembered the tense posture of witnesses and police officers as they leaned over the metal railings near the fifth-floor hearing rooms, waiting nervously to testify. There were the subtle, silent signs that were read only by the people familiar with the activity in the building and who spread the word on each board's outcome. The elevator operators watched carefully as accused officers left their penalty hearings, checking to see who was carrying the accused's gun. If it was in the advocate's hand, it meant the officer had been terminated.

The administration of LAPD justice churned relentlessly in the building, leaving bits and pieces of its victims' lives bobbing like scattered garbage in its wake. Like the Tower of London, it was way too beautiful a place for all the beheadings that occurred there.

Shane got on the elevator, rode to the third floor, and moved up to the heavy glass-paneled, wood-frame door of the Advocate Section. After taking a deep breath, he pushed it open and walked inside.

He was back in the narrow, gray and brown space fronted by three reception desks, where secretaries directed business to the twenty advocates seated behind them. Across the hall, on the opposite side of the open atrium, were the investigating officers, known as IOs. They were regular detectives assigned to IAD who did background interviews and took affidavits from "wits." All of Shane's memories of the place came rushing back. From where he was standing, he could see back to the advocates' cubbies located on the far side of the office. The advocates were all sergeants or lieutenants and worked in five-by-five clutter at small desks, cardboard "case" boxes filled with affidavits and IO reports clustered at their feet.

Shane remembered the chief advocate, a tall, vanilla milkshake named Warren Zell. Shane moved to one of the secretaries, a black woman with a remarkable body, and smiled at her.

"I'm Sergeant Scully. I've been assigned here. I'm supposed to report to Commander Zell."

"Hi," she said, "I'm Mavis. Take a seat. I'll tell him you're here."

While she buzzed in, Shane sat and picked up the LAPD newsletter, *The Blue Line,* that was on the table along with a stack of Chief Brewer's newsletters, a glossy white four-sheet called *The*

Beat. He assumed *The Beat* was required reading in this political squirrel cage. He was looking down when he heard the female voice that distressed him the most.

"Mavis," the voice said, "can you send all these 301's on the Scully deps out to the subpoena control officer and tell him I need them served as soon as he can get them issued? Also, make sure this charge sheet gets sent to Pam Davis in the District Attorney's Office. They're monitoring his board for a possible murder indictment."

He looked up and saw Alexa Hamilton standing with her back to him, wearing one of her severe, tailored gray suits. Her shapely calves and tight, rounded ass were only a foot from his face.

"Work, work, work," he said softly.

She turned abruptly and, for the first time, saw him sitting there.

"It's not work when you're having fun," she replied.

"Don't forget to subpoena Barbara Molar; she's an eyewitness and supports my statement word for word."

"We always include exculpatory evidence, despite what you think, Scully. This division exists to try and keep the department clean. We're not down here doing hatchet jobs."

"This division exists to destroy hardworking cops so people like you can get an E-ticket ride to the top of the department. You know it. I know it. Everybody on the job knows it. But don't take it from me, go ask any uniform sitting in the front seat of a Plain Jane."

Alexa stood there and tapped her thumb against a file folder. "Y'know, Scully, you mighta been an okay cop, except you've gotta do everything your own stiff-necked, jackoff way. You're always trying to be the smartest guy in the room, always cutting corners and blaming others. This is a division that is set up to defend the rules and mandates of this department. Since you have your head so far up your ass, you only see things through your navel; it's understandable your view is clouded. That's your problem, not mine." She turned to Mavis. "On second thought, Mave, I'm gonna walk this stuff over to the subpoena control desk personally. Nothing's too good for Sergeant Scully." She turned away and, carrying the paperwork, moved back to her desk behind the counter. Her hips swayed seductively as she walked. Shane felt nothing. She had turned his balls to ice.

The phone buzzed, twice.

"You can go in now," Mavis said.

Shane got up and headed down the long rectangular space between the east wall and the three reception desks. He entered Zell's office at the end of the room.

Seated behind a slab of oak was Commander Zell. He had his jacket off; a huge Glock automatic in an upside-down shoulder holster hung under his arm like a sleeping bat. It is a proven LAPD street-cop axiom that any officer in plain clothes who wears a shoulder rig is, by definition, an asshole. If it's upside down, then he's a puckered, purebred asshole. Zell looked up and pushed a stack of signed papers away as Shane entered.

"Sergeant, don't bother to sit, you won't be in my office that long." It was starting out worse than Shane had expected. "You're under my direct supervision," Zell went on, but while he spoke, he turned his attention to another stack of papers. "I expect you to report for duty at eight-thirty every morning, without fail. You have only half an hour for lunch, so I suggest you bring it. You punch out at five. It's a straight eight. No overtime will be approved. Questions?"

"Well, sir, I have to drop a fifteen-year-old boy at school every morning. I have to get him there by eight-fifteen. Eight-thirty is going to be pretty tight."

"Then here's your solution, Sergeant. You drop him off at eight instead of eight-fifteen." Zell finally looked up, fixing his gaze on Shane, as if to determine what sort of lame idiot wouldn't be able to figure that out by himself.

"Sir, if I might ask, what will I be doing?"

"You're the unit discovery officer."

"I'm sorry?"

"On every case going through here, the accused officer has the right to look at all statements and affidavits taken by our IOs. It's called *discovery*," Zell said, his voice dripping with sarcasm. "In order for the accused to get those documents, somebody has to Xerox the material, or make tape copies if it's a voice or video recording. The discovery officer works at the Xerox machines located on the second floor. There are four machines and some audio/video duplicating equipment. You make copies of everything, including personnel investigations, addenda, and any supplemental findings of proposed disciplinary action. Also include the response of the accused and the reply of the commanding officer, photographs or laser reproductions, rough field-interview notes, chronological records, case summaries, and the department wit list." He was ticking them off from memory, showing off. "Every case folder will tell you how many copies and where they are to be sent. They go out by registered mail to the accused officer's defense rep."

"I'm a Xerox machine operator?" Shane asked. He couldn't believe this was his new job.

"You are the unit discovery officer. Your job is to operate Xerox and electronic duplicating equipment. That's it. That's the job. You're excused."

"Wasn't there a crummier job you could have given me?" Shane asked, anger creeping into his voice.

"If you don't want the job, just tell me."

"Why? So you can hit me with a negligent-duty slip and put me in for insubordination?"

"Then go do what you've been asked to do."

"Yessir."

Shane moved out of the room and walked back down the hall. He stopped at Mavis's desk. "What room does the discovery officer use?"

"Room 256," she said. "It's locked. Here's the key." She handed him a key attached to a square wood block. It reminded Shane of a gas-station lavatory key. Appropriate. He was definitely in the toilet. As he moved out of the Advocate Section into the open corridor, he saw Alexa Hamilton coming back from the ladies' room. She passed him, her gaze straight ahead, as if he didn't exist or, more to the point, as if she knew he was about to disappear.

He punched the button for the beautiful old wrought-iron box. The elevator arrived and he got on. An elderly black gentleman in a dark blue blazer was running the lift.

"You must be new here," the old man said. "Whatchu gonna be doin'?"

"I'm the new discovery officer."

"Boy, good goin'. That sounds pretty darn important."

"Yeah," Shane said sadly. "No doubt about it. I am de man."

UNIT DISCOVERY OFFICER

AFTER CALLING Harvard Westlake and leaving a message for Chooch that he'd be late picking him up, Shane spent the morning Xeroxing cases in the narrow one-window office on the second floor. It was the only office that Internal Affairs had rented on two. Except for the occasional secretary who came in and dropped more cases on his stack, he was alone with his thoughts while the Xerox hummed and coughed up copies, passing its white light over the endless pages.

Shane wondered how much longer he should stay on the job. He'd pretty much run out of police department highway. He couldn't believe that the district attorney would ever bring murder charges. That was just being orchestrated by Chief Brewer to put pressure on him. But being terminated by Alexa Hamilton at his upcoming board was a distinct possibility. Except for Bernie Cookson, the judges were stacked against him. He would probably lose his tin and be kicked out, his seventeen-year pension going down the drain with the verdict.

He thought about Barbara Molar, how he wanted to hold her and make love to her, but this was immediately followed by a puzzling feeling of dispirited grief for something he couldn't identify. Moments later he was aware of a thickening depression. As the Xerox machine hummed and kicked pages into a tray, he tried to work it out.

He knew that pursuing a relationship with Barbara was stupid under these circumstances. Beyond that, something else was nibbling at his subconscious. He finally slapped it down and held it up.

It was a simple five-word question.

Why had Barbara married Ray?

What had led her to walk away from him and find solace in the arms of the most brutal cop on the force? She said that it was sweet to see tenderness in such a huge, seemingly brutish man.

Shane had known Ray almost from the day he'd joined the force, and he had never seen tenderness. Ray Molar was buffalo meat. His temper was always close to the surface, hiding there, waiting to explode. So why had Barbara married him? Why had she made such an obviously miserable choice?

With that question came another.

What weakness in her had caused her not to see Ray for what he was? Of course, Shane had also been fooled at first. But he'd had Ray as a partner. Having a kick-ass partner was considered a life-insurance policy in police work. Shane had misevaluated for reasons of his own survival. Why had Barbara been fooled?

His mind left that half-chewed thought and began on another. He had physical desire for her. He had once thought he loved her, but yesterday afternoon at Shutters, she had seemed to be trying to start up their relationship on the heels of Ray's death. He could understand cerebrally why this might be: she was lonely and scared, and Ray had been abusing her. She had come to hate him, but . . .

Ray had been her husband for twelve years. She had once slept in his arms. Yet his death seemed to hold no consequences for her. Shane had despised Ray, but he had not felt the same way since he'd squeezed off the round from his Mini-Cougar and watched his bullet explode in Ray's head. The picture of that death was on a macabre bulletin board in his psyche. He could not do anything without walking past it. Yet Barbara had no remorse, no guilt, no misgivings. To her, Ray's death was the doorway to her future. *What did that say? What did it mean? Had he been too young, immature, and blinded by lust to see any of her shortcomings back then? Had she changed . . . or had he?*

Shane looked at his watch. He was surprised to see that it was just a few minutes to twelve. He finished the case he was Xeroxing, then, following instructions, he put the copies in a manila envelope and addressed them to the defense rep involved. Then he put the packet in the OUT basket, where it would be picked up and sent off by registered mail.

He shut off the Xerox, locked the office door, dropped the key with Mavis, and headed out of the Bradbury Building on his lunch hour—make that *half hour*.

Shane wasn't hungry, so he decided to check on his Scientific Investigation Section request. He began to walk the four blocks to Main Street, where Parker Center was located. He needed to clear his mind. He made it a brisk outing, his arms swinging hard, his stride even and quick. When he got halfway there, he ran into another movie barricade. He badged his way through, walking along the sidewalk while wary assistant directors with head-mikes and walkie-talkies clipped on their belts glared at him. He was ignoring their barricades, trespassing on their superiority.

"You're in our shot, sir," one of them yelled.

Shane hurried along. Arnold was across the street with the

director, engaged in an animated discussion. There was a lot of gesturing and arm waving. Tourists and downtown office workers stood behind the barricades, holding their cameras at port arms, hoping for a shot while streetpeople angrily cursed this invasion of their living space.

Shane got to Parker Center and moved quickly to the Scientific Investigations Section on the seventh floor. He went down the corridor, hoping to remain invisible. Occasionally somebody would look at him, grab the arm of a companion, and start whispering. Shane could write the dialogue: *"That's him, right over there. Can you believe it? He shot Lieutenant Molar . . . they used to be partners."*

He got to SIS and asked for the results of his laundry tag analysis. A middle-aged woman with thick, red-rimmed Sally Jessy Raphaël glasses leaned across the counter with the results. "We got lucky. Most of the laundries in the database are local; this one is a ways away, but was still inside the sample area."

Shane looked at the printout. "Mountain Cleaners, Lake Arrowhead," he read aloud.

"That's what the computer says," she replied. Then almost as an afterthought: "I don't know if you missed it, but on the inside of the tag is a date, April tenth."

"Thanks," he said. "You're right, I missed it."

He moved away from the desk with the printout. The address was on Pine Tree Lane in Lake Arrowhead. He left Parker Center for the walk back to Broadway and Third, wondering why Ray Molar was getting his shirts done in Lake Arrowhead, and whether it really mattered.

Arrowhead was a two-hour drive up in the mountains. Shane had been there once or twice before. He remembered that the town sat in wooded splendor, around the ten-mile circumference of a beautiful freshwater lake. The community was picturesque, catering mostly to artists, writers, and L.A. refugees. A lot of old

Hollywood royalty had built huge mansions on the lake in the thirties, and some of these houses still existed—out-of-place old European-style homes with their stone walls and slate roofs.

When he got back to IAD, he picked up his key and trudged back down to the Xerox room. He unlocked the door and saw that a new case had been shoved through the mail slot. He picked it up and glanced at it as he walked across the room to drop it on the IN pile. Just as he was setting it down, he saw the name on the face sheet: PATROLMAN I JOSEPH CHURCH.

Shane stopped and looked at the sheet again. Joe Church was the patrolman who had escorted him yesterday morning, red light and siren, to see Chief Brewer. He flipped through the file, reading quickly.

According to the charges, three weeks ago Patrolman Church had been in a Code Thirty burglary car. He had accepted a call on a "hot ringer" in Southwest. A Hoover Street jewelry store was being robbed. It was a "There Now" call. Church had "rogered" the transmission but had not shown up for almost forty-five minutes. His Mobile Data Terminal showed him as being three blocks away. When he finally got there, the owner of the store had been beaten almost to death, and was still in the USC Medical Center. The IOs on the case stated that Church claimed he had never received the call, despite the fact that he had rogered it, and all of his communications and times were logged on his MDT as well as in the Communications Center.

Shane dropped the case back on the pile, not attaching much significance to it, except for one stray thought: *Why would an officer whom the chief of police had just personally directed to an IAD Board of Rights be given a special assignment by the chief to pick up and escort Shane to his office?* It didn't make sense. But then, nothing that had been going on lately made much sense.

He turned on the Xerox machine and spent the rest of the day burning copies in the hot, narrow room.

Shane punched out at five-thirty, walked back to his car next door, and headed to Harvard Westlake.

Chooch was sitting alone on the curb. Everyone else had been picked up. He stood slowly, then dragged both his book bag and ass over to the car and got in.

"Sorry. We're gonna have to make new arrangements for the pickup. I can't get back here till five forty-five. I sent you a message. I hope they gave it to you."

Chooch was strangely quiet. He just nodded.

Shane put the car in gear and headed up onto the freeway, back to Venice.

"Did you have some kinda talk with Mr. Thackery?" Chooch finally asked after almost ten minutes of silence.

"No, why?" Shane said, glancing over at him.

"I don't know. He pulled me out of study hall. It was like he was a different guy, wants to be my bud. He said I was gonna get another chance, that he had gone to bat for me."

"I'll bet your mom called and set him straight. Sandy did pretty good, huh? I'm telling ya, you got your mother down in the wrong column, Chooch."

"Yeah . . . What column is that, the 'Don't bother me, I'm always busy' column? She's had me in boarding school since second grade. Up at Webb School in Ventura, I never even got to come home at Christmas. I was the only kid left in the dorm over the holidays. I was being watched by custodians . . . had to eat at the headmaster's house. Sandy's some mom, all right. We gotta get her a Mother's Day award."

"People aren't always what they appear to be," Shane persisted. "Your mom has reasons. Her job takes her away a lot. She's trying to give you a great education. She wants you to have a good start in life."

"Thackery said if I have any problems, or if I want to talk, I should look him up," Chooch said, changing the subject. "As if I'd even tell that dickhead which way was due north."

"Look, Chooch, if he's changing his tune, don't hawk a lugie at him."

"He's a prick."

"Yeah, maybe. Or maybe he's had a change of heart. If he's trying to cut you some slack, take it."

"And you believe him?"

"Yeah. Yeah, sure, I believe him. Hey, look, Thackery may be okay underneath all that Latin he quotes. Maybe he's just a guy who's scared, like us."

"I ain't scared a' nothin'."

"Then you're the only one on the planet, Chooch. Everybody is scared."

"Were you scared when you shot that guy?"

Shane looked over. He had not discussed the incident with Chooch, and he didn't have a TV. He was foolishly hoping it would never come up.

"It's all over school," Chooch said, reading his look of dismay. "So tell me. When you offed him, were you scared?"

"Yeah. Yeah . . . I was scared to death. I was shitting bricks."

Chooch sat there for a long moment thinking. "Physical stuff doesn't scare me. I'm not afraid a' getting bombed on or fucked over that way. But"—he hesitated for a moment, his eyes on the road ahead—"sometimes I'm afraid that what I believe in isn't true, that everything I think is true was just set up by somebody to fool me."

Shane nodded. "Yeah, I've been getting some of that myself lately."

"And sometimes, just once in a while, I want to be the most important, instead of the least. . . ." He paused for a long time, his face in a wrinkled frown. "Sometimes I'm scared I'll never have anybody who gives a shit."

They rode in silence.

Finally they got back to East Channel Road. Shane pulled the car into the garage, and they went into the house. Shane closed the door and watched as Chooch dragged his book bag into his room, to sit there with desperate, lonely thoughts that probably matched his own.

 A.K.A.

SHANE SAT in his living room listening to an occasional siren, which always seemed to come from the east, where the gangbangers held their nightly life-ending turf parties. It was six o'clock and the sun had just gone down. He put his mind back on his problem.

Any police detective worth his salt always started a case by arranging known or probable facts in chronological order. Shane took a piece of paper off the table and began making notations:

1. Late Feb. or early March, Ray Molar gets a job driving for Mayor Crispin.
2. March, R.M. begins not coming home.
3. April 2, Joe Church fails to respond to Hoover St. robbery (related?).
4. April 10, R.M. gets shirts done at Mountain Cleaners.

5. April 14, B.M. gets phone call from mystery woman/tape coming.
6. April 16, 1:30 A.M., R.M. gets home, beats B.M.
7. April 16, 2:35 A.M., R.M. shot (no tape found in house).
8. April 16, 5:17 A.M., T. Mayweather does DFAR (S.S. secure files in IAD possibly accessed).
9. April 16, 6:00 A.M., S.S. threatened by Kono and Drucker, police garage.
10. April 16, Joe Church escorts S.S. to C.O.P.
11. April 16, C.O.P. threatens S.S. with murder indictment. Wants case material returned.
12. April 18, Samansky, Ayers break in and search B.M.'s house (no tape found). Warrant signed by Hernandez, Crispin appointee.
13. April 18, Letter of Transmittal arrives. S.S. suspended. S.S. motive for murder mentioned.
14. April 18, T. Mayweather walks 1.61 appeal through department. S.S. back on duty.
15. April 19, S.S. reports to IAD (DA intends to audit BOR).

He stopped writing and looked at the list. It was his first chronological log. There were huge holes in his time line. Aside from the missing tape, there was Ray's increasingly violent behavior toward Barbara. Also, the list made it even more obvious that there was some kind of link between Ray and the top floor of the Glass House, and that it might have to do with Mayor Crispin. The list directed him to where he had to look next. He needed to find out why Molar had his shirts done ninety miles away. He looked at his watch—seven o'clock. Shane turned on his desk lamp and picked up the phone. He got the number for the laundry on Pine Tree Lane in Arrowhead and dialed. After a few rings, a man's voice came on the line.

"Mountain Cleaners," the voice chirped.

"Yes. Who am I speaking to?"

"This is Larry Wright."

"Mr. Wright, I'm Sergeant Shane Scully, with the LAPD. I'm working a case and I have some dry-cleaned shirts that were done at your laundry. I'm trying to find out who dropped them off."

"I see, well, without looking at the tags, I wouldn't know. They're bar-coded; I'd have to run them through our scanner."

"This case is pretty important. If I got in my car, I could be up there in two hours. I know it's an imposition, but do you think we could make an appointment to meet about nine tonight?"

"No problem. I'm usually stuck here till nine-thirty."

"Great. I'll bring the shirts with me." He hung up and dialed Longboard Kelly.

"Yer tappin' the Source," the surfboard shaper answered. Kelly believed "the Source" was a magical place where great waves came from.

"It's Shane. You think you could come right over and keep an eye on Chooch for a couple of hours?"

"I'm busy crankin' off an eight-ball, dude. After I finish, I could make it."

"You're doing what?" Shane asked.

"I'm on the throne, takin' a shit. Gimme five."

"Great. I'll pay you."

"What for, man? One day, if I get busted, you play the 'Get Brian out of jail' card."

"Right. Only we took that card out of the deck. How 'bout I play the 'Put in a good word for Brian' card instead?"

"Agreed, dude! I'll be right over."

Shane hung up.

He went into the guest bedroom. Chooch was hunched over the desk, doing his homework. Shane had a momentary stab of "parental" gratitude. "It's great you're doing your studies," Shane said proudly.

Chooch looked over at him, and Shane saw that he had a Game Boy on his lap.

Shane's expression of gratitude was replaced with exasperation. "I'm gonna run out for a few hours. Kelly is coming over to be with you."

"Cool. He's kickin'."

"Right. When are you gonna get back to your studies?"

"I'm just takin' a break, man. You don't get breaks down at that duck farm where you work?"

"Yeah, I get breaks. I'll be back before midnight."

"Solid."

Shane left the room, got his coat, collected his badge, and grabbed one of the bagged dry-cleaned shirts, which he had hung in the closet. He headed out the back door.

As the garage door was going up, a car's headlights pulled in right behind him, blocking his exit. He put a hand on his belt holster and cautiously moved toward the driveway. As he rounded the back of his car, he could see Barbara Molar's red Mustang convertible. When she turned off her headlights, he saw her behind the wheel, a scarf tied around her hair.

"Shit, Barbara, whatta you doing here?"

"I had to come over. I couldn't reach you. Your machine was off and your cell phone is out of service."

"If they catch us together, *I'm* gonna be out of service," he said quickly.

"Shane, I'm getting phone calls at the house. Spooky calls. I'm being threatened."

"Go park a few blocks away. Lock up. I'll drive over and pick you up."

She nodded and followed his instructions. Shane got behind the wheel and backed the Acura out. He drove up East Channel Street to where Barbara was standing, her arms wrapped around her, shivering slightly in the cold marine air. She had put up the

Mustang's top and, he hoped, locked the car. Shane reached over and threw open the passenger door. Barbara got in. He put the Acura in gear and pulled off East Channel to a side street, keeping one eye on his rearview mirror.

"Who's calling?" he finally asked. He could tell she was panicked. Her features were drawn; she seemed even more pale than normal.

"It's a man's voice. He just says, 'If you've got what we want, turn it over, or you'll pay the consequences.' Stuff like that. Then a couple of calls where there was just breathing first, then somebody said, 'Do the right thing, bitch,' and hung up."

Shane pulled to the curb and parked. "That means they still haven't found what they're looking for."

"I'm scared."

"So am I."

She looked at the shirt between them on the front seat. "Is this one of Ray's?"

"Yeah. The laundry is in Arrowhead."

"Arrowhead?"

"You got any idea why he'd have his shirts cleaned all the way up there?"

"None."

"It doesn't make much sense," Shane said. "He was driving the mayor. Arrowhead is two hours out of L.A."

"Maybe the mayor had personal business there."

"Maybe."

"What are you going to do?"

"I was just heading up to Lake Arrowhead to talk to the cleaner. I wanna see what I can find out from the guy. They have customer information on the bar code of this laundry tag." He held up the shirttail with the purple tag attached.

"I wanna go with you. And don't tell me no. I'm scared. I can't go home. Those calls are terrifying me."

"Barbara, the DA is contemplating indicting me for murder.

My motive, they think, is that I killed Ray to be with you. If we get caught riding around together, I will be trying to explain it in court."

"Take me with you," she said again. "Please. I need company. I'm shaking."

Kinetic thoughts were buzzing around, bouncing off unanswered questions with pinball energy. Then without really weighing his answer, he just nodded.

"Okay," he said impulsively, and put the car in gear. They headed up the street.

Shane turned right onto Washington Boulevard, which took him to the 405, then north to the 10, which would lead them east toward San Bernardino and Lake Arrowhead.

• • •

The road was narrow and winding. His headlights swept across shadowy tree trunks that lined the two-lane highway in the Angeles Mountains. Shane had his eye on the road, but his mind was on Ray Molar.

Barbara sat silently beside him. She had started the trip with a lot of chitchat, then had tried to swing the conversation to her future, what she would do with her life now that Ray was gone. Then she made the leap to how Shane was feeling, how he felt about her and about them.

Shane had deflected it all, keeping his answers short. He was beginning to suspect that Barbara had some hidden agenda, but he couldn't yet tell what it was. Maybe it was just his cop instincts that distrusted everything. But something was telling him to pull back—to defend his perimeter.

While she talked, he had been thinking about the night of the shooting: the two critical minutes from the time he'd gone into that bedroom to the moment he had peeled the Nine at Ray. Something in his Letter of Transmittal had stuck in his mind. The department had accused him of inappropriate use of force, of bad judgment, which had escalated the situation out of control. *Had he fucked up? Why had he taken his gun? Had he anticipated shooting Ray? Had he acted out of policy? Was there a way he could have prevented Ray's death?* The only other witness to the event was sitting next to him, so after weighing the consequences, Shane gingerly broached the subject.

"Barb . . . the night I shot Ray . . . how well do you remember it? You looked almost unconscious, as if he had stunned you with that blow to the head."

"I remember it all. It's indelible. It's branded in my memory," she said bitterly.

"Do you think I had any other choice but to shoot him?"

"What are you talking about?"

"If I'd called in some uniforms, would it have made a difference?" he asked.

She turned in her seat and looked directly at him. "You mean, if you had called in a 415? Would it have changed things?" she said, using the cop's radio code for a general disturbance, the majority of which ended up being domestic disputes.

"Yeah. What if two blues had come through that door instead of me, Ray's ex-partner, your old boyfriend . . . do you think it would have changed anything?" He was straining to hear her answer as he drove, straining to evaluate any nuance in her voice.

"Are you joking?" she said, snorting the words derisively. "He was insane." She was incredulous now. "Ray was crazy. *You* know it. *I* know it. He went nuts on spec. Once he snapped, he didn't care what he did or who he did it to. It wouldn't have mattered if Robocop or Pope John Paul himself had come through that door."

"Do you think if I'd held fire that he—"

"If you'd held fire, Shane, you and I would both be dead, and somebody else would have the fucking coffin decorations. You can't be serious."

He looked over at her and could see that she was almost angry about it. Finally he nodded. "Yeah, okay," he said. "I was just wondering."

She shook her head in amazement, and they remained silent the rest of the way to Lake Arrowhead.

The two-lane highway led into a small, lush, wooded valley and then descended into the beauty of Lake Arrowhead. A-frame houses and log-cabin architecture dotted the roadside.

The buildings on the main street were rustic, the sidewalks narrow. They found Pine Tree Lane, and Shane pulled up to Mountain Cleaners. He and Barbara got out, entered, and found Larry Wright.

After Shane showed his badge, he gave Mr. Wright the shirt. The man walked into the back, leaving Shane and Barbara standing alone in the neon overhead lighting, looking into the area where the finished dry-cleaning hung on a moving conveyor belt. In less than two minutes, Mr. Wright returned.

"Got it." He smiled at them. "These were done for Jay Colter. He lives at 1276 Lake View Drive.

"Then they're not Ray's?" Barbara said.

Shane waved her off, then reached into his pocket and pulled out an old photograph he had brought of himself and Ray when they were both working together in Southwest. The picture had been taken in a bar. They were EOW in plain clothes and had their arms around each other's shoulders, grinning drunkenly at the camera. "Is this Jay Colter?" Shane asked, handing the picture to Mr. Wright.

He looked at the shot and nodded. "Little heavier now, but that's him."

"You know what he was doing up here?"

"Well, I only talked to him once. Seems to me he said he was a builder, or in construction, maybe. . . . A builder, I think it was."

"Okay, thanks, Mr. Wright. That's a big help."

They moved out of the cleaners and stood on the curb under

a streetlight. "What's going on?" she asked. "Jay Colter? Why would he change his name?"

"When we were partnered, Ray told me once that if I ever worked undercover and was going to use an alias, I should choose a name that sounds close to my own. So if somebody calls out to you using your assumed name, you will react to it, instead of forgetting it's your alias. For instance, a good a.k.a. for Shane Scully might be Lane MacCully."

"And Ray Molar would be Jay Colter. But why?"

"Let's go see who lives at 1276 Lake View Drive," he said.

BADGER GAMES

THEY FOUND the address on Lake View Drive. Shane drove the black Acura slowly past the house. The small cabin-style bungalow was lit up. They could see men moving around inside.

"What do you think they're doing?" Barbara asked as Shane slowed the car but didn't stop. He pulled up the street and turned left at the first intersecting road. He drove half a block up, parked, and turned off the headlights.

"Who are they? What're you gonna do?" Barbara pestered as Shane got his zoom-lens camera out of the trunk.

"Stay here," he ordered, and quickly moved down to Lake View, then crept along the sidewalk toward the target house. He heard something behind him and spun around. Barbara was hovering nearby.

"Go back. This could be dangerous."

"Maybe I know one of them," she said.

Shane realized that it was a good thought, so he nodded, then put a finger up to his mouth for silence. They crept along, slower this time, finally getting to a position of advantage behind a hedge across the street from the lake cabin. Shane put the zoom-lens camera to his eye and adjusted the focus, bringing the small house closer.

Through the front window he could see men moving around, carrying boxes and emptying drawers. He snapped a few pictures with the flash off, hoping that if he pushed it in the lab, he would get adequate resolution in spite of the low light. Through the viewfinder, he could see the men clearly. He didn't recognize any of them.

"What d'you see?" she whispered in his ear.

"They're tossing the place, looking for something, same as at your house," he said softly, handing her the camera. "You recognize anyone?" After a minute she shook her head and handed the camera back.

They continued to watch the house for another twenty minutes. Several times one or two of the men carried a cardboard box out and set it near the back door. Shane used up an entire roll of film, and then finally the men turned off the lights, locked up the house, and carried the boxes down to the little dock on the lake.

Shane moved out from behind the hedge, with Barbara at his heels. He ran in a crouch until he got to the side of the house, in time to see the men load the boxes into a small, old-style, wooden reproduction Chris-Craft, with varnished sides and teak decking. They all jumped aboard, and the boat's engine roared. It pulled away from the dock and sped off across the lake, leaving a white-foam wake that glistened in the mountain moonlight.

"Shit," Shane said, "I was hoping they had a car parked around here so we could follow them."

He turned and moved back to the house. He tried the doors. They were all locked. Then he took out a pocketknife. He crept onto the wooden back deck that overlooked the lake, and inserted the blade into the sliding glass door. Slowly he pushed the latch up, then slid the door open. He and Barbara stepped cautiously into the small two-bedroom house.

Shane moved to the back hallway and turned on a light. It threw a low glow into the front room and would slightly illuminate most of the rooms in the small house. He didn't want to light up the whole place and call attention to their presence.

"What're we looking for?" Barbara whispered.

"Evidence that Ray lived here or used this place," he said.

"Y'mean like this," she said, picking up a small framed photograph off the living-room TV. It was Ray with his arm around a very pretty dark-haired woman. They were both laughing, holding up glasses of champagne. Slightly out of focus in the background was a small wooden church with a sign that read:

THE MIDNIGHT WEDDING CHAPEL
LAS VEGAS, NEVADA

Barbara looked at the picture, and her expression turned dark. "Is this what I think it is?" she asked sharply. "Is this a fucking wedding photo?"

"I don't know." He removed the picture from the frame and put it in his pocket.

They moved through the house. The cottage appeared to be some kind of party pad. Both bedrooms sported huge king-size waterbeds, complete with ceiling mirrors. Shane looked around, opening drawers, searching closets. All were now empty; everything had been removed. When he got to the guest bedroom, he noticed that the closet seemed very shallow, with no hanging rods. He tapped on the back wall. It sounded hollow. He searched around the edges of the closet wall until he found a small kick-plate near the floor. He touched it with his toe, and the back wall of the closet opened on a spring hinge. He pushed "the wall" and found that he was in a small, dark area, about six by ten feet. From where he was standing, he was looking through a glass window, directly into the master bedroom.

"Barbara," he called to her, "go into the master bedroom and stand by the bed."

"Okay," she called from the kitchen, where she had been searching the cupboards. She went into the bedroom, and he could see her clearly through the window in the wall in front of him.

"Go to the mirror over the dresser," he said. She walked to the dresser and was now standing only a few feet away, looking directly at him through a one-way mirror.

"Where are you?" she asked.

"In here, in the guest bedroom."

She moved away from the mirror, exited the master bedroom, and in a minute was pushing the wall open and entering the small back closet he had discovered. Shane found the overhead light and flipped it on. The room was empty except for a vacant book-shelf.

"What is this?" she asked.

"Glory hole," Shane said, using the cop term for any opening used for sexual spying. He began looking around the secret room. Finally he pulled an empty bookshelf away from the wall. He found two videotape boxes that had slipped down behind the shelf and had been missed. He picked them up—they were empty. One of the boxes was not labeled, but the other had a name written on the spine:

CARL CUMMINS

"What were they doing?"

"Looks like some kind of variation on the Badger Game. They get a guy up here, have a party, videotape the funny stuff, then blackmail him."

"Ray was doing this? Ray and that girl?"

"I don't know. I'm not sure. Early in an investigation, it's best not to jump to any conclusions," he said. "Are there any Baggies in the kitchen?"

"Yeah, that kitchen is completely stocked," she said.

They moved out of the videotape room and into the kitchen. Barbara found a large Baggie, and Shane dropped the videotape box into it while she held it open. Then he pulled the photo out of his pocket and dropped it in, too. Suddenly they heard the back door open, and froze.

"In there," he whispered, pointing to the pantry.

A breathless moment, then the light Shane had turned on in the back hallway went off. The house was thrown into darkness.

As they crouched in the darkened pantry, Shane slipped his service revolver out of his belt holster and pulled the hammer back. He held the Smith & Wesson .38-caliber roundwheel out in front of him with both hands, using a two-hand Weaver grip. He could hear three, maybe four men conducting a careful search, looking for them. One of the men moved into the kitchen.

"In here, Cal," the man called out. The kitchen lights went on, exposing Shane and Barbara cowering in the back of the pantry. Shane aimed his revolver at the overhead light and put a round in the fixture, shattering glass and throwing the kitchen back into blackness.

Then all hell broke loose.

Gun muzzles flashed in the darkness. Shane pushed Barbara down, grabbed a can off the pantry shelf, and threw it out into the kitchen. It landed on the counter across the room, and where it hit, shots rang out, breaking glass.

Shane grabbed Barbara's hand and pulled her out of the pantry, into the kitchen. He ran full into one of the men, knocking him down, then heard the man's gun hit the floor and slide on the linoleum. Shane dove into the dining room, pulling Barbara. When they landed, two more shots lit the kitchen with their muzzle flashes as the slugs slammed into the dining-room wall over their heads. Shane rolled off his back, came up into a sitting position, and blindly fired all five of his remaining shots into the kitchen. He heard somebody yell in pain, then there were footsteps running. The back door was thrown open. He could hear people fleeing along the side of the house.

"Barbara, you okay?" he whispered.

"Uh-huh," she replied.

Shane got to his feet. His gun was empty, so he knocked open the revolver, tilted it up and dropped the hot brass into his palm, then quickly dumped the shells into his jacket pocket. He pulled his quick-load off his belt and pushed the six-slug package into his open revolver, then snapped it shut. A speedboat at the dock started, and he heard it roar away.

"Stay there," he said, and stepped into the kitchen, his gun out in front of him, combat-style. He moved slowly across the room and finally found the light switch in the pantry. He flipped it on. Whoever he had hit had left about half a pint of blood behind, but somehow had managed to escape. Then he heard a siren's distant wail across the lake.

"These bohunk sheriffs have even better response time than we do," Shane said. "Let's get outta here."

He had dropped the bagged videotape box in the gun battle, and it took him almost half a minute to find it. On his way out of the kitchen, he saw an answering machine sitting on the counter. He grabbed the entire unit and yanked it out of the wall. Then, leading Barbara, he ran out the side door of the house.

The siren was dangerously close. Shane ran up the street, pulling Barbara along. Suddenly he stopped, reached down, and stuffed the videotape box, camera, and answering machine into an overgrown hedge, wedging it way down, out of sight.

Shane and Barbara sprinted to his car. He got behind the wheel, and they took off. As he streaked out of the side street, he ran right into the headlights of the arriving sheriff's car. Shane jerked the wheel, hit the gas hard, and powered past the black-and-white. The sheriff's car spun a U-turn and came after them.

"What're you doing? Why don't you stop? You're a cop!" Barbara shouted.

Shane didn't answer. He had his hands full and his foot on it, trying to take as many corners as he could to get out of sight of the pursuing police unit.

Finally he made a skidding right turn and accelerated down a narrow street. Bad choice. He had picked a residential cul-de-sac and slammed on the brakes. He started to turn around when the sheriff's car squealed in behind them. The two cops were out instantly, crouching behind their squad-car doors. One had a shotgun resting in the window frame.

"On your stomach, assholes!" the shotgun officer yelled. "Do it now!"

"Do as he says," Shane ordered Barbara. He opened the door, dropped his revolver, and kicked it across the pavement toward the sheriff's car. "LAPD!" he yelled.

"On your stomach, now!" the man repeated. Shane and Barbara did as they were told. In seconds he could feel a sheriff's deputy's hot breath on his neck, and cold steel handcuffs on his wrists. They were ratcheted down hard. In L.A. it was what they called an "adrenaline cuff." His hands were pinned painfully behind his back, then he and Barbara were jerked up onto their feet and shoved into the back of the sheriff's car.

COP SHOP

16

THE ARROWHEAD SHERIFF'S DEPARTMENT was wedged in between a gas station and a small country market. The parking lot behind the station had three empty Plain Janes.

Shane and Barbara were unloaded from the back of the patrol car and shoved angrily into the station. The two arresting officers were still burning off their chase adrenaline.

Shane was pushed into a chair at the booking desk while Barbara was taken into another room. Separate interviews were always the rule in any half-decent police department. All cops quickly learned that most criminals never expect to get caught. As a result, they rarely have a cover story. One would tell you he was going to the market to get beer; the other would say they were picking up a sick aunt. Separating suspects to take statements was pro forma.

Shane was pissed at himself for making the same dumb mistake as every deadhead felon he had ever busted. He didn't know what Barbara would say, so he planned to tell them the exact truth.

The Arrowhead Sheriff's Department was in turmoil. Earlier that day they had found a dead body in the lake. From what Shane could pick up, it was so decomposed that they hadn't been able to make an ID. In L.A., a dead body was no big deal, but up here an unexplained death was the kind of unusual tragedy it should be everywhere. Shane watched as the tall, balding, fifty-five-year-old sheriff of Arrowhead made multiple calls to the coroner's office. After five minutes he hung up and walked over to Shane. His nameplate read SHERIFF CONKLYN.

"Sorry to add to your problems, Sheriff," Shane said pleasantly.

"What's your story?" Conklyn asked angrily.

"I'm LAPD. I'm up here working on a case."

The sheriff nodded to one of the deputies, who handed Shane's leather ID wallet to Conklyn. He opened it and looked at Shane's tin.

"If you're a cop, why did you run?" the sheriff said, looking at him critically.

"I'm out of my jurisdiction and I didn't take the time to check with you guys like I should have, so I just decided to get small," he said. "Bad choice. Your guys were magnificent."

"Put away the jar of Vaseline," Conklyn said. "You got a CO we can call?"

"I'd really appreciate it if we didn't have to do that," Shane said. "He's not going to be happy."

"It's a big club. I'm not happy." He pointed to his deputies. "They're not happy. You're up here on Lake View Drive, busting caps, and now I've got lots of unhappy people in houses up there. All of a sudden it's like Mexican New Year."

"My captain is Bud Halley," Shane relented. "He's in Southwest Division Robbery/Homicide."

The sheriff took one of Shane's business cards out of his wallet and went to the phone. He talked softly for a minute, waited, then hung up and dialed another number. The second call was taking entirely too long, and Shane's danger lights started flashing. After another minute Sheriff Conklyn moved back and unhooked Shane's cuffs.

"He wants to talk to you," he said.

Shane went behind the counter and picked up the phone. "Captain?"

"It's Tom Mayweather," the deputy chief said in his resonant baritone voice. "Halley transferred this to me 'cause you're in my division now. What the fuck are you doing in Arrowhead, Scully?"

"Sir, something is definitely not right. Ray had a second house up here and another identity, maybe even a second wife."

"Says who?"

"Sir, a dry cleaner identified his picture and gave us the alias he was using. His picture was inside the house, on top of the TV."

"Scully, you are really pissing me off. Read your fucking badge; it says LAPD. You're ninety miles out of your jurisdiction with Ray Molar's widow, engaging in a gun battle with who the hell knows who. Then you have the stones to try and tell me Lieutenant Molar had two identities and a second wife. He was assigned to the mayor, for God's sake."

"Sir, I—"

"Shut up!" Mayweather said. "Here's what you do. I'm gonna alibi your fucked-up story with Sheriff Conklyn. He'll cut you and Mrs. Molar loose. Then I want you to leave Arrowhead and drive directly to Los Angeles. I want you to park your car in the Parker Center garage, then turn yourself in to the Homicide Division duty officer. Send her home in a cab. I want this all to happen in less than three hours. Are we straight on this, Sergeant?"

"Yes, sir."

"Put the sheriff back on."

Shane motioned to the sheriff, who took the phone, listened for a minute, then nodded. "No problem," he said, and hung up.

Fifteen minutes later Shane and Barbara were back in the parking lot behind the sheriff's station. Barbara rode in the front seat as one of the arresting deputies drove them back to the Acura and let them out.

"Good luck solving your John Doe murder," Shane said pleasantly.

"Want some advice from a fellow badge carrier?" the deputy said.

"You bet." Shane smiled, trying to be as nonconfrontational as possible.

"Don't ever come back up here."

"Okay, sounds reasonable." Shane put out his hand, but the cop just looked at it.

"All right, then. Good deal," Shane said, pulling his hand back.

He and Barbara got into the Acura and drove away, staying five miles below the speed limit. Shane kept his eyes on the rearview mirror. The squad car was going to follow him all the way out of Arrowhead. He drove slowly down the mountain, until the black-and-white finally turned off and headed back toward town.

Shane pulled over and parked. He looked at his watch.

"What're you doing?" she asked.

"Giving this guy fifteen minutes to forget about us."

"Only fifteen minutes?"

"Small-town cops have short attention spans," he answered, then added, "I hope." They sat and listened to the motor cool.

"What is it?" Barbara said, noticing a frown on Shane's face.

"Those guys in the speedboat? I was thinking, how did they know we were in the house?" Barbara shrugged. "I think the place is bugged. They heard us searching, then they came back, maybe drifted back to the dock, then jumped us."

· · ·

Fifteen minutes later Shane started the Acura and turned around. This time he constructed a cover story.

"Here's the deal. We came back to get gas. We only have half a tank." He pointed to the gauge, and she nodded.

He drove quickly through town, made remembered turns, then found himself back on Lake View Drive. He drove up to the bushy hedge, jumped out, and retrieved the videotape box, camera, and answering machine. He locked them in the trunk, then got back behind the wheel and drove quickly out of the mountains, returning to L.A.

ELECTRONIC
EVIDENCE

SUSAN AND I can't come to the phone right now, but leave your name and number and, as soon as we can, we'll return your call." *BEEP*. Ray's voice sounded happy and unthreatening. Then there was another beep. "Ray, it's Calvin. Where the fuck are you, man? You gotta call me now." *BEEP*. Then: "Ray, it's Calvin again. The powers that be are asking questions. Don't fuck with love, man." *BEEP*. "Ray, it's Don and Lee. We're on for Saturday night. The Web after dark. Bring the jerseys." *BEEP*. "Ray, it's Burl. Call the special number." Then there were two hang-ups without messages.

Shane and Barbara were listening to the tape in his kitchen. He turned it off after the last message played.

"Burl—that's Chief Burleigh Brewer. . . . He knows about the house in Arrowhead. Shit," Shane growled. "Ray was the mayor's driver; I guess it makes sense that Brewer would be close to what

Ray was doing." Shane was looking down at the answering-machine tape.

"Who are all these other people, and who the hell is Susan?" Barbara asked angrily.

"I don't know. . . . Don, Lee, and Calvin. I never heard of them, either." He thought for a minute. "There were two cops who braced me in the Parker Center garage at six A.M. the morning I shot Ray. I think one of them was named D. Drucker— maybe that's Don. The other was a Hawaiian guy named Kono. Maybe he's Lee or Calvin. I don't know. 'Don't fuck with love.' And 'the Web' . . . 'Bring the jerseys' . . . What's all that?" he said as they traded blank stares.

They stood over the kitchen counter, where the answering machine was plugged in. Finally, Shane changed the subject. "Barbara, look . . . you gotta go home. I'll drive you down to where your car is parked."

"I'm afraid to go home. I can't take any more of those calls."

"There's a good hotel a few miles south of here, in Marina del Rey. I can't remember the name, but you can't miss it. It's on Admiralty Way. Why don't you go check in there?"

"I get the feeling you're throwing me out."

"I'm not throwing you out. I've got Chooch in the guest room. Longboard is sawing z's on the sofa. It's like a men's dorm around here. Just check into the hotel. I'll talk to you in the morning."

She turned her face up and kissed him on the mouth. When he didn't fully respond, she pulled back and looked at him carefully. "Are you sending me a message, friend?" she asked with an edge in her voice.

"Barbara, let's not confuse this more than it is. We need to focus on what's going on—who's behind this."

"If you promise that you'll let us happen again, once it's over."

"Of course I promise," he said, forcing it. "You know how

much I want that." His words hung in the kitchen, bright and empty, like a broken piñata.

"What're you going to do?" she finally asked.

"I'm gonna get this tape analyzed by the Electronics Section at SIS."

"You don't need a voice print. It's Ray's voice, believe me. I recognize it."

"I know it's Ray. I'm more interested in seeing what else is on here. Answering-machine tapes are used, erased, and rerecorded on. Sometimes there are old messages hiding there. I'm gonna see what the ESIS can pull off the erased portions," Shane said, referring to the Electronics Scientific Investigation Section.

"Oh," she said softly. Then she squeezed his hand for luck, and they headed out the back door of the house.

He drove her to her red Mustang, parked a block away. She got out of the Acura and unlocked her car door, then leaned down into his open passenger window and smiled at him sadly. "Why do I get the feeling this is over?"

"It's your imagination, Barbara. It's not over. It's on hold."

She kissed her fingertips and gently put them on his cheek. "Night," she said sadly, then got into the red Mustang and drove away.

...

Shane drove back to his house and locked up. He decided not to wake Longboard, who was snoring loudly on the sofa. He turned off the light and moved into his bedroom, stripped off his clothes, and wearing only his Jockey shorts, dropped heavily onto his bed. His head felt like a forty-pound medicine ball, worn, seamed, full of cotton and lead. He looked up at the ceiling, closed his eyes, and fought a wave of intense self-pity: *Why can't I catch a fucking break?*

"When did you get home?" Chooch's voice sounded suddenly,

pulling him up from useless thoughts. He opened his eyes and saw the teenager standing in the doorway, wearing a Lakers shirt and baggy shorts.

"I thought you were asleep," Shane said.

"I woke up."

"Well, go back to sleep. You've got school tomorrow."

Chooch didn't move; he had an expression that seemed both frightened and sad.

"What's wrong?"

"Nothin'. It's just . . ."

"What?" Shane turned on his side and looked at Chooch carefully.

"Sandy called. She wants you to call her first thing in the morning."

"Why? What's up?"

"She didn't say."

"She probably just wants to tell me how she smoked your geek principal."

"She didn't call St. John, I asked her. She said she's been involved in a big deal and hasn't had time to get in touch with him yet."

"Right. Well, okay." He lay back on his pillow. "So I'll call her in the morning."

"That means old Thackery musta talked to you, not her. You made him keep me in school."

Shane looked over at Chooch again, then rubbed his eyes and sat up on the bed. "Let's go outside for a minute. I can't sleep with this fucking headache."

"We could light up, toke some bang?" the teenager said hopefully.

"We're through getting high together. I wanna talk to you."

Chooch shifted his weight uncertainly, then nodded. "Okay, sure."

Shane got up, put on his pants and an old sweatshirt, then the two of them moved quietly past Longboard into the backyard. Shane pulled up chairs, and they both sat under a fruitless tangerine tree, looking out at the still canal. The reflection of an almost full moon wavered on the glassy surface.

"What is it?" Chooch asked cautiously.

"I'm in a lot of trouble," Shane started.

"Trouble's the exhaust of life," the fifteen-year-old said surprisingly.

"The trouble I'm in could get dangerous. Some of the people I'm sideways with could decide to make a play. I don't want you to get hurt."

"I'm not afraid." Chooch smiled. "Got your back, bro."

They were silent for a moment, then Shane continued. "I also think it's time for you to get to know your mother. Maybe you haven't given her a chance."

"I hate her," Chooch said softly. "Let's drop this, okay?"

"You can't stay here. When I talk to her tomorrow, I'm going to make arrangements for her to take you back for a week or so."

There was a long silence. Suddenly some crickets started up in the hedge between Shane's and Longboard's yards. They sawed holes in the silence with their back legs.

"I think it's time you gave your mother a break," Shane persisted. "Make me a promise, give it a week. Just five days."

"You're fulla shit, just like Thackery and all those other dickwads. I thought you were never gonna lie to me. I thought we had a deal."

"I'm not lying to you, Chooch. I'm trying to keep you from getting hurt."

"I'm not stupid. I get what's going on here. I've become a problem, an inconvenience, so you wanna throw me out, simplify things for yourself."

"Just one week, till I can get my problems sorted out."

Chooch got up and started into the house. Shane grabbed his arm to stop him, but Chooch yanked it free.

"Look, it's not . . . I'm not trying to get rid of you."

"Eat me!" the boy said, defiance and pain shining in his black eyes.

"I care what you think," Shane said. "It matters to me. We need to talk this out."

"You came close. You almost had me fooled, but I got it straight now. I finally got it . . . nothing's changed. It's just like it always was—I can only count on myself. So fuck off."

Chooch walked back into the house. Shane's head was still pounding. No matter which way he turned, he saw disaster. He didn't know what to do next, so he went inside and wrote a letter to his father.

THE
ARROWHEAD
LETTER

Dear Dad,

I hate to admit it, but I'm really scared. Something big and dangerous is going on, and I have the feeling if I don't figure it out soon, I will be destroyed by it. The answer is in that Lake Arrowhead house. Why would Chief Brewer call a location where Ray was committing some kind of sexual blackmail? Who is Carl Cummins? That name isn't in either the Arrowhead or the L.A. phone book. I need to get the answers to some of these questions fast. I'm running out of time. Why do I feel it all closing in? Dad, I'm losing it. I sense disaster coming. I need to talk to somebody.

I know my problems are the last thing you need right now, but please give me a call.

I love you, Dad, and miss you. I'm scared and lonely. You're all I have left.

Your son,
Shane

CLERICAL DIVISION 18

THEY PULLED UP in front of the Harvard Westlake School at eight the next morning. It was half an hour before the other students would arrive. Chooch got out, dragged his book bag off the front seat, and walked away from the car without looking back. He hadn't spoken all the way there. He had completely tuned Shane out.

Three times before leaving the house, Shane had tried to get through to Sandy but had reached only her machine. As he pulled away from the school, he dialed her number again.

"Hi, you've reached 555-6979. I'm not in, but you know what to do," announced the recording in her furry contralto voice. Shane didn't leave a third message. He closed his phone and headed back to Internal Affairs.

He pulled into the parking structure adjacent to the Bradbury and used his newly issued employee-parking card. The arm went up, and he found his assigned space on the third level.

He was just getting out of his car when he saw Alexa Hamilton five spaces away, removing a heavy cardboard case-file box out of the trunk of her plainwrap. A few Metro sergeants and special players in the department still had these prized vehicles instead of the hated slickbacks. Alexa's was a new dove-gray Crown Victoria with blackwalls and red velour upholstery. Crown Vics were senior staff vehicles, and hers was prima facie evidence that Sergeant Hamilton had top-shelf department "suck."

She slammed her trunk lid and started carrying the box to the elevators. Shane didn't want to ride down with her, but she had seen him and they were both heading toward the elevators, destined to arrive within seconds of each other. For him to veer off now or pretend he forgot something and divert back to his car would be a chickenhearted admission of weakness, so he kept walking and arrived a few seconds behind her. She had balanced the heavy cardboard box full of case files on her knee so she could push the elevator button with her free hand. She looked over at him with those slanted, exotic chips of laser-blue ice—poker player's eyes that cut holes through him but revealed nothing in return.

"Need help with that?" he asked, hating himself for even offering, the question inadvertently slipping out of him in an anxious attempt to fill the awkward silence.

"Wouldn't that be sorta like asking a condemned man to carry his own ax to the chopping block?"

"Hardy-har," he said sourly. It surprised him that the box was so full. She'd been on the case for only forty-eight hours. "That can't be all me."

"All you. And this is just '92 to '96. 'Ninety-four seemed like a fun-packed year, all those civilian complaints . . . the second unit-destroying traffic accident coming in April after the first-of-the-month kick down to Southwest Traffic."

"You had to be there."

The elevator arrived and they got in. The door closed, and as they rode down, Shane kept looking into the open box with the morbid curiosity of a freeway rubbernecker passing a fatal accident. All of his mid-nineties career pileups were collected there. He spotted a bunch of his old 7.04 ADAM control cards, which were identification sheets for radio-message logs. It shocked him. She was actually reading his old radio transmissions. He couldn't believe it. He also saw two manila envelopes from the Traffic Division that he assumed detailed the two unit-wrecking collisions he'd had while he was in Southwest Patrol. Wedged down in the side of the box were dozens of 8.49 out-slips, which were like library cards from Records and Identification. She was pulling all of his old arrest reports. The rest of the box was littered with field-interview cards and DR numbered witness statements filed by the IOs working his case. He was staring down into the box with growing dread.

"Jesus Christ, what's with the fucking rectal exam?"

"And you don't even have to grab your ankles," she said, shifting the box away from his stare. She was still balancing the heavy box on her knee as the elevator door opened.

Shane moved out without looking back at her. He had a tinny taste in his mouth as he pushed open the double doors at the back of the Bradbury Building and hurried through. He heard them swing closed behind him, right in Alexa Hamilton's face. She must have been trying to slip in with the file box before the doors closed and mistimed it, because he heard the heavy oak frame hit her hands, which were clutching the leading edge of the box.

"Shit!" she said as the door bounced off her knuckles.

Shane now had his own key to Room 256; he let himself in and turned on the stark neon overhead lights. They blasted a harsh, unfriendly blue-white glare down on the three Xerox machines. He dropped his coat on the back of the chair and glanced at his watch. It was 8:32. Since no deputy chief ever got in before nine, he took a chance and picked up the phone, dialing the number for Parker Center.

"LAPD Parker Center," a cheerful woman's voice greeted him.

"Deputy Chief Tom Mayweather," he said, and a few seconds later got Mayweather's secretary.

"Is he in?"

"Who's calling, please?"

His heart was beating fast. Once he identified himself, if Mayweather was in, he'd either have to talk or hang up; neither was an acceptable choice. What he wanted was just to leave an ass-covering message. "It's Sergeant Shane Scully," he finally answered, holding his breath.

"I'm sorry, Sergeant, he's at a breakfast meeting."

"Breakfast meeting" was department bullshit for "not in yet." Shane let out a chestful of air.

"It's really important that I talk to the chief," he lied, laying it on a little.

"I'm sorry," she said. "Can I give him a message?"

"Will you tell him I've been trying to get in touch with him, please? Tell him I was unable to get to Robbery/Homicide last night as he ordered because I fell asleep driving down from Arrowhead. Crashed the car, broke my front fender. It was dangerous to drive when I was that tired, so I stopped in a motel. I just woke up. I have some errands to take care of when I get home, so tell him I'll get in touch with him later."

"I'll be sure he gets the update." She hung up.

Shane hoped the phone call would give him a little cover.

He looked at his IN box and found half a dozen new cases that had been left for him to copy. He started to pull them out, and as he was arranging them in stacks on the worktable, his eyes scanned each face sheet.

He was surprised to see that Don Drucker had made this morning's lineup. Apparently Drucker was scheduled for a full board as well. Under the face sheet was an internal notification slip that informed Drucker's defense rep that his board had just been postponed from April 20 until April 23, as requested. The face sheet had the IAD case number and had been signed by the head of Special Investigations Division, Deputy Chief T. Mayweather.

"What the fuck?" he said softly, thinking, *Why was the head of the division signing these charge sheets instead of Warren Zell, here at IAD?* Then he picked up his phone and dialed the Clerical Division. He asked for and was transferred to a civilian employee who was a longtime friend.

Sally Stonebreaker was nothing like her name . . . a sparrow of a woman with a Transylvanian complexion, translucent skin, and thin white hair. Shane had met her in municipal court nine years ago. He'd been testifying in a robbery case, and she was getting a restraining order against her ex-husband in the courtroom next door. Al Stonebreaker had beaten her twice and had been threatening her over disputed alimony payments. That same night Shane had looked him up and explained the new rules. The "discussion" had taken place in the alley behind a neighborhood bar and required Al to get half a dozen stitches and some new bridgework. After that, Al Stonebreaker had left Sally alone.

Shane got Sally on the line. Once he identified himself, he could hear a little pause before she went on.

"I'm sorry about what's going on," she finally said. "Ray Molar was some piece of work."

"Sally, I need you to do a computer run. I'm sort of locked off the system now, and I don't want a record of this search anyway."

"Shane, I'm busy right now." She paused, then added, "Besides, they've got new DataLocks on our consoles and it's real hard to access the mainframe without a case clearance number," she said, trying to shake him. He was already department poison.

"Sally, I need this favor. You've gotta come through for me."

Another long pause, during which he could hear her breathing. "Okay, but only this once. After that, I can't do it again."

"Thanks. I've got an IAD complaint investigation CF number for a Board of Rights on a policeman one in Southwest, named Don Drucker. I need to find out what IAD is trying him for. The number is 20-290-12."

"Just a minute."

He could hear computer keys clicking, then she came back on the line.

"He's been charged under a 670.5 of the PDM," she said.

"What is that? Six hundred codes are like booking and prisoner-escape violations, right?" There were hundreds of numbered codes listed in the five-hundred-page LAPD manual.

"Yeah. Escaped juvenile. Drucker lost him in transit, prior to booking. Gimme a minute to read this," she said. Then a moment later she came back on the line. "Okay. Prisoner was a teenage Hispanic named Soledad Preciado, arrested in Southwest. According to Drucker's Internal Affairs complaint, he left the arrestee unattended in the back of his squad car while he went into a drugstore. Drucker claims he was having a migraine and needed to fill a prescription, said he couldn't drive with the headache and was getting nauseous. While he was in the drugstore, Sol Preciado got out of the unit and walked away."

"Was this kid, by any chance, a Hoover Street Bounty Hunter?"

"Just a minute," she said, and her computer keys were clicking again. She came back on. "A suspected Bounty Hunter, age fifteen. He claimed he's not in a gang, but he's listed in the Gang Street Alias Index under the name Li'l Silent, so at the very least he's a TG or a known associate." TG stood for "tiny gangster" and was basically a killer in training. Shane knew you didn't usually get a street name unless you'd already been "jumped in the set," so it figured he was probably a full member.

"Can you punch out another name for me?"

"I gotta go, Shane. My supervisor's a great white. All he does is swim and eat. Right now, he's cruising this floor."

"Sally, I need help. I hate to put it this way, but I helped you once, now you gotta do this for me." He could hear her sigh loudly on the other end of the phone.

"Okay, gimme it." She was getting mad.

"A policeman one, his name is Kono. I don't have his first name. Check him to see if he's got an Internal Affairs complaint." He was shooting with his eyes closed, firing on instinct.

"You got a CF number?" Sally asked, frustration in her voice. "It'll make it a lot easier."

"I'm sorry, this is just a hunch. There may not even be a board pending on him."

He could hear keys clicking again, then: "Yeah. Kris Kono. He's got a CF number, 20-276-9."

"No shit," Shane said, his heart beating fast now. He wasn't sure what was tugging on the end of this line, but he'd definitely hooked something. "What's IAD got him for?"

"It's . . . lemme see . . ." She was quiet as she scanned the file for a few minutes, then: "It was a gang fight, also in Southwest. Two bystanders got shot. A store owner died. Kono got the BOR 'cause he lost some key evidence. In this case, the murder weapon disappeared from the trunk of his squad car. The case got pitched by the judge at the prelim. The dead store owner's wife complained, and this complaint has a bunch of community affidavits attached. A city councilwoman in that district is on a tear. I process Southwest complaints on my terminal. The division started heating up about six months ago. Gang-related crime is soaring. The community is getting pissed down there."

"Was the Kono blown bust also H Street Bounty Hunters?"

"Yeah . . . same as Drucker."

"Two more names: Lew Ayers and John Samansky. I think they're operating in Southwest, too."

"I can't. I gotta go. I'm gonna get in trouble."

"Just tell me if these guys all worked on the same patrol shift or if you see any other common denominators."

"It's Southwest. That's all I can tell you. Look, Shane, I can't—"

"Okay, thanks, Sally. You've been a big help."

He hung up and sat silently in the Xerox room. His mind was chewing it, looking for the connection. Joe Church, Don Drucker, and Kris Kono were all first-year cops, emotionally distraught over Ray's death, and all had fucked up on cases involving the Hoover Street Bounty Hunters, a Hispanic gang in Southwest Division. Ayers and Samansky were policemen working Southwest, but had searched Barbara's house in Harbor Division, using a warrant supplied by a Mayor Crispin–owned judge. They were also highly emotional over Ray.

He sat in the wooden chair and tried to put it together. *What had he stumbled into? Was this just a bunch of stupid coincidences, or something much more sinister?* His phone rang. He looked over at it as if it were a coiled snake. Finally he picked it up.

"Yeah."

"Chief Mayweather calling Shane Scully," the chief's secretary said.

"Scully just left. He wasn't feeling good. Got the flu, I think. If I see him, I'll tell him the deputy chief was trying to reach him," he said, and after she bought it, he hung up quickly. He grabbed his coat and left the Internal Affairs Xerox room, locking the door behind him. He passed up the slow-moving elevators and hurried down the stairs. In less than a minute he was back in his Acura and driving out of the parking structure on his way to the Records Division on Spring Street.

DEN

O N HIS WAY across town, Shane dropped off the roll of film he had taken at Arrowhead. He told the man at the Fotomat that he wanted one set of normal prints and, if they didn't come out, a set with the negative pushed two stops. He was told that pushing the negative could permanently destroy the film, but he okayed it. The man behind the counter told him the film would have to be sent out and wouldn't be ready for six to twelve hours.

Shane drove to the Records Division and parked in the big asphalt lot on Spring Street. He locked the Acura and moved around the front, trying hard not to look at the bashed-in fender. He walked through the door of the large three-story brick building and climbed the stairs to the Criminal Division, where he sat at a table and filled out a records release request.

In order to access Soledad Preciado's criminal offender record information (CORI), Shane had to fill out a right-to-know/need-to-know CORI release form. Those persons defined in the California penal code with right- and need-to-know authorization included the juvenile court, Social Services, and members of the Special Investigations Section, which now, technically, included Shane Scully, its new unit discovery officer. Since it is specifically mandated that automated and manually stored CORI information not be electronically distributed, Shane had to be at the Spring Street building to tender his request in person.

Juvenile records are further restricted by the Department of Public Social Service (DPSS) and can be reviewed only by order of a juvenile court judge or the Los Angeles County Children's Services Department (LACCSD). However, the Special Investigations Division was exempted. . . . Shane was beginning to view his transfer to Internal Affairs in a more favorable light. Since Sol's case was part of Don Drucker's Internal Affairs investigation and had a Special Investigations CF number, Shane included that number and fraudulently listed himself as the case IO. He handed the paperwork to the clerk, a small, narrow-shouldered man with wispy blond hair combed over a yarmulke-sized bald spot. Shane hoped that the man was too bored to check the request against his badge number.

A few minutes later a manila envelope was passed over. Shane unwound the string tie, pulled out Soledad (Sol) Preciado's Criminal Records folder, and opened it. For a fifteen-year-old, Soledad had a very extensive yellow sheet. His arrest record included two CCWs (carrying a concealed weapon), one assault with intent to commit, and one attempted murder. He'd been down twice: once for a year at the Pitchess youth camp on the attempted murder, once for six months at CYA on a parole violation. Sol Preciado had definitely been out there flagging with the homies. Shane kept reading and finally came across the incident involving the escape from Drucker's patrol car, which was there by virtue of the department's Alpha Index Criminal History cross-reference system. He scanned Drucker's commanding officer's review. At the end of the page he saw that Preciado had not been originally arrested by Don Drucker. He had been called in later only to handle Sol's transport to Los Padrinos Juvenile Hall, which was all the way across town at 2285 East Quill Drive, in Downey. It was unusual for the arresting officer not to transport his own prisoner. Shane wondered why it had happened. He started flipping back, looking for the original arresting officer's report. He finally found it; Preciado had been arrested on November 12 by Sergeant Mark Martinez. Shane scanned the arrest report.

Sol Preciado, a.k.a. Li'l Silent, had been alleged to be committing multiple assaults outside the L.A. Coliseum (court appearance pending). The crimes occurred at about 12:30 P.M. as people were streaming in for the USC–Oregon State football game. He had assaulted several women, knocking them down and snatching their purses. Events escalated when a man trying to stop him was knifed in the abdomen, allegedly by the enraged fifteen-year-old. Preciado had been apprehended by Sergeant Martinez, a member of the Coliseum Division police unit.

Since Martinez was working a duty station and could not leave, Drucker had been dispatched to the Coliseum to pick up Soledad Preciado, then subsequently lost him on his way to the city jail with the ill-advised stop at the drugstore for a headache prescription. The report said that Preciado had somehow managed to open the handcuffs and escape.

There was a statement by Drucker describing his chronic migraine headaches, which had become unbearable and had caused him to stop for medication. He had listed several police officers who could attest to his medical problem. At the very top of that list was Lieutenant Raymond Molar, whom Drucker identified as his LAPD den leader.

Shane put down the arrest report and picked up the phone on the scarred wooden desk. He redialed the Clerical Division and, after a moment, had Sally Stonebreaker back on the line.

"Aren't you happy it's me again," he said, trying to put a friendly smile in his voice. It didn't work.

"Good-bye, Shane."

"Sally, don't hang up. This will just take a minute. Nobody else can help me."

"You've gotta leave me alone, for God's sake. I can't do this."

"One little, teeny favor. Just one. Take you thirty seconds. Take you fifteen."

"Oh, shit," she groaned, but he knew he had her.

"I just found out Ray Molar was a den leader, and I need to know who was in his den." He could hear a loud sigh for emphasis.

"Okay, but this is absolutely it. You call me again, I'm hanging up."

"Thanks, Sally, and don't get hit by the flower truck 'cause it's on its way."

"Don't send me flowers, just stop calling."

He heard the keys clicking as she entered Ray's name into the computer. After a moment she came back on the line. "He had a den in Southwest. Get a pencil, these are his cubs . . ."

Shane grabbed a pen out of his pocket and turned over the manila folder. "Go."

"A full pack. There's six: Lee Ayers, John Samansky, Coy Love, Joe Church, Don Drucker, and Kris Kono. Don't call again." And he was listening to a dial tone. No good-bye, no good luck, just a click and a buzz.

But he'd hit the lottery. The connection between all these first-year officers was Ray's police den.

A few years back, the LAPD had instituted an innovative concept called den policing. The department had discovered that it was difficult to go from civilian life into police work. After graduation from the academy, rookies were assigned a den leader to help them make the transition. As civilians, many of them had never experienced the discrimination and hatred that some elements of society aim at its sworn badge carriers. Often, particularly in the first year on the job, officers were totally unprepared for the abuse heaped on them. It was difficult not to respond when someone called you a pig and spit on you or your police car. Many cops ended up losing their tempers and resorting to violence. The idea of a den was to have a veteran officer who had perspective on the problems of police work assigned as a kind of emotional coach to help these rookies through their transition year. Den leaders were not commanding officers or watch commanders; they were not responsible for the officer's performance, only for his emotional stability.

Suddenly Shane could understand why these cops were hovering over Ray's death. He had been their coach; their confidant, their police department godfather. It was a piece of connective tissue that jerked the hostile emotional attitudes of the six officers into focus.

But it still left several more difficult questions unanswered: Why was Chief Brewer using Ray's old den to lean on him, and why were they all facing charges at Internal Affairs? What was the Hoover Street Bounty Hunter connection, and why were these six officers all involved in broken cases concerning that one Hispanic Southwest Division gang?

Shane sat there at the table, deep in thought. After a minute the narrow-shouldered wisp of a man who had given him the folder was hovering again. "You through with that?" he asked.

"Yeah." Shane handed back the folder, with the names of Ray's den still scribbled on the back. The clerk hurried away with it.

Shane was not sure what to do next or where to go. He couldn't return to IAD; he was dodging Mayweather. He didn't want to go home and just sit, taking the chance that the deputy chief would send a patrol unit out there to arrest him.

Finally, because he couldn't think of a better course of action, he decided to check in with DeMarco Saint.

It was not even ten-thirty in the morning when he got there, and DeMarco was already drunk. Shane was standing in the defense rep's living room, watching him struggle to get up off his sofa. He almost made it but fell awkwardly, catching himself painfully by an elbow on the coffee table.

"Whoa . . ." the defense rep said as he tried once more, this time managing to stumble to his feet. Two young boys, about fifteen, were lounging on the sofa on each side of him, watching the proceedings with glazed indifference.

"The fuck's wrong with you?" Shane asked, looking at his teetering defense rep. "How can you be wasted? It's not even noon."

"Had a few bubblies. Hit me harder'n I thought." DeMarco grinned. "Shane, meet the guys—Billy an' Mark. Guys, meet Shane. They just moved in. Been sleeping under the fuckin' pier. I'm helpin' 'em out."

They looked right through him, no change of expression. He wasn't even a blip on their radar. Anybody in a tie over thirty was in a parallel dimension and didn't exist for them.

"We gotta talk. Let's go." Shane grabbed DeMarco's arm and tried to drag him out of the house. The two fifteen-year-olds rose up to protect their new landlord.

"Sit down!" Shane growled menacingly, and they did.

"S'okay," DeMarco slurred. "Lez go . . . jus' don' yank on me."

They left the house and walked out onto the sand. It was a bright Southern California day. DeMarco groaned painfully as the sunlight hit him, and he shaded his eyes, wavering badly as he walked. They were twenty yards away from the house when Shane spun him and faced him.

"How can you be fucking drunk, man?"

"Relax, will ya? I was up half the night workin' on your case.

Haven't even been t'bed yet. No food . . . s'why the brews snuck up on me."

"Have you interviewed Barbara, prepared a witness list, contacted Mayweather or Halley to get their sworn affidavits and a copy of the DFAR, sent anything to the subpoena control desk?"

"I . . . I'm . . ."

"The answer is no, 'cause I've been with Barbara and you haven't even called her yet. She's gotta be priority one 'cause if she changes her statement, I'm dust. You gotta lock her in with an affidavit, secure her testimony before you mess with the rest of it. Since I know you know that, you've done nothing."

"Hey, Shane . . . will y'calm down? Okay, just calm down." DeMarco took a step forward and lost his balance and fell down. "Oops," he said, grinning. "Somebody's moving the beach."

"Dee, I was down at IAD this morning. I bumped into Sergeant Hamilton, who is running through my life with spikes on. She's got a box full of every mistake I ever made, even down to my old Patrol Division TAs. She's giving me a fucking sigmoidoscopy, while you're out here getting hammered. We only have eight more days, then we go in front of the board."

"Relax. Okay?" He was trying to get up and not having much luck, so Shane knelt down beside him.

"How can I relax? I'm on the block."

"I don't think Alexa Hamilton really wants to prosecute you. Okay?" He was smiling stupidly.

"That isn't what you said before. You said she'd been in Southwest supervising a patrol watch and came back to Internal Affairs specifically to take my case, that she volunteered for it."

"When I said it, I was trying to duck the case, but now that I have it, I think otherwise."

"She's the queen of the Dark Side. Whatta you mean, she doesn't want to prosecute me?"

"Why d'you think ya won the BOR sixteen years ago?"

"We won because you caught her key witness lying."

"We won 'cause Alexa threw the fuckin' case." He belched and then tried to stand, but again didn't make it.

"She what?"

"She threw th' fuckin' case, went in the tank, intentionally bricked it."

"You never said that before. If she dumped it, you would've told me."

"Hey, winning cases was how I kept my rep hard back then. I din' wanna share the glory. Wha' good's it to win a tough board if the prosecuting advocate throws the fuckin' case? 'Sides, she swore me to secrecy. . . . Said she'd get busted if I tol'."

"I want facts, Dee. I want the whole story. If you're bullshitting . . ."

"Not shitting." He sat back and took a deep breath to clear his head, then went on. "She comes to me like two days 'fore the board and tells me the chief advocate himself, the fuckin' Dark Prince, got a statement from Ray that was devastating to your case."

"Wait a minute. Ray was on my side."

"Grow up, man. Ray was on Ray's side. He didn't wan' any part of your problem, and his statement contradicted yours. Since he was your training officer, it was gonna flat fuckin' sink you." He took a deep breath and rubbed his eyes. "Alexa said she wasn't gonna include Molar's affidavit in the discovery material. Said since the DA took Ray's statement personally, he would insist Ray be called to testify, but Zell wouldn't be aware that Ray's affidavit had accidentally on purpose been left out of discovery." Now he was grinning stupidly again. "She said I should object an' get his testimony stricken, because she had failed to include it, makin' Ray's testimony inad . . . inad . . ."—he belched—"inadmissible at the hearing. Thas wha' happened."

Shane was confused. It didn't add up.

"Then she tells me she thinks the gas-station attendant was lying," DeMarco continued. "Tells me to polygraph him. She impeached her own fuckin' guy, and he was the best part of her case."

"Why? Why would she do that?"

"Maybe she wants your bod."

"Get up." Shane pulled DeMarco up to his feet.

He stood there, weaving drunkenly. "I'm figurin' there's a good chance she's gonna come across again." He grinned.

"You mean you're sitting around, sucking down beers, waiting for her to throw this case, too?"

"I'm not waiting around. I'm bustin' tail, bud. I'm all over this puppy. . . ."

"Okay, Dee, I'm stuck with you because they fast-tracked my board and nobody else will take it on such short notice. Right now I've got something to do, but I'm coming back, unannounced. You better be fuckin' clear-eyed and sober. Next time I'm here, I want a full review of this case, blow by blow. I want your subpoena list and I want to know who you're interviewing. I want to hear your case strategy."

"Done," he said, giggling slightly, shading his eyes, squinting into the sun.

Shane couldn't believe what he was seeing, couldn't believe what DeMarco had just told him. Alexa, with her box full of his career glitches, was hardly going to throw this board, regardless of what happened the last time. He glowered at the wavering defense rep. "We've gotta get our helmets on. If I catch you drunk again, I'll beat the shit out of you. Don't fall down on me, man." Then he turned, leaving the longhaired defense rep teetering badly in the bright sunlight.

THE BLACK WIDOW

AFTER HE LEFT **D**E**M**ARCO, Shane sat inside the hot Acura in the beach parking lot with the driver-side door open and called Sandy. Surprisingly, this time he got her; she picked up on the third ring.

"Sandy, it's me."

"Shane, it wasn't anywhere near as bad as you thought. I called the school, and they told me there's no problem. Chooch is back in classes."

"Yeah, no problem. What an alarmist I'm becoming. I need to see you today. We need to work out some stuff. I'll be there in half an hour."

"Today's really shitty for me."

"The whole week has been shitty for me," Shane growled. "You're meeting me at noon."

"Can't. I have a lunch engagement."

"Cancel it." He was pissed at DeMarco but taking it out on Sandy.

"It's not that easy," she hedged.

"Cancel the fucking lunch date. I'm gonna be there at noon." He hung up on her. It was eleven-thirty.

Sandy lived at the Barrington Plaza in Brentwood, in one of two gorgeous penthouse suites. Shane got there in thirty minutes. He pulled up to the overhanging porte cochere and handed the keys for the busted-up Acura to a doorman who had enough braid hanging off his uniform shoulders to lead a Latin American country or the University of Michigan marching band.

"I'll need to announce you, sir," the doorman said, frowning at the bruised Acura parked on his brick entryway, subtracting elegance like a turd on a serving platter.

"Shane Scully for Ms. Sandoval."

The doorman picked up the phone, had a short conversation, then walked with Shane into the lobby and key-carded the elevator for the penthouse level. "You can phone down before you return and I'll have the vehicle brought up." He pronounced the word "vehicle" like an ancient curse.

"Thank you," Shane said. The doors closed and he was alone in the fragrant oak-paneled luxury of the Barrington Plaza elevator, listening to a selection of orchestrated show tunes.

Shane marveled once again at what Sandy had been able to accomplish. When he had met her, he'd been on the job only a little over a year. It was just after he'd been separated from Ray and moved to West Valley Division. The first month in that division he'd been a floater, and because he was a "new face," he had been temporarily assigned to detectives working a bunco scam as an undercover. She had been a top-line L.A. call girl, working an executive clientele. The bunco detectives had been investigating a counterfeit bond trader, and Sandy happened to be balling the guy for a thousand a night. Shane, working UC, had arrested her for prostitution, but then instead of booking her, the bunco squad instructed him to try to "flip" her. He did, and she worked the case for him as an informant. Shane was her contact. She had skillfully pillow-talked the bond trader, allowing Shane and the Valley detectives to expand their investigation. When the bust went down, fifteen bond traders hit the lockup and Shane protected her, managing to keep her from being prosecuted. During that operation she proved that she had guts and savvy and could be counted on in a pinch. Shane became her friend, and one night, a week later over dinner, she suggested that she might be willing to work for the police if the price was right.

"How much do you guys spend to get a big player into court?" she had asked him. "How much overtime and special duty gets approved to bring down a big vice lord or drug kingpin?"

The truth was, often hundreds of thousands of dollars were spent trying to collar a predicate felon, and sometimes even then they failed to come up with an indictment.

Sandy's proposal was shrewd; it showed her keen business mind. She told Shane she would work any target they pointed her at and charge LAPD nothing up front. Despite the upscale nature of her clientele, she was tired of working one-night stands and wanted to expand her horizons. She had two conditions: if successful, she wanted half the amount of money the department had spent on that criminal investigation in the preceding year, and she would not work a target who had an annual police budget of under a hundred thousand dollars. She said she would trust Shane to divulge the correct amount. After almost a month of negotiating with her over terms and conditions, the department finally agreed.

Sandy proved to be exceptional in this new line of work. She was thorough and totally prepared herself before ever moving in on her target. First, she would study the criminal, research him like a doctoral thesis. If he liked Russian literature, she would memorize passages of Solzhenitsyn. If he was interested in Impressionistic art, she would become an expert on Gino Severini's essays, *From Futurism to Classicism*. Then she would set up shop somewhere in his field of vision. One day Mr. Big would be at his favorite country club bar and he'd look across the room and see a dusky, raven-haired goddess sitting at a table alone, reading an art pamphlet detailing the next Impressionist auction at Sotheby's. A conversation would ensue, and this unsuspecting criminal would find that, lo and behold, he had a soul mate, a drop-dead ten on the libido scale who miraculously liked everything he did, from van Gogh to ocean catamaran racing. She became so tuned in, she could finish his sentences.

Before long they would become intimate. Here, Sandy was on her home field. She was a Hall of Fame sexual acrobat. Mr. Big would think he'd won the quiniela. Then Sandy would slowly begin to work him for information. After sex he'd start bragging. He'd fill her beautiful head with his criminal exploits. She'd coo and tell him he was a genius. Once she had his criminal operation down, she would start looking around for a patsy. She knew that when the cops made the arrest, Mr. Big would know he'd been sold out. He might turn violent from his cell, might figure her for the informant and order her killed. To protect herself, Sandy would look around at Mr. Big's criminal companions for a stand-in who could fulfill this unrewarding role.

Before dropping the dime to the police, she would set up the patsy as the informant. She was careful to always pick someone worthy of execution, so the unsuspecting police department wouldn't put too much time into the scumbag's murder. Once she had selected her patsy, she would begin flirting with him, setting up a romantic triangle. Mr. Big would get furious at the patsy: "Stop hitting on Sandy. I catch you putting the make on her again, I'll drop you where you stand." But Sandy was worth the risk, and she'd work both men into steamy jealous rages.

When the bust came down, it didn't take Mr. Big long to figure out who had fingered him. The patsy would end up strolling the tidal basin in concrete loafers while Sandy sat in the jail visitors' room, crying her eyes red and promising Mr. Big that she would be there when he got out.

Because she always destroyed her targets, and a patsy always died, her nickname in the department was "the Black Widow." Like her namesake, she was a great but deadly piece of ass.

She would then present her bill to Shane for this valuable service, and he would be her bagman for the department's payoff. She was L.A.'s most successful consignment concessionaire. It was a fair deal. If she didn't get the goods, the LAPD didn't pay.

In the beginning Shane was the only cop she would trust to be her intermediary. The cases went down smoothly in court because the tip that led to the bust was always anonymous, so it couldn't be traced back to the department. Naturally, the arresting officers didn't even know about the arrangement. Since Sandy never testified in court or told anybody what she had to do to get the goods, it was, strictly speaking, legal. She was paid as an informant—something police do all over the country. It was a very efficient and profitable deal for everybody.

Inevitably, the feds got wind of her and, in their typical, claim-jumping fashion, moved in. Since their budgets were larger and she could make more money with them, they started poaching on the LAPD, and now she was working mostly federal cases.

■ ■ ■

The elevator doors opened, and Sandy was standing in the hall waiting for him. Every time he saw her, he was knocked out all over again. It was as if his memory wasn't able to retain her remarkable physical perfection. She was tall, almost five-ten, and had a spectacular, trainer-sculpted body. She had told him once that her mother was Mexican and her father Colombian, which was responsible for her Latin coloring. She had raven-black hair and coffee-colored skin. Her brown eyes twinkled and danced and said "Take me." She was one of the most attractive, sensual women he had ever laid eyes on. Although she was in her mid to late thirties, she could have easily passed for twenty-nine.

She was standing before him, wearing designer heels and a tailored white dress that revealed just enough knee and breast to cause him to lose concentration, but she was never overtly sexy. She was a strange, exotic mixture—classy yet seductive, expensive yet available—and somehow Sandy carried it off with incredible ease.

"Shane, you look tired. I hope you're not doing stakeouts, sleeping in your car," she said, reacting to the circles under his eyes.

"You always know how to make me feel so special," he said darkly as she took his hand and offered her cheek to kiss.

"Come on, stop it, you know I love you. I made us sandwiches." She was smooth, working him now, making him feel important. She was good at it. Men were her business.

The penthouse was huge, beautiful, and all white. White walls on white carpet, with white drapes framing an acre of plate glass. The antiques were all real. A black and goldleaf Louis XV desk and matching secretary unit were on opposite walls; white sofas and European accent pieces immediately caught the eye. Sandy stood in the middle of the entry with her hands on her slender hips, the most exotic decoration in the room by far.

"I think, now that I see you, you need some alcoholic CPR. How 'bout a beer?" She moved into the kitchen without waiting for a reply, got two Amstel Lights, and brought them back, along with the sandwiches on bone china plates. All of it was carried on an expensive antique silver serving tray. She set everything down on the white marble-top table near the windows.

The mirrored glass skyline of Century City twinkled in the clean air blowing in from the ocean a few miles away.

"You have to take Chooch back," he said without preamble.

"I can't, Shane, I told you, I'm on this thing for the DEA. I'm working almost every night. The target is a hitter. I stumble—I'm gone. Honest to God, this guy's a vampire . . . he plays all night."

"Sandy, I'm going to say this again, 'cause it's important. You need to spend some time with your son. I blew it. I almost got through, but I blew it. Now I'm afraid he's gonna take off, then we're gonna be out there looking for him. He's got some gang-bang friends in the Valley; he'll hang with bad company. He's pissed off, ready to run. I'm worried about him."

They sat with the beers and untouched sandwiches between them as Sandy bit her lower lip in concentrated thought. "I know you think I've just dumped him, that I sent him off to boarding school or left him with friends . . . but I'm trying to make enough money so he can go to Princeton or Yale. I want him to get the best education, maybe be a doctor."

"To begin with, it doesn't matter what I think. It only matters what Chooch thinks. You've gotta show him *you* care. You've gotta make room for him in *your* life, make him feel like he belongs somewhere, like somebody truly gives a shit. Forget about Yale, 'cause the way he's going, he's gonna be doing his postgrad study at Soledad State Prison."

"My plan is to get ten mil in tax-free munis and blue chips, stuff that will grow and throw off cash, then I'm gonna retire and move with Chooch to Arizona—Phoenix, I was thinking—settle down, be a regular mom. I'm a year away, maybe less."

"You don't have a year. You may not have a week."

"Shane, the sting on this drug deal goes down in two days. I'm right at the critical point, creating my exit strategy."

"You mean setting up your dead man," he corrected.

"Boy, are you in a shitty mood. Stop being so contentious. I'll take him once this sting is over. I promise. But I'm not taking him today, or tomorrow. . . . Maybe this will be over by Monday. Let's shoot for Monday."

Shane got to his feet, without having touched the sandwich or the beer. She didn't beg him to stay, either.

"By the way, who the hell is his father?"

"His name is Carlos Delmonica. I got careless with my pills. He was a drug dealer in Simon Boca's operation, and he's currently a resident of Leavenworth, Kansas, doing twenty-five to life in the federal pen."

"Jeez, no help there, I guess."

"The best thing we can hope for is that Chooch never meets his father. And don't tell him who he is. I don't want Chooch writing Carlos, who doesn't even know he has a son."

"Monday," Shane said with finality.

He started for the door, and Sandy scooped her purse off the sofa table. "I'll go with you. Maybe I can still make my lunch." She picked up the phone and dialed the bandleader with the braided shoulders in the lobby. "Darling, it's Sandy. I'm coming down with the gentleman who just arrived. Be a dear, will you?" She hung up and smiled brightly. "Our cars will be right up. Magic."

They exited into the hall. As she punched the elevator button, a phone rang. Both Sandy and Shane dug for their cells. It was Shane's. He popped it open.

"Yeah," he said.

It was Luanne McDermott, of the Fingerprint Analysis Unit at SIS. "The print lab lifted a set of pretty good latents off the videotape box," she said. "They came back to Calvin Sheets, 2329 Los Feliz, apartment sixteen."

"Calvin Sheets," Shane said, taking a pen and his small spiral notebook out of his pocket. "Spell it *ea* or *ee*?"

"Sheets—*ee*. Also, he used to be one of us."

"A cop?"

"Yeah . . . got terminated by Internal Affairs six months ago."

"Anything else?"

"That's it."

"Thanks." He closed the phone and tapped the pen on the spiral notebook, deep in speculation.

The elevator arrived at the penthouse level, and he and Sandy got aboard. This time they were listening to an orchestrated version of "Eleanor Rigby."

"I know Calvin Sheets," Sandy said, surprising him.

The doors closed and they rode down.

"You do?"

"He works for Logan Hunter—at least he used to."

"The movie producer?"

"Actually, Logan runs his own independent studio now, Starmax. Calvin Sheets is head of his security."

"How do you know Logan Hunter?" Shane asked, always surprised by the level of people Sandy knew. "Isn't he a big social deal, always doing some major fund-raiser or civic project?"

"Actually, that's how he keeps his reputation. He only works on stuff that will keep him in the press. Right now he's in the paper 'cause he's trying to get a pro football team to come to L.A. He's a football fan like I'm a microbiologist, but it's popular, makes him look good. If it's a news story, he's up for it."

"I hesitate to ask you how you met him."

"I was working Logan for U.S. Customs about two months ago. It went nowhere. He just wouldn't give me any play. One of my few wipeouts. I found out a few weeks later that he's a closet gay. To each his own . . ."

"What did U.S. Customs want him for?"

"They thought he was smuggling heroin into the country, using film magazines being shipped back from a production he had shooting in Mexico. They thought he was unpacking loads of Mexican Brown in the film lab, but like I said, I never got close enough to find out."

"And Calvin Sheets works for him now?"

"Yeah. And is he ever an asshole. A blister, that one. I'd hate to get caught alone with him in a dark place."

They got to the lobby and stepped out of the elevator. The doorman had already called up the cars; two Spanish-speaking men in white coveralls with BARRINGTON PLAZA stenciled over their pockets delivered the keys and stood by the cars waiting for their tips.

Shane slipped his man a dollar, while Sandy tipped hers five, then rattled some Spanish at him. He smiled and bobbed his head energetically up and down like a sparrow digging for worms. She got behind the wheel of her new bottle-green XJB convertible. They both drove off, heading their separate ways: Sandy in her Jag, to arrange some poor asshole's funeral; Shane in his battered Acura, to pick up her only son at Harvard Westlake before Mr. Thackery threw a shit-fit and started threatening expulsion, *ad summum bonum.*

21

B & E

I T WAS JUST after ten P.M. when Shane left a brooding Chooch Sandoval with Longboard Kelly. He was driving across town to the Bradbury Building, dressed for a burglary in 211 colors: a black LAPD sweatshirt, black jeans, and Reeboks. He had his .38 backup piece snug against his belt. His badge and ID card, picklocks, and penlight were stuffed in all available pockets.

He pulled off the freeway and drove down Sixth Street, right into the hovering helicopter lights of the Schwarzenegger movie. They were back downtown doing night work, barricades in place, assistant directors and klieg lights glaring. He had hoped he would be able to sneak into IAD, rifle the chief advocate's files, and get out unobserved. The last thing he needed to deal with was this fucking movie.

He got stopped two blocks from the Bradbury by a motorcycle cop, now a potential witness who could put Shane at the location.

He considered turning around and going home but then decided, *fuck it,* he was running out of options. He had to take the chance.

"Sorry, Sergeant, we're almost on a take," the old motorcycle cop said after Shane badged him. He had outgrown his uniform, which stretched over his belly like a Mexican bandit's faded guayabera.

The LAPD supplied movie companies with police assistance to control crowds and traffic on location, and many of the retired old-timers made some money by working movie gigs. Shane didn't know this officer. He never had many friends in Motors because the officers assigned there were basically "hot pilot" types—attitude junkies known on the job as "mustard cases."

"I need to get to my office," Shane explained.

"Lock up traffic. This is picture," the assistant director's voice came over the motor cop's walkie-talkie.

The officer was in his late sixties and looked slightly ridiculous in his too-tight shirt and worn leather knee boots. He held up his hands as if to say there was nothing he could do. The god of cinema had just spoken. "Sorry, we have to wait for the shot," he said.

"It's a good thing the corner bank isn't being robbed," Shane muttered.

They waited while the helicopter hovered loudly overhead. Suddenly a car squealed around the corner of Spring Street, roared down Sixth, skidded sideways, then disappeared around another corner.

"Cut. Release traffic," the AD said over the walkie-talkie, and Shane was finally waved through.

In L.A., movies had their own hallowed place in the subculture. God forbid anybody should fuck with a unit production schedule.

When Shane got to the Bradbury Building, he was greeted by another surprise. The entire north side of the building was flooded by a huge condor light suspended forty feet in the air from a crane. It lit almost the entire city block.

"Shit," Shane muttered. This was getting ridiculous. He was dressed in black, trying to do an illegal entry while a movie was shooting, and the fucking building he was burglarizing was lit up like City Hall. He had already decided not to use the parking structure, because he was pretty sure that the gate had a common security feature that would read his key card, then time-log it, so he parked in a private lot next to a string of honey wagons and dressing rooms.

He locked the Acura and walked past a line of chattering extras, out onto the brightly lit sidewalk. Hugging the bricks of the Bradbury, turtling his head down into his collar, he tried to hide, feeling stupid and exposed like a cockroach scuttling along a kitchen baseboard.

The building was open, as he knew it would be. Advocates often worked late, so the department kept civilian guards on at night. Usually they slept somewhere on the fifth floor.

He walked into the huge lobby and stood in the atrium. The guard desk was empty. He looked up at the advocates' windows on the third floor. The lights were off. He climbed the stairs, his tennis shoes squeaking on the tile floor. When he got to three, he headed down the corridor and stood for a moment in front of the advocates' offices, looking through the windows, past the reception desks to the cubbies beyond, where any late-working advocates might be sitting. The place looked empty, and the lights were all off. He knocked loudly on the door.

Shane had a cover story ready. If anybody was inside, he was going to abort and say that he had come back to finish some Xeroxing but first needed to pick up his key.

He knocked again, but nobody answered. Everyone had gone home. He looked up and down the exterior corridor, then pulled out a small leather case and removed a set of picklocks.

Ironically, picking locks was a criminal specialty he had learned from Ray Molar. A good set of picklocks contained an array of long, needle-shaped tools and one long, thin, notched metal strip. Shane slid the notched strip into the lock and jiggled it to find the first tumbler by feel. Then the smaller picks slid in behind it. The idea was to fill as many of the lock's keyed openings as possible so that you had enough leverage to turn all the tumblers inside the bolt. It was not as easy as it looked on TV, where some guy would just slide a credit card into a door and, bingo, he was in. It took Shane almost ten minutes before he could turn the lock and let himself inside.

He stepped onto the gray carpeted area just inside the door, then slowly withdrew the picklocks and returned them to the case. He closed the door and locked it from the inside. He moved down the carpeted hallway between the reception desks and windows, heading quietly toward the chief advocate's office. Shane knew that all of the active IAD cases were in a file cabinet there. He got to the end of the long reception area, pushed open the door to Warren Zell's office, took two steps inside, and stopped to adjust his eyes to the low light.

He had stood right in this same spot yesterday, when Zell had informed him that he was IAD's new Xerox machine operator.

He saw the file cabinet at the far end of the room. As he moved to it, he prayed that the cabinets weren't locked. He didn't want to spend any more time there than necessary. As he crossed the room, he took the small penlight out of his back pocket, turned it on, and stuck it in his mouth, gripping it between his teeth. The narrow light hit the top of the metal cabinet, reflecting the beam off its burnished gray finish. He put his hand on the top drawer handle and tugged on it. It slid open. The sound of the little metal rollers filled the room.

He looked down into a file crammed full with case folders; each one had a yellow tab with the officer's name and CF number. He cocked his head to aim the light on the tabs and, working alphabetically, quickly went through the cabinet. In the middle of the top drawer, he found a tab marked L. AYERS. He pulled the file out and opened it. Inside was a single slip of paper with the typed words:

FILE RELOCATED TO S.I.D.

He looked in the second drawer for Joe Church, the second name on the list, and found a file for him as well. It contained the same slip, indicating that the contents had been sent to the secure files over at Special Investigations Division in Parker Center. He glanced at several of the other case files in that drawer and found that none of them had been relocated, only Ayers and Church.

He knelt down and opened the bottom drawer, where he figured he would find Samansky's file, if there was one. It was right in the middle of the drawer, also empty, except for the same note.

What the fuck is this? he thought as he began looking for the Drucker and Kono files. He found both folders empty; the same note was in each. Coy Love didn't have a case pending. He was the only one of Ray's den not facing a Board of Rights.

Shane closed the drawer and stood up. He was just taking the penlight from between his teeth when he heard a gun cock behind him.

"Don't move," a woman's voice said. Then the lights were switched on.

He turned and saw Alexa Hamilton framed in the doorway, a black automatic gripped in both hands, her arms triangled out in front of her in a shooting stance. "You sure are one rule-breaking son of a bitch," she said.

"I'm just trying to—"

"Shut up, Scully! Where's your piece? Where're you packing?"

"Huh?" His mind was spinning, looking for a way out.

"Turn around. Put your hands behind your neck."

"Come on—this Dirty Harriet thing isn't working. I'm assigned down here, same as you. Put the gun down."

"Do what I say, asshole. Do it now!"

He turned his back to her and assumed the position; she quickly patted him down. She removed his clip-on holster, took a step back, and put it on the desk.

Shane assumed she didn't cuff him only because she didn't have her handcuffs handy. She was dressed in a blouse and jeans, her hair was slightly mussed, and he guessed she'd been working late, then fell asleep on the sofa in the back of the advocates' section. He'd awakened her when he'd broken in.

She shifted her gun to her left hand and held it on him while she picked up the phone, locked the receiver under her ear, and dialed three digits. "This is Sergeant Hamilton . . . requesting a Code Six Adam at 1567 Spring Street, third floor. I'm in the chief advocate's office. Notify the responding unit that they will be transporting a police officer under arrest to Parker Center, and notify Chief Mayweather, head of Special Investigations, to call me at 555-9878." She listened for a moment, then hung up the phone.

"You've gotta hear me out before you do this."

"It's done, Scully. You've just been yanked."

"I wasn't looking at my file—"

"I don't wanna hear it. I'm prosecuting you, so we're not having an ex parte conversation. Just button it till the backup gets here."

Shane was down to his last chance. She would either have to shoot him or listen to him, but he was not going to just stand there, mute, waiting to be arrested.

"Ray Molar was supervising a den of six guys. Five of them have cases going through IAD."

"Shut up. I don't wanna hear another word outta you."

"All of their case files are missing. They've been relocated to the secure files at SID. Why? I've never heard of that before, have you?"

"I said be quiet."

"Alexa, I need you to listen to me. Those files are missing because they contain dangerous information."

"Those files could be missing for a lot of reasons."

"Only the files on the guys in Ray's den are gone," he said incredulously. "Why only those guys?"

"I don't care. It doesn't matter. The chief advocate can relocate files anywhere he wants. They're his. Maybe he knows what a loose cannon you are, figured you'd pull this dumb-ass burg."

"Ray has a second home in Lake Arrowhead," Shane went on. "He had a second identity up there: Jay Colter. The house is owned by a real estate company, Cal-VIP Homes. I don't know who owns the company yet, but I have a search being done by the Corporations Commission. When I was up at Ray's Arrowhead house last night, I caught four guys cleaning the place out. After they left, I broke inside."

"So, you're averaging one illegal entry a night. This some kind of sideline for you?"

"Listen to me, will ya?" He was getting impatient. He told her about the one-way mirror, the glory hole, and the videotape box with the name Carl Cummins on it.

"None of this ties to anything," she said. "You're rambling, Scully."

"What're you talking about? A lot of it ties together. Ray's old den had some kinda deal going with the Hoover Street Bounty Hunters, possibly to blow arrests and let them off. Chief Brewer was on his answering machine at the party house. I can play the tape for you if you don't believe me. I think maybe even the mayor, who Ray was driving, is somehow involved."

"In what? Involved in *what?* You think it's some kinda buy-down? Some bullshit collars-for-dollars scheme?" she asked, referring to a situation in which a criminal shares his take with the arresting officer in return for a chance to walk. "Why would the chief of police and the mayor of L.A. be involved in some two-bit street hustle like that? You're delusional."

"I don't think it's a buy-down. I think it's something else, something much bigger. I got called into Brewer's office yesterday. He threatened me with this ridiculous murder charge, told me he thought I stole a videotape out of Ray's house, and if I gave it back, maybe all my problems would go away. If Ray was videotaping sex parties, maybe this Cummins character or somebody else was getting blackmailed, and if I lean on him hard enough, maybe he'll tell me what's going on. That is, if I can find him." He *was* rambling now, his own voice sounding desperate to him.

"This is weak shit, Sergeant—delusional and paranoid."

"Gimme some time. I've only been working on it for two days. Whatever is going on, it's sure got the top floor of the Glass House worried. They're threatening me with a murder indictment to get some tape they think I have."

"They're threatening you with murder because Ray's wife was your eighty-five. You used to date her, and my IOs say, like the stone-ass moron you're proving to be, you're still actually seeing her."

"Eighty-five" was police slang for girlfriend. Shane ignored it and went on: "All of these IAD cases involve the Hoover Street Bounty Hunters. Some ex-cop named Calvin Sheets is involved. His fingerprints were on the Carl Cummins videotape box I found up at Ray's house in Arrowhead."

When Shane mentioned Calvin Sheets, suddenly Alexa's body posture turned rigid. Her jaw clenched and her expression darkened. "Calvin Sheets is now head of security for the Starmax movie studio," he continued. "It's an independent studio owned by Logan Hunter, who U.S. Customs suspects of drug smuggling."

She was looking at him differently now. So he took a wild guess, trying to reel her in. "You know Calvin Sheets."

For a minute, he didn't think she was going to answer him.

"Another advocate, a good friend of mine, terminated him," she finally said. "He was a rogue officer, a dirty sergeant. How was he involved with Ray?" Shane had *finally* piqued her interest.

"I'm not sure. I've got his voice on that same answering-machine tape from Ray's house in Arrowhead. He said, 'Don't fuck around with love.' At first I thought they were talking about love in the romantic sense, but now I know they were talking about Coy Love."

He waited for her to respond, but she didn't, so he went on. "I'd like you to explain to me why my case jumped over the Shooting Review Board and went straight to a BOR, and why the district attorney is setting me up for this bullshit murder charge, when I have an eyewitness who backs me up."

"Barbara Molar is a shit witness. She's the motive for the murder. I should've punched your ticket sixteen years ago."

"Okay, since you brought that up, why didn't you?"

Her ice-blue eyes were sparking anger. "Why didn't I what?"

"You threw my board sixteen years ago. Why?"

"Who told you I threw it? That's ridiculous."

"DeMarco told me. He said you impeached your own witness and withheld Ray's sworn affidavit."

Now they could hear men's voices downstairs; they echoed in the hollow atrium. The backup unit had arrived. The elevators were shut down for the night and, after a minute, they heard footsteps marching up the tile stairs.

"You might have me on this low-grade B and E, but I'll get you for throwing that Board of Rights sixteen years ago," he threatened. "DeMarco will testify that you gave the case away. You'll probably be getting your own CF number down here. Give you a look at this division from the other side."

"I wish I'd never laid eyes on you," she said sharply.

He could see the beginning of indecision in her eyes. She was a career cop, high on the lieutenant's list.

There was a rattling at the front door of the Advocate Section.

"Anybody in there?" a cop's voice called into the office.

"What's it gonna be, Sergeant?" he asked. She stood frozen, holding her gun in one hand. Finally she lowered her weapon, turned, and walked to the door, then opened it.

Two uniforms moved in. Shane could see them through Warren Zell's open office door.

"It's okay, Officer. My mistake," he heard Alexa say. "It was just one of our sergeants. He works here."

To punctuate the point, Shane pulled out his badge and flashed it at them.

"Sorry for the call," she said. "If you could do me a favor . . . Cancel my Code Six A and ask Communications to cancel my call to Deputy Chief Mayweather."

The cop nearest to her touched his shoulder mike and started broadcasting a Code Four, which was a stand-down. Both uniforms turned and left. Alexa closed the door and walked back to where Shane was standing. "We're even. Get outta here," she said angrily.

"Not until you hear the rest of it," he said softly. "And not until you tell me why the hell you threw my board sixteen years ago."

EX PARTE
COMMUNICATION

THEY WALKED DOWN Third Street, through the glare of the movie lights, and settled on a small, dingy bar called the Appaloosa, two blocks south of the Bradbury. The proprietor had made a half-assed decorating attempt at a Mexican motif: table candles with corny glass sombreros, badly painted pictures of Appaloosas with stoic Mexican cowboys or dusty regal hombres from Santa Ana's army looking across prairies or valleys, their heads held high, reeking Hispanic nobility.

"That fucking Schwarzenegger movie is driving me nuts," she said as they slid into a cracked vinyl booth and waved at a Mexican waiter wearing a dirty white coat about the same color as the gray linoleum floor. Mariachi recordings hissed and popped through a bad speaker system. The place was a refried dive.

"Scotch and water," she said.

"Two," he added.

The waiter left and they sat there, each waiting for the other to start. She was pushed back on the ruptured red vinyl seat, as if she were trying to get as far away from him as possible.

"This is your party," she finally said.

"I want to know why you threw my board."

"Ancient history."

"I wanna know, just the same."

"I wanna know why Christie Brinkley can't keep a husband. It's a mystery. Leave it at that."

"You threw my board sixteen years ago, and now you volunteer for this one?"

"I didn't volunteer. I was ordered. I've been out of Internal Affairs for ten years, running a patrol shift down in Southwest. I wanted to stay in the field, but because of you, I ended up getting called back by Tom Mayweather to handle your board. Don't ask me why."

"Tom Mayweather?"

"Yeah. Heard of him?" Cutting sarcasm now, laying it on with a trowel. "He's head of Special Investigations Division. Read your department administration list."

"I heard you volunteered."

"Look, Scully, for whatever it's worth, you don't even remotely interest me anymore. I'm gonna try your BOR in seven days because the Glass House wants me to. Then I'm going back to Southwest Patrol, where I can actually do some honest-to-God police work."

"Why would Tom Mayweather pull you back to handle my board?"

"If I tell you what I think the reason is, it'll just piss you off."

"I'm already pissed off."

"Because I hold the record. I'm the best advocate they ever had down there. I only lost your case and a few others in the time I was in that division. Mayweather wanted the best, so he ordered me back. If that seems egotistical and self-serving— tough. That's what I think."

"You know what I think?"

She didn't answer, but sat staring at him with those remarkable laser-blue eyes.

"He pulled you back because you tried me before. Sparks flew back then, and he knew it would piss me off. He's trying to pressure me to turn over that videotape he thinks I have. He thought putting you on the case would up the stakes." He paused while the waiter set down their drinks and left.

"That's your take, because you always put yourself at ground zero," she said. "To everyone else, you're marginal business, just another dumb mistake that needs to be handled in due course. This has been fun. We've had our one drink. Meeting's over, see ya." She took a long swallow, then set the glass down and started to leave.

"Hey, Lexie, I'm not through yet."

"I don't go by 'Lexie,' asshole. The name's Alexa."

"I don't go by 'asshole,' Alexa. The name's Shane."

They sat in silence for a moment.

"So, why did you throw my board?"

"You won't get off that, huh?"

"It's pretty unusual. You're the best advocate down there, the Black Witch of the Division, yet you intentionally let me slide? I want to know why."

"Because I knew Ray Molar was using you. In the years I'd been at IAD, I'd seen a handful of probationers take violence beefs for him . . . guys he'd handpicked out of the Academy and teamed up with. It became pretty obvious what was happening. He was busting heads and holding court in the street, then getting you dummies to take the heat for him if complaints came down. It was starting to piss me off. Then, when Ray gave the chief advocate that bullshit statement behind my back, saying that you had emotional problems and that he'd been worried about your mental stability, I sorta lost it. Furthermore, I was sure my key wit, that gas-station attendant, was dirty. Ray musta threatened him to get him to say he saw you beat that kid, because he flunked the poly I gave him. The case was an air ball, so I called DeMarco and told him where the holes were."

Shane sat there for a long moment and looked at her. She seemed different, somehow softer, more vulnerable. Maybe it was the low light, or the scotch, or maybe it was what she'd done for him sixteen years ago at some risk to her own career. But he was being compelled to view her in a different way, so he sat there, turning dials, trying to regain some focus on her.

"You just throw cases if they seem wrong to you?"

"Listen, Scully, I know you think Internal Affairs is a sewer full of ladder-climbing politicians who don't care how many cops' careers they wreck."

"And it's not?"

"No, it's not. Don't you think we're drowning in all the politically correct bullshit that goes through this division? The Gay and Lesbian Alliance gets pissed because some cop gets tough trying to bust a two-hundred-pound angel-dusted bull dyke who's brandishing a hammer. The arresting officer ends up putting the bracelets on but has his head opened up in the process. Instead of filing a resisting-arrest charge on the hammer-wielding debutante, the cop gets accused of gay bashing. It's a big news story. Lots of angry meetings in West Hollywood. The *L.A. Times* does a blue-death dance on the front page, and our fearless leaders dump the whole thing into our basket. . . .

"Or some gangbanger caught standing over a dead body with a smoking MAC-Ten accuses the arresting officer of beating him in the station I-room. The EMTs are called, and the banger doesn't have a mark on him. But the special-interest groups take it to the press—racial violence, forced confessions, cops on the rampage. It's a big deal, and everybody knows all the banger is doing is getting back at the cops who busted him. It's total bullshit. My own IOs are telling me the board won't float, but the perp's a minority. The Glass House and the mayor fold like deck chairs, and the whole mess is back in my office.

"After a while you start to sort out the really bad ones, maybe drop a few key pieces of manufactured evidence overboard, impeach one of your own lying wits if you have to, lay back a bit, try and even things out so good cops don't end up paying the price for somebody's political agenda.

"Then along comes a Rodney King, where the cops were dead wrong, and you gotta go to war, kick some ass. The police need policing. A department without self-investigation is bound to become corrupt."

She drained her drink, the ice cube clinking on her teeth. She set the glass down hard on the table, telling him the lecture had ended. "Is that all? Can I go now?"

"Tell me about Calvin Sheets."

"I told you. Calvin was terminated by a good friend of mine, a current advocate named Susan Kellerman. Susan and I were both sergeants in Southwest Patrol, and I recommended her for Internal Affairs. She's not there two weeks and she gets Calvin's board. He was threatening her life with anonymous phone calls all during the investigation, but she couldn't prove it was him. She called me and asked what she should do. I took a ride out to Calvin's house and gave him a heads-up talk. It wasn't pleasant."

"What happened?"

"I just said it wasn't pleasant. Okay?"

"Did Susan tell you everything about his case?"

"In detail. As a matter of fact, I got so mad at Sheets, I worked it for free. Did some IO work in my off-hours to help her."

"What was he charged with?"

"He was shift commander on the Coliseum detail and was keeping bogus time sheets. He had officers listed as 'on duty' who weren't even there. They were kicking back salary and overtime to him. It was a mess—more than ten cops involved. His whole shift was signing their own arrest reports 'cause Sheets wasn't around. On top of all that, he was off working a second job at the movie studio, doing security work."

"For Logan Hunter."

"Yeah. The cops on his detail called him Dream Sheets because he was so tired when he finally got to the Coliseum, he would just sleep in his office. He was running the sloppiest PED team I ever saw. His Prostitution Enforcement Detail at the Coliseum was watching the games while the hookers were running wild. There were more blow jobs going on in the parking lot than at a swingers' convention. The Coliseum Commission was enraged. We had dozens of letters from those guys. Calvin's board took two days, and Susan got his tin. Eight of the ten cops he was supervising got terminated with him. Two rookies survived but were given six-month mandatory suspensions. It was a disaster for the city. Calvin called me up after he got terminated . . . told me he would pick a time when I wasn't looking and pay me back with interest. I can hardly wait for him to try. Total sleaze."

Shane sat across the table, absentmindedly twirling a red swizzle stick between his fingers.

"Stop playing with that, will you? It's making me nervous."

He put the stick in the ashtray. "Doesn't any of this seem strange to you? Add what I have to what you just told me, and it starts to reek. All these Internal Affairs cases, Ray's den and the H Street Bounty Hunters . . . a banger named Sol Preciado was doing assaults at the Coliseum; Calvin Sheets was failing to supervise his PED team down there, his fingerprints were on that videotape box, in an Arrowhead house where I think prostitutes were screwing guys that Sheets and Ray were blackmailing . . ."

"You've gotta connect the dots, Shane. You haven't done that. It's called police work."

"I know, but don't you think a lot of this is damn strange?"

She sat looking at him for a long moment. Finally she nodded her head slowly. "Drucker's case is going to a board tomorrow."

"No, it's not. Mayweather just got an extension pushing it back to the twenty-third. If you're so concerned about policing the police, why not work on this?"

"Because I'm on the other side of *your* case. I'm prosecuting you. How on earth can I help you?"

"I won't tell if you won't." He grinned.

"Tell you what, tomorrow I'll ask a few questions, just for the hell of it."

"I think we should talk to Sol Preciado. He's a witness in Drucker's case. Why don't we go out to juvie and sit him down."

"When were you planning for us to do that?"

"Now. Let's do it now. You've got an advocate card; the jail warden won't question it. Let's get him in an I-room at juvie hall and play 'I've Got a Secret.' Bluff him, see what he knows."

She sat looking at him, not answering or reacting to the suggestion.

"If we get nothing, I promise I'll leave you alone." Then he added, "You won't have to see me again till my board."

"We've gotta get one thing straight first," she said. "I want an unequivocal promise that you're not gonna use what I just told you about your old BOR against me."

"Alexa, I was never gonna use that. You may think I'm an asshole, but at least I'm an asshole with principles. You did me a favor. I won't forget it. Whatever you decide now, as far as I'm concerned, nothing happened back then."

"Okay, then let's go do some jailin'," she said.

They each took a car and followed each other all the way out to the juvenile jail in Downey.

Trouble was, once they got there and asked that Sol Preciado be brought to an interrogation room, they found out he was no longer a guest of the city. Earlier that afternoon a door had been mysteriously left open in the back of a court transport vehicle and the fifteen-year-old gangbanger had escaped again.

Shane and Alexa took the creaking elevator back down to the lobby and walked out of juvenile hall into the harsh Xenon lights of the parking lot.

"This kid has more jailbreaks than Dillinger," she said.

"They pushed Drucker's board back to get time to arrange for this. They let him go so he wouldn't be around to testify," Shane said. When she looked over at him, he added, "I'm telling you, it's been like this ever since I shot Ray. Somebody is pulling strings, making shit happen. It's been orchestrated better than the Philharmonic."

"You're being paranoid," she concluded.

"I'm being framed," he corrected.

CROSSROADS AND
23
CROSSFIRE

I'M MAKING ARRANGEMENTS for you to go back to your mom on Monday," Shane said.

They were sitting in his backyard chairs, Chooch with his feet up on the low picket fence, leaning way back, trying to look as though he couldn't give a shit. "Make any arrangement you want, but I won't be here on Friday," Chooch snarled. "You can go quakin' about it with the cave bitch all you want, don't matter, 'cause I'm gone."

"You think that I'm dumping you, that I don't want you here, but you're wrong. I'm telling you the truth, Chooch. I feel shitty about this."

No response.

"Tell you what. I should be clear by the end of next week. Whatta you say you and I get outta town, go do something together."

"What're we gonna do? Score some tasty together? Do some

jay?" He was smirking now, letting Shane know he was back on the other side.

"I told you no drugs. How 'bout a weekend at Disneyland?" Shane said. "We'll stay at the hotel there, ride the Matterhorn, Space Mountain; do the Log Ride, all that stuff."

"You think I'm some little kid? You can't bribe me with a trip to Disneyland."

"You ever been to Disneyland?" Shane asked.

Chooch shrugged, not answering.

"If you've never been, you don't know what you're turning down. And if you wanna score some tasty, there're girls all over Disneyland," letting Chooch know he understood rap lingo.

But Chooch said nothing.

"You told me once that you wanted to be the most important instead of the least. And I get that, man. I really do. But lemme ask you something. If I let you stay here, knowing that I was in some real danger and that you might end up hurt, what kinda guy would that make me? And how important would you be to me if I just flat disregard your safety?"

"Whatever . . . You're gonna do what you wanta."

"You want me to understand, to care about your problems, but you don't want to understand or care about mine."

"Is this gonna take much longer?"

"You're going to Sandy on Monday. Sorry you and I can't talk about it."

"You say you're in danger, that someone's gonna ride on you? And I'm supposed to believe this?"

Now it was Shane who didn't answer.

"Well, I don't. Okay? I see it as total doo-rah. You're a fuckin' liar."

Shane got up and moved toward the door. Before going in, he turned and talked to Chooch's back. "There are defining moments in a man's life, Chooch. You're at one. You can deal with this like a man, or you can run from it like a kid. If you run—if you take off and go hang with a buncha street bravos, you're gonna regret it."

" 'Cause why? You're gonna get me booked on a juvenile court detaining order?" he said, surprising Shane that he knew the exact document, and further proving he'd been hanging with some very unsavory people.

"You're at an important crossroad. Read the signs carefully before you choose what direction you want to go. You're fifteen. Nobody can tell you what to do anymore, certainly not me. You're gonna make your own decisions, no matter what Sandy or I say. You're almost a man now, so you stop getting the juvenile discount. But you also gotta pay adult rates—be careful."

Shane went inside and undressed for bed. It had been a strange night. He had left Alexa not knowing what she would do, or whether she believed any of what he had told her. Then he had come home to this draining conversation with Chooch. He lay on his pillow, looking at the cracked ceiling, wondering where it was all heading.

In his wildest imagination, he never would have expected what happened next.

...

Shane heard something outside the house.

It woke him.

He didn't know whether it was part of a dream or someone in his yard. He lay still, his heart pounding, his senses tingling; then he rolled out of bed and crept slowly to the dresser, where he had put his gun. He retrieved it, snuck out of the bedroom, padded down the hall in his underwear, and checked the guest room. Chooch was asleep in the bed next to the wall, so Shane went back up the hall.

He wasn't two steps into the front room when a machine gun opened up, blowing out the entire front window. Glass rained in on him, taking part of the drapery with it. Shane dove for the floor as the machine gun kept firing, stitching holes in the wall behind him, breaking plaster, shattering pictures. He worked his way toward the front door on his stomach.

Another burst from a second gun came through the side window. Nine-millimeter slugs tattooed the living room's east wall. He was pinned in a deadly cross fire. Shane rolled over and sat up, firing blindly out the broken side window with his .38. Then he heard a car start in the alley.

Chooch ran into the living room, and Shane launched himself at the teenager, taking him down seconds before another barrage of bullets screamed just above their heads, breaking a lamp and turning an end table into splinters. Shane pinned Chooch under him, protecting the boy with his body.

"Let's go. Let's get outta here!" somebody shouted.

A car door slammed; an engine roared. There was the chirp of rubber and then the sound of a car speeding away.

"Stay here. Stay down," Shane ordered Chooch. He wormed his way out the front door, slid down the front steps on his belly, and rolled behind a low wall. He didn't want to risk sticking his head up until he had a chance to check out all possible lines of fire. He strained to hear in the dark, to identify any warning sound, trying to be sure all of them had left. Then he rolled up and scooted back on his ass until he could feel the side of the house against his shoulder blades.

His neighbors were starting to shout: "What's going on!?" "What the fuck's happening?!" "Call the police!"

Shane couldn't remember how many shots he had squeezed off, so he flipped open the cylinder . . . three cartridges left. He snapped the revolver shut and got to his feet, quickly making a lap around the house. He ran into Longboard in the backyard and almost shot him.

"Get back inside, Brian," he ordered.

The surfboard shaper turned and ran back into his house.

After Shane was certain the house was secure, he went back inside.

"Let's go," he said to Chooch.

"Where?"

"You're going to your mother's. You can't stay here. Get your clothes, now! Meet me in the garage. We're outta here!"

They could hear sirens approaching, way off in the distance.

"Let's go. I don't wanna be here when the cops arrive. Move it!"

Shane grabbed his clothes out of the bedroom and, not waiting to put them on, bolted for the garage. He was already pulling the Acura out when the teenager arrived, carrying his shirt, shoes, and pants; Chooch jumped into the passenger side. The police sirens were now only a few blocks away.

Shane shot up the alley behind the east canal, made a left away from the water, and floored it. Miraculously, he didn't choose the same streets as the arriving squad cars. Five minutes later they were on the freeway, both clad only in their undershorts, heading toward Barrington Plaza.

Chooch sat quietly in the passenger seat, shaken by the experience. Finally he looked over at Shane.

"I thought it was bullshit," he said.

"Now you know," Shane answered, but he hadn't been prepared for the ferocious machine-gun attack. He had never imagined that somebody would stand outside his house pouring lead into his living room. His hands were shaking; he was glad he was gripping the steering wheel so it didn't show.

"Who were those guys?" Chooch asked. "They ride down on you with fucking machine guns. . . ."

"I'm not sure. Bad cops, I think."

When he looked over at Chooch a second time, he saw a strange expression on the boy's face, too complicated to read.

They got off the freeway at Sunset. Shane found a dark spot

and pulled to the curb so they could change into their clothes in the car. Then they drove around the corner and pulled in at Barrington Plaza. Shane badged the doorman with the braided shoulders. Sandy was standing in the living room wearing a silk robe belted around her slender waist. Her hair was tousled. She looked composed but concerned, an actress playing a scene.

"I can't believe it," she said after Shane filled her in.

"This isn't going to be a discussion, Sandy. You're taking Chooch."

"My God, who do you think they were?"

"I'm not sure, but I have a few hunches." He stood there, feeling a wave of fatigue. Then he looked at Chooch, wearing the same strange expression Shane had seen in the car. In the better light of Sandy's apartment, it looked a little like regret, or maybe it was guilt.

"Okay, here's the deal, Chooch . . ."

The boy jerked to attention and faced Shane.

"Disneyland, next weekend. You stay here till then, and I'll be back for you. It's a promise."

Chooch nodded.

As Shane moved to the door, he heard Chooch call his name, and he looked back. "I'm sorry," the boy said. "I thought you were lying, but I was wrong."

THE POLICE
BILL OF RIGHTS

WHEN SHANE GOT BACK to his house on East Canal Street, it was sunup. Five black-and-whites and a crime-scene station wagon were blocking the street. He edged the Acura past them and pulled into the garage.

There were ten cops standing in his living room. When he entered, they turned, clearly surprised to see him.

"Where the hell you been?" Garson Welch asked. The fact that the old detective had been called out on this told Shane that he was still a murder suspect in the criminal investigation surrounding Ray's death.

Welch had been given this call because he was investigating Molar's shooting and this machine-gun attack was most likely connected. The old detective looked at Shane with his basset-hound expression and tired brown eyes. "We just put a bulletin out on you."

"I had something personal to take care of," Shane said.

"What the fuck *was* this?" Garson said, pointing at the destroyed wall where Crime Section techs were busy digging 9mm slugs out of the plaster and bagging them as evidence for a ballistics comparison later. That is, if they ever found the weapon, which was right up there with the odds on Shane's next promotion.

Shane was sure that the machine guns were illegal street sweepers: AK-47s, maybe MAC-10s, most likely taken from the vast array of confiscated weapons held in the Firearms and Ammunition Section's secure property room, destined for eventual burial at sea.

"Who did this?" Garson asked.

"Don't know," Shane said. "The lights were out, and I was flat on my stomach eating carpet."

"Okay, let's go. You got an appointment at Parker Center."

"Shit . . . do we have to do that again?" Shane asked. The remark was greeted by a flat stare.

Shane was taken from his house and again made the early-morning ride across town to the Glass House. Garson Welch stayed quiet as they drove. He had the case but didn't want it. As far as Welch was concerned, the brass at Parker Center could ask the questions. They pulled into the parking garage next to the huge lit police building, then rode the elevator up to the ninth floor. This time Shane found Deputy Chief Tom Mayweather standing in the hallway waiting for him, looking very *GQ* in his black pinstripe suit, white shirt, maroon tie, and matching pocket accessory. His bald head was gleaming, his handsome face theatrically troubled. He didn't say anything but motioned Shane down the hall. Garson Welch stayed in the lobby, glad to be out of it.

Shane followed Mayweather into his office. The room was not as large as Chief Brewer's by half but had a picture window with a Spring Street view. The shelves were littered with Mayweather's old basketball trophies, game balls, and team photos, along with the more standard police memorabilia: his Academy class picture, civil-service awards, and plaques attesting to his superiority as a police officer.

Mayweather stepped behind his desk, using the large, light oak piece of furniture as a barricade to separate them and define their roles. Shane stood while Mayweather sat in his tan executive swivel chair. The overhead ceiling spot kicked white light off his shaved head.

"You are an amazing piece of work, Sergeant," the deputy chief finally said.

"Thank you, sir."

"I wasn't complimenting you. Why the hell didn't you come back from Arrowhead and report in here, as instructed?"

"I left you a message."

"Right . . . the 'I had an accident/fell asleep at the wheel/stayed in a motel' message, left with my secretary at eight-fifteen A.M." He shook his head in wonder. "You must think I'm one stupid son of a bitch."

"How would you like me to respond to that, sir?" Shane was getting mad now, wanting to fire back but on tender ground professionally.

Mayweather leaned back in his chair, the knife-sharp creases in his pants now visible over the desktop. "Take off your gun and hand me your badge. You're suspended from duty without pay pending your Internal Affairs Board of Rights."

"Don't you have to write up a 1.61 before you can suspend me?"

"Consider it written."

"The Police Bill of Rights really seems to have its limits where I'm concerned, doesn't it?"

"The 1.61 will be in your hands before nine o'clock. Take off your gun and give me your badge and ID card."

Shane removed the clip-on holster from his belt, then pulled his badge and ID in the brown leather fold-over out of his pocket.

"Put them on the desk, please," Mayweather commanded.

Shane did as he was instructed. "Now what?"

Mayweather seemed puzzled by the question, so Shane added, "Doesn't the district attorney show up about now with a murder warrant and cart me off to the lockup?"

"You really have an active imagination."

"I didn't imagine the nine-millimeter machine-gun slugs in my living-room walls. Chief Brewer has been threatening me with a murder indictment. Since you're not doing that, something else must be happening. Maybe you just want to leave me on the street without my gun and badge, where I'll be easier to get at?"

"You are a sick, paranoid man, Sergeant Scully. There are other ways to view what just happened."

"Let's hear."

"I think you're involved with the wrong people, vice or drugs . . . some other street action. You were taking a 'patch' and you took too much." A "patch" was police argot for a payoff to a cop for letting a crime happen, differing from a "buy down," which was a bribe to turn an arrestee loose or book him for a lesser crime. "People you thought you had fooled, or had under control, got tired of paying and threw you a party," Mayweather added.

"You surprise me, Tom," Shane said, using the deputy chief's first name to show he had lost respect for him. "The word in the department is you're a good guy, a smart guy, but what's happening here right now, between us, isn't smart at all. If you really don't know what's going on, then you're being used—played for a patsy. Either way, it marks you."

"I see." Mayweather seemed to consider this, sitting still, thinking, his big trophy-filled office and black Armani pinstripes dissing Shane—making him small. Then the deputy chief seemed to make up his mind and sat upright. "Get out. Check in every day with Captain Halley. Go home and leave this alone."

"Go home? Should I sit in the window?"

"That will be just about enough of that. Go home. Stay put. If you know what's good for you, you'll stop making trouble."

"You can suspend me, but you sure as hell can't tell me not to work on my own defense. Somebody made a big mistake. They thought I took something out of Ray's house and they over-reacted. Now they're pretty sure I don't have it, but Chief Brewer leaned too hard and got me looking in the wrong places. Suddenly I have too much of it and have to be neutralized. Whoever's behind this had one easy shot and missed. I won't be stumbling around, half asleep in my undies, next time. It's gonna be much harder."

Shane turned and walked out of the office without looking back, leaving his badge, gun, and career in police work behind.

Once again, he was stranded downtown without his car. He didn't trust anybody enough to ask for a lift, and as a suspended officer, he couldn't check a slickback out of the motor pool . . . so he walked four blocks east to the Bradbury Building and waited in the parking garage for Alexa Hamilton to arrive.

PRINT HIT

S EVEN THIRTY-FIVE A.M. Alexa pulled the gray Ford Crown Victoria into the parking structure and parked in her spot. She was early, as usual, getting a jump-start on the day while DeMarco slept late.

She got out of the car, dressed for success in a dark charcoal pantsuit tailored to her trim, twenty-three-inch waist. She was carrying another cardboard box full of files, her bulging, faded leather briefcase hanging from a strap over her shoulder. She headed toward the elevators and stopped when she saw him standing next to a concrete pillar in the shadows of the huge, underlit parking garage.

"You shouldn't be here," she said.

"I know, I should be in a slumber room at Forest Lawn."

She walked toward him now, closing the distance, stopping two feet away. He could smell her perfume. He'd never thought of her as wearing perfume.

"What happened?" she asked. "The chief advocate called me at six. He said somebody shot up your house."

"Shot up . . . My house was massacred. I got enough lead in the walls to go into strip mining. On top of that, I got suspended this morning by Mayweather. He took my gun, badge, and ID, kicked me loose. So I'm back on the street running around, a moving target. It's been way too entertaining. I was expecting to get hit with a murder one indictment, but for some reason it didn't happen. I guess things were bound to slow down sometime."

"The warrant's coming. The writ got signed. I saw it yesterday. Looks like they're holding it in reserve. . . . Let's go back and sit in my car," she said unexpectedly.

They walked to her car. She put the box in the backseat, then they both slid into the Crown Vic and closed the doors.

"Look, I don't understand what's happening. I agree, something's going on. I don't get it myself . . . but I'm compromised here," Alexa said with some anxiety.

"Lemme see if I got this straight," he said. "I've been threatened by Chief Brewer and most of Ray's old den. Somebody blew the shit out of my living room, Mayweather just suspended me, I got a murder warrant pending, but we're worried *you're* 'compromised'?"

She sat quietly, deep in thought. He sensed there was something she wasn't telling him.

"What is it? You know something else," he said.

Finally she opened her briefcase and pulled out a sheaf of papers.

"Those are the missing files from the Chief Advocate's Office. On my way in this morning, I stopped by the Office of Administrative Services. They supervise the Officer Representation Section at Parker Center. I have a friend down there. She pulled the duplicates on all missing case folders from the discovery files and made copies for me."

Shane took the missing files and looked through them. "Jesus, look't this, it's just what I thought. All of them involve Hoover Street Bounty Hunters. Lee Ayers was beefed by a store owner just like Drucker; slow response to Code Thirty calls. Kris Kono is also accused of a slow response. Joe Church failed to Mirandize a banger after a street homicide. The case got pitched." He looked up at her and, for the first time, saw indecision on her chiseled face. "Why would Ray's old den be kicking gangsters loose?" he asked.

"I don't know, but it's not my case. You're my case. I'm supposed to be prosecuting *you*."

"Well, excuse me," he said, anger filling the space between them.

"Look, Shane, I just said I agree you may have stumbled into something, but—"

"But you don't wanna see your career go in the bucket with mine."

"What do you want me to do? If I start messing with this, they're going to pull me off your case. The district attorney will file against you anyway. It won't change anything."

"Yes, it will, because you'll be doing the right thing. Alexa, I'm down to just you. Nobody else in the department will even talk to me. With no badge, I'm locked out. I can't even access the computer system."

"And you want me to sacrifice myself for you?"

"All that righteous shit you were giving me last night, the Rodney King speech about IAD policing the police, kicking ass when there's corruption—that was just bullshit. Sounds good, but what you really meant is, as long as you can do it without hurting yourself or putting yourself in jeopardy."

"That's not fair."

"Then help me."

"I can't help you. I'm prosecuting you. Don't you get that?" She sat in the car, glaring at him. Shane wondered how it happened: this woman he had despised so recently now seemed like the only chance he had left.

"I'll resign from the department, okay? I'm gonna get terminated anyway, so I'll save you the trouble. I'll send a letter of resignation, and then you won't have to prosecute me. You won't have this monumental ethical problem."

"Don't resign," she said softly.

"Why not?"

"Because . . . just because."

Then her beeper sounded, and she pulled it out of her purse. She looked at it, then quickly put it away.

"What is it?"

"Prints and Identification. I dropped off one of those empty folders from Zell's files. They're calling me back."

Shane didn't say anything, but he thought it was a good move to see whose fingerprints were on those empty file folders. He was surprised he hadn't thought of it.

She pulled her cell phone out of her briefcase and dialed a number. "This is Sergeant Hamilton, serial number 50791. I got paged to this number. I have a fingerprint request, number 487, April twenty-third," she said, reading off a slip of paper from her purse.

They sat in the still air of the parked Crown Vic as she waited. Then: "Okay . . . right. Okay, I've got it." She hung up and put the phone back in her purse.

"What?" he asked.

Indecision was tightening her lips, bending them down. "I've been a cop for seventeen years. It's all I ever wanted to do," she said sadly.

"Alexa, whose prints were on the file? They weren't Commander Zell's, right?"

"Zell's were on there, of course. But there was another set, fresh ones."

"Whose were they?"

"Why is the fucking head of Special Investigations Division personally clearing active case folders out of the Chief Advocate's Office?"

"Mayweather?" Shane said.

They sat in the Crown Vic, both realizing the answer was obvious. Mayweather had been doing damage control. There was no way she could ignore it, he thought. Mayweather was actively involved. The deputy police chief was personally emptying sensitive files because he didn't trust anyone else to do it. Shane looked at her and waited. Would she finally admit he was right? Whatever was going on, it was frightening and went straight to the top of the department.

ESIS

ALEXA HAMILTON sat in the Crown Vic for another minute, saying nothing. Then she opened the door and stepped out, retrieving her box of files from the backseat. She kicked the back door closed with her foot and stood looking over the roof of the car at Shane, who had also exited the vehicle.

"I don't know what you expect me to do," she said, her voice ringing in the cold, empty structure.

"I don't, either," he said. "If the district attorney files that 187 warrant, I'm going to be sitting this out in jail. I've got a lot of ground to cover, six cops to check out."

She stood there, reluctant to stay, unable to go. The heavy box was balanced on her slender knee. "What're you gonna do?" she asked, finally sliding the box up onto the trunk so she wouldn't have to hold it.

"On the tape in Ray's Arrowhead house, Don and Lee left a message. It said, 'We're on for Friday night, the Web. Bring the jerseys.' I don't have a clue what that means, but it's Friday, so tonight I thought I'd tail Drucker or Ayers, see what and where the Web is."

She listened but said nothing.

"Then I've gotta find out about Cal-VIP Homes . . . research who owns that company."

A car came up the ramp in the garage and pulled past them.

"I can't stand around here talking to you. Give me your cell phone number. I'll call you," Alexa said impatiently.

"When?"

"*When I'm through.* I've got six affidavits scheduled for today, starting with Bud Halley at eight-fifteen this morning. I've gotta go to the Patrol Division and dig out your old TA reports, then over to the Traffic Coordination Section and pull the reckless-driving sheets. You sure busted your share of city vehicles."

"You can't be serious?"

She pressed the alarm activation button on her car key, and the Crown Vic chirped loudly, cutting him off, ending the argument. Then she pulled the file box off the trunk and headed away from him toward the elevator. He watched as she stood in front of the elevator, balancing the heavy box; then the door slid open and she stepped inside. Just as it started to close, she stuck her foot out and stopped it.

"Meet me at the Appaloosa after work, five-thirty. We'll follow Drucker and Ayers together." Before he could answer, the door closed, taking her from view.

■ ■ ■

Shane spent the morning getting himself settled. He rented a room in a building called the Spring Summer Apartments, picking it because it cost only two hundred for one week. It was also within walking distance of the Bradbury.

The room was small but clean. He sat on the faded blue bedspread and dialed Budget Rent-a-Car. He reserved a Mustang from the rental agency located a few blocks away on Third, and walked over to pick up the car.

As he started down Third Street, he could see signs posted on telephone poles and buildings that notified residents and store owners that there would be no parking permitted on Saturday, by order of the LAPD, as a motion picture would be shooting on these streets. Schwarzenegger, no doubt.

When he got to Budget, they showed him to a red Mustang convertible, a year or two newer than Barbara's but totally unacceptable for a tail job. He turned it down in favor of a dull-brown four-door Ford Taurus.

He drove the Taurus back to the Spring Summer Apartments, parked, went back up to his room, and checked in with the Corporations Commission on his request for a printout of corporate ownership of Cal-VIP Homes. He was informed by a cold female voice that his request was in line but had not been processed yet. Maybe sometime after noon. He gave his cell phone number to her, stressing the urgency, and the woman promised to call back.

He hung up and sat in the room, feeling restless and caged. After pacing for almost half an hour, he called the Electronics Scientific Investigation Section (ESIS) to check on Ray's answering-machine tape analysis. He got a clerk there, somebody named Boyd Miller, who told Shane that ESIS had picked up fragments of old voices on the tape.

"Some of this is kinda jumbled," Miller said. "On one message, our best fragment sounded like 'If this is Susan Burbick or Burdick, we have your . . . something.' I couldn't make out the rest."

"Anything else?" Shane said, writing it down.

"No. That's it. You want to pick this up or shall we send it back to your office?"

"Hold it for me. I'll pick it up."

He hung up and sat there for several moments before reluctantly calling Barbara Molar at her house. He got the machine, so he tried her new cell phone. After he identified himself, she brightened.

"Hi, stranger. How you doing?"

"Terrible. How 'bout you?"

"Well, actually, pretty good. It's nice you finally called. I was worried."

"Have you ever heard of someone named Susan Burdick or Burbick?" he asked.

"What do I get if I say yes?"

"You get to find out if Ray was actually married to her or not."

"Oh . . . well, I'll have to think about it. I'll look in Ray's address book. How 'bout we get together for a drink, talk it over?"

"I can't, I'm meeting someone at five."

"Don't play hard-to-get with me, Shane. I don't like being dumped."

"Neither did I," he said softly, and hung up.

He sat in the transient apartment with its chipped, broken bathroom fixtures and fly-speckled wallpaper and wondered what to do next. Finally he got the number for the Arrowhead Sheriff's Department, called, and asked for Sheriff Conklyn. After a few minutes the tall, middle-aged sheriff was on the phone.

"Sheriff, it's Sergeant Scully. Remember me?"

"Whatta you want?" He was angry now, or maybe just impatient.

"When I was up there, you had a murder, a body you pulled out of the lake and couldn't identify. I never heard if it was a man or a woman."

"Woman."

"You ever ID the corpse?"

"Nope, still a Jane Doe." There was a sliver of interest in his manner now.

"Check out a woman named Susan Burdick or Burbick. I don't

know which. I also don't have an address, but maybe you can get a line on her through her marriage license. I think she was married to Ray Molar using the name Jay Colter. They tied the knot at the Midnight Wedding Chapel in Vegas six months ago. If that checks, you could get a dental match and maybe pin it."

"Why do I get the feeling I'm doing your footwork?"

"Hey, Sheriff, I'm trying to help you. If you don't wanna ID your icebox cases, don't bother with it."

"But if I do, you'd probably be interested in who she is and where she came from."

"I'm a curious guy."

"Okay, this will probably take a day or so. Call me back."

After he hung up, Shane drove back to the Fotomat to pick up the Arrowhead pictures. He was told by the clerk that they had to push the negative four stops to get an exposure. Shane opened the envelope and looked at six grainy snapshots of the men inside Ray's house. He could see most of their faces but didn't recognize any of them. He wondered which one was Calvin Sheets. Since his camera was in the Acura back in Venice, he bought a new Canon with a zoom lens and some film. He was loading the film when his cell phone rang. It was Sandy.

"Chooch ran away," she told him straight out.

"I was afraid of that."

"You've gotta find him."

"How'm I gonna find him, Sandy? All I can do is put a 'run-away juvie' out on him, and he's gonna get arrested. Then you'll be fooling around with the LACCSD—that's children's social services. If they find out what you do for a living, they'll take him away from you. Then he's gonna be a ward of the court."

"Well, what can we do?"

"I don't know. I'll try and find him, but I don't even know where to start. It's not going to be easy."

But it was easier than he thought. As soon as he hung up from Sandy, his phone rang. It was Chooch.

"I'm in a phone booth over by UCLA, the Texaco just off the freeway on Sunset," the teenager said. "I gotta see you."

"On my way." Shane got into his rental car and headed back to West L.A.

27

DEAL

H E WAS SITTING on a low wall that framed the perimeter of the Texaco station one block west of the 405. He seemed small sitting there, diminished by events, his head down, staring at the sidewalk as if the answer to his life might be hiding in the scrub weeds growing between the cracks.

Shane pulled the rented Taurus into the gas station and tapped the horn. Chooch got off the wall, moved to the car, and slid in, pulling the door shut. He sat there, silent, looking like he'd lost something he couldn't replace.

"Your mom's worried."

"Yeah. Okay, let's go," he said.

"You had lunch? There's a good place in Westwood, over by UCLA. Got subs and a great deli."

The boy shrugged, so Shane put the car in gear and headed that way.

The place was called the Little Bruin. Shane and Chooch got a booth in the back surrounded by chattering college students and lunch-break shopkeepers. Chooch ordered the special; Shane, pastrami on rye. They both had Cokes.

"I thought we had a deal. You were gonna stay put, and I was gonna try and get my stuff settled, get back to you by next weekend at the latest."

Chooch was looking out the window at the passing traffic so he could avoid Shane's eyes. "I been thinkin'," he said. "I know it's like a problem all the time havin' to have somebody look after me, but like you said, I'm a man. I make my own choices now, right?"

"Right."

"So, if I moved in with you, you wouldn't have to baby-sit me anymore or have Longboard come over and sit. I don't need to be supervised. I'm sorta beyond that. Like you said, right?"

"Yeah, I guess," Shane said. "But I got guys shooting up my place. We'd have to get Kevlar jammies."

"You're not sleeping there, either. I'll go wherever you go."

" 'Cept I'm not your legal guardian. I can't make that choice for you. Sandy has to."

"Yeah, well, the thing is, Sandy and me, we're not gonna happen."

"You sure of that?"

"Yeah. I'm sure. It didn't work."

"You gave it a whole nine hours."

"You know what she does for a living?"

Shane didn't know how to answer that. "Do you?" he finally said.

"Yeah. She's a hooker. I found her trick book. She has over fifty guys in there. It lists what they like, what kinda sex." He was having trouble talking about this, watching the traffic out the window, studying the street with manufactured interest.

"She's paying for my school and shit by fucking guys. She's a whore." He turned back, and Shane could see the anger in the boy's black eyes.

"Chooch, your mom—"

"Yeah?"

"When I first met her, she was young, alone in L.A. She made a bad choice, but she doesn't do that anymore. She's an informant for the police department. Federal, as well as LAPD."

"How does that pay for anything?" he challenged. "The private school and that penthouse."

"She dates guys that law enforcement wants to bust, works 'em for information, then sells it to the cops. She does real well. She's trying to save up enough to retire, live with you in Phoenix, be a regular mom."

"Some real mom."

The waitress, a college girl in shorts and a UCLA T-shirt, delivered their lunches, set down silverware wrapped in paper napkins, and left. Shane unwrapped his knife and fork and put the napkin on his lap while Chooch continued to look out the window, brooding.

"Whatta you want, man?" Shane finally said. "It is what it is. I can't change it; neither can you. You've gotta move past it."

"Easy for you. I got nobody now. Least you've got somebody you can talk to."

"Yeah? Who's that?"

"I found all the letters you write to your dad. They were in the desk drawer in the living room. I was looking for paper for my homework."

Shane put down his half-eaten sandwich. Chooch watched him closely, focused on him hard.

"You shouldn't read other people's mail," Shane said softly.

"You write them but you never send 'em."

"He's sick. They were downers. I didn't want to distress him. I don't want to talk about this with you. It's not right you reading my private mail."

They sat in silence for a moment, then Shane's cell phone rang, interrupting an awkward moment. It was the guy at Parker Center checking the Cal-VIP Homes with the Corporations Commission.

"Go," Shane said, grabbing a pencil.

"Spivack Development Corporation, Long Beach, California, owns Cal-VIP and paid the real estate taxes on the Arrowhead address you gave me."

"Anthony Spivack? That Spivack Development? The big corporate developer?"

"It just said Spivack Development, 2000 Lincoln Ave., Long Beach, California."

"Thanks," Shane said, and folded the phone.

"I can't go back to Sandy's place. I won't do it," Chooch protested.

"Okay, okay, I'll work out something. But I've gotta call and tell her you're okay."

"Fine. I don't care. I just don't wanna go back."

"Okay. We can try, but I can't promise that's gonna stick."

They sat quietly in the booth and ate their sandwiches. Chooch, still deep in thought, only picked at his.

"Shane," he said, and Scully looked up at him. "Did she ever tell you who my father was?" The question had been waiting there building up pressure, needing to be asked.

"Yeah," Shane said, "but she didn't want you to find out who he was."

"Because he was one of those guys, one of the crooks she plays to the cops?"

"Chooch, come on . . ."

"I wanna know. Was my old man a criminal?"

"She'll have to tell you. She made me promise, but it's not really gonna change anything, because he's not coming back for a long time."

"He's a crook . . . I know it. Some legacy, huh? No wonder I get into so much trouble."

"Hey, Chooch, criminal behavior isn't genetic. You don't pass it on, father to son, like blue eyes and freckles. You can make whatever you want of your life. It's up to you. Your father's mistakes are his. Everybody gets to make their own."

"That's what you keep telling me," the boy said. Then he gave Shane a rueful smile. "And you don't ever lie, right?"

"Right," Shane said. Then without really knowing why, but realizing it was the right thing to do, Shane finally unburdened himself of something he had kept hidden for years. "You wanna know why I never mailed the letters?"

Chooch nodded.

" 'Cause I don't know where to send them."

"It says Florida."

"I don't know where he is, or even who he is. I was left at a hospital. 'Infant 205,' in 1963. I got named by City Services. It's silly. I write the letters when I need to get my thoughts down. And my father . . ." He stopped, unable to finish for a second. "My father is an idea I can talk to."

"Somebody you wish you had, who can be whatever you want him to be," Chooch said, knowing exactly what Shane meant, feeling all the same things . . . the loneliness, the disenfranchisement, the emptiness coming from the same hole in their personal histories.

"Yeah." Shane's voice was husky.

"I wondered why you agreed to take me. That's why."

"I don't know why, Chooch. I don't know what I was looking for."

The waitress came to the table and asked them if they wanted anything.

"Yeah," Chooch said. "But I don't think you've got it in the kitchen."

Shane smiled. "Let's get going. I've got an errand to run. You want, you can come with me."

He paid and they left the Little Bruin and headed to the brown

Taurus parked at a curbside meter, dazed by what had just happened.

"Thanks for telling me about your dad," Chooch finally said.

"I won't tell about your dad if you won't tell about mine," Shane said.

"Deal," Chooch said, and smiled. They got in the car and left Westwood, both wondering what this strange new connection held for them.

CONNECTING
THE DOTS

28

THE FIFTEEN-STORY steel-and-glass building on Lincoln Boulevard was named the Two Thousand Building by a large monument sign that marked the entrance. Under that in gold letters:

A SPIVACK DEVELOPMENT

It was also on top of the building in five-foot-high lit letters, leaving no doubt about who owned the place.

Shane and Chooch parked in the underground garage, got out, and moved to the elevator, taking it up to the management floor at the top of the building. They exited into a huge architectural lobby decorated in monochromatic colors, dominated by too many sharp edges and angular lines. Steel-and-glass furniture dotted the interior. Futuristic recessed lighting laid down a cold blue-white glow. A huge gold sign behind the receptionist again announced that this was:

SPIVACK DEVELOPMENT
CORPORATE HEADQUARTERS

Shane left Chooch by the elevator and approached a striking, unfriendly white-blond receptionist who looked cold enough to have been delivered with the furniture. Shane opened his wallet and took out his police business card. Since he didn't have his badge, the business card was the best he could manage. He was hoping it would get him past the blond goddess who was guarding the floor, stationed behind her huge, semicircular, two-inch-thick green glass desk, like a turret gunner.

"What's this regarding?" she asked, speaking coolly, not intimidated by his card or manner.

"Police business," he replied.

"Mr. Spivack isn't here. Perhaps someone else can help you?"

"How about Calvin Sheets?" Shane said, wondering if Logan Hunter's head of security was also working for Spivack.

"He's down at the city council meeting with Mr. Spivack. Sorry . . ."

"The Long Beach City Council?"

She ignored his question and smiled an icicle at him. "Would there be anybody else . . . ?"

"Coy Love."

"We don't have a Coy Love."

"I'm not doing too well, am I?"

"Sometimes if you make an appointment in advance, it works wonders." Freon.

"I may just have to get a search warrant and start emptying everyone's desks. . . . Do a couple of body searches."

"Anything else?" She had grown tired of him.

"Pamela Anderson Lee wouldn't happen to be around, would she?"

"Just left." But at least this earned him a smile.

He picked up his business card, tucked it into his wallet, then took a Spivack Company brochure off the glass desk and walked across the lobby, the ice-blonde watching him all the way. He retrieved Chooch, got into the elevator, and went down. He left the teenager in the lobby, then found the staircase to the basement. It took him five minutes to find the service utility room. Inside was a huge gray panel box with a dime-store lock that took Shane less than thirty seconds to pick. Now he was looking at a startling array of colorful wires. "Shit," he said, then slowly went to work unraveling the building's complicated alarm system.

■ ■ ■

"I wonder where the city council meets. Probably city hall," Shane said as they settled back into the Taurus. He picked up his almost fried cell phone, called Information in Long Beach, and got the address for city hall on Front Street just before the phone quit.

They drove away from the Two Thousand Building and, with some help from a gas-station attendant, found Front Street. The huge domed city building loomed two blocks ahead. . . .

As they pulled up the street, they could see quite a demonstration in progress—thirty or forty pickets were congregating around in front of city hall. It was a strange mixture of people. Some were old men in American Legion uniforms, holding duplicate hand-lettered signs that read:

VETERANS AGAINST LONG BEACH
LAND-FOR-WATER DEAL

Other pickets carried more traditional union placards:

AFL-CIO OPPOSES NAVAL YARD WATER SWAP
THEY GET THE DOUGH, WE GET THE,HOSE

Others protested with:

GIVE US JOBS, NOT SOBS
SPIVACK-EVACK—WE DON'T WANT YOU HERE
WE SAVED THE WHALES—YOU SAVE OUR JOBS!

Shane and Chooch had to park a block away in a city parking lot and, after locking up, moved across the shimmering, heated asphalt to where the demonstration was taking place.

"What's going on?" Shane asked a tough-looking woman with inch-long hair wearing a plaid shirt and carrying a sign that read:

BEACHFRONT FOR H$_2$O?
OUR CITY COUNCIL SUCKS!

"These idiots are trading the Long Beach Naval Yard to Los Angeles County for a bunch of fuckin' water rights," she growled.

"Naval yard? I thought the navy shut it down years ago."

"Yeah, they did, and now we're giving it to L.A."

"Isn't it federal property?" Shane persisted.

She shot him a withering look. "Where you been, buddy? This is all over the fuckin' news."

"I don't have a TV," Shane answered.

"It was leased land. Now Long Beach's gonna trade it for some dumb water rights."

Shane moved past her and, along with Chooch, climbed up the steps and entered city hall.

The Long Beach Municipal Building was a large brick structure that had been built in the forties. It had a high, two-story rotunda, now overflowing with TV news crews who had set up there for a press conference.

"I'm gonna try and find this guy Spivack," Shane said to Chooch. "Stick close, okay?"

"Got it."

Shane moved past the news crews but got stopped at the door to the City Council Chamber by a uniformed Long Beach police officer.

"Sorry, we're maxed out. Fire regs," the cop said.

"LAPD, I'm working." He handed the cop his business card.

"Okay, Sarge, but it's a madhouse in there."

"He's with me," Shane said, indicating Chooch; then they entered the meeting hall.

The council room was a theater-sized, cavernous hall with a sloping floor and raised dais. The room was packed. They could hear a contentious argument being staged over microphones:

"How the hell can you say that the property can't be used by Long Beach?!" a woman yelled from the floor. "I worked at that yard, I was an employee of the Metal Trades Council for thirty years. I thought we were being reamed in '94, when the government closed the only profitable shipyard in the navy. But that's nothing compared to what's going on here. You're taking a huge city asset and trading it for chump change!"

The crowd shouted its approval. The president of the city council banged his gavel for order, then replied, "To begin with, the yard was closed in '94 because it was badly situated, too close to the big refitting yard in San Diego. What's going on here now is *good* for the city of Long Beach. Mr. Spivack is going to clear all the old military buildings off the site, regrade the property, and develop it. Okay, it's going to be ceded to the city of L.A., but I might remind you that the shipyard borders L.A. on the north and Long Beach on the south, so it's contiguous with them as well as us."

"Who cares? I'm not talking about geography. I'm talking about jobs!" the woman fired back, to a chorus of cheers.

The city council president was prepared. "Long Beach residents *will* get the jobs because the yard is much closer to our main workforce than to L.A.'s. There'll be hotels, shopping malls, restaurants—all employment for Long Beach citizens. And we don't have to float bond issues or construction loans to develop the site. We won't have to pay for its construction; L.A. will. But we will get the major work benefits, plus much-needed water from L.A."

Shane was looking for Anthony Spivack somewhere down front, not paying much attention to the argument going on between the Long Beach City Council and its angry residents. He had the Spivack brochure open to a picture of the CEO. Spivack was a heavyset man with a thick head of close-cropped, curly gray hair. The woman at the mike raised her voice in response, cutting through the background noise with electronic shrillness. "And who, may I ask, gets the municipal tax revenue on all this commercial property, Mr. Cummins?"

Shane spun around and looked up at the president of the Long Beach City Council. He was a slender, hollow-chested man with horn-rimmed glasses, identified by a plaque in front of him on the elevated dais:

CARL CUMMINS

PRESIDENT, LONG BEACH CITY COUNCIL

"Son of a bitch," Shane said.

Chooch looked at him. "What is it?"

Just then, some kind of disturbance seemed to be taking place in the back of the hall. A chant began: "AFL-CIO . . . Tony Spivack, you must go."

About thirty protesters had broken into the hall and were trying to march down the aisle, carrying placards. The agitated audience soon picked up the chant.

Carl Cummins started banging his gavel, trying to regain order. "We can't conduct this hearing under these conditions!" he said, screeching it into his mike, getting loud boos and electronic feedback. "The discussion period on City Resolution 397 is concluded. The board will retire to chambers to take its vote. We're adjourned." He angrily banged his gavel and rose.

The chorus of boos grew louder. Suddenly people in the front rows stood up and started throwing fruit at the stage; pulling oranges and plums out of carry-bags, brought in anticipation of this demonstration.

Carl Cummins and the nine other members of the city council bolted from their chairs as they were pelted with fruit, making a hurried exit from the stage.

The pushing and shoving was getting increasingly intense in the auditorium, threatening to turn into a riot.

"Let's go!" Shane said, grabbing Chooch. "Stay close to me. Hold on to my belt."

He felt Chooch grab hold of his belt in the back, and then Shane pushed through the melee to the fire exit on the same side of the room that Carl Cummins and the city council were using as a retreat. By now most of the frightened council members had left the stage.

Shane got to the fire exit, but it was guarded by another Long Beach cop. "Sorry. This is an alarmed fire door," the policeman said.

"Long Beach Fire Marshal," Shane bullshitted. "I'm authorized to open it under Regulation 1623. Excuse me."

He handed the startled cop his official LAPD business card and jostled him, hoping he couldn't read it in the commotion. In that moment of hesitation, Shane pushed down on the silver bar and opened the door. The alarm bell sounded. People were panicking as fruit continued to fly. Shane pushed past the Long Beach cop, dragging Chooch into the hot sunshine.

Up ahead, he could see a black limousine waiting with several chase cars. Then Shane spotted Anthony Spivack beside the limo. With him were several of the men Shane had photographed in Arrowhead. He assumed one of them must be Calvin Sheets. The people with Spivack started piling into cars. Carl Cummins arrived with one of the other council members and jumped into Spivack's limo. Like the last politicians leaving Saigon, they slammed car doors and squealed away from the angry mob pouring out of the doors behind them.

"Stay with me!" Shane said, trying to get an idea which direction the fleeing cars were headed while simultaneously sprinting for the Taurus, parked almost a block away.

He and Chooch finally reached the car. Both were out of breath as they jumped in. Shane put the car in gear and sped across the lot, cutting between parked cars. He bounced over the curb, shot out onto Front Street, and took off heading south, after the speeding limo and its four chase vehicles.

"What's going on?" Chooch asked.

"Some of these guys were in the house up in Arrowhead," he said, fearing he couldn't catch up with them.

Shane had lost sight of the cars but was now driving along a frontage road that bordered the Long Beach Airport. On a hunch, he turned into one of the executive terminals, past an open bararm at the end of a ramp, driving out onto the tarmac that bordered the runway. As he sped along past a row of FBOs (flight base operators) that lined the west side of the field, several ramp attendants and cargo loaders started screaming and waving their arms at the brown Taurus. Shane just ignored them, racing past parked Lears and Gulfstreams.

He thought he saw the black limo in the distance parked near a large Sikorsky helicopter, idling with the rotor turning slowly.

He drove around more executive jets—transportation necessities of the megarich.

Finally he could see the helicopter more clearly. Spivack and Cummins were getting into the idling chopper with the rest of the men from the Arrowhead house. He was close enough to the helicopter to read SPIVACK DEVELOPMENT on the side door as the huge green-and-white nine-passenger Sikorsky lifted off.

Shane got there half a minute too late. He watched in frustration as the chopper hovered for a minute a few feet above the tarmac, then the rotor changed pitch, and the helicopter streaked away, climbing to the north. Soon it was just a speck in the bright blue cloudless sky.

29

TAIL JOB

A T A FEW MINUTES before five in the afternoon, Shane was back inside the Appaloosa, watching a cockroach trying to hide under the molding that framed the tabletop, one feeler reaching out, tentatively tapping the Formica. He was in the same cracked vinyl booth in the back, nursing a Coke grudgingly supplied by the same greasy-coated Mexican waiter. "Das all chu gonna haf?" the man said.

"Yep," Shane said. "Working." The waiter left. Shane kept a wary eye on the barricaded cockroach and while "Malaguena" played through ruptured speakers, he was thinking about Chooch, whom he had left ten minutes earlier at the Spring Summer Apartments with the TV blaring. Shane had convinced Longboard to stop by the Venice house, get Chooch's book bag with his homework assignments, take it to the apartment on Third, and stay with the boy until Shane got back. In return for this service, Shane had given up his Lakers-Trailblazers tickets for the weekend. He made a mental note to call by six to make sure Longboard had gotten there okay.

Surprisingly, with trouble and chaos swirling around his own life, Shane found himself worrying about Chooch's back home-work assignments as well as his emotional well-being. Something about this newly found concern for someone else's future seemed to settle his own emotions in a way he couldn't understand. Underneath the boy's grumbling and bitching about the extra supervision, Shane suspected that he appreciated the concern. Earlier in the hectic day, when Shane had turned around unexpectedly and caught Chooch staring at him, the expression on his face was one of wonder. It said more than any words could convey.

Perhaps Shane could work out something more permanent with Sandy. She had her hands full right now with the DEA, but after that, she'd change teams and be on to some other predicate felon. He, on the other hand, was in the checkout line. If he didn't end up in prison or the grave, he was certainly through being a cop. Once he was off the force, he could devote more time to Chooch, stop farming him out to Longboard. Chooch didn't know who his father was, and although Shane couldn't fill that role, he sure as hell could be a big brother. Then he looked up, and she was coming through the door.

Alexa stood backlit in the late-afternoon sunshine, holding her briefcase under her arm, the shoulder strap tucked inside. She let her eyes adjust to the cavelike darkness of the windowless bar-restaurant. Finally she spotted him and moved across the room, her hips swaying seductively with the motion.

She slid in and smiled wanly at him. "Our spot," she said dryly.

"If it is, we've gotta either train these cockroaches or start killing them." She looked puzzled, so he lifted the sugar shaker, and the eight-legged German roach took off like a shot.

She let out an involuntary feminine squeal, then returned to form, slapping at it bare-handed and missing. The roach dodged, shooting across the table as Alexa slammed her palm down again—the only thing she hurt was her hand. The roach went off the end of the table, hit the floor, and was gone.

"Sign him. Good broken-field run." Shane smiled.

She checked around the perimeter of the booth, looking for relatives, then glanced at Shane. "Strong survival instincts. We should take lessons."

He took out the Arrowhead pictures he'd had developed and slid them across the table to her. "Know any of these guys?"

She went through them while he waited.

"Yep. All of 'em. This one is Calvin Sheets." She pushed a picture over and showed it to Shane. It was of the medium-built man with the ash-blond hair, setting a box down at the back door. Shane realized he'd been right, that Sheets had been the man standing with Tony Spivack at the limo.

"This is Coy Love," she said, sliding another photograph over to Shane, who could see why you wouldn't want to "fuck with Love." He was large, over six feet, with a huge, jutting jaw and a cruel, angular face. He had a thin, lipless mouth, straight as a ruler.

"These other two guys were cops on Calvin's Coliseum detail. They both got terminated with him on his bullshit time-sheet hustle." She pushed those shots over. "Lon Sherwood and Carter something, I can't remember his last name."

She looked up, and the waiter was back, hovering like a dragonfly over a lake, waiting for her order.

"I'll have what he's having."

"Chu makin' my day." He left, grumbling.

"Cummins is president of the Long Beach City Council, and I found out Spivack Development Corporation owns Cal-VIP Homes." Shane filled her in on the Long Beach City Council meeting; the dispute over the transfer of the naval yard to L.A. for water; the chase through Long Beach trying to catch Sheets,

Spivack, and Cummins; and their eventual helicopter escape. She was holding her briefcase on her lap in both hands, ready to strike in case another cockroach took off on an end run around the Mexican condiments.

"You had a busy day," she said.

"I won't ask how your day went, for fear it'll severely depress me."

"I hope DeMarco is staying busy, 'cause I'm getting good prima facie stuff," she said, needling him.

"Don't worry about DeMarco. The Saint's all over this. He says with what he has, we'll probably want to to file a civil action."

"Good. 'Cause I'd heard he'd become an alcoholic—a blackout drunk—and that's why he pulled the pin."

"Don't worry about Dee. He's kicking ass."

Blackout drunk? I'm fucked, Shane thought.

She looked at her watch as the waiter set down her Coke and left. "I ran both Drucker and Kono through the Office of Administrative Services at the Personnel Group," she said. "Drucker just got reassigned from Southwest to Hollenbeck. He's working street patrol—day shift. Kono has a worrisome nickname. They call him Bongo. I'm hoping that's because he's of Hawaiian ancestry, and not because he beats people like a drum."

She picked up her Coke and drained it. "Thirsty," she apologized. "Anyway, Kono's still in South Bureau, but now he's working day watch in University Division. That means we're going to have to split up if we want to follow both guys." She glanced at her Timex. "We better get moving. Day watch breaks in forty minutes. Which one a' these raisin cakes do you want?"

"Ladies first."

"Chivalry always knocks me out," she said drolly. "Okay, since he's closer, I'll take Drucker."

He put some money down on the table for the two Cokes, and they both stood.

"Let's communicate on a tactical frequency," she said. "One of the high ones nobody uses. Organized Crime is on tac ten, and that division doesn't have much going now. Let's use that."

"I don't have a police radio; my car's in Venice. I'm using a rental."

"You really bring it all to the table, don't you, Scully," she said sarcastically.

He needed her help, so he let it go.

"We can pick up a handset at IAD. I saw a whole bunch of them in a box in the IO's section," Shane suggested

She nodded. "We better move it, or they'll both be EOW before we get there."

■ ■ ■

The University Division station was an old concrete four-story building located on South Adams Boulevard, near USC. Shane left the Taurus in the only available spot he could find, half a block up the street. He fed the meter, moved away from it, and sat on a bus bench across from the station. From there he had an unobstructed view of the station parking lot. He had on an L.A. Dodgers cap, pulled low over his eyes, and a dull green-and-brown camouflage windbreaker he had picked up that afternoon at a surplus shop downtown for fifteen bucks.

Shane felt invisible and ready for action: Mr. Brown-and-Green in his camo jacket and dirt-brown Taurus. He had the police handset in his lap and was watching as the day watch started streaming out in civilian clothes, on the way to their private vehicles. It was 5:45.

"Six to Five. Target D is in motion." He heard Alexa's voice coming over the radio on tactical frequency 10. They had chosen their radio code numbers in the parking lot outside the Bradbury while doing a quick equipment check. He picked up his handset.

"Copy, Six. I'm still parked and waiting."

"Roger that," she said. "Target D just left Hollenbeck, heading up onto 91. He's westbound."

"Roger. Standing by on tac ten." He laid the radio on his lap and sat on the bus bench waiting for Kris "Bongo" Kono.

Officer Kono was one of the last ones out the station side door. He was dressed in jeans and a T-shirt and was carrying a duffel bag. He sprinted to his car, obviously late. He jumped into a blue '76 Camaro with racing stripes and a primered left front fender, then pulled quickly out of the lot, burning rubber.

Shane was caught leaning. He was half a block away from the Taurus and late getting back to it, fumbling to unlock the door as the Camaro made a sharp turn out of the parking lot. The 455-cubic-inch engine and blown mufflers on the muscle car roared angrily past and sped up the street.

"Shit," Shane said, finally piling into the Taurus and starting it up. He found a hole in traffic and pulled out, already danger-ously behind. He watched, frustrated, as the Camaro went through the intersection up ahead on the yellow light. Shane tried to make up ground, spinning his wheels, chirping rubber, trying to get around slower traffic. When he got to the cross street, the light was against him, so he leaned on his horn and broke reck-lessly through the intersection against the red light, causing an eastbound truck on Atlantic to slam on its brakes. The angry traffic started screaming at him, blaring their horns and flipping him off.

As Shane shot through the red light, he could see the blue Camaro one block ahead, speeding through another light on the yellow.

"Slow the fuck down!" Shane yelled at the Camaro as he was forced to stop at the second light, trapped behind a row of cars, unable to get around them. He could see the Camaro a block ahead, turning right, heading up onto the 110.

"Come on, come on, come on . . ." Shane begged the five-way light that was trapping him. Then it turned green, but an old woman in a rusting Subaru was making a cautious left, blocking traffic, afraid to go. "Come on, lady. You got the fuckin' right-of-way!" he shouted at his windshield.

"Six, I'm on 91, heading west, passing Olive," Alexa's voice announced. Static, then: "Six, do you copy?"

Shane had his hands full as the woman finally completed her turn. He was flooring it, illegally passing a city bus on the right, shooting past the line of traffic, hanging a right, going up the on-ramp. His tires squealed on the sun-hot asphalt.

He hit the 110 going way too fast for the flow of rush-hour traffic that loomed before him on the packed freeway. He had to hit his brakes to keep from plowing into the right side of a Ford Escort, startling the two hard hats inside.

"Six, this is Five. Do you copy?" Alexa's voice persisted. "Six, you are Code One. Copy, please." Code One was a command to respond and was given only when a unit did not answer a radio call and was perceived to be in difficulty. It was imperative to respond to a Code One, if at all possible.

Shane impatiently snapped the radio up off his lap. "I copy. I've got my hands full, for Chrissake. Gimme a minute." He threw the radio back down on the seat and managed to get around the Ford Escort. He couldn't see the blue Camaro anywhere. "Fuck!" he said, but kept heading west on the 110, going as fast as he could, dangerously passing cars, trying to make up lost distance, driving on the right shoulder, getting angry horn blasts from a whole line of drivers.

"Six, Target D is transitioning to the 710. I'm making that freeway change now." Alexa's voice, pissing him off, was cool and in control. *Fuck her.*

Shane was sweating. A river of perspiration ran down under his arm, slicking his shirt and rib cage. People around him were screaming through their car windows as he passed them on the shoulder illegally. He was running out of room, so he veered back into the right lane, forcing the Taurus between a sixteen-wheeler Vons Grocery truck and a green Chevy van. Both drivers yelled obscenities at him. The grocery truck blew its heavy six-tone air horn, scaring the shit out of Shane, but he forced his way in, now catching a glimpse of the blue Camaro in the far left lane. Kono was transitioning off the 110 to the 105.

Shane was fucked. He slammed the heel of his hand on the steering wheel. He was fenced off by four lanes of bumper-to-bumper traffic and was pushed helplessly along by the slow flow, past the 105 transition, heading uselessly in the wrong direction. The tail was completely blown. He snapped up the radio.

"Five, this is Six," he said.

"Roger," she said.

"I lost K. He was on the 110. I got trapped, missed the transition. He's southbound on the 105, running clean." Shane waited for Alexa to curse him out or belittle him for losing his man. But she didn't do either.

"Okay, I copy," she said. "My guy just left the 710 at Ocean. We're down by the water. I'll talk you in."

"Roger that, coming your way," he said, feeling like a complete rookie.

For the next ten minutes she was silent, then: "I'm Code Six at 2300 Ocean Boulevard. Take the 710 to the end of the freeway and turn left. I'm in a gas-station parking lot."

"Copy that," he said.

It took him another ten minutes before he pulled up Ocean Boulevard and saw Alexa's gray Crown Victoria parked in a Texaco station across the street from a vast piece of fenced property.

Razor wire ran for miles in both directions. He could see two big gates, each with a private security guard. The sign over the drive-through arch had been torn down.

Shane pulled into the darkened gas station, parked near the Crown Vic, got out, and slid into the front seat next to Alexa.

"Sorry, I got totally jammed on the 110."

"It's okay," she said. "All roads lead to Rome."

"Huh?"

"Your boy just pulled through that gate five minutes ago. A blue Camaro with racing stripes and a bondoed front fender, right?"

"Yeah."

He looked through her windshield at the five-hundred-acre piece of land across Ocean Boulevard next to the bay. On the east side of the property, the buildings were still standing, but to the west there were piles of rubble where the structures had already been knocked down. It looked a little like pictures of Berlin after the bombings in '45.

"Is this place what I think it is?" she asked.

"Yep," he said softly. "The Long Beach Naval Yard."

CHOIR PRACTICE

THE SUN SET slowly and magnificently over the Pacific Ocean. Scattered clouds that were strung across the horizon in steel-gray formations suddenly turned deep purple, riding above the dark blue sea like a colorful celestial armada until the sun was gone and night claimed its final victory.

Shane retrieved his new camera from the trunk of the Taurus, grabbed the heavy lens and some film, then walked with Alexa along busy Ocean Boulevard, across the street from the old naval yard. They were both looking for a good place to climb the fence. With cars streaking by in both directions, they picked a hole in the traffic, sprinted across the busy four-lane street, then continued west, looking through the fence at the property beyond.

There were security lights located inside the old naval yard every block or so, illuminating sections of the torn-down facility. This part of the huge yard had already been completely razed.

Behind them, on the east end of the property, the surviving naval buildings loomed.

Shane reasoned that they had a better chance of getting inside unobserved if they went west, where there were no structures left standing and, hence, nothing to steal and less need for security.

"Where do you want to try?" she suddenly asked.

He pointed to a place up ahead where the razor wire had come down, making it possible to get over the fence without ripping their hands and clothes.

"With all this traffic on Ocean, we'll be spotted; somebody's gonna call it in," she said. "Let's try over there." She pointed to the far end of the property, where the fence seemed to turn a corner and head south toward the bay.

There was a huge lit structure looming down there that Shane didn't like the looks of. "Except, what the hell is that?" he asked, pointing at it, but she didn't answer.

They kept walking and finally got close enough to see that it was an active Army Reserve post, with its own entrance located at the far end of the naval yard. A bunch of weekend warriors were standing around in the parking lot, milling in front of the post HQ.

"Okay," she said. "You're right. Let's go back and try your place."

They returned to the spot Shane had seen, and then waited for the line of traffic to pass. Once the light down the street turned red, Shane touched her arm.

"Now," he said.

He and Alexa hit the fence simultaneously. It was an eight-foot-high chain-link; Shane scrambled up and over fast, surprised to see that they hit the ground on the other side at about the same time.

They sprinted away from Ocean Boulevard as the light down the street turned green and the headlights of the approaching cars came toward them. They crouched in the dark unobserved as the traffic streamed past on the far side of the fence.

"When Drucker and Kono went in, you sure you couldn't see which way they turned once they got inside?" Shane asked.

"They were stopped by the plastic badge guarding the east gate, but once they drove through, I lost 'em. I was half a block away, across the street. I didn't want to chance getting spotted."

"If they went in there, then they're probably still on the east side of the property," Shane reasoned.

"Probably."

They took off along the paved road inside the fence, this time heading east, back the way they had just come. The two-lane base road they were on was identified by a sign as COFFMAN STREET.

They were both struck by the vastness of the old shipyard. Shane had heard about the property ever since he was a kid growing up in L.A., but he'd never been down there before.

"This place is huge," he said, stating the obvious as they quickened their pace, doing a speed walk. "No wonder those people at the city council hearing were pissed. This place has gotta be worth billions of dollars. Prime waterfront, right on the border between L.A. and Long Beach; the *Queen Mary* is half a mile from here, Fisherman's Village a stone's throw away."

She nodded but said nothing.

They were coming to a part of the yard that had not been demolished yet. They began passing huge covered docks, once used to refurbish naval vessels. Faded signs hung on every kind of structure, from wood-frame officers clubs and enlisted-personnel mess halls to poured-concrete warehouses and five-story-high covered sheds. They passed blast foundation plants; the compressor boiler plant loomed next to an air compressor building; then some hazardous-waste staging areas. There were mammoth towers leaning against a dark sky, marked COLLIMA-

TION TOWER and PUMPING STATION TWO. Neither Shane nor Alexa had a clue what they were used for.

They passed the old naval credit union building, the sheet
metal shop, and the asbestos removal headquarters, which was
part of the current demolition operation and consisted of a flock
of portable trailers.

The property was beyond anything that Shane had ever imagined. Now they were at the end of Coffman Street, where it
turned into Avenue D.

Up ahead they could see some bright light streaming out of a
huge warehouse. They were moving slowly now, trying to hug
the shadows created by the occasional streetlamps.

They finally got close enough to see ten or twelve cars parked
in front of a huge lit warehouse. Shane and Alexa could see the
open loading door with a sign overhead that read:

BUILDING 132

MACHINE SHOP—PIPE AND COPPER

They crept across Avenue D and found cover behind a two-
story-high cylindrical tank. When they looked around the rusting
tank, Shane and Alexa could see directly into the mouth of the
warehouse through the raised loading door.

A party with more than thirty people was going on inside.
Some tables had been set up full of food and buckets of beer.
Men and women were dancing on the cold concrete floor, which
was lit by lights from two gray police plainwraps that had been
pulled inside. Both Crown Vics had the doors open; stereo music was coming from the car radios tuned to the same FM station.

Shane was looking through his telescopic lens at the partyers.
"Most of these guys are cops. . . . I know some of the girls. I
busted a few when I was in West Valley Vice."

"Hookers?" Alexa asked. "Gimme it."

He handed her the zoom-lens camera, and she squinted through the eyepiece, panning around inside the lit building. "You're right, it's a regular coyote convention in there," she murmured. "Those are Beverly Hills pros—thousand-dollar girls— Angelica DeBravo, Deborah Kline, Donna Fleister, plus the rest of our police-department cast of characters." She was referring to Ray's den: Joe Church, Lee Ayers, John Samansky, Don Drucker, and Shane's blown tail, "Bongo" Kono. Calvin Sheets and Coy Love were not there, but the other guys he'd photographed up at Arrowhead were. Alexa identified them as ex-cops terminated from "Dream" Sheets's Coliseum detail. Then she caught her breath. "Shit—don't like this," she said, her eye pinned to the camera viewfinder.

"What?"

"There're two guys from the mayor's staff in there—his legislative assistant, Mark somebody, in the suit by the door; and Rob Lavetta, his press-relations guy, the one standing next to Drucker." She handed the camera back to Shane, who took a picture of both men.

The party was in full swing, everybody drinking beer and dancing to the music, although "dancing" was a conservative description of what was going on. It was more like a group grope in 4/4 time. Dress was optional, with the thousand-dollar girls opting for maximum exposure.

Shane wanted to photograph everyone, keeping a mental count of whom he had already shot and whom he still needed, waiting for the right moment when the dancers would spin, giving him a good angle of one or both. When he finished, he sat next to Alexa, leaning back against the rusting cylindrical tank.

"They oughta put these shots in the departmental brochure," he finally said. "We'd end our recruiting problem."

Alexa volunteered a slogan: "Not just long hours and cold coffee. Police work—a changing profession."

"Whatta you wanna do?" he asked.

"I don't know. . . ." She winced, then pulled something out from under her. It was a sign she'd been sitting on. They both read it:

ABRASIVE TANKS
MAINTAIN 50-FOOT SAFETY PERIMETER

They both looked up fearfully at the old rusting tanks they were hiding behind. Then Shane realized that his hand was in something wet, pulled it up, and looked at it.

"Shit," he said, shaking it dry.

"Let's move back, get outta here," she said.

Suddenly they heard laughing nearby. A man's voice: "You're on. Let's do it."

Shane and Alexa cautiously leaned out and looked at the party. It had now spilled out of the huge building; people were standing around the back of one of the cars parked outside, while Drucker pulled two cardboard boxes out of the trunk. He ripped them open and started handing out shirts to everybody.

"What the hell are those?" Alexa asked.

"The jerseys," Shane replied.

Black football jerseys with red numbers and letters on the back that read:

L.A. SPIDERS

The shoulder trim was done in a pattern resembling a red spider web. The cops started moving in a pack up the street with handfuls of beer and their arms draped casually around the hookers.

"I gotta see this," Shane said.

He and Alexa followed from the shadows, staying at least a hundred yards behind the group, which was drinking and grab-assing its way along Avenue D until finally they came to the old base athletic building and adjacent field. Shane and Alexa found themselves at the far end of the old field, the grass long dead from lack of water.

Someone had brought a football, and after more drinking and groping, a very fundamental game of tackle ensued. Slow, looping passes drifted to giggling hooker wideouts who gathered the spirals in without too much interference. The playful tackles were short on violence but long on rolling around on the ground and piling on. The beer kept flowing. The game looked to Shane like a hell of a lot of fun.

"How do you get a jersey and a place in the lineup?" he wondered.

"You don't want in that game, Shane. You'd get tired of all the AIDS testing."

He nodded and smiled. He realized it was the first time she'd used his first name.

They watched for quite a while and finally decided that everybody was so drunk, this was where the evening would end. They backed out, got over the fence, and returned to the gas station.

"I hate spiders," she said once they got to their cars.

"So the jerseys are football, but is this place the Web?"

"I don't know, must be," she said. "But I can tell you this much: these cops are having choir practice with first-string girls and two guys from the mayor's staff." "Choir practice" was an after-hours police drunk, usually in a park or some deserted place.

"Gimme the film," she said. "There's an all-night drugstore half a block from my apartment. I'll have the proofs back in two hours."

He hesitated, then unloaded the camera and gave her the two other exposed film containers.

They got into their respective cars and started to pull out when Alexa sounded her horn. Shane rolled down his window. She leaned across her front seat, talking through her passenger window. "For whatever it's worth, I believe you. Something big and shitty is going on here. I'm in."

"Thanks," he said gratefully. Then she waved at him and drove off. It had been more than a week, and she was the first one.

THE PITCHES
MOTION
31

SHANE WAS ON the 405 on his way back from Long Beach when he saw the transition ramp for the Santa Monica Freeway. He wondered whether DeMarco had been working on his case or whether he'd spent the day drinking and listening to rap. He decided to find out. He put on his blinker and made the turn onto the 10. Seven minutes later he was standing on the bike path outside DeMarco's house.

He hesitated a moment, almost afraid of what he would find. Finally he pushed open the gate, walked up to the front door, and knocked. One of DeMarco's new surfer roommates opened the door. He looked right through Shane and, without saying a word, stepped back and let him in. The boy was wearing surf trunks with no shirt and had an athlete's build. The eyes were where the problem was: empty, hollow tunnels of distrust.

"DeMarco around?"

The boy didn't seem to want to waste even one syllable on Shane. He jerked a thumb in the direction of the hallway, then flopped back down on the sofa, where his buddy was lounging with the TV remote. MTV's *Real World* was on the large Sony. Two teenage girls were on the screen arguing about their gay male roommate's new rottweiler, who apparently was shitting all over their London flat. One of life's smelly little problems. Shane moved through the hall and knocked on the end door. His defense rep called out angrily: "What?!"

Shane pushed the door open and looked in. For the first time, Dee was hard at it. He had law books and police department manuals open on the cluttered desk in front of him, his half-glasses perched on the end of his nose. He was a blue and gray vision in a faded LAPD sweatshirt and jeans. He had taken his long gray hair out of the knot in back, and it now hung on his shoulders, Cochise-style.

"How's it goin'?" Shane asked.

"Don't you wanna give me a Breathalyzer first?" he groused.

"Come on, Dee, gimme a break."

The defense rep leaned back in his squeaking swivel chair and swung around to face Shane. "Basically, it ain't getting any better," DeMarco said.

"You talkin' about the 1.61 Mayweather sent through this morning? I haven't seen it yet. I haven't been home."

"Copy right here," DeMarco said, picking up a fax and waving it at Shane. "But it's worse than just the 1.61. I found out this afternoon that Donovan McNeil, the only friendly face you had on your judging panel, is no longer able to attend the hearing." DeMarco rooted around his paperwork, found another fax, and held it up. "He's been transferred as of yesterday to the command chair at Administrative Vice in Central Division. Big fucking job. And since that transfer is effective immediately, it has been determined by the Special Investigations Division that, under these extreme circumstances, he does not have the time available to serve on your board. He's been replaced. I guess these Dark Side pricks finally found out you two used t'sling bait together."

"Who'd we get this time? The chief's brother-in-law?"

"Nope. The chief's old driver, Leland H. Postil."

"Fuck," Shane said. "Don't we still get to throw one out?"

"Yeah, they gave me two choices. The other was Peggy York, former head of IAD. In your absence, I chose Postil."

"Things can't get much worse," Shane growled.

"Wanna bet? Check this. I've been trying to restrict Alexa Hamilton's demands for your personal background file. It's full of a buncha unsustained complaints, CO's tardy slips, ridiculous stuff that every cop gets the minute he starts hooking up scumbags and dealing with this nitpick four-hundred-page LAPD Manual. The stuff in those background files is always just unproved bullshit, but it looks bad if you string it out in front of a board hearing."

Shane was pissed. "Old, unsustained complaints can only be used *after* the board convicts, *if* they convict, and then it can only be used as part of the penalty phase of the hearing to help determine past history and state of mind," he said.

"I see you've been reading Section 202," DeMarco said.

"I sleep with the fucking thing, for all the good it's doing me."

"Well, buddy-boy, once again, the powers that control the Special Investigations Division have ruled against you. Alexa filed a Pitches motion to overturn that section of the Police Bill of Rights. The panel granted her motion, and the package went over to her at four this afternoon."

They sat quietly in the room. Finally DeMarco got up, went to a small refrigerator in the corner of the office, and pulled out a beer. "You want one?"

"Dee, you've gotta stay off the Bud Lights. Okay?"

"Fuck you. I'm through listening to that shit from you." He ripped the tab off and took a swallow.

"I'm hearing around that maybe you have an alcohol problem," Shane said. "I hear that's why you pulled the pin."

DeMarco looked at him and smiled, then took a long fuck-you swig. "I won't even favor that with an answer."

"Look, Dee, I'm into something here. I think I've got the mayor tied into a blackmail scheme to trade billions of dollars' worth of property from Long Beach over to L.A. Ray and his den were blackmailing people in Arrowhead so this would happen, most notably Carl Cummins, who's president of the Long Beach City Council. I followed some guys out there to the old naval yard. I've got—"

"You got shit," DeMarco interrupted, slamming the beer can down on his desktop. "Maybe if you'd stop running around, accusing all these high-profile guys of bullshit crimes, we wouldn't be facing all this administrative flack. We wouldn't be losing the Pitches and all our other motions."

"But—"

"No! Don't 'but' me. Ever since I took this fucking case, you've been accusing me of not trying. The reason we're getting hosed here, buddy, is that you have proceeded to piss off the chief of police, Deputy Chief Mayweather, Ray's rookie den, and everybody in between. Add to that the fact that you're acting like you're fucking guilty. What kinda asshole breaks into Warren Zell's office and goes through his files?"

"Who told you that?" Shane asked.

"It's all over the department that Alexa Hamilton caught you in there, you dumb shit!"

Shane stood there, feeling slightly dizzy and stupid as hell. *Had Alexa lied? Had she told the department what he'd done?* "I . . . I don't see how—"

"On top of all that, you're about to get arrested for first-degree murder," DeMarco interrupted. "I got a call from the warrant control desk today. They wanted to know if you were here. They've been checking your house and said you're not living there. I think you'd better get in touch with them—turn yourself in."

Shane spun and moved out of the office, back into the hall. DeMarco followed him through the living room and out the front door.

"If you run, you're making a huge mistake," DeMarco said, standing in his doorway, peering over his half-glasses at Shane on the sidewalk.

"What else can I do, huh?" Shane answered. "I got nobody but me. If I get arrested, I'm gone without a ripple. Nobody will try and find out what's happening here. If I don't figure it out, I'm gonna go down in front of this rigged murder case." Then he turned and walked up the path. When he arrived at the parking lot two doors away, he got into his car and pulled out onto the highway.

He decided to go up the coast and cut across town on Sunset, afraid that DeMarco might call the cops down on him. He tried to get his head clear and to organize the facts. But one thought kept coming back.

Why would Alexa tell about his break-in at Zell's office? Shane could end her career with the information about her throwing his old BOR. Something had to be wrong.

Less than an hour ago, Alexa had said she believed him.

Now Shane needed to decide if he could believe her.

THE MONEY SHOT 32

I T WAS TEN-THIRTY when Shane got back to the 110, heading downtown toward the Spring Summer Apartments. His pager buzzed. He pulled it off his belt and read the printed message on the LED screen:

911 to IAD
A.H.

A.H.—Alexa Hamilton. She wanted Shane to go to the Bradbury Building immediately. He wondered what she wanted, or whether he should even trust her. Maybe the warrant was there and she was drawing him in so he'd be served and end up spending the night in jail. He picked up his cell phone, dialed her cell number, and got a not-in-service recording. He tried her apartment, no answer. Despite his suspicions, he had almost no choice. He had to take a chance on her. He knew the switchboard at the

Bradbury was closed, so he fumbled in his pocket for the number of the Spring Summer Apartments. He dialed and after a minute got Longboard Kelly on the phone.

"Yeah," the surfboard shaper said softly.

"It's Shane. Everything okay?"

"Yeah." Again, a whisper.

"What's wrong? How come you're whispering?"

There was a long moment, then: "Chooch is asleep."

"Look, I've gotta go run an errand on my way home. It's only a few blocks outta the way. Are you guys cool?"

"Yeah."

"See you in about an hour. If that changes, I'll call."

" 'Kay," and then Longboard was gone.

Longboard Kelly sounded strange. He was usually a nonstop talker. Shane wondered whether he and Chooch had started toking together. He almost called back, but then he had to change lanes to make the off-ramp on Sixth Street. In a few more minutes he was downtown.

It was just before eleven and Schwarzenegger was back.

· · ·

"Sorry, absolutely nobody gets through on Sixth. We're shooting a big stunt," the motorcycle cop said. "Back up, go four blocks over to Wilshire."

"I gotta get to Spring and Third," Shane said.

"Can't. It's inside the restricted area. You'll have to park it here and walk. This area has been posted for three or four days." The cop was another old-timer, a forty-year veteran, in his mid- to late sixties. He was standing on Spring Street, behind his yellow barricade, glowering in his knee boots and dark blue shirt with its thirteen hash marks, each one representing three years of service. The entire eight-block section from Wilshire to Seventh had been closed. There was a helicopter sitting in the middle of Sixth Street; klieg lights and a condor had the buildings lit up almost like daylight. Stunt people were milling about. A Brinks armored truck was parked in the middle of the street, near a camera on dolly tracks. The director and some assistant directors were pointing at extras with briefcases, directing them where to stand.

"When are you guys gonna be outta here?" Shane said darkly.

"Don't know," the motor cop replied. "But we got special permission tonight for this big shot, 'cause we had to land the bird in the middle of the street and then do the chase with the armored car down Spring. It's some lash-up," he said proudly, eager to display his film expertise. "We're using Tyler mounts on the camera ship to photograph the stunt exchange from the picture bird to the roof of the speeding armored truck. Arnie is gonna be on top of the moving truck, do the fistfight with the stunt captain while they're heading down Spring. Then Arnie jumps and catches the bar under the picture chopper and does the car-to-helicopter exchange. We cut, rerig, and the stunt double hangs there on the flyaway. It's a money shot," he said proudly. Everybody in L.A. talks the talk. Arnie had to be Schwarzenegger. It never even occurred to the bragging cop that half of downtown L.A. was ready to strangle this entire cast and crew.

Shane got out of the car and started to move past the barricade, toward the gathering of assistant directors and stunt people standing near the idling helicopter.

"Hey, you can't just walk through here, buddy. It's restricted," the cop warned.

"I'm not parking here and walking a mile."

"You gotta go around. This is a danger area. Nobody can be in there who's not cleared or been to the stunt safety meeting."

"Sarge, I'm on the job. I gotta get to Internal Affairs at the Bradbury." Shane dug into his pocket, pulled out his last business card, and handed it to the cop.

"You got a badge?"

"Left it at home. I was out on a boat when I got the call."

" 'Cept you could a' got this card from anybody," he said suspiciously.

"When did you stop being a cop and start being a movie PA?" Shane was getting pissed. He started around the barricade, and the old cop reached out and grabbed Shane's arm just as an assistant director came running up.

"What's the problem, Rich?" he asked the motor cop.

"Guy says he's a cop. Wants t'drive through." He handed Shane's card to the assistant director, who looked at it.

"We're still a bit away from the shot," the AD said to Shane. "Lemme see if I can set this up. Hang on." He turned and ran back to the group of men huddled near the armored car, handing the card to a tall man in a safari jacket. The man looked at the card, then up the street to Shane, and nodded.

The assistant director waved his arm at Shane to come ahead. The motorcycle cop was pissed off and didn't look at Shane as he moved the barricade.

Shane got back in the Taurus and pulled up the street, right into the activity of the movie set. He was trying to get around the idling helicopter when a man stepped out from the group by the armored car and motioned him to stop, then leaned in his passenger window, smiling.

"Hang on a minute," he said.

Suddenly Shane felt something cold and hard press on the left side of his head.

"Howdy-do," a low, soft voice said with a country twang. "Y'all wanna slowly get out of the car?"

Shane tried to look back, but the second man had positioned himself to the left of Shane and behind him, pointing the gun through the driver-side window, placing it against the left side of his head. Shane didn't have to see the gun to know what it was.

"This is pretty dumb, whoever the fuck you are," Shane finally said.

"Hey, dipshit, we been lookin' all over for you. You're the dummy. I sent you the nine-one-one. We was down here anyway, and you stumble right on in here, nice as can be." Then the man with the gun suddenly shouted at the man in the safari coat.

"Dom," he yelled. "What if, when Arnie leaves the car, we stage Sandra's abduction like this. Lookee here." Then he opened the door to the Taurus. "Out," he growled at Shane. "We're gonna get in that chopper. You're sitting in the back right side."

"You're gonna kidnap me in front of all these people?"

"This ain't a kidnapping, it's a rehearsal," he said. "You're gonna be Sandra Bullock. Don't fuck with me, pal. You make trouble, I'll clock you and carry you over. It'll look like blocking to these idiots." Then he pulled Shane out of the car, led him twenty feet to the helicopter at gunpoint, and shoved him into the back. Shane saw that it was Calvin Sheets.

Waiting in the helicopter was another piece of muscle Shane had never seen before. He was holding a gun low, out of sight. Shane settled in, and the man's cold eyes never left him. Calvin looked back down at the director, who shouted, "Yeah, maybe that could work, Cal. But I gotta deal with this first."

Calvin shouted back, "Hunter just called. We'll be back in half an hour, if that's okay."

"Go ahead," the director shouted. "We're an hour away, but we need the chopper back by eleven."

Calvin waved, climbed into the helicopter, and motioned to the pilot, who revved up the motor.

They lifted up off the pavement, hovered, then veered over the street and climbed away from the movie company.

Shane looked out the window and saw the fully rigged and lit street with the hundred or more movie people who had just witnessed his kidnapping without realizing it. They became miniatures as the chopper rose.

"So this is a Logan Hunter film," Shane said.

"Huh?" Calvin shouted back over the roar of the chopper.

"Forget it," Shane said.

Then the helicopter turned north and flew toward the mountains, picking up altitude, leaving the L.A. basin far behind.

33

THE HAT

"I'M GONNA PUT her down in the Valley of the Moon," the pilot yelled over the rotor noise. "I'll call the house; they can meet us there."

Calvin responded with the okay sign. They were flying low, streaking through the San Bernardino Mountains, following a river-cut canyon about fifty feet off the ground. Occasionally Shane could see the moon shadow of the helicopter against rock outcroppings of the granite cliffs on the west side. Suddenly the helicopter rose and veered right, then flew around a mountain peak.

"Arrowhead Peak!" the pilot yelled at Sheets, pointing at the pinnacle, acting like a tour guide instead of a fucking kidnapper.

They skirted the mountaintop and cleared the east face. Shane could see Lake Arrowhead shimmering off in the distance directly ahead. A few miles closer was a smaller body of water five or six miles west of Arrowhead, which Shane remembered was Lake Gregory.

The helicopter streaked low, skirting the shore of Lake Gregory, until finally they were hovering over the appropriately named Valley of the Moon . . . no trees, no rocks, just acres of brown dirt.

The helicopter engine picked up rpms as it hovered. Out of the window below, Shane could see a late-model Land Rover streaking along a dry riverbed, its headlight beams bouncing against the ground. The pilot pointed to the black four-wheel drive racing toward them, and Sheets nodded.

They found a flat spot in the center of the riverbed, and the pilot lowered the chopper until it was just a few feet above the ground. The black Land Rover came to a stop a few hundred feet away. Dirt flew out in every direction, sandblasting the shiny new vehicle, pitting its ebony surface. Then the helicopter touched down its skids. The pilot didn't kill the engine; the turbine whined and the rotor flashed overhead as Sheets and the man sitting opposite Shane opened the door.

"Out!" Sheets commanded. Shane looked out of the helicopter at the desolate terrain, wondering if he was going to get a seat in the Land Rover or become an eternal resident of the Valley of the Moon.

Before he could protest, he felt cold steel on the back of his head as Sheets pushed the weapon against his skull. Shane didn't move.

"Just gimme a reason, and I'll put one through your wet wear."

"This hard-ass routine you got ain't working, Sheets."

"You know who I am?"

"Everybody in Southwest knows you. You ran the French embassy in the Coliseum parking lot."

"Get the fuck out," Sheets snarled.

"Calm down," Shane growled, but he got out of the chopper before Sheets could sucker punch him. He ducked his head reflexively as the rotor spun safely above him and the silent man. Sheets got out last, and they pushed him toward the Land Rover. Dust was flying, getting into everybody's eyes.

They scrambled to the SUV, driven by a shorthaired, bull-necked man. Before they could get the Land Rover turned around, the helicopter revved its engine and lifted off, pelting them with sand and destroying what was left of the paint, starring the back window near Shane's head with a flying rock.

"Shit. Fucking guy . . ." Sheets said, glowering at the chopper as it spun around and flew away, hurrying back to Spring Street, Arnold Schwarzenegger, and the money shot.

Shane was glad to be in the SUV, moving out of the Valley of the Moon. The fact that they were taking him anywhere gave him some hope. If he was being brought here to be disposed of, they probably would have gone ahead and chilled him in this desolate valley.

Calvin Sheets sat next to the bullnecked driver, looking out the front window, the .38 snubby still in his right hand. The silent man from the helicopter sat in the backseat next to Shane, never taking his eyes off him.

They raced along the creek bed in four-wheel drive, bouncing through rain ruts, and after five tire-pounding minutes, shot up onto the paved highway. The driver shifted out of four-wheel and sped past a weathered sign that identified the road as North Drive.

Soon they came to Bay Road, which Shane knew went all the way around the perimeter of the Lake Arrowhead shoreline. He watched the shimmering lake appear and disappear, peeking out from behind buildings and trees as the Land Rover sped around the lake, finally turning onto Peninsula Road, making a left onto Long Point.

They pulled up to a dock at a deserted camping area. Shane

could see a man with his left arm in a sling standing next to the same classic reproduction Chris-Craft inboard that had delivered his assailants to Ray's dock two days before. The varnished sides glistened against soft teak decks.

Sheets went through his rough-guy routine again, poking at Shane with the gun. "Let's go, asshole," he growled. Shane got out of the Land Rover and moved ahead of the ex–LAPD sergeant, toward the boat.

Now he was struck by another gruesome possibility: maybe, instead of a dirt nap, he was about to go swimming with a forty-pound anchor. He didn't have much time to worry about it, though, because as he stepped up to the boat, the man with his left arm in the sling stepped forward as if to help him aboard, then, unexpectedly, threw a right hook, knocking Shane back against Sheets. His vision starred; he bit his tongue; his mouth filled with blood.

"Cut it out, Marvin," Sheets growled. "Rich, get the lines."

"Motherfucker," Marvin said, snarling at Shane, who was trying hard to clear his vision. The blow had landed high on his cheek. His eyes started watering badly. This was probably the guy who stopped his bullet and left the two pints of blood on Ray's linoleum floor.

"You know what they say, Marv. The kitchen is the most dangerous place in the home," Shane said.

"Fuck you," Marvin growled.

Rich untied the boat as Marvin got behind the wheel and turned the key; while the engine burbled and growled, they all took a moment and listened like teenage boys to the throaty rumble of the blown 257 flathead. Shane was pushed into the enclosed backseat of the boat, which was separated from the front by a teak deck and a second chrome windshield. He found himself wedged in tightly next to Sheets and the silent man named Rich from the helicopter.

Marvin angrily slammed down the throttle with his good hand

caught the wheel, and the boat roared away from the dock, picking up speed as they headed across the lake in the shimmering light of a three-quarter moon.

Shane could see Arrowhead Village twinkling across the water, about half a mile to the right. Finally Marvin slowed the boat and turned the wheel. Ray's party house and dock were ahead, about a hundred yards away. Seconds later they were slowing down, and Shane could feel the heavy inboard bumping softly against the wood dock.

"Out," Sheets ordered, again jamming the pistol in Shane's ribs.

They walked up onto the porch. The door was unlocked and they went inside.

Coy Love was waiting in the living room. Shane had only seen his picture, and the photo didn't begin to capture the essence of him. At least six foot six, he towered over all of them, wearing a blue windbreaker and jeans. His thin, lipless mouth, oversize head, and stringy, muscled neck dominated an overpowering physical presence. He stood Lurch-like and speechless until they all got inside and closed the door. "This doesn't have to end badly," he said. His voice was rough—hard and dusty, like boots marching through gravel.

"That's good news," Shane replied.

"I want to show you something," Love said. "Follow me." He turned abruptly and led them through the hall into the master suite.

The lights were all on in the room. Shane tried not to look at the mirror, which, he knew from before, fronted the hidden room with its glory hole. A small suitcase was open on the bed, and it was full of cash. The used bills were stacked and banded. As soon as he saw the money, Shane was sure that he was being videotaped.

It seemed that Coy Love was in charge, which momentarily

surprised him, because Love had been only a rookie patrolman when he'd been terminated. Sheets had been a sergeant, a watch commander. Yet Sheets seemed content to stand in the background and do his funky gun-poking routine while Love ran the show. Shane figured the shift in roles was primal—the law of the jungle. Love was more dangerous and brutal and, therefore, the alpha male. "Don't fuck with Love" the message machine had said. Love was the hammer.

"We need to come to terms," Coy Love said, his bloodless lips stretched tight across tombstone-shaped teeth.

"Good," Shane said. *A one-word answer—keep it thin; don't volunteer anything.*

"That's yours," Love said, indicating the cash in the suitcase on the bed. "A hundred grand in tens and twenties."

"Lucky me. Did I win the lottery?" Shane asked.

"Yeah, you were down to your last ticket, and then you got lucky, hit the number. If you start acting smart now instead of just running around like a hard-on with dirt for brains, then maybe there's another suitcase like that one in your future."

"I like this so far."

"We got some rules that go with giving you this hat." Police terminology for a bribe.

"Rules? Okay."

"One. You go home, you sit in your house, and you stay there."

"Trouble with my house is, it's full of nine-millimeter federals. The Major Crimes dicks have been digging them out of the walls like fruit seeds."

"That was a mistake. We apologize."

"I accept." Shane was beginning to think that maybe he might actually get out of there alive.

"Two. You stop messing around in Long Beach. Stop going to the naval yard."

"No problem there. I didn't like it much anyway."

"Three. Whatever you think you've figured out about Mayor Crispin or the top floor of the Glass House—forget it."

"Okay . . . it's forgotten."

"Let me explain to you why you are being offered this hat instead of a plot at Forest Lawn."

"Okay."

"Since you shot Ray, you have been in the press a lot. We're trying to keep a low profile. You get to live as long as you play ball." Love moved around Shane, forcing him to turn sideways to the mirror while keeping his own back to it. This was definitely being videotaped. Shots of Shane Scully taking a suitcase full of cash. Damning evidence if he ever changed his mind. On the plus side, it also probably meant the murder one charge wasn't coming. If the DA had what he needed, these guys wouldn't be doing this.

"Okay, since we're playing ball, I assume I'm the catcher," Shane said.

"That's what you are. You just caught a break. If you're smart, you won't catch a bullet."

"I'm gonna be smart. I'm gonna just take my suitcase of un-traceable cash and go home and sit in my bullet-riddled living room until you tell me it's okay to come out."

Love closed the suitcase, snapped the clasps, and handed it to Shane, spinning him slightly so that he was looking more toward the glory hole. Love kept his back to the bedroom mirror the whole time.

"Is that it?" Shane asked. "Is our business concluded?"

"Not quite yet. Come in here." Love moved out of the bedroom and back into the living room. Shane followed him, carrying the suitcase, thinking the hundred thousand in small bills was surprisingly light. Sheets, Marvin, and Rich stayed behind him.

In the living room Coy took a videotape box off the TV, opened it, slid the tape into the VCR, then turned his frightening, bloodless smile on Shane.

"I think it's important that you do not mistake kindness for weakness," Love said as he grabbed the remote off the TV and turned the set on. He punched PLAY.

Suddenly Shane was looking at Chooch and Longboard Kelly on the videotape. They were tied to wooden chairs in Shane's rented apartment on Third Street. He recognized the faded wallpaper and frayed blue drapes. Both Brian and Chooch had silver duct tape across their mouths. A man was offscreen holding a shotgun, the barrel of the weapon sticking about an inch into the frame.

Shane felt his guts tighten into a knot. Bile instantly flooded the back of his throat. "He's a fifteen-year-old kid," he protested weakly. "Brian Kelly is just a surfboard shaper. He doesn't know shit."

"You go home and stay quiet for two or three days. Then, if everything goes right, you get them both back. Otherwise, I'm gonna put these cowboys on the ark," Love said.

On the tape Chooch was struggling against his ropes. Longboard looked dazed and had blood on the side of his head.

"Seen enough?" Coy said, and when Shane nodded, he turned off the TV and handed Shane a set of car keys. "There's a department car parked in the driveway. Take it back and leave it in the motor pool at the Glass House. Then take a cab home and pull the grass up over your head."

Shane took the keys and the suitcase and walked on wooden legs out of the house. They all followed. There was a gray Crown Victoria with blackwalls in the drive. He got behind the wheel, started the car, and pulled out of the driveway. The headlights swept across the four ex-cops as he backed into the street, turning right. He was operating on autopilot . . . his mind on the sickening video images of Chooch and Brian tied to the chairs.

He drove down Lake View Drive, the black suitcase full of cash jiggling on the seat beside him. He took the correct turns from memory and found himself back on I-7, heading out of Arrowhead toward L.A.

As he drove, he could picture Chooch's black Hispanic eyes staring out at him from the recesses of his memory. He remembered the boy's swarthy, handsome features as he sat in the Little Bruin deli in Westwood, looking out at the traffic, his gaze averted so Shane wouldn't see his pain.

"Do you know who my father is?" the boy had asked. *"Did Sandy ever tell you?"* Hurt and longing in the question.

Shane had wanted to fill the void in Chooch's life, just as he had wanted to fill it in his own. But he had been slow out of the blocks and running two steps behind, a clown in swim fins, flapping along, heels down while the rest of the field breezed past him.

Almost without thinking, he picked up his phone and for the second time in twenty-four hours asked Alexa for help.

By the time he got to the San Bernardino Freeway, he had explained to her in detail what had happened and what was on the videotape. "I'll meet you at the Spring Summer Apartments," she said. "Maybe we can pick up something there."

An hour later he was back in downtown L.A. He found a spot at the curb on Third Street, across from his rented room. He could see Alexa's gray Crown Vic at the curb across the street. He quickly got out of his borrowed car and hurried into the building, afraid of what he might find in the cramped rented single on the third floor of the dingy rooming house.

THE THREE-FLUSH RULE

34

HE FOUND HER kneeling by the toilet in the bathroom, wearing latex gloves and brushing black granite powder from her field-investigation kit onto the toilet handle with a fine bristle brush. Every detective and patrol officer carried a crime-scene investigation kit in the trunk of his or her car.

"You got gloves?" she asked, glancing back at him, not bothering with a greeting.

"No," he replied woodenly. Alexa reached into her open kit and pulled out an extra pair. "I'm gonna need a set of elimination prints from you. We've also gotta get a set of Chooch's and Longboard's from somewhere."

"Right," he said, and looked around the bathroom. "You get anything yet?"

"Hard to tell. A lot of this is junk, smudged or overlapped. I got a partial palm off that kitchen chair, where somebody must've grabbed it by the back and carried it. I think, from what you described on the phone, the videotaping took place in the center of the living room. They moved the chairs back to the kitchen, but there are fresh indent marks on the living-room carpet. I marked 'em with chalk, so don't step on 'em. I'm gonna take pictures. I emptied the kitchen trash into a towel in the sink, but I haven't gotten to it yet."

Shane moved out of the bathroom and looked at the small living room. "You try the TV?" he called out to her. After a minute she came out of the bathroom with a yellow four-by-five fingerprint identification card in her hand. She leaned down on the dining-room table and labeled a partial print she had just lifted off the toilet flush handle.

"We'll never get a print run with these," Alexa said. "They're mostly partials and smudged. The best we can hope for, if we even catch these perps, is maybe a match on a few of the basic Galton classifieds—maybe connect up on some of these ridge endings. The loops, arches, and whorls are pretty smudged."

"Chooch used the TV; maybe the remote has a set of his you can use for elimination," he said.

She took the channel changer, holding it by its side, and started dusting it, dipping the brush into the glass vial of black powder, then softly brushing the fine camel-hair bristles across the remote, looking for graphite residue that would indicate the oil of a fingerprint. She found a few good latents on the underside of the channel-changer, then took the clear tape out of her field kit and lifted the prints, stuck them on the card, and pressed them down, labeling the back of the card, "Channel Changer Right Index and Middle Finger."

While she worked, Shane moved through the apartment. There were no signs of a struggle, no blood, but lots of dirty black powder. She had been working there for quite a while and had left graphite everywhere—on the doorjamb at shoulder height, where somebody might lean with a palm, against the wall, on the cupboard doors, on the countertops.

Shane put on his latex gloves and began, halfheartedly, poking through the trash collected on the towel lying in the deep kitchen sink. He found a cardboard roll about an inch in diameter and plucked it out, using a pen from his pocket. Then he saw an empty bag of M&M's. Longboard was an M&M's freak. He pulled it out as well and took both items back into the living room. He handed the cardboard roll to Alexa. "Looks like the core from the roll of silver duct tape," he said.

"I saw that, too," she said. "We can try, but there's so much gummy shit on it, I doubt we'll lift anything." She took the powder and brushed it on the cardboard core, but as predicted, it was too sticky. Powder clung everywhere, turning the core graphite black and revealing nothing.

He told her about Longboard's candy addiction, so she went to work on the M&M's wrapper.

"Was there anything on the videotape you can remember that might be helpful?" she asked as she brushed the surface of the wrapper.

"No," he said. "Except there was a shotgun in the side of the frame . . . a riot pump. Looked like an Ithaca."

"Department issue." She said what he'd been thinking. "I don't think we're gonna find anything. If those guys were cops, they wouldn't leave evidence behind. They were probably all wearing gloves and picked up or flushed everything."

"Speaking of flushes, did you check the trap in the toilet?" he asked.

"No," she said, looking up. "I always hate that job, but I guess we oughta give it a try." She finished with the M&M's wrapper, lifting three good prints. "We're gonna need wrenches to get to the toilet trap," she said.

"I'll go see the manager."

"Don't bring him in here," she said sharply.

"Don't worry, I'm not a total idiot," he snapped back, then

went down to the front desk, rang the night bell, and got the manager out of bed.

"Trouble with the toilet," Shane lied to the bleary-eyed man, who looked as if he hadn't shaved in two days. Rumpled, tired, and angry, he glowered at Shane from under the harsh light above his desk.

"Shit," the man said.

"You got a pipe wrench? I used to be a plumber. I can clear it for you."

The manager looked at him and computed the odds that Shane might break his toilet against the cost of calling a regular plumber. Money won . . . South of Main Street, it usually did. The manager moved into the back room and returned with a toolbox.

Shane took it up to the third-floor apartment. He closed the door and put on his gloves, then he and Alexa moved to the bathroom and removed the commode. He took off the porcelain top and plugged the flush valve with toilet paper. Then they began to remove the metal elbow from the back of the toilet.

One of the little-known truths about modern plumbing is that it takes at least two, sometimes three flushes to completely get rid of a bowl load. On more than one drug raid, the perps had flushed the dope with the cops coming through the door, not bothering to repeat the procedure, then were shocked to learn that two or three grams of cocaine remained in the water in the elbow and trap. Liquid samples had rolled up more than one drug dealer. The Drug Enforcement teams called it "the Three-Flush Rule."

They got the elbow off, and toilet water spilled onto the floor. Shane kept from kneeling in it by squatting as he worked. The elbow looked pretty clean, so he went after the trap, which was below the elbow and was there to keep larger obstructions out of the plumbing lines until they dissolved or softened.

"The things one learns in law enforcement," he muttered as he finally got the trap out and took it to the sink, emptying the four-inch cylinder into the basin. The last thing out was fat, round, and dark brown. It landed on the white porcelain like a turd on a wedding cake. The object had a shiny gold band around it.

"Cigar," he said triumphantly, picking it up with his latex gloves. It was a three-quarter-smoked panatela. The gold band said DOMINICAN REGAL.

"I think this is what's commonly called a clue," she said, smiling. "We have us a cigar smoker." She was holding out an evidence bag.

He dropped the mushy stogie inside the glassine pouch, then washed his gloved hands.

Five minutes later they had replaced the toilet fixture, taken the living-room crime scene photos, and were sitting on the cigarette-burned sofa, trying to figure it all out.

"There was no forced entry, so Longboard must have just let the guys in. If they were cops, they probably just flashed a potsy," she said.

"Maybe." His mind was circling a worrisome thought, but he pushed it aside. "Coy Love told me to go home and wait for two or three days. That means whatever it is they're worried about, it goes away after that."

"Makes sense," she answered.

"He also said to forget about the Long Beach Naval Yard and Mayor Crispin."

She nodded, but said nothing.

"These guys aren't gonna turn Longboard and Chooch loose, are they?" he blurted, putting the distressing thought into words. "They're gonna kill 'em."

"Probably," she said. "They'll hold 'em for leverage in case you get restless, but once this is over, they can't leave a kidnapping charge and two vics on the table."

"Shit," he said, rubbing his eyes. "I've fucked this up so bad. It's always like . . . if I knew yesterday what I know today . . ."

"Shane, I think we need to tell his mother."

"Yeah. I guess I've been putting that off." He looked at his watch. "It'll be sunup in an hour. Sandy is having sleepovers with some DEA target. She won't be there till sometime after eleven. I'm whipped, but I can't sleep here. How's your place sound?"

"I got a couch you can use," she said, then gathered up all of her stuff and stood in the doorway, looking at the dusted room. "If we leave it like this, you're gonna forfeit your security deposit."

"Fuck it. Let's go."

They closed the door and locked up, heading downstairs. Shane deposited the toolbox behind the counter without ringing the night bell, and they walked out into the street.

"I gotta drop this department car back at the Glass House. I don't wanna disobey any of their instructions. Follow me, then later we can go to Sandy's in your car," Shane suggested.

"My car's at home. I was with a friend when you called. I had him drop me off here. I figured we'd use your car."

"Then who owns that plainwrap?" he said, pointing to the gray Crown Vic across the street. "That's gotta be department issue. No civilian is gonna buy a stripped-down gray sedan with no air and blackwalls."

They moved across the street and looked through the windshield of the locked car. They could see the telltale wires hanging down under the dash, identifying the recessed police radio.

"Yep," she said, "but it's not a detective car. No coffee lids on the dash."

She was right. Since detectives had to do lots of stakeouts, they drank gallons of coffee. The cars were department-owned, so the cops had no pride of ownership. The common practice was to peel the plastic lids off the Styrofoam Winchell's cups and throw them up onto the dash. Shane had never been in a detective's plainwrap that didn't have half a dozen or more plastic lids up there. If the motor pool ever cleaned the interiors, the old, wet rings from the tops stained the dash and remained behind as a permanent testament to the practice.

"Staff car?" he said hesitantly.

They both walked around the Crown Vic, looking through the windows. It had beem immaculately cleaned. All the cars in the staff motor pool were automatically washed and vacuumed once a day by inner-city gangsters dressed in jailhouse orange.

Alexa took out her cell phone and punched in a number. After a minute she got the Communications Center.

"This is Sergeant Hamilton, serial number 50791. I found one of our plainwraps parked in a bad spot. It's a 548E," she said, giving the radio code for a vehicle parked illegally across a drive-way. "It should be moved. Could you give me the officer's name so I can contact him to move it?" She listened, then said, "City plate, DF 453." Another wait, then, "Thanks," and she closed the cell, a troubled look on her face.

"Shit, I don't even want to ask," he said.

"It's a Triple-O staff car," she said.

Triple-O stood for the Office of Operations, which reported directly to the chief of police. Shane remembered that the admin-istrative staff of the Office of Operations contained about five men and women, all captains and above. The office acted as an adviser to the chief of police and exercised line-of-command over-sight in all divisions. In short, Operations was Chief Brewer's right hand.

"It could have been left here because of the movie," she said hopefully. "Triple-O handles press relations."

"You packing?" he asked.

"Yeah, of course."

"Gimme it. Mine's gone. I've been losing guns faster than winos' teeth."

"What're you gonna do?"

"Break into this thing. I don't wanna fuck around with the lock, standing on a street corner. Lemme have it."

She dug her Beretta 9mm out of her purse and handed it to him. He dropped the clip and handed it back, then tromboned the slide to make sure the chamber was clean. He held the automatic by the barrel, looked both ways for potential witnesses, then broke the side window of the car, shattering glass onto the maroon velour upholstery.

"Dominican Regals are expensive smokes," he said. "I don't know many line cops who can afford ten-dollar cigars."

He opened the door, leaned inside, and started rummaging around. The ashtray was clean. He opened the glove box. There were three objects inside: the departmental registration, indicating that the car was indeed the property of the Los Angeles Police Department; an L.A./Long Beach Thomas street guide; and in the back of the compartment a sealed Baggie containing three fresh Dominican Regal cigars.

THE COURTESY REPORT

THE UNOFFICIAL NOTIFICATION of a crime to a civilian was known in police work as a courtesy report.

Shane had revealed Sandy Sandoval's identity to Alexa over breakfast in her neat duplex apartment on Pico, two blocks east of Century City. He had slept fitfully on her living-room couch, and now, marginally refreshed, they left her place and drove across town. It was Saturday morning, and Barrington Plaza loomed, a tower of sunlit granite.

Shane pulled up, and Alexa badged the shoulder-braided band-leader who announced them, then keyed the elevator. Show tunes from the Boston Pops serenaded their arrival at the penthouse level. It was eleven-thirty A.M.

"So this is the famous Black Widow Nest," Alexa said, looking at the magnificent hallway on the eighteenth floor.

Most of the LAPD knew about her and knew that Shane had once been the Black Widow's handler, but her real name had been in the possession of only two Special Crimes detective commanders. Shane had deliberated hard before telling Alexa. In the end, it was the fact that Chooch's life was involved that made the decision for him.

Shane rang the doorbell to Sandy's penthouse apartment, dreading the job of telling her what had happened. He was sweating, but it was flop sweat, cold and clammy as wet clothing.

The mahogany door opened, and Sandy was standing there in a tailored black sheath that fit her size-four frame like a second skin—skin that was dusky, the color of dark sand; her eyes, golden-brown amber; her long raven tresses swirling around her shoulders with planned abandon. A single strand of pearls dangled with fuck-you elegance. She was dressed to party. She stood in the doorway, a questioning look on her gorgeous face. Then she shot a quick glance at Alexa.

"What is it? This is a terrible time, Shane. I'm bushed, I just got home."

"Chooch is gone," Shane said. "He's been kidnapped."

"I . . . I thought you said you had found him," Sandy finally stammered, her liquid amber eyes losing focus, clouding like a fighter hit too hard.

"He's been kidnapped, Sandy. By men who are trying to stop an investigation. I'm afraid . . ." He stopped. "I think by cops," he finished.

"Cops?!" she said, and involuntarily her hand went up to her mouth.

"This is Sergeant Hamilton. She's my—" He looked over at Alexa. *What exactly was she? His department prosecutor? His only believer? His nemesis? What the hell else was she?*

"I'm Shane's partner," she said, answering his question and filling the void.

Sandy spun abruptly and headed back into her apartment. Alexa and Shane followed. She walked slowly ahead of them, fluid as a dancer, her hips swaying seductively. Shane would have preferred a more leaden gait. Even in the face of this news, she radiated sexual grace. When she turned and faced them, he saw distress bordering on hysteria in her eyes. Instantly his heart went out to her, and guilt overwhelmed him.

"Why? Where did it happen?" she asked.

"An apartment on Third Street, a safe house I was renting. I guess they followed the sitter over from my place in Venice. I can't think of any other way they could have found him," Shane said.

"We aren't exactly sure who," Alexa said. "But it appears to be high-ranking police officers who are calling the shots."

"You should go to the chief. Go to Burl. Tell him what you suspect."

When Alexa hesitated and looked at Shane, Sandy sank down on the sofa. "You're telling me you think Burl's—"

"We don't know exactly who is involved," Shane said. "But it goes way up. Maybe all the way to the mayor. It involves Logan Hunter, Tony Spivack, and the Long Beach Naval Yard."

"The 'why' is easier to understand. They took Chooch to keep us from continuing an investigation into it," Alexa said.

Sandy looked down at the white plush pile to hide her devastation.

"Sandy . . . I'm sorry. I'm really sorry. I didn't see it coming. If I could change this, I—"

She waved this away with her slender hand, sat absolutely still for a moment, then looked up. Her expression had hardened, the vulnerability had vanished. "How can I help? There must be something we can do." He watched in fascination as she tucked the loose strands of panic away, grabbed hold of her plummeting emotions, pulled hard, and darted up quickly, climbing hard, like a kite in a strong wind.

"Do you know any of these girls?" Alexa asked as she reached into her purse and handed over two packets of pictures from the party at the naval yard. Sandy spread them out on the white marble coffee table. She picked up a small antique magnifying glass with a carved ivory handle and examined each picture.

"I know one or two of these girls," she said, looking at them slowly, studying the shots, separating out the pictures of the two girls she knew. "Scarlet Mackenzie is the red-haired one. This one here—this blonde—changed her name from Gina Augustina to, what the hell was it . . . Avon Star. Used to have black hair. I think some of these others used to work with Madam Alex until Heidi took over the L.A. market. They all work the executive trade."

"What about the men? We know a lot of them are cops," Alexa said.

Sandy looked through the pictures again but shook her head. "To be honest with you, I'm not working much with LAPD anymore." She shoved the pictures of the two girls she knew toward Alexa, never once looking over at Shane. "I only know these two."

"These girls might know what's going on," Alexa said. "We need to find somebody who can help us, somebody who can tell us who took Chooch."

Sandy studied Alexa for a moment, then looked back at Shane. "I'm going to have to shut down this thing I'm doing for DEA. I'll tell 'em I need two days, that my brother got sick in Connecticut." She got up, moved to the phone, then punched in fourteen or more digits, which Shane knew was probably a number for a satellite beeper that the feds all used now.

After she finished, Sandy hung up and returned to the table. She sat down and looked at them, biting her lower lip. "Maybe I could convince Scarlet to duke me in with this crowd."

Duke me in, Shane thought. Sandy was even beginning to talk like a cop. It was definitely time for her to get out of the business.

"I could call Scarlet, say I just got out of a bad marriage and want to get back on the stroll. Nobody knows what I've been doing all these years. I haven't seen these two girls in ages."

Shane had to get out of there. He was starting to feel trapped. He got up abruptly. "Here's my beeper number," he said, giving Sandy one of his cards. "It's on all the time."

Alexa took out a pencil, wrote hers down, and handed it to Sandy.

"Okay," Sandy said. "I'll check back with you tomorrow. I should be able to get in touch with her by then. I'll set something up. If she knows anything that will help us get Chooch back, I'll find it."

"Good," Shane said.

They all walked to the front door. Sandy seemed cool and in control again. After she opened the door, she looked hard at him, and Shane knew he had to say something.

"I was trying to do you a favor when I took Chooch," he said. "It didn't work out, and I'm sorry."

What she said next was very strange. "You weren't doing me a favor, Shane, I was doing one for you."

He saw the dark, strange look again, and then her amber eyes opened for a moment and he was seeing her uncovered core . . . a self-loathing and sadness deeper than he could have ever imagined. Then the look was gone, replaced in a heartbeat by shrewd cunning and the cold gleam of sexuality. She closed the door, and he found himself looking at brown mahogany, the exact color of her eyes and almost as hard.

S AND J

IT WAS NOON, and they were back in Shane's borrowed Crown Vic. Alexa had turned on the police radio, and they were listening to staccato radio calls detailing the menu of violence and death, all of it described numerically in a flat monotone: "One X-ray twelve. A 415 at 2795 Slauson. Handle Code Two." Human carnage was a day-and-night routine.

"I don't know what the next move is," Alexa admitted.

Shane looked over at her. He knew what he was going to do, but it was a felony and he didn't think he should confide in her, for fear she'd hook him up on the spot.

But she was good, and she read the look in his eyes. "Let's hear what you're planning," she said suspiciously.

"You don't want any part of it. I'll drop you home."

"Lemme guess. You wanna go pick up Drucker or Kono or one of Ray's other hamsters . . . then go give them some S and J."

S and J stood for "sentence and judgment." Cops used to call it "holding court in the street." Either way, in this case it would be kidnapping and assault, both Class A felonies.

"Right idea, wrong guys," he said. "Kono and Drucker are small players; they may not even know what's really going on. I think they're just getting envelopes."

"It doesn't matter, 'cause we aren't going to kidnap and threaten anyone. That's a bonehead play." She stared hard at him in the dim light. He didn't look back. "Who, then?" she finally asked, her curiosity boiling over.

"You're gonna hate it." And then for some unknown reason, he told her.

After he had finished explaining his idea, she sat silently in the car for almost five minutes. The police radio underscored their separate thoughts, broadcasting misery while each of them pondered the personal cost if his dangerous plan went wrong.

Shane knew he had nothing more to lose. Any way he looked at it, odds were, he was headed to prison, where as a cop in the joint, he would last about as long as ice cream on a summer day.

Alexa, on the other hand, was only on the edge of this. She hadn't been put in play yet. Nobody except Sandy knew she'd been helping him. She could still go home and sit it out, saving her career and maybe her life.

He finally looked at her and saw those chips of blue staring out the front window, her brow furrowed in stubborn concentration, frustrated and confused like a fifth-grade algebra student.

For Shane, it was only about Chooch. It was his fault the boy was gone, and if he had to end his own life behind the secure perimeter of Vacaville State Prison, at least it would be for trying to put this mess right. Deep down he had formed a fraternal attachment to Chooch Sandoval. He couldn't exactly explain why, but it had happened.

Then he felt Alexa's weight shift on the seat beside him. He looked over at her. She had turned to face him.

"Okay," she said slowly, "I'm in."

...

The marina was strangely quiet for a Saturday afternoon. Shane thought the boat was a ketch or a yawl—whatever the hell they called them when the second mast was taller than the first.

"Schooner," Alexa said, reading his thoughts perfectly. The stern of the fifty-five-foot sailboat carried the boat's name.

"*Board and Cord*—cute name for a sailboat," she said.

He assumed she was thinking it stood for the wood of the hull and sail lines, so he set her straight. "It's a basketball expression. Means a bank shot off the backboard and through the net."

"Oh." She smiled. "In that case, he should have called it *Cheap Shot.*"

They were parked in the lot next to the slips at D Dock in Marina del Rey, looking out the front window of the car at the boats tied up forty or fifty yards from them, baking in eighty-degree sunlight. Both were wearing drugstore baseball caps and wraparound sunglasses—a minimal disguise.

"I heard he's down on this thing every weekend," Shane said, focusing a new pair of binoculars he'd found under the seat at the boat's portholes, looking for movement inside. "He's probably sleeping late."

Shane shifted his field of vision, concentrating on the yachts to either side of Mayweather's schooner. It appeared that most of the boats around the *Board and Cord* were empty.

"You sure you want to do this?" he asked. It was hard for him to believe she was about to risk her career and maybe even her freedom for Chooch Sandoval, whom she didn't even know. Of course, he had completely missed the point, so she set him straight.

"You claim I didn't believe what I said about keeping the job free from corruption, that I didn't want to risk it when the chips were down, and maybe there's some truth there. This is hard for me, I admit it, but these guys are committing crimes. They're kidnapping children. So, if I know this is happening and I walk away, that makes me as guilty as they are."

"Still, we're talking about committing a Class A felony."

"Shane . . ."

"Huh?"

"Shut up, will ya? Let's go roll up this shitwrap."

She opened the door and got out of the car. He followed her to the concrete path.

"I hope he's here. I wish I knew what his POV looked like," she said, changing the subject so he wouldn't pursue it, looking out at the twenty or thirty parked cars in the marina lot.

"Listen, you've gotta hear me on this," he said, turning her around, holding her arm as he talked, feeling the tight muscles in her biceps. "This means a lot to me—Chooch has become important—Brian, too, but Chooch . . . Chooch and I, we . . . it's like he's the piece of me that got lost growing up. It's hard for me to explain exactly, but I'm never gonna be able to pay you back."

"No shit, Sherlock." She smiled, then turned and moved off toward the slips.

They walked quietly along the concrete path and down onto the dock, light-footing it. They had already decided how they would do it, and as they got to the stern of the boat, Shane found some cover one boat away as Alexa moved up to the cockpit.

"Hello, anybody there?" she called out. "Anybody home? Chief Mayweather? Request permission to come aboard."

The back cabin door opened, and Deputy Chief Thomas Mayweather stuck his gleaming black head out. "Yes?" he said. "What is it?" He had on a striped polo shirt and white pants.

"You alone, sir? It's Sergeant Hamilton, IAD. I need to talk to you."

"My wife and kids will be here in an hour. What is it, Sergeant?" he said impatiently.

"It's about the Scully prosecution, sir. I've got a big problem, but I don't think we should talk about it out here. May I come aboard?"

"Okay." There was some hesitancy in his voice, almost as if he smelled deception. He came out of the cabin, reached up, and helped her down into the cockpit, then into the main salon. Once they were inside, he closed the rear hatch.

Shane had been hiding, lying flat on the dock one slip away. Now he got up and moved around until he was standing behind the schooner. They had planned to take Mayweather in the main salon, where they could control the capture and not be observed. Shane knew that he had to be very careful getting aboard. Mayweather would feel the sway of the boat if he rocked her when he stepped on.

Shane slowly lowered himself down and hung his feet carefully over the deck, gradually getting his footing on the upholstered cockpit seat. But to his dismay, the moment he put all his weight down, the boat shifted with the load, and a few seconds later the salon door flew open. Mayweather glared out at him.

"Permission to also come aboard?" Shane said stupidly.

"What the fuck?" Mayweather blurted.

Then they both heard Alexa chamber her 9mm behind the deputy chief. The sound froze Mayweather.

"Assume the position, asshole," Shane snarled, switching to street demeanor. They would have to take him out in the open. Shane moved farther onto the boat.

Deputy Chief Mayweather glanced back at Alexa in the middle of the salon, holding her gun, glaring blue ice over the barrel.

Shane was unarmed and presented Mayweather's best avenue of escape. Suddenly the deputy chief charged. Shane had been ready for it and had already screwed his heels awkwardly into the padded seats for traction.

didn't think Chief Mayweather, with his shelfful of basketball trophies and high-profile sports background, had ever spent much time on the street. He probably went right from the Academy to Press Relations or the Chief Administrative Staff. Hopefully, he would be disoriented and frightened enough to buy the act.

"You wouldn't dare kill me. You wouldn't dare," Mayweather said, but he sounded now as if he was trying to convince himself, not Shane.

"You don't think I'll kill ya; watch this, asshole." He pointed Alexa's Beretta at the wall beside the deputy chief's shaved head. He aimed it wide so that the shot would ricochet off the concrete a few inches from Mayweather, then fly harmlessly up the tunnel, into the dark. But he wanted the bullet to be close enough for Mayweather to feel its draft.

Shane fired the gun. The echo of the 9mm pistol was deafening in the enclosed space. Chief Mayweather actually yelped when the gun fired. The slug hit inches from the side of his head, throwing plaster and dust in all directions, then whined away up the tunnel into the dark. Speckles of blood suddenly appeared on Mayweather's face where some flying concrete chips had hit his left cheek.

"Shit, Alexa, this thing pulls right," Shane said, keeping it loony and loose.

"Whatta you doing?" she shouted. "Are you nuts? Stop it! You can't kill him. . . . *You can't!* I don't wanna go down for murder!" Picking up her cue perfectly, she turned on the camera without having to be told. Shane heard it whir softly behind him, and just like Coy Love, he stayed to the side, out of the frame.

"Okay, okay . . . I won't. You're right—you're right. Jesus, what's wrong with me. . . . It's just . . . Ahhh, fuck it! This guy is *going!*" Shane pointed the gun at the chief and pulled the hammer back. The metallic *click* echoed in the silence.

"Don't, Shane. Please!" she shouted, in standard Actors Studio over-the-top fashion. Mayweather was too panicked to spot their bad performances.

"Please . . . please stop him. Don't let him shoot me," the deputy chief begged Alexa. This was a new Tom Mayweather; no longer the officious police commander, this one was shitting his pants, pleading for his life.

"How can I stop, Tommy? You're such a hopeless prick. I can't believe all the worthless shit you've been pulling, starting with screwing me for Ray's death, going all the way up the penal code to double felony kidnapping."

"What're you talking about?" he said, his lips quivering, blood beginning to run down the side of his face where the cement chips had cut him, staining his collar.

"What I'm saying, Tom, is I want answers. Don't you get it? *I'm fucking pissed off!* I'm through taking your *shit.* You don't walk away from a bad FI down here. You get buried in this fucking wash!" Shane was taking time on his performance now, first working on his loony sound, then screaming, making it unstable and completely out of control.

"Look, I don't know what's going on," Mayweather blurted.

"Come on, you think I'm a fucking moron? You're the deputy chief, *asshooole,*" he said, dragging the word out, leaning on it. "You're Burl's guy. You think I'm gonna believe that? You took all those files outta Zell's office. Your fuckin' prints are all over the folders." He was pacing madly back and forth, strobing the floodlight, keeping his head turned from the lens but throwing a moving shadow against Mayweather and the sweating concrete tunnel wall. The effect was eerie.

"I just get money. I don't ask questions. I do what I'm told." His voice shook badly.

"Is that how you can afford that shiny new sailboat?" Shane asked.

"I . . . I . . . Yes."

"And you know what? You know what? You know what I'm feeling?" He was rolling his words around like marbles in a tin dish. "I'm thinkin' you and Brewer and Ray and his whole fuckin' den are just *scum-sucking pieces of shit!* You sold out the fuckin' job for a fuckin' sailboat."

Mayweather was breathing through his mouth now. His fear was so pronounced, he'd forgotten to swallow; drool started coming out the right side of his mouth, running down his chin. He was close to snapping. Close to the edge of temporary insanity.

"Hey, Shane, calm down, for Chrissake. Whatta you doing?" Alexa said, seeing the dangerous change in Mayweather, not wanting him to snap and start babbling. "The man wants to talk—why don't you let him?"

"Tom, you gonna talk?" Shane said, sounding a little more in control. "You talk, maybe you could live to go sailing again. . . . Maybe—just maybe. But I need answers, man. I can't take no more shit! I can't . . . I just fucking can't." A little insane exasperation.

"Let him talk, for Chrissake," Alexa persisted. "Go ahead, Tom. Just tell us."

"What . . . what is it you wanna know?" His voice was close to tears.

"I wanna know what's going on with the H Street Bounty Hunters. How come Ray's den was letting those bangers run free in Southwest?" Alexa asked.

"I don't know."

"This is just more fucking *bullshit!*" Shane screamed, and cocked the gun again.

"No, no . . . Please . . . Please stop it. What I'm saying is, I know they're being allowed to rob down by the university." His words tumbling out now . . . "The gangbangers were told to do whatever they want from Exposition Boulevard to the freeway, and the police would look the other way."

"Down by USC?" Alexa said.

"Yeah, the old University Division."

"Why?"

"I don't know. For the love of God, I'm telling you all I know, I swear it."

"*Why* are those Gs being told it's okay to caper south of Exposition?" Alexa continued.

"I don't know. I don't . . . All I know is Brewer, once when I asked him, said that he wanted to drive the crime stats up in that part of town."

"The chief of police wants to drive the crime stats *up?*" Alexa asked from the darkness behind the camera. "Why? His job performance depends on driving the stats *down.*"

"I don't know. It's all he said."

"Tommy, this is all fucking, runny yellow *bullshit.*" Shane shoved the gun out in front of him, right into Mayweather's face, the barrel pressed against his right cheek.

"Shane—NO!" Alexa shouted.

"Stop it," Mayweather sobbed, his eyes bugging, straining to get away, the cuffs rattling against the metal ladder. "I don't know—I swear it! All he said was he was trying to increase the number of uncleared crimes in that section of the city. Molar's den was setting it up, running it. They transported the H Street bangers after the arrests and turned them loose. Sometimes they blew the busts by not reading the Miranda or by losing evidence." He was glistening with sweat under the floodlight. Shane didn't answer, but recocked the gun. The sound echoed menacingly in the concrete tunnel.

"Scully . . . Calm the fuck down," Alexa ordered.

There was a moment when all Shane could hear was the three of them breathing. Then Alexa moved out from behind the camera.

"Stop him. . . . Make him stop," Mayweather pleaded. Tears were suddenly running down his cheeks.

"Tell me about Calvin Sheets," Alexa said. "He worked the Coliseum detail down there. He was letting hookers and petty thieves run wild. Was he part of it?" She was taking over "point" on the interview because Mayweather had begged her. She probably seemed like his only chance. Shane let her have him, taking a step back.

"I don't know why, but yes, I heard Sheets was in on it."

"So that's why all Ray's den members have cases going through IAD," Alexa reasoned. "But why send them to full boards where they'd be tried in the open, in public hearings? The chief could have disposed of the charges on his own, in private, under Section 202."

"Because the community down there was getting pissed. Their shops were being held up, people beaten or killed. They were filing complaints. That city councilwoman, Alicia Winston, is making a big fuss, her and Max Valdez. They want the bangers stopped, so the chief sent all those cases to open boards to appease the community. The panels were gonna be rigged. I was in charge of picking them. The officers were all gonna be acquitted or get modulated penalties—days off without pay, but no terminations. If that happened, they'd get envelopes to make up the difference. Burl wanted to control the timing of the boards so they wouldn't fall one on top of the other."

"And that's why Drucker's board was just postponed?" she asked.

Mayweather now seemed uncomfortable. He shifted his weight, averted his eyes.

"Something wrong with that, Tommy?" Shane asked, stepping in again. "Did I get that wrong? *Spit it out!*"

"Uh . . . uh . . . uh . . . please . . . please . . . make him . . . I'm trying to . . ." the deputy chief said inarticulately.

"Was Li'l Silent making trouble?" Alexa persisted. "Did he want something that you couldn't give, so you couldn't trust him on the stand in Drucker's case? Was he shaking you down?"

"Look, I've told you all I know."

"Are we ever gonna see Sol Preciado again?" Shane asked softly. "Or did Li'l Silent break jail and dive into a pit full of lye?"

Mayweather licked his lips and said nothing, but it was as good as a confession.

"How did you ever get to be a deputy chief?" Alexa said softly.

Mayweather was sobbing heavily now, standing there, psychologically stripped, cuffed to the ladder and sweating like a field hand, his chest heaving, tears streaming down his handsome face. "My dad was a cop, y'know. He was a uniform in Lake Falls, Illinois. When I went to UCLA to play ball, he used to save up, come to the games. . . . He loved watching me play. He was proud. . . . He was . . . he . . . he . . ." Mayweather was so lost and out of control, he couldn't get the words out.

Shane closed his eyes. He didn't want to hear this man's bullshit story.

"When I didn't make it in the pros, I wanted to make my dad proud . . . so I . . . so I . . ."

"Shut the fuck up, or I'll kill you just for being a pussy," Shane shouted, not performing now, truly pissed.

"You kidnapped a boy named Chooch Sandoval. With him was my next-door neighbor and friend, Brian Kelly. I want them back. If I don't get them back, you die."

"Honest, honest . . . I know nothing about that. I told you, I know nothing about any kidnapping."

Shane took the cold barrel of the gun and again laid it up against Mayweather's cheek and held it there. The man's eyes got wide, trying to look down to see it.

"Why should I believe you?" Shane asked softly. "Make me a believer, Tom."

"Sol Preciado is dead," he whispered. "They let him out of

that jail-transport vehicle, then took him out and shot him. That makes me an accessory before the fact in a first-degree murder. You think I'd confess to that with a tape running and withhold information on a kidnapping?"

Shane took a deep breath and a moment to get level, turned away, then shut off the videotape and sun gun, packing up the camera. Alexa reached out and uncuffed Mayweather. Shane could barely see him but knew the deputy chief would not make trouble. He was beaten.

"Go home, Tom," Shane said softly. "Think about what you've done, the lives you've hurt or destroyed. Not just mine or Sol Preciado's, or Chooch Sandoval's or Brian Kelly's, but all the shop owners who had their brains kicked loose or were murdered. Think about all the old ladies who got knifed or beaten for their welfare checks so you could have that pretty new sailboat. If you believe in God, you better start working on a good excuse, 'cause you're gonna need it."

He turned and, carrying the video box, walked out of the tunnel with Alexa.

When they were outside, he paused and handed her gun back to her. They could hear Tom Mayweather splashing around in the tunnel, slowly making his way out.

"You wanna drop him somewhere?" she asked.

"Let the prick find his way home. Maybe some H Street gangster will pick him up and finish the job for us."

They scrambled up the concrete incline and finally got back to the car. Shane locked the video box and tape in the trunk. Tom Mayweather's confession was obtained illegally and under duress. It would be useless in court but would surely keep him on the sidelines. The last thing the deputy chief wanted was to see it on the six o'clock news.

They sat in the front seat of the Crown Vic for a long moment, both changed by what they had just done.

"That was brutal," Alexa finally said. Shane nodded, and she added, "What now?"

"What now? We've just pulled off a pretty successful kidnapping and felonious assault," he said. "Wanna try your hand at forced entry and burglary?"

A BEGINNING?

SHANE DIDN'T WANT to attempt a B&E in broad daylight, so they went back to Alexa's apartment to wait for the sun to go down.

He felt dirty and tired as he sat on her snow-white sofa. Mayweather's confession had darkened his mood, driving his spirit down without producing Chooch.

Shane had always considered police work a noble calling, where Blue Centurions defended the public, upholding society's laws. The slogans reverberated in his mind: *Protect and Serve; Reverence for the Law; Integrity in Word and Action.* His oath made seventeen years ago while holding his head and right hand high now seemed hollow and meaningless. *"I recognize the badge of my office as a symbol of public faith and I accept it as a public trust to be held so long as I am true to the ethics of police service."*

Years on the job had shown him that police work was a flawed occupation at best, its participants on a narrowing, cynical path toward destroying the very thing they had pledged to uphold. Mayweather's crimes made Shane as dirty as if he had committed them himself.

"Is it okay if I take a shower?" he asked Alexa, hoping that maybe a long, hot soaking would wash the feeling away.

"Sure," she said. "I was just thinking the same thing, but you go first."

Shane heard a sadness in her voice that matched his own. He got up and walked into the bathroom, closed the door, and looked at himself in the mirror. The face staring back at him was tired and craggy and didn't resemble what he'd come to expect. The change worried him. He stripped off his shirt, pants, shoes, socks, and underwear, then turned on the shower and waited for it to get hot. Shane stepped in and stood under its steaming spray. He looked up at the nozzle, his eyes squinting as the spray bounced hard off his face and hot water filled his mouth. He was dirty in places it could not reach.

"You want, I'll do your laundry. I'll throw it in the machine with mine," he heard Alexa call from outside the bathroom.

"Good. Thanks. I tossed 'em next to the sink," he shouted back. Then, through the frosted shower door, he saw her step into the bathroom, retrieving his clothes. He turned his back, pinching his eyes shut, trying to blank out his troubled thoughts, when, almost before he knew what was happening, the frosted glass door opened and Alexa was in the shower with him, standing there naked, the steam turning her beautiful body slick with its moisture.

"Move over, you're hogging the spray," she said.

"What're you doing?" Shane's mind was doing flip-flops.

"I feel . . . I feel . . ."—she stopped, then looked up at him—"like I don't exist . . . like I don't even want to."

"Me, too," he said softly.

"I thought if we . . ." She stopped. "Bad idea . . ."

Shane didn't say anything, just took her into his arms and held her. As her wet body slid up against him, for the first time in days he felt the tension disappear; the knot in his stomach released as they stood locked in a cathartic embrace. They remained like that for a long time—holding each other, feeling each other's comfort and warmth. Then Shane felt his desire for her swelling and pushing between her legs, proving that he was still alive, still a man; perhaps all his failures of the past week could somehow be forged into a new beginning. He desperately wanted to start over. Then he felt her clutching him, pulling him closer, and was overtaken by a desire for her that was so intense, it brought tears to his eyes. "Is this right?" he said, asking for absolution, permission, and maybe directions all at the same time.

"Shut up," she whispered.

And then they were caressing each other in the steaming shower, Shane's mouth covering hers, his body pushing her back against the wet tiles on the wall of the small shower, kissing with abandon, feeling each other's warmth. Suddenly she pulled herself up, wrapping her arms around his neck, bringing her legs up around his waist. While she clung to him, he entered her, slowly at first, then thrusting more deeply. As her moans of pleasure washed over him, he felt changed and reborn.

Shane didn't know how long it lasted; time, in that small place, had become endless. They were in a wet cocoon of human ecstasy, and then he heard her cry out as he released inside her. She kissed him hard on the mouth, her breath mixing with his in the steaming shower.

Shane finally set her down, and they remained under the hot spray in a desperate embrace, almost afraid to let go, afraid to return to their individual fears and loneliness. Finally she took the bar of soap and began to wash his back, his arms, lathering him in erotic places. After she was finished, he did the same for her. They held each other in a sweet fragrance of body and soul. Shane felt different, stronger, more alive.

He looked down into her laser-blue eyes, which now seemed softer and filled with caring.

"Now we can start over," she said, putting his exact thoughts into words.

■ ■ ■

Later she made dinner and they sat at her kitchen table. She was wearing a white terry-cloth robe; he was wrapped in a towel.

After dinner she handed him his clothes, fresh from the dryer; they felt soft and were still warm as he put them on. When he walked into the living room, he noticed that there was renewed energy in his stride and a spring in his step.

They said very little, but as they locked her front door and headed to her car, she reached out, took his hand, and squeezed it.

THE HOT PROWL

HE WAS BACK in the parking lot, studying the fourteen-story steel-and-glass building in Long Beach. They had waited for the sun to go down. It was 8:05 on Saturday night, and they were still using the staff car Shane had been given up in Arrowhead. Across the street, roof letters announced Spivack Development Corporation in five-foot-high blue neon.

"I feel like Bonnie and Clyde. Do you have this effect on everybody?" Alexa said. She was sitting in the Crown Vic next to Shane, putting on a pair of latex gloves so she wouldn't leave her prints behind, both of them feeling a sense of awkwardness from the passionate lovemaking they'd engaged in a few hours before.

"Y'know, you're the last person I would ever have thought I'd be pulling a second-story job with," he finally said. She ignored it.

"You said you were here before. Did you scout it? You got a way into this place?" She was all business, putting that memory out of reach, taking the binoculars out of the glove box, unwinding the strap and training them on the building.

"Look, things have changed. We both know it," he said softly.

"Yes, but . . . Shane, it's dangerous. We have to be either cops or lovers. We can't be both. You've seen what a mess that turns into when it happens. . . . For now, we gotta do the job."

He knew she was right and finally nodded.

"So, did you scout it?" she asked again.

"Yeah . . . we can get to the roof by way of the fire stairs. Go down through a special staircase up there for the helicopter pad. It leads right down to Spivack's floor. The fire doors have interior bolt locks except on the first floor."

She nodded. "Y'know what pisses me off?"

"Ummmn," he answered, putting on his own pair of gloves.

"These binoculars piss me off—Bushnell 16x35s with a waterproof case. I worked Southwest Patrol for three years with a cracked pair of six-power prewar Lens Masters with one side out of whack. Couldn't focus the right eyepiece, asked for new binocs ten, twelve times, was told it wasn't in the budget. And here, in this staff car, they leave 'em under the seat like throwaways."

"Yeah, and we don't get sailboats, either."

She didn't answer but continued to focus the binoculars on the building. "You think we try for the roof? Go up through the fire stairs, pry the lock up there, then go down one floor, hope the interior doors aren't wired?"

"You're a fun date," he said, finishing with his gloves, snapping the wristbands while she lowered the glasses.

"Spivack builds shopping centers and commercial real estate all over the place, right?" she said.

"Yeah, malls, sports complexes, city buildings—anything where you've got high budgets and low administrative supervision costs."

"Tony Spivack, Logan Hunter, Chief Brewer, Mayor Crispin, and Ray Molar—quite a five-man team," she said.

"With Tom Mayweather still at point guard. Seems pretty obvious they stole this land in Long Beach—the naval yard—to build something. Hotels or a huge resort would be my guess. It's right on the bay. . . ."

"Why would Logan Hunter be part of it? He's a movie guy."

"I don't know. He likes press . . . maybe it's gonna be his new studio, with a theme park like Universal's . . . call it the Web. Lotsa rides, lotsa fuzzy cartoon characters greeting you at the gate in chipmunk costumes. Who the fuck knows?"

"Let's go," she said. "This isn't gonna get any easier the longer we wait."

They got out of the car and moved across the parking lot.

"If we get stopped, flash your tin," he said.

"Always *my* tin, *my* gun."

"You collected mine already, remember?"

"Stop bitching," she said, but they were both smiling.

Strange how that can happen, in the midst of losing Chooch and Brian. Despite feeling devastated in the face of that loss, he had first had a moment of uncontrolled sexual passion with her and now he was grinning like an idiot, adrenaline driving his emotions, skewing his senses while keeping his vision bright . . . both of them acting like kids snatching a pie off a bakery-shop windowsill.

They got to the side of the building and began walking around it, looking for the fire door. There were several private security guards inside. Shane and Alexa could see them in the lobby looking out through the glass at them.

"Gimme your hand," he said.

She immediately reached out and took his, strolling lazily beside him, putting her head on his shoulder. They looked like two lovers going nowhere special, nuzzling and feeling it again: a new sense of closeness.

Shane was acutely aware of her perfume, and in that moment, while they were pretending to be lovers, he felt something strange and confusing and powerful stir inside him. The feeling was undeniably strong but totally inappropriate in the middle of a hot prowl, so he bundled it up, stowed it on a top shelf in the back of his mind, slammed the cupboard shut, and saved it for later. He turned his thoughts instead toward the fire door coming up on the left.

She took her latex-gloved hand away from his and tried the door. It was locked.

"I have keys," he said, removing his little leather pouch of picklocks.

"No way," she said, looking askance at the burglar tools.

"Stand back. I'm not as good as Ray was, but I'll have this open in a sec." He went to work on the lock while she turned and watched the terrain behind him, making sure no slow-moving Long Beach patrol car came upon them unexpectedly.

After a moment he manipulated the last pick in the lock and felt it hook down into the tumbler inside the door. He was ready to turn the knob. "Okay, all set," he said.

She turned back to him. "What about the alarm?" she asked.

"What about it?"

"Won't it go off when we open it?"

"Here's the way I have this figured," he said. "If there's an alarm on this door, then when I open it, it will damn sure go off. If there isn't one, then my thinking is, it won't."

"Asshole."

"Of course, if it rings, we need to fall back and think up a new strategy. I'm not good with alarms; I haven't had time to perfect that talent yet."

"Let's go. Do it," she said, and watched breathlessly as he put his hand on the knob.

He felt the lock turn and then pushed the door open.

Nothing!

They ducked into the dimly lit concrete stairwell and closed the exterior door.

"That's amazing," she said. "Why wouldn't they have this door rigged?"

"They did. I unplugged it yesterday afternoon when I was here. The unit box is in the sub-basement." He smiled while she glared. "Come on, lighten up. I wanted you to experience the whole thrill."

Then he turned and ran up the stairs, taking the first flight two at a time.

It took them almost five minutes to get up to the roof, then they were standing in the reflected glow of the five-foot blue letters while Shane went to work on the roof door.

"This leads right down to the lobby on the top floor," he said.

"Is this alarm unhooked, too?"

"I hope so. The panel was a little confusing down there. I had to straight-wire a lot of shit."

"So you *are* an expert on alarms."

"Ray always said the picks are worthless if you set off alarms."

"Some probation training you got."

He finally had the door open, and the two of them went down the one flight to the fourteenth floor. The interior door to the helicopter stairs was unlocked, and in another minute or so, they were inside the steel-and-glass offices of Spivack Development Corporation. The only thing missing was the blond ice goddess behind the reception desk.

They moved through the lobby into the back, where they found themselves in a long, narrow hallway decorated with artistic schematics of past Spivack developments. Huge hotels and major airport buildings hung in stainless-steel frames. The renderings were crisp line drawings with pastel watercolors. They passed out of the corridor into a huge drafting area. "I wonder where Tony Spivack lives," Shane said.

After a few more minutes of searching, they found his office, fronted by a vast secretarial area and a set of mahogany doors with ANTHONY J. SPIVACK engraved on an antique silver plaque.

Shane turned the doorknob and pushed it open. They entered an ornate, palatial office: red carpet, embroidered drapes, and a mixture of furniture styles; French armoires and steel-and-glass tables populated the room. Shane moved to the immense plate-glass window that overlooked the city of Long Beach. He could see the domed city hall and, way off to the west, the *Queen Mary* sparkling with lights. Beyond that, he knew, was the Long Beach Naval Yard, which was magnetic north because everything pointed to it.

"We've gotta go through his files, see if we can find the project drawings," he said, still looking out the window, struck by the view: the shimmering Pacific Ocean beyond a ribbon of moonlit sand.

"Shane, look at this," he heard her say.

He turned, and she was no longer in the office.

He found her standing in the adjoining conference room. There was a magnificent 1:16 architectural model on a ten-foot-long side table. It covered the entire tabletop and was ten by five feet. Shane approached the huge model and saw that it was the architectural layout for the five-hundred-acre Long Beach Naval Yard project.

The plaque read:

THE WEB

A NEW CONCEPT IN ENTERTAINMENT

The centerpiece of the development was a football stadium with two rings of luxury suites. It was perched on the property, a big concrete oval, its escalators arching away from the perimeter like eight long spider legs. It dwarfed everything. Engraved over the stadium's modern entry was a tiny sign:

THE WEB

"The L.A. Spiders. A football team," Shane said. "Sandy told me Logan Hunter was trying to bring an NFL franchise to L.A."

"This is about *football*," she said, appalled, sounding exactly like every housewife in America.

"It's really not about football, it's about real estate." He studied the rest of the development. The thirty or more architectural models placed on the site plan were beautifully made and exquisitely detailed. They dotted the five-hundred-acre site. There was an amusement park with roller coasters and Ferris wheels; five luxury hotels, each one next to the water; shopping malls and restaurants. Little catamarans were stuck in the "water," racing along motionlessly up on one pontoon, their tiny sails billowing orange and red against aqua-blue plaster waves.

Shane was trying to put it together. "Okay," he said slowly, using her words. "It's called police work. . . . Connecting the dots . . . Ray Molar and his den blackmail the Long Beach City Council with hookers at the party house in Arrowhead. A video festival occurs that forces Carl Cummins and the embarrassed city officials of Long Beach to give the naval yard over to L.A. and Mayor Crispin in return for some bogus water rights. The mayor gifts the property to Spivack in return for Spivack's promise to develop it for the city of L.A. as a home base for a new sports franchise. Spivack funds the actual physical development in return for the property. Logan Hunter gets the NFL to award L.A. a new football franchise, and everybody, from top to bottom, gets silent ownership in the deal and walks away multimillionaires."

"And the H Street Bounty Hunters were just a fun idea that got included for ethnic diversity?" she said.

"Okay, that's a wild piece. I don't have that connection yet, but I like the rest of it."

"Could be . . ." She sounded less sure.

"I remember reading once that the real money play on these

sports franchise deals is the land, not the team. These guys get billions of dollars' worth of land from L.A. for free in return for financing the project and building this thing. Most of the public doesn't bitch, 'cause they don't care about the land; they want the team and a class A stadium to go with it. Sure, you end up with a roomful of environmentalists and hotheads protesting, but it's on page ten of the Metro section. . . . Nobody gives a damn about them because pro football is coming back to L.A.!"

"They can do that? Just give the land away?"

"Yeah, happens all the time. Years ago the city of Anaheim gave Georgia Frontiere hundreds of acres around Anaheim Stadium to get her to move the Rams there. Then, even when she carpetbagged the team off to St. Louis, the land was still hers. The O'Malleys were given Chavez Ravine for Dodger Stadium—the city condemned it, moved out all the Hispanics who lived there, then gave the O'Malleys the property, free and clear, in return for building Dodger Stadium. That way they wouldn't have to try and float a bond issue."

"Do you mind if we get out of here?" she said. "This is all quite fascinating, but I'm not as comfortable doing hot prowls as you are."

"One more thing first," he said, and moved out of the conference room and over to Spivack's desk. He opened the center drawer and took out Tony Spivack's appointment calendar while Mrs. Spivack and two dark-haired children eyed him suspiciously from behind a silver frame on the corner of the desk.

He opened the leather-covered book and started flipping pages.

"What're you doing?" she asked.

"Wanna see if he's in town. Last time I saw this shitbird, he was flying off in a green and white helicopter." Shane flipped the calendar to April. "Here it is; Sunday, April twenty-sixth, Miami Beach, NFL, eight-thirty A.M."

"Lemme see that," she said, and he spun the calendar toward her.

"Alexa, he's in Miami Beach right now, meeting with the NFL at eight-thirty tomorrow morning. You likin' my theory any better?"

They moved out of the office, but she stopped at the secretary's desk and looked around at the slips of paper that Spivack's secretary had pasted up neatly on a bulletin board: lots of yellow Post-its, reminders, important numbers and addresses.

"I thought you wanted to leave."

"If we're gonna do this, let's do it right," she said, still looking. "I worked as a secretary once, during a summer vacation in college. You keep the boss's temporary numbers up near the phone if he's traveling." She reached up and pulled a Post-it down. " 'Coral Reef Yacht Club.' That sound like Miami to you?" she asked.

"Take it. Let's go," he said.

Seconds later they were on the roof, then back inside the concrete fire stairs; a few moments later they were in the Crown Vic and gone.

40
BACKGROUNDING

DON'T WORRY, I'll get us there."

It was just after ten P.M. and the last flight to Miami had departed LAX, so Shane drove to the Long Beach Airport. He found the executive jet area and drove along Executive Terminal Row until he found a busy-looking FBO called Million-Air Charters. He pulled into the parking lot next to the mostly glass one-story building, then he and Alexa got out.

"Private jets cost big money," Alexa said

"I've got a hundred thousand in small bills, but we're gonna look like drug dealers, so get your tin ready."

He opened the trunk and retrieved the suitcase with Coy Love's cash bribe inside. They walked into Million-Air Charters, and Shane plunked the leather bag down on the counter.

"We'd like to charter a jet to Miami," he said.

The girl behind the counter was young but no dummy. She took one look at Shane and Alexa's off-the-rack clothes, stole a quick peek at their fourteen-dollar Timex watches, and knew these two were not customers.

Alexa pulled out her LAPD identification and laid it on the desktop. "If you need to talk to a manager, this is police business. We're with the Drug Enforcement Task Force and we have got to get to Miami before morning."

Shane snapped open the suitcase and spun it around, revealing the stack of cash.

"Confiscated drug money," Alexa explained. "We'll need you to receipt it for us." All bullshit, but comforting words when a civilian is looking at a suitcase full of used bills.

"Let me talk to Mr. Lathrope," she said.

Mr. Lathrope wanted to be called Vern; he had hunched shoulders, wireless granny glasses, and hair that had the general shape and texture of a number-nine paintbrush. He looked at the cash and Alexa's badge speculatively, then made a few calls. His weary attitude said he didn't like them, but business was business. "I can have two pilots here in half an hour, then I'll put you in 868 Charlie Papa," he said to Shane.

"What's 868 Charlie Papa?" Shane asked, showing total ignorance of jet charters.

"Tail number. It's the white Gulfstream Three with green stripes," he said, nodding his head toward the window where three or four executive jets were parked.

Shane didn't know a Gulfstream 3 from a palomino pony, but he nodded anyway. " 'Bout how much is that gonna run?" he asked.

"It's fifteen each way, thirty for the whole trip. We won't charge you for hangar time up to five hours; after that, the ground rate is one-half the hourly."

"Not giving us much of a break here, are you, Vern?" Shane said.

"Our prices are competitive. Make as many calls as you want—check it out. However, if you're interested in an opinion, it is a bit unusual to be getting paid with used bills out of a suitcase."

Stalemate.

Shane moved to the sofa, put the open suitcase on his lap, and began counting out stacks of banded cash. Each packet had fifty twenty-dollar bills in it. Shane counted out thirty stacks, snapped the suitcase shut, then walked up and handed the money to Vern Lathrope, who couldn't get his right eyebrow down from the middle of his forehead.

"I usually have a brown paper bag for transactions like this," Shane said as he shoved the cash over.

Shane and Alexa sat and waited on the expensive calf-leather couches, now clients of Million-Air Charters. Shane made two calls to Sandy, but she didn't pick up and her answering machine was off.

Half an hour later two young pilots in uniforms led Shane and Alexa to the Gulfstream 3 that Shane now realized was the biggest plane sitting on the flight line.

"Vern didn't like taking used cash, but he sure didn't mind renting us the most expensive piece of iron he had," Shane groused.

They stepped on a small rectangular red carpet before climbing the ladder and entering the jet. Then the copilot quickly rolled it up and stuffed it in a luggage compartment, with a "so much for that" smile on his face. He climbed up the stairs and pulled the door up after him. A few minutes later the Gulfstream jet, with Shane and Alexa and nine empty seats, was out on the end of the Long Beach runway, waiting for the tower to green-light the takeoff.

Shane found a beer in the refrigerator and brought one back to Alexa, who had kicked off her shoes and was reclining in the seat.

The plush interior was heavily scented with the smell of English leather. Rich, polished burlwood glistened in the Trivoli lighting. There were Baccarat crystal glasses in slots over a full bar.

"Okay, Shane and Alexa," Bob, their friendly pilot, said. "We're cleared for takeoff, so we're gonna do our thing now. Anything we can get you along the way, we're on channel three on the intercom."

"Thank you," Shane said to the empty cabin.

"I think you have to pick up a little receiver first," she said, smiling at him.

"For thirty grand, Bob can come back here when I want to talk to him." Then he kicked off his loafers and put the seat back. He had chosen to sit across the aisle from Alexa, facing backward so he could look at her.

Suddenly the plane was hurtling down the runway, its wheels coming up immediately on takeoff, climbing fast. They flew out over the ocean, then the pilot made a slow turn and headed east.

Shane and Alexa sat in the luxurious executive jet, sipping imported beer while the plane climbed to altitude and the lights of Long Beach gradually slipped away below the starboard wing.

"I'm gonna try to get some sleep," she said, putting her head back and closing her eyes.

Shane could smell her perfume again; it drifted across the aisle like a carefully thrown net.

"Mayweather's dad was a cop in Illinois," she said unexpectedly, without opening her eyes. "I didn't know that."

"Yeah," Shane said. "Just another grunt in a blue suit, out there hookin' and bookin' assholes for the city."

"My dad was a cop in Hartford, Connecticut," she said, her eyes still closed. "He was a patrol cop but never made sergeant. Couldn't take tests. He froze every time he went up for the exam."

"Oh," Shane said, trying to picture her father. What must he and Mrs. Hamilton have been like to have produced this iron-willed yet exotic-looking creature?

"Did you have brothers or sisters?" he asked, hoping she would open up. After a long moment:

"Two brothers." She started slowly, then it seemed important for her to tell him more. "I was the youngest. My mom died in childbirth. For a long time I thought that was my fault. We had pictures of her all over the house. It was like a shrine. My brothers and I, we tried to imagine what it would have been like to have her around. I used to wonder if she was in heaven looking down, mad at me for causing her death, so I tried to make her happy by doing all the chores: cleaning up after Dad and my two brothers, doing dishes, washing clothes, trying to take her place but knowing I never could." She stopped, the memory somewhat painful, then went on. "Dad remarried when I was fifteen, and we got Karen, who was nice but kind of distant. It was like Dad's three kids were some sort of mistake that she was forced to accept in the deal. I went to college on a track scholarship at UCLA—sprints and hurdles. I was there about ten years after Mayweather, but they still talked about him on Bruin Sports Radio, particularly during Bruin basketball games. He was a big deal, even years after he graduated. They all said he should have made the pros, but he ended up on the police force instead. . . .

"It felt shitty watching him plead and beg down there. . . . Somebody special that everybody looked up to turns out to be a self-centered shitball. Down there in that tunnel, I lost something. I don't know why it should affect me, but it does."

He was looking at her, wondering if she was ever going to open her eyes.

"Is that enough personal history?" she said, shining her blues at him again.

"Are you mad at me for some reason?" he asked. "You seem pissed off."

She sat still for several moments.

"Yeah . . . I guess I am. I wanted this career, wanted to believe in it. I wanted Mayweather to be stand-up. I actually liked him once. Respected him. Life is full of disappointments. I'll get over it. I wanted Santa Claus to come down the chimney with toys made at the North Pole especially for me."

He studied her, his dark, intense eyes trading her amp for amp.

"But just so you don't get the wrong idea, Shane, I don't think it's your fault this is happening. You just got put in the soup. You didn't ask for this any more than I did. It happened to you, and I'm in this with you because to do anything else is unthinkable."

There was a long silence. He was trying to think of the right thing to say. Finally he just smiled.

"Thank you," he said.

"You're welcome."

They didn't speak again until they landed.

Before he closed his eyes and tried to sleep, he glanced over at her. Her shoes were off, feet up on the seat facing her, those restless ice-blue lasers sheathed now. She was breathing rhythmically, sleeping peacefully.

He tried to picture her as a child, a little girl wondering if she'd killed her mother during her own birth, carrying that burden around with her. Just as he'd carried the idea that he had not meant enough to his own parents to have them hold on to him even for one day. He'd been left at the hospital like trash put out by the back door.

He had often tried to picture his parents. . . . Who were they? Did they go to college? Were they just teenagers who got careless and conceived him in a drive-in movie and decided to run? Were they hicks from Alabama, driving a pickup and drinking sour mash from a jug, with no money to raise him? Was he part Jewish or Italian or Irish? Did his mom and dad ever think about him and feel bad about what they'd done?

Why had they left him without even a first name pinned to his shirt?

He'd spent his life struggling to move past it, struggling to overcome it, finally using Chooch as a way to pull himself up, until he discovered that Chooch had become more important to him than the whole tired problem that had been weighing him down in the first place.

Alexa had been struggling, too. Internal Affairs was the perfect place for her. Weeding out the bad ones, making another house clean, all the time looking up, wondering if her mother hated her . . . wondering if she was good enough to be forgiven.

He admired her for it, but it also made him sad.

The sound of the huge jet engines hypnotically hummed in his ear. *I wonder if, despite all that's happening, I'm actually beginning to feel something important for this woman.*

Then Shane Scully, whose first given name was Infant 205, finally closed his eyes and went to sleep.

Shane dreamed about Chooch. The boy was on a vast beach, flying a kite over the ocean, but the kite was all black and dipping dangerously, diving toward the surface before straightening up again. Each time it seemed to get lower and lower.

"Shane, help me!" he was yelling. "It's going to crash!" Shane was moving toward him, but the faster he ran, the farther away Chooch seemed to be. If Shane didn't stop the kite's wild flight, he knew it would all end in disaster.

THE LAST DOT

MIAMI WAS BAKING in heat, the temperature in the mid-nineties, the humidity intense. They walked down the steps of the Gulfstream 3 into an invisible wall of moisture. A rent-a-car arranged by the FBO in Miami was waiting for them—a bright yellow Thunderbird. Shane signed for it; then, after locking the suitcase containing the rest of the money in the trunk, he got the map of Miami out of the glove compartment and looked for the Coral Reef Yacht Club. It was a large piece of property marked on the map in orange, located east of Highway 1, south of the wealthy town of Coral Gables.

"You navigate, I'll drive," he said to Alexa, getting behind the wheel.

The car was a hardtop, and somebody had been chain-smoking in it. The unpleasant smell of old tobacco hung over them, wet and onerous. The air conditioner needed Freon and put out a stream of tepid air. They pulled out, and she directed him to Seventh Avenue, which turned into Cutter Road.

The sky was that special tinsel-blue that you can only get in Miami, where the land is so flat that no pollution can stay trapped above the city, instead blowing across the state, dissipating in the ocean breeze, leaving Miami glistening in bright sunshine and mirrored glass architecture.

Clouds floated by intermittently, huge white formations of indescribable beauty moving slowly across the flat horizon like whipped-cream galleons.

The Coral Reef Yacht Club was just down the road from the U.S. Department of Agriculture's Plant Introduction Station. The yacht club sat on man-made levees and fronted a dredged ocean cut that was enclosed on three sides. Nestled among this lush marine setting were clusters of old Florida-style buildings made of coral bricks, with overhanging eaves. Boats of all shapes and sizes were moored at dock fingers in front of the exclusive club.

Shane pulled through an open gate with a guardhouse but no guard. The parking lot was jammed; he finally found a spot way down by the docks. There were several news vans parked a hundred yards away, by the main building.

Shane and Alexa got out of the Thunderbird and moved up a crushed-gravel drive, where they found a man leaning against one of the mobile units, having a smoke.

"They inside?" Shane asked vaguely.

"Yep. It's going down right now."

"Yeah? The . . . uh . . . NFL owners' meeting?"

"No. The owners' meeting was in July. This is the new team announcements," the man corrected, taking a closer look at him.

"Right, that's what he meant," Alexa said; then they moved past the man into the yacht club.

There was a large hall off the entry called the Trophy Room, and it was packed. There were a dozen news teams—network as well as local Miami stations—with cameras and mikes marked

CNN, ESPN, and WNS (World News Service). There were also radio and print media. Close to two hundred people were milling about in the room under exposed beams and slow-turning paddle fans.

Without having to discuss it, Shane and Alexa separated. If one got thrown out, the other probably wouldn't. They took up positions on opposite sides of the room.

There was an NFL banner behind a makeshift stage. All around the room were yachting trophies and pictures of past commodores of the club, smiling out of their lacquered frames, wearing their captain's hats with too much braid on the visors. The room was elbow to elbow. Shane's cop mind noted that they were dangerously over the fire regs.

Up on the stage, a man was droning on. Shane tried to catch the flow of his remarks:

". . . as they said . . . which, of course, made us very sure we had embarked on the right course as far as that program was concerned . . ."

Shane looked around for Tony Spivack or Logan Hunter, whom he remembered as a slim, somewhat handsome blond man from pictures he'd seen in the newspapers.

". . . So, Don and Fred, who will be speaking to you in a minute, took all of those factors into account. These decisions, at their core, are difficult at best, because community pride is always involved. That's why we have been so deliberate on this issue."

Shane waited, crushed in between a florid-faced man in a Hawaiian shirt and a news crew from WKMI-TV.

". . . That having been said, I'd like to present, with great pleasure, our very own commissioner of the NFL, Mr. Paul Tagliabue."

There was a smattering of polite applause. Shane was scanning the podium now. There were twenty-nine men and two women seated in leather club chairs behind the main speaker. He was beginning to recognize some of the faces from TV or the sports pages: Wayne Huizenga, owner of the Miami Dolphins; Alex Spanos of the San Diego Chargers; Jerry Jones of the Dallas Cowboys. All the owners of the thirty-one NFL teams were up there.

"Thank you, Lee," the commissioner said. "Okay, now for the moment we've all been anticipating. We have, as you all know, decided to award three new expansion franchises to three deserving cities: Houston, Los Angeles, and Oklahoma City. We have picked three facilities and ownership structures to be the homes of these new franchises. In Houston, we are proud to announce that we are awarding the NFC expansion franchise to the syndicate headed by Keith Fowler and Martin Fisk."

There was a gasp from the room, and then a whoop went up from the back of the hall. Shane turned and looked as the two men went up onto the stage.

The Houston winners had named their new expansion team the Houston Blaze and were holding up uniform jerseys and doing their photo op as news crews swarmed.

Shane looked over at Alexa on the far side of the room, just as a gray-haired man with a belt buckle the size of a small serving platter stepped to the mike and started throwing out Texas homilies:

"Now that we got this here thing safe in the corral, guess it's time ta wash off the war paint and throw us a shindig," he said. "We're set up like pigs in a mud bath over at the Four Seasons Hotel, so y'all come on over and help us raise the roof." He went on to thank half a dozen people.

Shane finally spotted Logan Hunter. He was dressed in a tan suit tailored to his wispy frame, without one sag or wrinkle. He had an abundance of too-blond hair and was wearing a mint-green shirt with no tie. There was something exotic in his carriage. Logan Hunter wore his millionaire film-mogul status like imported cologne; it wafted around him. He was boyish and, except for the wrinkle lines around his eyes, would have appeared to be in his mid-thirties instead of the fifty that Shane had read he was.

"In L.A. we had a terribly difficult choice." The commissioner was now back at the mike. "We had two competing franchises— one from Bill Kaufman, who proposed a restoration of the L.A. Coliseum. Bill has made a wonderful presentation, showing how that grand old lady could be brought up to millennium stan- dards. And I've gotta say, a lot of incredible thought went into that plan. The other group, headed by Logan Hunter and Tony Spivack, have proposed a fresh site, a new development at the now-deserted Long Beach Naval Yard, which has recently been ceded to the city of L.A. I'm pleased to add that the mayor of Los Angeles, Clark Crispin, is with us today, and I'm going to let him announce the winner of the new L.A. expansion fran- chise. Clark . . . ?"

A door opened at the side of the room, and Clark Crispin came onto the stage. Shane had seen him at many official L.A. gath- erings and had even worked his security detail one weekend dur- ing his second election campaign. He was tall and angular, and when he smiled, his face always radiated warmth. He was dressed in hit-man black, his Armani pinstripe relieved by a festive red tie.

"Thanks, Paul. What a day for L.A. We, of course, have missed having a pro team in our city since you took the Raiders back north, Al." He smiled at Al Davis, who barely returned it. "Or since Georgia moved my beloved Rams to St. Louis and won a championship . . ." She smiled warmly, but there seemed to be a definite "fuck you" in the mixture.

"So now we have a new opportunity. Will it be the Coliseum, with Bill Kaufman, or the Web, with Tony Spivack and Logan Hunter? The envelope, please," he said, grinning, and there was a mild groan in the room.

"It is my honor to announce that the new Los Angeles AFC expansion franchise, and soon-to-be Super Bowl football team, will be the L.A. Spiders, playing at the Web. Tony? Logan? Come on up. Tell us how it feels."

Suddenly, as the two of them made their way to the stage, a side door opened and ten Spiderettes, dressed in their new black and red minicostumes, came onto the stage. Music played through a speaker system as they began to dance, waving black and red pom-poms. The crowd loved it.

The TV crews were circling, gunning footage, and then as the music stopped, the girls fell back, and Logan Hunter went to the mike.

"Thank you, Clark. Well, who would've thought this day would come?" More cheering and applause.

"Please," Shane said derisively under his breath; then the nickel dropped, and he knew what the missing piece was.

"I'm delighted we're going to be bringing football back to L.A.," Logan Hunter said. "We're going to deliver a top-flight product. We'll spare no expense to build a first-rate franchise at the Web. If you buy season tickets today, we'll guarantee you a spot in the stands when we kick off in our new stadium in the fall of 2001. We're gonna be up and ready. We break ground tomorrow. Tony, you wanna say a few words?"

Spivack, who had just put on a new Spiders football jersey over his suit and tie, came to the mike. "I don't have much time to talk. I better get back and grab a shovel if I'm gonna meet Logan's date."

There was a ripple of laughter.

"Commissioner Tagliabue . . . one question!" Shane shouted. "How come you didn't choose the Coliseum? That's a national historic landmark, built for the '32 Olympics. . . . Plus, the people with businesses in that neighborhood count on Coliseum events to survive."

The room fell silent. Spivack stepped back and handed the mike to Paul Tagliabue. "There were other factors involved. It was a complicated decision," the commissioner said. "We don't want to get into that right now."

"Was it the high crime stats down there?" Shane persisted, rolling the idea up to the stage like a live grenade.

"The growing crime rate around the Coliseum certainly entered into our decision," he said. "But there were many factors. We'll have a question-and-answer session after the announcements are concluded. Now, moving on . . . We come to the last franchise, in Oklahoma City—"

"Why do you suppose crime in that neighborhood rose so dramatically?" Shane was pulling the pin now.

A police officer appeared at his elbow. "May I see your pass, sir?"

"Don't have one," he replied.

"Whatta you doing here?"

"I'm a mental patient. We sorta wander around."

"Not funny. Let's go." He led Shane out of the room, walking with a firm grip on his elbow. They moved past Alexa, who was standing next to a WMI Radio team. She caught his eye and smiled as he was ejected from the room.

Once they were outside, the cop glowered at Shane. "You can leave, or you can take a ride with me. Your choice."

"Why don't I just leave . . ."

"Why don't ya," the cop said.

Shane walked to the yellow T-bird, took a piece of paper out of his pocket, and wrote Alexa a note. He shoved it under the car, got behind the wheel, and rolled over the note, then drove out of the parking lot, up the winding driveway, and parked on the street outside. He sat in the front seat in the oppressive heat, with the lousy air conditioner blowing a foul tobacco smell, until he couldn't bear it any longer. He got out of the car, threw his coat off, and looked down at his sweat-soaked shirt. He tried to get cool under a Japanese banyan tree while he contemplated what he had just learned. It was maddeningly simple once you had all the pieces:

The NFL wouldn't put a team in an area where violent crime and prostitution were out of control, so they awarded the franchise to Logan Hunter and the new entertainment/stadium complex being built at the old Long Beach Naval Yard. That was the last dot. He didn't know what he was going to do about it, but after ten days of eating everyone's exhaust, Shane had finally caught up.

For the first time since this all started, he actually knew what the hell was going on.

42

HALF AN HOUR LATER she came out of the Coral Reef Yacht Club and, shading her eyes with a four-by-five card, stood amidst milling news crews.

Shane could see her from the road, a slender figure standing defiantly in the entryway, looking toward the empty space where the yellow T-bird had been parked.

Shane had just tried to get Sandy on the phone again, but with no luck. He folded his cell and watched from the road, three hundred yards away, as Alexa walked uncertainly to the empty parking spot, reached down, and picked up his note. Then she turned and headed toward the main road, quickening her pace when she saw him, walking out the main gate and approaching the car. She frowned when she saw Shane's sweat-plastered shirt.

"Did you decide to take a swim?"

"I can't handle this steam bath they got down here." She nodded and handed him the card in her hand.

"What's this?"

"Logan's having a barbecue. He borrowed Elton John's house to celebrate. I'm invited. I can bring a guest, but I'll be damned if I'm showing up with a guy who looks like he's been playing in the sprinklers."

"I'll stop on the way and buy a new shirt. Let's go." They got into the T-bird and drove off.

They actually made two stops, first at a drugstore for deodorant and a razor, then at a small department store, where Shane bought a new white shirt and Alexa bought a simple cocktail dress. After he washed up and shaved in the employee bathroom, Shane felt 50 percent better.

He walked out and got into the idling T-bird, joining Alexa in the lukewarm stream of tobacco-scented air. "That looks good on you," he said, glancing appreciatively at the way the short pale blue dress fit her trim, athletic body.

"Thanks," she said noncommittally.

They drove up Cutter Road, back toward Coral Gables.

The beautiful Japanese banyan trees hung overhead, strobing leafy shadows across the T-bird's hood. They turned right on Casuarina Concourse and drove east, toward the water.

Elton John's house was not hard to spot. The press was already there. Shane turned into the winding drive and waited in a long line of cars while the guests showed their numbered invitations and were checked off a list.

"By the way, I'm Whitney Green, WMI Radio. Whitney does the noon show and couldn't make it."

"How the hell did you get invited?"

"I promised Whitney's husband, Don, I'd have a drink with him later."

"Yuck."

"Double yuck. You haven't seen him."

They pulled up to the man checking invitations. Alexa leaned across Shane and handed over her engraved card. "Whitney

Green and guest," she said as the security guard wearing a tailored blazer checked the invitation, then nodded. Two valets opened both doors. Shane and Alexa got out as a man in a red jacket ran up, jumped into the car, and pulled away.

As they joined a line of people heading up the drive toward the house, they could hear a band playing. They walked under a large balloon arch stretched across the driveway, done in red and black Spiders football colors, with a large sign that read:

L.A. SPIDERS 2001

Waiters in white coats circulated with trays of champagne and hors d'oeuvres. The grounds were magnificent. The huge Florida antebellum house stood at the end of the drive like a turn-of-the-century dowager; lace curtains and wicker chairs framed a sloping porch.

"Do you get the feeling that winning this franchise wasn't much of a surprise to Mr. Hunter?" Shane said.

"Even Martha Stewart couldn't lash this together in two hours," she agreed.

They got to the house and climbed the wooden steps, moving inside.

People were clustered in the magnificently furnished living room, but the flow of the party was being directed through the house and into the backyard, where the bar and the band were set up.

Shane and Alexa walked under more slow-moving Florida paddle fans out onto the veranda and stood for a moment on the back porch, looking out at the sparkling aqua-green water of Biscayne Bay.

There was a huge hundred-foot yacht called *Rocket Man* moored at the concrete dock. Palm and banyan trees hung over the grassy lawn. The twenty-piece orchestra was dressed in white tuxedos.

"Some barbecue," she said.

He nodded, but his eyes were wandering, checking out guests.

"How do you want to do this?" she asked.

"The play's at any base."

They moved down and joined the line at the bar. Four or five mannequins dressed in Spiders football uniforms, complete with helmets, had been set up in different parts of the yard in the Heisman Trophy pose. When they finally got up to the bar, Shane ordered a ginger ale; Alexa had a glass of Evian with a lime twist. Just as Shane was turning away, the bartender smiled. "Cigar to celebrate the franchise, sir?" and held out a box of Dominican Regals.

"Got anything else?" Shane asked, looking down at the box suspiciously.

"Mr. Hunter owns this company, so we only have Regals."

"In that case, give me one." He took a cigar, and they moved away from the bar, stopping a few feet away, looking at the panatela identical to the one they found in the toilet trap at the Spring Summer Apartments.

"You don't really think Logan Hunter was at your little fleabag on Third Street, supervising that videotaping and kidnapping . . . ?"

"No. But somebody who works for him was, and as far as I'm concerned, this stogie ties him in directly."

"That's theoretical, not evidential."

"Fuck evidence. I'm way past worrying about that."

As Shane moved toward the house, Alexa grabbed his arm and pulled him back. "We gotta worry about that. We're hanging out a mile here. We gotta get something worth taking to the DA, or we're dust."

"Yeah, sure."

"I'm not kidding, Shane. I'm in this with you, but you've gotta run everything past me first."

"I think we oughta find Mr. Hunter, invite him to a quiet spot in the garden, and have a little talk," Shane said, changing the subject.

"*Find? Invite?* Define your terms."

"I'm gonna kidnap the little prick, stuff this stogie up his ass, and make him smoke it rectally until he tells me where they're holding Chooch. It worked with Tom Mayweather."

"We got lucky with Mayweather. That doesn't mean we can throw a bag over Logan Hunter in the middle of this soiree and get away with it."

"Sure it does. All we've gotta do is find a good quiet interview room before we take his statement. Don't worry, you don't have to do it. I'll pick this daisy. Believe me, he's gonna tell me what I want to know."

"Shane, he's got forty security guys here, most of them packing."

"If you wanna wait in the car, go ahead. . . ."

"Shit! You are one stubborn son of a bitch," she said angrily, but he just looked at her for a long moment and nodded. "Let's stop arguing and do it, then," she relented.

They moved slowly around the party, looking for an appropriate spot. Shane recognized one or two of the girls they had photographed at the naval yard. They were dressed in slinky evening gowns, wearing hostess tags and escorting the press. Shane thought the main house looked too crowded. The gardener's shed was too close to the pool. Finally they found themselves down by the dock, where the hundred-foot yacht was tied to the wharf. There was a rope across the boarding ramp that warned: OFF LIMITS.

Shane removed the rope and they walked up onto the fantail of the yacht, where they were screened off from the party by the huge triple-deck superstructure.

"Some barge," Alexa said as she looked inside the main salon.

Shane had already tried the door and had his picklocks out.

"Not again," she said.

"Unless you can find a key, this is the best I can do." He worked for a few minutes while Alexa stood on the fantail, out of view of the party on the grassy lawn. They could hear the band playing an instrumental selection of Elton John hits. The music was mixed with the low murmur of party conversation.

Shane got the door open quickly and looked back at her. "I'm getting better at this, refining my technique," he said.

"I'll add it to your charge sheet."

"I'm gonna find a nice quiet place below. Why don't you see if there are keys in that thing? We may need to make a fast exit," he said, pointing over the rail at a small red-hulled Scarab speedboat tied to bumpers against the side of the yacht.

"How'm I supposed to get down there?" she complained, looking over the rail at the Scarab ten feet below.

"Climb over the side, stand on the rub rail, then lower yourself down. Lotta people keep the spare ignition key in the engine compartment, hanging on a hook. Lift the cowling and take a look."

"The nautical equivalent of the back-door flowerpot?"

"Exactly."

He paused inside the main salon while she pulled up her short dress to climb over the side. Her toned, shapely legs were straddling the rail. She glanced up and caught him staring. "What're you looking at?"

"Nothing," he said too quickly, then ducked inside. He heard her drop down into the small boat as he moved through the magnificent yacht. Beautiful antiques and silk fabrics adorned the classic interior. He went below to the crew's quarters.

A few moments later he found the engine room behind a pair of soundproof double doors. It spanned the whole width of the boat. He turned on the lights. White-painted machinery glistened in the strong bluish neon. A hook, used to winch up heavy equipment so it could be worked on, hung between two large 2300-horse Caterpillar engines. Shane found a coil of rope on the engineer's bench, stowed it nearby, turned off the lights, and left.

When he got back to the rear deck, he found Alexa with a strange expression on her face. "You find the key?" he asked.

"Yeah, it was there, right where you said." She held up the ignition key.

"What's wrong, then?"

"I think I just saw Sandy. I went off the boat for a minute. I was trying to spot Logan Hunter . . . and I think I saw her with Calvin Sheets, walking up the path. She didn't look too happy about it."

"Sandy must've hooked up with her friend Melissa," Shane said. "Got herself invited to this party. But how the hell did she get all the way to Florida in ten hours?"

"Logan Hunter has his own jet," Alexa volunteered.

Shane nodded and walked out onto the fantail. "Let's see if we can find her."

They moved off the boat, rejoining the party, then walked along the carefully manicured path across the lawn, toward the house. Shane and Alexa were both scanning for familiar faces. Shane spotted Tony Spivack with a group of men and women, still wearing his quarterback jersey. He saw Coy Love over by the bar and grabbed Alexa's arm, turning her away.

"What?"

"Coy Love."

They got to the path that Sandy and Calvin Sheets had taken moments before, then started down it. The path wound around and finally ended about a hundred yards from the dock, down by a chauffeur's stone house on the east side of the property. The two-story stone house was connected to a six-car garage and separated from the rest of the property by a stand of mango trees. As they moved around the side of the house, they heard moaning. Shane stopped and looked at Alexa, who raised her eyebrows.

They couldn't determine the nature of the sound yet, so they stood by the house and listened. Suddenly they heard a hard slap, and a woman cried out in pain. Shane recognized the voice.

Alexa pulled her Beretta as they moved toward the front door. Shane, without a gun, felt vulnerable and exposed. He paused by the back door.

"Okay," he whispered. "Standard SWAT kick-down. I'm going right—on three. One . . . two . . ."

Then he stepped back, kicked the door, and dove inside to the right, sideways and low. He hit the floor and was unable to see the room as he rolled, but he heard Alexa dive in behind him, going left and yelling, "Freeze, asshole!"

Then two shots blasted from the opposite side of the room. Shane finished his roll and came up behind a couch. The bullets thunked into the wall over his head. Alexa rolled to the left, then fired twice. Her first shot took Calvin Sheets high in the chest. He flew backward and hit the far wall, leaving a streak of blood on the white plaster as he slid down.

Shane came up in time to see Don Drucker move into the room, pulling his gun. Sandy was darting right just as Drucker fired. She passed through his sight and was hit in the back, screaming in pain. Shane watched in horror as the bullet went directly through her abdomen, exploding out the front, leaving an exit wound the size of a softball. Sandy looked down in abject terror as blood and stomach contents streamed out of her, staining her light-green cocktail dress. Then she slumped to the floor, groaning.

Drucker turned his gun on Shane, who dove right just as the rookie cop fired. Shane felt the 9mm whiz by, inches from his head. He heard Alexa's gun discharge twice more, then Drucker flew out of Shane's field of vision and hit the floor. It was quiet for a second, but as Shane came up, he could see Drucker lying on his back, his mouth gaping open, dead. Alexa had hit him in the center of his forehead.

She was still low against the wall on the left side of the door, grim-faced and sweaty. Suddenly they heard footsteps on the path.

"Bolt the door," he ordered.

Alexa slammed it shut and threw the latch while Shane checked Drucker and Sheets. "These two are history," he said.

Shane snatched up Calvin Sheets's Smith & Wesson and tucked it away in his belt, then moved to Sandy, who was lying in an expanding pool of her own blood. It was widening beneath her, staining her dress a dark crimson, soaking the sides around her waist. He knew instantly that she probably wouldn't make it. The wound was fatal; she was already shivering, turning cold as her blood left her.

"Sandy . . . Sandy . . . it's me. Can you hear me?" he said, kneeling beside her.

When Sandy looked up, her face had lost its shape; her eyes were dimming as blood pumped out of her onto the tile floor. "I know . . . where . . . Chooch . . . is . . . Calvin told me . . . after we . . . we had sex and . . . and . . . he told . . . " She was shaking badly, struggling for breath. "Then . . . Clark Crispin came . . . seen my file . . . knew I was . . . Black Widow . . . " She started to choke, blood flowing from her mouth now, running down her chin.

"Shit," Shane said. "Let's get you outta here, to a hospital."

"No. . . " she said as he tried to lift her. "No . . . Please . . . listen. In Arrowhead . . . Sheets said . . . they're holding him there . . . "

Sandy's strained words were overwhelmed by a heavy pounding on the front door.

"Open the fucking door, Cal! Open up!" Coy Love shouted.

"Give that asshole something to think about," Shane barked. Alexa turned and fired her fifth shot through the bolted wood door.

"Shit," they heard Coy say angrily from the porch outside.

"Shane . . . you've gotta listen . . . " Sandy whispered.

When he looked back down at her, she seemed smaller than she had just a moment before, as if she were losing volume, a pint at a time.

"Shane . . . you get him back . . . you take . . . take care of Chooch . . ." she rasped.

"I'll get him."

"He's yours . . . Shane . . . yours and mine." She was almost whispering now, her voice so small that he had to bend down to hear her.

"I was wrong . . ." She reached up and clutched his collar, pulling him down closer. "I didn't think you'd want him. . . . I wanted him but couldn't raise him. . . . You gotta do better." Her voice was so weak now, he placed his ear almost on her lips to hear. "He needed . . . his father . . . It's why . . . I made you take him . . . It's why . . . it's why . . . I . . ." And then she was looking at him, but her gaze had turned empty. Her heart had stopped beating. Those flashing black eyes went dead and stared up at him, damp and blank as licked stones.

Shane slowly lowered her to the floor. When he looked up, he saw Alexa staring at him from the door.

"Shane, we've gotta get outta here," she said.

Suddenly, Coy Love's face appeared at the window. Then his gun came up, aiming at Shane, who snatched Calvin's .38 out of his belt and fired twice just as Alexa peeled her last two rounds at the ex-cop. The window shattered as four bullets hit Coy Love, blowing him backward into the brush outside the chauffeur's cabin.

"Let's go!" Alexa screamed, and Shane got to his feet.

They could hear more voices screaming outside. They found the back door and threw it open. It led into the six-car garage. A black Lincoln Town Car was parked inside. Shane grabbed the keys off the pegboard, then he and Alexa jumped into the car; he started the engine, pulled the garage-door opener off the visor, and pushed the button. The door opened while Alexa was digging into her purse for a spare clip. She jammed it into the grip of her Beretta just as he floored the Lincoln, hurtling out of the garage and onto the driveway.

Armed men in black suits blocked their path but scattered as he plowed through them.

Out the front window, he could see security men running at them from several directions, all digging under their coats for weapons. Shane yanked the wheel and bounced the car up over the curb and onto the newly sodded front lawn. They shot across it, taking the direct route to the front gate, tearing up chunks of grass before finally bounding back over the curb onto the main driveway.

With four men chasing them on foot, they sped out the front gate, Alexa holding her gun at port arms. The Town Car skidded onto Casuarina Concourse, then a mile and a half later rounded the corner onto Cutter Road. Soon they were speeding under the leafy banyan trees, heading toward the airport.

"Get Bob at the flight center. Tell him we gotta get moving."

While Alexa turned on her cell phone and dialed, Shane got a Miami all-news radio station. It had been only five or six minutes, but the story was already breaking.

"Our field news team covering the plush NFL party Logan Hunter is throwing at Elton John's Coral Gables mansion has reported a shooting," the announcer said. "We're still awaiting more details, but as we have it so far, several people have been gunned down. A man and a woman are identified as the shooters and have fled the scene in one of Elton John's personal vehicles. Stand by as we get more information."

Shane let Alexa off at Million-Air Charters, then parked the car around the corner and up the street in a dense growth of oleander bushes, out of sight of the road. He wiped their prints quickly, using his old shirt, not forgetting to do the back of the rearview mirror, the place most car thieves miss. Then he walked around the corner and met Alexa. They entered the office and found Bob in the pilot's lounge, filing his FAA flight plan.

"Ready to go?" Bob said. "That was quick."

"Can't afford the hangar time." Shane smiled, but the grin felt wide and shiny and about as genuine as an Amway salesman.

"Be right out," Bob said.

They quickly boarded the plane, this time without waiting for the red carpet. Shane and Alexa sat in tense silence as the two pilots finally got aboard, shut the door, and smiled warmly. "We've got a slight tailwind for a change," Bob said happily. "Should get us back in four and a half hours or so." He settled into the right seat and wound up the engines.

Moments later they were rolling down the runway, taking off, leaving Miami and four dead bodies behind.

Shane sat stoically in the cabin, unable to deal with his thoughts. Alexa reached over and took his hand. "You okay?" she asked. "What did Sandy say to you?"

"Nothing," he answered. He couldn't tell her yet, couldn't quite admit it to himself.

His mind went back almost sixteen years, recapturing a memory long forgotten: it was his second summer on the job, right after the first arrest Sandy had arranged on the Valley bond trading case. They'd gone to dinner several nights later, to celebrate. Sandy had made her pitch to him, offering to work for the police as an informant. They'd had too much to drink, and in the car outside her apartment, he had shucked her out of her dress, then in awkward, thoughtless passion had entered her. There had been no tenderness in the coupling, and surely no love. It had been pure sex for him, raw and unadorned, an act he thought held no consequences. For Sandy, it was like a handshake to close their new deal. He had been just twenty-two years old.

The next morning he had felt cheap and ashamed of himself. She was a prostitute, and since he had always demanded more from his intimate relationships, he had never made love to her again. Instead, they'd gone into business together. Over the years he had managed her informant's career, making her rich while getting his share of class A busts in the bargain. The drunken romp in the backseat of his car was all but forgotten.

All these years later, the consequences of that mindless act had finally come due. If what Sandy had told him was true, she had changed his life forever with her one dying sentence.

Then he remembered what she had said in the doorway of her Barrington penthouse two days before. It had made no sense then, but now it spoke volumes: "You weren't doing me a favor," she had told him solemnly. "I was doing one for you."

DEAD END

THE ROAD was dark and winding, and he was going too fast, overdriving his headlights.

"For Chrissake, slow down. We're gonna die on one of these curves," Alexa barked at him.

Shane momentarily lifted his foot off the gas and then, without realizing it, slowly sped up again, impatient to get there.

They had turned off the car radio because he and Alexa had just been named as the shooters at Elton John's Florida home and were now dominating every national newscast. Somebody at the party in Florida had made them, probably one of the ex-cops from Sheets's old Coliseum detail. They were the subjects of a national manhunt. Shane knew it was only a matter of time before their sleeping pilot would get up, turn on his TV, and see the story. He would inform the police that Shane and Alexa were back in L.A., thereby narrowing the manhunt.

The national news story was snowballing, becoming as big as

when Andrew Cunanan shot Gianni Versace, each broadcast digging deeper into their pasts. Shane was now being described as a rogue cop prone to violence. His moment of self-defense when he protected Barbara and himself from Ray's insanity was now being called the cold-blooded murder of an exemplary police officer that launched a coast-to-coast crime spree. The news media was having a party with Alexa's involvement, calling her his Internal Affairs prosecutor, accomplice, and partner in crime. Her Bonnie and Clyde joke had come true.

Shane had chosen to take the back road up to Arrowhead. They were on I-18, known as "the Rim of the World Highway," heading through the mountain town of Snow Valley. There were patches of snow visible at the highest elevations, distant reflections glimmering faintly in the moonlight.

Shane took another turn too fast, and the tires on the Crown Vic screamed in protest.

"For Chrissake, Shane, slow down!" she repeated, then reached out and switched on the police-band radio but got only static. They were too far up in the mountains to get anything, so she turned it off.

They slowed down to drive through the small town of Running Springs. At Crest Park Drive they took 173 along Burnt Mile Creek and finally dropped down into Lake Arrowhead. Shane knew the route to Ray's house and quickly found his way there.

He drove slowly past the party house on Lake View Drive. It looked dark inside. If they were holding Chooch and Brian, he reasoned, they would probably try to make it look deserted. Shane turned the car around before parking it. He wanted no cul-de-sac mistakes this time.

Shane had found a sporting goods store in South Central on the way in from Long Beach. The owner-manager made it a point to mind his own business as Alexa bought a box of FMJ 9s and Shane a box of .38 hollow points. She had changed back into the clothes she wore to Miami: jeans, tennis shoes, and a turtleneck.

Alexa pulled her handcuffs and reload case with the extra clip out of her purse and slid them into her belt with her cell phone. Then she and Shane got out of the Crown Vic and moved down the street toward the Arrowhead party house.

As they approached, his heart was beating fast. Shane knew he had to do this just right. He couldn't take a chance that Chooch would end up in a cross fire as Sandy had. He pledged to rescue Chooch and Brian, or die trying.

The problem right now was that Shane and Alexa couldn't get backup. If they showed their faces in any police station, they'd be arrested on the spot. Nobody would listen to them, and Chooch and Brian would simply become part of the untold history of the new L.A. football franchise.

They were across the street from the house, crouched down behind the low hedge, looking at the property carefully. "I hate to say this, Shane, but that place looks empty. No cars out front, nothing," she whispered.

"They use a boat to get here. A Chris-Craft inboard."

"Okay, let's go, then," she said.

They moved like shadows across the street, their guns out in front of them, staying low as they went.

They got to the side of the house, creeping through the old rosebushes, trying to ignore the thorns. When they were within view of the dock, they could see that there was no Chris-Craft tied there. They made their way to the back porch, where, after checking the windows and seeing nothing, Shane shimmied up under the porch rail, then wormed his way across the deck on his stomach. Alexa covered his approach, her gun at port arms, looking right, then left, scanning the area, straining her night vision.

Shane was finally at the sliding glass door. He looked into the living room but could still see no lights or movement inside. Then he knelt, taking out his pocketknife, and pried open the door as he had done before. He motioned for Alexa, who came quickly and lightly up onto the porch, using the steps on the far side.

They entered, breathing the stagnant air of an empty, shuttered house. They went through the place efficiently, moving fast—Shane going one way, Alexa the other, no longer creeping silently but throwing open doors SWAT-style, training their guns through the thresholds, calling out to each other.

"Master bedroom and bathroom clear," he heard her call from the back of the house.

He threw open the guest bedroom and was looking at another empty room. "Guest room clear," he shouted. Then he made his way to the secret room. He pushed the door open, hoping—praying—that Chooch would be there, alive, waiting. But the room was empty.

"Kitchen and pantry clear!" he heard her shout from the back of the house. Then she yelled, "We're secure!"

The entire house was empty.

They met in the living room and looked at each other. Shane's face was pulled tight. "You think they got here ahead of us and moved him?" Shane asked.

"No. There's no sign of anybody having been here. No garbage in the kitchen trash. Nothing. This isn't the place."

"Sandy said he's in Arrowhead," Shane protested.

"But not here. He's someplace else. . . ."

"Alexa, we've gotta find him." His voice was thin. Even he could hear it screeching in the still house.

"I wanna find them, too. It's how we get out of this. But ever since Miami, you've been different. You're not right, Shane. You're not thinking straight. You gotta calm down." And then she asked softly, "What did Sandy tell you? Whatever it was, your face dropped when she said it."

When he didn't answer, she took a guess. "Did you used to sleep with her?"

He still wouldn't answer.

"He's your son, isn't he?"

When he looked up at her, his expression told her it was true.

"Okay. But you've still gotta calm down, okay? Calm the fuck down. We can figure this out, but we gotta think it through."

" 'Kay," he said softly.

"All right. You said they owned an old boat—that they used a boat to get here. *Who* owned it?"

"I don't know. It's not really old. It's a reproduction of one of those classic Chris-Crafts with two windshields like they used to make in the thirties or forties."

"Maybe there's a dealer. . . ."

"Shit, that's gonna take forever. They know we talked to Sandy in the chauffeur's house and that she got the location out of Calvin Sheets. That's gotta be the reason they were hitting her, trying to find out how many people she told. If they know Sandy knew where Chooch was, they're gonna move him. He won't be up here anymore."

"We've gotta take this one step at a time," she said evenly. "Let's start with the phone book. There's one in the kitchen." She walked away from him, into the kitchen, turned on the light, and grabbed the Arrowhead directory. Then she started looking in the Yellow Pages, under "Boat Dealers." "Here. Butterfield Boats, an authorized Chris-Craft dealership."

"It's nine o'clock at night, Alexa. They're closed."

She was already flipping to the *B*s in the white pages. "Leo Butterfield, Lake View Drive. Can't be too far from here. We can call him or pay him a visit. Connect the dots. . . . What's it called?"

"Police work," he said dully. "Our faces are all over TV. We'll probably do better on the phone."

"Okay. Who makes the call, you or me?" she asked.

"The head of the department up here is a guy named Sheriff Conklyn. Let me. . . . Let's hope these guys don't go fishing together."

Shane had pulled the phone out of the kitchen four days ago, so they returned to the one in the living room. He dialed the number and after a minute a woman answered.

"Mrs. Butterfield? This is Sheriff Conklyn at the substation. I need to talk to your husband," he said.

"Just a minute." Her voice sounded puzzled.

So far, so good. She didn't seem to know Conklyn personally. Chances were her husband didn't, either.

"This is Leo Butterfield. What is it, Sheriff?" a baritone voice said.

From his tone, Butterfield didn't seem to know Sheriff Conklyn. "Mr. Butterfield, sorry to bother you at home, but I'm trying to run a trace on a classic reproduction wooden Chris-Craft. You deal in that line of boats, I understand."

"That's right."

"I can't be too specific, but I'm looking for somebody who lives up here who may have bought one of those classic designs in, say, the last two or three years."

"We got a few of those boats on this lake. It's a rare item. They're beautiful, but not for everyone. I service most of them myself."

"Can you give me the owners' names from memory?"

"Think so . . . Let's see . . . Carl Nickerson bought one last June. . . ."

Shane made a writing sign in the air, and Alexa grabbed a pen. "Carl Nickerson," Shane said. "Go on."

She jotted it down on the back of the phone book.

"Bert Perl has one. . . ."

"Bert Perl," Shane repeated, and she wrote it down.

"Logan Hunter," Leo said. "The movie producer."

"Logan Hunter," Shane said, and Alexa closed the book and looked up.

"Does he have a dock? Where's he keep it?" Shane asked.

"It's the old mansion on Eagle Point Drive on the Shelter Cove side. The one built by Clark Gable in the forties, looks like a Transylvanian castle."

THE CODE SIX MARY

THEY PARKED off the road and got out of the car. The house was down by the water, two blocks away.

Shane and Alexa walked down Mallard Road to Eagle Point Drive, where they found the public dock that accessed Shelter Cove. They walked out on the wooden float and stood on the blue and white platform, looking back across the moonlit waters to the huge house that loomed majestically against the distant snowcapped mountains. Its slate roof was glistening in silver light, its four roof turrets, each crowned with metal spikes, punching holes in the cloudless sky. The twenty-thousand-square-foot mansion had been designed in the forties and resembled a medieval castle, complete with stone arches and dormer windows.

The lights were on downstairs, and from the distance, across the cove, they could see occasional movement inside. From time to time people passed in front of the first-floor leaded-glass windows. Parked on the grass, near the water, was the same Bell Jet

Ranger that had brought Shane up to the lake after he'd been kidnapped in front of an entire movie company on Spring Street.

Tied to the dock was a classic reproduction wooden Chris-Craft.

"Sandy told me that Logan Hunter was a closet gay. This must be his getaway house. Good place for slam-dance weekends."

"Boy, do I hate this layout," she said, still studying the mansion carefully. "The house sits on high ground, acres of grass all around. Porches and too many windows . . . Tactically, we're fucked."

"Come on . . . don't be so negative. We lickety-split across the lawn, slip through an open window, find Chooch and Brian, make the rescue, bust ass, and we're gone—zim, zam, zoom."

"Shane, we need backup."

"Who did you have in mind, the Power Rangers?"

"If Chooch Sandoval and Brian Kelly are being held here and we get them out, they make the kidnapping case for us, and we're halfway off the hook. If we get caught, we're dust anyway. I think we need to call in a Code Six Mary." She was referring to the LAPD radio designation for officer assistance required due to extreme militant activity. "We'd have to time it right, but once we know Chooch and Brian are there, let's just dime ourselves out, let Sheriff Conklyn sort the frogs from the princes."

"What if Chooch and Brian aren't here," he said, "and we don't get killed, but arrested? Then we're sitting in jail, trying to talk our way out of four killings in Florida."

"No plan is without some operational deficiencies."

He shot her a withering look.

"Okay, let's go in, scout it, then back out to a safe spot and do a nine-one-one," she said, revising her idea.

He thought about it for a long moment, then said, "I'd rather take it one step at a time and see what develops. But, either way, I think we should tee up the Code Six Mary before we call it in."

"Good idea . . . but how?"

"Gimme your phone."

She handed the cell phone to Shane. He got Information, then called the Arrowhead Sheriff's Department. After asking for Sheriff Conklyn, he was transferred, then got the tall, balding man on the phone. "Guess who?" Shane said.

"I don't have the faintest idea. . . ."

"Turn on your TV. I'm starring in every newscast."

"Shit . . . Scully?"

"I'm looking for you to take me in, Sheriff. I want you to make the bust. You'll be famous. It's probably at least good for a shot or two on Oprah, but I have a few conditions. . . ."

Conklyn paused, and then Shane heard a *click*, so he knew the rest of the conversation was being T and T'd—taped and traced.

"Why me?" Conklyn asked.

"If you're tracing this call, it's just gonna come back to a cell station in Arrowhead. I'm up here now, but I'm not quite ready to turn myself in yet. I want you to make the arrest because I've got problems with some of my brother officers in L.A. and I don't want to stop a stray bullet by mistake."

"Not to mention all the dead bodies you left in Florida."

"There's a story that goes with that, Sheriff. Extenuating circumstances."

"If you're smart, Scully, you'll tell me where you are now. Otherwise, this will go down hard."

"I want you to call Bud Halley, my old CO in L.A. He's a good cop. Tell him what's going on. Tell him I need to see him and to get his ass up here."

"Where are you, Scully?"

"Stick by your phone. I'll let you know." Shane hung up and looked at Alexa.

"Pretty good," she said, nodding. "He'll have his flak vest buttoned and be ready to roll."

They moved off the dock and skirted the water's edge until they got to a wire fence that went ten feet out into the lake and separated the castle's property from its neighbors. Shane climbed out on the fence, U-turned around the end post, then came back toward shore, and dropped off onto the sand inside the grounds.

After a minute Alexa repeated the maneuver, landing on the sand beside him.

They crept away from the shoreline and ran up toward the house, both silently cursing the full moon as they sprinted under its silvery glow. They hurried across the vast expanse of lawn, then hugged the wall, moving around the castle house slowly. They could see a row of ground-level windows throwing streaks of light out across the dew-wet lawn. They moved in that direction. Once they got to the windows, Shane dropped to his stomach and looked through a narrow glass pane into what looked like a huge billiards room.

"Uh-uh," he whispered, rising again and moving on. Alexa followed quietly in his footsteps.

On the south end of the house, he found the ground-level window he was looking for. When Shane glanced inside, he saw that it opened into a basement laundry room. He took out the .38 S&W and tapped loudly on the window with the gun butt.

"Whatta you doing?" Alexa hissed. "Why don't we just ring the fucking doorbell?"

"If somebody's down here, I'd rather find out now. Better to be outside than trapped down there in the basement. I'm gonna break the glass. If we get a ringer, get small."

She nodded, then watched as he slammed the gun butt hard into the pane, breaking it. The sound of tinkling shards hitting the cement floor froze them. They lay prone on the grass for several long minutes, waiting.

Nothing.

Shane reached through the glass, unhooked the latch, and swung the window open. They slipped into the laundry room and dropped onto the basement floor. Once inside, they could hear the faint sounds of opera music playing upstairs.

"Okay, let's work our way through this place, starting with this side, then moving east," he whispered.

She nodded, and they opened the laundry-room door and found themselves in a narrow, concrete-walled corridor with a vaulted ceiling. The corridor had no carpet, windows, or wall decorations. They crept along the tile floor, trying to keep their shoes from echoing on the polished surface. They checked doors as they went, mostly storage rooms and a basement bathroom. Then they were back at the poolroom Shane had seen from outside. The room was medieval in design, with old lances and shields on the walls. Two full, man-sized suits of armor on stands stood guarding a pair of double doors.

Movie posters hung on every wall, each one featuring a well-known Logan Hunter film. A red felt pool table loomed like a mahogany crypt in the center of the huge rectangular room.

They slipped out of the poolroom through a side door, still heading east. Shane and Alexa found themselves transiting through a part of the basement that was beginning to resemble a dungeon— bars and studded steel doors, ornate metal hinges with brass church locks. At the end of the center hall was a wooden door with a small, eight-by-ten-inch barred window set at eye level. Shane looked through the bars into an even narrower, underlit hallway. The door was locked. He reached in his pocket for his picks.

"What would we ever do without those?" she quipped.

It was a simple two-tumbler lock, designed more for looks than function. He got it open quickly. The door creaked ominously as he pushed it wide.

They crept down the three-foot-wide stone-block hallway. The first door on the right was unlocked, so he pushed it open and found that he was standing in a replica of a medieval torture chamber, replete with fourteenth-century stretching racks, wall restraints, and steel wall hooks holding every imaginable kind of leather apparel.

"This kink is into S&M," Alexa said.

Shane felt a chill go through him and prayed that Chooch and Longboard had not been subjected to a dose of that madness.

He passed through the dungeon toward a door on the far side of the room, opened it slowly, and found a hallway that ran farther underground. It stretched for about forty or fifty feet on a gentle slope. At the end of the corridor was another large wooden door with metal trim and steel studs.

"Hold my back," he said, then ran down the concrete tunnel. When he got to the end, he tried the door. It was unlocked.

He pushed it open and found himself looking at Chooch and Longboard. They were blindfolded, gagged, and handcuffed to pipes in a small room that contained three giant water heaters. Shane ripped the blindfold off Chooch, then pulled the wadding out of his mouth. "You okay?"

"Shane," the boy said; tears started flowing from his eyes. "I knew you'd come. . . ."

"Shhhh . . ." Shane said. As Brian *umph*ed behind his gag, Shane checked Chooch's handcuffs before quickly turning and removing Brian Kelly's blindfold and fishing the gag out of his mouth.

"Shit, am I glad to see you," Longboard said weakly.

"You guys okay?"

"I guess," Longboard said. "Frickin' scared, but okay."

"Stay quiet. I'll be right back. Gotta get a key for those cuffs. They look like standard LAPD issue."

Shane sprinted back up the ramp to the dungeon room, where Alexa was guarding the hallway.

"They're down there. They look all right. I need your cuff key."

She reached to her belt, pulled it off, and handed it to him.

Shane hurried back to the heater room and unhooked both sets of cuffs.

"How many guys are here? How many guns?" Shane whispered.

"There's about four guys who are packing," Brian said.

"Shane, that movie producer is here," Chooch said. "He owns the place."

"That kink didn't put you on any of those tables up there, did he?" Shane asked.

"No. They just cuffed us to those pipes," Brian said. "Seems like we been here almost two days."

"Okay, listen up. We're on our way out. There's a woman with me. She's an LAPD sergeant. Once we're out of this dungeon, I'll go first, she'll bring up the rear. Stay close. Don't make any noise. What I want to do here is just disappear. I don't wanna fight our way out." Shane's words echoed softly against the walls of the stone room.

He led Brian and Chooch up the corridor, rejoining Alexa. Silently they retraced their footsteps out of the dungeon and back into the connecting hallway. Shane paused by the door, looking into the billiards room. It was still deserted, so he pushed the door open and they headed out across the tile floor, past the suits of armor, and back to the laundry room at the far end of the house.

They slipped inside; then Shane locked the door and turned to Alexa. "You're first. Once you're out there, scout both sides. We need a good exit line."

"Got it," she said.

He put his hands around her slender waist and lifted her up to the open window. She grabbed the ledge and shimmied out. She was amazingly light, which surprised him. Her intellectual weight had become so huge, it didn't seem possible that her physical weight was only 115 pounds.

Next he lifted Chooch. Once the boy was out of the window, Shane turned to Longboard and cupped his hands. "Hop aboard. You're outta here."

Longboard stepped in, and Shane boosted him out the window. Then Shane grabbed the ledge and pulled himself up and out onto the wet grass.

The cold, moist lake air filled his nostrils as he regained his feet and looked at all of them.

"Somebody just pulled in. They're in a truck in the drive. There're people in the big front room now. They'll see us moving across the grass," Alexa said. "Our best bet outta here is that speedboat. We need keys, but if they aren't in the boat, we could get trapped down there on the dock, out in the open."

"Don't need keys," Chooch whispered bravely. "I'll hot-wire it. Car theft is my Vato specialty."

"Okay then, that's the plan," Shane whispered. "Alexa, you look for the keys. If they're not aboard, Chooch, you get it going. Brian, you're on lines. I'll hold the back door and lay down cover fire if we get spotted. Everybody straight?"

They nodded, their faces grim.

"Okay—let's do it."

They slipped away from the house, staying close to the west side of the property, moving like shadows against the fence line.

They finally got to a spot where, in order to reach the dock, they had to make a final dash across an open stretch of moonlit lawn. They huddled down in the dark and checked the house. There were a few people visible in the windows. Nobody was on the porch.

"This is as good as it's gonna get. Let's go," Shane whispered.

They started running in a group. They moved fast and low, across the open area, but quickly spread out. Alexa, the sprinter, took the lead, with Shane a few steps behind. Chooch and Longboard were losing ground. They all finally reached the pier and headed out to the dock.

"Who's out there?!" a male voice yelled from the house.

"It's blown. Move it! Move it!" Shane shouted. He was out on the small dock, standing by the ramp leading down to the float, motioning to Chooch and Longboard, windmilling his arms, trying to get them to go faster. They ran by him heading for the boat.

Now all but Shane were on the boat.

Alexa was looking for the keys when Chooch and Longboard got aboard.

"No key in the ignition," Alexa shouted. She was pulling the engine cover up, looking for a key on a hook inside, when the first shot rang out. The bullet pinged off the top of the concrete piling next to Shane's head, then whined angrily away into the night.

Shane, still holding his position on the dock, fired blindly up at the house. He couldn't see anyone, so he popped only one cap—firing for effect—turned, and ran to the boat.

Chooch was under the dash pulling out ignition wires, and Longboard ducked down low in the backseat. As Shane jumped into the boat, two more shots rang out from the sloping lawn. One of the bullets thudded into the boat's hull. Alexa pulled her pistol and returned fire.

"Save your rounds!" Shane yelled. "Unless you can see 'em, don't fire."

Suddenly the boat engine started, and Chooch backed out from under the dash. Longboard came up from his hiding place and started throwing off lines.

They could now see two men running down toward the dock. Both stopped halfway out on the wooden pier, aimed their pistols, and fired down from a position of advantage. Shane felt a bullet tug at the sleeve of his sport coat. He dropped into the seat behind the wheel and slammed the throttle all the way forward.

The Chris-Craft roared away from the dock amidst a hail of gunfire. He heard Alexa's Beretta bark near his left ear, then the distant sound of return fire from the dock.

"Shit," she said, and dropped onto the seat beside him. He glanced over at her, alarmed.

"I took one," Alexa said, looking at her side. She couldn't see the blood in the moonlight because of the dark turtleneck.

"How bad?" Shane shouted over the roar of the engine.

She pulled up her shirt and checked the wound. "Looks like a through and through. The right oblique. Just drive. If I start fading, I'll let you know," she shouted.

They heard two more shots, but they were distant popping sounds. One bullet ricocheted off the metal windshield, and then they were out of range.

Longboard and Chooch were lying prone on the backseat. "Did we make it?" Longboard asked tentatively as he sat up.

Shane looked back at the dock, a receding structure in the distance.

"They're out of range," he said. All of them had wide smiles on their faces. It was a well-known police axiom that nothing is more exhilarating than being fired on without serious result.

The little speedboat streaked across the lake, its metal-tipped bow parting the moonlit water, leaving a frothy, expanding wake behind them as they headed toward the lights of Arrowhead Village two miles away.

"We've gotta get to a place where Sheriff Conklyn won't panic making the arrest. Someplace out in the open. I don't want one of his trigger-happy deputies ruining this perfect rescue," Shane shouted to Alexa over the wind and engine noise.

"How 'bout the main dock in town?" she suggested. "It's open from all sides. He can make an arrest easily there."

"Good idea," Shane agreed. She pulled out her cell phone to call, but before she could dial, the odds abruptly changed.

It was coming at them low and fast across the water, its rotor blade flashing streaks of reflected moonlight. The blue and green helicopter was ten feet off the surface, approaching quickly. By the time they heard it, it was way too close. The throaty roar of the speedboat's engine had camouflaged its deadly approach.

The Bell Jet Ranger swept low across their speeding bow. Two men leaned out the open door with police shotguns aimed down at them, and seconds later the men let loose. . . . The teak deck and left windscreen were peppered with buckshot. Exploding safety glass flew back in pebble-sized pieces. Chunks of pellet-riddled teak flew up, caught the air, and were whipped away over their heads.

Shane jerked the wheel right, to change the angle, taking away the Bell Jet's point-blank line of fire. Now the speedboat was heading west, away from the town. The chopper banked, its engine whining as it turned, and in seconds it was behind them again, closing in. Two more blasts from the shotguns, and the rest of their windshield was gone.

Shane felt sharp pain on his ear and cheek where several pellets from the widening shot pattern had nicked him. Blood started running down the right side of his face. He spun the wheel again.

Alexa turned and was now facing back. She had her knees on the leather seat; her body was prone across the center deck. She had her 9mm Beretta in both hands, aiming up at the approaching helicopter. She took her time sighting. "Slow down, you're bouncing too much!" she shouted.

Shane eased the throttle back, slowing the boat and subtly drawing the chopper in closer. Then, sighting carefully, she fired twice. Suddenly the chopper veered right and pulled up fast, exposing its belly. She fired again. The pilot, feeling the hits, banked the helicopter away. He pulled back to avoid further gunfire, but was now also way out of shotgun range.

Her shots had not disabled the Bell Jet Ranger.

Shane sped up. The chopper paced along a hundred yards to the right, skimming low across the water, tracking the speedboat from the side at about forty miles an hour.

The boat was bouncing badly, hitting the larger chop in the center of the lake. The waves slammed against the varnished hull, throwing water wide to each side.

"Don't shoot! Don't waste rounds—we're pounding too

much!" Shane shouted. "They can't reach us with those twelve-gauges—save it for when they come in close."

Alexa nodded as they sped across the center of Lake Arrowhead, the chopper flying sideways now, the nose aimed at them. Four faces were staring out from behind the bubble-glass windshield.

Shane was headed toward Blue Jay Bay.

Alexa pushed redial on her phone. A moment later Shane heard her shouting at Conklyn. "Sheriff, it's Alexa Hamilton. I'm with Shane Scully and two others. A male Caucasian and teenage Hispanic. We're Code Six Mary in a speedboat heading across Lake Arrowhead, taking gunfire from a helicopter above us. We're at Blue Jay Bay. We need help. Get here fast, or notify the coroner." She threw the phone down on the seat without waiting for a reply, then aimed her gun at the tracking helicopter.

They streaked past a sign marking Village Point, then past two poles planted in the lake that warned:

SHALLOW WATER—SANDBAR

"Shit," Shane said. He was going almost forty. If he went aground at that speed, they would all end up as part of the dashboard. He pulled the throttle back, slowing to about twenty. The helicopter veered again, vectoring toward them. They could see distant flashes of fire from both shotgun barrels, then heard the slower sound of the blasts. Simultaneously the varnish on the side of the boat exploded and turned chalky white as the pellets tore holes in it.

The body of water narrowed abruptly ahead; they were running out of lake. Shane saw Totem Pole Point coming up on the right, marked by a hand-painted sign. Suddenly they were in the narrow and unforgiving waters of Paradise Bay, heading for the mouth of Little Bear River.

"Fuck," Shane said. If he turned back now, he would be forced to slow way down to make the turn in the narrow inlet, making them vulnerable to a withering shotgun attack. So he eased back on the power, cutting his speed to ten miles per hour, then headed up the narrow mouth of the river. Occasionally he could feel the boat hesitate as it scraped bottom.

The helicopter came in close now, making another pass. Two men were leaning far out of the door of the chopper. Alexa fired three more times. One of the men screamed, his voice faint and distant, barely audible over the racket of the competing engines. Then the man tumbled out of the helicopter door and splashed into the shallows below.

Shane could see the end of the ride coming up ahead. A sandbar was stretched across the narrowing river. He sped up momentarily so he could run the heavy boat up onto the sand.

The Chris-Craft shot up onto the bar. He felt the sand scraping beneath, heard the propeller pin shear. The engine screamed as the propeller flew off. As soon as the boat slammed to a stop, it leaned right against its bottom, white smoke and a high-rpm whine coming from the exposed shaft.

"Out! Out! Get out!" Shane shouted, and yanked the .38 out of his waistband. He trained it on the helicopter that was now hovering and watching, waiting for them to run away from the grounded speedboat, where they would be easy to pick off.

"Stay put. Use the boat for cover!" Shane yelled. They all huddled behind the beached hull, keeping the Chris-Craft between them and the chopper. The overheating inboard engine finally coughed and quit.

Then the nose of the Bell Jet Ranger dropped and, like a bull in an arena, made its deadly charge. Shane unloaded the .38 as the chopper streaked over them. He could hear the shotguns firing, in a steady *ka-boom, ka-boom, ka-boom!* He knew they were using police-issue, Ithaca pump-action 12-gauge riot guns. As the shots continued, the engine compartment on the beached boat blew open . . . the last shot hit the exposed gas tank.

The next thing Shane knew, he was flying through the air, the sound of the exploding gas tank ringing in his ears. He landed ten feet away and saw that Alexa, Chooch, and Brian had also been blown off their feet by the blast.

Shane had been nearest the tank, and he now realized that his clothes were on fire. He got up and made a stumbling run for it, then dove into the shallow Little Bear River. While he was rolling in the water, trying to extinguish the flames, the helicopter turned back and made a low pass at him. He was now sitting upright in the middle of the shallows, an easy, stationary target, when the shotguns started again. The first pattern went wide, turning the river water to the left of him foam white with the pellets. In his peripheral vision, he could see Alexa splashing across the open ground toward him, limping slightly, favoring her right side. She was slamming her last clip into the Beretta, chambering it as she ran.

The helicopter flashed over her now, getting closer to him. As it went over, she peeled the full clip straight up into the belly of the chopper, hitting the Bell Jet Ranger with all nine shots.

Shane didn't know what the hell she hit, but it was certainly something vital, because the helicopter immediately began spinning on its axis, wobbling around like a slowing top, going out of control. Then it slammed, nose first, into the water and went down fast.

Shane got up out of the river, his burnt clothes steaming in the cold night air. He joined Chooch, Longboard, and Alexa at the water's edge. They looked out at the spot where the chopper had crashed. The engine housing and rotor were all that was still above water. There had been no explosion and no attempt by anyone to get out. Then it disappeared, sinking quickly.

"Fuck you," Shane said softly to a bubbling spot in the water where the helicopter had been.

A few minutes later, while they were still watching the Bell Jet's last air bubbles rising to the surface, exploding trapped air, they saw the black-and-white Hughes 500 approaching, coming in low over the lake. The belly-light on the sheriff's chopper snapped on, and they were caught in its blinding glare. Shane and Alexa immediately threw down their guns and assumed the position, placing both hands behind their heads. Shane instructed Longboard and Chooch to do the same.

They were all standing out in the open as the sheriff's helicopter hovered overhead, churning up rocks and river water. "On your stomachs. Facedown on the ground!" they heard Conklyn's voice shout over the bullhorn.

All of them proned-out on the sand and waited.

It was only moments before the first squad cars arrived. They drove off the road, their tires squishing on the wet river sand, their cherry-colored bar lights flashing. Then, as patrol officers swarmed them, the police chopper landed.

"Watch it, she's been wounded," Shane said as sheriff's deputies cuffed Alexa and dragged her to her feet. They ignored his instructions and pushed her roughly toward the squad cars. Shane was cuffed and pulled to his feet, then found himself looking at the jacked-and-flacked Sheriff Conklyn. "Glad to see you, man," Shane said.

"What the fuck? What chopper? She said there was a chopper shooting at you. . . ."

"There was," Shane said, nodding to the spot in the river where the Bell Jet Ranger had gone down. "But you're gonna need to come back with divers, a crane, and some body bags if you wanna see it."

Shane watched as Chooch and Longboard were roughly cuffed, then put into squad cars. "They're victims. You don't need to throw them around like that. They were kidnapped," he complained, but Conklyn didn't seem to care.

"You're really some kinda jerkoff, Scully. This is a quiet town. Every time you come up here, I gotta throw a fucking cherry festival." Conklyn pushed Shane toward the squad car. "I can hardly wait to hear this one."

"Right," Shane said softly. "But you better send out for pizza, 'cause it's a long and complicated story."

EXCULPATORY
EVIDENCE

POLICE MISCONDUCT is defined under Section 805 of the LAPD Manual and falls into one of four categories:

1. Commission of a criminal offense
2. Neglect of duty
3. Violation of department policies, rules, or procedures
4. Conduct that may tend to reflect unfavorably upon the employee or the department.

After their arrest, Shane, Alexa, Chooch, and Longboard Kelly were taken to the Arrowhead substation. Alexa's bullet wound was stitched up and bandaged by EMTs in Sheriff Conklyn's office. Then she was returned to a holding cell.

A pissed-off Bud Halley arrived at two A.M. and reluctantly

did Shane's DFAR. They were in one of two windowless FI rooms.

After he heard it all, Halley leaned back in the wooden chair and glowered. "Shit, Scully, I'm supposed to believe that the mayor of L.A., the Super Chief of our department, and one of the largest developers in the state of California, along with a dozen or more sworn or terminated LAPD personnel, are involved in murder, blackmail, kidnapping, fraud, and a buncha other criminal misconduct," Halley said, looking at Shane through tired eyes. He didn't want any part of it. This was the ultimate red ball.

Shane had asked for Captain Halley for three reasons: One, with Tom Mayweather sure to get indicted, he was Shane's most recent CO. Two, the captain was well respected in the department, and Shane needed a trusted "rabbi" as his advocate. And three, he knew that Halley was deeply religious, with a highly developed sense of morals and ethics. Underneath all the police bullshit, he was a stand-up guy. If Halley could be made to believe Shane's story, he would come aboard, regardless of the consequences.

Shane had started his DFAR talking about the kidnapping of Chooch and Longboard, finally convincing Halley that they had been hit over the head, tied up, videotaped, and abducted from his Third Street apartment. They had then been taken to Logan Hunter's mansion in Arrowhead and held there for two days by current and former LAPD officers.

Shane, Alexa, Chooch, and Longboard all volunteered to take lie-detector tests, and after Halley agreed, Conklyn rolled a big, new Star Mark polygraph machine into the FI room. One by one they were given the test, and one by one they passed.

Shane could see the building frustration in Bud Halley's hazel-green eyes as night turned to day.

By ten o'clock the helicopter had been pulled out of the Little

Bear River. Inside were the remains of the pilot, as well as Logan Hunter and Joe Church. Kris Kono had been found in the shallows with Alexa's 9mm slug buried deep in the Hawaiian officer's chest.

It was all exculpatory evidence, further sustaining Shane's statement.

Alexa and Shane described the events that occurred in Miami, starting with their attempt to rescue Sandy Sandoval and ending with the attack by Drucker, Love, and Calvin Sheets. Alexa handled their escape from Elton John's Biscayne Bay estate, then Shane explained about Ray's Arrowhead house and how Molar had been blackmailing the Long Beach City Council so Los Angeles could get control of the naval yard. Halley listened, took notes, and groaned as the scope of the corruption grew larger, reaching all the way up through the chief of police to the mayor's office.

Halley kept the startling events under wraps as best he could, but of course Logan Hunter's death had leaked out. News crews from L.A. were arriving in vans and helicopters. The newsies were already picking up other shreds of the story, sharking for details, sensing that much more was at stake.

"I don't know what to do with this," Halley admitted to Shane and Alexa after he'd heard it all. They were no longer being kept in holding cells and were seated in Sheriff Conklyn's office. He had promoted them from suspects to witnesses.

Out the window they could see a small TV uplink antenna farm being constructed on the vacant property across from the police station.

"I'm gonna call in Erwin Epps," Halley finally said, referring to the Baptist minister and political activist who had just been elected head of the L.A. Police Commission. "Under Section 78 of the city charter, the board of commissioners has the power and responsibility to supervise, control, and regulate the department." Halley quoted the section from memory.

"Good idea," Shane said.

Shane asked for and was given a chance to talk to Chooch. The boy was staying in the Arrowhead Motel with a sheriff's matron. Shane was driven over and let himself in.

Chooch was watching the news, his legs stretched out on the bed. He snapped off the television as Shane came through the door.

"Man . . . can you believe the coverage this is getting?"

"Chooch . . . I wanna talk to you about your mom."

"I know about Sandy . . . it's on the TV." His voice was guarded.

"I'm sorry you had to hear it that way. I wanted to tell you, but they wouldn't give me a chance until now."

Chooch nodded, his black eyes showing little. "I'm sorry she's dead," he said. "I didn't want that to happen. . . . I just wanted her to . . ." He stopped, then shook his head in frustration. "You know what I mean." He looked up. "You and me are the same, Shane. I got nobody, same as you." The way he said it, Shane couldn't tell what he was thinking. Chooch, like Shane, had become good at hiding his emotions.

"I want you to know something—something important about your mother."

"That she loved me?" the boy said, but his tone said he found it hard to believe.

"Yeah, she loved you, and she died trying to save you. She gave herself up for you, Chooch."

Chooch got up off the bed and moved to the window, his muscular body silhouetted in the morning sunlight streaming past him into the room.

"You were the one who saved me," he said softly.

"I never would have known where to look if your mother hadn't gotten that information for me. She gave up her life to get it."

There was a long moment, then finally Chooch turned and

faced Shane. "I want to cry for her. . . . It seems like I should. Am I being an asshole?"

"No, Chooch. I just wanted you to know. Whatever you feel about Sandy, in the end, when it counted, she was there for you."

Chooch nodded; suddenly his eyes filled, and he moved quickly to the bathroom and closed the door.

■ ■ ■

At two that afternoon, Chooch was picked up by the Child Protection Section of the Social Services Department and whisked away. Shane was back at Sheriff Conklyn's office and found out about it an hour after it happened. They said that since Chooch had no mother or father, he was being remanded to Juvenile Hall.

Shane knew he couldn't claim Chooch without a DNA test, and that would take time. Besides, the more he thought about it, the more he was beginning to suspect that Sandy had lied about his being Chooch's father. It was just what she would do—just like her to say that to get Shane to look after Chooch once she was gone. Either way, he couldn't get a DNA analysis up in Arrowhead, so it would have to wait until he got back to L.A.

Three hours later, Reverend Epp arrived and conferred with Bud Halley. He was a tall, dignified African American in his fifties who had tremendous credibility in the black community and had been put on the L.A. Police Commission to help deal with the charges of racism that had plagued the post–Daryl Gates department.

The two devout Christians listened all over again as Shane, Alexa, and Longboard Kelly retold their story.

Slowly, over a period of hours, it became distressingly clear to both Captain Halley and Reverend Epps that much of what Shane and Alexa had been describing was undoubtedly true.

The two tired sergeants were finally allowed to move into the Arrowhead Motel to get some sleep. They had rooms right next to each other but were too exhausted to even say good night.

One by one, other members of the L.A. Police Commission quietly arrived in town. They had decided to hold their meeting in the Arrowhead Lodge, away from the sheriff's department and the hovering press corps.

At the end of their first meeting, after Shane, Alexa, and Long-board had retold their stories, Sheriff Conklyn got a district judge to issue a search warrant.

On Monday evening they broke the front-door lock and entered Logan Hunter's lakeside mansion. What they found in his office files pretty much confirmed everything Shane and Alexa had been saying.

At ten o'clock on Tuesday morning, Reverend Erwin Epps chaired a meeting in his Arrowhead Lodge hotel room. Shane and Alexa were both present, along with Captain Halley, Sheriff Conklyn, and the entire seven-member L.A. Police Commission.

"I think we now have to consider Section 79 of the L.A. city charter," Epps said gravely. Then he took that bound document out of his briefcase and opened it to a paper clip marking the section.

"Let me read this to refresh you: 'A simple majority of the Police Commission is necessary to enact the provision of Section 79, which grants the commission the right to *appoint,* as well as to *remove,* the general manager of the department. However, the chief of police shall only be removed under the terms and conditions in city charter, Section 202.'" He flipped to that section and read the paragraph pertaining to the removal, suspension, or demotion of sworn police officers, then:

"I think we need to instruct the head of the Internal Affairs Division to draft a resolution to suspend the duties of Chief Brewer and bring him up on administrative charges. The head of IAD should further notify the district attorney of the possibility of criminal misconduct."

Shane couldn't help a small smile thinking of the panic that "resolution" would bring to the vanilla features of Commander Warren Zell.

The news was leaking from Lake Arrowhead to Los Angeles, and, little by little, shreds of it were showing up in the press and on TV.

The case went further into frenzied hyperspace when Tom Mayweather's body was found in the main salon of his boat anchored off Avalon Harbor in Catalina. He had put a police-issue shotgun into his mouth and blown his head off.

The subpoena control desk at Parker Center was flooded with paperwork issued by Warren Zell and the fifteen IOs he had assigned to the case. John Samansky and Lee Ayers, the two surviving members of Ray's den, had hired criminal attorneys and were both clamoring to cut a deal.

Samansky won that ugly contest and became the department's star witness against Chief Brewer, Tony Spivack, Mayor Clark Crispin, and the surviving officers. The district attorney petitioned the department for the right to sit in on the upcoming BORs under Section 21.2 of the L.A. city charter—a sure sign that criminal charges would be forthcoming.

One day after Logan Hunter's helicopter was fished out of the river, Mayor Crispin was arrested at the airport on his way to a "vacation" in Mexico.

Chief Brewer staged a press conference after his subpoena was served. He denied any wrongdoing had taken place and promised a victory in court. Nevertheless, at the district attorney's request, two detectives from Special Crimes were assigned to his house, and he was ordered to remain at home, pending further investigation.

A day later the district attorney finally filed murder one charges against them all.

Alexa and Shane had been released, then went back to L.A. and watched the rest of it on her TV, since he didn't have one. She had cooked a remarkably good Italian dinner for them, and after they had two glasses of red wine, Shane was lying on the sofa in her anally neat living room, watching Dan Rather talk about him. Alexa was in the kitchen doing dishes, hoping her mother was watching over them all.

Shortly after the news ended, an investigator from IAD knocked on the door to pick up the files Alexa had gathered for Shane's BOR. The IO notified her that she was no longer the advocate prosecuting Scully's case.

"What case?" Shane asked, coming up off the sofa like a Harrier jet. "You mean, after all this, they're still planning to terminate me?"

"Just because you two turned this department upside down doesn't mean your unnecessary use of force on the Molar shooting goes away," the IO said. Then he took the four crammed case-file boxes and left.

"When will it end?" Shane growled.

"Shane . . . you'll prevail at that board. With all this going on, believe me, their case won't stick."

He looked at her and again felt something stir inside him. She saw it in his eyes. "I know, but this time let's wait," she said. "Let's not do anything again until all this calms down and we know if it's real, or if we're just pulsing 'cause we're glad to be alive."

"It's real," he said. But she was right, now was not the time.

Shane had heard that Chooch was being held under IDC—Intake and Detention Control—at Juvenile Hall. So he called Captain Halley and had Chooch moved to PNP—USCMC, which was the patient-not-prisoner section of the Juvenile Detention wing of the USC Medical Center. They were talking about assigning him to a foster home.

Shane slept on Alexa's couch, and the next morning, after she cooked him breakfast, he had her drop him off at the police impound garage, where he reclaimed the rented Taurus he had left on the movie set the night he got kidnapped. Then he drove down and gave blood at the USC hospital. He couldn't see Chooch, by order of the district attorney, who was still interviewing him as a witness, so Shane found an old friend named Ellen Webb, who worked in PNP as a nurse. He gave her his blood sample number and asked her to get a match from Chooch.

"How come?" Ellen asked, brushing a wisp of honey-blond hair out of her eyes. "According to the news, he's Hispanic."

"His mother was, but I think I may be the father."

She looked at Shane for a long moment and smiled. "Can't keep the little head from controlling the big head?" she said playfully, so Shane stuck his tongue out at her and left.

He had one more stop to make before he went home and slept for a year.

The freeway was crowded, and he was locked in bumper-to-bumper five o'clock traffic. He finally got to the end of the 10 and found himself back on the Coast Highway. He didn't have his badge, so this time he had to pay for parking. He left the Taurus, walked onto the bike path and up to DeMarco's house.

For once it was quiet out front. The blond beach ornaments were all gone, off playing with somebody else's mind. Shane passed through the gate and walked up to the front door. He tried to look through the front window, but the blinds were pulled and he couldn't see anything. Finally he reached into his back pocket and fished out his trusty collection of picks. The lock was an old brass Yale and was a bitch to open, but after five minutes he turned the tumblers, went into the house, then closed and relocked the door behind him.

He stood in the living room, looking around, remembering his trip here two weeks days ago. . . . He had stood in this very same spot, watching DeMarco play with his speakers while Snoop Doggy Dogg spewed race hatred. It seemed as though that had been in another lifetime. He walked softly through the place, looking into each room. No one was home, so he entered the office at the end of the hall, walked across the room, then sat at DeMarco's desk. His defense rep's case material was sitting there in one half-filled file box. DeMarco had been on Shane's case for almost ten days, and as Shane went through the material, he was surprised by the lack of evidence he'd collected to support Shane's position. The defense rep hadn't yet received all of the discovery items, and there wasn't even a copy of Barbara Molar's statement. There was a halfhearted, half-full spiral notebook. . . . It was all damned puny compared with the mountain of stuff that had been carted out of Alexa's house.

He finally stopped looking at the case files, leaned back in the chair, and waited.

An hour later he heard the front door open; DeMarco was talking to someone. He heard a young boy's laughter, and then the music came on. Shane waited for a minute, then got out of DeMarco's chair and continued silently down the hall, into the living room.

What he saw didn't surprise him as much as it sickened him. On the living room sofa, DeMarco Saint and one of the fifteen-year-old surfer boys were lying in a romantic embrace. They were both naked.

"What a total shitbox!" Shane said.

DeMarco snapped his head around and glowered up at Shane. Then he scrambled up into a sitting position and grabbed for his underwear. The boy made no move to cover himself. Instead he remained lounging on the sofa, glaring his indifference.

"You didn't get thrown off the job for drinking. You got thrown off for pedophilia," Shane said.

"Nobody ever proved anything," DeMarco said, now reaching for his beach shorts.

"I should've seen it. First you turn me down, then a day later, all of a sudden, you're taking on my case. Mayweather got you to do it, didn't he? He wanted somebody on the inside of my defense. He wanted to find out what I was up to. He knew about this thing you've got for underage boys. He could've still filed criminal charges and gone after your pension. He forced you to reconsider."

"That's nonsense," DeMarco sputtered as he got his shorts on and rose to his feet. He was flushed, his complexion a ruby red. Sweat was slick on his skinny white chest.

"Nonsense?" Shane said reflectively. "I only told one person that I went to the Long Beach Naval Yard. Two hours later I'm kidnapped and taken up to Arrowhead, and Coy Love knows about it. The person who told him was you!"

"Whatta you . . . whatta you . . . gonna . . ." DeMarco's lower lip was quivering.

"Do?" Shane finished the sentence for him. "I'll show you." He grabbed DeMarco's arm and jerked him off balance. As his defense rep fell forward, Shane swung, landing a left hook square on the side of Dee's face.

DeMarco went down in a slump and began to weep. The naked teenager was on his feet now, his hands up, fists balled.

"Don't try it, Jocko. I'll make fucking hash outta you." Shane walked to the door, then turned. "By the way, Dee, you've got a subpoena coming. I'm putting you in the mix." Without saying another word, he left.

Shane drove back to Venice. The incident hung with him and poisoned his mood.

He worked hard to shift his thoughts and finally tried to contemplate his future. He thought about his life, about Chooch, and whether he was truly the boy's father. Shane had been looking for a deeper meaning in his life. Chooch had begun to fill that emptiness.

In the past two weeks, Shane had had two big surprises, both from unexpected places. Chooch had been one; Alexa, the other.

He was paralyzed with fear that the blood test would prove that his one intimate moment with Sandy would turn out to be just what he'd always believed it to be—a mindless mistake—instead of what he hoped it was now, a chance for a different kind of future. He parked the Taurus in the garage at his Venice house on East Canal Street, walked past his ruptured Acura, and went into his kitchen. Longboard had slipped a note under the door:

Shane,
I got some cold beer and steak.
I'm tapping the Source.
You're invited.
Longboard

He put the note on the counter and slowly walked through the house, taking stock of his minimal emotional and physical existence: the furniture—remnants from broken love affairs; the bullet-riddled plaster walls in his front room, reminders of his fragile mortality. He picked up a pen and paper, then went outside and sat in one of the old rusting metal chairs.

He looked out at the setting sun just dipping below the horizon, dragging the last vestiges of the day across the shallow channels like a burnt orange memory.

He was in a new place, starting a new chapter in his life. He was not sure where he was going or how long it would take to get there, but for the first time in a long time, he was looking forward to the journey.

Then he uncapped the pen and wrote a long, personal letter to Chooch.

46

THE NEWS VULTURES were on the sixth floor of the Bradbury Building, leaning over the rails, blowing white streams of cigarette smoke into the huge glassed atrium. The ancient wrought-iron elevators went up and down, making unhurried stops, measuring each trip with a tailor's precision.

Shane was seated in the witness room on the fifth floor because he didn't want to stand out in the corridor and be pestered by news crews asking about the whole breaking Long Beach story. The NFL had just rescinded the L.A. Spiders' franchise along with the Web, and the Coliseum was now the likely choice to get the nod.

Burl Brewer was awaiting trial in County Jail, and the LAPD had a new chief named Tony Filosian, from New York. A short, round man who wore huge pinkie rings and spoke with a Brooklyn accent, he showed up for work in a shiny suit and was instantly dubbed "the Day-Glo Dago," but he seemed like an excellent choice because of his background of turning around troubled departments.

Barbara Molar got off the elevator and walked down the hall. Shane saw her through the window. He hoped she wouldn't come into the witness room, but when she saw him, she smiled and quickly came through the door, her blond hair shining, smile radiant, dancer's calves flexing as she took a chair next to him in the empty room.

"Boy, talk about a cluster fuck," she said, opening the conversation in typical in-your-face Barbara fashion.

"Yep, it's assholes on parade," he said, not showing her much.

"I'm here to back you up. I did the IO interview last night. I've been out, so I stopped by and signed it this morning on my way over."

"That's good. Thanks."

"So who's your new DR?" she asked. "I heard you canned DeMarco Saint."

"I'm gonna try my own board," he said.

"Is that smart?"

"I've been getting that question a lot, so I'm beginning to wonder." He smiled at her.

She fished a cigarette out of her purse, lit up, and started smoking in the small room. Shane wished she wouldn't; he'd never completely gotten over his desire for cigarettes.

"I figured I know the case better than anybody," he went on. "Since the department didn't want to give me more than a four-day postponement, I figured, what the hell . . ."

"Right. What the hell," she said. "Are we finally at a place where we can talk about the future?" she asked, smiling through the smoke.

Shane thought it'd be bad timing to piss her off just before she was going to testify. On the other hand, the IO had told him that she'd backed his story in her deposition, and he knew she pretty much had to stick to her statement.

He turned and faced her. "Y'know, Barb, I don't think we're gonna get a chance to see that happen." He watched her as her expression turned sour. "I've got some new responsibilities," he continued. "I took a blood test to see if I'm Chooch Sandoval's father. I'm expecting the results today. Then I'm picking him up and taking him home for the long weekend. We're gonna talk it out. After that, who knows? I may decide to raise him. I mean, if everything works out."

"Y'know, Shane, our timing was always pretty damn shitty, but you're not giving this a chance. Now that Ray's gone, it can work. And a kid? You wanna raise a kid?"

"Well, yeah, I sorta do," he finally said. "He and I hit it off."

"Kids are a drag," she said, stubbing out her cigarette. "Ray and I never wanted kids. You never said anything about wanting kids . . . baby-sitters, homework, car pools . . . You can't be serious?"

"Listen, Barbara, thanks for being there for me."

"Yeah. Well, I'm gonna see if they've got coffee. See you inside." She got up and left.

Over and out.

Then Commander Van Sickle arrived, and a uniformed police officer announced the commencement of the Scully Board, in hearing room one.

Shane walked out of the witness room and entered room one. It was the largest of the hearing rooms, and there were news crews in all the available chairs in the back. Internal Affairs Boards were public hearings, so there was no way of keeping the press out. They would have to suffer through his clumsy presentation of the defense.

The room was rectangular, with large arched windows that streamed in sunlight and backlit the three-man judging panel. The two sworn and one civilian panel members were seated in leather swivel chairs at a long table at the head of the room. The American and LAPD flags decorated opposite ends of the stage. A court reporter was in a chair off to the side.

Warren Zell was prosecuting the case for the department, and there were four IOs clustered around him. Shane was alone at the defense table; his one assigned investigating officer was still out, taking statements and collecting last-minute depositions. Hopefully he would be back by noon.

Commander Van Sickle opened the proceedings. "Sergeant Scully, are you ready to proceed?"

"Yes, sir."

"To start with, I'm going to read you your rights, from the Police Disciplinary Manual. Okay?"

"Yes, sir."

"You have the right to appear in person and present a defense to the charges against you. You have the right to be represented by a department defense representative. You may produce witnesses to testify on your behalf, including character witnesses. You may cross-examine witnesses testifying against you. You have the right to testify in your own defense. You have the right to be present when board members examine your personal history and records. You also have the right to have all sworn testimony at this hearing reported and transcribed by a hearing reporter. You shall be entitled to a copy thereof." He looked up. "Do you understand your rights?"

"Yes, sir."

"This board has been convened to determine if unnecessary and escalating force was used in the fatal shooting of Lieutenant Raymond Molar. There are five counts of misconduct, all listed in your letter of transmittal."

The door in the back of the room opened, and Alexa Hamilton walked into the hearing. Everybody turned to look at her. She was wearing a tailored black suit coat and skirt over a white silk blouse. A red scarf decorated the collar.

"Excuse me, Sergeant Hamilton. You've been replaced as the advocate on this case," Warren Zell said. "I thought you'd been told that."

"Could I have a moment with Sergeant Scully, Commander?" she asked the board chairman.

Commander Van Sickle heaved a sigh and nodded. She moved briskly across the room and sat down in the empty chair beside Shane, resting her purse on the defense table. She leaned in to whisper to him.

"Since I can't prosecute you, I'd love to defend you," she whispered in his ear.

"Are you serious?"

"You can choose anybody in the department below the rank of captain; the last time I checked, that included me. I know this case from top to bottom. I prepped it for ten days. I know where every piece of bullshit is. Warren Zell is a mediocre administrator and a worse trial advocate. Just say the word, and I'll kick his vanilla-milkshake ass."

"Alexa, will you please represent me?" he whispered softly.

"Honored."

"If you're through with your little discussion?" Van Sickle asked with irritation. "I'd like to get started."

"And I'd like to notify the board that I'm taking over as Sergeant Scully's defense rep," Alexa announced.

"I'm afraid you can't do that," Zell said, rising to his feet. "She's a member of the Advocate Division and, as such, is prohibited from acting as a defense rep."

"To be precise, I'm currently assigned to Southwest Patrol," Alexa said. "I was brought back to try this one case. Once I was replaced as the advocate, I was immediately reassigned to my Southwest Patrol commander, freeing me to fulfill Sergeant Scully's request that I represent him."

Commander Van Sickle looked over at Zell.

"It's completely improper, sir," the chief advocate protested.

"But not outside of department guidelines," Van Sickle said. "Sergeant Hamilton is accepted as defense rep."

"I'd like a recess for fifteen minutes to get my files on this case out of my car and up here into the hearing room. I reproduced the entire case history and have been working on it all night. Maybe you could get a few officers to help me? There's a bunch."

• • •

They adjourned, then reconvened fifteen minutes later. For the rest of the day, Alexa shredded every piece of evidence that Zell put forward.

The board had been scheduled to go for two days, but by five o'clock that evening, Commander Van Sickle had heard enough.

"If you have something substantive to add that will make your case, would you put it on now, Commander Zell? Otherwise, I'd like to entertain a motion from Sergeant Hamilton to dismiss this case."

"Sir . . . Due to obvious circumstances, this case has been fraught with monumental difficulties."

"This case should never have been brought here in the first place," the commander scolded. "It should have gone to a Shooting Review Board, which would have resulted in a finding of appropriate use of force. So, unless there is some statement or evidence to the contrary, I'm suggesting that this board immediately dismiss the proceeding. And let Sergeant Scully get back to work."

Alexa so moved.

• • •

He stood in the parking lot outside of the Bradbury Building and waited for her.

She came down at about six-thirty, carrying a stuffed briefcase and a box of paper supplies. He took the box and walked her to her car in the adjoining parking structure. They stopped at the trunk of her Crown Vic, and he put the box inside.

"I have something that belongs to you," she said. Then she reached into her purse and retrieved his badge, gun, and ID.

"I want to get to know you better," he said awkwardly.

"We killed half a dozen guys together . . . what does it take with you?" She smiled and then saw that he was serious, so she nodded her head. "I'm free most evenings unless I'm on night watch."

"Tonight I'm barbecuing dinner for Chooch. I'm picking him up at the Med Center and we're going home. We'd love to have you join us."

"No . . . that would be wrong. You should do this one alone."

"Tomorrow night, then?"

She nodded, and he stood there in the garage, not sure what to do. Then he reached out and took her hand.

"Are you going to kiss me?" She smiled.

"Probably not good form for the accused to kiss an advocate in the IAD parking garage. . . ."

"But it's okay for him to kiss his defense rep," she said.

So he took her into his arms and kissed her. The electricity that he felt again surprised him. It made him feel warm inside. His breath got short, his legs weak.

They finally separated, and she looked up at him. "Wow, you're a good kisser."

"Let's find another verb," he said, grinning.

Then he turned and left her standing there, looking after him, a smile on her beautiful, exotic face.

THE

LETTER TO

CHOOCH

Dear Chooch,

I told you once that you were an adult and that you were in charge of your life.

A man makes his own decisions but is also forced to live with the quality of his choices.

Your mother wanted a lot for you. She wanted to see you grow up to be strong, valuable, full of integrity and vision. Unfortunately, wanting something isn't the same as achieving it, but her heart was in the right place. Everything she was doing, she was doing for you. I know that's hard to envision when you're spending Christmas vacation alone in the prep school dorm, but I believe she wanted the best for you.

Sandy had parts of it right, but maybe she didn't have the whole deal figured.

Now she's gone. She died in my arms, asking me to take care of you. Making me promise that I would.

Even before that moment, I've been wanting you in my life, but I've also been wondering if I'm the right person to attempt it. Is it fair for me to mess up, when you've been given so little up to now?

And, of course, in the long run, as an adult, it should be your decision anyway. These questions have been on my mind. Since you've come to mean a great deal to me, I want you to carefully consider my offer to move in and live here, before you give me your answer.

I'm not skilled at sharing. My life has been about grabbing and holding. It's a long way from the back door of the community hospital to this house in Venice. It doesn't represent much wealth or status, but it's the best I could do, and I feel blessed to be here.

You asked me once if I knew who your father was, and I told you that you would have to find out from your mother, that she had sworn me to secrecy. She once told me that your father was a criminal, a drug dealer that she had helped to put in jail.

Before she died, she told me why she had asked me to take you for this month. She said she felt it was finally time for us to get to know each other.

They say that things are never the way they appear, and I guess in this case that is certainly true. Sandy loved pulling all our strings, and now we're both faced with her last request.

I know the responsibility of looking after you goes much deeper than advice or guidance or suggestions to do your homework. It's about being a worthwhile role model. I'm not sure I can do that well.

Sandy had dreams of glory for you; she wanted you to go to Princeton or Yale, to be an attorney or a doctor. I have different goals. I want you to be a man of substance. I want you to know how to be a good friend and how to love without reservation. I want your word to be your bond.

So, Sandy and I have different goals now, just as we did when she was alive.

If you decide to take a shot with me, I will try hard to make this part of your life enriching. Can't say we won't argue or that I won't be wrong, but I can promise I'll try to always be honest with you.

Chooch, it's a much shorter journey we're on than it appears to be at its beginning. You can accept this ride or flag down another. It's all choices. It always will be.

Love,
Your father,
Shane

. . .

He heard the door open behind him and sat quietly on the metal chair. After a moment he heard footsteps coming across the grass. Then Chooch sat in the metal chair beside him. He was holding the letter and looking out at the still water. The three-quarter moon was coming off the horizon, hiding behind a drifting cloud, lighting its lacy edges. They sat in silence and watched it float slowly by.

Shane was almost afraid to speak; his heart was beating fast in his chest. "So, whatta you think?" he said softly.

Chooch sat looking at the still canal, his face strangely set, breathing deeply. Then he dropped the letter on the grass, reached out and took hold of Shane's shoulder, and squeezed it.

"I want to stay here," he finally said. "This is where I belong."

THE

VIKING

FUNERAL

DEDICATION

I was sitting having lunch in a Hollywood restaurant with my friend Bill Gately, a lean, dark-haired, intense man who often speaks in whispers. Suddenly Bill leaned forward and said, "Hey, Steve, you ever hear of the parallel market?"

Bill had recently pulled the pin after a distinguished career at the U.S. Customs Service, where he ended up as the Assistant Special Agent in charge of the Los Angeles office. The year before, he had supervised the now-famous Casablanca bank sting. In that covert operation, which was run inside Mexico, he ended up busting dozens of Mexican bankers who had been secretly laundering billions of dollars in Colombian drug money, escaping detection by wiring funds bank to bank.

In my opinion, Bill Gately is one of America's heroes. He has spent his life holding the fort against international crime syndicates, often risking his career and life, to bring dangerous criminals to justice. So naturally, when Bill talks, I listen.

I told him I had never heard of the parallel market.

What he explained to me at that lunch two years ago eventually became the basis for this novel. Without Bill, I would not have been able to write *The Viking Funeral*, because I would have been just as blind to the devastating effects of the parallel market as I'm sure the rest of you are.

While this is a work of fiction, it is based on fact. These facts have been overlooked or scrupulously hidden by our own government.

The stated reasons for this oversight defy logic.

When you read this, I hope you will become as outraged as I am.

For

WILLIAM GATELY

Friend, Colleague,

American Hero

Police officers must agree on a certain set of philosophies, because there cannot be a rule for everything.

L.A.P.D. Management Guide
to Discipline

JODY

1

Looking back, it was pretty strange that just the night before, they'd been talking about Jody Dean. Shane and Alexa had been in Shane's bedroom in the Venice house; Chooch was in the front room doing his homework.

Here's how it happened. . . .

It was six in the evening, and the conversation took place after they'd been making love, Shane draping his arms protectively around Alexa's narrow waist, smelling the sweet scent of her, feeling her soft rhythmic breathing on his neck. He was still inside her, both of them trying to sustain the afterglow of lovemaking for as long as possible, staring into each other's eyes, communicating on levels much deeper than words could convey.

He'd been building up to it for months, but it was right then, at that particular moment, that Shane decided he would ask this incredible woman to be his wife, to share his life and help raise his son, Chooch. All he needed to do was determine the timing of the proposal. Maybe Sunday night, after the awards ceremony. But soon, because he now knew he had to add her to his life . . . to his and Chooch's.

A swift series of connect-the-dot thoughts followed, and his mind was suddenly on Jody: Jody Dean, who wouldn't be at the wedding, standing at Shane's side, as they had both once promised each other. Jody wouldn't be standing up for Shane as Shane had for him, his raucous humor making everything funnier and more exciting, pouring insight and personality over Shane's special day. "Jodyizing the deal," he would have called it. And then, tumbling over this thought, a tidal wave of sadness and loss.

Alexa was looking into his eyes and must have seen his gaze gutter and dim, because she suddenly asked him what he was thinking, and that was how his best friend's name came up the day before Shane's whole world changed.

"I was thinking about Jody," Shane said, not explaining how Jody had entered his mind during postcoital sex, when his thoughts should have been on her. She lay in his arms and nodded, maybe frowning slightly, but it was hard to tell because they were so close together. He could see only her eyes and they had not changed, still soft with love.

"Oh" was all she had said, but she shifted slightly and Shane came out of her.

"I was thinking how he would have been happy for us," Shane had tried to explain, still not confessing his real train of thought.

Alexa hadn't known Jody, not really . . . station-house war

stories, mostly, and opinions; there was certainly no short-
age of either where Jody was concerned. Jody had been assigned to the Special Investigations Section—SIS—when . . .
when he . . . well . . . when he did the unthinkable.

Alexa had been running the Southwest Patrol Day Watch
back then. Of course, she knew how the event had busted
Shane up, how it still deeply affected him. After all, Jody had
been like a brother. Jody's family had been like Shane's family.
The Deans, with their wealth and position, never once made
Shane feel like what he knew he was—a socially inept, un-
claimed orphan from the Huntington House Group Home.
They had cared about him when Shane had nobody who cared.
Jody had been like a brother all through elementary school,
high school, and the Marines. Actually, if you wanted to be
absolutely accurate, all the way from Little League through the
Police Academy.

But there was something else about Jody, something even
harder to define, which Shane had often thought about but
never completely understood. He had finally come to accept it
simply as Jody's aura, or Jody's "mojo"—some force of personality that made his ideas seem better, his jokes funnier, his
world slightly brighter. It had even been there at the very beginning, when they were only seven or eight, back at the very
start, from that first day at Ryder Field, that first Pirate Little
League practice.

Shane had been dropped off by the volunteer driver of the
Huntington House van and had joined the team. He didn't
have a father or mother to cheer him on, or a family to buy
his uniform—Jody's father stood in on both counts. Jody had
had a startling effect on him from that very first day. He had
it on everyone, children and adults alike—almost hypnotic.

You knew that if you did it his way, it would just be more fun, more exciting and that in the end it would come out all right, even though sometimes it didn't. Sometimes Jody's way produced disaster. But with Jody, even disaster could be an E-ticket event, where if you held on tight, you could come off the ride, adrenalized and miraculously unhurt. Shane had been Jody's best friend, right next to all that pulsing, hard-to-define excitement; ringmaster of the Jody Dean Circus. Everybody always came to Shane, trying to get him to do their commercials, to sell their ideas to Jody. Everybody knew that Jody was destined for greatness, until that August day in the police parking lot, when . . . when it . . . well . . . when the unthinkable happened.

Alexa rolled away from him and sat up on the side of the bed, cutting off that string of painful recollections. "Jody's dead, honey. He's been dead for three years." She said it softly, but there was concern in her tone, as if no good would come of this.

"I know. . . . It's just . . . I was thinking he'd be happy for us, that's all," eager to change the subject now, almost popping the question right then, to refocus the energy in the bedroom. If he had, it all probably would have come out differently. But something . . . maybe all those dark memories, stopped him.

"It's enough for me that *we're* happy for us, and that Chooch is happy."

"I know. . . ." But his voice sounded wistful and small. He knew that she was jealous and frightened of these Jody thoughts—feelings and memories that she had never been a part of, that had once led Shane to the edge of a dangerous crack in his psyche, then to his spiraling depression in the months just before they met. It was hard to explain to her what

Jody Dean meant, what an important part of Shane's personal history he was. She couldn't understand what the loss of Jody had done to Shane and how it had changed him. Until Chooch and Alexa came into his life, he'd been ticktocking along, heading slowly but surely toward his own dark end.

Alexa got out of bed and started to dress. Her suitcase was open on the bedroom sofa, and she had already finished packing her things, getting ready to move out of Shane's house for the week that her brother was in town.

"Buddy comes in on American Airlines tomorrow morning," she said, changing the subject.

"I'll be there, ten o'clock. Then dinner at the beach at seven. I got it all down," his tone still hectored by a confusing recipe of Jody thoughts that he couldn't completely decipher, even after all these years.

She turned and looked at him. "You all right with this?" she suddenly asked, picking up on his sharp tone, but not the reason for it. He knew she wasn't talking about Jody now or picking up her brother, but rather the awards ceremony this coming Sunday afternoon. She was going to receive the LAPD Medal of Valor for a case he'd originally discovered, then ended up working on with her. He was not being recognized. Of course, during that investigation Shane had broken more rules than the West Hollywood Vice Squad. The case and Shane's misconduct had been written up in the *Los Angeles Times*—twenty-five column inches, with color photographs describing all of his transgressions. In the face of that, the department couldn't award him the medal.

During the week they worked the case, Shane had taken a confusing emotional journey from pure hatred of Alexa Hamilton to grudging respect, to finally knowing that she was the most special person he had ever met. The case had turned his life around. Not only had he fallen in love, but Sandy Sandoval, a beautiful police informant he had once managed, confessed just before she died that her fifteen-year-old son, Chooch, was Shane's love child. Suddenly, his life had new meaning. In the end, the mayor and the police chief had both been arrested, along with a famous Hollywood producer and a real-estate tycoon. That was why Alexa was getting the M.O.V. on Sunday and why her older brother was coming to town to watch her receive it.

"I've got to get the budget review for DSG wrapped up before the end of the week." She was talking fast now, quickly getting dressed, inserting her small, department-approved brass stud earrings while trying to switch off the dark energy of Jody Dean.

She was referring to the annual budget for the Detective Services Group, where she had just been assigned as the executive officer. Normally the XO at an Administrative Operations Bureau would be a lieutenant, but Alexa, though still a sergeant, was on the lieutenant's list, third tier. She was probably less than a month away from getting her bars.

Shane got off the bed, his thoughts of Jody Dean left drifting in the wake of this new conversation.

"I'm gonna go say good-bye to Chooch," she said as she ran her fingers through her shoulder-length black hair, then turned and snapped her suitcase shut, presenting him with her classic profile for a moment. His heart clutched. . . . *God, she is beautiful.* Then she carried the suitcase out and set it down in the hall next to the front door. A moment later Shane trailed her out of the bedroom.

Chooch was not studying for his final exams at the desk in

the den, where he did his homework. Shane looked out the back window and saw that Alexa had already found him in the backyard, seated in a metal chair, going over a vocabulary list for tomorrow's test. Shane watched through the window as Chooch stood and Alexa reached out and took his hand. His sixteen-year-old son was tall and had his deceased mother's Hispanic good looks. The waters of the Venice, California, canals dappled late-afternoon sunlight across their features. Alexa was looking up at the six-foot-tall boy, who seemed intense and serious, nodding at whatever it was she was saying. As he watched them, he thought they seemed perfect together, standing, talking earnestly in the backyard of his little Venice canal house. He liked what he saw, what he felt—liked the sense of calm that all this laid against his once turbulent interior. Then Alexa leaned forward and kissed Chooch on the cheek, and he hugged her.

Shane's mind flipped back once again. *Too bad Jody isn't here to see this*, he thought.

Then he opened the door and went out into the yard to join them.

THE IMPOSSIBLE HAPPENS

• • • **S**O COACH FRY says that they have this camp every year. It's up by San Francisco, and he says he's gonna call and find out if there's still a place. That is, if it's okay with you," Chooch said, looking over at Shane, wondering which way it was going to go. They were in Alexa's powder blue Subaru, on the way to Harvard Westlake School the next morning, the morning it happened—Friday morning.

"How long is the camp?" Shane asked.

"Coach said it's about a month. It starts next week, June seventh. After school gets out."

Shane nodded. He was worried about expenses, but Sandy's estate had left money in trust for Chooch, and part of his new responsibility as a parent was to provide enriching life experiences. On the other hand, he wasn't sure that the Jim Plunkett Quarterback Camp in Palo Alto, California, qualified as life enrichment. But Chooch had a great arm, and the football coach said he would probably start at quarterback his sophomore year.

Shane had spent afternoons after his therapy sessions standing on the sidelines at Zanuck Field, watching spring ball. Chooch in practice pads, his silver helmet shining in the afternoon sun, taking his five-step drop, setting up, rifling passes to streaking wideouts on long fade or post patterns. He had to admit that his son looked good, but he was hesitant to let him go, to lose him for even a few days, let alone a month. Sandy had raised him for the first fifteen years of his life, and Shane had no idea he was the boy's father. Now, after Sandy's death, Shane was Chooch's sole parent. The newness of this obligation produced a degree of anxiety. Indecision enveloped both of them, swirling around in the front seat of Alexa's car like a sandlot dust devil.

"Why don't you ask him to make a call, find out what the deal is," Shane finally compromised.

"Solid." Chooch grinned at him.

Shane had just transitioned to the 101 Freeway and edged Alexa's car into the right lane to get off at Coldwater, where Harvard Westlake School was located. Sandy had enrolled Chooch there, and Shane was now paying the tuition—more than ten thousand dollars a year—from Chooch's trust account.

"Bud," he said softly. "Not to change the subject, but I need to get your take on something."

"The Chooch Scully Store of 'Sagacious' Advice is open," he said, using one of his new "vocab" words Shane had tested him on last night, after Alexa had left.

"I know you like Alexa. I know she's important to you, right?"

"She's the other level, man, you know that."

"Yeah," Shane said. "I was wondering . . . how would you feel about putting her into our deal, full-time?"

"You mean you're gonna knock off this light-housekeeping thing you've been doing and finally give her a long-term contract?"

"That's the idea," Shane said, smiling. "But I don't want to ask her unless you're okay with it."

"If you can get her to say yes, then get after it, dude. 'Cause you an' me won't ever do any better."

Shane smiled and looked over at Chooch, who was grinning openly.

"Okay, okay, good deal," Shane responded with relief.

Soon they were in the line of cars in front of Harvard Westlake. As they pulled up to the drop zone, Chooch grabbed his book bag from the backseat, then hesitated. "Don't screw up the proposal," he said. "Get a good ring, no zirconias. And I wanna preview the pitch. I wanna hear how you're gonna say it. You can practice on me, y'know, so you don't boot it."

"Come on, whatta I look like?"

"Like you're in over your head." Chooch grinned. "I don't want you t'blow us out on some whack move."

Shane raised his right hand and Chooch high-fived it. "Good luck on your English final," Shane said, and Chooch nodded his thanks. Then he was out of the car, still smiling as he walked up the path toward the classroom. He was instantly joined by two friends, both girls.

Shane pulled the Subaru back onto Coldwater, got on the 101 heading west, on his way to the 405 South. He would probably arrive at LAX an hour early to pick up Alexa's brother Bud, but Shane figured he could get some coffee at the American Airlines terminal amid the passenger rush, and plan this new part of his life. He was breezing along in the middle lane up over the hill, passing Sunset. He had his left arm on the open window, feeling the warm June air in his face, hidee-hoeing along, his mind freewheeling, when he glanced over and saw the Al Capone Ride—the lowered orange and black muscle car with a strange, thin layer of black dust all over it. The car was tracking along next to him in the fast lane. The man behind the wheel was looking straight ahead, up the freeway, his curly blond hair and short beard whipping in the slipstreaming wind.

Shane's heart actually stopped . . . like when you're about to get very lucky or very dead. The driver looked over at him.

It was Jody Dean.

They stared at each other for almost ten seconds, racing along, door handle to door handle, at sixty, sixty-five miles an hour, both of them frozen by the complicated moment.

Shane was filled with thoughts too mixed up to fully deal with, thoughts that started out as questions but boomeranged back as unbelievable dilemmas. His dead best friend was ten feet away, speeding along, staring over at him from the fast lane. Jody Dean, who had committed suicide, shooting himself in the Valley Division parking lot three years ago, leaving his fly-specked, stiffening corpse sprawled in the front seat of a

Department L car for the shocked officers of SIS to discover. Shane's mind double-clutched, missed the shift, and redlined dangerously. How could Jody Dean be alive? It was impossible. Jody had eaten his gun, put it in his mouth and pulled the trigger, turned his brains into blood mist. Shane Scully, his best friend, his Little League catcher and soul mate, had carried the coffin, watched it go into the furnace, cried over the urn as he handed it to Jody's grieving widow. In the months that followed, before Alexa saved him, Shane had started circling the drain himself, getting closer and closer, following Jody into the same suicidal vortex.

So how could Jody be in the fast lane of the 405, driving a dirty black and orange '76 Charger, not ten feet from him? Suddenly, Jody's expression changed, became hardened with recognition and resolve. Shane's attempt at a logical explanation was unhinged by that determined look on Jody Dean's face.

You see, Shane *knew* that look. There was no mistaking it. He'd seen that look a thousand times, going all the way back to Little League. Ten-year-old Jody, on the mound staring in at nine-year-old Shane behind the plate. *That look on his face, and in his eyes, stone cut and insistent.* Shane, crouching behind the plate, clad in his catcher's gear, each sending the other thought vibes. A silent conversation nobody else could hear. *We gotta give him the rainbow curve, man . . . or give him the slider. . . .* Jody, reading these thoughts and shaking his head even before Shane's fingers flashed the sign. *Nothin' doin', Hot Sauce . . . gonna throw the heater,* he telepathed back as clear as if he had walked up and shouted it at Shane. That was what was happening right now. Jody's thoughts shooting across the painted lane dividers from the Charger's front seat, shooting a vibe . . . a warning, plain as if Jody had shouted it: *Forget this, man. Forget you ever saw me.* And then, some kind of good-bye: *See ya. Sorry. . . .*

Suddenly, Jody floored the dust-covered Charger, shooting ahead, changing lanes around a slow-moving truck.

"No!" Shane's voice was a strangled plea. "Don't go! Not again!"

Shane pushed the pedal all the way to the floor, but Alexa's Subaru was underpowered, winding up slowly like a twenty-year-old air-raid siren, taking its time to reach full power, its thin whine lost behind the Charger's four-barrel roar. Finally, Shane was going almost a hundred, chasing the vanishing muscle car between semis and soccer moms, businessmen and airport taxis, weaving dangerously in and out amid a chorus of blaring horns and unheard curses.

The Charger was ahead, gaining ground, its loose but empty chrome license-plate holder winking morning sunlight back at him.

Suddenly, Jody cut off a Ryder van and the top-heavy rent-a-truck, with its inexperienced driver, started pinwheeling across all four lanes. In seconds, it was directly in front of the Subaru. Shane had a scary two seconds as he tried to avoid death at a hundred miles an hour. Alexa's car, broke loose, swapping ends. Then he was carouseling wildly down the freeway: the landscape strobing past his windshield—dangerous, disembodied glimpses of trees, guardrails, and concrete abutments. A kaleidoscope of images on spin cycle . . . Around and around the Subaru went, metal lint on the busy L.A. freeway, until he saw the end coming. A bridge abutment spun into view like a huge concrete iceberg.

Shane fed the little Japanese car some gas, trying to

straighten out the spin. He caught some traction, and the car made a try at straightening out, but he was still crooked and sliding sideways when he hit the wall of concrete, slamming into it hard. He felt the whole right side of Alexa's car explode, as door handles, side mirrors and paint all disintegrated or flew free, followed a second later by the whole left door—all of this accompanied by the scream of tortured metal. Shane was staring at blurred concrete graffiti and tagger art grinding and strobing past the doorless opening like the scenery wheel in an eighth-grade play.

The Subaru finally shuddered to a halt, and then it was over. He was sitting in the car, stuck in the fast lane, facing the wrong way, his heart jackhammering in his chest.

Shane spun around and looked out the back window. The black and orange Charger was nowhere to be found.

Jody Dean was gone as suddenly as he had reappeared.

YOU'RE OUTTA THERE

OKAY, SO HOW do I bullshit my way out of this one? I'm
a police officer, trained to make split-second observations but also regarded by the department as something of a
head case. I'm forced to sit in a cracked vinyl La-Z-Boy three
times a week while an overweight, balding therapist looks
across at me over templed fingers, saying, "Uh-huh," "I see,"
and "How does that make you feel?"

His career was already in big trouble. This little story
about seeing a dead man on the 405 Freeway would make
him look as though he'd started carrying his shit around in a
sock.

Shane sat in the office of the towing company, waiting for
the cab he'd called, looking out the window at a crumpled

gallery of traffic mistakes, the latest of which was Alexa's little Subaru. Aside from the destroyed right side, the car looked badly torqued to him. If the frame was bent, it was a total. Right on top of this sobering realization, his cell phone rang. He dug it out.

"Shane, where are you? Bud just called, and nobody was at the airport. He had to take a cab." Alexa sounded annoyed.

Shane had completely forgotten about Bud, the breakfast-food salesman. Shane had never met Bud but had talked to him once or twice on the phone. His booming "Hey, pal" voice always seemed jovial while still managing to convey displeasure.

"I'm sorry, honey. I hate to tell you this, but I had an accident in the Subaru."

"Are you okay?" Instant concern.

"Yeah, I'm fine." But of course, he wasn't. He was close to hysteria, his whole body shaking, his nerves buzzing like a desert power line. "I'm great," he lied, then added, "I need to talk to you. We need to sit down. I'm taking a cab over to the Glass House. I should be there in half an hour."

"Shane, I—"

"Look, I'm sorry about Buddy and the car. I'm afraid I really boxed it."

"I don't care about the car, Shane. As long as you're okay, that's all that matters."

Through the fly-specked office window, Shane saw the Yellow Cab pull into the tow company's parking lot. A round-shouldered Melrose cowboy, wearing a plaid shirt and a silver buckle the size of an ashtray, got out and started looking around for his fare. Shane motioned to him.

"Cab's here. I'll be there in forty minutes."

"Shane, you know I'm swamped getting this financial review finished."

"I need help. Something just came up. I can't go into it on the phone."

"Okay, then let's try meeting at the Peking Duck. It's fast. We can grab something while we talk, but gimme at least an hour."

"Okay," he said, and closed the phone. He heaved himself up and walked on stringy, oxygen-starved muscles out of the tow-service waiting room, then got into the Yellow Cab.

They were on the 405 heading back to L.A., Shane sitting quietly in the backseat behind the driver, looking for his bridge abutment, finally seeing the crash site sliding by across six lanes of traffic at Howard Hughes Parkway. A pound of rubber and a powder-blue slash of paint. His accident, like a thousand others, was now immortalized on freeway concrete, insignificant as a sauna-room butt mark.

A block from Parker Center was the Peking Duck, which was actually now called Kim Young's. It had been sold by the original owners after an armed robbery attempt, but the old sign was still hanging out front. Kim Young had bought the restaurant from his cousin, who retired, giving up his American Dream after four dust bunnies in ski masks had tried to take the place, unaware that half the LAPD Glass House Day Watch lunched there. This criminal brain trust of highwaymen had just pulled their breakdowns out from under cool street dusters when they were surprised to hear half a dozen automatics trombone loudly behind them. They spun around and in seconds ate enough lead to qualify as the second-largest metal deposit in California. It took a crane to lift them into the coroner's van.

Shane took a booth in the back. The restaurant had linoleum floors and was always noisy. He sat alone, waving at a few friends who came in but not over.

He thought about Jody—or more correctly, how he would explain what he had seen to Alexa. His mind was already hunting for a way out: shifting details to make them seem more acceptable, eliminating facts, pulling them this way and that. Piece by piece, he was trying to arrange the event so that it would become at least digestible, removing one crumb at a time, working to make it disappear, his thoughts like ants struggling to carry away a picnic. However, this was too big. He had to deal with it. But how? What should he do? How could he explain it?

Ten minutes later Alexa entered the place, and Shane heard the volume of conversation dip as forty or fifty guys whispered her arrival across tables stacked with egg rolls and dim sum. Then again, maybe that was just his jealous imagination—he wasn't sure. She walked toward him, her hips swaying slightly, her slender calves flexing.

She slid in, reached across the table, and squeezed his hand. "You sure you're okay? No whiplash?" she asked, concerned.

"Yeah, but your car is junk. A sea anchor."

"If it saved your life, it did its job." She smiled. "I'll cash the insurance and get a red one. I was tired of powder blue anyway."

Then, almost without knowing how he started, he was telling her, talking about seeing the Charger, seeing Jody Dean looking back at him across a lane of traffic, the heart-stopping moment of recognition . . . And then, Jody, taking off, leaving Shane in the dust; the Ryder van pinwheeling in front of him until the Subaru finally ground to a halt under the bridge on the Howard Hughes Parkway.

Alexa didn't say anything while he was telling it. "Shane," she said after he had finished. "Jody is *dead*. We talked about it last night. What is it? Why do you insist on? . . ." She didn't finish, but instead, let go of his hand.

"His suicide never made sense to me. . . . I couldn't believe he'd kill himself," Shane said. "He wasn't the kind of guy who eats his gun."

"Yet cops who seem normal do it all the time. . . . When it's a good friend, it's just harder to accept."

"Alexa, I may be going through a psychiatric review, but I'm not a psycho."

"Jody is dead," she repeated. "You carried his box to the furnace—gave his ashes to his wife. You *know* he's gone."

"Then who did I see on the freeway? He ran, Alexa. Took off. I crashed because he cut off a truck and it almost hit me. Why would he run if it wasn't Jody?"

She sat there quietly, looking at him, for a long time, trying to find the right thing to say. Then she lowered her voice and leaned toward him. "I want you to let this go. Okay? I want you to keep quiet about it and let it go."

"Don't think it'll look good in my package? Help dress up my psychiatric review?" he said sarcastically.

She smiled a tight smile. "I'm sure there's some explanation. Jody's body was identified by his wife and by his commander at Detective Services Group . . . who was it back then?"

"Captain Medwick."

"Right. Carl Medwick. He and Lauren wouldn't identify the body if Jody wasn't dead."

"Yeah . . . yeah . . . of course. Probably not." The conversation stopped, but these ideas lay between them, festering malignantly.

"You just saw somebody who looked like Jody," she added.

Ants working hard, tugging at crumbs, still trying to make this untidy idea go away.

"Of course, you're right," he said, with more enthusiasm. "That's gotta be it. Gotta be. And he ran because . . . because . . ." He looked up for help.

"Because, sometimes, Shane, when you stare at people, you can look very ferocious. The driver of that Charger just got scared."

A big piece, an important piece, dragged . . . hauled, actually, to the edge of the blanket, but not gone . . . not quite yet.

"You're right," he said. "Shit, I probably scared the poor guy, whoever he was, half to death."

"I've seen you do it."

"He probably thought I was some lane-change killer about to pull a gun and start blasting."

They both sat there anxiously, trying to buy it, hoping for the best, like family members waiting for a biopsy.

"Yeah . . . God, what was I thinking? The guy sure looked like Jody, but it wasn't him. Couldn't've been," Shane said.

Alexa nodded.

But as he sat there in the Peking Duck trying to convince himself, he remembered that look again—Jody's look. In his memory he saw little ten-year-old Jody, standing on the mound, shaking off signs in frustration, sending Shane his own brand of telepathy . . . Jody-thoughts coming in on their special frequency. With this realization, the self-deception ended. It *was* Jody in that Charger, talking to Shane without having to speak, just like in Little League. *Stop screwing around, man. . . . I'm gonna throw the heater.* Rearing back, going into his windup, burning it in there . . . Shane, knowing the pitch without even flashing the sign. Cowhide slapping leather. Fastball. Right down the old pipe.

Strike three, asshole. . . . You're outta there!

QUESTIONS 4

WHAT HAPPENED NEXT made no sense at all.

Since Shane had missed his psychiatric appointment because of the accident, he decided to kill the early afternoon pursuing this dilemma. He'd promised Alexa that he'd forget about Jody, forget about seeing his dead best friend tooling along on the San Diego Freeway instead of doing what he was supposed to be doing—gathering dust in an antique urn.

Shane broke his promise to Alexa because he had to. He got Jody's old commanding officer's address from the department newsletter mailing roster, then cabbed home to Venice and picked up his black Acura. Chooch's last spring practice wouldn't finish until six P.M., and Alexa had agreed to pick him up in a department car. Shane had lied, telling her that his shrink appointment had been pushed back and that he'd be late getting out of the psychiatrist's, freeing himself to go see Jody's old captain.

Captain Carl Medwick lived in a *Leave It to Beaver* neighborhood in the West Valley: maple trees, picket fences, tricycles parked unattended in the driveways, as if L.A. hadn't become the bike-theft capital of the world, not counting Miami and Singapore.

Shane parked out front and looked at the wood-frame house painted a light blue—Subaru blue. He was beginning to loathe that color.

He rang the front doorbell and then, after the door opened, found himself staring into the bloodshot, tear-filled eyes of a handsome middle-aged woman wearing a loose-fitting cotton-print dress and comfortable shoes.

"Excuse me, ma'am. Is Carl Medwick home?" he asked. The question caused the woman to bring a lace handkerchief up to her eyes. It fluttered there and landed hesitantly, like a delicate white butterfly. She didn't answer. He tried again.

"I'm looking for Carl Medwick."

"We all are," she said, her voice weak, almost a whisper. "He's not here. He didn't come home last night."

"Didn't come home?"

"He went to the store and didn't come back. We talked to the police, called all his friends, checked the places he goes, we even checked the hospitals." Rambling all this at Shane, not even knowing who he was but needing to say it to somebody . . . to anybody . . . ticking off the details of her search to convince them both that nothing had been forgotten.

"I'm Shane Scully, a sergeant in the department," he said, stretching the truth. He was really suspended Sergeant Scully. Psychiatrically disoriented and temporarily unassigned Sergeant Scully. But the fib worked, because the woman reached out and clutched his hand. "I'm Doris Medwick, his wife. Please tell me you found him."

Shane held her hand, looked into her bloodshot eyes, and shook his head sadly. "I'm afraid I'm not a part of the Missing Persons Bureau," he said.

"Oh . . ." She hesitated, then went on. "He . . . he was in his woodshop, working . . . building a birdhouse for our grand-daughter. He said he needed some materials and would be back in twenty minutes. Then he drove to the store. They found his car in the parking lot at the Hardware Center, but he didn't . . . he wasn't . . ." The handkerchief came up again, fluttering around her face, wiping her eyes, blowing her nose. She was a stout but attractive gray-haired woman in her late sixties with almost translucent white skin.

According to information Shane had collected from several of Medwick's friends, the captain had retired, having pulled the pin two months ago.

"Could I take a look at his shop?" Shane asked.

"What possible good could that do?"

"I'm a detective," he fudged. "Sometimes I find it's a good idea to study the events that occurred just prior to an incident."

"Oh," she said. "The other policemen didn't ask about that." She led him through a house filled with discount furniture. Despite her husband's disappearance, the room was freshly vacuum-tracked and dusted. Shane had witnessed this behavior before. The families of a victim often busied themselves with chores, as if the mere performance of those every-day acts restored order and normalcy. *Look how nice the carpet looks for when he gets home, and I've polished the furniture. Everything is all right.*

Doris Medwick turned on the garage lights and left him alone. Shane found himself looking at a very professional woodshop area. He moved to Captain Medwick's workbench and glanced down at the skill saws and jigs, the power sanders and drills. In the corner, vise-clamped to the bench, was an almost completed prefab birdhouse. The box it came in called it a Squirrel-Proof Robin's Roost and Feeder. The sides were glued and the screws countersunk. The roof had been assembled but not attached, and a plastic water dish was fitted into a wooden feeding tray. It was made of fresh-smelling, unpainted pine and was about two feet square, not counting the pitched roof. It was easy to confirm what had happened: Carl had run out of brass screws. The empty box was on the bench, and two drilled holes in the underside of the birdhouse remained empty. The project lined up with Doris Medwick's story.

Shane stood there, looking down at the unfinished birdhouse while a feeling of deep-seated unease swept over him. Carl Medwick had been Jody's commander at Detective Services Group. Carl had identified Jody's body. He'd finished his tour on the LAPD, pulled the pin, and, thirty-four months after Jody's suicide, had started his retirement. Then yesterday, the day before Shane saw Jody on the San Diego Freeway, Carl runs out of screws, goes to the hardware store, and mysteriously disappears.

The timing of these two events, like the unfinished Robin's Roost, was for the birds. He turned off the lights and left, pausing at the back door to say good-bye.

"You will call if there's anything, anything at all? . . ." the distraught woman pleaded, still not registering the fact that Shane was not part of her husband's missing-persons investigation. He had a strong feeling that Carl Medwick was going to stay lost.

"Absolutely," he said, adding, "who did you talk to at the Missing Persons Bureau?"

"A woman, Detective Bosterman."

"Thanks. If I get anything, I'll be in touch."

He left, in a hurry to get away from there, lickety-splitting down the trimmed driveway, past the gardening shack by the garage with its neatly stored rakes and hoes and top-folded bag of Lawn-Grow. Mrs. Medwick tracked him from the back porch until he got around the corner. He could feel her blood-shot eyes on him, steady as government radar, pinpointing a spot directly between his shoulders.

■ ■ ■

It took Shane half an hour to get Lauren Dean's new address, finally finding it through his old Homicide Division, getting Sergeant Bill Hoskins to grab it off the computer for him.

Lauren had moved since Jody died and was now in a small, one-bedroom duplex in a run-down section of Downey.

By the time Shane pulled up, it was already three-thirty in the afternoon and he was scheduled to be at Moonshadows restaurant in Malibu by six forty-five. It was going to be tight.

Shane parked in front of an old, weathered-concrete two-story building with paint-chipped shutters and tried to come up with an approach. How would he tell Lauren that he had seen her dead husband on the freeway just that morning? He sat there, trying to find a subtle opening, finally realizing there just wasn't one. He decided he had to ask straight-out if she'd viewed her husband's body as everyone claimed she had. He could see Jody's old green Chevy Malibu in the drive, so he figured she was home.

Shane climbed out of the car and walked into the courtyard. The building was badly in need of maintenance. The drainpipes were broken at the gutter spouts, the wood trim unpainted and termite-eaten. *What the hell is Lauren Dean doing living in a dump like this?* But in the next instant, he realized the answer: because Jody had committed suicide, the widow wasn't entitled to any Department loss-of-life death benefits.

He rang the bell and stood there while fear swept over him. *What am I afraid of? This is all going to make sense eventually.* It had to. There are no ghosts, no paranormal events. Facts were just missing, and those missing facts were creating a distorted picture. When he filled in the blanks, it would all make perfect sense. . . . *It better start making sense,* he thought.

Lauren Dean opened the door. Since he'd last seen her two years ago, she'd gained forty pounds and looked twenty years older. Cynicism and disgust had pulled the once happy curve of her mouth down into a permanent scowl that she seemed completely unaware of. Once beautiful—stunning, in fact—Lauren Dean was now plump and used up: her skin mottled, her clothing dirty, her fingernails a nerve-frayed war zone of nibbled cuticles. It was as if he were looking at somebody else—the ghost of Lauren Dean, or her ugly older sister.

"Shane?" she said, and he could smell scotch on her breath.

"Lauren, I need to talk to you about Jody."

She looked at him for a moment, not moving or breathing. "Jody?" she finally said.

Again, he could smell the liquor. "Could I come in?"

A hard question for her. He could see indecision seesaw back and forth in her pale green eyes. Then she stepped back reluctantly and let him into the apartment.

The place was a mess. Round pizza boxes dotted the living-room furniture like giant tomato-stained mushrooms. Shane picked a spot on the sofa and sat across from Lauren.

"What about Jody?" she challenged.

"Lauren . . . I need to find out something. It's gonna sound a little strange, so hang with me here, but I think I saw someone today on the San Diego Freeway who looked a lot like Jody. In fact, exactly like him."

"Oh, Jesus, gimme a fucking break." She snorted a puff of stale scotch at him.

"I know . . . I know . . . but it's bugging me and I just wanted to get clear on this. When they called you after he . . . after he . . . did the . . . did the . . ." Shane couldn't say it, even now, almost three years later.

"You mean after he blew his fucking head off?" Lauren finished the thought for him, bitterness and anger stretched across her face, pulling her mouth down farther, flattening her features like a nylon stocking mask on a drugstore bandit.

"Yeah, after they found him. They called you down to the ME's office. Did you get a good look at the body? Was it him? Were you absolutely sure? 'Cause the guy I saw . . . I didn't talk to him, but it looked like he recognized me. . . . I could sorta read it in his eyes."

"I always used t'wonder about you two guys finishing each other's sentences, like you were hooked together by cable," she said, not answering his question. "After I first married him, before Jody ate the nine and turned my whole life to shit, he used to say he thought you and he had both been the same person in another life, said he could tell what you were thinking, say it before you said it."

"He could—sometimes he could."

"And now . . . it's hard for you without him, you miss him. So subconsciously you're trying to bring him back."

Shane started to answer, but stopped. Was that what he was doing?

"Let him go, Shane. Let Jody go. He's dead. Believe me, I know. D-E-A-D. Dead." And then she smiled at him. A ghastly smile it was, too. Her teeth were tobacco-stained, and her new double chin quivered. "Let the motherfucker go. Hasn't he done enough to the both of us? Hasn't he?"

"Did you identify the body like it says in the death report?" he persisted.

"Yeah. Yeah, I looked at him. The back of his head was gone, but it was him. It was our precious, go-to-hell Jody, no doubt about it. I don't know who you saw on the freeway, but it wasn't him. Jody walked out on us, babe. The selfish prick put that cannon in his mouth and blew all three of us away with one shot."

Shane looked at the wreckage that was now Lauren Dean. He wondered how she could have let this happen.

"I'm sorry, but you can't stay," she said abruptly. "I was just going out. . . . I have an appointment." She slurred the word *appointment,* missing most of the consonants.

She stood and led him to the entry, anxious to have him out of her house. She opened the door and stood by it as he walked behind her in the underlit hallway.

As he was about to pass by her, he saw something that stopped him, made him reevaluate everything she had just said. Jody Dean had zeroed himself out—taken a pine box retirement. Yet there, on the table in the hall, was an unopened envelope just like the one Shane got every two weeks from the City Payroll Department.

She led him out into the late-afternoon sunlight and closed the door without saying good-bye. He stood there on the porch, his mind reeling. "What the fuck is going on here?" he whispered softly. One more in a series of unanswerable questions. *If Jody committed suicide like everybody says, why is his widow still getting paychecks?*

DINNER

MOONSHADOWS SAT ABOVE the rocky beach in Malibu. Waves rolled under it in sets, crashing on the rocks below, throwing a fine sea mist up into the air that refracted in the setting sun.

Buddy, the breakfast-food sales and marketing executive, was already there with Alexa and Chooch, telling a story. Buddy was round-shouldered and pear-shaped with a bushy head of hair, which salt-and-peppered his massive head. ". . . so the sales rep is telling me he can't sign up the tri-state area, 'cause the little guys, the minimarkets and such, won't compete with the huge category killers—the chains like Ralph's or Vons—on new product lines. I tell the guy: Stop crying, this is a candy store problem, 'cause our money is just as green as theirs, and all you gotta do is find the right palm to grease. Give the local rack-jobber his blood money."

Alexa looked up and saw Shane approach, jumping to her feet to give him a hug.

"Buddy, I'd like you to meet Shane." Alexa was trying to orchestrate everything.

Shane shook Buddy's big fleshy hand. Buddy was soft and out of shape, but he was big, almost six-four.

After the introductions, they all sat down to a tense meal where Shane felt more and more like the main course.

"So how bad did Alex's car get mashed?" Buddy asked, getting the conversation rolling. He seemed to call her Alex instead of Alexa, as if it somehow made her one of the boys.

The evening crawled by like a half-crushed bug dragging itself across a four-lane highway. By nine o'clock, Buddy had eaten his main course and half of Alexa's and was just finishing the third basket of complimentary bread, ordering his sister to get a new basket after each one was emptied.

When Buddy wasn't treating Alexa like a servant, he was patronizing her. Never once did he bring up the Medal of Valor award she was going to receive on Sunday. His sister was being given a huge honor, the LAPD's highest, yet he didn't seem to care. It was hard for Shane to believe that someone he loved and looked up to would allow herself to be so overrun by this loud breakfast-food salesman.

Chooch stayed quiet, trying to keep out of the cross fire, while Buddy switched from the subject of Alexa's car to questions about Shane's medical leave.

"So, it's like some kinda shrink deal?" he asked, a concerned frown pulling two caterpillar-shaped eyebrows toward each other. "But, you're okay, though, I hope?" Smiling now. "You're not gonna snap and start comin' at us with a razor?"

"I'm fine. It's no big deal," Shane said, choking back several more confrontational replies.

"In police work, psychiatric reviews are standard," Alexa explained less than truthfully.

"But it's with a shrink, right? A psychiatrist," Buddy persisted. "The LAPD *makes* Shane go and see a head doctor. That's what got me worried, 'cause you don't see that happen in business unless the guy's parked out in the ozone, where the buses don't run."

By ten o'clock, it was mercifully over. Alexa drove Buddy to his hotel. Shane drove Chooch back to their house. Alexa showed up half an hour later and met them in the backyard.

"So, what did you think?" she asked anxiously, wanting his approval.

"Quite a guy," he said evasively.

"But did you like him?" she persisted.

"More to the point, do you think he liked me?" Shane said, hedging.

"He's a little judgmental sometimes, I admit. But you'll learn to love him. He just wants what's best for me."

"He sure orders you around a lot," he finally contributed.

"I'm used to taking care of him. Mother died, so by the time I was ten, I did all the housework, all the cleaning, for Dad and Buddy. I guess he just got used to me doing things."

"Alex, can you get us tickets to *The Producers*?" Shane mimicked. "Can you go ask the waiter to get us more bread? He doesn't have a broken leg, does he?"

"So, you didn't like him?"

"Yeah, I liked him. It's just . . . He treats you a little like hired help."

Then Chooch saved him: "What Dad is saying is, we're used to seeing you be in charge. You're everything around here for us, and we always want to do stuff for *you*. It's a little different seeing you with your brother . . . but we think it's neat the way you take care of him. That's what he meant."

"Exactly what I meant." He smiled at her.

Chooch went inside to do his homework while they sat in the backyard, looking out over the Venice canals.

Venice was located halfway between Santa Monica and Marina Del Rey. It had been built by Abbot Kinney in the thirties, to resemble the canals and bridges of Venice, Italy, but the eight-block area had gone downhill. Just two blocks from the ocean, it still managed to retain a sense of quaint, rustic charm, but the once grand houses and reproduction gondolas had been replaced by fiberglass rowboats and a mixture of stucco houses and wood-frame tilt-ups.

Regardless, Shane loved his little house. It spoke to him in ways he found hard to describe. He and Alexa sat in his metal lawn chairs, watching the moonlight waver on the still waters of the shallow canals.

"Aside from wrecking my car and seeing Jody's ghost," she said, trying to be lighthearted about it, "how was the rest of your day?"

"Fine."

"I hope you didn't do something else—start running around investigating the Jody thing."

He didn't answer.

"I'm just interested," she said softly. "And a little worried."

"Captain Medwick is missing. He was building a birdhouse for his granddaughter, then went to the hardware store for brass screws yesterday and didn't come back."

She sat quietly, her cop instincts buzzing with this fact, just as his had. "Doesn't have to be connected," she finally said.

"I know."

After that they both fell silent awhile. Then he gave her the rest of it: "I also went to see Lauren Dean. She says that it was definitely Jody on the coroner's tray. She said the back of his head was blown off."

Alexa didn't say anything.

"Only thing wrong with that is, I think she's lying," he said.

"Why would she lie about something like that?"

"Because she's still getting paid by the city. There was a City Payroll Department envelope on her hall table. If Jody shot himself, why would the city be paying her death benefits?"

"There could be lots of reasons. She could owe money to the credit union and be getting statements, or it could be tax material . . . or she . . ." Alexa stopped and looked over at him critically as he leaned down and pulled out a blade of grass, then stuck it in his mouth.

"You're not gonna give up on this, are you?"

"I'm just telling you what I saw."

"I'm gonna set up a meeting for you with Commander Shephard."

"Why are you gonna do that?" Shane asked, instantly wary.

"I want him to show you Jody's autopsy report and crime-scene pictures. He could get those for you. He heads the Detective Services Group. They supervise SIS. Jody was in Special Investigations when he died, so Commander Shephard can pull all that stuff from the custodian of department records at the Personnel Division. He can get it for you without turning it into a three-act play. You've gotta get this off your mind."

Shane sat there, chewing on the grass stalk, turning it between his teeth, feeling it tickling his tongue. "Good idea," he finally said. "Thanks. I'd really like to see all that."

"How soon do you want to go see him?" she asked.

"How 'bout tomorrow," he answered softly.

THE GOOD SHEPHERD

AFTER YOU GET used to it, it's not so bad here," Jody said. "It's not heaven, but it's not hell. You'd like it, Shane. We got everything we need." Jody was talking to Shane, but he was lying in his casket. The back of his head was missing and he had on his old Pirate's Little League uniform. It was stretched tight over his adult body, his pitcher's mitt laid ceremoniously across his chest.

"Everything you need?" Shane asked. He was wearing his old catcher's gear but was having trouble keeping the mask on straight. It kept sliding around on his head, blocking his view.

"Everything we need, 'cept one thing . . ."

"What's that?"

"Coca-Cola. Can you beat it? No Cokes here, and me with my sugar jones raging all the time."

"No Coca-Cola?" Shane asked, dumbfounded. "I never thought about the hereafter not having Cokes. You'd think they'd have 'em if you asked."

Then Jody sat up, leaving his brains behind. "Dammit," he said, looking down at the bloody mess on the white satin pillow. "That keeps happening."

Suddenly Shane woke up. He lay in his bed, staring up at the ceiling. It took him two hours to get back to sleep.

■ ■ ■

Mark Shephard's office was on the sixth floor of Parker Center—the administrative floor.

Shane and Alexa got off onto the seafoam-green carpet, then walked down the corridor, past the blond-paneled doors, where the four deputy chiefs and the super chief had their offices.

The Detective Services Group, which Shephard commanded, was in the Office of Operations and supervised five detective divisions: Bunko-Forgery, Burglary–Auto Theft, Detective Headquarters, Robbery-Homicide, and the Detective Support Division, which included the controversial Special Investigations Section (SIS), where Jody had been assigned when he took his life.

SIS had come under a lot of fire in the press recently because it was a super-secret section, with a very unusual operating technique. Their critics claimed they would target predicate felons, usually parolees just out of some Level 4 institution. All of their targets had long, violent criminal histories. It was alleged that they would set up surveillance on the scumbag, often lying back and just watching while the ex-con bought illegal street artillery at some gun drop (a fresh felony and parole violation) or hung out making criminal plans with some other "yoked" and "sleeved" ex-cell soldier (also a parole violation). They wouldn't bust the target for these violations but would wait until he and his ex-con buddies finally pulled some major Class A felony: a holdup, armed robbery, kidnapping—you name it. The members of SIS would follow the targets away from the crime and exercise their patented car-jamming maneuver. This consisted of speeding up in two or three department plainwraps, then jamming the target vehicle to the curb . . . whereupon six or seven adrenalized, heavily armed cops would do high-risk takedown. As a result, SIS had bought a large percentage of these assholes seats on the ark. Because of the high body count, and growing number of incidents where civilians were accidentally injured or almost killed by stray gunfire, city activists were constantly gunning for the unit, and SIS was always in the pot, on slow boil.

Jody had been in SIS for almost a year before he ate his gun in the division parking lot. A lot of people said it was the pressure of the unit that brought him to suicide, but Shane knew that Jody relished the work there. He said he loved the rush, the adrenalized risk taking. But most of all he loved "capping assholes."

They had discussed SIS a month before Jody died. It had turned into one of their few really bad arguments. Shane hated the unit and everything it stood for. SIS was holding court in the street and, to his way of thinking, was little more than a death squad. Shane had left Jody's house moments before the argument got violent.

• • •

Alexa's office was down the hall, on seven. She was the XO of the Detective Services Group and the only sergeant officed there. She'd been given a small room, with no window and a shared secretary. As Shane and Alexa waited in her office, they heard Mark Shephard come in and get his coffee. They were told by his secretary that he would see Shane after he went through his mail.

"What'd you tell him about why I wanted to see the file?" Shane asked while they waited.

"I told him the truth, that you saw somebody who looked like Jody on the freeway and that you wanted to set your mind at ease."

"Jesus, Alexa, I'm in the middle of a ding-a-ling review. That's all I need right now."

"What else can we tell him?"

"I was gonna say Lauren asked me to look at the file. That she needed some information for his life insurance or something and couldn't bear to see that stuff again."

"He's not a moron, Shane. He wouldn't go for that. Besides, we can trust him. He's a friend."

"He's *your* friend. I barely know him."

"They don't call him the 'Good Shepherd' for nothing," she smiled. "He's good people; he won't blow you in."

A uniformed lieutenant in her late twenties appeared in the doorway. "The commander is ready now."

■ ■ ■

Mark Shephard was a climber in the department, but he was an unusual mix—a uniform-friendly commander who also had Glass House suck and deft political skills. He reminded Shane a lot of his first Boy Scout leader: tall and good-looking, with a tan complexion and blond hair. Mark Shephard's blue eyes crinkled with what seemed like ever friendly amusement.

"Sorry to keep you waiting, Sergeant," Shephard said. He wore his blue-steel revolver on his belt in a Yaqui Slide holster, the flap snapped down over a black checkered grip. A lot of Glass House politicians, who had done the minimum amount of street work, packed chrome-plated, custom-gripped artillery—but not the Good Shepherd. This was a no-nonsense piece. He had his coat off, and Shane could see that he stayed fit.

"Thanks for seeing me," Shane said.

"Any friend of Alexa's . . . I'm really proud about the ceremony, her getting the MOV. As her commander, I'm honored to be reading the citation this Sunday, before Tony gives her the award." Tony was the new chief of police—Tony Filosiani—a street cop from New York who had applied for the job of top cop in L.A. after Chief Brewer was arrested. He had been chosen over other candidates because of his record of turning around morale in troubled departments. Los Angeles had had a string of police crises, from Rodney King to the Rampart Division scandal to the Naval Yard disaster.

Chief Filosiani was short and round and talked out of the side of his mouth in New York Brooklynese. As a result of this and his penchant for large pinky rings, he had been dubbed the Day-Glo Dago.

"I guess the best thing is to just take a look at Sergeant Dean's death package," Shephard said, interrupting his train of thought.

Shane nodded.

Commander Shephard pushed the folders over. Shane sat down in the chair opposite the desk and opened them.

Shane had never seen Jody in death. He'd pictured it in his mind, of course, but his subconscious had neatly sanitized it. His imagination was nothing like the photographs. As he opened the folder, his stomach lurched. His throat constricted.

It was worse than he expected. In the pictures, Jody was sprawled in the front seat of a department plainwrap.

The details were graphic: the puckered blood-drained lips, the huge hole blasting away half of the back of his head, the green flies feasting on heavy arterial ooze. Shane could see Jody's gun, the big Israeli Desert Eagle he'd been using at the end. The .44 magnum automatic was light in weight but 30 percent bigger than the old army .45. It dangled in death, at the end of Jody's broken finger, like a child's forgotten toy. The recoil had obviously snapped his index finger, and as a result, the gun hadn't flown from his hand as was normal in most suicides.

Shane went through the autopsy and crime-scene pictures carefully, forcing himself to study them: Jody slumped in the front seat leaking fluid fatally; Jody on the coroner's table. The clinical labeling screamed from the bottom of each photo: anterior angle, medial angle, proximal and midline photos; right side, left side, overhead. Jody, naked on a steel autopsy tray, bathed in sterile lighting and antiseptic brutality.

Finally Shane went to the autopsy report itself. The ME's phrases jumping up, posting themselves forever on his memory: "massive trauma," "self-inflicted gunshot wound," "destroyed distal portion of the cerebellum." Then the death terms: "cadaveric spasm," "adipocere," and "acute cyanosis."

Shane read it all, finally closing the folder. He looked up at Commander Mark Shephard, who had turned his attention to the mail on his desk but now felt the gaze and lifted his friendly blue eyes to meet Shane's. "Well?" the Good Shepherd said. "What do you think?"

"I must have been wrong," Shane answered softly.

NIGHT 7 MUSIC

THE PHONE SCREAMED in his ear. He clambered up out of a restless sleep. *Where's the damned clock? What the fuck . . . ? What time is it?* Focusing now on the lit dial, trying to read it: a few minutes after two in the middle of the night. *You gotta be kidding.* He grabbed the phone, fumbling it out of the cradle.

"Yeah?" his voice raspberried.

"How they hangin', bro?" Jody's voice was grinning, having fun with this back-from-the-grave moment.

Shane bolted upright in bed, his heart immediately slamming with adrenaline, banging unevenly, a four-barrel engine with a bad cam. He was gripping the receiver hard, his knuckles turning white, his palm instantly slick on the instrument. "Jody? Is this Jody?"

"Back from the Great Department in the Sky. Thought you and I needed a little night music," his term for the late-night talks they had during sleepovers as kids.

Shane was wide awake in less than thirty seconds; sleep was quickly broomed away like corner cobwebs. He swung his feet off the bed. Got them down onto the floor for stability.

"Why? . . . Why? . . . Why did you do it? Why did you make us think you were dead? I cried, man. It really fucked me up."

"Hey, it's just police work, Salsa. I'm doin' a job." Jody had nicknames for everyone; nicknames were a "Jody" thing. He'd called Shane "Salsa" or "Hot Sauce" almost from the beginning, because in the old days when they were children, Shane had a short fuse and often couldn't control his temper.

"You're still on the job?" Shane said, trying to pin down that fact. "With the department?"

"Yeah, but you didn't hear it here. I'm working UC."

"You're undercover?" Astounded, still trying to find the edges of it. In his heart he had known that Jody was alive from that first moment he saw him on the freeway last Friday, but hearing his voice was different—spooky, surreal.

"It's a big laydown, so a few of my old road dogs and me been bustin' moves and doin' doors on some serious assholes." "Doin' doors" was an old term referring to cops stealing from drug houses but more recently had come to mean any activity where cops cheated to get busts. Shane took a deep breath to settle down. It was unbelievable . . . Jody on the phone, in the middle of the night, talking trash, sounding wired. "We found out there are a few moles in the Clerical Division who would've given us away if we got regular paychecks. This is a big hustle,

Salsa. Lots of chips on the table. We needed to work the bust from the inside."

"What bust?"

"Hey, come on . . . You know better than to ask that."

"Jody . . . I . . . Look, Jody, I have to see you."

"Ain't gonna happen. Can't happen. Reason I called is, I know you'll pull on this thread till you unravel the whole sweater, and that could fuck me up. You gotta chill, brother. You gotta leave this behind. Forget you saw me. Don't 'plex up on me, Salsa."

"Plex up"—a prison term meaning to get complex. *Why is he using con lingo?*

"Does Lauren know?" Shane asked.

"No, I cut a deal with my CO. . . . Told 'em she wasn't solid . . . she'd give us up. I needed to get out of that. It took a while, and I had to pull some juice downtown, but in the end, the department went along. She thinks I'm dead." But he said all of this slowly, as if considering it a word at a time. Shane figured it could mean anything.

"She's not doing well, Jody. She's gained weight. She's become an afternoon drinker."

"Hey, Salsa, shit happens. I made a mistake with her. I thought it was love, but it was just my dick. She's okay. She's got my police pension. I got a medical pass on the suicide. They said it was caused by psychiatric stress, so it protects my death benefits. 'At's the best I can do. After this job, I'm gating out . . . gonna get small, shake off the drag line."

More prison lingo. "Gating out" was release from custody. "Drag lines" were prisoner restraints, linking cons together.

"So, Shane . . . I called 'cause I didn't want you to mess me up. A lot of people could get fucked unless you keep this to yourself. I hadda eat some shit to get my people to stay frosty. A few guys wanted to send you some GBH." More prison talk: "grievous bodily harm."

"Jody, is this sanctioned?" he heard himself ask. But he knew it didn't matter how Jody answered. He knew he couldn't trust anything he said.

"I'm not working off my badge, Hot Sauce. I'm just working off the books. Do yourself a favor and forget you saw me. Forget we were both on the 405. It didn't happen. Do that, and everything stays right side up."

"And if I don't?"

"Don't even suggest it, man. I Jodyized this deal! Make me a hero with my troops. I told 'em you'd see it my way—*our way*. I told 'em you were good people. And, Salsa, don't tell anybody about this call. With your current problems, those squints in the Glass House are gonna black-flag what's left of your career."

"Where's Carl Medwick?" Shane asked suddenly.

"How the fuck should I know. Home in bed, I guess."

"He disappeared the day before I saw you."

"Now you're acting like a complete asshole. If you keep this up, it won't come out good."

"So you're threatening me now?" Shane said, his voice turning cold with anger and betrayal.

"I'm just passing along information. Use it, or don't."

Then there was a long, tension-filled pause. Shane could hear Jody breathing. Both of them were waiting to see what would happen next. Finally, it was Jody who broke the silence.

"So, that's all I wanted to tell you. Miss you, man. Sorry we can't lay in together."

"Lay in"—prison lingo for a meeting.

"I'll see ya, Salsa. You're still my catcher, like always. Dig this pitch outta the dirt for me. Go Pirates!" And then he was gone.

Shane sat on the corner of his bed for a long time, stunned. The receiver finally started beeping in his hand. He dropped the handset back in the cradle, got up, walked out, and sat in one of the white metal chairs in the backyard. He felt the cool ocean breeze drying the sweat on his face. He stared at the moonlit canals, trying to sort out what Jody had told him.

Is it possible? he wondered. Could the LAPD be working a deep sting so dangerous and sensitive that they would fake the deaths of Jody and several other officers? Would they take them off the books, so some criminal snitch working in the Clerical Division wouldn't spot a paycheck coming through and sell the information to a crime syndicate? Was it possible that these guys would leave their wives and that the department would arrange for their families to be paid with death-benefit checks and then just let them disappear? It was almost too bizarre to contemplate. Except for one thing . . .

Shane was pretty sure the new chief wouldn't have anything to do with it. The Day-Glo Dago might talk out of the side of his mouth and wear a New York pinky ring, but his reputation for honesty was well known.

Burleigh Brewer, the old chief, whom Shane had caught with his hand in the money jar, was a rule bender, and rule benders always hired people who go along and don't ask questions—people like Deputy Chief Mayweather. Only Mayweather was dead—a suicide after Shane broke him on the Naval Yard case. Chief Brewer was still alive; however, he was on trial and wasn't going to admit to putting an illegal unit into deep cover, paying their wives with death checks. Even if Brewer was in on it, which he may not have been, and even if Shane could prove it, Brewer would blame it on Mayweather or some other cop who wasn't around to argue. The old chief wouldn't say anything that would adversely affect his case in court. That door was closed. Even so, it was possible that the corruption that spawned the Naval Yard disaster could have also given rise to this.

He sat there, his mind chewing it over. What should he do? How should he play it?

Tomorrow afternoon Alexa was getting the Medal of Valor. Maybe after the celebration dinner, after he had taken Buddy back to the airport, maybe then he could ask her advice. Alexa had political savvy without being a politician. She'd know what to do.

Shane had no evidence of the call from Jody. He'd get AT&T to print out his phone records, but he knew Jody would have used a public booth—a number that was untraceable.

Don't plex up on me, Salsa, his old friend had said.

"Well, fuck you, Jody," Shane whispered into the night wind, the anger and betrayal so intense that acid reflux burned in his throat. *If you didn't love me enough to say good-bye . . . if you could let me carry your coffin and cry into your ashes, if you didn't trust me or Lauren, the people who loved you, then bring on the GBH, buddy. . . . 'Cause I'm gonna find out what the hell you're up to. . . .*

He was still sitting in the metal chair, churning and making plans, when the sun came up Sunday morning.

MORE THAN THE EYE CAN SEE

CHOOCH AND SHANE went shopping for Alexa's ring on Sunday morning. Murray Steinberg opened his store in the Jewelry Mart on Spring Street at ten, turned on the lights, and began showing them diamonds. Murray was tall, rail-thin, and nerdy. He always seemed to be rubbing his palms together like a huge skeletal insect but had a heart the size of Minnesota.

Shane had been the primary on Sharon Steinberg's rape/murder. She was Murray's sister and only living relative. It had been a particularly gruesome crime that had happened almost three years ago. Shane had promised Murray that he would never let it slide to the back of his too-crowded homicide folder. Sharon Steinberg had been tied up, mutilated, and raped in her own bed before she finally, mercifully died from loss of blood.

The twenty-four/twenty-four-hour rule dominates most homicide cases. This unwritten rule states that the last twenty-four hours of a victim's life and the first twenty-four hours after the murder is committed are the two most important time periods in the investigation. The reason being that a victim's actions just prior to the crime are just as important in determining the killer as mistakes the perp makes in the first twenty-four hours after the murder. If nothing happens during these two time spans to help solve the investigation, chances are good that the crime will go uncleared.

Because of the vast workloads in L.A. Homicide, with two or three fresh murders hitting the duty board every day, most homicide detectives put old, unsolved cases on the back burner. Because of administrative pressure to keep clearance percentages up, cops always focus on the fresh crimes, where the likelihood of success is higher. The unsolved cases are technically still active, but not actively policed.

In the case of Murray Steinberg's sister, Shane had become so incensed by the level of perimortem violence that he refused to stop working the case. He knew that the perp was in the psychiatric category of "sadistic rapist," a man who had tortured and humiliated Sharon Steinberg before her death, dehumanizing her during the rape, making her an actress in his sexual fantasy. Shane had given up his days off for almost six months, working without overtime. Finally, he had managed to turn a witness that eventually led to the arrest of a thirty-year-old carpet cleaner and weekend dust bunny named Grady White. Grady was a hot-prowl burglar who cased his jobs when he cleaned carpets. He had entered the house to steal appliances but, after seeing Sharon asleep, had descended into glazed sexual rage, finally torturing, raping, and killing her. In Grady's house there were Polaroids neatly pasted into a memory book of not only Sharon's rape-murder but ten others. Shane got him prosecuted and convicted on six of the ten. Four women pictured in his book remained unidentified. Grady was currently awaiting a July 10 execution at San Quentin.

That was why Murray had opened his store on a Sunday and was now showing Chooch and Shane VS-1 diamonds at wholesale prices. Technically, Shane probably should have refused the bargain, but somewhere in the back of his head, he reasoned that it was the right solution. Murray was finally paying Shane back for months of tireless work on Sharon's murder, and Shane was getting a ring he could otherwise not afford.

Shane finally settled for a perfect stone at slightly over two carats, which would have retailed for around five thousand dollars. Murray refused to take a cent more than cost, which he maintained, was thirty-four hundred. The old jeweler left the showroom with a platinum setting to make up the ring so Shane could take it with him.

Chooch and Shane sat silently, looking at the other diamonds glittering on the black velvet show cloth. They looked like stars in a cloudless night sky.

Finally, Murray returned with Shane's ring, now twinkling in a classic setting with two diamond baguettes on each side, which Shane had not paid for.

"My wedding gift," Murray said when Shane asked about them.

Shane thanked the embarrassed jeweler, who said, "Acht, is nothing. I'm wishing I could do more, my friend."

Soon Shane and Chooch were back on the street with the box burning a hole in Shane's pocket, the ring inside waiting to be slipped onto Alexa's slender finger.

"When you gonna give it to her?" Chooch asked nervously.

"At a romantic dinner tonight, after Buddy leaves."

"Good move," Chooch agreed. "Wait'll he's outta town. That guy could sink a Carnival Cruise."

"You don't think it's too soon?" Shane asked, suddenly nervous. "The Medal of Valor and this ring, all in one day."

"Go for it, man."

•••

The Medal of Valor ceremony took place at three in the afternoon, in the Jack Webb Auditorium at the Police Academy, where the LAPD had their biannual graduation ceremonies. The academy was a cluster of Spanish-style buildings located in Elysian Park in the foothills, at the end of a long, two-lane drive. Shane always thought the Police Academy looked like a Spanish hotel or a Franciscan mission, sprawled on its ten landscaped acres, including a full athletic field, swimming pool, and shooting range.

Shane and Chooch got there half an hour early and parked in the reserved-parking lot, already almost full with TV news vans. The annual awarding of the Medal of Valor was always a big deal in L.A. Besides Alexa, there were four other officers receiving the honor, but it was Alexa the press had turned out to see.

The high-profile case that she and Shane had broken eventually made the cover of *Time* magazine, a full picture of an LAPD shield with a black ribbon across it. The article was titled "Grieving the Police."

There were stories in the issue about the Detroit and Philadelphia police scandals as well as NYPD's problems, but the Long Beach Naval Yard case turned out to be the granddaddy of them all. Alexa's picture was in a sidebar describing her incredible heroics.

Shane and Chooch walked into the auditorium, which was already almost full. He saw Buddy up near the front. Shane waved at him, but Buddy either pretended not to see him or had decided to ignore him.

A tall, good-looking lieutenant in plain clothes from Press Relations grabbed Shane moments after he arrived.

"Sergeant . . . good. I was hoping I'd spot you. We have a special place for you," the lieutenant said. His ID was in a badge holder hanging upside down in his suit pocket like a Spanish leather bat.

"What about my son?"

"He can sit here. We thought you'd want to be up close."

"Go ahead, Shane," Chooch said, grinning. "I'm cool." Then he plopped down in the back.

Shane was led out of the auditorium, along a side corridor, and into a small room with a TV monitor that showed a picture of the empty podium.

"You can see it better from here."

"Whatta you kidding me, Loo?" Shane said, using the nickname reserved for all lieutenants while glowering at the handsome recruiting-poster officer. "I'm supposed to watch it back here, on TV?"

"Look, Sergeant." The Press Relations officer was now talking slowly, as if addressing an irritating child. "The last thing we need today is to have the press make *you* the story." He looked at Shane hopefully. "I'm sure you want Sergeant Hamilton's day to go smoothly."

Shane knew in his heart that the man was probably right, so he finally nodded, but it still pissed him off. Shane was being hidden away like a leper. He reached into his pocket and secretly wrapped his fingers around the jewelry box containing Alexa's diamond ring. "Okay," he finally said. "But will you tell Alexa I'm here?"

"Of course. Absolutely." It sounded like bullshit rolling smoothly out of the handsome press officer's mouth.

"Hey, Loo, no kidding . . . she needs to know I'm here."

"I wouldn't kid about this, Sergeant. I never kid about anything," he said, revealing a shred of his humorless personality. Then he turned and left Shane alone in the room.

That was when the third strange thing happened.

Shane watched on the color TV in the isolation room as the event was postponed for almost fifteen minutes. He slipped out of his makeshift holding cell and found out that Commander Shephard, who was scheduled to read Alexa's citation, had not yet arrived.

As a result, the award ceremony began half an hour late, and the other four officers received their MOVs first. Their commanders all read their commendations, then the chief awarded the medals. Then it was Alexa's turn. Since Mark Shephard had still not shown up, Chief Tony Filosiani stepped to the microphone and ad-libbed some remarks:

"Obviously, I was still back East, running da Rye, New York, department, when all dis happened," he said in Day-Glo Dago Brooklynese. "Now dat I'm here in Los Angeles and have had the opportunity of dealing with all of you, I wanna say, I'm humbled by the extreme bravery Sergeant Alexa Hamilton displayed in the completion of her assigned task. We all should take pride in her profound dedication to her duty, and to the people of dis city." He turned from the podium and faced her.

"Sergeant Hamilton, you are among the finest officers I have ever been privileged to command, an it is with great pride dat I present you with dis, our department's highest honor."

Alexa blushed, standing at attention in her blue pressed and starched uniform, her black hair shining.

Shane had not returned to the Press Relations room; he was standing in the auditorium's wings, looking out at her. He, like Chief Filosiani, was also very proud of her, while at the same time experiencing a sinking feeling of concern for the missing Commander Shephard.

Has he disappeared like Captain Medwick, his predecessor at DSG?

Chief Filosiani read the citation. It described how, while she was at Internal Affairs, Alexa became aware of a high degree of police malfeasance involving a Hispanic gang named the Hoover Street Bounty Hunters, whose turf was located around the L.A. Coliseum. She discovered that arrested gang members were easily escaping from the police cars in that division. They were often not Mirandized, so their cases were thrown out of court. On one occasion, an arrested Bounty Hunter had been left unattended and just got out of the back of a squad car and walked away. The citation explained that these police screwups had been sent to IAD, where Alexa had noticed that police officers in these incidents were all involved with Shane's dead ex-partner, Ray Molar. Alexa had followed the trail of this investigation to a huge real-estate scam involving the defunct Long Beach Naval Yard. LAPD Chief Burleigh Brewer and L.A. Mayor Clark Crispin had been silent partners in that venture and were arrested two weeks later. The citation further stated that in the apprehension of the criminals, Sergeant Hamilton had been severely wounded. Of course, Shane, who had originally brought all of this to Alexa's attention and had helped solve the case, was not mentioned in either the citation or the chief's portrayal of her heroism.

As he stood in the wings, Shane had a fleeting moment of jealousy and anger directed at Alexa. How had it come to pass that no matter what he did on the job, he always seemed to come out a loser? He knew the answer as soon as he asked the question. He tended to grate on his superiors. Shane had, on occasion, tried to be politically correct, to kiss ass, but it never came off right; plus he hated the taste it left on his lips. Alexa, on the other hand, never kissed ass but seemed to have the ability to get her points across without rancor. She was tough and uncompromising; somehow, unlike Shane, she didn't irritate everyone in the process.

He ultimately had to admit that his failure had been more a question of style than substance. He stuffed these ungallant thoughts away, then watched as Alexa stepped forward after the citation was read and the chief hung the medal around her neck. It glistened there, shining in the TV lights, as the room full of people applauded.

A press and media buffet in the Police Academy cafeteria followed. In its typical killjoy fashion, the department served soft drinks instead of champagne. People stood around in clusters, stealing looks at their watches and saying what a wonderful ceremony it had been. Shane hugged Alexa, then, while she accepted congratulations from staff rank officers, he moved through the room, again looking for Commander Shephard, who had still not arrived.

The Press Relations lieutenant worked Shane like a sheep-dog, screening him from the media, herding him here and there, trying to keep him away from anybody holding a mike or a camera. Shane, of course, obliged willingly, not wanting to begin another round of negative press coverage on the case or embarrass Alexa.

Finally, Shane and Chooch were back in the Academy parking lot, looking at the rear door of the Jack Webb Auditorium, waiting for Alexa to come out.

"That was cool," Chooch said, not realizing that Commander Shephard's no-show was a potentially dark omen.

"Yeah," Shane said, holding the leather ring box inside his pants pocket, gripping it, feeling the corners digging into his palm. "Listen, Chooch, I'm gonna go for the quarterback camp. I think that's a good deal. I called the coach, and he's setting it up."

"You sure we can afford it, man?"

"Yep. Gotta do it."

"It starts in two days. I could probably go up a few days late."

"Nope. You gotta be there when it starts. I'll figure out the plane reservations when I take Buddy to the airport." Shane let go of the ring box, reached out, and put his hand on Chooch's shoulder. "But I'm gonna miss you, man."

"Maybe you can come up and watch."

"I'll try," he said, but he already knew what he was going to be doing. The quarterback camp would put Chooch in Palo Alto, safely out of Jody Dean's reach, because he didn't know how ruthless Jody had become. Right now, Shane wouldn't put anything past him.

Alexa walked out of the Jack Webb Auditorium and over to

the car. She had changed out of her dress blues and was wearing a plain black skirt, white blouse, and heels, carrying the uniform in a hanging bag, smiling as she approached the car. The MOV was in a gold-lettered leather box stuffed under her arm, significantly larger and more elegant than the box in Shane's pocket.

"Great ceremony," he said giving her a hug.

Chooch did the same. They stood in the Police Academy parking lot, all shifting their weight awkwardly.

"Next stop, dinner with Buddy," she said. Buddy had left the ceremony shortly after it was over. "He had to go back to the hotel and get packed," she alibied.

"So what happened to Mark Shephard?" Shane finally asked. "That was strange, wasn't it?"

"I don't know. I called his office and his house, but there was no answer," she said.

A heavy cloud passed overhead, further darkening the parking lot and the moment.

"Listen, I think on the way to dinner, we should swing by Shephard's house," Shane said. "There could be more here than the eye can see. This guy is a Glass House commander. I doubt he'd miss a chance to make the six o'clock news."

"It *is* pretty strange," she agreed.

"So, let's do it." Shane said. And that decision took them on step further down the road to disaster.

DUTCH TREAT

SHANE AND CHOOCH followed Alexa's department-issue Crown Vic to Commander Mark Shephard's house in the Valley. It was strange, Shane thought, that Alexa knew exactly where he lived. They pulled up in front of a small Spanish-style bungalow—typical L.A. construction from the mid-forties. The house had a red-tile roof, arched doorways, and a small, neatly trimmed front lawn. A spill of purple bougainvillea garlanded off a garage trellis.

"This is it," she said, exiting her car and joining them at the curb.

Shane stole a glance at her. "How many times you been here?" he asked with forced casualness, trying not to come off like a stiff-necked jealous boyfriend.

"Had to drop some budget stuff off once or twice," she said, not looking at him.

"Okay, let's go see if he's home." He got out of the car, and Chooch scrambled out of the backseat. "Stick out here by the car, will you, Chooch?" Shane asked.

"How come?"

"Just wait by the car, okay? I'm not sure what we're gonna find."

"I think you're being overly dramatic," Alexa said, but her voice seemed guarded.

They left Chooch and moved up to the front door of the house. It was locked, so they rang the bell. No answer. No key under the pot, over the jamb, or in any of the other no-brainer hiding spots.

They rang the bell three more times.

Shane moved around to the garage and looked in the side window. A dark green, department-issue Crown Victoria staff car was parked inside. "Car's here," he said. *Not a good sign.*

Next they tried the back door—also locked. He decided he'd have to break in, so he took out his small set of lock picks.

"Those things again?" she said, wrinkling her nose at them.

"We could just stand out here until the neighbors report us," Shane said.

She nodded, so he slipped the picks out of the little leather case. The set contained half a dozen slender needles with widened ends, and one larger shaft piece. The trick was to work the pick's wide shaft into the lock, then slip the needles in under it, twisting them so they'd fill up the spaces inside the tumbler lock. Once he had enough purchase inside the dead bolt, he could turn the collection of picks to throw the lock. Shane had seen several newer-style lock-picks used by state-of-the-art B&E men. The most recent consisted of long strips of a new metal alloy attached to a heating coil. They were first slipped into the lock, then heated up by the coil until the soft metal melted into the lock. The alloy dried quickly, hardening and allowing the bolt to be turned. But Shane liked his old-fashioned Sam Spade set better. It took a little longer, required more skill, and appealed to his sense of police noir.

He got the door open and smiled tightly at Alexa; then they moved into a small, white-tile-and-wood-trimmed kitchen.

Mark Shephard lived alone. For a bachelor, he was uncommonly neat: dishes washed and stacked on the drip tray, washcloth folded neatly over the goosenecked faucet that hung over an old-style metal sink. They passed out of the kitchen, into the dining room.

Shane could smell him before he saw him. The sweet, sick odor of flesh decaying in a self-liquefying bath of butyric acid.

The Good Shepherd wasn't looking so good today. He was sitting in his Archie Bunker armchair, directly in front of the TV, wearing gray slacks and a white dress shirt, his shoes laced neatly on his feet. His head was thrown back with his mouth wide open, as if he had fallen asleep in front of the tube. Except for two green flies crawling in his mouth, he looked peaceful. His .38-caliber Smith & Wesson was halfway across the floor behind him.

He had shot himself in the temple, or so they were supposed to believe. The entrance wound was round and neat. Purple-black blood and cerebral spinal fluid had oozed from the hole, staining his shirt collar and shoulders. There were what looked like second- or third-generation maggot larvae festering inside the wound. Shane knew that each generation represented approximately twelve hours, indicating that he had been dead somewhere around thirty-six hours, or at least since yesterday evening.

"Oh, my God," he heard Alexa whisper. "No . . . no . . . please, no."

Shane glanced at her and saw a look of shock and pain tightening her features. She seemed pale and frightened—not exactly Medal of Valor crime-scene behavior. However, Mark Shephard was her friend, he reasoned. The Good Shepherd had arranged for her to be his XO at Detective Services . . . arranged it early, even before she had made lieutenant. So they were close. It was hard to witness a close friend in terminus situ, oozing blood and hosting fly larvae. Even though they were cops and had seen it before, she would find this difficult; that's why she seemed emotionally wrought.

He reached out and touched the body. It was loose, the flesh jiggled . . . rigor mortis had already come and gone, confirming his rough estimate of TOD.

"Suicide. Why would he commit suicide?" he heard Alexa say.

"Yeah," Shane said, now noticing some more disturbing pieces of the crime-scene puzzle. Shane was a homicide detective, so right off, three things bothered him—two small, the other large. First, and least important, was the fact that Mark Shephard had his shoes on. Most suicides, approximately 80 percent, remove their shoes before killing themselves. The why had never been adequately explained to him, but they did it nonetheless. It was troubling only in conjunction with his two other observations. The large event was the bullet itself. It had entered Mark Shephard's right temple, but had not come out again. The gun was on the floor where it had supposedly been thrown from his hand by the recoil after the shot. It was the same checkered-grip .38 that Shane had seen on his belt in Shephard's office Friday morning. Shane knew that a full-load, 110-grain .38 caliber slug traveled at a velocity of 995 feet per second and had 240 foot pounds of muzzle energy. These were manufacturer's stats. So the big, hard-to-explain piece was why the bullet had not exited the other side of Shephard's head, taking half his skull with it like it was sup-posed to?

The third thing Shane noticed was that at the edge of the wound, there was "tattooing" from the exploding gunpowder coming out of the barrel. Most tattooing from guns held close to the head made a tight pattern around the wound. The tat-tooing around Mark Shephard's wound, however, was about an inch from the exterior circumference of the bullet hole, in-dicating that the bullet Commander Shephard had used to take his life was most likely a standard-police-issue, light-load car-tridge. Light loads were the hated ordnance of all street cops because they contained half the gunpowder of a full load. The reasoning was that if a police officer got into a gunfight in the street, the bullet would carry only half as far and not kill an innocent civilian feeding a parking meter a mile away. It also had damn little velocity, so when fired close-up, it left this wider tattoo.

Mark Shephard was a cop. Cops were issued light loads. A light load wouldn't necessarily go all the way through Shep-hard's head and out the other side. It would cause this wider tattoo. That's physics. That's the way the cartridge is designed. So what's the problem? What's wrong with this picture?

Only one thing.

Shane had been on the job for almost twenty years, and in all that time he'd seen or heard of hundreds of cops screwing their service revolvers into their mouths or ears and doing a Dutch Treat. But in all of those cases—every single one—the cops used full loads. Not one of them had tried to kill himself with a light load, and the reason for that was obvious: there was a high degree of probability that a half load wouldn't get the job done, like in the street, where it sometimes failed to even slow down an enraged assailant. Half loads, most of the time, managed only to maim or cripple.

Why had Mark Shephard used the underpowered cartridge? Was this a suicide, or could it be a murder? Had somebody used the commander's gun to kill him, unaware that it contained Remington Lights? While these thoughts were going through his mind, the situation became even more complicated when he heard Alexa sobbing.

He looked over and saw her sitting on the sofa, her head in her hands, crying. He'd only known her well for half a year, but she was not a weepy woman. Why was this street-trained police officer who had witnessed the worst of man's inhumanity to man sitting on the sofa crying like a heartbroken relative?

Shock? Yes.

Dismay? Of course.

Anger and depression? You bet.

But tears, uncontrollable tears, at a crime scene?

What the fuck is going on here?

AFTERMATH

THEY DIDN'T GET out of Mark Shephard's house for hours. Buddy had to take a cab to the airport, and Chooch drove the Acura home. Shane and Alexa stood on the Good Shepherd's neatly trimmed lawn while the ME and lab techs did their gruesome work: bagging the corpse's hands, photographing the body with its growing colony of fly larvae.

Alexa watched in silence. Somewhere around six, the body was wheeled out and put into the coroner's wagon. The windowless, black Econoline van pulled slowly away from the little Spanish house, taking its resident away for the last time.

Shane looked at Alexa, who had regained her composure but seemed drained, almost shrunken, standing in front of Mark Shephard's house, watching his corpse leave.

"Tough, huh?" he finally said.

She nodded but didn't say anything.

"Listen, I think we need to go someplace and talk about this," he suggested softly.

She looked at him, her gaze unfocused, her features pulled tight in an expression that seemed trapped somewhere between a frown and a squint, reflecting her emotional devastation. She nodded but still didn't speak.

"You hungry?" he asked.

This time she shook her head.

Jesus, for the love of God, say something. I'm dying here. But Shane said only: "I could use some food. Lemme buy you some coffee."

She finally spoke. One word, only two letters; sounding hesitant and unsure.

"Okay."

Shane had told the ME that he suspected the fatal shot was a light load. The ME concurred, also referencing the wider tattooing and the lack of an exit wound. Shane told the ME they were leaving and left his pager number, then drove Alexa's Crown Vic back toward Venice while she looked glumly at the passing neighborhoods.

They hadn't spoken about it, but with her downer brother safely out of town, Shane had intended for her to move back in, to spend the night in his bed at 874 East Canal Street. He stopped a block away from his house at a small restaurant on the beach.

The place was called the Hungry Termite, which always struck Shane as an unlikely, unappetizing name. He had never been able to find out why it was called that, but the cover of the menu had a stick drawing of a termite eating a sandwich.

They sat at a patio table and listened to the surf crashing on the sand a few hundred yards away.

"I'm sure Buddy got to the airport okay," Shane offered, to get the conversation rolling.

"Good . . ."

"I'm afraid I didn't turn out to be much of a taxi service for him."

Again she just nodded.

"Alexa, we need to get the needle off deep grief for a minute and start thinking more like cops," he said, angry at the way she was behaving. It was almost as if she'd been sleeping with the guy.

"Christ, Shane, gimme a little time to deal with this. He was a good friend."

"Right. He was a good friend. I get that, but I'm not so sure this isn't somehow connected to Jody being back."

"*Jody?*" She seemed appalled at the suggestion. "Good God, Shane, Jody again? We're still on that?"

"I don't think Commander Shephard killed himself," Shane said, and the remark sat there between them, a big unwashed idea with absolutely no hard evidence supporting it.

"I beg your pardon?"

"I'm just doing police work here, okay? I'm trying to make sense of this."

"Right. Jody is alive. Got it. Makes great fucking sense."

"Alexa, you've been with me during a pretty intense investigation. In fact, it was a good enough investigation to win *you* the Medal of Valor." *Shit*, Shane thought, he was now sort of bitching to her about not sharing the award. But she didn't react, so he went on: "You know I can look at facts and construct truth, or at least sometimes I can." Hating the way this was going, sitting here, doing his own dumb-ass commercial while she swirled her coffee around in a chipped Hungry Termite mug using a stainless-steel spoon. "There's a lot of stuff on this unnatural death I don't like the look of."

"Let's call it suicide since that's what it is," she said. When he didn't answer, she added, "I'm listening." But there was a dead, listless quality to her voice.

"Okay, why would he shoot himself with a light load?"

"Distraught."

"Come on, I don't buy it. He's gonna take a chance on coming out a vegetable? You ever see a cop do a Dutch Treat with a light load?"

"Shane, people do stupid things in times of stress. Mark was obviously stressed. He . . . he . . . God. . . . Do we have to talk about this?"

"Yes, we have to. Jody is alive, Alexa. He called me last night. He told me he was working UC on some high-profile case, said he was 'doing doors' on predicate felons and that the department had supplied him with a new ID and faked his death so that his crew wouldn't get busted by moles in the Clerical Division. In Payroll. They're actually paying death benefits to the wives of the guys in his unit. That's how they're getting their police salaries."

She sat there, with anger in her eyes. At least the dead indifference had disappeared. Anything was better than that. "How would they ever pull that off?" she said. "The department isn't going to be involved in cops doing felonies, committing crimes to get criminals, then faking death payments, Shane. That's the most insane thing I've ever heard."

"Not Tony Filosiani, but the old department. Chief Brewer might have done it, or Deputy Chief Mayweather, before he killed himself to avoid jail. This thing predates Filosiani. It started back with Chief Brewer. Mayweather was head of Special Investigations Section. He was supervising the Criminal Intelligence Group and the Organized Crime Division. Do you, for a minute, put it past him to recruit a buncha walk-alones out of SIS or some of those testosterone cases from SWAT, guys who wouldn't mind scoring points the old-fashioned way? You know Mayweather might have sanctioned a group like that."

"And put it under Mark Shephard, a decent, honest cop?"

"Yeah, maybe," Shane said softly.

"No fucking way. Mark wouldn't do that."

"Okay, Alexa, we also need to talk about you and Mark. I know this is a shitty time for it, but I'm sensing more than professional respect here." His hand was back in his pocket, tightly gripping the little box containing Alexa's perfect VS-l, two-carat engagement ring. He knew she wouldn't lie. The answer to this question might determine whether the ring would ever end up on the third finger of her left hand. "Was there more going on there?" he asked, his voice tight.

Alexa sighed, and took a sip of coffee. She seemed to be steeling herself in preparation for Shane's reaction. "You're right. Mark and I were more than just friends," she said quietly.

The sentence arced around inside him like loose volts of electricity. His right hand flinched; his stomach rumbled dangerously, threatening to erupt.

"We used to date. Nobody in the department knew, because

he wanted it that way. He was a commander; I was a sergeant . . . and two years ago he asked me to marry him. I turned him down, but I came close, Shane. I almost said yes."

"And why didn't you?" He was numb with this, not thinking, just reacting.

"I didn't marry him because something told me not to. . . . Something told me that even though I found him extremely attractive and sexy, even though he was sweet and considerate, and had a great sense of humor—"

"Okay, okay. I get the point," he interrupted. "Go on."

"Something told me that he was close, but not the one. In the end, I respected him a lot but didn't love him quite enough."

"And so, when he asked you to take over as his XO at Detective Services Group, that was his chance to be around you so he could get the romance going again."

"Maybe he saw it that way. I can't speak for him . . . but I told him I was seeing you and that I wasn't looking to have an affair with my commanding officer. I wouldn't consider sleeping with the boss on management principles alone. Mark said he understood but wanted me there anyway because I was the best person for the job. And, dammit Shane, I think I am."

Shane sat there, inert, unable to find the right words to express his emotions.

"I won't deny I had strong feelings for him," she went on. "I still do. I'm sorry I lost it at the crime scene. That was unprofessional. It just hit me hard. I wasn't ready to see him that way."

"It's okay," Shane said, but it wasn't. He had almost crushed the little box in his pocket. He didn't expect Alexa to be a virgin, but the idea that she'd recently been so close to marrying another man agonized him. "Look, Jody is alive," he said finally, to get his mind off it. "I know 'cause I talked to him. SIS was Jody's division when he disappeared. My guess is that this secret unit, whoever they are, is being run out of Special Investigations, because I get the feeling from what Jody said that he's in charge."

"How do you know that?"

"Because Jody was always in charge. It's just his way. He wouldn't be in the unit unless he was running it."

She nodded. She'd heard enough stories about Jody Dean to know that was probably true.

"If this crew was being run out of SIS, then Mark Shephard would have been the unit supervisor, their administrative division commander. Most of these deep-cover units have only two or three contact people, staff officers who know they exist. My guess is Mayweather was one, but he's gone. Medwick ran Detective Services until two months ago, and now he's missing. And trust me, he won't be coming back from the store with his box of brass screws. . . . He's in a shallow grave somewhere, curled around a bag of lye."

"And now Mark," she said.

"Yeah, Commander Shephard completes the trio. So if these three are gone, who's the department CO? Who's running this bunch a' kazoonies?" When she didn't answer, he answered for her: "You are, Alexa. Whether you know it or not, you're the XO, so you're now in charge. I think they're constituted under some subgroup in SIS under DSG. You're acting head of Detective Services until Chief Filosiani appoints a new head."

"You're serious about all this, aren't you?"

"Alexa, he's *alive*. Jody is alive. I don't know who doctored those crime-scene photos and the death report Shephard showed me, but with computer-generated imaging, you can do almost anything with photographs today. I'm telling you, Jody's death was rigged. Lauren Dean is either in the dark or lying, but either way, she's so screwed-up about it, she's turned into a lush. Everybody else who knew about this unit at DSG is dead or missing. I think we've got a huge problem here."

She sat looking across the table at him, taking all of this in. "If you believe that, then you need to take it to the chief. . . . You need to tell Filosiani."

"The Day-Glo Dago? This guy talks out of the side of his mouth like a Brooklyn cabdriver. You're acting head of DSG. . . . I'm telling *you*."

"I'm just a sergeant. If you believe all this, you need to go to a staff-rank commander or above, and for reasons of security, I suggest the chief. Filosiani didn't get to the LAPD in the front seat of a cab. He was one of the best street cops in New York. He's cleaned up three departments and has been honored at the White House. He's a smart, tough, in-your-face police officer, so if you think Jody is running a criminal conspiracy and is killing his commanders, then you better take it to him and not just your girlfriend because you don't trust anybody above the fifth floor at the Glass House."

They sat there looking at each other, chewing on this for a long time.

"If I decide to do that, would you go with me?"

"I don't think Jody is alive. I think you're—"

"What?" he interrupted. "Making it up?"

"Why do you want me to go with you?"

"Because it's your responsibility as XO and because you've got heat. Today you won the Medal of Valor . . . and because you owe me." *There. He'd finally said it, but he knew it had come at some cost to their relationship.*

She looked out toward the ocean, her beautiful profile to him. Finally, she turned back, but she didn't answer. She sat there, pondering thoughts too difficult for him to read or for her to relay. Loss and despair completed the mask of confusion on her face.

11

TOMATO FARMING

ALEXA CAME BACK to Shane's house with him, but she was quiet most of the way. He pulled her Crown Vic into the garage next to his Acura. They got out and went into the house, where they found Chooch asleep on the living-room sofa, his algebra book across his chest. Alexa slipped out the door to the backyard while Shane shook Chooch's shoulder.

"Hey, bud," he said.

Chooch opened his eyes and looked up as if Shane had just beamed down from the teleport room of the *Enterprise*. Then recognition dawned as he yawned. "Just resting my eyes," he said "Last final tomorrow."

"I think you should rest the whole machine," Shane said, taking the book off Chooch's chest. "You know this stuff.

Once you've got the formulas, you can't study for algebra. You should get a good night's sleep."

Chooch cocked a wary eyebrow. "Yeah?" he said. "And just what'd you get when you took this course?"

"Doesn't count." Shane grinned. "Statute of limitations ran out on that crime." Shane helped Chooch to his feet. He glanced out the window and saw Alexa on the lawn, her back to the house, staring at the canals, both arms wrapped around her as if she were cold on that warm June night.

"You give her our rock?" Chooch asked, following Shane's gaze out the window.

"No, not yet. Something came up. It didn't seem like the right time."

"Don't screw this up."

"Don't worry. Now get to bed," he said, and Chooch shambled off to his room.

■ ■ ■

Later that night Shane and Alexa made love in his cluttered bedroom. It started off well enough: some gentle caressing at the beginning, with Shane moving his hand over her soft, tight body, finding the place between her legs, rubbing her while her arms encircled his neck, her breath warm on his ear. But somewhere between the beginning and the end it turned competitive, with both of them on top of the sheets, bathed in sweat, thrusting their hips at each other, climax finally coming in a ferocious moment that more closely resembled anger than love.

Instead of closeness, loneliness followed the event.

"I've been thinking about it, and I changed my mind," Shane said as they lay on his bed in the dark room. "I can't go to Chief Filosiani. If I do that, my career is over. I have zero evidence. I can't prove that I saw Jody or that he called me. If

I try and bring all this up—Medwick and Shephard—I'm gonna look like a jerk."

She rolled toward him and looked at him carefully. "I think that's the best way to handle it," she said, softening as he held her. "Honey, if you insist on pressing this Jody thing, it will turn out bad. . . . You're almost through your psychiatric review. Once that's done, you're back on the job. Maybe then, if you still feel this way, you could look into it. But if you do it now, you could get pushed into forced retirement."

"But let's suppose I'm right. Let's just say, for the hell of it, that I did see him, and let's suppose he *is* doing doors. Don't we need to stop him?"

"It's a matter of timing, Shane. Now is the wrong time."

"I'm not going to the chief anyway," he said, knowing that she was right. A move like that would be an event Filosiani couldn't ignore. Without a shred of evidence to back up what he saw, his career would be over. He didn't trust the Day-Glo Dago, despite all the stories going through the department about the legend of Tony Filosiani, the "policeman's policeman." Shane wasn't yet ready to put his entire twenty-year career into the hands of the short, round-faced man who talked out of the side of his mouth and looked as though he should be in the corner market, cutting up flank steak.

Chief Filosiani had hit the LAPD like a shaft of white light from the first day he took over four months ago. His first day on the job he had witnessed four cops trying to wrestle a crazy old homeless man through a metal detector at West Hollywood Division. The man had been arrested for walking naked down Santa Monica Boulevard, wearing only a silver biking helmet. He said that he was from the planet Argus and wanted an audience with the President. There were four large uniformed cops fighting with this deranged and panicked old man in front of the booking cage, trying to force him to put on a city jail jumpsuit and go through the metal detector into the holding-cell area. The four uniforms were rolling on the floor, trying to cuff him, when a short, balding man in a shiny suit stepped forward and gave a space salute, slamming his fist onto his chest.

"Welcome to the planet," Filosiani bowed. "It is with great honor and respect that we welcome visitors from your galaxy." The man jumped to his feet and returned the salute, standing naked in front of the four sweating cops.

"I am the interplanetary ambassador for Earth people, and I will be your escort while you are a visitor here. Is this your desire?" the new chief continued in Brooklynese.

"Yes," the old man said.

"It is our custom that visitors to the Earth Senate and Presidential Chamber wear the honored robes of the Interplanetary Guest Council. Would this be acceptable?" Filosiani bowed again.

"Yes . . . I will wear your robes," the man said, bowing in return. Filosiani reached out and took the orange city jail jumpsuit out of a startled cop's hands. The old man shinnied into it, pulling up the zipper. Then Tony bowed once more to the old man, who bowed back.

"Now, as is our custom, it is necessary to take you to our Interplanetary Medical Center where you'll be screened for diseases and bacteria from the planet Argus that may be harmful to the people a' Earth. Will this be acceptable?"

"Yes . . . I understand."

"Our galaxy medical officer here will escort you," he said. Tony gave the old man another space salute, which was returned, then they bowed a fourth time, looking like two Japanese businessmen. One of the cops led the homeless man quietly through the metal detector guarding the entrance to the West Hollywood Division booking cage. He walked peacefully into the holding cell, wearing his new orange Earth clothes and silver biking helmet.

The old man was booked without further incident and taken to the mental ward at County Hospital.

The four cops had by now figured out who the short, round man in the shiny suit was. They stood and listened as Tony gave a lecture on how to handle deranged or disoriented people: "This old man is sick," he told them. "You guys don't fight or wrestle with a sick person. Y'buy into his fantasy and he'll follow ya anywhere. Do it right, fellas," he said, smiling. "Save all this rough-and-tumble stuff for the hard cases."

The story spread like wildfire. After Chief Brewer, L.A. was ready for a top cop with a shrewd streak of humanity. But still, Shane wasn't ready to go in front of the little man with his Jody Dean story, at least not yet. Not until he had something more—one piece of concrete evidence.

Alexa elected not to sleep over, and Shane didn't try to stop her. She took her car back to her apartment in Santa Monica. They were badly out of sync and needed time to get past it.

Shane put the little leather box containing her engagement ring inside the top dresser drawer and finally went to bed.

He didn't dream of Alexa and he didn't dream of Jody. Strangely, he had a dream about tomato farming. He was sitting on a huge green tractor, trying to plow a straight furrow so he could plant his tomato seeds. But the tractor kept going its own way, despite his efforts to steer it. The huge green machine left a wavy, drunken furrow behind him. "Dammit," Shane kept saying, as the tractor wavered. "Dammit, stay straight, will ya." It was a difficult night of farming.

THE CANOE FACTORY

THE NEXT MORNING Shane went to Mark Shephard's autopsy. The ME performing the examination was Dr. Clyde Miller, a notorious civil-service character. He wore tie-dyed T-shirts under his white medical smock and sang old Beatles tunes while he cut up corpses.

"It's been a hard day's night, and I been working like a dog," he warbled at ten A.M. to the accompanying screams of a bone saw in the autopsy room. The procedure was taking place in operating theater three of L.A.'s huge medical examiner's facilities. The next-in-line corpses were on rolling gurneys in the narrow basement corridor, all waiting under ironed green sheets, with red name tags wired festively to their bloodless toes. They were bumper to bumper under the fluorescent tubes, surrounded by the throat-clogging cologne of the newly departed—formaldehyde mixed with preserving chemicals. It was a sad little parking lot of last night's traffic and gun mistakes.

Commander Mark Shephard was the only self-inflicted gun-shot death that morning. The physical inspection of the body was just getting under way as Shane arrived.

"Hey, Sarge, welcome. Another opening, another show," Miller caroled, switching momentarily to Cole Porter as Shane entered the room. "Was this poor guy a friend?"

"No, I found the body."

"Hard way to go," Miller grunted, and switched back to the Beatles, altering a lyric here and there as he continued his physical inspection of the lower extremities. "Hey, Jude, don't make it bad / Take a sad song and make it better / Just don't hide the reason you're gone, and this Doc will find the answer, answer, answer, answer." He broke into the "na, na, nas" as he went over Commander Shephard's legs and feet, inch by inch, looking for any exterior abnormalities before making his Y-cut at the sternum, then emptying and weighing the Good Shepherd's heart, liver, and kidneys.

Shane was standing at the head of the table when Dr. Miller suddenly stopped singing and turned to his medical assistant, a black woman Shane had never met, who was functioning as his "diener" during the autopsy. "Whoa, Nellie. Whatta we got here," he said, raising an eyebrow.

Both Shane and the tall African American woman moved to the foot of the table to see what he had found. There, on Commander Mark Shephard's left ankle, on the inside just above his medial mallealous bone, was a small, two-inch, hand-drawn tattoo of a Viking head in profile. A horned helmet dominated the artwork.

Shane looked at the tattoo, then took a small camera out of

his pocket that he always brought to autopsies to photograph anything of note for his case folder. He carefully shot the tattoo from different angles.

Two things about the tattoo bothered Shane: First, most police officers would rather cut off one of their fingers than get a tattoo anywhere on their body. They viewed tattoos as a mark of the criminal underclass. Cops who already had one prior to joining the force usually invested in laser surgery to remove it.

Common folklore on the streets was that if you were a criminal, always look to see if your cohorts in crime were tattooed—or "sleeved," as the cons called it—because any guy without a tattoo was immediately suspected of being the Law.

The "no tattoo" rule among cops was relatively inviolate, so it bothered Shane that Mark Shephard had this Viking on the inside of his right ankle. But there was something else about the tattoo that bothered Shane even more.

About three years before, the L.A. County Sheriff's Department had discovered a band of rogue officers. This group called themselves "the Vikings," and they all had Viking tattoos on their ankles. They were suspected of forcing confessions, usually by administering a little chin music in some dark place. The Vikings were eventually broken up, but this tattoo looked exactly like the ones worn by that bunch of officers. It was in the same place on the body, low on the right ankle, where it could be covered by a sock.

When this rogue group of deputies was first discovered, Sheriff Sherman Block tried to stage an inspection. He wanted to examine every sheriff's deputy's right ankle in search of Viking tattoos. But the Sheriff's Department Law Enforcement Union filed a lawsuit, claiming that such an inspection without probable cause violated the officers' civil rights. It became a big deal, and eventually the sheriffs' union prevailed. The physical search never took place, but ten deputies were eventually terminated from the original core group.

Mark Shephard had the same tattoo, or at least one a lot like it. Shane wondered if the culture of the Vikings had somehow migrated from the Sheriff's Department to the LAPD. He made a mental note to try to get someone to pull Shephard's file to see if he had ever been loaned out to the sheriffs or had ever been part of one of the cross-pollination task forces. There had been several over the years, and a few were still operating: The Cobra Unit in the Valley was one; L.A. Impact was another. Even some of the big serial-killer task forces qualified. On the Hillside Strangler Unit, the Sheriff's Department and LAPD worked closely together because the murders occurred in both the city and county.

One other strange thing turned up as a result of the autopsy, and also caught Shane by surprise. But it didn't happen while Doc Miller was sawing up Commander Shephard and singing selections from the *Sgt. Pepper's Lonely Hearts Club Band*. It arrived an hour later, when the preliminary blood work came back from the lab. Shane was stunned to learn that the Good Shepherd had been stoned when he parked the Remington Light in the central lobe of his cranial cavity. He had high traces of marijuana in his bloodstream.

"Shit," Shane said as he stood outside the ME's office in the hazy mid-morning sunshine, trying to decide what to do with this new piece of information. How would he tell Alexa, or should he even tell her at all? Since it would eventually find its way into the press, maybe it would be better to let the *Los Angeles Times* deliver the bombshell. Shane didn't need to be the one to further distress Alexa with negative facts about her old boyfriend.

He decided to take some time and think about it. He went across the street and had a Heineken in a tavern called the Canoe Factory. The place was a hangout for medical examiners and their staff after long days of opening corpses and turning them into what they referred to as "body canoes."

As he sipped his late-morning brew, he realized he had no choice but to tell Alexa, even if telling her would drive them further apart. She was acting head of DSG, and it was her responsibility. She had to know about the tattoo, about Shane's suspicions. Furthermore, he was determined to find out if his old best friend, Jody Dean, was out there committing multiple homicides on his former commanding officers.

At eleven Shane left the bar and just barely made his rescheduled psychiatric appointment, only five blocks away.

He sat in the reclining chair while the psychiatrist asked him how his last four days had gone.

"Very well," Shane lied. "Exceedingly well, in fact."

"Uh-huh . . . I see. Go on," the fat doctor said.

MORE TROUBLE

ALEXA GOT OUT of her department-issue Crown Victoria in front of Mark Shephard's house, where Shane was waiting. "I really don't have time for this," she said. "I'm trying to get the budget stuff finished and take over down there." She was dressed in a tan skirt and green blouse. Her lustrous black hair was pulled back, clipped with a barrette glinting in the late-afternoon sunshine.

He was standing by his Acura, which was parked nearby. In the backseat, jumping around with boundless enthusiasm, was Officer Krupkee, a one-year-old German shepherd he'd just borrowed from the West Valley Drug Enforcement Team. He let the dog out of the back of the car, took his leash, and led him toward the driveway.

"We need to go through the house. You need to be here," he said, ducking under the yellow crime-scene tape, which was still strung up, moving around to the back door so the neighbors couldn't watch him break in. He was walking ahead of Alexa so she couldn't stop him.

He was already on the porch, lock pick out, when she finally caught up to him. Officer Krupkee was jumping around, barking and sniffing wildly.

"What's this about? Is that a drug-enforcement dog?" Alexa's questions were apprehensive.

"Meet Officer Krupkee, West Valley Canine Hall of Fame. He's discovered more drugs than Dow Chemical."

"Shane," she said ominously, "why are we bringing a drug dog into Mark's house?"

"You remember the Vikings, that old Sheriff's Department club, or whatever it was?"

"Yeah, sure. Guys who had tattoos on their ankles and held court in the street."

"I went to Commander Shephard's autopsy. He has one of those on his ankle."

"Not when I was dating him."

"Then it's more recent than that," Shane answered stiffly.

He pulled the photo he took at the autopsy out of his jacket and gave it to her. He'd had it developed at a Photo-Mat an hour earlier. She gave it a quick glance, then handed it back without comment.

He stuffed it away and began feeding his picks into the back-door lock. He finally got them in, but his hands were sweating. When he tried to turn the lock, his fingers slipped, or maybe it was Officer Krupkee tugging and jumping in circles at the end of his leash; whatever the reason, the picks fell out of the lock onto the wooden porch. Shane bent down to retrieve them and started over again.

"What's the second thing?" she asked as he went back to work on the dead bolt.

"He had marijuana in his bloodstream," Shane said, avoiding eye contact while working on the door.

"Mark didn't do drugs."

"Go tell the ME."

She was silent, considering this. Then: "So, now we're over here with a DED to do what?"

"Alexa, I know this isn't going to go down well between us, and I really do regret it, but I think it's possible Mark Shephard knew Jody wasn't in that urn on Lauren's mantel, and that's why Shephard is dead. I think Jody's undercover unit may be going bad, and I think it's possible Mark knew what Jody was doing—maybe tried to stop it."

"Think, think, think . . . Isn't Shane a thinking policeman? Of course, a little evidence would sure be nice."

"And you can stow the sarcasm, okay? I'm not trying to run down the memory of your friend."

She was pissed; he could see it even in her sharp movements.

Mercifully, he finally got the back door open, and they walked into the house, Officer Krupkee leaping around at the end of his handler's chain like a demon possessed. Shane reached down and unhooked the leash. The dog took off, running around the kitchen, sniffing, pawing; then, unrewarded, he dashed toward the living room while Shane followed. Alexa was a few feet behind.

"We're looking for his stash, is that the drill?" she asked.

"If Shephard used drugs, he would probably have a stash

here somewhere," Shane admitted. "When I used to work drug homicides, way back before I became the leading department kook-a-boo, I found that hypes would often hide confidential stuff with their works: hot merchandise, murder weapons, dirty pictures, right there next to their happy bag."

"And that's what we're looking for?"

"If somebody forced Mark to smoke a joint before killing him, this place will be clean. We need to know either way."

"Why?"

"Alexa, stop chewing on my foot, okay? I need a witness. You're it. If I turn up anything and I'm here alone, they'll probably say I planted it. My word is about as good as a junkie's promise right now."

Suddenly, Officer Krupkee started barking. Shane and Alexa went into Mark Shephard's bedroom and saw the dog sniffing and pawing at the heating grate in the wall down by the floorboards, across from the bed.

Shane looked at Alexa, whose face and features were tense. He dropped down on his hands and knees. The screws on the vent were loose, so he began pulling them out with his thumb and fingernails. One by one, he extracted them while the leaping, barking dog jumped and lunged around, eager to help, pawing and growling at the heating grate.

"Good going, Krup," Shane said. "Alexa, lock him in the bathroom, will ya?"

She grabbed the chain, dragged the dog off. Shane heard her give the dog a "sit/stay" command. Then he heard the bathroom door close. He waited for her to return before pulling the heating grate away from the wall. She kneeled and they both looked inside.

Shane could see something way in the back of the exposed

opening. He put on a pair of rubber gloves, reached into the small hollowed compartment, and pulled the contents out of the wall. What came first was a large black metal box, about a foot long and six inches high. Shane set it down in front of them and glanced over at Alexa, who nodded. He opened it and inside found a very sophisticated high-frequency radio of some sort. It was set to 367.23 on the UHF band. The radio was turned off. Shane looked up at Alexa, who nodded again, so he turned it on. The batteries were working, but nothing was broadcasting: static hissed. He switched it off.

"Ever seen one of these before?" he asked.

"No . . . looks scrambled. I don't think it's department-issue."

Shane peered back inside the opening in the wall, took a penlight out of his pocket, and shined it inside. There was another box in the hollowed-out vent. He pulled it out. This one was mahogany, or some kind of polished wood, and was much smaller. He lifted the lid, and inside was what looked like a few rocks of cocaine, some marijuana, and a bag of pills.

"Shit," he heard Alexa say under her breath.

"I'm sorry," he murmured, but didn't risk a look at her. Instead, both of them just stared at the box.

When he finally looked up, he saw nothing on her beautiful face, no expression of any kind.

"I think we can go see Chief Filosiani now," Shane said. "I finally have something to show him."

"He's out of town until tomorrow, at a police chiefs' conference in San Francisco," she said softly.

"Tomorrow then, as soon as he gets back. Set it up." Shane took out his camera and photographed the heating grate. He and Alexa bagged the radio and wooden box, then loaded them both into the trunk of her Crown Vic. She got into the front seat, and after Shane put Officer Krupkee into the back of his Acura, he went to her driver's-side window and squatted down so he could look in at her.

"Alexa, we can't let this destroy us. I don't want this to wreck what we have."

"It's not you, Shane. . . . I love you. It's me." Then without saying another word, she drove off.

BLACK DUST 14

AND SINCE I think this guy could be dangerous," Shane said, "I'm not going to take a chance on what happened last time happening again."

They were driving to the airport. Chooch was heading off to quarterback camp. His duffel was stuffed; his helmet and pads were on the backseat.

"No way what happened last time can ever happen again," Chooch said.

They were talking about the Naval Yard case, when Chooch had been kidnapped in an attempt to get Shane to back off.

"So why didn't you give Alexa the ring?" Chooch asked, to change the subject.

"Don't worry about me and Alexa. Things always happen for the best."

"Shane, you're screwing this up."

"Maybe, but you don't have all of it."

"So, tell me."

"No."

"Why?"

" 'Cause I haven't got it completely figured out myself yet. And you may be right. I may be screwing it up, but you've gotta let me and Alexa work it out. This stuff can't be forced."

"You know, I love her, too," Chooch said.

"I know. I know you do."

When they arrived at the airport, Shane left his car parked at the LAPD substation. He got Chooch's stuff out of the backseat, and they walked to the Southwest Airlines terminal. Security was intense since the World Trade Center disaster; it took almost two hours to get to the counter. Shane helped Chooch check in and get his seat assignment, then they sat outside the metal detector in the lobby while people milled around, full of their own life's worries.

"Chooch, look, I'm not gonna mess it up. Okay?"

"She's the best person we ever knew, and I'm urging you— shit, man, *I'm begging you* . . . give her the fucking ring."

"Don't swear so much," Shane said. "Your mouth is getting terrible. Swearing doesn't make you an adult."

Chooch smiled. "Okay," he finally said. "I'll work on it, but give her the frickin' ring."

It was time for Chooch to go, and his son stood. Shane was surprised lately to see that he and Chooch were exactly the same height. At six feet, they were eye to eye when they gave each other a hug.

"I love you, man," Shane said.

"Me too, Dad." Then Chooch grabbed his pads and helmet,

which he had elected to carry onto the flight, and walked to the end of the line. Shane stood and watched as he got through the entrance, then turned back. "Give her the ring, Shane," he said once more.

"Is that your last comment on the matter?"

"That's it." Chooch smiled, then he was gone.

...

After that a strange series of events occurred.

As Shane was standing in the parking lot by the substation, about to get into his car, he noticed that on the trunk lids of most of the squad cars was a fine black dust. It reminded him of the black dust he'd seen on the trunk and hood of Jody's Charger as he looked over and saw his "dead" friend speeding along next to him on the San Diego Freeway Friday morning. Most dirty cars had brown dust, not black.

A uniformed police officer, a sergeant, moved past him on his way out of the substation, and Shane stopped him. "Hey, excuse me, Sarge . . ."

The man turned.

"I'm Shane Scully, detective three at Robbery-Homicide," he said as the man turned and walked toward him. Shane dug out his badge and showed it to the man.

"I heard about you. You got a lot of ink last year."

"Right." Shane smiled, trying to disarm what seemed like a negative attitude. "I notice all these Plain Janes here have a black dust of some kind all over them."

The sergeant wrinkled his brow. "You working for the motor pool now?"

"No," Shane said. "I was just wondering what it is."

"It's burned jet fuel. These jets take off every minute or so, and they spew black exhaust. Gets all over the cars that live around here."

"No kidding," Shane said, looking at a plane that was just taking off, climbing out past the terminals, trailing dark smoke out of four huge engines. "Got it," he said. "Thanks."

Shane got into his car and pulled out of the parking lot. He didn't know what he was looking for, or even what he was doing. Maybe it was just the vast amount of free time he seemed to have on his hands these days. He drove aimlessly around the Los Angeles airport, picking neighboring streets, looking at cars parked at the curbs. The ones that looked like they'd been there for a while all had the same layer of black dust on their hoods, trunks, and windshields.

Then Shane saw the green-covered fence.

It was at the end of one of the streets near the airport and seemed to run for several blocks. He parked, got out, and moved up to the chain-link, which was covered with Highway Department green plastic so you couldn't see through it. He took out his pocketknife and cut a hole in the plastic.

Inside the fence was a vacant neighborhood, just like the one he was in, only there were no cars on the street, no tricycles or toys strewn around on the brown, unwatered lawns.

"Whatcha doin'?" he heard a voice behind him demand.

Shane turned and saw an old man with a long, string-bean neck. His Adam's apple looked like a ball bouncing up and down on the end of a rubber band when he spoke.

"What is this place?" Shane asked.

"Noise-abatement area," the old man said. "They condemned all a'them houses 'bout two years ago, 'cause they sit right at the end a'the runway and the people who lived in them was all the time complaining about jet noise. Not that it's any better out here," he said. Then, as if to make his point, a jet took off, rising overhead, its engines screaming, trailing black exhaust.

"See," the old man shouted over the racket.

"Shit, that's loud."

"They say you get used t'it, but y'don't. Fuckin' drive y'nuts. Can't never sell these here houses 'cause only a deaf moron would buy 'em. We built here in the thirties, 'fore there was an airport."

"So, nobody lives inside this fence?"

"Nope," the old man said. "Three square blocks, empty as a hooker's heart."

"Nobody ever goes in there?" Shane asked.

"Once or twice, some cops. Showed us badges; said they was using the neighborhood to practice clearin' barricaded suspects house to house. Only seen 'em go in there a couple a'times."

"Any way to get in?" Shane asked.

"There's a gate right up the street on the Florence side, but it's all padlocked."

Shane nodded, thanked him, then got into his car and drove up the street to have a look.

What he found inside that fence defied all reason, as well as most of the core values he believed in.

15
CRIBBING

THE FENCE WAS topped by barbed wire.

Shane slid the picks into the heavy Yale padlock and flipped the tumblers. The padlock jumped, clicking open in his hand. He removed it from the chain that was wrapped around the center posts, then pushed the gate open enough to get through. He could see recent tire tracks in the black dust at his feet.

Shane reached down, withdrew the Beretta Mini-Cougar from his ankle holster, chambered it, and repacked it, tucking the weapon into a handier place in his belt. He moved into the deserted four-block neighborhood, then closed the gate behind him and relatched the lock the way he had found it.

Every two minutes a low-flying jet screamed overhead, shaking the ground and the houses with a deafening roar.

Shane steeled his nerves against the racket, slipping into the fenced noise-abatement area. A broken sign announced the street he was on as East Lannark Drive. He was moving slowly, cautiously from house to house, staying out of sight of the few unboarded windows, seeking cover behind chipped, unpainted garden walls or dead hedges. The effect of the neighborhood was startling: the houses had long been unattended, the lawns brown—bone-dry from lack of water; hedges and trees were skeletal and dusty; only a few hearty weeds clung stubbornly to rock-hard flowerbeds. The entire neighborhood was covered with the same fine black exhaust powder, turning everything dingy and gray.

Another jet screamed over him. Shane jumped in response to the shrieking roar of its four huge engines passing just a few hundred feet above his head.

Shane followed the tire tracks on the dusty pavement, running from hedge to house to wall, his senses quivering, his eyes darting back and forth, searching for any movement—any sign of life.

Could this be where Jody and his undercover unit are cribbing?

The tire tracks he was following turned right into one of the driveways. The house was a standard forties wood-frame, shake-roof number that had once been cheery yellow with white trim. But the yellow had faded to a dirty cream and the once-white trim was now gray and peeling. Shane sprinted across the dead grass to avoid leaving footprints on the dusty pavement; he pressed flat against the east wall of the house. Somebody had removed the plywood that covered the front bay window looking out onto East Lannark Drive.

Another jet took off and he jumped again, his frayed nerves

unprepared for the earsplitting roar. "Shit," he muttered. This was going to take a little getting used to.

Shane crept up to the locked front door. He could see that it had a shiny new brass dead bolt. He felt exposed and didn't want to stand there trying to open the lock, so he left the porch and continued down the driveway, ducking under the kitchen windows, past the locked garage door, pausing to look in through the dirty windows. Cobwebs dominated the empty space inside. Nobody had been in the garage for a long time.

He turned and moved silently up onto the back porch, where he found another new Yale lock. He pulled out his picks and in a few seconds had the back door open. Shane moved silently into the kitchen, closing the door softly behind him.

Another plane screamed overhead, rattling his nerves and the kitchen cabinets.

Late-morning sunlight streamed through dirty windows. A lone drinking glass was sitting in the sink next to a large noz-zled bottle of Arrowhead water propped up on the counter. Shane tried the sink faucet, but as he had suspected, the water in the neighborhood had been turned off long ago. He picked up the glass, placing his fingers on the inside to preserve any fingerprints, and held it up to the window. He could see some latents smudged on the surface, so he put it down, reached into his pocket for an ever present detective Baggie, which all cops carry, then popped the glass inside, putting it in his jacket's flap pocket.

Shane crept slowly out of the kitchen. He could not hear any movement in the house but pulled the Mini-Cougar out of his belt as he slipped into the small dining room.

A large slab of plywood, which had probably come off the front window, was laid across two sawhorses, forming a crude dining-room table. It was littered with maps. Some were of a portion of South Central L.A.—the tangled narrow streets south of Manchester. In a separate box at the end of the table were half a dozen folded maps, all in Spanish. Shane picked them up. He couldn't determine what Latin American country the maps depicted. He hadn't heard of any of the cities. Somebody had written *San Andresitos* on one of the maps. Most of them appeared to be of rural desert areas. He opened them and saw two towns marked with a circle: Maicao and Culcata. He set the maps back down in the box where he had found them, then continued out of the dining room into the living room. It was almost completely empty, except for one small camp stool and two Coleman lanterns. A small hibachi for cooking was set into the hearth where the smoke would go up the chimney. There was a corner-hanging lamp. Shane tried the light switch, but the power was also off. Shane kept his gun handy as he moved silently down a dark hallway into the bedroom, where he found a sleeping bag laid out on the threadbare carpet. Nothing else was in the room.

The jackpot was in the bedroom closet.

When Shane slid the mirrored sliding door open, he was looking at an arsenal of illegal weapons propped up against the back wall: an Uzi, complete with a Grumman laser sight, and two Heckler & Koch fully automatic machine pistols stacked next to two fully automatic AK47s. On the top shelf were boxes of 9- and 7.62-millimeter ammunition and a collection of thirty-round banana clips. Also in the closet was a black radio identical to the one he'd found at Mark Shephard's house. Shane took it down, set it on the floor and examined it. The dial was set to the same high-band UHF frequency: 367.23.

He switched it on; a whispered voice immediately staccatoed in the small bedroom but was overcome by another takeoff. The jet engines rattled the windows in their frames as the plane screamed overhead. Once it was gone and silence returned, Shane heard:

"Copy, W-6. There's a bird in your attic." A man's voice, whispery and coarse, followed by a hissing sound. Then a second voice crackled: "I saw him. Tell Sawdust we're in and watertight. Move the truck to the tip of the triangle. Hot Rod is holding the Alley. Inky Dink, gimme an update." Then he heard a black-sounding voice, low and resonant: "Pimp Daddy's in the house. Where's he get the white disco boots and them funky purple hats? Man, I gotta get me some a'dat."

Then unmistakably, Jody: "Hey, Inky Dink, cut the cross-talk. Take care of business. We don't take these guys till they come out with the package."

"Affirmative," the African American replied.

"Hot Rod, gimme your twenty," Jody demanded.

This time, a man with a Mexican accent: "I'm parked in the gas station across from the house."

"Okay. Till the party moves, stay back. Everybody hold position. Be ready to jam."

"Roger that . . . I'm parked and dark and ready to bark." The black voice again.

Shane had heard this sort of broadcast hundreds of times on police tactical frequencies. It was some kind of field surveillance, probably on a drug deal. This radio, like the one in Shephard's house, looked as though it had some kind of scrambler attached. It weighed almost twenty pounds—too heavy to lug around while he searched the house, so Shane switched it off and put it back in the closet, placing it up on the top shelf with the ammo and banana clips. There he noticed several boxes of earplugs like the ones they handed out at the Academy shooting range, answering his question of how anybody could live in these houses with the constant noise pollution overhead. Shane momentarily debated inserting some to deaden the racket, but he immediately rejected the idea. It was better to have frayed nerves than a deadly surprise.

He took out his small digital camera and photographed the arsenal in the closet. In the back, way down at the end, were two suits of Kevlar body armor. He slid the closet door closed, then moved through the rest of the house, photographing it all. The bathroom contained another jug of bottled water and some toiletries. When he finished, he exited the house and re-locked the back door.

Shane darted across the street, where he could see that another set of tire tracks had turned into the driveway of a house there. He walked toward the gray stucco Spanish-style bungalow, again staying off the pavement to avoid leaving footprints in the fine black powder.

The back door was unlocked, so he pushed it open and walked into the pantry, then into the kitchen.

Just as with the first house, it looked to Shane as if only one person was living here. But this place was a mess: paper plates and plastic cups were thrown on the floor; McDonald's wrappers and stale fries were kicked into the corner. Again, no furniture, but another hibachi was in the hearth. It didn't look as if these guys cooked and ate their meals together. The same general setup existed, except in this bathroom Shane found a hand mirror with what looked like a residue of powder on it.

"Shit," he said softly as he ran a finger over the white dust, touched it to his tongue, experiencing the sharp, bitter taste of cocaine.

Shane left the house and, following more tire tracks deeper into the neighborhood, found another, one block over on Sutter Street. Then he found a fourth and a fifth house. Crystal meth, cocaine, and uppers were in three of the last four bathrooms; more weapons and Kevlar vests were in the closets. He also found one more black UHF radio. Several of the weapons he discovered still had LAPD evidence tags wired to their trigger guards with old case numbers on them, telling him that this ordnance had been stolen from the munitions locker downtown, where confiscated street weapons were held after being used in court prior to being destroyed.

He lost track of time as he wandered through the last house on Dolores Street. Every two minutes, without fail, another plane took off, rattling windows, roofs, and Shane's confidence.

Suddenly, out of the corner of his eye, he saw movement, then heard the sound of a car engine. He looked out the side window of the house and saw a gray van pulling up the street, followed by several cars. One of them was the orange-and-black Charger he'd seen Jody driving on the San Diego Freeway.

"Damn!" he said under his breath, cursing his lack of vigilance, as one of the cars pulled into the driveway of the house where he was hiding. Shane crossed to the front door. Through the small glass eyehole, he saw a tall, muscular African American man wearing a baseball cap get out of a Chevy pool-cleaning truck. He was carrying an assault weapon and a Kevlar vest. The man moved slowly up the walk toward the house. Then he heard somebody yelling from across the street:

"Hey! Somebody's been inside my crib!"

Shane turned and ran toward the back door, flung it open, and sprinted into the backyard.

"Muthafucka's over here!" he heard the African American shout.

Suddenly an assault weapon let loose close behind him, and as Shane darted across the yard, he felt a stream of lead stir the air by his head just as he ducked around the garage. He spun back in time to see the entire rear corner of the wood building turn into chunks of flying debris and stucco dust as more automatic gunfire chewed into it. He fired three shots blindly in the direction of his assailant, to slow him down and give him something to worry about. Then Shane turned and ran between the garage's back wall and a ramshackle grape-stake fence. He leaped up, grabbed the top of the wood rail, and flipped over, landing in another weed-ridden backyard. This one was also deserted, except for a rusting swing set on a cracked concrete patio.

"Cut him off! He went over the back fence! Block the alley!" the voice behind him yelled. Shane heard footsteps slapping concrete in the driveway of the backyard where he was now trapped. He aimed his Mini-Cougar at a spot where he esti-mated the running man would appear, and waited. His heart was slamming so hard in his chest, he could see his gun pulsing at the end of his triangled grip.

In a moment a huge man came around the corner of the house. He saw Shane and quickly brought a MAC-10 auto-matic pistol up to fire, but Shane was ready and got his round off first. The muscle-bound man went down screaming, his right thigh blown open, now firing his MAC-10 wildly, bullets sparking off plaster and concrete.

Shane ran directly at him and kicked the man savagely in the head. Then he snatched the MAC-10 out of his weakened hand and sprinted up the driveway.

Surprisingly, despite the gunfire, there was nobody out on the street. A red Ford Fairlane was at the curb, still idling. The fallen giant must have just left it there.

Shane ran to the car, jumped in, put it in gear, and took off. He accelerated up the street just as three men appeared at the intersection behind him and opened up. The Fairlane bucked and shook as magnum-force weapons fire poured into it. Suddenly, his back window and two rear tires exploded. He spun the wheel, taking the corner at the end of the block, squealing on ruptured rubber and sparking rims. He was now heading toward the padlocked fence at Florence Avenue.

"SHIIIIIIT!" he yelled, flooring it. The car wobbled on blown, flapping tires. As it hit the chain-link fence, Shane was thrown into the dash. The car bowed the metal gate, then the tortured hinges popped free and the gate flew open. The Fairlane rumbled through, coming to a stop on Florence Avenue.

Shane was immediately out of the car and running toward his Acura. In the excitement, he realized he had left the MAC-10 on the Fairlane's front seat. Behind him he could hear several men shouting in confusion.

"What the fuck's going on?" the old man with the stringbean neck asked, still holding his garden hose.

"Get inside and call nine-one-one!" Shane yelled as he dove into the Acura, and took off in reverse. He shot backward down Florence, spun a reverse 180, then floored it again. The Acura's torqued engine and tires whined as he sped up the street, finally turning the corner at the end of the block.

THE DAY-GLO DAGO

SWAT WENT THROUGH the houses," Filosiani said out of the side of his mouth. "Even called the Tech Squad to dust, but so far, it's clean as the board a'health."

Shane reached into his pocket and withdrew the memory strip with the digital photographs he had shot inside the airport houses. "You have my word, *and* these pictures," Shane said as he handed it to the short, round, balding police chief.

"Good going, Sergeant. This is what I like t'see." Filosiani was standing behind his desk in the chief's office at Parker Center.

Shane looked around for a place to sit down. The last time he had been here, the office had belonged to Burl Brewer and was decorated with classic antiques. An amazing array of expensive charcoal line drawings depicting police officers doing their duty had adorned the walls. Shane had been told that the artwork was done by a famous L.A. artist from the thirties and that Chief Brewer had described them as a PR expense, paying more than thirty thousand dollars from the Police Department Public Affairs budget. Now they were gone . . . sold by Filosiani at auction. The money, Shane learned, had gone to the equipment fund to order new second-chance Ultima flack vests—the latest and lightest body armor on the market. Now there was only a metal desk placed in the exact center of the room, with a secretarial chair behind it. No sofa, no occasional chairs, no artwork. Filosiani had put his phone and computer on a metal rolling table next to the desk. The walls were empty except for two framed diplomas: one containing his doctorate in criminology from New York University, the other his night-school law degree. A large bulletin board was leaning against the wall with the five LAPD division crime-stat sheets and an array of Polaroid pictures of the five division commanders, as well as shots of the administrative staff officers with their name and rank printed neatly below each one. Shane had seen military barracks with more amenities. Filosiani was a no-bullshit guy.

The chief saw Shane looking for a seat. "No chairs, Sergeant. This ain't a place t'sit n'chat. Y'state your business and go."

Shane had heard that the chief was rarely in his office anyway, preferring to be out touring the department, making unscheduled stops. Filosiani had posted office hours for those seeking meetings, but he spent at least three hours each day in the trenches, available to his troops. At first, the Blues in the field had remained skeptical, but slowly, one cop at a time, the Day-Glo Dago was winning converts.

A buzzer on the chief's phone rang. He picked it up and listened, then said: "Send her in."

The door opened and Alexa walked into the office, carrying a manila file folder. She crossed the office and delivered it to the chief. "That was in a wall safe behind a picture in Commander Shephard's office," she said. "I thought a hidden office safe was sort of unusual, so I checked to see who authorized the installation. I couldn't find any record anywhere. I checked the Furniture, Equipment and Transfer Log, along with the Equipment Budget Request for DSG, even the Maintenance and Repair Log. . . . Nothing. The safe must have been put in on the sly, on a weekend or something. We had to drill it to get it open. That file was all that was inside."

The Day-Glo Dago rubbed his mouth with his right hand, inadvertently flashing his diamond pinky ring in the light streaming through his huge office windows. "Okay, then . . . ," he said, opening the folder, "let's see what we got here." He squinted at the first page, flipped a few . . . read . . . squinted again . . . flipped some more . . . Now he was frowning. Then he closed the folder. "It doesn't say nothin'; just a bunch of numbers," he growled, looking at her. "Gibberish."

"Yes, sir," Alexa said. "It looks like some kind of arithmetic code." She still didn't look over at Shane, not wanting to admit that he might have been right, that Mark Shephard had somehow been involved in an illegal conspiracy.

"You get this over to the Questioned Documents Division?" Filosiani asked, referring to the section of the Scientific Investigations Division that broke codes and did handwriting analysis.

"Yes, sir, I sent them a copy; they're looking at it now, scanning it into their computer. Captain Franklin over there said they would probably be able to break it, but he couldn't estimate how long it would take."

"Sir, this unit is going to go further underground," Shane said. "Jody knows I found his crib. He'll be twice as hard to find now."

"Where's the radio you two took outta Shephard's wall?" Flosianii asked.

"In my office," Alexa said.

"Bring it in," he ordered.

She turned and left the room. Shane and Tony Filosiani traded stares but didn't speak. A few minutes later Alexa returned with the twenty-pound black UHF radio. She lugged it in and put it down on Filosiani's gray metal desk.

The Day-Glo Dago looked at the dial. "You say this is set on the same frequency as the one you saw in the noise-abatement house?" the chief asked in his distinctive New York accent.

"Yes, sir," Shane said. "Same frequency."

"It's got a built-in scrambler . . . and a satellite transmitter—very expensive and almost impossible to triangulate on," Alexa added.

"Dusted?"

"Yes, sir. We got a right-hand index and thumb off the faceplate. They're over at Latent Prints with the ones we got off the glass Shane found in the kitchen," Alexa said. "We're running them against Jody Dean's file; then, if that fails, we're gonna see if we can get a cold hit from the Police Academy class records."

Filosiani nodded. He leaned over the radio and put his pudgy fingers on the ON/OFF button. After a moment, he flipped the switch. The radio hissed to life, but there was no one using the frequency. The radio was monitoring dead air, so after listening to the hiss for a minute, he shut it off.

"They probably have those radio units turned on only when they're on surveillance," Shane volunteered.

"Okay, I'm gonna assume the worst here," Filosiani said softly. "I'm gonna assume we got a rogue squad throwin' bricks and tryin' t'fly under the radar."

Alexa's expression told Shane that her defense of Mark Shephard was starting to crumble. "Sir, I'm not at all sure that—"

"Yeah, yeah," Filosiani interrupted her. "Me, either; but if we assume the worst, then we ain't gonna get schmucked."

The phone on his desk beeped, and the chief picked it up. "Yeah . . ." He listened without speaking for over a minute. "Okay. Got it." He hung up and stared at them. "Latents just got a cold hit. The prints from the radio were Shephard's, but the ones on the water glass belong t' an LAPD sergeant named Hector Sanchez Rodriquez. He was a member a'Cobra, workin' special crimes in the Valley Division. He supposedly died in a drug-house fire two years ago. The story is, he was workin' a Mexican drug ring, undercover, and SIS didn't know he was ours, tried to take down a crack house he was in, lobbed some canisters, and the place flamed. Sergeant Rodriquez went up in the fire. Records is sending his file over."

"Sir, Cobra is one of the LAPD units interacting with the Sheriff's Department. The Vikings were originally Sheriff's Department rogues. Commander Shephard had a Viking tattoo. Jody was in SIS, and since I got that glass two hours ago, we know Rodriquez is still alive, just like Jody. This is a criminal conspiracy."

There was a strange silence in the underfurnished office.

"This ain't gonna be easy," the Super Chief said. "Matter a'fact, it's gonna be tricky and dangerous as hell. . . . But if you two are willin' t'play a little loose, I think maybe we can reel this bunch in."

"Let's hear it," Alexa said.

"I'd tell ya t'pull up a chair, but since I don't have one, how 'bout we all go across the street and get a cuppa coffee?"

So that's what they did.

•••

Shane didn't get home until almost ten-thirty that night. His mind was picking up the dangerous pieces of Chief Filosiani's plan and then putting them back where he found them. Jigsaw pieces that had made a convincing picture an hour ago now didn't seem to fit. In theory it could all come together, but the plan was physically dangerous for both him and Alexa. But despite his nervousness, it seemed as if it might be the only way to lure Jody out—the only way Shane could get Jody to trust him enough to let him infiltrate his secret squad.

Shane had the black UHF radio under his arm as he entered his Venice house from the garage. He could feel the reloaded Mini-Cougar heavy on his ankle. He had filled the nine-shot clip with light loads that would protect Alexa when he eventually fired at her per Filosiani's plan. He set the radio down on the kitchen counter and switched it on. Shane had to wait until the rogue unit went hot again; then while they had the UHF satellite radio on, he would step on their transmission, trigger the mike, talk to Jody, and make his pitch. He hoped Filosiani had given him enough information to get Jody to agree to meet him. As the radio hissed softly from the kitchen counter, Shane fished a beer out of the refrigerator and held it up to his face, rolling it along his forehead to cool his throbbing brain.

Then he sensed movement behind him.

He spun around, but he was way too late.

17
COMING CORRECT

THE FIRST THING Shane became aware of was a fetid, throat-constricting stench. He was still unconscious; the smell had started in the middle of a confusing, kaleidoscopic dream. The odor filled his nostrils, becoming stronger and more unpleasant as consciousness gradually returned. Getting his eyes open was a little like prying up a manhole cover with his fingernails.

He was finally looking at a damp, rusting metal wall; his hands were locked painfully behind him. Finally Shane realized he was sitting on a metal floor, handcuffed to some kind of structural support . . . all of this drifting through his thoughts without making much of an impact. The back of his head throbbed where he had been hit, and a sharp pain pulsed behind his eyes, threatening to explode with each heartbeat. Suddenly a moment of panic and a surge of adrenaline. His thoughts focused; his senses returned.

Cold, bluish light hissing from a Coleman lantern hanging from a knotted rope on the ceiling; the radio he took from Shephard's house, on a nearby table, on the edge of his peripheral vision; three . . . no, two men, talking low.

"Was me, I'd come correct on the man." The sentence had a Mexican lilt. The second voice was deep and rumbling. Shane recognized the same African American speech rhythm from the UHF radio broadcast he had overheard from the house on Dolores Street. He had to concentrate hard to translate the rich ghetto idiom.

"We all be flossin'. You hear what I be sayin'? Jody's all'a time treating us like we just studio gangstas hangin' round, tryin' t'get served. He ain't da only one bustin' moves here. Know what I'm sayin'?"

"You a tough cabeza when Jody ain't in the room, but you just doin' fake jacks, nigger." A chair scraped.

"Ain't afraid a'Jody—fuck Jody," the black voice said, then added: "I think Casper's over there lyin' in the cut. Check him out."

Shane heard footsteps, then a face loomed into view. The man had tangled shoulder-length hair and a bushy black beard laid up against dark, swarthy skin. He looked Hispanic, but his eyes were an odd color for a Latin, a strange light gray— hooded eyes, set deep under massive, bony brows. He shoved his chin down in Shane's face and studied him.

Could this be the late Sergeant Hector Rodriquez?

When the man spoke, the Mexican idiom disappeared. Now his tone was condescending, more like a cop talking to a street criminal: "How's things down there in Shitsville, Scully?"

Shane heard another chair scrape, and a second face swung into view. This was the African American who'd exited the pool-cleaning truck when Shane was trapped in the noise-abatement house. He was ebony black, and now that the man had his baseball cap off, Shane could see that he had shaved his head. From his right ear hung a long chain with a cross dangling at the end of it. His tank top was ripped and dirty.

"How long you been listenin', Scully?" the African American said.

Shane could smell booze on his breath. "Where's Jody?" Shane's pinched voice echoed weakly in the windowless space.

"Ain't here," the Mexican said.

"Are you cops?"

The black man looked at Shane and gave his answer careful consideration before he spoke. "We was makin' weak-ass music, y'know? Hadda leave da jam. You come along and be tryin' t'collect for the trip. 'Cept now all you be doin' is waitin' on the big bus."

The confusing ghetto-speak made Shane's head throb. "Get Jody. I got something he'll want to hear, something important." Shane was trying to focus, to collect his scattered thoughts. He didn't know how long he'd been unconscious. He couldn't see outside and didn't know if it was day or night. As his senses cleared, he began to feel the gentle lapping of water against the outside of the metal wall he was cuffed to. He thought maybe he was on a big rusting boat, somewhere down by the harbor. "I got something important to tell Jody," he repeated.

"You don't tell nobody shit. You assed-out big-time, mutha-fucka," the African American said softly. "You shot Victory. Fuckin' guy is moaning and cryin'. We hadda smuggle him down t'Mexico t'get him fixed."

"Victory?" Shane asked.

"Peter Smith. Man calls hisself 'Victory' 'cause he say he never loses. He's the—"

"Hey, Inky Dink," the Mexican interrupted. "Shut up. Yer mama ain't here, so who you tryin' to impress?"

"Don't matter . . . Fuckin' guy's dead anyway."

Then, either because he had been disrespected or to make his point, the black ex-cop stepped forward and grabbed Shane, jerking him up violently. Shane's hands were still cuffed to some kind of structural support, so his wrists exploded in pain as he came abruptly to the end of the chain. His head and torso were only three feet off the floor, his shoulders aching, barely able to keep his legs under him.

"I told Jody we shoulda capped you when you went to see his old lady . . . when you talked to the Good Shepherd," the black ex-cop said angrily. "But he says no. He's got some fuckin' issues with you. Like what you two white boys did in Little League makes a shitload of difference t'anything. But he ain't here t'cover ya, so guess what? We gonna come correct on yo' white-slice ass."

He hit Shane with a thundering right cross.

Darkness swarmed, and Shane was knocked back inside his head. For a second he was still conscious, peering out through a tiny hole of light that quickly narrowed.

Then he was swimming in black . . . dreamless . . . unattached . . . alone.

THE WINDUP

"YOU AMAZE ME," the voice said.

Shane kept his eyes closed; his head was down on his chest. His jaw felt dislocated. He was trying to get his jumbled thoughts in order, standing on the front porch of a disaster, rehearsing opening lines like a teenager on his first date.

Jody's voice droned: "You runnin' all over, talkin' to Glass House brass. I always held your back, Hot Sauce. How come ya' couldn't hold mine?"

Shane still didn't answer.

"Give it up, man. I can see ya thinkin' in there. I read you like the funny papers. Open yer eyes, or I'm gonna set your socks on fire."

So Shane opened his eyes and looked up.

Jody was still greyhound-lean, his stringy muscles flexed and bulged under an old LAPD T-shirt that read SIS . . . WE MAKE HOUSE CALLS. Copper hair hung in long, untended ringlets around his head. His tangled beard had not been trimmed. But Jody's X-ray eyes were drilling, piercing holes in Shane's paper-thin psyche.

"I was countin' on you, Salsa, but you didn't come through. It was all I could do to keep my crew from swingin' by your house and giving you a shiny new set of nine-millimeter nipple jewelry."

"You're hanging out with very frank company," Shane mumbled softly; his throat was sore, his jaw was popping cartilage painfully when he spoke. "Your crew thinks you're a piece of shit."

"Two weeks more and none a'that matters. I can hold it together." He smiled, and for a second, Shane saw the old Jody from Little League, smirking after a tough out, joy mixed with sarcasm, as if his charmed life were still just a practical joke on everyone.

It was time to make his pitch. Shane felt weak and dull, not up to the task, but he had no choice. He wondered what day it was . . . how long he'd been unconscious. . . . He wondered if he needed to adjust the Chief's carefully worked-out time-table.

"You got something you're about to lay on me, Hot Sauce. So, get to it." Jody was back inside his head, browsing, uninvited.

"What time is it?" Shane started. "What day?"

"Two A.M. Tuesday morning."

"Tomorrow at nine A.M., the department is gonna know all you guys are still alive."

"I don't think so."

"Commander Shephard had a secret safe in his office. He kept a file on your unit behind your back. Alexa found it. She's taking it to Filosiani tomorrow morning." Shane watched Jody for a flicker of interest or concern but saw nothing. "The whole thing is written in some kinda number code," Shane continued. "Once Filosiani gets it, he's gonna send it over to Questioned Documents. They're gonna scan it into their computer and they'll probably be able to break it in a day or two. Then everything you did to Medwick and Shephard is gonna be for nothin'."

"Medwick and Shephard?"

"You killed 'em."

"I what?" Jody smiled. "Why would I kill those guys?"

"Because they were the only two left who knew that you and this squad of yours exists."

Jody was squatting before him, Indian-style. Shane remembered that Jody could squat on his haunches like that for hours; his thighs, like steel, never seemed to tire. He was looking at Shane carefully, reading him like always but never giving away his own thoughts. Jody's face was granite, so Shane had to push his bet. He shoved more chips out. "If that file says you and these other guys aren't dead, then the department is gonna figure you killed Shephard and Medwick so you could disappear. Once they believe that, there isn't a town high enough up in the Andes or far enough out in the bush for you to hide."

A long, tense moment was punctuated by the distant moan of a foghorn. Shane was now pretty sure he was inside one of the old deserted freighters he'd seen chained to the docks in Long Beach or San Pedro.

"I think you still got something else you want to tell me. This ain't all of it," Jody finally said.

"Jody, I've been fucked over by the department." Shane repeated the lines they had all come up with in the coffee shop across from Filosiani's office.

"No shit."

"I made that Naval Yard case, not Alexa, but they gave all the credit to her, gave her the Medal of Valor while I got a psych review. While she makes lieutenant, I'm stuck in a basket-weaving class. At first I was pissed. Now I'm just looking to get paid." Jody didn't respond, so Shane pressed his bet again—threw in some more chips. "When I saw you on the freeway, I was hurt," Shane continued. "You should've told me what was going on—that you were alive. I was like your brother. That's why I went to Medwick's house and to see Lauren. I couldn't believe you'd do this to me . . . let me think you'd killed yourself."

"I had no choice, Shane. It was a department-sanctioned deep-cover op. Medwick set it up. Got the phony coroner and death-scene photos made. CGI, they call it—computer-generated imaging. He got us all undercover driver's licenses out of ATD, where they bury 'em with high-security numbers. Only Medwick and Mayweather could access them." ATD was the Anti-Terrorist Division; among other things, it supplied bogus IDs for undercover cops on deep-cover stings. "I couldn't tell you, Salsa. . . . It was a black ops case."

"Bullshit. You told Lauren."

"Right. And look what it did to her."

No turning back now. "Whatever it is you got goin', I want in," he said. "I know you're about to score, and I know it's gonna be big."

"Yeah?"

"Yeah. You're not doing doors for the department anymore . . .

you're way past that. You're running some kinda high-dollar conspiracy. For you to be taking this big a risk, it has to be huge."

Jody was still squatting before him, elbows propped on knees, hands straight out, not moving, studying him intently. Shane tried to make his thoughts neutral so Jody couldn't crawl back inside his head and read the lies.

"I was gonna use that UHF radio I found at Shephard's to contact you," Shane continued, "to set up a meet . . . but you moved first. I wanted to tell you, I think I have a way to save this for you, but if I do, I want in. I want an equal share."

"You're dreamin', Salsa."

"Jody, the department is going to find me unfit to return to duty and they're gonna take back my pension. Twenty years on the job goes in the shitter. . . . They're gonna gig me, I can smell it."

"I warned ya," Jody said. "In police work, it's all about CYA."

"Covering your ass. Yeah. . . . So you better listen to me and cover yours. Since Shephard died, Alexa Hamilton is the temporary head of DSG. I told her I saw you on the freeway. She's goin' to Filosiani with it tomorrow. Since she's just won the MOV, he's liable to believe her."

"Good goin', Salsa," Jody growled. "How's this supposed to help me?"

"I call her up, tell her I figured the number code that Medwick's file is using. Tell her the numbered file she found in his secret safe is not an arithmetic sequence but a key-book code and that I found the key book. I'll set up a secret meeting with her in some deserted spot, tell her if she brings the file, I'll bring the key book, so we can break the code together. She's an ambitious bitch. She'll come because she'll want to claim the credit."

" 'Cept it's probably not a key-book code," Jody said. "Medwick was in DSG, and DSG always uses alphabet number codes."

"She doesn't know what it is. If I say it, she'll assume I'm right," Shane answered, "and she'll know Questioned Documents will never be able to break a key-book code. She'll *have* to play ball with me to get the book."

A key-book code was a simple and almost unbreakable code developed by the Germans in World War II. In order for it to work, both the sender and receiver had to have the same book. If the word you wanted to send was *apple*, and it was the third word on page 200 of the key book, then you would write *200-3*. The person receiving the code would read the third word on page 200 in the same book, where he would find the word *apple*, and so on. Without the key book, the Scientific Investigations Division would never be able to break the code because it didn't correspond to the frequency of letters used in the alphabet, like most codes, but to a page in an unknown book. Shane could see this realization dawn on Jody's face.

"Without the key book, she'll know she's got nothing," Shane continued. "That secret file was originally set up by Medwick and Mayweather. Mayweather died during the Naval Yard case, leaving Medwick. He retired and turned it over to Shephard. If the department knows you guys are alive, they'll know you killed those two captains. Your picture will be at every airport and border crossing. You'll spend the rest of your lives running."

Jody's intense blue eyes kept drilling, compelling Shane to look away.

"She used me, man . . . fucked me over," Shane growled. "I hate her guts." Shane was aching all over. His head was throbbing even worse than before. This story had sounded foolproof when he, Alexa, and Filosiani had discussed it over coffee earlier that evening, but now, handcuffed in the dark hull of the rusting freighter, he hoped Jody would go for it.

"Lemme think about it, Hot Sauce," Jody finally said, then rose gracefully to his feet without having to put his hands down for balance or to push himself up.

"I can get her to meet me and bring the file before it goes to Filosiani. I know I can."

"Would you kill her for it?" his old friend asked softly.

"Yeah, I could kill her, you bet I could."

" 'Cause if I go for this, that's what you're gonna do."

"Jody . . . it could be like old times."

Jody stood over Shane. "I'll get back t'ya," he finally said, then turned and walked out of the cargo hold, closing the rusting hatch behind him.

The distant foghorn moaned, a morose note, low and dark, as Shane's plunging spirit.

THE PITCH

SHANE HAD BEEN dozing.

Somebody was touching him under the chin, pulling his face up. His eyes opened and he was looking at Jody. The Mexican with the gray eyes loomed in the background; the Coleman lantern hissed and sputtered.

"Make the call."

"Thanks, Jody."

"Shut up and listen. You lure her out; you take the file; then you light the bitch up."

The Mexican stared.

"Hot Rod, here, and Inky Dink wanted to pull your drapes. I still might let 'em, so you're on strict probation." Jody glanced at his watch. "It's just after three A.M. You call her at home around four and get her moving. I want this to go down before sunup. Gimme the cuff key, Rod," Jody ordered.

The big Mexican stood still, his gray eyes burning with contempt.

"I said gimme the fucking key, Rodriquez," Jody repeated. "You gonna make me take it from you?"

That confirmed it. *The gray-eyed Mexican was Hector Rodriquez.*

Reluctantly, Rodriquez reached into his pocket and pulled out the key.

Jody snatched it from his hand, reached behind Shane, and uncuffed him. "Get up," he commanded.

Shane's legs were weak under him as he rose. Jody spun him around and quickly recuffed him.

They led him out of the rusting cargo hold, clanging up a set of metal stairs, onto the deck of the old freighter. As he came out of the hatch, Shane saw a million stars twinkling in a windswept sky. He filled his lungs with fresh ocean air. They led him off the dank freighter, down a makeshift wooden gangplank, and over to the same gray, windowless van that had pulled into the noise-abatement area. Shane was shoved into the back, down onto the floor. Rodriquez got behind the wheel, and Jody, carrying the black UHF radio, slid into the passenger seat facing back, never taking his eyes off Shane.

"You got my gun?" Shane asked, noticing his ankle holster had been removed.

"Right here," Jody answered, holding it up. "Why?"

"If I'm gonna take her out, I wanna use it. I qualified Marksman with that piece."

Jody smiled but said nothing. Rodriquez put the van in gear.

Shane heard the tires crunch on the gravel as they pulled away from the rusting freighter. Then they jounced along on the rutted, paved roads down by the San Pedro docks until they got on surface streeets.

They drove for almost forty minutes while Jody made him rehearse his call to Alexa, going over it several times, adjusting a word or thought here and there until he was finally satisfied.

Shane could not see out of the windows, but he knew from the speed that they were now traveling on one of the L.A. freeways. Occasionally, he could see a lit sign streak by overhead, but from his position on the floor he couldn't read them. He had no idea which way they were going. Rodriquez's cold gray eyes never left him for long, constantly frowning back from the oblong rearview mirror.

Shane wondered where the rest of the members of the unit were. Victory was in Mexico, getting his wound attended to, but where were the others?

Finally they came to a stop, and Rodriquez turned off the engine.

"Okay, Salsa, we get out of the van. Hot Rod, here, is gonna lead the way. You follow. I'm in the rear. We go single file . . . head down . . . no talking."

"Right," Shane answered.

Jody got out of the van and pulled open the sliding back door. As Shane exited, he sneaked a look. They were at some low-end motel in a shabby, half-built, one-story neighborhood. Fields of weeds and low cactus plants completed the rest of the landscape. It seemed to Shane that they were in the far West Valley, perhaps Sunland or maybe even as far out as Valencia.

"I said head down!" Jody said harshly, and slapped him

hard with the palm of his hand in the exact spot where Shane had been blackjacked earlier. He winced but managed not to cry out.

They followed Rodriquez into a small motel room through a chipped red door.

The room was threadbare and decorated like Pee Wee's Playhouse: ratty orange drapes fought with faded olive-green club chairs and a yellow bedspread; the vinyl furniture had hosted a hundred forgotten cigarettes. Jody closed and latched the door, then spun Shane around and uncuffed him, stepping back to put a few feet between them. "Okay, call her. Use that phone. I'm gonna be listening from the bathroom extension."

"Okay."

"And, Hot Sauce . . . here's the 411. I love ya, but that horse don't happen t'be runnin'. You get cute, I'll kill you right here and let Rod piss on your corpse. You should also know I sent Inky Dink over to Santa Monica. He's parked across the street from her apartment. So if this is a setup, he'll spot a tail, and then it's lights out for everybody."

"I'm down, man. Stop threatening me." Shane was trying to manage both fear and anger.

After a second, Jody nodded and handed Shane a typed address. "That's where she needs to go."

Jody moved to the extension, unscrewed the receiver, emptied the speaker element into his palm, replaced the handset in the cradle, then nodded.

Shane picked up the phone and dialed Alexa's number. Jody waited near the second phone until Shane signaled that it was ringing, then Jody picked up the extension and pulled the cord out to a spot in the dressing area where he could watch Shane.

On the third ring, Alexa answered the phone.

"Hello." Her voice sounded clogged with sleep, but Shane knew she'd been waiting for his call.

"Alexa, it's Shane."

"It's the middle of the damn night," she complained groggily.

"Yeah . . . Yeah. Look, something just developed. I think I'm onto something here."

"Huh? What? Jesus, what time is it?" A pause for theatrics, then: "It's four-fifteen in the fucking morning!"

"I think I found 'em, Alexa. Better still, I think I maybe found the code they're using. It's a key book. If I'm right, we got a Class A collar here. These guys are cop killers. It'll be our bust."

"Key book?" She was sounding more awake now. "A key book can't be cracked by the computer." Pensive and cautious—reading her lines like Meryl Streep.

"Exactly."

"Okay . . . Okay . . . Where are you? Don't do anything till I get there."

"We gotta make a deal first."

"I don't make deals, Scully."

"You do if you want a piece of this. You jobbed me on the Naval Yard case and you gave me up to Shephard when I saw Jody. This time, we do it one hundred percent my way."

"You've turned into a complete dick, ya know that?" she snorted. Then there was a pause, and she added, "Okay . . . what's your deal, big shot?"

"You do this exactly the way I say. No arguments, no revisions. Right now we both have a bargaining chip, so you bring the file you got from Shephard's office; I'll bring the book."

"That file's evidence! I don't even have a copy yet."

"We need it to make sure I really found their crib. If my book decodes your document, then we know I'm right."

"Where are you?"

Shane looked at the typed sheet Jody had given him.

"I'll meet you at 1623 Glen Oaks. Near the old deserted airfield in San Fernando out by the wash."

After a long silence, she asked: "Where's Jody's unit now?"

"They're on a field op. It sounds like an all-nighter. I'm listening on the radio we found in Shephard's house—monitoring them. If you hurry, we'll be out before they get back."

"Okay, stay put. I'll be there in twenty-five," she said, then hung up.

"Let's go," Jody said. "It's only ten minutes from here. Tremaine will tail her from her place."

Shane figured that meant Inky Dink was Tremaine.

When they got back into the van, Rodriquez slid behind the wheel again. Jody sat in the passenger seat, Shane on the floor in the back as before. This time they left the cuffs off.

"Get rollin'," Jody instructed. Rodriquez put the van in gear and pulled away from the motel.

They drove for three miles to the old abandoned airfield. It was on a hundred acres, but had only a twenty-five-hundred-foot runway and was right next to the Van Nuys wash. The underdeveloped site had become too valuable for a "propeller only" landing strip, so it had recently been sold to a big developer. A sign on the rusting wire fence proclaimed it as the future site of the Dominico Gardens Condominium Project.

They parked near a culvert. Jody began fiddling with the radio, finally tuning in a rap station. Synthetic drums and black anger filled the van.

"When'd you start listening to this shit?" Shane asked. "You used t'like jazz."

"Funny, but now I puke when I hear jazz. I need some 'tude with my tunes."

"Can I have my gun?"

Jody looked at him for a long time.

"Hey, Jody, you want me to cap this bitch or not? If I'm gonna do it, I'm gonna need a piece, or am I supposed to just kill her with a rock?"

Jody just smiled. "Calm down, Salsa. . . . Here." He reached into his belt and handed Shane's nine-millimeter Mini-Cougar back to him. Shane nodded as he pulled out the clip and checked it. The Remington Lights glittered in the pale moonlight. He slammed the clip back, then stuck the automatic into his belt.

"Okay, we're in the bushes," Jody said. "And, Shane . . . much as I hate to say this: You take her, or I'm taking you."

Jody nodded at Rodriquez; they got out of the van and walked across the road. Shane watched them until he lost them in the dark.

Twenty minutes later Shane saw Alexa's headlights pull up behind him.

COP KILLERS

ALEXA ARRIVED IN her Crown Victoria, pulling around and parking in front of the van. Shane stood by the open driver's door, glancing off, trying to see, without luck, where Jody and Rodriquez were hiding. The rising sun was just beginning to light the edge of the horizon. Shephard's radio was on the seat near him, turned down low. Jody and Rodriquez had handsets and were planning to broadcast a phony surveillance.

"Whose wheels are those?" Alexa asked, nodding at the van as she got out of the Crown Vic.

"Rental. Didn't want to use my car—Jody knows it," Shane answered.

Alexa approached him with the manila file in her hand. She was dressed in jeans with a blue LAPD windbreaker and had skinned her black hair back and fastened it with a clip. She wore no makeup, and he could see tension pulling at the corners of her mouth.

Suddenly, Jody's voice came over the radio, startling both of them: "Snake, this is Gopher. . . . Hold your position. I'm comin' to you."

"Dick-brain is still in there with his dealer. They're probably gonna inhale the retail," Rod's voice answered. "If these assholes are chalked up, it could get screwy."

"Roger," Jody said. "We're holding the back door. Let 'em come out. We'll do the takedown on the street. Out."

Shane smiled at her. "Sounds like they're gonna be occupied for a while." She nodded. Jody and Rodriquez were doing the scam broadcast for Alexa's benefit, but she already knew it was bullshit. Shane and Alexa didn't dare break cover for fear that there was a mike hidden in the van—the ultimate game of cheating the cheaters.

The file in her hand was the original. The copy had been scanned into the computer and was in a safe at the Questioned Documents Division. Filosiani had wanted them to use the original in Shephard's ballpoint pen, so Jody wouldn't become suspicious.

"That it?" Shane asked, pointing to the folder and reciting his first line, not knowing whether Jody could even hear him, but taking no chances.

"Yeah. Where is this place you found—how far from here?" she responded.

"It's right on the other side of the fence; the blue and white hangar by the gas pumps. The whole place is deserted. I'm not gonna lug this thing," he said, and switched off the radio.

Then he led her a hundred yards up the road to the pad-locked gate.

"There," he said, pointing through the fence at the hangar. "The big blue and white one. I've been through it. They got sleeping bags, Coleman lanterns, ice coolers. . . . Place looks like an ad for *Field and Stream*."

"That's private property. Did you even bother to get a search warrant?"

"No, where'm I gonna get a warrant in the middle of the night?"

"You need a warrant, dummy. We can't go on private prop-erty without one. Anything you find there will be inadmissi-ble."

"Fuck court. This isn't about court; it's about me an' Jody. That fucker lied to me. I'm gonna bring him down." Shane was almost screaming at her, hoping the argument would be overheard.

"That was it all along, wasn't it?" she said. "You don't care about prosecuting these guys; you just want revenge. You're a bleeding sore, Scully . . . no wonder you're going through a Pattern of Conduct Review. Gimme the book," she demanded.

"I left it in there."

"Why on earth did you do that?" she challenged.

"Because if they got back before you arrived and the book was gone, they'd know somebody tossed the place. Jesus, how many of these have you been on?"

"Okay . . . it can still work," she said. "We won't touch any-thing or leave our prints around. We'll check out the book together. If it translates, we'll back out, call for a warrant and SWAT. Nobody has to know we went in there illegally first.

That way we can still use the evidence." Lines written by the Day-Glo Dago.

Shane and Alexa had now arrived at the chain-link gate. After Shane picked the lock, they moved onto the deserted air-field, past a windsock long ago eaten by the toxic L.A. air. It hung at the end of a rusting pole, like the shredded skin of a dead animal. They had agreed earlier to say nothing unscripted, to avoid surreptitious communication for fear they might be under high-powered directional mikes and a telephoto lens. Shane thought this choice of an open location might have been designed by Jody to give Shane and Alexa a chance to reveal themselves to some long-range listening device.

Once they got to the hangar, Shane picked another padlock. He swung the door wide, and they walked into the huge, seem-ingly empty space.

The timing was now very critical.

Filosiani's idea was simple but dangerous: Shane was to lure Alexa out and then shoot her with a light load. The Day-Glo Dago explained that she would be wearing Kevlar. Filosiani wanted to know who they were working for, what crime they were about to pull off, and how deep the corruption went in-side the LAPD—from possible Glass House commanders all the way down to the suspected moles inside the Clerical Division. If Jody thought Shane had murdered another police officer to acquire Shephard's file, the hope was that he would eventually accept Shane into the conspiracy and give him its entire scope.

The critical part of the timing came right after Shane fired his light load into Alexa's Kevlar vest. SWAT was supposed to arrive immediately after the gunshot, before Jody would be able to check Alexa and see that she was wearing body armor.

They were then going to let Shane and Jody escape amid a hail of nonfatal gunfire. It had to look good and go down fast.

Shane glanced around the hangar's interior, but because it was windowless and dark, he couldn't see if anybody was hiding in the blackness. He knew that SWAT had tailed Alexa's car from a distance, using a GPS sending device attached to her bumper. They should be a mile or more back, so Tremaine would not be able to spot them. Shane hoped that Jody had sneaked inside to witness the "killing."

"Hand over the file," Shane said.

"I want the key book first."

"There isn't one, you dumb bitch," Shane said, then pulled his gun, ominously aiming it at her.

"You piece of shit. You cut a deal with Jody, didn't you?" she shrieked.

"Gimme the file," he repeated, cocking the gun for emphasis.

"This is a dumb play, Scully. I called in SWAT. They followed me. You didn't think I was gonna wander in here without cover, did you?" Alexa said. This sentence was supposed to keep Shane clean when SWAT did in fact arrive.

"Whatta I do, Jody?" Shane called into the darkness.

"It's bullshit . . . a bluff," Jody's voice called back from somewhere inside the hangar. "What the fuck you waiting for? Give her the pill."

Shane and Alexa gave each other tight smiles. The trap was set; Jody was inside the hangar with them, watching.

Shane stepped forward, snatched the manila file out of her hand, and checked it.

"Cap her!" Jody ordered. "Do it now!"

Shane aimed his gun at Alexa, but even though all of this

was rigged and she was wearing Kevlar under her windbreaker, he was afraid to fire.

"Do it, man! Whatta ya stalling for? She's bluffing. . . . There's no SWAT team!" Jody screamed from somewhere above. "Blow the bitch away, or I will!" They heard him trombone the slide on his automatic weapon.

Shane had no choice. He fired.

The Mini-Cougar bucked powerfully in his hand, surprising him with its kick.

It felt like a full-load recoil. How could that be? The clip contained Remington Lights.

Alexa flew backward, blood spurting from her chest where his bullet had entered.

He couldn't believe what he was seeing: His round had punched through the Kevlar. "Shit!" he screamed.

Suddenly, all hell broke loose. A machine gun started chattering outside, then two others joined in.

"Let's go! Let's go!" Jody screamed. "She brought backup!"

Shane was standing over Alexa's dead body, looking down at a growing pool of blood spreading out around her shoulders. "No . . ." he murmured in shock. More gunfire outside. Jody's footsteps pounding down a set of stairs somewhere behind him. At least ten weapons were now working outside.

Shane was still looking down at her, dumbfounded, when Jody grabbed him and pulled him across the hangar. Shane stumbled over his feet while his stomach leaped toward his throat. He barely avoided vomiting.

A door flew open on the far side of the hangar, and Rodriquez appeared. "Let's go, man! It's a fuckin' SWAT meet out there—they got ten guys and a step van!"

Shane was dragged along by Jody as they followed Rodriquez through connecting doors into an adjoining building. He could see a red-and-gray Bell Jet Ranger with skids and no FAA numbers parked inside on a rolling platform under a center light. Both side doors had been removed from the chopper. A blond man Shane had never seen before was in the pilot's seat; he already had the helicopter whining to life. The big rotors began to turn slowly overhead. Jody snatched a garage-door clicker off a nearby table and aimed it at a huge set of electric elephant doors. He pushed the button. Immediately, the metal slats of the doors began rattling, creaking, and clanking as they went up. Rodriquez moved to the opening door and stood just inside, pouring lead into the predawn darkness. Hot brass clattered and chimed at his feet. Jody pushed Shane into the back of the chopper, then dove in behind him. They could hear a constant barrage of machine-gun fire as SWAT team officers and rogue cops swapped 9-millimeter ordnance.

"Pick it up!" Jody shouted at the pilot.

The helicopter, with its engine at full roar, lifted up slightly and hovered inches above the portable pad. The rotor wind set up a perilous cross-draft inside the hangar, buffeting the Bell Jet Ranger from all sides. It began rocking dangerously but crept forward. When it was halfway out of the building, Tremaine jumped onto one skid and the gray-eyed Mexican hopped onto the other. The pilot pulled the collective back, and the helicopter rose while both men stood on the skids firing MAC-10 pistols at the SWAT officers below.

They were climbing rapidly, crossing the dirt taxiway. Shane could see three police cars and a black SWAT van falling away quickly beneath them as they pulled up. He could see sparks of gunfire aimed at them, but the chopper was moving too fast and SWAT was aiming low. Then they were heading north, leaving the police gunfire behind.

"Fuck you!" Jody yelled triumphantly out the open helicopter door at the distant line of black-helmeted police.

Tremaine and Rodriquez, still hanging on the skids, emptied their clips until the slides locked open. The airfield was now far away, out of sight.

"Mexico," Jody said, grinning at the pilot. The helicopter turned south to meet the Pacific coastline.

Shane sat numbly in the backseat wedged beside Jody, who suddenly grabbed the file out of his hand.

"We're clean," he was looking at the file full of pages crowded with numbers.

Rodriquez and Tremaine swung inside the helicopter and found seats, forcing Shane to slide over, pinning him to the bulkhead next to the door opening.

"Good catch, Salsa," Jody shouted triumphantly. "Way t'dig it outta the dirt."

He reached over, took the gun out of Shane's grip, and popped the clip. "You see the way she flew when your slug hit her? That's 'cause she was flacked, man. Good thing I put one of these in the pipe for you." He pulled a bullet out of his pocket and held it up. The Remington Lights Shane had checked were still in the clip, unfired. "Black Talons. Cop killers! I put one in the breech. Bastards explode on impact." Jody smiled at Shane, who just sat there, unable to get his mind around it. "You never woulda got the job done with that light load."

Shane was reeling.

He had shot and killed a woman whom just two days ago he had decided to marry.

"Hey, lighten up," Jody yelled over the helicopter roar. "You said you wanted her wet. It's done. You made your bones, man. Don't fuck it up. Don't gimme a reason to have second thoughts now."

Shane looked at Jody and forced a smile onto his face, but it felt as wide and ghastly as the grille of an old Buick.

21

THE VIKINGS

THEY FLEW STRAIGHT out over the ocean, staying under the radar, skimming the whitecaps kicked up by a gusty Santa Ana wind. Once they were six miles out to sea, they banked south toward Mexico. Occasionally, Shane could see a large fishing boat off on the horizon, drifting lazily in the chop, packed to the rails with beer-drinking day fishers.

They streaked over a school of dolphins, twenty or more, humping playfully along in the same direction.

Then after an hour, Jody screamed something at the pilot that Shane couldn't make out over the roar of the engine and slipstreaming air that was rocketing in through the missing side doors. It must have been a shouted direction, because a minute later the pilot altered his course and headed northeast, until they passed over the rugged shoreline of Mexico. Then they were flying low over the open sandy beaches of the Baja Peninsula, streaking along above the windblown surf, the seven o'clock morning sun climbing out of the mountains to the east, lighting the frothy tips of waves and throwing long streaks of sunlight across the white windblown beaches. The helicopter's shadow chased beneath them on the sand, catching up to them a foot at a time as the sun began its slow climb.

It was morning on the worst day of Shane's life.

He sat stoically, the racket of the engine and the buffeting wind mercifully killing Jody's normal inclination to talk.

Shane was trying to find a way to deal with his devastation over Alexa. He knew if he didn't get his head working, he would end up just as dead.

He was suddenly struck by the realization that his own death could be a release. Death would take him out of this pain, and transport him to another place. He would be free of himself, away from this soul-destroying guilt.

Or would he?

There was still Chooch to think about. He could see his handsome son in his memory, standing on the other side of the airport metal detector, holding his pads and duffel.

Don't fuck this up with some whack move, Chooch had warned.

Shane had destroyed it beyond their wildest dreams. It was off the scale. But didn't he still owe it to Alexa to see the mission through?

Or should he just dive out the open door—DFO into the sand at eighty miles an hour, snap his neck, cartwheel into the black, leaving it all behind?

In the end, he knew he couldn't give Jody an easy way out. If he was going to die, he'd take Jody with him. He'd have more honor as a kamikaze than as a suicide. He would bring Jody down . . . for himself and for Alexa. He would do it without mercy or regret.

Then, as if he could sense Shane's murderous pledge, Jody shivered and zipped up his windbreaker.

"There!" Jody yelled, and smacked Shane on the shoulder, pointing at a deserted beach at the mouth of a river.

Shane nodded as the pilot again altered his course, shooting across the beach and up a narrow wash, slowing as the hills narrowed on both sides of the low flying chopper. The Bell Jet Ranger continued a few hundred yards up the gully, swapped ends, then hovered over a patch of grass.

A short way off, Shane could see a dusty new blue-and-white, thirty-six-foot, double-axle Vogue motor home parked on a dirt clearing—an expensive rig with all the extras. A satellite dish poked up from the roof. Two men were standing in front, shielding their eyes, shifting and turning away from the swirling rotor sand as the helicopter settled. Even at that distance, Shane could see that one of the men was gargantuan, leaning on crutches, his left leg bandaged from ankle to hip. The last time Shane had seen him, they were faced off over gun barrels behind the noise-abatement house. Shane felt the skids touch ground, and the pilot started flipping switches as the engine wound down.

"Let's go." Jody was out of the helicopter first, followed immediately by Tremaine and Hector Rodriquez. As Shane started to exit, he looked into the expressionless, hazel eyes of the pilot, who wore his weathered complexion like a snake's skin.

"David VanKirk. Jody calls me Lord of the Skies," the man said. "I was in the Police Air Unit until IAD terminated me for flying drugs up on weekends. Now I drive this taxi for the Vikings. Personally, I don't give a shit whether you get a piece of this or not. I'm on a flat deal. But you got trouble here. Watch out for Rod, and Sawdust."

"Sawdust?" Shane asked.

"Yeah. The tall thin guy over there by the motor home. Sergeant Lester Wood—Sawdust. Get it? Jody's got nicknames for everyone."

"Always did."

"See the steroid case on crutches, next to Sawdust? That's Victory Smith. His real name is Peter. You shouldn't a'shot him. . . . Jody thinks he can control them but most a'these guys are doing heavy drugs now. My guess is, you won't last the day."

David VanKirk turned away and finished shutting down the helicopter.

"Thanks for the heads-up." Shane got off the backseat and reluctantly followed Tremaine, Rodriquez, and Jody over to the two men waiting by the Vogue coach. Jody turned to him as he approached.

"This is Hot Sauce," Jody said, laying a protective hand on Shane's shoulder.

All four men glowered at him in silence. Shane found himself trading eye-fucks with the barrel-chested monster on crutches. When they'd exchanged gunfire, Shane had been so jacked on adrenaline that he'd missed Victory's overpowering brutishness. Now, standing in this Mexican wash, he took a better inventory. Viewed piece by piece, he was impressive, but the combined effect was awesome.

Victory Smith was propped up on crutches, the massive slabs of muscle on his shoulders rising and falling slowly with each breath like plates on a weight-lifting machine. His neck triangulated down on overdeveloped trapezius muscles. A MAC-10 was tucked in his belt, and a webbed bandolier full of magnum nines was stretched across a sixty-inch chest; his biceps flexed at least twenty-five inches. Riding atop this angry tower of muscle was a narrow face, pinched and mean, with a complexion as rough as lunar lava, pockmarked and rutted by steroids. Prehistoric, reptilian eyes never moved off Shane, tracking him mercilessly. He was predatory, deadly, and barely in control.

"Our code name is Vikings," Jody was saying. "It was given to us originally by Captain Medwick. I kinda like it, so we've kept it. Hector Rodriquez and Peter Smith are 'Hot Rod' and 'Victory.' They're both ex-SWAT. Tremaine Lane, here, is 'Inky Dink,' and this too-tall, half-mute Texas motherfucker dressed like Clint Eastwood is Sergeant Lester Wood: 'Sawdust.' They were in SIS with me."

Shane had hardly noticed Lester Wood, he'd been so focused on Victory Smith. Now he glanced over and saw a man who radiated silent disapproval. Wood was close to six-four and unnaturally thin, dressed in dusty, worn cowboy clothes. A silver rodeo buckle divided faded jeans from a denim work shirt. He had on a new windbreaker vest, rough-out bull-rider boots, and old-style Ray-Ban aviator sunglasses that were coldly studying Shane from under the brim of a custom-made Charlie Tweddle cowboy hat.

"Shane, I know you two had a little run-in a while back," Jody said, indicating Victory Smith. "But I want you guys to get past it."

Shane didn't say anything; a few more amps of pure hatred spread across the weight lifter's steroid-cratered face.

Jody put his arm around Shane. "This is my old Little League catcher. He's in for an equal share. Nobody fucks with Hot Sauce, or they deal with me, *personally*. Now, let's break out that beer an' get a fire going. We got plans to make. Bring all that shit down to the beach." Pointing at three coolers sitting on the ground near the motor home, he opened the door and disappeared inside.

Shane found himself looking at four seething ex-cops. Nobody spoke.

"In literature, this is called a pregnant moment," Shane finally said, trying to break the tension.

"Hey, asshole," Victory Smith whispered, "I don't know what you think you got goin' here, but far as I can see, you're just a walking corpse."

"Maybe you should take that up with Jody," Shane answered.

"Fuck Jody," Victory growled. Moments later Jody bounded out of the motor home and set down a cooler of beer. He saw the anger, hesitated, then started pulling cold brews out of the ice chest and flipping them around at the circle of men.

Smith made no move to catch his. It ricocheted off his crutch and landed in the sand.

Jody tried to talk their anger down. "To begin with, let's get a few facts straight. This ain't his fault. He saw me on the freeway. My mistake—not his. He did what any one a'you woulda done if you saw a friend you thought was dead. He looked into it."

Now they were all glaring at Jody.

"He shot an LAPD sergeant for us. Killed the acting head of DSG and took this file." He reached into his back pocket, pulled out the folded manila folder, and waved it at them. "Hot Rod and Inky Dink were there. Right? Tell 'em what you saw."

Reluctantly, Tremaine Lane and Hector Rodriquez nodded, but the nods were so subtle, they were almost imperceptible.

"This file is in code, but it says we're all still alive. Fortunately, it's the original and there are no copies. Right, Hot Sauce?"

"Right," Shane answered.

"It was only hours from being sent to the Questioned Documents Division. We were all about to get made. Without Scully, our whole deal was dust. So, in my opinion, that gets him a piece."

"Then give him your piece," Smith said darkly.

"And what're you gonna do, Victory? You gonna lead cheers and be in charge a'that fuckin' crutch? Who's gonna handle your end of it, now that you're draggin' one leg?"

"I wouldn't be draggin' it if yer buddy here hadn't shot me," Victory said, but his eyes shifted briefly away, then came back.

"You're supposed t'be a SWAT Home Incursion Specialist, so how come you're the one ended up stopping a round?"

Victory didn't answer, but he leaned down, and with a long arm, scooped his beer out of the sand. He ripped the tab off; the can chirped and hissed foam.

"Okay. Let's go have this cookout. Sawdust, get the tattoo kit. Since Hot Sauce is a Viking, we gotta give him his leg piece."

Nobody moved.

"Is somebody gonna have to shed blood over this?" Jody asked softly.

"I ain't down with this shit, and I ain't sharin' my end with this peckerwood," Tremaine growled, but the rest of the Vikings turned, and Tremaine finally followed them toward the beach.

After they left, Jody smiled. "Give 'em a little time, Hot Sauce. They'll get over it."

"Right . . . " Shane said softly. "I'm gonna count on you to make that happen." Then he followed Jody down to the beach, feeling intense emotions directed toward his childhood friend—frustration, disillusion, and murderous rage.

22

THE VIKING FUNERAL

THE SMALL GAS generator hummed.

The tiny ink-filled needle whirred.

Tears filled Shane's eyes.

Lester Wood hunched over Shane's left ankle while Jody held it against a driftwood plank to stabilize it. Slowly, Sawdust drew the crude Viking helmet, freehanding the tattoo without a stencil, the horns reaching up the inside of Shane's foot unevenly, curling around his ankle bone.

Sawdust leaned into the needle, painfully blunt-ending the job. Shane could see a dark, sadistic smile twitching at the end of the ex-cop's bloodless, ruler-straight mouth. Shane clenched his teeth, determined not to cry out.

They had been on the beach all day, drinking. Shane had

tried to keep away from the alcohol, realizing that his survival depended on a clear head, but the ache inside him continued to grow. Finally, about noon, depression overcame him. He consumed beer after beer until sometime late in the day he realized he'd finished more than two six-packs and now felt bloated, sick, and unruly.

As the morning sun came up, the Vikings had stripped off their shirts, and Shane could see the insanity of Sawdust's body art; most of it done with standard stationery-store black ink. Hot Rod was sporting what street parlors call a Fullback Royal—a badly proportioned hand-drawn eagle emblazoned across his shoulder blades. It was still red and looked as though it was getting infected.

All of the Vikings except Tremaine Lane had the same free-hand Viking helmet on the inside of their ankles, with additional designs on their arms and shoulders. It was low-grade prison-quality art, done in black ink with Sawdust's amateurish scrawl. For some reason, the African American ex-sergeant had no tattoos.

"There she be. . . . All done," Lester Wood said in his West Texas drawl. Shane looked down at his ankle: red, raw, and bleeding from dozens of deep new puncture marks.

"That's a tattoo?" he said angrily.

"Right now, it looks like beef day at the Injun Agency, but you wait an hour, then git it in the ocean, wash her off. It'll look fine when she heals." Sawdust snapped his kit closed, got up, grabbed a beer, and wandered off.

Shane's ankle throbbed as he stood. Most, if not all, of the Vikings seemed either wired or wasted. Shane watched as they drifted up the beach, away from him. Throughout the day he caught glimpses of their stash and saw fresh needle marks hiding in tattoo ink. Only Jody seemed to be drug-free, but he had been guzzling beer after beer.

Shane noticed that the unit was divided. Lester Wood sat at the north end of the beach with Tremaine Lane. Smith and Rodriquez stayed at the other end. More than once Shane caught the steroid junkie and the gray-eyed Mexican whispering, making plans and looking in his direction.

The end of the day finally came. At sunset, when Jody and Shane walked down the beach away from the others, Jody pulled a bottle of tequila out of his pocket. "How 'bout a shot a'Mexican courage," he said, handing it over.

Shane took the bottle, telling himself he would take only a sip, but once he got it up to his lips, he found himself swallowing hungrily, trying to burn loose the tangled knots inside him. His eyes were closed as he gulped it down, until he felt Jody's hand tugging at the flask.

"Hey, hey, Hot Sauce . . . save some for me." Jody pulled the bottle down to find it half empty.

"Yeah, right," Shane said. "Sorry."

"You hit the number this morning . . . put that round right through the ten ring. Clean shooting, Salsa." Jody was talking about Alexa's murder as if it had been a firing-range event.

Subliminal memories flashed:

Alexa flying backward, arms extended.

Blood spurting.

Eyes lifeless.

Shane winced inwardly and his face contorted. Jody saw the flinch. "Fuck her, man. . . . Give it up. She deserved what she got."

Shane nodded, but Jody's eyes were drilling—reading his thoughts, seeing his devastation.

"Don't do this grief thing, Salsa. Get over it." Jody ordered.

Shane nodded again. "You're right. Fuck it," he finally said. They walked on in silence for a few feet, then: "You got a disaster here, Jody. All these guys are cranked up."

"I know they seem a little fractured, but I'm trying to keep things in balance," Jody said.

"Balance . . . Yeah, right." Shane took a deep breath. "Victory Smith is popping Arnies like they're M&M's. He's got 'roid-rage'; it's the reason he wants to rip the shit outta everybody. The guy's got enough gym juice in him to bench-press a school bus. And Lester Wood . . . I saw his Baggie: cocaine and pills. Tremaine is just an alcoholic, and I think Rodriquez is candy flipping—heroin and Ecstasy. The only straight guy you got is VanKirk, and he just sits in that fuckin' helicopter playing Game Boy. You got a mess here, Jody."

"I gotta cut 'em some slack. I can't ride 'em too hard anymore, or they'll mutiny. The only one I'm seriously worried about is Victory. . . . He used t'be a good hammer, but you're right . . . lately his brains are on tumble dry. He quit functioning even before you shot him. But I'll handle it. Leave him to me. We'll all be straight when the deal goes down." He paused and leaned back against a rock outcropping.

What deal? Shane thought, but didn't ask.

"Back in the beginning, before we started doin' doors for Medwick, I had a tight group," Jody continued. "These guys were the best—handpicked. But once we began committing felonies, the LAPD Rules of Discipline and Engagement didn't cut it anymore. At first Mayweather just had us doin' low-grade stuff, and only against big-time organized criminals. We'd break into some shot caller's house and go through his desk, find out what his action was. Then we'd either dime him out to the appropriate division in the department and let them make a bust they could take to trial, or we'd swing down outta some tree and start capping the assholes, handle it ourselves, y'know? The drug-use thing started slow. At first I didn't know they were using, 'cause they did it in their own cribs at those damn airport houses. But once I thought about it, it made sense."

"Cops using drugs? . . . That's never gonna make sense."

"These guys were warriors, man—the best of the best—and the department had them committing crimes. It was fucking them up. So after some low-grade B&Es, a few started doing a line of coke here and there, maybe a little Mexican grass . . . nothin' too nasty, just a little chemical help after a confusing day. But after we took down Medwick and Shephard, a couple a'guys started seriously freaking. I even had t'lose a guy. He went completely haywire. We buried the poor motherfucker on a beach up in Oxnard. Right now I'm just trying to keep some balance here. I only need to hold it together for a little longer."

"Jody, you've been hanging with 'em too long. You've lost your perspective. These guys don't give a shit about anything. . . . Not money . . . Not life or death. They don't want what you want."

"You got 'em all figured out, huh? You're here six hours and you got the whole thing scoped," Jody said angrily, but handed Shane the bottle. "Give it a rest, Salsa."

They sat on a rock and watched the sun go down. A quarter moon came up and rode low on the horizon, reflecting on the silver-black ocean. Shane looked over and saw Jody staring out to sea; his expression was fixed but strangely wistful.

"I'm not saying it's not my fault. . . . I shoulda seen it coming." Jody was silent for a minute before turning toward Shane.

"When you cut to the chase, we all just got sold a buncha shit—end of story."

Shane wasn't sure what he was talking about. Whatever was going through Jody's mind, Shane couldn't fathom it. Somewhere along the way, Jody Dean got lost and this new person he didn't even recognize had taken his place.

The almost-empty tequila bottle slipped from Jody's grasp, then clattered onto the rocks and broke. "Protect and serve . . . Respect for individual dignity, compliance with lawful orders, duty to report misconduct . . . courtesy, gallantry, and morality in the service of the public trust. What a crock, huh?" Jody sounded drunk. "These Glass House swivel-chair commanders write this shit up. They put it in *The Management Guide to Discipline*. They force-feed it to us at the Academy, and we swallow it whole, like a buncha brain-dead assholes. It's a worthy ideal, but it's ill-conceived because you can't give life-or-death power to a bunch a'eighteen-year-old testosterone cases and not have a recipe for disaster. And the strange part is, the bosses in the Glass House don't give a shit; otherwise, they wouldn't sanction units like SIS or SWAT and fill them up with adrenaline junkies."

Shane remembered the discussions they'd had at the end, just before Jody faked his death and disappeared. Back then, Jody had argued that the department needed these two controversial units. He said it was cutting-edge law enforcement like the Special Investigations Section and Special Weapons and Tactics that held back the tide of criminal pollution.

"I thought you loved SIS."

"I was wrong. They finally let me see what a crock a'shit the whole deal really was." He paused, took a deep breath, then went on: "Right after the Vikings were formed, we were working a big drug laundry out of Southwest. We had forty Mexican bankers bagged and tagged and ready for the bus. Had these guys dirty, on videotape . . . big guys, white-collar crooks, at big banks like Bancomer and Banco ProMex. We had the pricks. The case was solid, so we took it to the bosses, Medwick and Mayweather . . . and guess what?"

"They cratered the investigation."

"Worse. They farmed it out to Justice because they were afraid of the political repercussions. If we arrested all these white-collar crooks in the Mexican banking system, they were afraid of the international pressure that would come down. Then, of course, Justice shut down the investigation to avoid the political turmoil. The same people who keep preaching about how we have to protect our children from drugs limited the scope of the investigation so it wouldn't become an international banking scandal for our NAFTA buddies in Mexico.

"When over a year's work hit the wall, we were already set up on this new sting, the one we're working now. It's even more potent. But instead of working it for the department so they could throw it away when it was time to book the perps, we decided to go ahead and work it ourselves. We had already stumbled onto an independent criminal contractor who was into something too good to turn down. We . . . How do I put this? We moved in on him and took over his action. We eventually had to lose him, too, but now we're runnin' his operation and interfacing with his criminal targets. Only this time, nobody gets busted. This time, we're keeping what we make. We're gonna say good-bye to that pile a'bricks up in L.A., split up and live on the Riviera or some damn place. . . . Anonymous millionaires."

"You had to *lose* him?" Shane asked. "You mean you killed him."

Jody turned and smiled suddenly at him. The smile seemed wide and loose and tinged with madness.

"So what is it?" Shane finally asked, changing the subject to get that scary look off Jody's face. "What's the new play?"

"Not yet, Hot Sauce . . . not yet." He pushed himself away from the rocks and stood. "We're outta here soon as I make a phone call and get the okay. Come on . . . I don't like to leave 'em alone too long to plot against me." He was grinning, but they both knew it was true.

...

It was after midnight.

Shane was on the beach, trying to sleep, but hadn't been able to shut his mind down. He had his head buried in the crook of his arm, while thoughts of Alexa tormented him. His ankle tattoo was throbbing. Twice earlier that evening, he had asked if he could check the locked motor home for bandages, but the Vikings just looked at him with dead eyes, as if they didn't want to waste precious medical supplies on a walking corpse.

Jody had been up the beach arguing with somebody on a portable satellite phone, so Shane didn't bother him. Finally, he had just torn off the bottom of his shirt, wet it in tequila, and wrapped his lower leg.

Shane was looking up at the stars, the ache of Alexa's loss deep inside him. Then he heard something. . . .

He lay still and heard it again: a rustle, like a puff of wind blowing dry grass.

He felt movement on the packed sand nearby. Although Jody

still had his Beretta, Shane had found a palm-size granite rock earlier and had put it next to him for protection. He reached out and slowly curled his fingers around it. The round, smooth surface filled his palm. His heartbeat quickened; neck hair bristled. He knew without looking that the man who was snaking up from behind was about to strike. He waited until he felt the ground quiver.

Shane lunged violently to his right.

A knife thundered down exactly where his chest had been. He scrambled to his knees and tried to spin around, but Hector Rodriquez lunged forward and grabbed him. The Mexican's muscular arms locked around Shane's neck, his gray eyes shining. The knife fell out of his hand onto the sand.

"Motherfucker," Rodriquez grunted, bearing down now, closing Shane's windpipe.

Shane dug his heels into the sand for traction as Rodriquez shifted his grip, going for the police choke hold. Shane had to move fast before his carotid artery was closed, shutting off the blood supply to his brain.

"Die, motherfucker," Rodriquez rasped into his ear, ratcheting down even harder. Shane felt consciousness dimming. He was out of options. He swung the rock in his right hand as hard as he could.

It hit with a mushy thud, and Rodriquez screamed. The Mexican let go of his throat, so Shane struggled up onto his knees, then spun around to face the big Hispanic, whose crushed nose was now spread across his face. Blood, lit by moonlight, appeared almost black and dripped from his chin, splattering in ugly Rorschach patterns on the white sand.

Rodriquez went to his belt with his right hand, pulled out a mini-Uzi, and chambered it. "Cocksucker!" he roared.

Then the muzzle flash of automatic gunfire lit the dark beach.

But it was Rodriquez, not Shane, who flew backward. Most of the Mexican's head was missing when he flopped onto the sand a few feet away.

Shane, startled and exhausted, looked over and saw Jody standing in the dark, holding a short-barrel Heckler & Koch machine pistol.

After a moment of silence, Jody walked over and pried the mini-Uzi out of the dead man's hand. "Dig a hole. . . . Let's get him buried." For the first time since he'd known him, Shane thought his old friend looked shaken.

Shane's eyes found Victory Smith behind Jody. . . . The weight lifter's pockmarked face was stretched into a grimace of hate. Shane knew that Smith had somehow managed to talk Rodriquez into the attempt on his life. Now, with Hot Rod dead, Victory Smith was not going to be held in check, no matter what Jody said.

■■■

Shane watched from the doorway of the motor home as Tremaine Lane dug the shallow grave, then Lane and Wood dragged the near-headless body of Hector Rodriquez over and laid him at the edge of the fresh pit. Victory Smith teetered on his crutches in smoldering silence.

Jody came to the motor home, opened a side compartment, and pulled out a five-gallon can of Coleman lantern fluid. "We're gonna give him a Viking funeral. No invitation required. Come on," he said.

They walked to the edge of the hole where the three other Vikings stood, expressionless.

"Okay, let's get something straight," Jody said. "Rodriquez

died because he couldn't focus on the problem. I talked to Papa Joe this afternoon, and the plans have changed. He wants us up in the Springs tomorrow night to meet the other players. That means we gotta get movin' now. We've got a week, maybe less, before we cash in. After that, we don't ever have to see each other again. But I can't pull this off if we keep losing people." He looked around at their sullen faces. "Starting tonight, no more drugs. This guy's dead 'cause he couldn't keep the spike outta his arm. I'm friskin' everybody 'fore you get on the coach. If you don't ditch your stash, you don't leave with us. The Lord of the Skies will fly you back, and you lose your cut." Nobody spoke, but they all stood there, glaring. "Okay, let's plant him."

Tremaine Lane and Lester Wood rolled Rodriquez into the hole. He thudded when he hit the bottom, three feet down.

"Anybody wanna say anything?" Jody asked.

"Motherfucker sure used a lot of X," Tremaine finally murmured.

Jody emptied half a can of Coleman lantern fluid onto the body, then dropped in a match. The body exploded in fire. They stood there, around the flaming grave, watching Hot Rod burn until they could no longer make out the shape of him.

As Shane watched, he felt another wave of soul pollution that darkened his world and deadened his senses. The moment stood as a dark premonition of the path his life had taken. The depression brought with it a listless loss of self that made everything seem unimportant—even Alexa's murder.

The body crackled and burned, until finally all that was left was glowing ash.

"That concludes the service," Jody said softly.

23
LISA

SHANE SAW THE distant lights of Palm Springs shimmering on the horizon like a counterfeit jewel. The motor home was crusted with brown sand from the rutted dirt roads they had taken in Mexico before finally crossing the border at Mexicali, then turning northwest toward the Cochella Valley.

The entire way across Baja and into California, nobody had mentioned the shooting of Rodriquez, but the memory certainly lingered.

Then they were driving through downtown Palm Springs, on North Palm Canyon Drive, past Arby's barbecue joints and faux French restaurants, past golf courses and Bentley dealerships.

They left Palm Springs proper and started to pass through neighboring towns, strung back-to-back along Highway 111 like brightly painted beads. They passed Smoketree Village and Palm Springs Heights, with their estate homes built low on the desert hillsides . . . then drove through Cathedral City, the only tarnished bead on this expensive necklace of resort towns. Used-clothing stores and taco stands stood side by side like passengers at a skid-row bus stop trying desperately to ignore one another.

They drove through Rancho Mirage and Indian Wells, finally arriving at the exclusive development community of La Quinta.

The same three architects must have been making a killing in the Cochella Valley. Everywhere he looked, Shane saw Spanish arches and terra-cotta tile. In La Quinta, every palm tree was bathed in its own 2,000-watt xenon "up-light." All of this costly, brightly lit architecture was draped in colorful purple and red hibiscus and bougainvillea.

La Quinta was upscale housing that stretched along several world-class golf courses.

Jody had driven the last leg of the journey and now turned the big, dusty motor home into a new "behind the gates" development project called La Quinta Esperanza. He pulled up to the guard shack and tapped the horn. An octogenarian in a crisp brown uniform decorated with shiny yellow shoulder patches came out of his flower-draped shack with a clipboard and limped over to the driver-side window.

"Howdy," Jody said, grinning. "I'm Lewis Foster. I think I'm expected. I'm a guest of José Mondragon's."

The man scowled at his clipboard as if it contained the results of his last prostate exam. "Can't see with these glasses," he muttered. "Gotta get me a new prescription."

"Lemme help," Jody said, reaching for the clipboard. He

found his alias and pointed to it: "Lew Foster. Right there," he said, handing over his phony driver's license obtained by the ATF Undercover Documents Section.

The old man grabbed the clipboard back and nodded. "Yep . . . Yep, sure 'nuff, there she is," he muttered. "I'll get the keys." He returned Jody's license, then limped painfully back into the shack.

"They musta got this plastic badge from Geezers 'R' Us," Jody growled. "If this dinosaur is our security, we're gonna have t'post our own watch. Inky Dink, you got the first duty."

There was a groan from Tremaine Lane in the back of the motor home, then the old man came back and handed Jody a set of keys. "It's the big Spanish one . . . very end of Desert Flower Drive."

The house was at least five thousand square feet and sat at the end of a cul-de-sac. Jody pulled into the circular drive and parked the Vogue coach in front of a four-car garage. Fairways from the adjoining golf course bordered the hacienda-style home.

The Spanish structure was two stories and, from the landscaping, looked as though it had just been completed. Topiary trees cut into veterinary shapes were lit by pale moonlight and haunted the perimeter of the house, rustling in the desert wind like restless spirits.

They climbed out of the motor home, then passed through the side gate into the courtyard, where a wing of guest suites horseshoed around an Olympic-size pool. A few shanked golf balls were submerged in the deep end.

One by one, Jody opened up the guest suites with his keys, and members of the Vikings picked their accommodations. All of the rooms were big, with kitchenettes, living rooms, and remarkable views of either the fairway or the mountains beyond.

Shane's room had a phone jack but no phone. Not that he would attempt to contact Chief Filosiani under these circumstances. He was supposed to get loose and call in, but so far he'd had no opportunity. Also, he didn't know what to say to the Day-Glo Dago, how to explain the "cop killer" bullet Jody had put in the breech of his gun that resulted in Alexa's death.

He undressed in his bathroom, then put his clothes in the suite's apartment-style vertical washing machine and dryer. He set the wash cycle; then wearing only a terry-cloth robe he found in the closet, Shane went outside to swim a few laps. He hoped some exercise would help get his head clear. He shrugged off the borrowed robe and dove naked into the water. His new, raw tattoo shot pain up his ankle all the way to his knee, but he ignored it and kicked hard to the bottom. Just for the hell of it, he retrieved a Titleist 4 golf ball with a huge smile cut in the side, then he frog-kicked the length of the pool under water. When he came up on the far end, he dropped the ball on the deck, and it rolled slowly to a stop between two patent-leather high-heeled pumps. He glanced up, looking into the jade-green eyes of a blond woman in a black-striped business jacket and matching skirt. A world-class beauty, she was standing at the edge of the pool, holding an ostrich briefcase, smiling down at him with open delight.

"José said this place was well stocked," she mused, studying his nude body, "but this is almost too good to believe."

"Jesus, lady. . . . Where the hell did you come from?" Shane blurted.

"Panama City," she replied, deadpan. "And you would be who? The famous but mysterious La Quinta Water Nymph?"

"Funny. You wanna turn around so I can get my robe?"

"Not on your life."

A man's voice called out: "Lisa, let's go! We're late! You can meet these people later."

Shane looked over the pool deck. Standing in the doorway of the lit living room, about twenty yards away, was a short but powerfully built dark-skinned Hispanic man dressed in a black suit. Despite the Palm Springs heat, he had an overcoat draped on his right arm.

"Coming, José," she called to him, then turned back to Shane, kissed her fingertips, and wiggled them seductively at him. "I guess, as the man says, we're going to have to meet later," she said, smiling. Then she turned and walked away, making a show of it, her calves flexing, her short, tailored skirt flipping playfully against sculpted thighs.

LAUNDRY

"COME ON, WE need to talk," Jody said, startling Shane. He had just dressed and spun toward the open door, but Jody had already left.

He grabbed his wallet off the bed, stuffed it into his pants, and followed.

Shane found Jody standing behind the house by the golf course, on the edge of the sixth fairway, staring out at the moonlit grounds. As Shane approached, Jody handed something to him in the dark. "Here."

Shane couldn't see what it was, but when he took it, he was surprised to find his Beretta still in its Yaqui Slide ankle holster.

"Figured after what happened in Mexico, maybe you shouldn't wander around without that. I reloaded it for ya. Full loads."

The gun that killed Alexa.

Darkness hovered, but Shane pushed it away. He sat on the grass and strapped the holster to his right ankle, which thankfully was not the one with the throbbing tattoo.

Jody squatted down beside him on his haunches, Indian-style. "Okay, Hot Sauce. You won't be much help to me if you don't know what's going on, so here's the deal. I already told you about these Mexican bankers, the ones we lost to the Justice Department. . . ."

"Yeah . . ." Shane waited, and finally Jody continued.

"Well, hiding out at the edge of that bust was this little guy we couldn't identify. Name was Leon J. Fine. Turns out he was an L.A. bail bondsman. He was trying to write some paper on one or two of these Mexican bankers. I got a friendly judge to shut that down fast. All of those guys were big-time flight risks—white-collar crooks with no priors. These Mexican bankers were all sitting in jail having anal-penetration nightmares. The judge agreed that if they ever bonded out, everybody woulda been back in Mexico before the first siesta. Anyway, so here's this little shitball bondsman, L. J. Fine, hanging around the edge of my bank case. Maybe he pissed me off, or something about him didn't add up. Either way, I got interested. After Justice took over our case, I had some time on my hands, so I put one or two days in on the guy just to see what his story was . . . and guess what this schmuck was doing?"

"Beats me."

"He was going out to airports, getting on private jets that belonged to Fortune 500 companies, and flying all over the place like he was Prince Abu Dabi or somethin'. So I'm saying to myself, What does my little low-rent L.A. bondsman have on these big corporations, and why are they flying him around in their twenty-million-dollar corporate jets?" Jody smiled at him. "Wanna guess?"

"Why don't you just tell me."

"You ever hear of something called the parallel market?" Jody asked.

"No, I haven't."

"Don't feel bad, neither had I. It's a little confusing till you get the hang of it, but basically, a lot of big Fortune 500 corporations are using their product to launder Colombian drug money. And it's bigger by a bunch than the Mexican bank bust, 'cause hundreds of these U.S. companies are doin' it . . . and have been for over twenty years. Any company with a product that's worth a lot, but doesn't weigh much—like cigarettes or booze or electronics—is prime for the hustle."

"You're shittin' me," Shane said, thinking he must have heard wrong.

"That's what I thought at first, but it's true. The deal we're working right now is with All-American Tobacco. I guess it's not enough these guys are killing us with their cancer sticks, now they're also laundering Cali cartel drug money."

Shane asked, "How do cigarettes or liquor products wash drug cash?"

"It took me a couple a'months to figure it out, but here's the headline on how it works. Let's say my little schmendrik— my bail bondsman, Leon Fine—wants some money to buy a new house, or a speedboat, or some other damn thing. He calls around to drug dealers he knows—guys he's written paper on, and he asks, 'Hey, Pedro, how much money have you got stored up?' Let's say, for easy math, Pedro has ten million in an L.A. collection house, and it's Cali cartel money, and he needs to get it laundered for his *patron* in Colombia. So he says to Leon: 'I got ten cartwheels, but I gotta do the deal with a black marketeer in Colombia, 'cause my *jefe* wants the cash to end up in Colombia. Then Pedro, the drug dealer, puts Leon in touch with some Colombian black marketeers. Actually there are six families in Medellín who specialize in parallel-market goods. After Leon sets up his deal with Pedro and the black marketeers he calls the Blackstone Corporation—"

"Who?"

"Blackstone. It's a big Swiss free-market trading corporation. There are a bunch of foreign trade companies who do this shit. Blackstone is one of 'em. They're the guys who run the duty-free shops in airports—they also run duty-free zones all over the place. And, Shane, you won't believe this, but these foreign duty-free corporations are running the biggest drug laundries in the world, and have been for two decades."

"How could that be? I been a cop for twenty years and I never even heard a'them."

"Me neither," Jody said. "Anyway, my bondsman, Leon, says to his contact at Blackstone: 'I got ten million in drug cash from Pedro in L.A. to buy cigarettes, and I have a deal set with Colombian black marketeers, so I need the smokes delivered to Aruba.' Aruba is inside the Caribbean duty-free zone and it's legal for All-American Tobacco to ship as much product there as they want." He paused. "Got it so far?"

Shane nodded.

"Okay, good . . . The Aruba duty-free zone stretches from Aruba across to South America, specifically to Caracas, Venezuela, which is, lo and behold . . . right on the Colombian border. Leon's black marketeer has his smuggling business in a little border town out in the desert, called Maicao." Shane remembered that Maicao was one of the towns circled on the map he found in the noise abatement house on East Lannark Drive. Now everything's set up and ready to go." Jody continued, "Blackstone calls All-American Tobacco and says: 'Ship ten million dollars' worth of Virginia Fives to Aruba for the parallel market.' "

"Virginia Fives?"

"Yeah . . . top-quality Virginia tobacco. See, a lot of the product sold in South America is shit: Turkish leaves or stuff grown in the South American jungle. The top quality V-Five is what everybody wants. So now the guy at All-American says, 'Okay, we'll take a meeting.' Then Blackstone puts a sales distribution executive from All-American in touch with my L.A. bail bondsman, Leon, and they cut a deal. Still with me?"

"Yeah. The bondsman is making a deal with a major drug dealer in L.A. for cash. Then he makes a deal with All-American Tobacco to buy the cigarettes with the drug money, using this Swiss duty-free company, Blackstone, as the middle man."

"Exactly. You got a real knack for this, Hot Sauce. Okay, next, Papa Joe Mondragon, who is Blackstone's head of Latin American Ops, gets in touch with the Cali cartel leader in Colombia. Let's say it's the Bacca family. Papa Joe confirms the deal. The cash is then handed over to Leon, who picks it up in L.A. using a step van, because that much cash is bulky as hell. Leon takes it to a compliant bank, where he deposits it and wires it to one or two other U.S. banks, to wipe out the paper trail. Then he wires it to a numbered account in a bank in Aruba, where it's held and earmarked to go to All-American

Tobacco to pay for the cigarettes when they finally arrive in Aruba. That gets both the cigarettes and the drug money to pay for them out of the U.S. and safely into the Aruba duty-free zone. You with me still?"

"Yeah. . . . Two bank transfers to throw off any suspicious bank examiner, and now the drug cash is in Aruba along with the smokes."

"Exactly. What makes this deal really sweet for the tobacco company is, normally AAT sells a case of cigarettes, which contains fifty cartons, for a base price of a hundred dollars in the legitimate market. But remember, they have to pay U.S. federal cigarette taxes, so that pushes their sales price per case up to three hundred dollars."

"The federal duty on a case of cigarettes is two hundred dollars?" Shane asked, surprised by the amount.

"Cigarette taxes are a bitch. Except on this deal, these cigarettes are gonna be smuggled out of the duty-free zone, into Colombia, and All-American is never going to have to pay the taxes. But AAT sells them to Leon for three hundred dollars a case anyway, just as if the taxes were attached. So instead of making a hundred dollars a case on these smokes, they're actually making three hundred. A much, much better deal for All-American."

"So the parallel market in Colombia is way more profitable for them than the legitimate market."

Jody nodded. "Then the cigarettes are shipped by All-American to Aruba and smuggled into Colombia, where they're sold. Then my little schmendrik, Leon, collects the drug cash, which is in the Aruba bank, and wires All-American Tobacco their money. He also pays Blackstone, which takes a three percent cut. Leon gets his percentage. Then the cigarettes are sold in the Bacca cartel black-market malls in Colombia. That completes the circle, because once Bacca sells them, he gets his L.A. street cash back. The Cali cartel loses about forty percent from the original ten million for this laundry service, but he can now say he's a legitimate cigarette broker and claim his income without fear of prosecution. Everybody goes away rich and happy."

"You're shittin' me."

"That's what this little bald geek, Leon, was doing. And get this: Leon's end of the deal is thirty percent of the gross amount. Off that original ten million bucks, he would be making three million. This little piece a'shit was doing better than the president of All-American."

"So what happened?"

"We picked him up, beat the snot outta him, and got him to introduce us to all his contacts . . . especially José Mondragon, who is head of Latin American Product Placement at Blackstone—the godfather, as far as all this is concerned. Papa Joe has to bless every deal, or AAT and the Colombian drug lords won't play."

"Why are you running the laundry? Why not just rip the drug dealers and take all the money?"

"That was my first plan, too, but if you rip these greaseballs, they'll never stop lookin' for you, and there's enough in this deal so our thirty percent is plenty."

He paused to let that sink in, then went on. "After we got Leon to duke us in with Papa Joe, we also got a list of Leon's contacts at all the other Fortune 500 companies he'd been dealing with. Once he told us all that, Leon didn't seem like such a critical element anymore, so we just took the business away from him and set him up with a six-foot hole and a bag of lye on Dead Man's Beach in Oxnard." Jody smiled. "If the tide changes, that beach is gonna spit up more bones than a Halloween horror flick. In the meantime, we're cutting our deal on those cigarettes tonight with José Mondragon and All-American Tobacco."

"Who's Lisa?"

"Lisa St. Marie. She's AAT's account exec on this deal. Bitch is a tough negotiator. She'll try and cut our percentage to improve All-American's take."

"But you can handle her, right?"

"Yep. Good-lookin' piece of trim, but she's cold as a polar bear's nuts. She's also something of a sport fucker and I'm told by those who've tried her out that she's a world-class lay. Just do me a favor: if you decide to haul her ashes, don't tell Victory. He's got a crush on her, and so far she won't give him any play."

Shane nodded his head. It was hard to believe that Fortune 500 companies would be engaged in this kind of criminal behavior, but he believed what Jody was telling him was true.

"So that's what we're doin', Hot Sauce. Only the deal we're cutting tonight's not for ten million dollars . . . it's for fifty."

"What's the split?" Shane asked.

"Thirty-three point five of the fifty million buys the cigarettes and goes to AAT, the other sixteen point five mil is commission. Three percent, or one point five mil, goes to Blackstone; thirty percent to us. Our end of this fifty million dollar deal comes to a cool fifteen mil. No taxes, no record of the deal . . . it's cash in a bag. After this is done, each of us is gonna get a little less than three million dollars apiece. David VanKirk gets a half a mil to fly the chopper."

Shane let out a low, long whistle.

"Now you can see why we crossed over; why Medwick, Shephard, and Hamilton had to disappear."

Shane said nothing.

"If I hadn't watched my little bail-writing shitball do this, I wouldn't've believed it myself. But it's for real, the payday of a lifetime, and as of now, you get Rod's share." Jody let out a long breath and smiled. "Welcome to the Vikings, Hot Sauce. And don't ever say I never gave ya nothin'."

25
PAPA JOE

EVERYBODY CALLED JOSÉ Mondragon "Papa Joe." Aside from the house at La Quinta, he also kept a villa at the Ritz-Carlton in Rancho Mirage, where he transacted his business. Tremaine Lane had security duty, but the rest of the Vikings left for the eight o'clock meeting at a little past six. They stopped on the way to pick up some food and new clothes, parking the motor home in a pay lot in Palm Desert. Then Jody doled out some money that Papa Joe had given him to buy the scruffy unit a more terrain-friendly wardrobe.

Shane wandered the shopping malls with Jody, but eventually they split up and he found himself at Don Vincent's Store for Men, on North Palm Canyon Drive. He selected a lightweight blue blazer, gray slacks, and a pale-blue shirt with a white collar, along with new underwear, socks, and shoes; then he rolled up his old clothes and put them in the store bag. Shane was just coming out of the dressing room when he was stopped in his tracks by a rayon nightmare. Lounging in a nearby chair, dressed in a new shimmering mint-green shirt, which stretched ominously across his overdeveloped chest, was Victory Smith.

"Hey, Scully," the huge weight lifter said. "Two hours I been wandering in these stores buyin' stuff, but I ain't happy, man."

"It ain't easy bein' green."

"Rod was my home slice. He and I rolled up scumbags together for two years in SWAT. I loved that guy. Because of you, he got dusted, an' it's pissing me off."

"Whatta you want from me?" Shane asked, setting down his bag so that both hands were free while feeling the comforting weight of the automatic on his right ankle.

Smith saw him freeing up and smiled: "Hey, dickwad, I'm not gonna try for you in a Palm Desert men's store. Gimme a little credit here."

"I don't want any trouble. Why don't we put this behind us?"

Victory Smith pulled himself to his feet. He had dropped one of the crutches somewhere and was now using only one. He propped it under his left armpit and leaned on it casually. "You know where the abductor canal is?" he said lazily.

"North Michigan, up by Lake Erie."

"Keep the jokes comin', asshole." They glared at each other. "The abductor canal is in the mid-thigh. That's where your slug hit me. You'd be surprised how much really necessary stuff goes through the abductor canal: you got your deep femoral perforation artery—carries blood to your feet; your femoral nerves—fuck with them and they hurt like a bitch. Then y'got all the other abductor muscles—your abductor minimus and magnus; plus a lotta tendons and shit, too numerous to mention. After you shot me, this leg looked like a plate a'spilt spaghetti—a fuckin' mess. Beyond that, my Beaner doctor musta got his license at the Tijuana School of Terminal Agony. How much of this is ever gonna work right again is anybody's guess."

"You trying to tell me something?"

"Just fillin' you in on what happened, Scully; what you did to me." He turned and hopped toward the door, then stopped and swung back. "I got one real bad habit. Even back on the job it kept getting me in trouble. Wanta guess what that was?"

"You fart in squad cars."

Smith ignored the remark. "I'd go outta my way to make things right. Didn't leave no negative balance on the books. Fuck with me an' you got some payback comin'. No exceptions, no reprieves."

"I'll consider myself warned."

"It's not a warning, Hot . . . Sauce," stretching it out, making the nickname sound ridiculous. "No, sir, not a warning."

"Then what?"

"A promise, a fact of life. Course, I gotta wait till I'm feeling a little stronger. . . . Couple a'days and I figure these stitches oughta hold. Then, after I see what's left a'my leg, I plan on givin' you my own Viking funeral . . . very small event . . . just you, me, Rod's ghost, some gasoline, and a match." He turned again and, using his one crutch, hobbled out of the store.

■ ■ ■

They all met back at the motor home at seven-thirty as agreed, but Smith was late. All of the Vikings except Shane were now dressed like breath mints. Jody had on a plain, light blue, spring-weight sport coat, aqua blue shirt and linen slacks, with a pair of two-tone brown-and-white shoes. He looked like a cartoon gangster. Even Lester Wood had shucked his Western garb in favor of tan slacks and a light-purple shirt. He had a new off-white linen jacket. The rough-out cowboy boots and aviator glasses were all that remained.

Jody studied Shane's conservative attire: "This is the Springs, Hot Sauce."

"I didn't realize we were supposed to dress like Disney characters."

"Where's Smith?" Jody grinned.

They heard the crutch poke-poking along on the sidewalk around the corner from them. Then the massive ex-cop limped into view, and stopped.

"Where you been?" Jody asked.

"Me an' Hot Sauce went shoppin' together."

Jody nodded, not registering the implausibility of that idea. "We gotta get up to Papa Joe's before eight. While I cut the deal with Lisa, you guys hang out by the pool and back me up. Papa Joe says there're only gonna be one or two other people from All-American Tobacco there, so this should only take half an hour. Then we'll find a bar and celebrate."

■ ■ ■

The Ritz-Carlton Hotel sat on twenty-four landscaped acres in the foothills of the Santa Rosa Mountains, overlooking the Cochella Valley. Jody drove the motor home to the front gate, gave José Mondragon's name, and was directed to the Palo Verde villa at the end of a road that skirted the hotel grounds. The view looked across Frank Sinatra Drive into the twinkling lights of Rancho Mirage. The Palo Verde villa, like everything else in Palm Springs, had sweeping arches and Spanish tile, all of it wrapped in flowering bougainvillea.

As they pulled up to the villa, they could hear a band playing swing music somewhere inside. The melody leaked out across the grounds. Valets in red Ritz-Carlton jackets were grabbing the car keys of arriving guests, jumping into the vehicles and running them backward up the drive at breakneck speed to park them in the overflow lot above. The motor home was jamming up traffic, causing a difficult parking problem.

"Half the fuckin' world's here," Victory complained. "I thought this was a private little deal with just one or two tobacco executives."

"So did I," Jody said, getting out of the motor home and handing the keys to the attendant. "Sorry, nobody up at the gate told me this was so tight down here," he said to the valet. "Who are all these people?"

"AAT executives and their wives," the valet answered. "They're having their Western Regional Sales retreat."

"How do we do a deal with all this goin' on?" Victory said as they headed into the villa.

The band called themselves the Majestics—a string quartet, plus piano, drums, and bass. They seemed stuck on forties music, which the mostly gray-haired men and women in dark suits and cocktail dresses danced to energetically. The Spanish-style living room had been emptied of furniture to accommodate the makeshift dance floor.

Jody was gazing down at his pastel outfit with concern. "Shit," he growled, "we look like a buncha ushers at a Mexican wedding."

After a minute the man who had called out to Lisa when Shane was in the pool walked up, and Jody introduced him as

José Mondragon. As Shane shook hands, he could see that the short, powerfully built man was dripping with pricey accessories; a twenty-thousand-dollar gold Cartier watch peeked out from under diamond-studded French cuffs.

As they released the handshake, Jody patted Shane's shoulder, "José, this is my friend Shane I told you about. Of course you remember Victory and Lester."

"*Mucho gusto.*" José shook hands all around, then smiled at Jody. "*Con su permiso, por favor.*" He smiled, dismissing them curtly as he took Jody's arm and led him off, leaving Shane and the other two Vikings standing there.

"*Bésame la pinga,* asshole," Smith growled. "Since we all know this fucker went to Harvard, why don't he speak English?"

Without inviting him to join them, Smith and Wood moved off, leaving Shane alone.

He pushed into the bar and ordered scotch on the rocks, then wandered slowly through the party, feeling out of place and suddenly very lonely. He desperately missed Alexa and Chooch. Finally, he wandered onto the veranda and leaned against the concrete rail, looking out across the twinkling lights of the valley.

"I liked your swimming outfit better." A rich contralto voice interrupted his thoughts.

Shane turned and once again found himself looking into the remarkable jade-green eyes of Lisa St. Marie. He wondered if she got that color by wearing contacts. She had changed out of her business suit and was now dressed for maximum effect. It was a high-fashion balancing act, teetering precariously between sexy and slutty. Her neckline plunged, her short dress was slit way up one side, all the way to her abductor canal.

She had on just enough jewelry to accent her alabaster complexion, but not too much to detract from her eyes. A single pearl rested between her swelling breasts, diamond earrings twinkled from behind shoulder-length wings of honey-blond hair.

"Is it too soon in our relationship to make a personal observation?" she smiled. Her teeth and personality glittered.

Shane didn't feel compelled to answer; she was working hard enough for both of them.

"You have a magnificent tush."

Shane gave her a slow smile. "I'm trying not to get into any trouble with you, Ms. St. Marie."

"I must have made a good first impression. You bothered to find out my name," she enthused, then moved closer to him and slid her right hand through his arm.

He pulled out of her grasp and put out his hand. "I'm Shane." She shook it formally.

"Nice to know you, Shane. Lisa."

"Aren't you supposed to be having a business meeting with Jody right now?"

"I might get around to Jody, but right now I'm more interested in you." She brushed up against him, pressing a breast against his arm.

"You always leave this many skid marks?" Shane asked. "We could both get whiplash. Why don't we start by trying to be friends."

She studied him for almost half a minute while the Majestics switched to "Stardust." Then she kissed the tips of her fingers; this time, instead of wiggling them at him, she gently touched his cheek. "Nobody can resist me for long, Shane." She smiled at him seductively. "Let me get you another drink; then we can get started on our new friendship. Or better still, why don't you keep me company? Come to my meeting with Jody."

Shane finished his drink to buy time. He didn't want to piss off Jody . . . at least not yet. But this was a heaven-sent opportunity to stand up close and watch the players in this deal. The ice cubes clinked against his teeth. As he set down his glass, he had a strange flashback.

Alexa was standing in his backyard, at the canal house, looking up at Chooch and talking earnestly. Shane's heart froze with the memory, followed by deep pain and intense longing. Then Alexa and Chooch were gone, and Lisa St. Marie remained, frowning at him. She had seen the painful look pass through his eyes.

"Whatever that was, I don't want any," she said.

"I was just remembering something," he muttered.

"Follow me, I'm betting we'll have some fun."

So he followed her . . . across the dance floor full of swirling executives and into the bedroom where José Mondragon, Jody, and three other men were waiting.

26
TRIPPING

THE BEDROOM WAS large, dominated by a king-size Spanish-style poster bed. Four men turned simultaneously as Lisa opened the door. A frozen tableau.

Jody, dressed in powder blue, with two-tone shoes, his drink halfway to his mouth, glaring; José Mondragon, by the desk, looking up from a sheaf of papers, startled, like a kid caught cheating on a test. And then there were three gray-haired AAT tobacco executives who were standing together by the plate-glass window. As the door opened, these three West Coast cancer distributors stared as Shane and Lisa entered the room.

"I don't think we need any more people here than is absolutely necessary," José said, now speaking in perfect, unaccented, English. He had completely dropped his bullshit *"como está"* act.

"I can vouch for Mr. Scully," Lisa said. "He's working with us on distribution. He's also an extremely qualified deep-end retrieval expert." She twinkled this nonsense at them, and the room tension dissolved in her smile like an Alka-Seltzer tablet in a sea of sexuality.

Only Jody seemed unmoved. In fact, there was a crazy tightness to his mouth and around his eyes, as if he had just been insulted and didn't know where to park the anger. Finally he nodded—a jerky, almost spastic movement not at all like him.

Lisa motioned toward one of the lung-cancer salesmen. "This is Chip Gordon, head of our overseas subsidiary, American Global Tobacco," she said, smiling at a tall, narrow-shouldered man whose face in profile had the shape of a quarter moon. "And this is Arnold Zook," she said, motioning to a nondescript, pudgy man with a laurel wreath of gray hair circling a shiny pate of open scalp. "He supervises some of our other Latin American duty-free transactions." She turned toward the third man, dressed in black: "And our host this evening, Louis Petrovitch." She didn't mention his corporate title, but it was obvious that Petrovitch was the power player. He had a Prussian general's military bearing—tin-colored short hair, a mile of jaw, and eyes the approximate color and texture of poured concrete. He didn't acknowledge the introduction.

"Shall we go out onto the patio, where it's safe?" José suggested, fearful of listening devices. He swung open a pair of double doors, and the group walked out onto a large deck, almost twice the size of the bedroom. Shane followed, finding a spot near the door where he could observe but would hopefully be forgotten. The rest of them walked to a glass-topped table ten or twelve feet away. The lit golf course stretched out, fragrant and verdant below them. Shane watched as Jody sat; he seemed stiff, uncoordinated.

Where was that old fluid grace . . . Jody's athletic elegance . . . where was the casual economy of motion?

Lisa was the last to join them. She slithered into a chair and wrapped her legs to the side, showing a lot of well-shaped thigh. Chip Gordon, Arnold Zook, and the formidable Lou Petrovitch stood nearby, holding glasses of melting ice. When Lisa crossed her legs, Shane heard Petrovitch inhale sharply.

He's sleeping with her, Shane suddenly realized.

Lisa smiled at Jody with jade-green confidence, while Papa Joe started the meeting.

"Lisa will conduct this transaction for AAT," José said. "As the representative for Blackstone Duty-Free Imports, I will act as a court of last resort in any dispute. My company will also control the drafting of the transaction, and the contract will be held at the Blackstone office in Geneva for obvious reasons. Acceptable?" The question was aimed at Jody, who simply nodded. Strangely, Jody's hands were trembling on the table-top.

What the hell's wrong with him? Shane wondered.

"Okay, Ms. St. Marie, you're on," José began.

"Señor Mondragon tells us you want to buy some duty-free, V-Five product and market it in Aruba," Lisa said. "Aside from distributing product, we can also handle all the shipping, warehousing, and insurance. I'd like to pitch a package deal."

"Skip that. Let's start with the cost per case." Jody's voice was shaky. "Since we're dealing in bulk, I think five percent to Blackstone and three hundred dollars a case to All-American is fuckin' nuts. You're not even paying federal taxes. It's way too high. We're gonna need a break on those numbers." Unexpectedly, Jody started rubbing his eyes. The people on the deck watched him with growing concern until he finished and squinted up at them. *"What?"* he said angrily, catching them staring.

"It's always bad form to look into someone else's pocket, Mr. Dean. I think if you want to do a deal, we need to transact it along traditional lines. Whether or not we have a federal tax burden just isn't any of your business," pudgy, dark-suited Mr. Zook said.

"Traditional lines? How many guys you do business with want to buy fifty million in V-Fives in one shipment? I'm looking for a discount and a lowered percentage for volume."

"Let's get back to who handles the product-shipment insurance and warehousing," Lisa said, smiling across the glass tabletop at Jody, trying to calm him down.

Jody didn't answer; instead, he rubbed his eyes again. It was almost as if he couldn't see properly.

"We'll ship for fifty cents a carton," Lisa said. "We'll insure for another dollar fifty. We'll warehouse in our building in Aruba for two hundred dollars a pallet on an amortized weekly rate."

Jody dug into his pocket and pulled out a folded paper with some math scribbled on it. He squinted as if he could barely read his own writing.

"Either that," Lisa said, "or you can get your break from José out of Blackstone's five percent. That's up to them, but All-American is not cutting our three hundred dollar per case base price."

Petrovitch nodded. He seemed proud of her.

"Leon Fine said there was room to negotiate on volume," Jody protested.

"Ahhh, yes, Leon. . . . Whatever happened to poor Leon? He sorta up and disappeared," Lisa said softly. "And since Leon isn't here to confront that issue directly, maybe we ought to leave him out of it."

"Who do you fucking people think you're dealing with?" Jody asked, his voice too loud and badly out of sync with the setting.

Shane took another hard look at his old friend: Jody was smarter than this, yet Shane saw something in his eyes that he had never seen before. Jody's eyes were on fire. Gone was the cold appraising confidence. Shane wondered if he was on something. He couldn't believe Jody would be stupid enough to get high and then come to this meeting, yet he seemed clearly out of it.

"There's no need for rude behavior," Lisa said.

"Fuck you, honey!" Jody responded hotly, exploding to his feet. "Just 'cause there's no history here, don't think you can fuck me over! You people act like this is a business transaction. It's not! It's a criminal conspiracy. Let's not forget that you're all money launderers. I make one call and this whole deal goes into federal court and back to the taxpayers."

The Prussian general cleared his throat: "Get this . . . this person out of my party." Petrovitch turned and left the deck, taking his two flunkies and most of the available oxygen with him.

Jody was left standing, glaring awkwardly. José Mondragon turned and followed Petrovitch.

Lisa finally rose from her chair while Shane put a hand on Jody's shoulder. "Come on, man. Cool down."

"Get your fucking hands off me!" Jody screamed and backhanded Shane's arm off with his fist.

"What'd you take?" Shane asked, looking at Jody closely. "You're on something. . . . This isn't you."

"No . . . no . . . I'm . . . I wouldn't . . . I didn't . . ." And then he fell backward.

Shane had to scramble to catch him before he cracked his head on the tile. "Somebody slipped him something," Shane said, looking at Lisa.

"Get him out of here," she replied. "Go back to José's."

"What's going on? Jody wouldn't use drugs. He's trying to get everybody *off* drugs."

"I think I know what happened. I need to do some damage control. Just do what I say. I'll be there as soon as I can." She turned and left the deck.

Shane got his hands under Jody and half dragged, half carried him off the patio. He laid him down on the damp grass at the side of the villa. Jody was groaning. Inside the party, the Majestics ended "Begin the Beguine," finishing up with a corny drum riff. Jody rolled over and vomited on the grass.

"Always a music critic," Shane mumbled.

"Get me outta here, Salsa," Jody moaned. "I feel like shit."

A few minutes later Shane found Sawdust and Victory on the far side of the room, pounding down scotches like construction workers at a neighborhood bar.

"Let's go. Jody's outside," Shane said, and left without waiting for them to reply.

They found Jody on the grass where Shane had left him, but now he was unconscious, snoring loudly.

"What'd you do to him?" Lester growled.

"I didn't do anything to him. Somebody spiked his drink. It was weird . . . some kinda mood-altering substance, maybe GHB. He went nuts . . . blew the whole deal."

"What?" Sawdust said, then looked at Shane suspiciously. "Who would drug him? Everybody's in this for the money. These people need us to move their product. You did this to him!"

"It wasn't me," Shane said. "You want a guess? I think we got some competitors inside All-American who don't want this deal to happen."

Victory stood leaning on his crutch while Sawdust ran to the parking lot above and retrieved the motor home. When he pulled up, Shane and Victory dragged Jody inside. They drove back to José Mondragon's villa to wait for Lisa St. Marie.

But she was already there, standing with Tremaine Lane out by the pool.

THE REBOUND 27

WHILE THE REST of the Vikings put Jody into bed, Shane talked it over with Lisa.

"I think I can still save this," she told him. "I know what happened. At least I'm pretty sure I know. I think I can convince Lou . . . but we need to . . ." She stopped because Victory Smith had just come out of the house and was hopping around the deep end of the pool, over to where they were standing. He leaned in on his crutch, glaring.

One by one, the rest of the Vikings came out and formed a circle around them.

"You ain't supposed to talk to her. Jody does the deals," Victory growled.

"Somebody, and I won't mention who, dropped hydroxyl methylphenidate into Jody's drink," Lisa said.

"I'm not a fucking druggist. Talk English, lady," Smith said.

"MDMA-two, a form of juiced up Ecstasy. It's a big-time depressant, causes irrational behavior," Shane replied, and Lisa nodded. Apparently, Victory had been so busy at SWAT, kicking doors and doing kneecaps, he missed out on his drug tour in Vice.

"We don't have any time," she continued. "If you guys still want this deal, I have a chance to save it. Mr. Petrovitch is leaving on his private jet in two hours. I either put this back together by then, or it's dead." She was cool and in control. Her jade-green eyes seemed to twinkle with excitement. Or was it amusement? Shane couldn't shake the feeling that she was thoroughly enjoying herself.

"I need to cut a deal *now*," she pressed.

"If Jody's X-ing, he won't be up to anything for hours, maybe a day," Tremaine said.

"I need to take Lou a deal tonight, in the next hour. I know I can square things with Papa Joe. It's Petrovitch we need to capture. Jody threatened him, and frankly, Lou doesn't like being threatened. I may have a way to straighten that out, but I want one of you to cut the deal with me now. I need to bring him an offer."

"One of us?" Sawdust asked.

"Him," Lisa said, pointing at Shane.

"Fuck him. He not even scheduled t'live till Friday," Victory growled.

"It's him or nobody . . . and, whatever he and I work out, you've gotta make Jody stick to it."

"Maybe it was you, spiked Jody's drink so you could front up and kick Scully's ass on this deal," Tremaine Lane said lazily from a chair a few feet away, his feet propped up on a glass-topped table.

"Okay . . . have it your way. See ya around," Lisa said, then started to walk to the far end of the pool. They all watched, mesmerized by the hip action. Shane guessed she was probably not doing it intentionally. She'd learned that walk in high school when she first realized it turned every guy's brain to mush.

"Hang on a minute," Lester drawled. "We'll do it your way."

Lisa stopped and turned theatrically to look at them.

"What if Jody don't like the deal once he comes to?" Victory asked.

"Hey, boys," she said softly. "The big money is in the smuggle. You guys are gonna make your percentage off that. You wanna blow this over whether it ends up being two seventy-five a case or three hundred?"

They stood glaring at her, trying to decide what to do.

"What's it gonna be? Once Mr. Petrovitch's plane takes off, this is over. He won't revisit it. We're out of time."

Victory Smith leaned forward on his crutch and whispered softly to Shane, so nobody else could hear: "Okay, Party Boy, go ahead. But if you get shorted by this bitch, the balance comes out of your end."

"Y'mean I'm gonna be around for the payoff? I thought I wasn't gonna make it till Friday."

"Keep yer hands off her. I'm the one's gonna be doing her. You fuck her, you're dead."

"Is this on or off?" Lisa asked from the far side of the pool, where she waited impatiently, hands on her hips.

"Go on, gaffle with the bitch," Tremaine said softly, his deep ghetto voice rumbling.

Lisa crossed back, took Shane by the hand, and led him around the side of the house to the front drive, where her car was parked. It was a white Mercedes convertible with the top down. She slid behind the wheel and got it started.

"Where're we going?" Shane asked, still standing by the passenger door.

"I'm not gonna try and cut a deal here, with all these testosterone cases leaning on me. We'll find a nice quiet spot. Get in."

Just before sliding in beside her, Shane looked up and caught Victory glaring out of the living-room window. Shane shot him a wide grin, then grabbed his crotch. Smith was still there as they pulled away from the house.

■ ■ ■

"It's Arnold Zook," she said. "I can't prove it, of course, but I'm pretty sure he's the one who spiked Jody's drink."

"Who? You mean the little round short one who looks like he should be stacking cans at Ralph's?"

They were parked halfway between La Quinta and Rancho Mirage, off Bob Hope Drive, in a small, sculpted park. Up-lit date palms stood over them, swaying in the breeze like giant eunuchs waving fans.

"He was the product executive who was working with Leon Fine. When Leon disappeared, Jody preferred working with me. Arnold lost the account, and he didn't take it too well."

"What's the difference? Don't both of you work for All-American Tobacco?"

"Our individual financial arrangements are complex, but they're tied to product placement. If Jody made an ass of himself and pissed off Mr. Petrovitch, Arnold Zook wouldn't lose any sleep over it."

"Okay, so how do you get Petrovitch to come around?"

"Leave that part to me," she allowed. "I just need to know what we're talking about."

"And, like Tremaine said, you picked me because I looked like the biggest moron."

"I picked you because you're the only one who isn't fucked up on drugs. You can still think. I swear . . . Jody's let these guys get completely out of control. This is my first and last arrangement with him."

"Okay, let's hear your offer."

"I can't cut a deal on product price. Mr. Petrovitch won't go for it. Our parallel market is in place and has been operating along set guidelines for a very long time."

"Over twenty-five years, I hear."

"Yeah, maybe. And if word gets out that I cut you a discount price on product, it's gonna haunt me on every other deal I make in the world."

"So, you smuggle tobacco and launder drug cash in places other than just Colombia?"

"I don't like to use words like 'smuggle' and 'launder.' I'm a tobacco-company account executive, negotiating a deal with you to supply the Blackstone duty-free zone in Aruba with cigarettes to be sold there. Period. End of discussion."

"Lisa . . . you're laundering Colombian drug money for the Cali cartel."

"I'm not laundering anything."

"The Vikings set this deal up with a Cali cartel drug dealer in L.A., then Jody cut a deal with Papa Joe at Blackstone. They brought All-American in to supply the cigarettes, which get shipped to Aruba, paid for with drug cash, and smuggled back into Colombia, where they're sold by the Cali cartel, who then gets its money back. If that's not a laundry, then I'm Pippi Longstocking."

"Where Jody or anybody else gets the money to buy our product is their business, not mine. Listen, Shane, I'm cutting you a lot of slack here. Don't make this impossible."

"Okay, so you won't negotiate on the cigarettes. How 'bout the shipping and insurance and warehousing—all that other stuff you were talking about?"

"I'll give you ten cents per case off the shipping, and forty cents on the insurance—"

Shane put up a hand and interrupted her, "Slow down. I don't even know what we're talking about."

"We're talking about all the ancillary expenses."

"Hell, I don't even know what's good or bad . . . or what competitive bids on those services might be. I'm negotiating blind here."

"So, then, how are we gonna make a deal?"

"You have rate cards on all this shit? For your legitimate deals? The shipping and insurance and warehousing?"

"Yeah."

"Okay . . . fifty percent off on the entire package, per your rate card."

"What?"

"I want those services at cost."

"I heard you, but that's ridiculous. I'd be cutting my price by over . . ." She reached into her purse and pulled out a calculator and began poking at the keys, her lacquered nails clicking as she punched in numbers. Shane watched her while she worked, her features shimmering in the moving lights from the swaying date palms. After a minute, she looked over at him. "Thirty percent. Best I can do."

"Fifty percent, Lisa. Don't fuck with me on this. If I cut too bad a deal, Jody's just gonna tank it. You can sell this to Mr. Puffenguts, I know you can."

"Petrovitch," she said, smiling.

"You guys will be running your shipping, insurance, and warehousing at no profit, but you're still getting a full three hundred dollars a case on the smokes; like Jody said, it *is* a huge shipment."

She looked down at the computer in her hand. "Fifty percent off." She punched in a few more figures. "That comes to a little more than seventeen dollars a case."

"Okay, that's the deal then. Yes or no."

She tapped her thumb on the Texas Instruments computer, which had a twelve-digit LD screen instead of the normal ten.

"Okay. But if I can't sell this to Lou, I'll need you nearby. I want you to wait for me in a place where I can get back to you without having the rest of Jody's animals contributing their opinions."

"Where?"

"AAT rented me a separate villa at the Ritz-Carlton, down by the tennis courts. How 'bout there? Lou should still be at the hotel, packing. That way, if we need to adjust anything, you'll be handy."

"Okay."

She put the car in gear. They pulled out from under the date palms, shot down Bob Hope Drive, and turned right again on Highway 111. Lisa St. Marie was holding her head erect, her shoulders straight. She seemed lost in thought while she drove: intense, hard and beautiful, no flirtatious nonsense now. She had turned back into a very busy executive on an important lung-destroying mission.

Shane wondered if she was planning to blow the Prussian general to get the deal done.

28
CANDY KISS

HER ROOM WAS full of shiny masonry, Italian terra-cotta, and Spanish tile. Expensively framed but marginal abstract art hung on the walls. Like everything else in the desert, this junior-executive suite had a pastel-peach color scheme. Except Lisa's suite was without the magnificent views of the valley or the golf course. Shane could see a lit tennis court out the main window and hear the steady *thunk-thonk* of a singles match, mixed with energetic grunts and squeaking shoes. The match was obscured behind a green screen that hung on the chain-link fence a few yards from the window. The shadows danced and lunged on the colorful canvas like ghostly memories.

Lisa was still with Petrovitch. Shane looked at her telephone and again considered making a call to Filosiani. But he didn't want the LAPD number to show up on her bill, so he decided to wait. Instead, he took the opportunity to get to know her a little better.

He started his search where most cops do—in the bathroom, where you often learned personal secrets. Lisa's bathroom was no exception. She had the standard beauty aids: eye shadow, makeup brushes, and Vaseline; two round metal hairbrushes, each tangled with honey-ash strands. He pulled several loose. There were no dark roots—a natural blonde. Lipsticks by Lancôme: Iced Amethyst and Bronze Fire. No eyewash or contact-lens case, so it seemed the jade-green color came direct from the factory. Then he found two small, brown plastic compacts stuck way down in the webbing of her cosmetic travel case. The powder inside was not from Revlon, but Colombia. Fine and white, it dusted the mirror. Shane ran a wet index finger across the stuff and tasted it. . . .

Bingo. *El diablo!*

Lisa St. Marie kept that high-strung motor of hers redlined with toots of Inca whizbang.

Shane closed the compact and put it back where he found it.

Well, he mused darkly, *there are worse things than snorting coke . . . you could always punch a round through your girl-friend's heart.*

He moved through the rest of the place.

The closet contained mostly expensive designer stuff. She either did very well at All-American Tobacco or General Puffen-guts bought her a lot of high-priced collectibles. The shoes were strictly from the Imelda Marcos shelf: Prada, Charles David, Manolo Blahnik.

Her jewel case was locked inside the flimsy key-locked room safe, which Shane opened easily with his picks. The case was just a small leather box, but with impressive contents. Shane wasn't much at appraising jewelry and wished he had Murray Steinberg there to scan them with his loupe, but they looked authentic—expensive settings glittering with designer elegance.

He closed the safe and kept snooping.

The refrigerator was where he found Lisa's moonwalking kit. The heavy artillery was tucked in the freezer compartment behind the ice trays: amphetamines, methamphetamines, and, oh yeah . . . some $MDMA_2$. So maybe Tremaine had called that one right. Maybe Lisa had sabotaged the deal with Jody so she could knock down the price with Shane.

There were also some tabs of something that Shane thought looked like LSD, making them the only ingestibles. This was gyro-hydro, but there was no needle. Lisa didn't do her cooking in a spoon. She didn't violate that perfect alabaster skin with track marks. Everything in here but the acid and the Ecstasy went up her nose.

He closed the refrigerator and wandered back into the living room. The tennis game had finished, so Shane slumped into the big, overstuffed club chair by the window. He was bone-tired, and without planning to drift off, he was suddenly somewhere else . . . asleep, but maybe not; dreaming, but it felt terribly real . . . like he had passed into some other dimension intact, summoned there for an audience and a scolding.

She was dressed in her sergeant's uniform, the one she had worn at the Medal of Valor ceremonies, and she was still holding the medal in its beautiful leather case.

"Shane, we can never make this work. . . . You know that, of course." She was scowling at him, but there was also disappointment.

"Why, Alexa . . . why can't we?"

"*Because there's darkness in you. Whether it's because you were abandoned by your mother . . . left at that hospital as an infant, or because police work made you cynical isn't important anymore. Darkness is darkness, no matter where it comes from. And it's been there as long as I've known you. Even when we laughed, it was there, hiding behind your smile, frightening me.*"

"*Alexa . . . no . . . please . . . I can change.*"

"*It never would've worked. Never. We were kidding ourselves.*"

"*No . . . no, it could have, because I loved you. I still love you.*"

"*God decides these things,*" she said sharply, standing in the beautiful pulpit now, preaching down at him. He remembered that pulpit. As a child, he had gone to the Episcopal church each Sunday with the Deans, looked up in wonder at its carved perfection, studied it while sermons droned. It was ornate and encrusted with symbols. Angels with their wings outstretched held the corners of the desk aloft. On its polished surface rested the powerful book of words. A scroll was carved on the front face of the pulpit. He'd wondered what important truths were on that document, what overpowering wisdom. He went up and tried to read the scroll, but the letters were only tiny scratches in the polished wood; like so much of his early life, only there for effect. "*God makes these choices for us,*" Alexa continued. "*You went your way, I went mine.*"

"*No . . .*"

"*It's done. The deal is closed.*"

"No, Alexa, not yet."

Suddenly, somebody touched his shoulder.

He opened his eyes. It was Lisa. She was standing over him, dressed in a black linen coat.

"I said, The deal is done, and who the fuck is Alexa?"

"Hi," he said, still troubled by the nature and content of the dream. "Nobody . . . old friend. She's dead."

"Mr. Puffenguts will do the deal as negotiated." Lisa smiled. "Papa Joe is writing the contract over in Lou's suite. If you sign it before you leave, the ball is back in play."

"Oh . . ."

"And now for the celebration." She held out a bottle of champagne she'd been hiding behind her back.

"I don't like champagne much." His head was clogged; the heavy sleep and troubling dream lingered.

"How 'bout this, then?" she said, and let the coat fall off her shoulders. She was standing naked in front of him, wearing only her high-heeled pumps.

"Jesus," he said, and struggled to sit up in the heavily up-holstered chair.

"You showed me yours. . . . How do you like mine?"

She turned and showed him her gym-trained glutes. Sexy and very beautiful . . . no denying that.

"My . . . I . . ."

"Your what?" she said, smiling. And then, before he could say another word, she dropped into his lap and put her arms around his neck. "You can touch. Go on . . . feel me here," she said, then took his hand and placed it between her legs. He started to pull away but she held it there. "I need to feel you. I need for us to know each other this way."

"Why . . . why is? . . ."

"Now for the candy kiss." Then her mouth was on his, open

and hungry. She pushed her tongue between his lips; he suddenly felt something on his tongue . . . bitter and stinging, it was dissolving, being quickly absorbed.

A candy kiss? . . . Cocaine? . . . LSD? He started to pull away, to spit it out.

"No," she said, never taking her mouth off of his. "Go with it, baby. Go with it—you'll fly." He felt the substance running off his tongue, around his tonsils, down his throat. She had her hands on his belt and was undoing it, stripping it off.

"I need to feel you. I need to touch you, to taste you," she whispered as her hand reached into his pants, stroking him.

"Goddamn," Shane thought, or maybe he actually said it. He wasn't sure. He tried to pull away—at least he thought he tried . . . *wanted* to have tried.

"Alexa . . . Alexa!" his mind screamed, but all he heard were her dream-remembered words.

"Shane, we can never make this work. . . ."

"Why, Alexa . . . Why can't we?"

"Ahhh . . ." Lisa purred. "That's better. You're so hard. Let me help you . . . ," and his pants were coming down, sliding around his thighs. She took her mouth off his and found him down there . . . found his traitorous erection.

"It never would have worked. We were kidding ourselves," Alexa scolded.

"Isn't that better? Doesn't that feel nice?" Lisa whispered.

"It could have worked because I loved you. I still love you." He felt her lips on him, her tongue on his hardened shaft.

"There's darkness in you. Even when we laughed, it was there, hiding behind your smile."

Lisa rose, adjusting herself on his lap to face him, her hips rising up slightly, then she slid his erection deep inside her. "There," she

panted. "There . . . there . . . harder . . . harder . . . harder . . .
Fuck me, you bastard!" Her voice guttural and craven.

Shane felt the drug inside him, spreading fire and ice.

"You went your way, I went mine."

He wanted to scream—*No!*—but his mind blurred with carnal darkness.

"Now, now . . . Do it now!" Lisa commanded.

So he did. He released, spasming inside her. She threw her head back and rode him, moaning out loud with unabashed pleasure.

It was a chilling moment for Shane, as if the depravity that had been hovering, beating its dark wings, had finally settled on him, devouring his morality and self-respect all in one lustful encounter.

Unfortunately, it was the best sex he'd ever had.

29

THE LOOK

SHANE'S FRAGILE PSYCHE fell in on him. He remembered Lisa's kneeling over him, feeding him something . . . maybe more pills, or tabs; he wasn't sure. He vaguely recalled signing the agreement, the paper swimming in blurred vision, and Lisa's voice, musical but furry. He wasn't sure how he got back to Papa Joe's house. He had a momentary recollection of Lisa's dashboard clock, wondering if it could really be four A.M. He guessed she'd driven him. His mind buzzed and snapped like a broken speaker.

A few memories stood out.

The front door, with Tremaine standing in the threshold holding a .38 snubby, muttering, "You're fucked up, too?"

Jody, sprawled in a lawn chair in the bright midday sunlight, moaning and crying, then suddenly leaning over and vomiting into the pool.

Victory Smith standing over him, whispering softly: "It would be so easy now, motherfucker . . . so easy."

The fog he was swimming in didn't clear until almost six that evening. When it did, it was all at once, as if somebody had yanked up a shade. He was suddenly back behind the wheel, driving a swerving, disabled brain.

He was with Jody in mid-sentence when he snapped back, and Shane had no idea what they'd been discussing. His own words lingered in his head like a remembered dream: ". . . I could do . . ." was what he had just said. One moment he was nowhere, and the next he was stretched out on the sofa in Papa Joe's borrowed room, feeling like shit while Jody, sitting on the bed, scanned a two-page document.

"The best you could do?" he said, throwing the papers back onto the bedspread. Shane could see his signature scrawled on the bottom. "She jacked you up, man. I hate this deal . . . it was signed under duress. You're still babbling like an idiot."

"I'm okay. . . . I'm better now." Shane's head was pounding, but the real pain, the one deep inside him, was an unbearable feeling of loss—this time not for Alexa or Chooch, but for himself.

"This bitch got the full three hundred dollars. Leon Fine said he bargained her down to two seventy-five. Leon woulda got an extra twenty-five bucks a case on his deal."

"Yeah, Leon's doing great. Let's hear it for Leon."

Shane sat up, then stood and went into the bathroom, washed his face, and glanced at himself in the mirror. He looked as bad as he felt; three days of stubble under furtive eyes that belonged to a frightened loser stared back at him. Shane couldn't bear to look at the wreck he had become, so he left the bathroom and returned to the living room. Jody was still holding the papers, scowling down at them.

"I ain't gonna do this deal. Call her back."

"Jody, she says Petrovitch won't renegotiate."

"*She* says? Like I give a shit what she says. Fuck her . . . but of course, you've probably done that, too."

"Jody, remember what Captain Clark always told us?"

"Y'mean that prick from the Fiscal Support Bureau who kept running audits on our expense sheets in Southwest?"

"He said dollars are fungible. And they are." Shane's head was at least functioning now.

"What does that mean?"

"It means, it doesn't matter where they come from as long as you get to the same number in the end. We got a seventeen-dollar-a-case discount on ancillary services. Leon says he woulda got twenty-five dollars off on the sale price, which, since he never closed the deal, is questionable. But he probably woulda paid full boat on all this other shit—the warehousing, insurance, and shipping. That means, if he wasn't lying to you, he mighta done eight dollars a case better than us. Who fucking cares?"

"I care," Jody said as he stood up. "These people are crooks. They're laundering money for scumbags, putting it back in the hands of greaseball cartel bosses who're using it to sell more drugs to kids."

"So are we. Let's just take the deal and get on with it."

Jody walked to the east window and looked out at mountains that were slowly turning purple in the evening light. "Yeah . . ." he said, softly, "so are we." Then Jody turned and faced Shane, changing the subject abruptly. "You're still fucked up over shooting Sergeant Hamilton, aren't you?" Shane's muscles froze; somewhere deep in his psyche, survival instincts took over.

Jody didn't wait for an answer. "At first that pissed me off. I wanted you not to give a shit, but I've been thinking about it, and now I know if you weren't fucked up over it, you'd a'been faking. Since you're unwinding, taking drugs and balling a skank like Lisa St. Marie, I know you're on the level. Otherwise I'd be suspecting a setup. I can see inside you, man. You're eating yourself up, just like you always did when things weren't John Wayne perfect."

Shane didn't answer.

" 'Member all that night music . . . back when we were kids . . . planning what we were gonna be?" Jody went on.

"Yeah . . ."

"You always knew. 'Cept at first. At first it was a fireman, remember? Then you switched to a cop, and you never changed. I never knew what I wanted. I became a cop because you did. Dumb fucking reason, huh?"

Shane's head was killing him. He could barely think.

"It's funny . . . when you grow up with everything, you don't know what to wish for." Jody was studying Shane while he spoke. "I mean, pitchin' for the Dodgers . . . what kinda bullshit dream was that?"

"Maybe you could've done it if you'd tried."

" 'Cept I never wanted anything bad enough to put out for it. Things just sorta always happened for me. You worked selling ice cream at Huntington Beach t'get that old piece-a-shit Ford you loved so much; hand-washed that pile a rust three times a week. I got a new Mustang convertible for my sixteenth birthday. I never washed it once, 'cause I never really cared about it."

"Right." Shane didn't want to hear any of this. Worse still, he suspected Jody was working up to some kind of soul-cleansing confession.

"You always had a code. When you fought for shit, it was for honor or something corny like that. You never just beat on some kid for his lunch money. Underneath all my jokes, I guess I admired that."

"Can we give it a rest?" Shane muttered.

"I never told you this, Salsa, but I always envied you. I wanted things to matter for me like they did for you. I wanted them to be more important. But they never were, and the funny thing was, the less I cared, the more people seemed to do what I wanted. You were the only one who didn't completely buy into my bullshit. I had to really work to capture you, 'cause you had all those lofty ideas. Used to piss me off, too, 'cause I never could understand what the big deal was . . . and then one day, I found out why I could never care." He turned slightly and was now looking out the window at the mountains. It was almost half a minute before he continued: " 'Member that course at the Academy on criminal psychology?"

"Yeah."

"That was a real wake-up call for me 'cause I fit one of the criminal classifications dead on. You know which one?" He turned suddenly to look back at Shane.

"No."

"Sociopath. That was me. No feelings, no emotions, all the time pretending; acting emotions I couldn't feel, but knew I was supposed to . . . pretending sorrow when my dog died, pretending love on Mother's Day . . . never feeling anything. Not one damn thing. We were from opposite ends of the spectrum. What a team—the bleeding heart and the sociopath, the ultimate high-low block. No wonder we always kicked ass."

"But here we are in the same room, both doing this same shit, so let it go. Please . . . I don't need to hear this." Shane desperately wanted to end the conversation; he was afraid of it.

But why?

A few years ago, when they had the arguments over SIS, Shane suspected that Jody had lost his conscience, but it had never occurred to him that Jody never had a conscience to begin with.

So, does it really matter now if Jody felt anything back in sixth grade?

But it did. It was critically important, because Jody's boyhood friendship had been one of the only pillars of strength in Shane's youth. It had formed a significant part of his value system.

More night music: "Y'know one of the other reasons I fucked up?" Jody said softly. "It was my dad . . . good old easygoing Fred Dean. What a world-class jerk." Jody shook his head in wonder. "What a train wreck that guy turned out to be."

"I loved your dad. Your parents treated me like I was their own."

Jody shrugged and turned again to look out the window. "When he went broke, he left me hanging out there with no fuckin' values . . . nothin'. You didn't have money or parents, but you had everything. You had beliefs. You had your code, corny as I thought it was. I cared about nothing. Worse still, I couldn't settle for less than we'd always had, and couldn't find any legal way to get that standard of living back."

"So you make this score and then all your problems go away?" Shane's headache was pounding, but Jody's confession was even worse.

"You always loved being a cop," Jody continued.

"Yeah," Shane answered softly. "Yeah . . . It seemed like a great profession. I thought it was noble . . . blue knights standing up for the innocent. I thought the battle was about right and wrong. But it wasn't about right and wrong; it turned out to be about legal and illegal, rules of evidence . . . the Police Discretionary Clause . . . the Miranda. Make some tiny technical mistake, and a confessed child molester goes free. I loved it until it turned me into a cynic."

"I never loved being a cop," Jody said quietly, turning back to study Shane's reaction. "I loved what it let me do. Turning on my gumball, and running a red light to get to a ballgame on time. I loved being able to get some asshole down on his back in an alley with nobody watching, then shove my piece in his mouth and listen to him beg. I loved seeing that look in his eyes. The look, man . . . better than sex or drugs. It validated me, y'know? The look said, 'I know you can do it. You can light me up and walk away, and nobody will even ask why.' The look said: 'I know you're all that's between me and eternity. I'm alive for only as long as you allow it.' Shit, nobody had to say anything. It was there, pure and clean . . . no misunderstandings, no technicalities, just a beautiful fact." His eyes were almost glowing as he spoke. Then he paused and studied Shane. "You never felt that on the job, when you pulled down on some asshole? Never felt the pure joy of that?"

"No," Shane said. "I was in it for something else."

"Yeah." He snorted. " 'Service in the public trust.' "

"Maybe we could've stood for something, Jody. Maybe we still can. Chief Filosiani's different. He wants to try and put it back the way it should be."

"Chief Bada-bing? You're dreaming, Salsa. You trust Filosiani and he'll fuck you over just like the rest a'them swivel-chair heroes on the sixth floor of the Glass House. And that's not cynicism; it's *truth*. But, hey . . . go ahead and fantasize. That's what I always liked most about you. You knew how to have dumb-ass dreams." He turned and, without another word, walked out of the bedroom, snatching Papa Joe's contract up off the bed as he passed.

Shane turned on the TV news.

He never should have, because Alexa's funeral was the headline story. Shane sat, mesmerized, as Chief Filosiani spoke about her courage under fire:

"It is with tremendous regret that I am here this afternoon," the chief said to almost two thousand of L.A.'s finest, who were standing in their dress blues on the Police Academy training field. Even Chooch was there. Shane caught a glimpse of him standing with his head bowed as the TV shot panned over to Buddy. Chooch looked as though he was crying. Shane put out his hand and touched the TV screen.

The blond female news anchor came on camera, continuing the story with a slide show over her right shoulder: "Sergeant Hamilton, a recent Medal of Valor recipient, was gunned down by her ex-boyfriend, Detective Sergeant Scully."

No! What is this? Shane was on his feet.

He leaned forward and stared. Shane's picture appeared over the shot of the Police Academy memorial service. It was his

Academy graduation picture. He looked youthful and proud. "Sergeant Scully had been undergoing a psychiatric review and was deemed by his LAPD commander to be emotionally unstable when apparently he was driven to murder."

No . . . It was an accident. Why are you saying this?

The shot switched to the police brass band playing "Taps." There were shots of a Helicopter Air Unit fly-by: five black-and-white Bell Jet Rangers and a Hughes 500 passed low over the field. Then more shots of Buddy dressed in a black suit, somber and grief-stricken . . . shots of the ceremony later, at Forest Lawn, as the casket was lowered with a twenty-one-gun salute. Buddy was handed the flag off the coffin, folded into a tight, career-ending package.

Shane stared in disbelief at the screen until the newscast switched stories.

His mind kaleidoscoped. His thoughts tumbled. Images flashed before him:

Lisa on top of him, her head thrown back—guttural and feline: "Fuck me, you bastard!"

Chooch standing in the airport, carrying his helmet and shoulder pads: "Give her the ring, Shane."

Jody, just a minute ago . . . his words soft, but horribly prophetic: "You trust Filosiani and he'll fuck you just like the rest a'them swivel-chair heroes."

And finally, Alexa . . . in her dress-blue uniform, standing before him, disapproving and remote: "There's darkness in you, Shane. It would never have worked. You went your way, I went mine."

WHO AM I?

THE SPEEDOMETER ON the Vogue motor home hovered near seventy while its tires sang in the rain cuts on the concrete highway. The ornate grille reflected the dotted white lane markers on the chrome bumper, hoovering up lines like a Main Street junkie.

Shane was trying to sleep in the big blue crushed-velvet club chair, forward of the galley. Jody was stretched out on the bed in the rear compartment. Tremaine and Lester Wood were up front, engaged in whispered conversation, while Victory Smith was in the booth nursing a beer and brooding.

But Shane was restless. His mind kept touching the edges of new, soul-defining realities: Alexa's death, Chooch left in the wake of this catastrophe, the powerful memory of sex with

Lisa—a woman he knew was corrupt and dangerous but whose darkness he was inexplicably drawn to.

When he thought about everything that had happened, he knew Jody was right.

If Tony was on the level, why would the LAPD be calling him a murderer on TV and making him a shoot-on-sight fugitive for every law-enforcement agency in America? The Day-Glo Dago had picked a scenario that eliminated Shane from the equation. It was now pretty obvious to Shane that Filosiani didn't want to face the consequences of his own mangled plan. A plan that had resulted in the death of a police officer under his direct supervision. With this news story, he had cut off Shane and forced him to run. Shane was completely alone.

The weird thing was, it didn't seem to matter much. His perspective had changed. He felt like someone else. His world had lost the vivid colors that had always characterized his thoughts and feelings. In their place, a gray mist had descended, taking the volume way down. Shane suspected he no longer had very many things he really cared about. Maybe he had become like Jody. Although the treasured memory of Alexa and Chooch lingered, even these once powerful performers in his life failed to fully penetrate this new fog of listless disinterest.

He began to realize that the ache inside him was really more of a craving. He needed something . . . something to brighten this reality.

How had Jody put it?

A little chemical help after a confusing day.

He was looking at Lester Wood's travel case sitting on the blue carpet, not five feet away. He wondered if Wood had found a way to smuggle one of his little Baggies past Jody's inspection. Or maybe he had found a connection in Palm Springs and hooked himself up, scored some *polvo blanco*. So Shane stretched his foot out around the case and began to nudge it closer.

"You banged the bitch, didn't ya?" Victory interrupted his thoughts, dropping into the chair in front of Shane. "I told ya t'leave her be."

"Get away from me," Shane said softly.

"I told ya not t'fuck 'er."

"I don't take my orders from you, Vic. 'Sides, with all those anabols and oxys you pop, you couldn't lay a carpet."

"Gonna teach you a lesson, then blow yer worthless head off." Smith was sitting with his huge legs spread out in front of him, leaning back in the chair, acting as if all of this was his choice and on his terms.

Shane shifted his right foot and let it fly . . . kicking the steroid junkie right between the legs.

The weight lifter screamed in agony, doubled over in the chair, then dropped to his knees on the carpet, moaning. His left hand cradled his balls, but his right was snaking toward the Uzi tucked into his belt.

Shane yanked the Mini-Cougar out of his ankle holster, pushed it toward Smith, thumbing off the safety as he slammed the muzzle hard into the man's simian forehead. Shane beat Smith's draw by a full second. Victory was caught with one hand on his nuts and the other on his half-drawn Uzi.

"Go on. Bust a move. Let's see what ya got," Shane whispered. He could actually feel the weight lifter's heartbeat pulsing through the muzzle of the Beretta.

Jody exploded out of the bedroom and in an instant was standing over them, his own Mini-Light pulled and chambered.

Shane could feel the motor home gearing down as Tremaine Lane slowed, turning around to see the drama that was playing out behind him.

"Put it down, Shane," Jody ordered.

"Him first."

"Unhook, or I'll lose the both a'ya right now," Jody commanded.

"This ape's been threatening me for two days. I want this over with," Shane demanded.

"Fuck you," Smith said.

Jody fired his Mini-Light. It was on auto-fire, and half a dozen bullets ripped holes in the carpet between them. The rounds blew chunks out of the floor of the motor home and ricocheted off the pavement below, then whined away across the desert. Somehow, miraculously, nothing hit the gas tank or driveshaft. The insanity of the event carried the moment.

Victory Smith let go of his weapon and put both hands out to his side.

Shane still didn't take the Mini-Cougar off the giant's pock-marked forehead. He found himself actually contemplating pulling the trigger, his fingers twitching inadvertently on the cold steel. Then he finally saw fear in Smith's eyes.

In that second, Shane knew he owned the man. He'd have to risk death to pull the trigger because Jody really might take him out, but Shane was seriously tempted to end it—kill Victory and let Jody shoot him for it. It was Shane's call in that split second, and everybody knew it.

And then Shane felt it.

Jody was right. There was a spark of pure joy in this simple equation. It emanated from Victory across the two feet of bullet-torn carpet into Shane. He saw the fear of imminent death register in Smith's pig-mean stare. Shane desperately wanted to seal his own fate. He couldn't remain caught between what he used to be and what he was becoming. He needed to be one thing or the other.

Jody reached out and slowly pushed Shane's wrist aside, shoving the gun away from Victory's sweat-slick forehead. "This ain't it, Hot Sauce."

And then it was over.

"This pile a'shit gets near me again, I'm gonna put him down." Shane's voice, as well as his whole body, was shaking.

Victory was still on his knees, rocking slightly back and forth on the bullet-ravaged blue shag carpet, cupping his balls in both hands. "Lose this motherfucker, Jody," the weight lifter whispered. "There's a five-state manhunt for him. He's poison. Get rid of him."

Jody didn't respond. Instead, he reached down and yanked Smith's Uzi up off the floor. "Let's have yours, too," he said sharply to Shane.

Shane shook his head and put the gun back into his ankle holster. Then he walked to the back of the motor home, into the bedroom, and kicked the door shut. He sat on the queen-size bed with his head in his hands. He could hear the others talking low, as the vehicle once again picked up speed. Jody's voice was louder than the others. Shane couldn't make out the words, but he could feel the vibe right through the paneled bulkhead. Jody was scared. They had started pulling guns on each other, and he was losing control. The mix had turned dangerous, with a strong suicidal flavor.

The gray mist settled lower, engulfing Shane inch by inch.

He had been half an ounce of a trigger pull away from murder. Half an ounce from putting a round through Peter Smith's head.

It was exactly what Jody had talked about: getting a guy down, seeing that look—the look making you feel pure and alive, but also driving you . . . pushing you. In Victory's weakness, he felt rage; in his total surrender came a surge of unreasoning violence.

He remembered a saying from somewhere but couldn't recall where it came from . . . perhaps a Sunday school lecture, or maybe just some barroom psychologist: *When a man is severely tested, only then does he discover who he really is.*

So who the fuck am I? Shane wondered.

HOUSE IN THE VALLEY

IT WAS ALMOST eight P.M.

Jody told them they wouldn't be needing the blue-and-white motor home, so they spent twenty minutes wiping their prints off every surface, then left it in a pay lot off Ventura Boulevard and walked four blocks to the Sherman Oaks Inn, on Valley Vista. As they climbed the stairs to the second-floor room, Shane could see the orange-and-black Charger in the adjoining lot, parked next to an unmarked blue step van.

The room Jody led them into was several notches up from the one in Sunland. The two-room studio apartment was colorless, decorated in beige and brown. The furniture was new and nobody had left cigarette burns on the wood or vomit stains on the carpet.

They had said very little since the incident in the motor

home. Victory Smith had remained silent, his eyes furtive and brooding. But the one time that Shane had locked stares with him, he saw hatred so intense that it froze him momentarily. Jody must have sensed trouble, because he'd kept Victory's Uzi locked in the motor home.

Lester Wood, whom Shane had learned was born in southern Texas and was fluent in Spanish, moved to the phone, took out a slip of paper with a telephone number scribbled on it, and dialed. He spoke quietly in Spanish, then a few moments later hung up. "That was one a'her Spic bodyguards. Juanita's on the way."

"Wait'll you see this bitch, Hot Sauce. Real *guapita,* but hard as asphalt. The spill on her is, she's already dropped six guys. She's Raphael Bacca's niece."

Jody turned to the other Vikings. "Because Rodriquez is gone, we gotta change the lineup. Inky Dink, you're driving backup. Stay at least two blocks back; use the GPS. Hot Sauce, you're with Tremaine. Victory, you're in the gray van with Sawdust."

"I don't wanna stay with the fucking monitors," Smith growled.

"I don't give a shit what you want, that's the way it's going down."

"What monitors?" Shane asked.

"The white step van parked in the lot down there is the one we're using to pick up the cash. It has three pin-cams mounted on it. Tiny little bastards're about the size of a shirt button. One is on the back of the rearview mirror, shooting out the front window. Gives us a wide shot. One's in the grille, pointing down; one is mounted under the bumper, looking back."

"Why?"

"I wanna know where they keep the cash. Since I'm gonna be a hostage and blindfolded, the cameras will tape the whole deal. Send the pictures to the monitors we got in the gray van."

"Once they give the money to us, what's it matter where they keep it?" Shane asked.

"A guy I know in SIS is gonna get the videotape mailed anonymously. We'll be long gone, but Juanita and her band a scumball *ladrones* are gonna face an SIS hard takedown. Most greaseballs don't survive those." He smiled at Shane. "I don't want any *cholos* left behind to point a finger at us, pick us outta some picture lineup."

Tremaine Lane suddenly walked out of the room, and Shane wondered where he was going.

They waited.

The Colombians arrived at a little past eight-thirty. There was a knock on the door, and Victory got up to open it.

"Hola," one of the men outside said softly.

"Yeah, right," Smith growled. "How's yer asshole?" He stepped aside, letting them into the room.

There were two men and a woman, and as Jody had promised, Juanita Bacca was quite a package: shoulder-length, shiny black hair framed a dusky complexion and deep almond eyes. She was wearing a long black skirt wrapped tightly around her slender waist, slit in the middle almost to her crotch.

Jody nodded to her. "Juanita. *Cómo está?"*

She didn't acknowledge him; instead, she rattled some Spanish at the two men standing behind her, who immediately separated and flanked her protectively.

It was then that Shane got his first good look at both bodyguards. The one on the right was going to be big trouble. He was six-foot-two, unusually tall for a Colombian, and had flat, uninteresting features. The tattoos on his neck ran down into his open shirt collar. His name was Octavio Juarez, and Shane had busted him three or four times when he'd been working with the Valley Vice team. As soon as Octavio spotted Shane, he nudged Juanita.

"*Ay, cabrón! Es cuico,*" he whispered.

In a second, everyone had a gun out, including Juanita Bacca, who squatted slightly and grabbed between her legs through the folds of her split skirt. A spring-release holster chimed loudly, a chrome-plated .45 caliber Hardballer suddenly appeared in her hand.

They all held position, glaring over gun sights. No one seemed jittery, either . . . just another day at the office. Then Tremaine Lane appeared from the corridor behind them and tromboned the slide on his auto-mag. The sound brought the first flicker of fear into the faces of the two black-eyed bodyguards, but they didn't turn or flinch. Only Juanita's and Jody's eyes hadn't changed; both were prepared to go down.

Victory Smith, unarmed, was standing in a crouch, his huge mitts helplessly out in front of him.

Juanita rattled something in Spanish to Octavio.

"*Sí,*" he replied. "*Esta cerote me puse en el bote.*"

"Hey, in English!" Jody demanded.

Shane spoke enough street Spanish to know Octavio had said, "This piece of shit put me in jail." And it was true. Octavio was a good bodyguard but a less-than-gifted street dealer who kept selling drugs to Valley Vice cops throughout the mid-nineties. Shane had roughed him up three times in one eleven-month period. A Valley Division record.

"Tu compañero es policía," Juanita said suspiciously to Jody.

"He says what? A cop? You're nuts!" Jody was stalling.

"Jody, go buy this bitch a newspaper 'cause I'm all over the front page," Shane said.

"That's right," Jody brightened. "Tremaine, we got these greaseballs covered. Go down to the lobby, get the *L.A. Times*." He motioned at Shane. "He's wanted by the cops for the murder of a police officer. Tell her, Sawdust." Lester Wood rattled the translation at Juanita.

"No . . . Miguel, vete!" Juanita said, motioning to a bodyguard who was holding a Tech 9 on Shane and Jody. She barked something else in Spanish, then Miguel backed out of the room past Tremaine.

"Inky Dink. Go with him!" Tremaine followed. They were all left standing in the room, gripping their iron, hoping nobody would get nervous and squeeze off a round by mistake.

A minute or two later, Miguel reentered the room with a copy of the *Los Angeles Times* and handed it to Juanita. Tremaine appeared in the threshold behind him.

On the front page, above the fold, was a picture of Shane, along with the story of the murder of Alexa Hamilton. Juanita scanned the paper quickly, looked at the picture, glanced up at Shane, then over at Jody, her beautiful face composed in a silent question.

"He's not a cop anymore," Jody explained. *"Jamás policía.* He's wanted for murder . . . he's with us now." He looked at Sawdust helplessly. "Is she getting any of this?"

Lester Wood rattled off a long sentence. Then all of them seemed to be talking at once. Finally Juanita lowered her Hardballer, and the others followed suit.

"Tienes los numeros? Te los dió mi tío?" she asked.

Shane knew about "los numeros" from other drug stings he'd worked. She was asking Jody for a secret number given by the cartel boss to both parties involved in a street transaction. Bacca was the cartel boss, and this was his money. The ID number was proof of his consent that the cash could be turned over to the Vikings. Since there were no contracts protecting the transfer, it was Jody's knowledge of this code that enabled Juanita to hand over millions of narco-dollars with no questions.

"The number? Yeah . . . It's 457, from Raphael," Jody said.

"Cuatro cinco siete por Raphael," Lester said.

"Okay. *Vamos. Usted solamente,"* Juanita ordered, pointing at Jody.

"Absolutely." Jody smiled. "Me only." The tension in the room had eased slightly.

"Vamos en su coche," she said to Jody. Adding in horrible English: "We load. For is done. You go back. *Es suficiente?"*

"Works for me." Jody smiled at her again. "You guys wait here."

"Dame los llaves." She turned to Miguel. *"Como se dice?"*

"She wants the keys to our car," Shane said.

"Sí," Juanita answered. "Keys."

"It's the blue step van in the lot downstairs," Jody said to Miguel as he handed him the keys. The bodyguard immediately left the room.

Through all of this, the still-suspicious Octavio Juarez never took his eyes off Shane, not for a moment believing that a cop who had hooked him up three times in one year was now a fugitive.

"Let's do it," Jody said.

Juanita and Octavio flanked Jody, and with no further discussion, they walked out of the room and closed the door, leaving the rest of the Vikings behind.

"Why're we waiting? Let's get outta here," Shane said after they were gone. He moved to the door, but Lester and Tremaine were still at the windows, watching as the step van, followed by a new black Cadillac, pulled out of the lot.

"Be cool," Tremaine said to Shane. "With this satellite rig, we can tail them from miles back . . . it shoots a tracking signal back to us from outer space."

They waited for almost three minutes before Tremaine nodded and Shane opened the door. They walked out of the apartment, down the stairs, and into the parking lot. Shane and Tremaine climbed into the black GMC truck with the pool-cleaning logo on the side. Victory Smith and Lester Wood got into the windowless gray van with the monitors. Tremaine had already switched on the dash-mounted GPS: a map of the entire West Valley downloaded onto the LCD screen. Then they saw a small blip moving near the center of the readout, indicating the route the step van was taking. It was heading east, down the Ventura Freeway toward Studio City.

"Let's go. That's them," Tremaine said. Then he pulled out. The gray van, with Victory driving, followed right behind them.

"Where'd you get all this high-tech stuff?" Shane asked.

"Rod stole it from SWAT. They got the best shit," Tremaine answered, his deep voice resonating in the sound-deadened cab.

They were on the freeway now, following the flashing dot on the GPS, heading east. The white step van was at least a mile ahead of them.

Shane looked over at Tremaine, his shaved head glistening, reflecting the passing freeway lights.

Of all the Vikings, Shane thought Tremaine was the most puzzling. The ex-SWAT sergeant had a cool intelligence and natural leadership that he masked with profound silences, mixed with spurts of ghetto-speak. But every time he spoke, Victory, Lester, and sometimes even Jody stopped talking and were suddenly alert, like street punks listening to a distant siren.

Tremaine glanced over and caught Shane looking at him. "Whattcha think you starin' at?" he demanded angrily.

"Nothin'." Shane shifted his gaze to the LCD screen. They rode in silence for a minute.

"Why don't you get it the fuck off your mind," Tremaine suddenly said.

"You know this is coming unglued," Shane said. "Two guys already dead and buried. Victory's a mess. Sawdust doesn't give a shit, and Jody's on autopilot. You saw him back there, ready to swap lead with a buncha street dealers."

Tremaine continued driving, and a slight smile passed across his face, then disappeared, barely visible, like a shadow on a dark wall. He shook his head slowly. "You got it all worked out, huh?"

"So when it all comes apart, then what?"

"You best slow yer roll, Chuck. You don't know me. . . . You 'bout t'make a bad mistake here."

"I'll tell you something else I'm wondering."

They drove in silence, the target vehicle flashing on the LCD screen between them, heading down the curving freeway map, being measured from deep space by a satellite while Tremaine drove and said nothing.

"All these other guys've got Sawdust's shitty pictures drawn all over 'em," Shane said. "You . . . you've got no ink . . . no nothin'. Not even the little Viking helmet. I'm thinking, Why is that? It raises questions."

Tremaine didn't look over at Shane, but he had lost the slight smile. His knuckles gripped the wheel hard as he drove.

"Tell you something else," Shane continued. "You hate being called 'Inky Dink.' Every time Jody calls you that, it's like you got kicked in the ass. So I'm wondering how come you put up with it; why you lettin' Jody 'Tom' you like that."

Tremaine looked over. His eyes had become cold black warnings.

"Here's my guess . . ." Shane continued recklessly. "You ain't completely down with the program, and if the rest of these guys weren't so zooted, they'd spot it."

The speedometer was ticking up in the seventies while the truck radials hummed.

"I ain't no Sega radio," Tremaine finally said. "Go play those tunes somewhere else, white boy."

Then, the beeping light on the LCD screen turned off the freeway. A few minutes later Tremaine made the same turn. The windowless van containing Victory and Sawdust followed like a gray shadow, sharking along behind them.

Ten minutes later they watched the map screen as the step van turned left on Shadow Drive, then right onto a street called Glen Haven. It stopped at the last house, at the end of a cul-de-sac.

A few minutes later Tremaine drove into the same high-income neighborhood with his headlights off and parked up the block out of sight of the house. The gray van parked behind them.

Tremaine switched off the GPS and got out of the truck.

They went over to the van. Tremaine knocked on the side door, then as soon as it opened, they jumped inside.

Victory Smith was already tuning in the three TV monitors, revealing that the white step van was parked in a hedge-lined driveway.

"Always the same deal," Sawdust said. "Expensive house at the end of the cul-de-sac with a view of the whole street. The Beaners living inside are just window dressing sent up here from Colombia. It's all on page one of the playbook."

They watched on the wide-angle lens coming from the camera stuck behind the rearview mirror as Jody, wearing a blindfold, was led into the house.

Once he was inside, Miguel opened the garage and Octavio pulled the step van inside. They could see the garage door come down behind it from the rearview camera. The grille-mounted camera now showed an expensive Spanish tile floor in the large, empty, four-car garage.

Octavio took off his jacket, grabbed a pickax out of the storage cabinet, then walked to a spot in front of the van and swung the ax high over his head, bringing it down hard, smashing the decorative tiles.

"Must have their money room under all that expensive tile," Sawdust drawled.

They watched on the monitors as Octavio, then Miguel, took turns breaking up the three square feet of flooring. Next they shoveled out four inches of subsoil, revealing a trap door. Octavio pulled the door up and turned on a light, exposing an underground room. Then, one at a time, the Colombians went down a short flight of stairs, disappearing off the monitor for a moment, only to reappear, carrying large rectangular canvas bags that looked to Shane to be about three feet long by two feet high and wide.

"Show me the money, boys," Tremaine rumbled softly in his rich baritone as the two drug dealers put the canvas bags into the back of the step van, then returned for more.

The whole treasure hunt took less than an hour. The step van was almost completely filled with bags of cash. Then Jody was led blindfolded out of the house and helped back into the front seat of the step van.

They watched on the rearview-mirror cam as the truck backed away from the house. In the process, the front-end cameras neatly panned the mailbox and the house number on the curb. Then the step van took off, up the street, again followed by the black Cadillac, its front license clearly photographed by the rear-bumper camera.

The two vehicles swept past the van, rocking it with slip-streaming air. "We'll let 'em get a block or two ahead," Tremaine instructed, then after a minute, added, "Okay, now."

Shane and Tremaine got out of the gray van and returned to the truck. They switched on the GPS and again followed the step van from several miles back, watching on the LCD screen until it stopped moving.

Both tail vehicles pulled over and waited. The beeping light on the GPS continued blinking but remained stationary. Five minutes later the cell phone in the truck rang and Tremaine pushed the speaker button. Jody's voice filled the truck cab.

"Okay, they're gone. I'll drive the van and meet you back at the Sherman Oaks apartment. We'll see what we got here."

What they got were thirty large canvas bags containing fifty million dollars in banded bricks of used cash.

RUSTY

J ODY HAD A deal with a crooked armored-transport company driver to move the thirty bags of cash to the Union
Bank in San Diego. They unloaded the step van and put the
cash in the back of an armored truck that had been borrowed
without permission from the transport company's service department. At a little past eleven P.M., it pulled out with Tremaine riding shotgun and headed toward San Diego.

"You ever heard of a guy named Giovanni DeScotto?" Jody
said to Shane as they rested in the back of the empty step van.

"Yeah, he's a banker or something, suspected of doing bank
wire transfers for the Cali cartel. I read a department one-sheet
on him. He was never busted."

Jody grinned. "Wrong! I busted the fuck. Got him dead-bang

during the Mexican drug case. Caught him on videotape, offering to launder twenty mil."

"You flipped him?" Shane asked.

"Amen, brother. Burned him and turned him. He's our guy now. He's working at a bank in San Diego as vice president of Latin American deposits." Jody was grinning. "He's gonna take delivery of this armored-truck shipment and pass it through his bank." Shane knew that once the money was deposited in a bank, Jody was home free. Bank-to-bank wire transfers were exempt from Treasury Department supervision. There was no federal record kept on these transactions. It was a major loophole in the Justice Department's anti-drug policy. This one fact alone was responsible for the existence of the drug laundries operating in both Mexico and Colombia.

"Tremaine rides in that armored truck down to San Diego and gets our money logged in to the bank there as a cash transfer from Bancomer in Mexico," Jody continued. "Giovanni writes up the phony paper to record the deposit, then he does the cybertransfer to a little bank I found here in the Valley where I got some serious leverage with the VP of regional operations. From there, it gets wired to Aruba." Jody smiled. "Two bank transfers, and the money is off-shore."

"Slick," Shane said, and watched Jody smile.

■ ■ ■

The West Valley Bank of Commerce was located just off Ventura Boulevard on Beverly Glen, nestled into a landscaped commercial park five blocks from some of the most expensive real estate in the Valley.

They left Victory in the car outside, with instructions to cover their backs.

Tremaine had called an hour before, to say that the transfer of funds to the San Diego bank was complete. He was headed back to L.A.

It was nine A.M. when Jody, Shane, and Lester walked through the swinging glass doors. The West Valley Bank had a minimalist decor and looked as though it had been designed by Frigidaire. A few black-and-white Impressionist paintings dotted the shiny white walls.

Jody asked a passing bank employee if Bob Miller, the vice president of regional operations, was around.

"You mean Rusty." She smiled. "I'll get him."

After five minutes Bob "Rusty" Miller walked up. Shane thought he was fifteen years and at least one hair transplant past his nickname.

Rusty led them to a private, windowless office in the back of the bank and closed the door.

"Both of these gentlemen are police officers as well?" he began without preamble. He seemed agitated and definitely in a hurry to get Jody out of there.

"That's right." Jody smiled. "This deal is going to work just like the Mexican bank sting. Same MO, only this time we're gonna wire slightly more cash . . . fifty million. It goes to a personal account in Aruba."

"*Slightly* more?" the pudgy banker exclaimed. "You can't be serious. That's five times more. . . . and isn't Aruba in the Caribbean?"

"The Lesser Antilles. Twenty five kilometers from the Venezuelan coastline."

"That's outside of the continental United States."

"Yep. Last time I checked."

"Sergeant, this branch is currently undergoing a federal bank examiner's review. It's going to be very difficult to handle that large a sub rosa transfer at this particular—"

Jody held up a hand and interrupted him. "You're going to do it because this is police department business, and a failure to comply will bring all kinds a'nasty shit down on you, Bobby."

"Jeezus, when is this gonna end?"

"Never," Jody snarled.

"I can't just keep doing this," he whined.

"Then you shouldn't a'been banging that teenage boy in the Valley, Bob. Shit like that has consequences. You know what happens to pedophiles in prison?"

"Look . . . I . . ."

"You're gonna be home plate at pole-vaulting class."

"Stop it, please."

"I'm just trying to reset the table for you. Let's not get stupid and lose our perspective here."

Rusty was perspiring dark half-moons under the armpits of his designer blue shirt.

"Another bank-to-bank transfer?"

"Right. The cash is in this numbered bank account in San Diego." Jody handed him a slip of paper with the number on it.

"Okay," Rusty wheezed. "Who's this go to?"

"Wire it to the First Mantoor Bank of Aruba, marked to Lewis Foster's account there," Jody said, using the same alias he had given the geriatric gate guard in Palm Springs.

Rusty's face had gone pale.

But Shane had no sympathy for him. Worse still, he was appalled that Jody had rolled this creep instead of booking him. In Shane's mind, there was no worse crime than pedophilia.

Yet Jody had apparently caught this guy and had let him slide in return for performing a banking favor on his Mexican bank sting.

In the wake of his disgust over doing business with Rusty Miller, Shane felt the old cop anger return, the sense of right and wrong that had propelled him toward police work in the first place. In that second, standing there in the back room of the bank, he felt for a moment like the old Shane Scully who cared about justice. He desperately wanted to be that man again. So he stood glowering angrily at the fat pedophile with a teenager's nickname, trying to turn back the clock . . . trying to be what he had once been, to reclaim feelings he had lost.

Then Rusty left the room with the account number to arrange the transfers.

"You rolled a child molester?" Shane asked as soon as the banker was out of the room and the door was closed.

"We caught this bozo by sheer accident." Jody grinned. "We were staking out the Mexican bankers, had a video trap set up to shoot through some glory holes in the motel rooms they had rented on Canyon Boulevard, not half a mile from here. We were waiting for them to get back from dinner, and unknown to us, the guy on the lobby desk was 'hot cotting' rooms, letting a buncha chocolate cowboys use already-rented suites for an hour or so, for cash. Rusty stumbles into our video trap with a fifteen-year-old male prostitute named Bunny. No shit, that's this kid's street name. When it turned out Rusty was in the banking business and we desperately needed a U.S. bank to wire our department-issued sting cash from . . . it was too good to let slide. So Rusty became our CI on that op."

"This guy victimizes children. How can you make him a confidential informant?"

"All the John Wayne bullshit's really starting to get old, Hot Sauce," Jody snapped.

A few minutes later Rusty Miller came through the door. The trip to the wire-transfer room had done him some good. His color had returned. He handed Jody a slip of paper. "Here's your wire confirmation," he said.

Jody looked at the slip, then pulled out his wallet, managing to flash his sergeant's badge for good measure as he put the receipt inside.

"You stay out of trouble, Mr. Miller. I don't wanna hear from any of my Vice contacts that you're out boning kids on the Strip. If I do"—he nodded toward Shane—"my man, here, is gonna chop-block your ass."

"Please, leave me alone," Rusty squeaked.

"Right . . . Lemme take that under advisement," Jody said, and led the frightened pedophile out of the room.

Lester looked at Shane after they had gone. "This guy turns my stomach," he drawled. "Was up to me, he'd be doing a telephone number in the joint." A telephone number was con lingo for a long sentence.

Then Lester exited the room, and Shane found himself alone for a moment. He wanted to speak to Chooch, even if it was just for half a minute. Without worrying about the consequences if he got caught, Shane reached out, picked up the phone, and quickly dialed his home number. One ring . . . then two . . .

Come on, Chooch . . . Pick up, please.

Then his answering machine clicked on.

"What the hell are you doing!" Jody interrupted, glaring at Shane from the doorway.

"Calling my machine."

Jody exploded into the room, grabbed the receiver and put it to his ear. Shane could hear his own voice recording leaking into the small room.

"Whatta you, nuts? They could trace this call through the phone-company records, come here, and roll Bob Miller. You don't talk to anybody. I thought we had that straight." He slammed the phone back in the cradle.

"I was just gonna leave a message for my son," Shane said.

"No messages. Nothing. You don't exist for that kid. You're history. Now let's get moving. They're waiting."

Shane didn't ask who was waiting. His heart was slamming in his chest.

In that moment, he had a premonition that he would never see Chooch again.

FLIGHT

"V ICTORY'S BACK ON steroids," Shane said, just loud
enough to be heard over the whine of the starboard engine. He was seated in a plush Gulfstream 5 that was owned
by All-American Tobacco. The jet was parked at the Peterson
Aviation private jet terminal in Van Nuys.

"You're dreamin', Salsa."

"Hey, Jody, I blew this guy's thigh to shit just under two
weeks ago. Look at him ... he's already walking without
crutches. Only way he could be healing this fast is if he's slamming steroids."

"Get off this, will ya?"

"The guy is fixing. Once his leg is solid, he's gonna try for
me. I can't do what you want and be watching my back at the
same time."

"We got less than three days and this thing is done. You'll never see him again. Don't make a problem now."

"Why don't you just go ahead and admit you can't handle him, that you're afraid to confront the guy."

Jody spun and glared across the narrow aisle at Shane. "Get off my jock, for Christ's sake. I told ya I'd take care of him, and I'll take care of him, but I don't need you all the time in my ear about it."

"You planning on doing that before or after he makes another play for me?"

Just then, a pretty young blond woman dressed in a blue uniform with shoulder boards came up the stairs into the plush jet. "Hi, I'm Lily," she announced happily to the Vikings, who were spread out in the comfortable club seats. "I'll be your stewardess. If any of you want to order a special meal, I can take care of that now, but it will delay departure. I suggest the selected menu on the embossed cards in the back of each seat."

"We're fine," Jody said, his voice still tinged with anger.

They heard footsteps on the jet staircase, and Lisa St. Marie came aboard, followed by José Mondragon.

"Okay, Lily," Lisa said. "Tell Matt and Carl we're all here." She was the only AAT employee on the plane and seemed to relish being in charge. She had chosen tropical colors for the flight, an off-the-shoulder Hawaiian print dress and matching sweater that she tied around her waist like a sash. José, in his trademark black Armani and glittering links, poured himself a drink from the chrome-and-crystal bar, then settled into an empty seat as the stewardess disappeared into the cockpit. Momentarily, a hydraulic mechanism hummed and the staircase came up, air-locking tightly into place.

The port-side engine wound up as Lisa walked down the

aisle, pausing at Shane's seat. "I thought I'd sit back there," she said, pointing to the sofa in the aft compartment. "It's more private, and I'd love the company."

"Sure," he said, shooting a look at Victory as he unbuckled his seat belt and followed her to the rear of the plane, where they both sat on the champagne leather sofa.

She took his hand and smiled. "It's a long flight. We generally cruise at around forty-five thousand feet, and you know what that means. . . ."

"No, Lisa, what does that mean?"

"You're about to become a satisfied member of the Mile-High club."

"I am?"

"We can be brave and do it here after everyone's dozing, or we can go to the lav, but once they're asleep, I'm planning to screw your brains out."

"Do I have any choice? Or is it always your call?" He could already feel the effect of her . . . her scent, her vibe, her wanton sexuality.

She reached down and felt his erection. "Look who's ready to go," she purred.

When she smiled at him again, he turned his face away. He promised himself he would not make love to Lisa again. But even as he made this pledge, he could feel lust beginning as a warm, sick feeling in the pit of his stomach, growing inside him, spreading to his loins like deadly poison. They took off and climbed quickly to their cruising altitude.

It was going to be a long flight, and Shane's resistance to her brand of spiritual darkness was low. After the stewardess served dinner and collected their trays, Lisa started in on him . . . teasing at first . . . reaching out to him, feeling him, pulling her dress off her shoulders, exposing herself, pulling his face down, her nipples already hard with passion. Shane glanced nervously at the others sprawled out in the forward cabin, sleeping in their reclining chairs.

What was it about this woman, whom he didn't even like or care about but couldn't seem to resist? Why did she have this carnal hold on him? Like an addict, he was no longer in charge of his impulses.

Suddenly, she was unzipping him, leaning down and placing her mouth on him.

"No . . . no . . . please, no," he mumbled feebly. She was dangerously close to his core, close to destroying the last valuable remnants of him, and yet he desperately wanted her.

She glanced up, delight twinkling in her jade-green eyes. "What do you mean, no? This is my gift. Everything else I do just fills up the spaces in between."

"No," he said weakly, pushing her away and zipping up.

And then, filling in for his faltering resolve, brutish Victory Smith was towering over them, stooping slightly in the six-foot cabin. "He giving you a problem, Lisa?" the steroid jockey asked softly. " 'Cause if he is, just say the word and I'll take care of it."

"Excuse me." She got up off the sofa with no further comment and, swinging her hips, walked all the way to the front of the jet, passing through the small door into the pilot's cabin.

A strange sense of gratitude for the weight lifter swept over him.

"Check it out," Victory said as he did a slow, deep-knee bend. Pain registered on his face, but Shane was shocked to see that he could squat all the way down and then rise up again. "Pretty good, huh?"

"Looks like the old abductor canal is back in business."

"Jody ain't gonna be here to protect you forever. I'm gonna pick a time when it's just you and me, no witnesses. This is your last day on planet Earth, pretty boy. Try and enjoy it." He turned and lumbered back to his seat in the front, and never looked back at Shane again.

Seven hours and three time zones later, they landed on the small Caribbean island of Aruba.

ONE HAPPY LITTLE ISLAND

34

QUEEN BEATRIX AIRPORT was on the eastern side of Aruba. They taxied up to a Customs shed located between the Mantoor executive-jet terminal and the regular commercial-jet boarding areas.

Out of the window of the private jet, Shane could see a handsome, forty-five-year-old dark-skinned man in white linen trousers and a flowered shirt leaning against the fender of a black, seven-passenger Mercedes SUV. His sandaled feet were crossed at the ankles, his arms laced comfortably across his chest.

Jody had promised that there would be no Customs or Immigration check, so Shane left his Beretta strapped to his ankle. Except for Victory, the rest of the Vikings were also packing. Shane wasn't sure what had happened to the weight lifter's Uzi.

He just hoped Jody hadn't returned it to him and that it wasn't hidden in his gym bag.

Shane followed Lisa, José, and Jody off the plane into the humid tropical morning. The rest of the Vikings trailed behind with their small satchels and stopped near the waiting man.

José gave the man a bear hug. Then Lisa took her turn, administering a couple of pecks on his swarthy cheeks. José turned toward the Vikings, who had arranged themselves in a semicircle, squinting in the nine A.M. tropical sun.

"This is Sandro Mantoor," José said. "Sandy is going to take us to the hotel." All of this was spoken in perfect Ivy League English. "Sandro and I attended Harvard Business School together." He added proudly, "We were in the same Eating Club."

They all exchanged names and handshakes, Sandro exposing two rows of porcelain-white, orthodontically perfect teeth. "I've arranged for our best villas at the La Cabana Beach Hotel. I think you will be quite comfortable there."

"Sandy owns the hotel." José smiled proudly. "But you'll come to see the Mantoors own almost everything on this island." Then, to prove his point, José grinned up at the Mantoor Aviation sign hanging on the front of the private-jet terminal.

"Isle de Mantoor," Lisa said happily.

"I've arranged for a second vehicle to take us to our accommodations. Customs and Immigration have already been dealt with, so we can leave without delay," Sandro informed them. "José, perhaps you and Ms. St. Marie could travel with me. I have a few things to discuss before the meeting this afternoon."

"Of course."

José, Sandro, and Lisa got into his Mercedes and pulled out

just as an identical SUV arrived. Shane noticed that both vehicles were brand-new, with dealer plates in chrome holders that read: MANTOOR IMPORTS. The island's motto was inscribed on the yellow and red license plate: ONE HAPPY LITTLE ISLAND.

They all got into the second SUV, Jody choosing the passenger seat next to the driver—a large, Germanic man who said his name was Eric.

Shane was jammed in next to Lester and Victory in the second row. Tremaine had slightly more room in the back.

The capital city of Oranjestad was only five miles away, and they arrived minutes later. The outskirts of the port town were surrounded by tin-roofed shacks, happily dressed in bright Caribbean colors—red with green trim, or yellow with blue. Boxed palms lined the streets and swayed in a brisk trade wind. As they neared the center of town, the red, tin-roofed houses gave way to traditional Dutch and Queen Anne architecture. The port was picturesque, with quaint, brightly painted, stern-tillered fishing boats anchored in the magnificent horseshoe harbor, waiting for dusk. A medieval fort and a lighthouse were on opposite ends of a pair of stone jetties.

Then they were in the center of town; they passed the First Mantoor Bank and Commerce Company, located in a two-story Dutch turn-of-the-century manor house. It dominated most of one block in downtown Oranjestad. Mantoor Travel, a Donatella Mantoor Corporation, sat on Main Street, along with the Fredrico Mantoor Shipping and Freight Forwarding Company. Farther down the street was the King Venezuelan Shipping Line—a Daveed Mantoor Corporation, and so on.

Eric kept up a running dialogue in a thick Dutch accent,

pointing out sights: "The Mantoor family is, how you say . . . tradition of Aruba. She is a business dynasty formed by late grandfather, Elias Mantoor, yah. Elias, he come here, was Lebanese Christian . . . migrated to Latin America over hundred years ago. He do . . . how you say . . . trading all along da Caribbean coast. Dere on corner is Mantoor Corporation headquarters." Eric pointed to a plantation-style house on two acres taking up an entire city block in the center of town. "Used to be colonial governor's mansion until Elias, he buy in 1896, for corporate headquarters. Da Mantoor family all become citizens of Netherlands, like me, with Dutch passports. Sandro Mantoor . . . one day soon, he make the control for all this. The great-uncle, Milos . . . he very ill." The spiel continued like that until Eric turned into a floral-landscaped, tree-lined drive.

The La Cabana Beach Hotel and Casino was a beautiful Dutch Colonial structure: rococo white wood railings, fronted slanting wooden porches like delicate lacework. Huge paddle fans turned in the open lobby, swirling hot tropical air lazily around inside the exposed-beam entry.

Shane was given the Orchid Suite. He went inside, closed the door, and set down his gym bag. The room was large, beautifully appointed, and done restfully in light blue and white. He looked through the sliding glass doors to the Caribbean waters just a few yards beyond. A twenty-five-knot wind was snapping the palm fronds just outside his window. The crescent white-sand beach was teeming with sunbathers. Bodysurfers competed for wave space with half a dozen streaking sailboarders who shot diagonally back and forth across the turquoise lagoon. Paddle balls and Frisbees flew recklessly. Sailing above it all were a few hang gliders, crisscrossing over this frantic activity like colorful winged creatures circling for a spot to land.

"Pretty cool, isn't it?" Lisa interrupted. He spun around and found her standing in his bathroom door. She had changed into white shorts, sandals, and a pastel orange blouse tied in a knot at the middle.

"Are we roommates?" he asked.

"Actually, my room is next door . . . but I scammed a key to yours, so I guess we get to be whatever we want." She crossed the room and kissed him lightly on the lips, then pulled away, spinning slightly to her right, showing herself to him. Certainly seductive and inviting, but Shane thought it was also a little too choreographed.

He was being manipulated. This suddenly seemed like the too-planned dance of a professional . . . and in that moment, the spell she had cast over him was broken. She suddenly seemed sad, comic, and slightly desperate.

"We'll have to save our party for later. I've got a meeting with the Harvard Marching and Chowder Society in ten minutes. When we do this again, I don't want us to have to rush." She smiled. "What did you think of Sandy?"

"The Mantoor family is something," Shane said. "What don't they own around here?"

"You don't know the half of it. Aside from their legitimate businesses, the Mantoors control the trans-shipping of all drugs and parallel-market product in this duty-free zone. They're the new pirates of the Caribbean. The Mantoors and Paco Brazos control most of the negotiations for black-market product down here."

"And who is Paco Brazos?" Shane asked.

"He's a Colombian nightmare—a 'San Andresito.'"

"A what?"

"The San Andresitos are the five families that control all the smuggling into Colombia. They get that name from black-market malls called San Andresitos that are located all over Colombia. The malls are owned by the Medellín cartels. Paco's malls are owned by the Bacca family, the same people that Jody's L.A. drug cash came from. Our smokes will be sold in their malls, and that's how the cartel gets its money back. The five smuggling families—the San Andresitos—operate out of a desert town called Maicao. Since we're running such a huge load of cigarettes, and no one or two families can place that much product, Paco Brazos has subcontracted the deal to include his competitors. But he's charging the other families a big commission, and this could cause a problem. The other San Andresitos don't want to pay him. That's why I'm off to meet Sandy, José, and Paco. We're trying to hose these guys down. Then at four, José and Paco are meeting with the rest of the San Andresitos to do the deal." She walked toward the door. "These smugglers make me a little nervous. I can hardly wait to finish this and get back to L.A."

"Do we all go to the four o'clock meeting?"

"No. Just Sandy and José. I won't be there, either, because—"

"Because as an All-American Tobacco executive, you don't really have a clue what's going on, right? You're just selling duty-free cigarettes."

"Don't be a shit, darling."

She smiled, planted another kiss on her fingertips, and wiggled them at him from the door, then turned and walked out of his room, a sexy package designed for trouble.

■ ■ ■

After she left, Shane sat on the bed and thought about what she had told him.

The problem was, he didn't seemed to care anymore. He felt a heavy layer of depression just off the edge of his psyche . . . a rolling fog of guilt and darkness. It was threatening to overcome what was left of him . . . to make him completely disappear.

THE DUTY-FREE ZONE

YOU LOOK LIKE Ricky Ricardo," Shane said to Jody, who was standing in the hall outside Shane's door, wearing a wild flowered island shirt. It was ten minutes to four in the afternoon.

"Just bought this in the gift shop. We're comped." Jody grinned. "Everything's on Sandy. Despite his greasy look, I'm beginning to really acquire a taste for that guy. This place a'his ain't bad, either. You should see all the A-caliber trim hanging by the pool." He smiled broadly, then added: "Let's go. Eric's waiting downstairs. We're supposed to be at the duty-free dock for a meeting with the Colombians in ten minutes."

"I thought we weren't invited."

"An hour ago we weren't; something musta changed."

They met the rest of the Vikings in the lobby and again

found themselves packed into the black Mercedes SUV, Shane wedged in behind the driver's seat, staring at Eric's Teutonic wrinkles. Lisa wasn't with them, and Papa Joe had taken the seat up front.

"We got a little problem," he said to Jody as soon as the vehicle was in motion. "Unfortunately, it's not something I can fix."

"Unfixable problems are a Viking specialty," Jody said, smiling.

"Paco Brazos decided to cut one of the San Andresito families out of this deal. The man he left out is Santander Cortez. Santa is not a man you get rid of easily. He's something of an enigma out in the desert . . . a black marketeer with a political agenda. He will undoubtedly make trouble."

"Don't worry," Jody said. "We'll take care of it."

José shook his head. "Don't be so sure. There are frequent kidnappings and murders surrounding parallel-market transactions in Maicao. It's out in the desert. There is no law, no police or civil government. Worse still, there is only one road in and out. Once you go in, you are in a trap. Making things more complicated, the leftist guerrillas and the right-wing death squads hide in that desert preying on each other and the San Andresitos' shipments. As white Americans, you will be easily spotted. Everyone in Maicao will know you are there from the first minute you arrive. There are no Anglos in Maicao. You will have only Paco Brazos standing between you and all this, and Paco cannot easily be trusted."

■ ■ ■

When they arrived at the port, Eric drove the Mercedes to a fenced-off wharf with a guarded gate. Signs identified it as the

MANTOOR SHIPPING COMPANY FREE-TRADE ZONE. NO TRES-PASSING warnings were printed on the gate in four languages. A uniformed guard with an out-of-date carbine swung the bar arm up and allowed Eric to drive the German-made SUV down the bustling pier. There were several old three-hundred-foot freighters tied to the wharf. All the ships were registered to different countries. English, Japanese, Dutch, and Venezuelan flags tugged at their halyards, snapping energetically in the stiff breeze. Crane engines roared as loaded containers swung from cables over the dock and above rusting freighters, creating a deafening racket. Green John Deere forklifts, piled high with boxed merchandise, were zipping around, scooting loads of duty-free in and out of ten huge warehouses located on the pier.

The wharf was immense, almost fifty yards wide, and swarming with people and product.

"How come they don't warehouse onshore?" Shane asked. "Why store all this stuff out on the dock?"

"Because none of it is going to stay here more than a day or two," José answered. "It's all contraband. Parallel-market goods heading into Colombia."

"All of this is going to Maicao?" Shane asked as he watched a forklift with three crated washing machines whiz by in front of their vehicle.

"Maicao and Culcata, Panama," José said. "It is no wonder the Mantoors control so many businesses, no? They have much money to invest."

Shane nodded as he again remembered the maps he had found in Jody's airport house. Culcata was the other city that was circled.

Eric drove the Mercedes into the last warehouse on the pier and parked. "This building contains only cigarettes and liquor," José told them.

Shane was looking at billions of cigarettes from every U.S. manufacturer: Phillip Morris, Reynolds Tobacco, Liggett & Meyers, and Lorillard. On the other side of the warehouse were the liquor products: huge wooden pallets were stacked forty feet high with cases of Seagram's, J&B, Early Times, and Beefeater.

"Our cigarettes came from Norfolk, Virginia, yesterday, on that Dutch freighter tied up across the pier. They are now on those pallets over there." He pointed to more than three hundred large shipping containers stacked near the door, with the AAT logo stamped on every box. Each carton also sported a big red duty-free sticker. "They will soon be loaded on a Venezulean ship to cross the channel."

"How many cigarettes is that?" Shane asked.

"There are twenty cigarettes in a pack," José began. "Ten packs to a carton, fifty cartons in each case, and nine hundred sixty cases in each of these containers. We have shipped three hundred fifty containers." He paused for effect. "That comes to ninety-six million cigarettes."

As soon as they got out of the SUV, Sandro Mantoor came out of a door a few yards away and headed toward them, his leather soles clacking on the shiny concrete. "This way, my friends," he said, and led them through another door and up a flight of stairs, into a plush suite of offices. They walked down an air-conditioned corridor, then entered a small conference room. A plate-glass window dominated the far wall, overlooking the bustling warehouse operation below.

There were four men standing in different parts of the room, and despite their expensive tropical clothing, they all looked like extras from the movie *Rio Lobo* . . . round, sweating men with crooked teeth turned brown by tobacco. Greasy smiles lurked menacingly under hungry eyes. If one of them had started cleaning his teeth with a knife, it wouldn't have surprised Shane. Tucked in their pants, under loose shirttails, he could see handguns bulging.

"Paco, mi amigo," Sandro said expansively as he embraced Paco Brazos, who was only five foot four and bald on top but wore his fringe hair long and pulled back in a ponytail.

He had on tan slacks and a Mexican guayabera with two Snickers bars stuffed into the breast pocket.

"Buenos días, mis compañeros," Paco said to all of them with something approaching two-faced warmth. Then Papa Joe introduced Jody, who introduced the rest of the Vikings.

"These are my dear friends and trusted business associates," Papa Joe said first in Spanish, then turned to Jody and translated it all into English.

"Bueno, bueno," Paco Brazos said, nodding and bowing all in the same motion, then introduced the three other men in rapid Spanish.

Spartacos Sococo was the tallest at around five-seven. He had the worst haircut Shane had ever seen. It looked as if he had attempted to cut it himself using garden shears. Emilio Hernandez was five-five, fat, and had a recent-looking red-welted scar that cut through his left cheek, running down his neck into his collar. Octavio Randhanie, the only skinny San Andresito, just smiled at them, never removing his straw hat or dark glasses.

The San Andresitos kept stretching their humorless grins over hard eyes that were expressionless as licked stones. Shane had done enough undercover gun and drug deals in Los Angeles to spot the deadly crosscurrents.

The six men began speaking rapid Spanish. Shane was struggling to keep up, but their Colombian accents sounded different from the Mexican Spanish he'd encountered on the streets of L.A. It appeared that the San Andresitos were arguing over how many containers of cigarettes each family would handle. At one point, Spartacos Sococo slammed his fat brown hand on the table. *"Ay te huacho!"* he said angrily as he got up and made an elaborate false exit.

"Tú no tengas miedo, vete," Paco replied sharply, calling Spartacos's bluff, challenging him to go ahead and leave.

Spartacos finally turned and went back to his chair. More shouted conversation was followed by more curses and posturing. Then, ten minutes later, the men stood quickly and glowered at one another. Nobody shook hands as Paco showed them out of the room.

"The deal's done." José sighed. "Paco got an additional ten percent of each of their profits, which they are all very unhappy about. He also got the most product—fifteen million dollars in cigarettes. Each of them got only five. They wanted an even split, but this is more than they would normally handle, so hopefully they will get over it."

■ ■ ■

They left the warehouse and drove to Sandro's bank to disburse the fifty million dollars.

The First Mantoor Bank of Aruba was magnificent. Brass and leaded-glass doors fronted the executive offices, which were done luxuriously. English antiques squatted on white plush pile.

Jody presented his wire-transfer confirmation slip from the

West Valley Bank of Commerce, then accessed the fifty million in L.A. drug cash that Rusty Miller had wired to the bank to be held under the name of Lewis Foster. Jody showed the bank president his phony ID, took possession of the account, then wrote out the instructions to wire thirty million dollars to American Global, which was All-American's European company in Geneva. It was payment in full for the cigarettes. Five million was wired to Blackstone in Geneva, which covered their commission for brokering the deal. Fifteen million was put in escrow to be jointly held by Papa Joe until the Vikings had delivered the cigarettes to Maicao, Colombia. Once the product was safely there and the four families had taken delivery, the money would be released to the Vikings. The Bacca drug cartel would be repaid its original L.A. drug cash once the cigarettes were sold in their cartel-owned black-market malls, completing the laundry.

BETTING THE HOUSE 36

"Look't that rusting bastard," Jody said to Shane. They were standing on the duty-free pier, studying the old Venezuelan freighter being loaded with containers of cigarettes. It was four P.M. that same afternoon. The only paint on the vessel's brown steel hull was some fresh white lettering on the stern that read *Subu Maru,* which Papa Joe had explained meant "bright star." Shane thought the rusting bucket looked more like a falling star. They had been told the ship was leased by the King Trading Company: a Mantoor-controlled Venezuelan shipping line.

"This rusting piece a'shit only handles contraband for the drug trade," Jody said.

The *Subu Maru* was at the end of her days, stuck in the service of the devil, making the short, twenty-five-kilometer run from Aruba to the port of Maracaibo, which sat just inside the Gulf of Venezuela.

As they stood on the dock, watching their containers of cigarettes being lowered into the black hold, something strange happened to Shane—a darkening of Shane's spirit, worse by far than any of his other episodes. It kept building throughout the afternoon, until his chest was tight with anxiety and he was short of breath. Suddenly, he felt he couldn't stand to go on for even another hour.

Although the rest of the Vikings had left the pier, Shane and Jody watched until the last containers were loaded on board. The sun had begun to set, treating them to a luscious, multicolored sunset, before slipping below the surface of the Caribbean Sea, bringing down the curtain of night.

"I'm gonna see if I can find a woman," Jody said with a grin. "How 'bout it? Wanna come? No pun intended."

"No . . . No . . . I think I'll get something to eat at the hotel, walk around a little," Shane said as a frightening notion began to haunt him.

"If you change your mind, call me."

"Gimme your cell-phone number," Shane said as he picked up a Spanish newspaper off the dock and handed it to Jody, who wrote down his number and handed it back. Shane folded it carefully, then put the newspaper in his back pocket.

He caught a cab to the hotel but didn't want to go to the room for fear that Lisa would be there, stripped down to her high heels, waiting to destroy what was left of him. Shane got out of the cab, and as he walked through the lobby, he knew that he was at the end . . . knew he couldn't go on. Spiritual darkness overwhelmed him. All of his thoughts, no matter the content, just served to drive him lower.

He wandered toward the pool, looking for something, any-thing, to free him from this suicidal grip. It was a few minutes past eight. Nobody was out there. The lights in most of the ca-bana suites were on. He could see guests moving back and forth in front of the curtains, getting ready to go out, their lives full of adventure and romance, while his was now only about loneli-ness and despair. He sat in a pool chair and rubbed his eyes.

There was nothing that mattered to him anymore—not even his pledge to destroy Jody. There were Jodys everywhere, men who lived violent lives without remorse. What was one Jody, more or less?

He felt himself sink deeper.

In desperation, he tried to lock onto something positive.

Chooch.

He focused on the feelings of love for his son. He loved Chooch desperately but now began to realize that his son would be better off without him. He sat on the corded pool chair, wondering how he had become so completely lost.

He got up suddenly and walked into the lobby. "Could I have a piece of paper and an envelope, please?" he asked the pretty island girl at the concierge desk.

"Of course, sir," she said, handing it to him.

He walked across the lobby, then sat at the small writing desk and began a short letter.

He couldn't address it to anyone in particular, because he had no one left at the LAPD whom he trusted, so he began:

TO WHOM IT MAY CONCERN:

   The following facts have been obtained regarding a massive money-laundering scheme involving the illegal sales of parallel-market V-5 All-American Tobacco products into Colombia . . .

Then Shane laid out the entire scheme, with every detail he could remember. The letter went on for three pages. He named all of the Vikings and included Jody's admission that he had killed the two heads of the Detective Services Group. Shane wrote about Leon Fine, dead and buried on the beach up in Oxnard; he named the All-American Tobacco executives: the Prussian general, Lou Petrovitch, and his two helpers, Chip Gordon and Arnold Zook. He described the Mantoors, how they used their power and influence in Aruba to subvert their own duty-free zone for illegal profit. He named the five San Andresito families, spelling their names as carefully as he could, hoping he had them right. Then he confessed to pulling the trigger on Alexa Hamilton in the Tony Filosiani–supervised plot, intended to set his cover for the Vikings, explaining how he fired, not knowing Jody had reloaded his gun with a Black Talon. Finally, he wrote about Lisa St. Marie, who probably, more than even Jody, had presided over his ultimate corruption. He asked the LAPD Scientific Investigations Division to scan the enclosed newspaper for Jody's fingerprints, proving that he was still alive at the date of publication.

He ended the letter with a message to his son:

Forgive me, Chooch. You will be better off without me. I did the best I could, but it was not enough.

He signed it:

LAPD Sergeant Shane Scully

He put the letter into an envelope along with the dated Spanish newspaper containing Jody's cell number and fingerprints.

Shane sealed the envelope, then walked back to the concierge, bought two stamps, affixed them, and addressed the envelope:

> COMMANDING OFFICER
> LAPD INTERNAL AFFAIRS DIVISION
> 304 SOUTH BROADWAY
> LOS ANGELES, CALIFORNIA 90007
> U.S.A.

"Would you please mail this for me?" he asked the concierge.

"Of course, sir," she said as she took the letter. "I'm afraid it won't go out till the morning. . . ."

"That's fine," he said.

She dropped it into a mail slot and smiled at him. "Have a nice evening."

"Yes," he said. "Of course." He turned and headed back out to the pool, but he didn't stop there. He continued toward the lagoon, walking on numb legs.

When he reached the beach, he turned right. It was deserted, no longer the colorful playground of a few hours ago.

He felt the weight of the Beretta on his ankle, heavier with each step. He walked almost a quarter mile from the lit seaside cabanas before he sat down and began untying his shoes.

I'm taking off my fucking shoes just like eighty percent of the dumb-ass suicides I worked, he thought.

He finished removing his shoes and placed them neatly beside him. Then he peeled off his socks, the weight of the Beretta heavier with each passing second.

His mind was lasering back and forth across this final decision, searching for one last handhold—one positive emotion that would save him.

But when he really examined it, there wasn't anything left for him. Chooch was going to be in college in eighteen months. With no one to vouch for him, Shane would be vilified by the LAPD and eventually caught and convicted of Alexa's murder. He couldn't face Chooch's reaction to that.

He had no friends left on the department. Alexa had been the last, and he had killed her.

He had once felt brotherhood and love for Jody, but now he knew that Jody was a sociopath and had just been using him all these years, pretending love and friendship but feeling nothing. Worse than that was the realization that Shane was becoming more like Jody every day.

All he wanted to do now was to get off the ride.

Slowly, he pulled the 9-millimeter automatic out of its slide holster.

He chambered it.

The unusually loud click rang in the empty night.

One last important decision: Where to place the muzzle?

Under the chin at the mandible? Aiming up through the horizontal palatine bone into the anterial cranial fossa—coroner's terms echoing back at him from hundreds of autopsies.

Perhaps he should stick the muzzle in his mouth, go for the medial soft palate uvula . . . drive that two-ounce pill right up into his cerebral peduncle. Usually a sure thing, but on one or two occasions, he'd seen that path produce total brain vegetation but not death.

Maybe he should just stick with the reliable old temple shot. Put the muzzle on his inferior temporal line, just above the ear . . . pull the trigger and hope for the best. Hope that the slug wouldn't ricochet around inside his cranium but leave him breathing through a tube for ten years, until he finally rotted from the inside out.

As a cop, he'd seen all of these muzzle positions fail to get the job done. His last meaningful decision.

What a dumb fucking problem, he thought ruefully.

The old homicide dicks called this dilemma "betting the house." Slowly, Shane brought the gun up and stuck it into his mouth. His hand was shaking. He could taste the Hoppe's gun oil on his tongue, pressed flat by the weapon. His teeth began chattering on the barrel.

"God help me," he said quietly, his words slurring on the cold metal.

He tried to pull the trigger, but something stopped him . . . some last-second doubt. And in that moment, everything changed.

Somebody came out of the dark and hit him hard from behind, knocking him forward.

The gun flew out of his hand, splashing into the water while Shane was thrown, face-first, onto the wet sand.

He felt a huge weight land on his back. A massive arm locked around Shane's throat. In that instant, he changed from a potential suicide to a potential homicide. With this change in category came a desperate will to survive.

He fought and clawed to get the man's arm off his windpipe, struggling to keep from being strangled on that deserted stretch of beach.

"This is for shooting me, and for killin' Rod, and for screwing Lisa," Victory Smith whispered, the gasps of hot air filling Shane's ear.

Shane managed to tuck his chin down and get his hands around the grizzled arm, which was slowly choking him.

Suddenly, Victory's grip slipped.

Shane got his mouth on the weight lifter's huge forearm and bit down hard.

"Fuck!" the steroid jockey screamed, letting go.

Shane rolled out from under Smith and came up on his knees, just in time to field a left hook that caught him on top of his head, ringing his ears, starring his vision, and knocking him back into the light rippling waves at the edge of the lagoon. Shane landed on his ass in two feet of warm tropical water. Pain shot up his spine. He had come down on something hard. Instinctively, he reached down and grabbed it—

His Beretta.

As Victory Smith ran toward him, splashing water, Shane brought the gun out from under him and pulled the trigger.

The Black Talon shell casing had resisted the seawater, and the gun fired, bucking loudly in his hand. The exploding slug took Victory in the center of his simian forehead, blowing it wide, but the weight lifter kept coming . . . cerebral fluid and brain tissue spilling down his pockmarked face as he ran. The muscled giant took two more faltering steps and fell toward Shane, his arms out in front of him, grabbing Shane in a lifeless hug as he landed. Shane felt Victory's heart beat twice before it stopped.

It was suddenly quiet.

All Shane could hear was the gently rippling surf and the distant sound of rustling palm fronds. He let go and pushed the huge man off, watching as Victory rolled onto his back into the churning surf. Seawater washed the sickening hole in his head, turning the swirling surf dark with blood and brain matter.

Shane staggered to his feet, then looked down at his fallen

adversary. Why hadn't he just let Smith finish the job he'd already started? What had made him fight so desperately to survive?

Shane stood over the corpse, watching it roll and turn in the light surf. A lifeless ballet. The swirling black patterns of Victory's strange personality washing out of his skull into the seawater. He knew this memory would be locked in his subconscious forever.

Finally, he reclaimed himself and pulled Victory up onto the beach, dragging the two-hundred-fifty-pound man . . . tugging, struggling to pull him up to the berm, where the white sand met with a ridge of low, tropical vegetation.

Shane got down on his knees and started to dig a hole, using his hands to paw up the granules until he got down where the sand was damp. Buried shells stabbed at his fingers as he dug, breaking his nails and making his hands bleed.

He could hear someone crying softly and looked around, afraid he was being observed. Then he realized he was the one crying.

He locked his mouth shut and forced himself to stop. Finally, Shane had dug a trench that was two feet deep and seven feet long; hardly big enough to hide this hulking giant for long. The first strong wind would uncover him, but Shane could dig no longer. He was completely spent. He took Victory's wallet and rolled the steroid junkie into the shallow grave, then covered him up until nothing was left but a foot-high mound of packed sand.

He picked up the murder weapon, wiped the Beretta clean on his shirt, then threw it as far as he could into the lagoon. He heard a faint splash somewhere way out there as it hit.

When Shane got back to his room, it was empty. Thankfully,

Lisa wasn't there, but he saw that there was something on his pillow, glittering and colorful. He walked to it, wondering what it was, and whether Lisa had left it there.

He picked it up and stared at it in confusion. It was a two-inch round medal, with a red ribbon attached.

The LAPD Medal of Valor.

"You were the one who really earned it, so it's only fair that you should keep it."

He turned, and she was standing just outside on the balcony.

She walked toward him, took him in her arms, and held him. Then he could feel her pressed against him. Suddenly he was kissing her, holding her head in both his hands.

But he had shot her, watched her fly backward . . . watched as the huge pool of blood spread around her. Yet somehow she'd come back. Somehow she'd survived.

Alexa Hamilton was alive.

RESURRECTION 37

I'M SO SORRY, so sorry," she said, holding him. Shivers ran through both of them.

"I thought I killed you . . . " he stammered.

"I wasn't hurt," she said softly.

He finally let go of her and stepped back, the joy of holding her overtaken by heart-wrenching fear that Lisa or Jody would suddenly return and that he would lose her all over again. "We can't stay here," he blurted.

"I've got a room up the beach. Come on . . ." She pulled a high-frequency radio out of her bag and triggered it. "This is Three. Are we clear out there?"

"Roger, Three. This is One. Come on," a man's voice said.

"Who's that?" Shane asked.

"I'm down here with federal backup. Tony set it up . . . DEA guys . . ."

"Shit, Tony's got half the free world out looking for me."

"We had no choice. I'll explain everything, but we've gotta get outta here first."

She led the way to the door, but Shane stopped her before she could exit. He kissed her one more time, her mouth soft on his, feeling such sweet warmth radiating inside that it brought tears to his eyes. He released her, then cautiously opened the door and peeked out. The corridor was empty.

"What's your backup look like?" he asked.

"Jo-Jo Knight—tall, black, linebacker type—fashion disaster . . . Dacron shirt and plaid Bermudas. The other one is a little round Cuban, Luis Rosario. They never stop rippin' each other, but they're pretty good guys. They're tasked outta Treasury."

They left the room and ran down the corridor into the stairwell, where a tall, wide-body African American was waiting with a radio.

"Howdy-do," he said. "I'm Agent Knight. Hang on a sec while I check in with Beaner Central." He triggered his walkie-talkie. "Two, this is One. How we lookin' out there?"

"Smooth as Cuban cookin'. Bring 'em on. Got ya covered," a soft voice with a Cuban accent replied.

"Where's Miss Shake an' Bake?" Jo-Jo asked.

"In the bar. Got the gringos in there all pitching tents in their pantalones. We'll go out the back, through the service entrance."

"Roger that," Jo-Jo said, looking up at Shane. "Your friend Lisa."

"Business associate," Shane corrected, wondering if Alexa knew about his relationship with the sexy tobacco executive.

They took the stairs two at a time, finally exiting into a service area, where they found a short, round Cuban with a dark complexion, infectious smile, and porkpie hat.

He glowered at Jo-Jo Knight. "Your people maybe got rhythm, but you got no timing? I'm gettin' flat arches out here, waitin'." Rosario turned and led the way through the service area and down a narrow corridor that was filled with laundry hampers.

They ran out the back door to where a car was parked. Jo-Jo got behind the wheel; the Cuban opened the back door and they piled in, then the car pulled out and headed across town.

Shane held Alexa's hand, squeezing it hard, afraid to let go. He couldn't believe he was sitting next to her again, couldn't believe she was alive and back in his life.

Her room was on the beach at the Divi-Divi Resort Hotel, on the outskirts of Oranjestad. Luis Rosario and Jo-Jo Knight took cover positions where they could watch the front and back of the hotel. Alexa opened her suite, then she and Shane entered.

Once the door was closed, she turned and they kissed again. Finally she pulled away, reluctantly.

"Fun as this is, we don't have much time," she said, still holding his hand. "I'm sorry for what we did to you, Shane. It wasn't fair. I didn't want to do it, but the DEA-SAC in L.A. insisted. Tony finally had to go along."

"Good old Tony."

"Don't blame him. He didn't want to. Sit down, I'll fill you in." She led him to the bed where they sat side by side.

She looked into his eyes and began her story. "After you didn't report in, we went to your house. We saw blood on the kitchen floor, the broken screen and window in the bedroom. We knew you'd been kidnapped. Tony picked me up and we had a meeting in his office. Right about then, the Questioned Documents Division broke the number code on the logbook we found in Mark's safe. It was Medwick's account of how the Vikings were formed, how all five of them were removed from the city payroll records. You were right. The whole experiment was set up under Deputy Chief Mayweather."

"There were six of them," Shane said. "Jody, Tremaine Lane, Victory Smith, Lester Wood, Hector Rodriquez, and some Hispanic cop they killed and buried up in Oxnard."

"The records say only five. There's no mention of anybody named Tremaine Lane . . ."

Shane thought about that for a minute, and a new idea started to form, but for the moment he filed it. "Okay . . . Go on."

"The whole parallel-market thing was in Mark Shephard's logbook, including the Fortune Five Hundred companies, Aruba—everything. It was undoubtedly written before Jody decided to go bad and take over Leon Fine's business. Once Jody made that decision, like you suspected, he had no choice but to kill Medwick and Shephard because they knew what the Vikings were working on. Chief Filosiani notified Washington and brought in a Treasury SAC from the L.A. office. Once those guys were aboard, everything started to play like a James Bond movie."

"Those two feds outside play more like a Cheech and Chong movie."

"They were Chief Filosiani's picks. He worked some joint-ops cases with them when he was in New York. They're best friends, and good guys once you get past the constant ethnic ribbing."

"I shot you with a Black Talon," Shane said. "How could you have survived that?"

"Remember those paintings in Chief Brewer's office?"

Shane nodded.

"He sold them to get new equipment. Flack vests."

"Yeah."

"Well, they weren't just ordinary vests. It was brand-new body armor designed at the Pentagon. They're level-three tech vests, called Ultimas, capable of stopping anything, including Cop Killers, Teflon loads, armor-piercing stuff—the works. Tony was afraid that Jody would switch guns on you, so he had me fitted for one as a precaution. And then, to make it look real, he got a friend of his, a Hollywood special-effects man, to rig a blood squib and give me a bladder full of cow blood. I had a pump I could squeeze down on under my arm."

"Why? Why would you do that? I was so fucked up, I almost—"

"I know . . . I know . . . I guess that was sorta my fault. I told them you thought Jody could read your thoughts. Then the Treasury SAC began to wonder if you could pull it off. He felt if you believed you really killed me, your reaction to my death would be more authentic. Your life was at stake, so Tony and I finally agreed. But when we lost you after the shooting, our plan got totally scrambled. We didn't count on a helicopter being in that hangar. We didn't think we'd completely lose contact with you. When we didn't know where you were, the

DEA decided we had to put on a full media funeral . . . because that's what would have happened if I'd really died two days after winning the MOV. They were afraid that if Jody was in L.A. and it wasn't a big media deal, he would know it was all bullshit, and he might kill you. We didn't know where you were, so I sat home and watched my own funeral on TV."

"And Chooch?"

"I told him. I forced them all to let him in on it. I couldn't let him think you'd killed me and gone bad. It wasn't fair. Buddy knows, too."

"For whatever it's worth, they were right," Shane said. "Jody told me he probably would have suspected something if I hadn't been as screwed-up as I was."

She nodded, then went on. "We knew that the Mantoors were part of this because it was all in the logbook. We hoped you would eventually show up in Aruba, so I came down here with Luis and Jo-Jo and we waited. This morning, when that jet pulled up at Mantoor Aviation and you got off, my heart broke, baby." She put her hand over his. "I could see how far down you'd gone. Sometimes I can see inside your head, too. Maybe I can do it even better than Jody. I knew you were close to the edge, so I begged them to let me contact you, and Tony agreed. He finally just overruled that tight-ass Treasury SAC in L.A. and did it without their approval."

"You were almost too late."

"I was waiting in your room, with Rosario watching Lisa, hoping she wouldn't come back before you did."

"I'm sorry about Lisa, I—"

"Shhh," she said softly. "You thought I was dead. You don't talk about Lisa St. Marie, I won't talk about Mark Shephard.

We'll mark it down as history and move on. Fair enough?"

"Fair enough."

"I love you, sweetheart," she said softly. "I can't tell you how bad I feel about the way this went down."

"It's okay . . . it's okay. It's over now. I have you back."

"But you've got to go. You can't be missing for too long."

"I need a gun," Shane said. "I had to lose mine."

"Here . . ." She opened her purse and handed him a Spanish automatic. It was a 9-millimeter Astra with a short barrel and an eight-shot clip. Shane chambered it and stuck it into his ankle holster. "I've only got one spare clip," she said, handing it over to him. Shane stuck it in his back pocket.

They stood up. "Hold it," she said. "I almost forgot something." She reached into her purse and handed him a bottle of pills.

He looked at the label: "Blood pressure pills?" He said as he unscrewed the bottle top and rolled one little white tablet into his palm. "What's this for?"

"It's not a pill. It's a satellite-tracking device; a satellite transmitter with microcircuitry. You take it as soon as you leave port. It lives inside you and broadcasts your position. I don't want to lose track of you again. It'll pass through you in twenty-four hours, but hopefully this whole thing should be over by then. That thing will tell us where you are within a yard."

"You're kidding me."

"Your tax dollars at work." She smiled. "The Frisbees have great toys. Now, get going. I don't want Jody looking for you, asking questions. We're less than twelve hours from the take-down. We'll save our reunion till then." She got him up off the bed and led him to the door.

He turned to face her. "Alexa, wait . . . There's something I need to ask you first."

"No time."

"No, I need to ask you now."

He pulled her closer.

"When I thought you were gone, it seemed like my life was over. Now I can't let you go without asking." He took a deep breath. "I love you. Will you marry me?"

She stood before him for a long moment, tears welling in her eyes. "Of course I'll marry you, you idiot. What took you so damned long to ask?" She kissed him. The kiss lasted almost a minute, and when it was finally over, she pulled him back into the room and led him over to the bed where she pulled him down.

"I thought there was no time." Shane teased.

"Changed my mind . . . female prerogative."

She made slow love to him, and in that moment came Shane's redemption and resurrection.

In that coupling, he was reborn.

MARACAIBO

SO, WHERE THE fuck is he if he's not in his room?" Jody asked angrily, looking at Tremaine Lane, Lester Wood, and Shane. But mostly he was glaring at Shane.

It was ten past eight in the morning; the black Mercedes SUV was a few feet away in the porte cochere with the trunk lid up and their canvas bags already inside. Eric was standing nearby, watching.

"You're asking me?" Shane said. "Since when am I in charge a'that steroid case? Like you advised, I'm giving that asshole all the room I can."

"Victory knew the *Subu Maru* was set to leave at eight. We're already late."

"We could split up and go lookin'," Sawdust drawled, not putting much energy into the statement.

"Okay, scout around; we'll meet back here in ten minutes," Jody said.

While Tremaine, Lester, and Jody took off, looking for Victory, Shane went to the reception desk.

"I gave the concierge a letter to mail for me last night," Shane said. "I changed my mind about sending it. Has it gone out yet?"

"Yes, sir. The mail left an hour ago."

Shane nodded and saw a Caribbean guidebook for sale. He picked it up, peeling off five U.S. dollars.

"How come I get the feeling you're not telling me everything, Hot Sauce?"

Shane spun around and found Jody standing right behind him.

"I really love this . . . " Shane said as his mind suddenly filled with the vivid image of Victory lying dead in the surf, his dark brain contents washing around in the light surf.

"You're thinking about some shit swirling around in the water," Jody said. "What's that all about?"

It was frightening how he did it. Shane forced his thoughts away, forced them on nothing . . . a trick he had perfected when they were kids.

Jody straightened up, and his expression changed. "It's gone," he said softly.

"Victory Smith is your problem. You wanna know how I feel about him going missing? I feel great. The guy was an unguided missile. Somebody probably did us all a favor and pulled his drapes."

"Papa Joe wasn't fooling about this Santa guy. He's an Argentine fugitive, a political terrorist, and he could be big trouble for us. We need Victory. He might be nuts, but he gives us a comfort zone."

"We should forget him and get moving."

Eventually, that's what they were forced to do.

. . .

Jody talked to them on the dock just before they boarded the ship. "I don't know what kinda bullshit we could be facing, so I got Sandy to score us some better firepower." He handed each of them a brand-new Polish MP-63 9-millimeter machine pistol. The weapon was compact, with a flip-down grip and retracting stock. Then he handed each of them two forty-round clips. The machine pistols fit easily into their gym bags. "If we get jumped by the whole town, we're pretty much fucked, but at least we'll take some greasers with us."

The *Subu Maru* pulled away from the Mantoor Duty-Free dock an hour past schedule. Its mostly Venezuelan crew gathered in heavy, oil-stained mooring lines as the gap widened between the freighter and the dock.

The old Caterpillar engines clanged into reverse, and the ship creaked in protest as the stern made a slow journey back and to starboard, pulling the ship away from the wharf.

Jody was on deck, somewhere aft as the bow of the *Subu Maru* swung slowly around and was now pointing toward the mouth of the harbor.

The breeze was ten knots on the stern and the slow-moving ship just managed to make up the difference, leaving them engulfed in a tropical stench, fouled by its own diesel smoke.

Then they cleared the jetty and were out of the harbor in a light following sea, the slow-turning propellers churning up a white wake, pushing them toward the southwestern horizon and Maracaibo, thirty miles away.

Shane stood at the rail feeling so content that even the clogging heat and stink of the ship didn't bother him. He was grateful to whatever divine force had prevented him from pulling the trigger, until Victory saved him for Alexa, Chooch, and their future together. Only yesterday at this same time he had felt empty and used up; now Shane was overcome with excitement and expectation. All he had to do was stay alive for one or two more days.

And that reminded him . . .

Shane reached into his pocket and took out the bottle containing the white transmitter pill. He unscrewed the top, then looked at his watch: 10:15 A.M. He shook the pill into his hand and was about to pop it into his mouth when Lester Wood materialized at his side.

"Got a cold, pard?"

"High blood pressure," Shane said as he popped the pill into his mouth and dry-swallowed it. He showed Sawdust the prescription bottle.

Woods looked at the label, then handed it back. Shane threw the bottle into the sea.

"Guess what?" Sawdust said.

Shane didn't answer but kept his eyes on the horizon.

"While I was out lookin' for Victory, I heard that some soft-drink vendor found a body up on the beach real early this morning. The corpse was buried in the sand."

"Why tell me?"

"I hung out down there and listened to them bean-eaters shootin' the shit. Kinda got the gist of it. The way they were talkin', the stiff was a big, ugly guy, lotsa muscle, flowered shirt, tattoos, American. Sound like anybody we know?"

"To these islanders all Americans look big and ugly."

"Appears this guy got on the wrong end of a corpse-and-cartridge party. Course, I didn't see the body, but they say he was built like Schwarzenegger. Tell me this don't sound like our own anabol-slammin', iron-pumpin' steroid case."

"Lotta big guys with muscles down here."

"I ain't making no accusations, Hot Sauce, but all them anabolics was makin' Vic buck real close t'the ground. I think maybe he finally came after ya, forced ya to burn some powder. But like I say, I'm not losin' no sleep over it." He paused, reached into his pocket, and pulled out a tin of chewing tobacco. "Course, Jody might see it differently."

"Is this a threat?" Shane said softly.

"A negotiation." Sawdust took a pinch of Skoal and put it into his mouth. "With Victory dead . . . that means we only got us a four-way split now. I'm thinking this information might, could stay between just the two of us."

"How much?"

"With Victory outta the mix, that means the fifteen mil now only gets divided by four. That makes each share worth three point seven-five mil, give or take a pony. I'm thinking, you kick back a mil to me. With Victory's cut thrown back in the pot, you still walk away with almost three million."

"You've got no proof," Shane said. "Your word against mine."

"Yer right . . . but we ain't in court here, pard. This ain't about proof, it's about anger and paranoia. Jody's stressed. Takes one phone call to the Mantoors back in Aruba. Dandy Sandy checks the body, finds a Black Talon parked in Vic's head, and you're in a heap a'grease, pard."

"Okay," Shane said softly.

"Good goin'." Sawdust was smiling, swaying with the rolling deck, his Ray-Bans kicking moving spots of tropical sunlight up and down Shane's face. "Nice tradin' time with ya."

Then he spit a line of tobacco juice over the rail into the ocean before ambling off.

An hour later Shane could see the faint outline of the Peninsula de Guajira, which made up the western end of the Golfo de Venezuela.

Ninety minutes later they were steaming into the Straits of Zapara, which narrowed until they were in the spacious Bay of Tablazo, passing anchored freighters flying hundreds of different flags, each one waiting for its turn to offload cargo at the main dock.

Amazingly, the rusting *Subu Maru* steamed right past all of them, heading straight to the front of the line. Shane mused that drugs certainly had their place in the Latin American scheme of things.

The huge Venezuelan shipping port of Maracaibo loomed on all sides as the *Subu Maru* groaned and moaned, then jockeyed her ugly bow toward the dock, first in slow forward, then slow reverse, backing down on the port engine, straining to pull her canoe stern up to the concrete wharf. Commands were shouted angrily in Spanish over the loudspeaker from the bridge. Monkey-fist knots that gave weight to thin strands of nylon line were heaved overboard by sweating deckhands and hit the dock, where other men in blue overalls grabbed them and pulled hard, dragging the heavy oil-stained mooring lines they were attached to ashore. The heavy lines were then hooked to dock cleats, winched tight, and spring lines were set.

The growling engines on the *Subu Maru* were finally shut down, but loud dock sounds immediately replaced them. Cranes hummed and men shouted in Spanish.

They were in the Venezuelan portion of the Aruba duty-free zone.

The Vikings were about to embark on an insane journey that none of them had bargained for.

TRUCKIN'

TREMAINE LANE AND Lester Wood stayed with the cigarettes while Shane and Jody found Paco Brazos in the shipping office on D Dock, where he was getting their cargo manifests logged in at the duty-free desk. A uniformed Venezuelan Customs inspector was banging his rubber stamp on countless egress forms without bothering to read them. Next to him was a uniformed Colombian colonel with shoulder patches that read EFECTIVOS DE COLOMBIA. Despite his nonresident status, the colonel seemed to be in charge of the trans-shipping of their cigarettes.

"Son seguros," he said sharply, indicating a stack of import invoices.

The Venezuelan Customs official nodded and kept stamping the forms furiously.

Paco finally glanced up at Jody and Shane. "You have nice the travel?" he said in his broken English.

"If you don't mind choking on diesel fumes," Jody answered.

"We go soon. Customs, she all fix, no?"

"What about the other San Andresitos?" Jody asked. "Hernandez, Sococo, and Randhanie. Aren't they supposed to be here to take delivery?"

"Ahh, is very good . . . yes . . ." Paco smiled. He didn't seem to have a clue what Jody had just asked him.

They moved out into the hot afternoon sunlight. A line of five trucks were just pulling through the guard gate on the duty-free dock—old Mexican Fords with chipped paint, broken headlights, and fenders redesigned by traffic. Wooden stakes held up stained covers that arched over the truck beds like dirty brown rainbows.

"Los camiones," Paco announced.

The trucks came to a stop, then ten or twelve private armed guards, known in Colombia as *celadores,* jumped out of the back of each vehicle. They wore threadbare, faded khakis tucked into shiny new paramilitary jump boots, and each guard carried an identical olive green machine gun—old Mexican Mendozas. The out-of-date thirty-ought sixes had wooden stocks and twenty-round box mags that loaded from the top. For a while the Mexican gangs in L.A. had been using these weapons, but as the drug business quickly became prosperous, they all switched to Russian auto-mags. Shane remembered that the old-style Mendozas were prone to jamming.

Paco rattled off a few sentences in Spanish. Jody looked over at Shane for a translation.

"I didn't quite get it. Sounded like he said you and he should ride in his bubble, whatever that means," Shane said. "He wants the rest of us in the back of the trucks."

"Your bubble?" Jody asked Paco.

"*Sì, sì. Mi bubble es mi carro. Tengo nuevo*—Land Cruiser." Paco pointed proudly at a new black Toyota that was parked nearby.

"A bubble." Jody grinned. "Yeah, looks kinda like one, don't it?"

Ten minutes later the other San Andresitos arrived, also in new Land Cruisers. The SUVs were all loaded with extras: chrome rims, whip antennas, and roll bars with deer lights. The custom interiors were tuck-and-roll. They all had TMX sound systems that could blow the fur off a rabbit.

An hour later the cigarettes were safely loaded and the caravan was turned around, ready to leave.

"Hokay," Paco said, pushing his ugly brown teeth out from between puffy lips. "We go. *Vamos a la ciudad de Maicao.*"

The Vikings retrieved their gym bags containing the comforting weight of their machine pistols and boarded the trucks, which were now full to the top with All-American's cigarettes: one truckload for each of the three San Andresitos families, two for Paco Brazos. Paco got into his Toyota Land Cruiser, with Jody in the passenger seat beside him, and pulled to the head of the line. Shane was assigned to the back of the second truck with two of Emilio Hernandez's teenage guards.

Shane's vehicle was so filled with cases of cigarettes that there was almost no room to stand. He looked at the guards and guessed them to be about seventeen or eighteen. Their smooth faces and round cheeks had not yet been hardened by adulthood, but their eyes were those of predators. These teenagers had seen death or had caused it—Third World eyes, burning with anger and determination, in faces only slightly older than Chooch's.

The trucks moved slowly off the dock and through the duty-free gates, into the old town of Maracaibo.

They rocked dangerously in and out of deep potholes, rolling down the narrow streets like a parade of lumbering elephants, past a seven-block-long green island that sat in the center of town like a huge grass runway.

"*Que es esta?*" Shane asked one of the guards, pointing at the rectangular grass strip.

"*Paseo de los Siglos,*" the teenage *celador* said sharply, and turned his back on Shane. The rough translation was "Passage of the Centuries." It meant nothing to Shane.

Finally, they reached Avenida 15 and hung a left. One after the other, the trucks and Toyotas rounded the corner, then proceeded north through the new part of Maracaibo.

Tall skyscrapers and flat-roofed, one-story shacks stood within yards of one another, giving the place a feel of unstructured growth.

Soon they were in the countryside, passing arid fields and slanting wooden fences, blowing road dust out from behind each truck as they headed into the desert.

La Guajara was described in Shane's Caribbean guidebook as a semi-desert, but to him it looked bleaker and hotter than Death Valley. Brown cactuslike vegetation clung to the few sandy washes, hoarding precious drops of moisture like thirsty castaways.

They passed straggling tribes of nomadic Indians herding half-dead burros along the dirt road. The nomads ran to get out of the way of the caravan, as the smugglers blasted the air horns in their shiny new Land Cruisers. The Indian men shouted at their frightened children, grabbed the halters of their braying donkeys, and glared with impotent hostility at the trucks that sped past, leaving them engulfed in a curtain of brown dust.

Shane tried to ask one of the guards about the Indians, but the boy just shrugged. "Wayu," was all he would say. Shane wondered if that was the name of the tribe or a curse, or both.

Soon they crossed out of Venezuela into Colombia. The border was marked by an old yellow sign shot full of bullet holes, outside the small town of Paraguación.

Paraguación seemed right out of a Sam Peckinpah western. The trucks slowed only slightly as they jounced down the dirty main street, past dusty cinder-block stores with broken glass windows. Rough-hewn corner posts supported tin roofs on buildings that leaned precariously. A dry fountain dominated the center of town, across from a general store.

The trucks and SUVs swept through Paraguación like a Panzer division. A few Indian children stood on the boardwalks, holding on to their mothers' cotton dresses. They watched with black-eyed wonder while a few of the trucks carelessly clipped the circular base of the fountain as they rushed past.

The convoy had just passed out of Venezuela, into Colombia. There were no Customs stops, no government officials, nothing.

Nobody in the town of Paraguación, or the two nations it separated, seemed to care that ninety-six million cigarettes had just been converted from duty-free product into illegal contraband. It had happened in the blink of an eye as they shot through that little village under the uninterested gaze of a few desert Indians.

They picked up speed again, heading across the "semidesert," scattering jackrabbits and rattlesnakes in their path, heading west toward a lawless hell town known as Maicao.

MAICAO

SHANE COULD ACTUALLY smell the town before it came into view, a malodorous combination of sewage and rotting garbage drifting east on the desert wind.

They soon reached what Shane assumed was the airport, according to the Colombian guidebook he'd picked up at the hotel. But it was unlike any airport he'd ever seen.

What had first been a meandering dirt road, rutted and treacherous, suddenly became a two-way, poured-concrete highway that ran for a mile and then miraculously widened into six perfectly straight lanes complete with runway arrows, footage markers and landing lights. The caravan of trucks rolled over old rubber landing marks left there by the four-ply jet tires that had touched down in both directions. After five miles, the six lanes narrowed again, becoming a two-lane highway and then, as if it had never been there at all, they were back on dirt bouncing along again. The field had no tower, no hangars, no gas pumps or support buildings. The Maicao International Airport was just six lanes of concrete, some telltale skid marks, arrows, and a few landing lights. Shane guessed that night flights put down unannounced to offload cargo and left just as quickly.

"*Aeropuerto?*" Shane asked a teenaged *celador,* whose scraggly new chin whiskers stubbornly announced the coming of manhood.

"*Sí, aeropuerto,*" the angry youth answered. Two words this time. They were having a verbal festival.

Shane's guidebook said that Maicao was a town that should not be visited. Shane could never remember seeing that kind of statement in a guidebook before. Under this startling warning, it said the town had a population of fifty-five thousand, all of it apparently living on the outskirts of town in slum housing with no plumbing or electricity. Shacks now dotted the sandy desert on both sides of the road, without the slightest hint of organization or city planning. The terrain was littered with shanty tilt-ups and lean-tos made out of wooden packing cases and discarded sheets of corrugated metal. Worse still was the smell that became more intense as they pulled into town. Every block or two they passed six-foot-high mounds of reeking garbage. Big greenback flies strafed the piles of refuse, prospecting ferociously.

Very few people could be seen standing outside, as the oppressive midday heat pushed into triple digits.

They bounced around a curve and saw a Colombian military garrison located on the east end of town, protected by a nine-foot-high razor-wire fence. Two white-helmeted gate guards stood in the sweltering heat but paid no attention as the five truckloads of contraband rattled into town.

They entered the business district, which Shane thought was even more depressing than the slum housing they had just encountered. The first and most remarkable thing about this section of Maicao was the prodigious amount of discarded packing material. It was everywhere.

It seemed that the boxes full of contraband, once opened, had simply been shucked out onto the street. Bubble wrap, as well as old wood and cardboard from broken-down containers, covered everything. A layer of white Styrofoam popcorn was blowing over it all. It scattered in the trucks' wake, finally piling up against the curbs. In a curious example of urban eco-balance, human waste ran in the gutters, rotting the packing material from the bottom, slowly making room for next week's load. Concrete lane dividers, once intended to be planters to enhance city beauty, were now just catch basins for old cardboard boxes and rusting metal banding tape.

The trucks slowed to ten miles an hour as they drove down Calle 16.

The few men walking on the heat-shimmering sidewalks turned to watch as the five-truck caravan with its Toyota SUV escorts rumbled into town.

Shane noticed that there were no women, and the men he saw were all packing dangerous-looking weapons. Pistols were stuck into webbed canvas belts. Machine guns of every make hung by faded leather straps.

They drove past the Heda Hotel, where there was supposedly a cantina called the Corraleja. The guidebook said it was named after a particularly dangerous bullfight where the spectators could come down from the stands, enter the arena, and take their chances with the bull.

The center of town was more of the same, except as they got closer to the warehouse district, the refuse and garbage grew in height, overflowing the curbs. The Styrofoam popcorn now dominated the landscape, swirling over everything, drifting like Rocky Mountain snowbanks.

They finally turned off Calle 16 into the warehouse district, and it looked like no place Shane had ever seen. Most unusual and out of place were the half a dozen or so untended and underfed cows that wandered aimlessly in the street, grazing on God knows what, blowing the popcorn aside with angry snorts to get at the rotting garbage below.

Each of the five San Andresitos families had magnificent warehouses there. The first one they drove past was located at the mouth of the street: a large, paranoid building that seemed designed to repel an invasion force. The windows resembled gun ports. Castle-type exterior doors were banded with heavy metal. CORTEZ LTD was written in silver letters across the side of the building.

Farther down, Shane could see four more mammoth buildings, two on each side of the street—one to each square block. In front of every warehouse was a modern, architecturally designed showroom that displayed the San Andresitos families' black-market products.

Santander Cortez's showroom followed his castle motif: steel and granite walls with narrow slit windows, each containing spotlit radios and watches. The glass looked thick enough to be bulletproof.

Emilio Hernandez had gone for a massive French Provincial

showroom. For Octavio Ramandi, it was Colonial. Greek Orthodox for Spartico Sococo. Paco Brazos had really gone fishing. His showroom was a black and red Japanese pagoda-style building, with Macy's-size front windows filled with merchandise. The glass was protected by silver alarm tape.

The canvas-backed trucks began to peel off, each one heading to its respective family headquarters.

The truck Shane was in stopped halfway down the street, and the engine shut off. He waited while the tailgate was dropped and his two teenage *celadores* jumped out, then Shane picked his way through the shifted cases of cigarettes and dropped down onto the street. He landed on two feet of compressed packing wrap in front of Emilio Hernandez's French Provincial showroom.

From where Shane stood, he could see the other four trucks parked in front of their respective warehouses. Paco Brazos was standing a block away in front of his large pagoda monstrosity, grinning broadly.

Jody was just getting out of Paco's black Toyota as Tremaine jumped down from Sococo's truck farther up the street. Two blocks ahead, Shane could see Lester Wood was already making his way carefully down the street toward Jody, his boot heels sinking in the muck.

"Qué está allá'?" Shane asked one of the teenage guards, who just turned and walked away without answering. "Eat me," Shane muttered softly.

Suddenly a door opened on the side of the warehouse, and a dozen more armed teenagers jogged out to stand in a semicircle around the truck. They weren't packing the old Mendozas. These guys were strapped with shiny blue-steel auto-mags, which they held at port arms. A pair of elephant doors on the warehouse clattered up behind them, and two battery-powered yellow forklifts hummed out and parked nearby.

"No es necesario que usted quedarse," Emilio said, dismissing Shane. His sweating round face showed disdain.

Shane could see Jody waving for him to come over. "Okay . . . *bien. Adiós,"* Shane said, then turned his back on the hate-filled eyes of fifteen heavily armed teenage boys and made a slow, treacherous journey across the garbage-filled street to join Jody and Paco and the other two Vikings in front of Brazos International.

He walked carefully past a dozen more *celadores* who were protecting Paco's two truckloads of cigarettes. They watched him like prison guards until Shane finally pushed open the two-inch etched glass door and joined Jody, who was standing just inside. Entering the showroom was like stepping back into air-conditioned sanity.

The room was cooled to sixty-eight degrees, and Shane's sweat-soaked shirt immediately began drying ice-cold against his skin. The stench of Maicao was left behind, and a sweet lilac scent of an expensive room deodorant took its place.

"Some little township they got here," Jody said softly.

"Jesus, I didn't know there was this much bubble wrap on the planet," Shane answered.

"You see Santander Cortez's place?" Jody asked. "From those gun-port windows on the second floor, he could control the whole street with less than ten guys. What's that about?"

"They got a whole new take on commerce out here," Shane answered.

"I don't like the way this feels. We need to complete our business and get the hell outta town before Santander gets back."

"Back from where?" Shane asked. "I thought he was up here, layin' in the cut, waiting to slit our throats."

"According to Paco, he had to go to Medellín on business."

"*Quieren mirar a mi tienda?*" Paco interrupted them as he entered the showroom.

Jody cocked a questioning eyebrow at Shane.

"He wants to show us his store."

"Yeah, *bueno,*" Jody said. "But let's not take all day."

Paco led them through his magnificent showroom with its glass cases full of radios from Motorola and TVs from GE. Electronic conveniences glittered under recessed lighting, each one on its own Japanese-style jade marble stand. Tremaine Lane and Lester Wood trailed behind, their eyes flickering across the incredible display of goods.

Paco walked them through the appliance room with its ultra-size Sanyo, Panasonic, and Sony TVs. Dishwashers from Westinghouse, microwaves from Revel, refrigerators and washer-dryers from Maytag and Kitchen Aid. Almost every make and brand imaginable was represented. The cigarette and liquor display was in a hallway about forty feet long that stretched between two appliance rooms. The corridor was walled with glass cases full of every U.S. cigarette brand. Bottles of Russian Stoli sat next to carved decanters of Chivas Regal—all of this twinkling merrily under recessed product lights.

From there, they walked out into the warehouse.

Shane didn't know how long they were in the cavernous concrete-block building, but the tour was a definite mind bender. The three-story, open-spanned structure was so full of goods that they had to often walk sideways to get down the aisles. Men in straw hats driving forklifts whizzed past on the center aisles, moving things around in the massive air-conditioned building.

It was hard to determine how much product was stored there, but if Shane guessed several hundred million dollars, he couldn't have been too far off.

Paco kept talking as he led them through his black-market kingdom, keeping up a fractured-English spiel worthy of a Disneyland riverboat guide: "General of Electric, *aquí*. Packard Bell, *allí*." But he saved the best for last. "*Y la plata está al todo derecho adentro.*"

Jody shot Shane a look off the last sentence.

"I think he's saying the money is inside." Shane smiled.

"I like that. Let's go see the money." Jody grinned back.

They climbed a flight of stairs. Paco opened a door, and they entered a plush suite of offices. For the first time since arriving in Maicao, Shane saw women—all young and pretty. Each sat in front of a computer, furiously clicking their mouses and scrolling inventory screens. Paco Brazos was thoroughly enjoying the effect his tour was having on them, and he had obviously saved the best for last.

He punched a code into a very sophisticated computer lock, swung open a three-foot-wide metal door, and turned on the lights; then all of them entered.

The room was about sixty feet square. There were several upholstered chairs, and in the center a computer monitor sat on an antique wooden table. The screen showed the peso exchange rates all over the world. Banded bricks of every kind of currency imaginable were stacked on the shelves that lined the walls, overpowering the room with the sweet, musty smell of paper money.

Each section had a label indicating the currency stored below: U.S. dollars, Swiss francs, Greek drachmas . . . Colombian, Venezuelan, or Mexican pesos. Floor-to-ceiling displays of cash dominated every inch of wall space.

"*Es mi cambio,*" the short, fat black marketeer beamed proudly. "My . . . How you say? Exchange for *todo de* business, no?"

"Yeah, yeah," Jody said, his eyes locked on the fortune in the room, his breath suddenly short with envy.

"Time to go. We must to meet others," Paco said, looking at a diamond-encrusted Rolex Presidente. "For to get delivery receipt. Then maybe *señorita,* some fucky-fucky, no? *Entonces vamonos a la Maracaibo antes de que Santander vuelva.*"

"This jerk-off thinks if we hurry, we might have time to get laid before Santander gets back," Sawdust drawled.

"Tell him we'll take a rain check on the pussy," Jody said.

"*Sí, sí,*" Paco chirped, getting the gist of that. "*No senoritas. Lo siento.*" He led them out of the room, carefully shielding the lock with his body while he reset it.

"You believe this, Salsa?" Jody whispered.

All Shane could do was shake his head in wonder.

"*Tengo sed,*" Paco said. "*Bebemos tan fuerte como los otros San Andresitos.*"

"He's thirsty," Shane said. "He wants—"

"I got it," Jody interrupted, looking at his watch. "Only one beer while we get the delivery receipts, and then, adios."

"*Sí, sí, está bien, mis amigos.*" Paco grinned, showing teeth the approximate color and texture of an old wooden fence.

Paco led them to his Toyota, then they got in and drove up the street.

Five minutes later they were parked next to the three other Toyota Land Cruisers in front of the Corraleja Cantina—the very bar Shane had read about in the guidebook.

It was just past two in the afternoon and the businesses in town had closed for siesta, but nobody seemed to be sleeping. Inside they could hear laughter and Mexican music playing on what sounded like an old scratchy forty-five. Then a glass broke, followed by hoots of laughter.

"*Ándale,*" Paco said, grinning, as he led them into the cantina. The Vikings took their gym bags with them as they got out of the Toyota and cautiously walked through the door.

Even though it was named after a Colombian bullfight, Shane thought the place looked more like the bar from *Star Wars*. Adrenaline and beer were being mixed in dangerous quantities. Sweating men were talking loudly.

Forty pairs of angry eyes swung toward them.

Suddenly the room went deadly silent.

BAR FIGHT

THIS JOINT DON'T feel too friendly," Jody said, one hand on his gym bag, the other fingering the hard place under his jacket where he kept his chambered Heckler & Koch.

"*Hola, mis amigos,*" Paco shouted expansively to the other San Andresitos, who were in a booth at the back of the cantina. Paco led the way through the bar full of Colombian misfits, to where Spartacos Sococo, Emilio Hernandez, and Octavio Randhanie were perched on hard, butt-polished vinyl, grinning like three hungry vultures on a split-rail fence.

Shane and Jody wedged in next to Emilio Hernandez and Spartacos Sococo, while Paco Brazos, Tremaine, and Lester found seats next to Octavio Randhanie. The San Andresitos forced smiles onto their faces while the background noise in the bar began to build again slowly.

The cantina was quite large, dominated on one side by a scarred wooden bar and mismatched furniture. The men in the place all seemed to be made of gristle and knotted twine. Their brown muscles glistened with sweat. There was no air conditioning; a big paddle fan with wicker blades turned ineffectively from the ceiling while an old Wurlitzer jukebox screeched American rock and roll through blown-out speakers.

"*Que bueno, no?*" Paco said. "Good pussy, *abajo. Pero tienes ningun tiempo por la fucky-fucky, no?*" He grinned, spreading his lips happily. His bullshit brown-toothed grin was really beginning to wear thin.

"Look, boys . . . *amigos*," Jody said. "We don't need to get laid, we need our paperwork—our receipts proving that the merchandise got delivered up here safely, so we can collect our money from Sandro Mantoor in Aruba. You got that for us?"

Five sets of stone-hard eyes met Jody's question, glaring volumes of guarded thought, but no hint of what was to come.

"Sawdust, tell 'em what we want."

Lester Wood rattled it off in Spanish, and the San Andresitos all nodded, sipping whiskey from shot glasses, but nobody made a move to hand over anything.

"I'm thinking we got us a little problem," Sawdust said. "These boys don't seem t'wanna ride in the wagon."

"Tell 'em we don't get our receipts, we're gonna take that info back to Sandy. And if they got some dick-brained idea about us not getting outta this town in one piece, then Sandy Mantoor isn't gonna send any more product up here. He's guaranteeing our safety."

Lester Wood translated this, but after he finished, all four of the San Andresitos just stared. Nobody was smiling any longer.

"Kinda like barkin' at a knot," Lester Wood drawled.

"Okay, what's going on? Where's our bottom line here?" Jody asked.

Paco rattled off some Spanish, and the other San Andresitos nodded.

Sawdust translated: "Seems we're being kidnapped. They won't let us go unless *we* pay *them*."

"You want us to give you money to let us out of here?" Jody growled.

"*Sí . . . sí, dinero*. Money for to go. *Es correcto*," Paco said.

"You fuckin' people . . ." Jody snapped. "I'll die here before I pay one fucking cent."

"Jody . . . let's think this through," Shane said softly. "Let's get a number from 'em. Why should anybody die if we're only talkin' about one or two grand."

"No," Paco said, understanding instantly when the subject was money. "*No es suficiente*."

"How much?" Jody was smiling now, but Shane knew that smile. He'd been dealing with it since the sixth grade. It was a deadly warning.

"*Te va a costar veinte por ciento*."

"He wants twenty percent," Sawdust drawled. "We need us a laugh track t'go with this."

"That's about three million dollars!" Jody said. "You sure that's gonna be enough, you fucking *ladrón*?"

The four San Andresitos froze. Shane realized most of them had taken their hands off the table where they were now dangerously out of sight.

"Jody . . ." Shane said. "Take a look around in here . . ."

Jody swung his gaze across the bar. Most of the men had silently risen off their stools and were now forming a loose circle around their booth. Shane continued: "I think I saw some of these people driving forklifts in Paco's warehouse. They lured us in here. We've been set up."

The bar had gone graveyard quiet, except for a bad version of "Blue Suede Shoes" screeching over the blown speakers, sounding more like a catfight than music.

Suddenly, Jody yanked his H&K P-7 out of his waistband and shoved it in Paco's face. Simultaneously, all eight men in the booth had guns in their hands.

Half the men in the bar had also found weapons in that split second.

Twenty pistols were cocked and aimed at the Vikings sitting in the booth. It had happened fast, but Jody had beaten Paco's draw. Paco Brazos was in no-man's-land, frozen, with Jody's gun an inch from his face, his own weapon not quite out.

"I'm ready! Go for it, asshole! Let's do the dance." Craziness lit Jody's face like the changing colors of a raging fire. It was all there—excitement, adrenaline, and a willingness to die, all of this registering in one crazy heartbeat. "Come on. Start blasting. But no matter what, you're on the bus. You're goin' first, greaseball."

They were all stretched out in deadly postures, each one shoving a gun across the table at the enemy opposite him. None of the Vikings had time to get to their Polish MP-63s but instead had gone for their handguns. Shane had snatched the Spanish Astra out of his ankle holster and was trading aims with Spartacos Sococo's huge Desert Eagle. They posed there for several dangerous moments before a slow, impish smile broke across Paco's dirt-brown face.

"No *quiero disparar* . . . no shoot. *Tomamos y comemos y luego tus papeles.*" He turned to the other San Andresitos. "*Mis amigos . . . no más . . . no más.*"

"He's changed his mind. . . . He doesn't want to shoot us. He's gonna give us our papers," Sawdust said, holding his Colt Commander on Emilio Hernandez, who had a blue-steel Beretta 9 aimed right back at him.

"Tell 'em to put their guns away," Jody ordered, and Sawdust did.

All of the San Andresitos slowly reholstered their guns. The Vikings didn't.

"Get the rest a'these shit burners outta here," Jody ordered, indicating the men standing in a deadly circle around them.

"*Veten, veten afuera,*" Paco said to the sweating contingent of armed men.

Slowly, the men in the bar shouldered their weapons or re-packed them in faded canvas holsters. They sauntered toward the door, trying to look tough in the middle of a retreat, dragging their pride like heavy sacks behind them.

Only then did Jody nod for the Vikings to put their guns away.

"*Muy bien, muy bien,*" Paco said, heaving out a tortured sigh.

Spartacos Sococo, Emilio Hernandez, and Octavio Rand-hanie stood angrily, then pushed their way out of the booth.

"Where are the fucking receipts?" Jody asked. With no need of translation, the San Andresitos reached into their pockets and pulled out the delivery vouchers, handing them to Jody, who in turn handed them to Lester Wood. He read them and nodded.

"Yep," he said, returning them to Jody, who put them in his back pocket.

Just then a phone started ringing. Nobody answered it. Paco shouted at the bartender.

"*Teléfono!*"

The old man behind the bar crossed and picked up the phone.

"*Como?*" he said, and listened for a long moment. "*Sí . . . sí.
Gracias.*" He hung up and looked over at Paco.

"*Que es?*" Paco demanded.

"*Cortez viene al pueblo.*"

"Santa's coming," Sawdust translated. "This might be a
good time t'blow town."

SANTA'S COMING TO TOWN

TREMAINE SAID, "THEY'RE plannin' something. We need t'break hard on these assholes before it gets outta hand."

They were standing on the curb outside the cantina. The San Andresitos were clustered over by their cars.

"How'd ya figure to do that, Inky Dink?" Jody said. "There's four of us in a town of fifty-five thousand gun-toting *pendejos.*"

Paco broke away from the others, approached, and slapped Jody on the back as he rattled some Spanish. Jody frowned and glanced over at Lester Wood.

"He says we gotta get going before Cortez returns."

"So, let's do it," Jody said.

All five of them jammed into Paco's Toyota. He turned his bubble around and headed back toward his warehouse on

Calle 16, leaving the three other San Andresitos standing in front of the cantina, staring down at designer-name watches as if their futures were ticking away on each dial.

"Where's he going?" Shane asked. "We should be heading west. That's the only way out of town."

Paco answered in Spanish, and Sawdust turned to Jody. "He says we need to pick up some *celadores* at his business, for our safety. He says Santander won't attack us if we have enough protection."

"Now he's worried about our safety?" Shane asked. "Five minutes ago this prick was trying to hold us for ransom."

"Good point," Jody said, then pulled the P-7 out of his side pocket and put it against Paco's rib cage.

"*Que es?*" Paco said, glancing at Jody, then down at the gun.

"So you don't go stupid on us, *amigo.*"

They made a right onto Calle 16 but had to stop as soon as they turned because they were stuck behind a strange column of armed men and vehicles. A sole man pushing a wheelbarrow was leading the parade. Walking on each side of him, guarding the wheelbarrow, were four *celadores,* their machine guns aimed in all directions. An empty flatbed truck rumbled along behind.

"What is this?" Jody snapped.

"*Por comercio* . . . How you say? *Dinero por* trade, *Hernandez no tiene* dishwashers, *de modo que va a comprarlos en mi tienda.*"

Sawdust said, "If one of them doesn't have what he needs for his market in Colombia, he buys it from one of the others."

"*Sí,*" Paco said.

"They going to your place?" Jody asked.

"*Sí, a mi tienda . . .*"

"What's in the wheelbarrow?"

"*Dinero Colombiano.*"

Paco managed to pull around the column, and as they drove past, Shane looked out the window. Sure enough, the wheelbarrow was half full of stacks of Colombian pesos.

Paco stopped the Toyota in front of his warehouse. A moment later the wheelbarrow full of cash and the empty truck arrived. Two yellow forklifts zipped out of Paco's warehouse with pallet-loaded boxes of Maytag washing machines stacked three high. A dozen *celadores* stood out front, facing Hernandez's *celadores* over glistening new auto-mags. The man with the wheelbarrow upended it unceremoniously onto the Spanish-tile sidewalk in front of Paco's showroom.

"Cha-ching," Jody said softly.

Three of the women whom Shane had seen in the office upstairs now rushed out of the building and bent over the bundles of cash, rifling through them, their nimble fingers counting. Calculators hummed and LCD screens printed out figures. Once again, Shane noticed that the calculators were the big twelve-digit Texas Instrument computers. He finally realized that when tabulating these huge sums in pesos, the regular ten-digit calculators ran out of decimal points.

Suddenly, from the end of the street, they heard the sound of big truck engines growling loudly. Shane looked over and saw two old army trucks with at least twenty men in them, rolling over the garbage-strewn street.

"*Adentro! Adentro! Andeles!*" Paco said as he began to move toward the warehouse.

"Not so fast, asshole," Jody said, grabbing Paco by the collar, now putting the P-7 to his head. "You're not quite through here yet."

All of the *celadores* swung and pointed their weapons at the Vikings, but Jody ignored them and pointed up the street at the approaching trucks. "Whose guys are those? Is that Santa?"

"*Sí, Santander viene,*" Paco said. Unreasoning fear was in his eyes and spreading over his face.

"Let's go," Jody said, jamming his gun barrel hard against Paco's temple, freezing the army of *celadores* on the sidewalk.

Paco shouted at them, "*No disparar! No disparar!*"

The women on their knees kept gathering and tabulating. They never looked up.

"Somebody get a piece on this guy," Jody commanded, and Sawdust put his pistol to the back of Paco's head.

Jody jumped out of the Toyota SUV. Then he ran around and got behind the wheel, pushing the fat San Andresito over into the passenger seat beside him. Tremaine broke out the glass of the two fixed windows in the rear of the Toyota, using the barrel of his pistol. Gym-bag zippers ripped open in the car, followed by a chorus of forty-round mags slamming home and sliders being tromboned.

"Only one way out and that's past those guys up there," Jody said. "It's gonna be reckless, so hold on." He backed up, turned, then headed up the street directly toward the approaching vehicles and twenty armed men.

"*No! No, es loco . . . somos muertos!*" Paco said, sweat pouring down his round face, drenching his shirt collar.

A happy madness distorted Jody's features: "We may die, but we're gonna take a few motherfuckers with us."

In seconds, the first bullets rocked the Toyota. Fired from a half a block away, they thudded into the grille and shattered a side mirror.

"Get busy!" Jody shouted.

Shane leaned out one of the broken side windows and aimed his Polish MP-63 up the street at the column of army vehicles. The badly rocking SUV distorted his aim as its tires spun, looking for purchase on a street covered with decaying garbage. He started blasting, aiming blindly with one hand, the bolt clattering maniacally as the machine pistol fired, spewing hot brass out into the street.

It was hard to assess what happened next because it was a blur of spinning tires, rotating landscapes, and chattering gunfire. Jody was heading right at the lead truck, then yanked the wheel to the left at the last second. The radial tires spun garbage out behind them, slushing badly in the rotting muck as the SUV hit a curb and bounced up then, somehow, they were on the sidewalk in front of Sococo's showroom.

Ten automatic weapons broke out simultaneously, shattering the remaining windows in the Toyota. Jody kept his head low while the entire front windshield starred and then rained chunks of glass in on them.

Shane dropped the first clip and jammed his last one home. Tremaine was firing out the window on the far side of the SUV. With the windshield gone, Sawdust was aiming straight out the front, his MP-63 barking loudly inside the car, throwing a stream of spent casings at Paco in the front passenger seat. The sweaty San Andresito screamed in panic as Sawdust's hot brass hit him, the bullets whizzing past his ear. They were now opposite Cortez's two army trucks.

Santander's men had taken cover behind the vehicles and let loose as the Toyota roared past on the sidewalk. The Vikings fired until the weapons were empty and the slides locked open. Heavy 9-millimeter bullet hits rocked the SUV but, miraculously, it didn't stall.

Shane grabbed his Astra and emptied his last clip until he was pulling the trigger maniacally, dry-firing, unaware that he was empty because of the booming retort of the Colt Commander that Sawdust was using right next to his ear. The chattering racket of ten incoming machine guns set up a deadly cacophony only twelve feet away.

"I'm dry!" Shane yelled. They were now past the column of men and trucks. Almost immediately, Jody's P-7 flew over the seat and hit him on the shoulder. Shane scooped it up, turned, and kept firing out the back window.

Somehow they got through the violent maelstrom and bounced back onto the street.

"Anybody hit?" Jody yelled.

"Yeah, I'm leakin' some," Lester Wood drawled.

"How bad?"

"Well, it's . . . it's . . . I think I'm okay . . ."

Jody was making a right turn, back onto Calle 16, heading out of town. The Toyota engine sounded as if it had been hit—running rough and getting worse by the minute.

Sawdust's face was drained of color, but his denim shirt was drenched in red. "This ain't good back here," Shane said. "Sawdust looks bad."

The SUV was losing speed, coughing and bucking.

"We gotta get to that garrison at the end of town," Jody said. "We'll deal with it then."

"No!" Paco said. "No militia."

"I'm through listening to you!" Jody shouted, spinning the wheel to avoid another wandering Hereford grazing on garbage in the middle of the street.

They headed back through town. The Toyota was barely moving when the garrison finally came into view.

Shane could see out the back window that Santander's jeeps had gotten turned around and were now behind them, closing fast. "They're four blocks back," he announced.

The SUV was lurching badly as it bucked and coughed down the street. Shane pried the Colt out of Lester Wood's hand and emptied it out of the broken back window.

"No! No militia!" Paco shouted again. Jody ignored him and lurched the Toyota onto the paved road leading into the military base. The two gate guards swung their weapons down on polished shoulder straps, aiming them at the Toyota as it pulled to a stop at the main gate.

"Police," Jody said, yanking out his LAPD badge and holding it out the window. "American *policía*."

"*Necesitamos socorro*," Lester Wood rasped.

Santander's trucks pulled into the driveway behind them but slowed down fifty yards away and inched forward like jackals at the edge of firelight.

"Fuck this," Jody said, watching them in the one remaining side mirror. Then he hit the gas. The Toyota bucked forward, smashing the wooden bar arm across the base road, shattering it.

"No!" Paco screamed.

An alarm started ringing, and almost immediately fifteen soldiers ran out of a wooden building slamming banana clips into a variety of automatic weapons, clicking off safeties as they approached. In seconds, they had the Toyota surrounded.

Jody got out of the vehicle with his hands up and his LAPD badge held high. "American *policía*," he repeated to the soldiers, who were staring in disbelief at the bullet-riddled vehicle. Shane looked back at Santander's trucks parked just a few feet outside the garrison. At first it seemed they were afraid to come closer. Then Shane began to wonder if perhaps they were parked there to block a possible retreat.

"Sawdust, tell this guy we demand political asylum," Jody said. "Tell 'em. Tell these guys we're American cops on a U.S. government mission. Go on, do it!"

Shane was studying the dusty look in Lester Wood's vacant eyes. "We're gonna have to find a way to tell 'em ourselves. Sawdust didn't make it."

THE WHITE ANGEL

IT WAS AN empty structure: no windows, a tin roof, wooden shelves, and a poured-concrete floor. It looked like a supply locker. Once the door was locked, Tremaine sat glumly on the floor while Jody and Shane began pacing.

"What now?" Tremaine challenged, his low voice turned flat and cold as slate.

"Okay, look, this is a Colombian military unit," Jody said slowly. "America has diplomatic relations with Colombia, so we try and get a message out to the U.S. embassy, get them to cut through all this, get the embassy to release us into U.S. custody." He looked up into Tremaine's angry, disbelieving stare.

"You're kiddin' me, right?" Tremaine glared at Jody. "Didja forget, we're supposed t'be dead."

"We're also laundering fifty million in Colombian drug cash," Shane said. "If we call the U.S. embassy, we're not gonna get released; we're gonna get extradited."

"Okay, Hot Sauce, then you tell me. . . . Whatta you wanna do?"

"I'll tell you one thing," Shane said. "There's something very wrong about this military base. Did you see the weapons those troops were carrying?"

"Yeah, what of it?" Jody growled.

"Some of it was prototype stuff, brand-new Beretta 92s. But I also saw some twenty-year-old Chinese assault rifles. I think one of those guys even had an antique Lee Enfield. He'd be better off using that thing as a club."

"So what?"

"Doesn't the army of a sovereign nation generally issue standardized equipment?" Shane continued. "Doesn't the Colombian government supply its soldiers with unitized ordnance? These guys are packing everything from auto-mags to sling-shots."

"He's right," Tremaine said, looking up with concern.

"So what am I supposed to do about it?"

"Nothing. I'm just wondering why. And what happened to Paco Brazos? They pulled him outta the car with us, but they didn't put him in here. How come?"

"Maybe he drinks beer with these assholes. Who the fuck knows." Suddenly Jody didn't have very good answers.

"This afternoon we rolled in here with almost a billion contraband cigarettes, right past those guards," Shane said. "Nobody gave a damn. You saw that building of Paco's. . . . How much contraband had to go past this base, unobstructed, to

fill up that warehouse, not to mention all the other San Andresitos?"

"Okay, so somebody's getting paid off," Jody said, frustrated. "Stop asking all these dumb questions."

"Let the man talk," Tremaine said, turning toward Shane.
"Whatta you thinkin'?"

"You were saying that José told you about the political situation in Colombia. I've read some department one sheets
about it—it's supposed to be treacherous," Shane said, still
pacing slowly in the locked room. He stopped and looked
over at Jody, who was a few feet away, a strange expression
on his face. "What is it? Do you know something?" Shane
prodded.

"Yeah, that's what Papa Joe told me, too," Jody said.

"What'd he say?" Tremaine demanded.

"To tell you the truth, when he told me, I wasn't paying a
whole lot of attention. He said something about—"

"What? Come on, man," Tremaine rose off the floor, moved
across the room, then grabbed Jody's shirt and yanked him up
close. "What did José tell you, man?"

"Get your hands off me, Inky Dink. Who the fuck you think
you're pawing?"

"I wanna know who those green jackets out there belong to."

"Then get your fuckin' hands off me!"

There was a long, electric moment before Tremaine finally
let go of Jody's shirt and took a step back.

"What did José Mondragon tell you?" Shane asked again.

"I don't remember, exactly. I'd been drinking. Something
about two Marxist armies fighting with the government, or
some shit. He said there's a lot of kidnapping out here. These

Marxist guerrillas snatch people, mostly U.S. oil-company executives working on desert drilling rigs, or any Anglo they can get their hands on. They ransom you back to your family or your company—whoever will pay the most money to keep you alive. He was telling me about this insurance you can buy, kidnapping insurance. He said nobody from Blackstone or All-American will set foot inside Colombia without it."

"You tellin' me we coulda got kidnapping insurance?" Tremaine said. Now he was right in Jody's face.

"Inky Dink, you put your hands on me again, I'll knock your lights out. How we gonna buy insurance? We're all supposed to be dead."

"We got aliases. We coulda worked somethin' out through José," Tremaine shot back.

"We're not a bunch a fucking oil-company pussies. Nobody's got the stones to kidnap us."

"Am I just imagining this, or are we all locked in a god-damned windowless room here?" Tremaine glowered.

"Fuck you," Jody growled.

Shane stepped between them. "What else did José tell you?"

"Just that there are these two leftist armies that prey on the San Andresitos and on each other. All the San Andresitos pay a percentage of their black-market profits to the guerrillas so they'll let the contraband go on into Colombia—a political contribution made at gunpoint."

"Who are the two armies?" Shane asked.

"They've both got acronyms . . . one is like RAFC. Stands for something like the Revolutionary Armed Forces of Colombia. And the other is NLA, the National Liberation Army."

"Sounds t'me like you paid more than a little attention. You got all this down pretty good," Tremaine challenged.

"What're you tryin' to say?" Jody threatened softly. "You got something on your mind, lay it down, asswipe."

"How 'bout we focus on the damn problem," Shane said. "If these guys aren't regular army, then is that good for us, or bad?"

"One other thing José told me . . . There's another guy up here. It's probably not important, but José said he's the joker in the deck, an ex–Argentine army colonel who leads a death squad—a right-wing fanatic with white-blond hair. He supposedly trained in the U.S. at the School of the Americas, in Fort Benning, Georgia."

"Never heard of it." Tremaine glowered.

"It's some kinda counterterrorist school, run by our Pentagon. Latin American army officers from OAS get nominated by their governments to go there. Instructors from the Pentagon teach greaseball commandos how to get info out of captured commies, how to pull out fingernails with pliers—shit like that."

"I love it," Tremaine said.

"Papa Joe told me this Argentine colonel gets off by torturing and killing."

"What's his name?" Shane asked.

"Don't know his name, but they call him the 'White Angel.' Papa Joe said The Hague finally charged him with war crimes committed while he was in Argentine Intelligence. He was sentenced to death in Argentina, but he escaped and fled to Colombia. He settled up here, in the desert."

"So I guess we got two choices," Shane said. "If these guys are regular Colombian army, we play the American embassy card. If they're Marxist guerrillas, we get down on our knees, start begging, give them a cut of what we got in the bank in Aruba."

"And if we been captured by this other dude, the White Angel?" Tremaine asked.

"It's not him," Jody said. "He's a right-wing extremist . . . an outlaw hiding from the government in the desert."

"But isn't the Colombian government a right-wing democracy?" Shane asked. "Wouldn't the White Angel be closer politically to them than to a buncha Marxist guerrillas?"

Nobody answered Shane's question. Finally Tremaine changed the subject.

"You're an asshole, ya know that, Jody?" he said. "We coulda had insurance. We had us some insurance, then we coulda got the fuck out of here."

Jody took a swing at him, knocking Tremaine back hard against the brick wall. In an instant, the two were at each other, snarling like animals.

"This is great," Shane muttered.

They came hurtling back toward him. Shane tried to get out of the way, but the room was small, so he was pinned as the two crashed hard against him. He caught an elbow in the head and went down under a pile of flying fists and sweating bodies. He finally managed to roll free and get up. He grabbed Jody, who had gained control and was now on top of Tremaine, pummeling him with both fists.

Shane yanked Jody off and threw him against the far wall. "We got enough trouble without this!" Shane shouted.

Tremaine wiped some blood off his mouth with the back of his hand, while Jody slid down the wall and sat on the floor.

"You fucking jerk-offs," Jody mumbled. "How'd I get stuck with such pussies?"

"You picked us!" Tremaine shot back.

They sat on opposite walls of the room, all staring at their feet.

An hour later the door opened and a tall, handsome Hispanic man they had never seen before entered the room. He was wearing a perfectly cut tan suit and a red silk ascot. He kept his jacket buttoned despite the oppressive heat inside the windowless, metal-roofed room. There were two armed guards beside him, but they weren't adolescent teenagers with bristling chin whiskers—these men had expressionless eyes like dark holes cut into cardboard.

"Good evening," the man said. His English was perfect, and he spoke with an American accent. "My name is Santander Cortez and I'm sorry you have been forcibly detained. I know you probably think that because of our business difficulties, I mean you harm, but let me assure you this is not the case. I hold Paco Brazos responsible for leaving me out of your cigarette transaction."

"You got that right," Jody said, standing.

"And you, I wager, are Mr. Dean?"

"Yes."

"I would like to discuss options with you, if that is convenient." He was smiling warmly.

"Sounds good."

"You other two gentlemen, if you'll please bear with me, I think everything can be amicably arranged. I'm sorry if this has been stressful. I'll be back to you two shortly." He motioned to Jody. "Mr. Dean?"

Jody moved across the room and exited with the tall, handsome man. The door was locked behind them.

"Maybe we finally caught us a break," Tremaine said.

"Yeah," Shane answered. But one thing troubled him about Santander Cortez.

The man had a full head of snow-white hair.

CHAT

FOUR HOURS PASSED, but Jody never returned.

The more Shane thought about it, the more he was sure that Santander Cortez was the White Angel. He sat in the dark, running their predicament over in his mind, studying it from every possible angle. The first thing he needed to do was pick up some coordination with the man silently brooding a few feet away.

"Tremaine . . . ," he said.

Tremaine raised his head and glowered at Shane.

"You and I need to work together if we plan on staying alive. We've gotta stop fighting and do some thinking."

"We're fucked," Tremaine said softly. "What we gonna do to change that?"

"For starters, how about the answers to a few questions?"

Tremaine stared at Shane but didn't respond.

"I still wanna know how come you're not inked . . . why you didn't get that Viking tattoo like the rest of us."

"I don't buy into that. That's white-boy shit."

"That's one reason, but you wanna hear another?"

Tremaine didn't answer.

"I think you're a department mole. Internal Affairs, or something."

Tremaine's lip curled into a snarl . . . or was it a grin? It was hard to tell in the dark room.

"I know you came aboard late, after Jody had already set up the Vikings," Shane continued. "Wanna hear my theory?"

Tremaine still didn't answer, so he went on.

"Somehow, you or somebody in IAD found out about the Vikings, so you got yourself assigned to SWAT. Then through your friendship with Rodriquez, you put a move on Jody and got picked to be the last Viking. But since you were workin' undercover, you weren't listed in Medwick's log. Cops hate tattoos. You didn't want a tattoo, 'cause you weren't really a Viking. You were only there to find out what they were doing and bust 'em. You were the only one in the unit who wasn't on drugs—same reason. How'm I doing so far?"

"You got a big imagination."

"Jody isn't coming back. He's gone. You and I are next. We're all gonna die. There's no police to protect us up here, and there's no government to save us, just criminals, flies, and garbage."

"You doin' fake jacks on me now. Tryin' t'fuck with my mind."

"I'll tell you something else that doesn't quite stack up. Your jive ghetto bullshit reads like street cover to me. Every now

and then when you get surprised, it slips. I think it's just camouflage for Jody, but Jody's gone, so you're wasting this hot-
shit performance on me."

"Zat right?"

"Yep. And laugh this one off if you can. . . ." Shane paused.
"I'm workin' undercover, too. I think we're both department
plants running games on each other. Problem is, there're no
Vikings left to bullshit. So maybe we oughta come clean with
each other—start from there."

"I saw you cap Sergeant Hamilton . . . saw her bleed out.
No fuckin' way you're workin' undercover."

"It was rigged. She was wearing a vest."

"Ain't no vest gonna stop a Black Talon."

"You're wrong. It's called a level-three tactical vest . . . developed by the Pentagon. I'm working a special undercover
assignment for Chief Filosiani."

"Bullshit."

"Listen, Tremaine, whether you're Internal Affairs or not,
we still need to work together. There used to be six of us. Now
it's just you and me."

"Okay, smart guy . . . so let's hear your plan."

Shane glanced around the room. "You suppose those shelves
will come down? We could pry loose those heavy two-by-four
supports underneath."

Tremaine looked up at heavy wooden shelves and the two-
by-four frames holding them. "Yeah," he said. "So?"

Then he gave Tremaine the rest of his plan.

45
CAT AND MOUSE

THE DOOR OPENED an hour later, and two of the hardened mercenaries entered the room. Shane and Tremaine were pressed flat against the wall. Each swung a three-foot-long two-by-four at his man. The two Colombians doubled over and went down. Shane and Tremaine sprung out and searched them for weapons but found none. Suddenly a volley of machine-gun fire exploded through the door from four backups positioned outside. The bullets whined and ricocheted around inside the small enclosure, sparking off walls like manic fireflies.

Shane felt hot pain sear in his thigh, then another slug hit him in the side of his neck. A moment later he was pounced on by three men and went down in a pile. Their blows rained down on him; he was clubbed with a gun butt until his vision blurred. Consciousness hovered against a black mist that finally descended and swallowed him.

When he awoke, everything ached. He was alone in the room; Tremaine was gone. He pulled himself into a sitting position and took a quick, fuzzy-headed inventory of his bruised, bleeding body. He had a nasty-looking through-and-through on his upper thigh that was still leaking blood and had completely numbed his left leg. The slug was close to his abductor canal. *Karmic payback*.

The second bullet had grazed his neck, and he had a furrow an eighth of an inch deep running across the right side of his throat. The blood had crusted, but that wound had stopped bleeding. His lip was split and two front teeth were loose; his head ached, and everything else felt horrible.

He slumped onto the floor, and for the next hour felt the temperature slowly drop as the desert night cooled the tiny tin-roofed room until he was freezing. Then he sat with his arms wrapped around him, his teeth chattering. He didn't know how long he waited. He dozed off once but awoke with a start when the door flew open.

Four men rushed in, grabbed him, stood him up, and laced his hands behind his back with wire. Using pliers, they twisted the wire tight until it cut painfully through his skin. Then they pushed him brutally through the door.

He was stumbling ahead of them, one leg almost numb, lurching across the lit compound. Every time he slowed, somebody would give him a hard push, knocking him forward. They herded him past the parade ground toward a small wood-frame building.

The house was painted white with green shutters; it had a peaked roof and slanting porch. A bright redbrick chimney completed an out-of-place Iowa farmhouse look.

He was dragged and pushed up the steps, then shoved through the front door.

The living room was American Gothic with a turn-of-the-century rocker and quilted chairs. Framed fox-hunting paintings of jumping hounds and horses dressed the walls. The mercenaries shoved him through an oak and glass door into a small, cozy den and pushed him down onto the floor.

"*Abajo solamente, no mueves,*" the guard ordered.

Shane nodded and waited for what would come next.

A few minutes later the tall Hispanic man walked into the room. He had removed the tan suit jacket; in its place was a blue three-quarter-length silk smoking jacket, belted at the waist. He wore sharply pleated tan pants and a white shirt. His bullshit red silk ascot was still peeking out from underneath. "This is not what I wanted. Please, will somebody remove those restraints?" he said in perfect American English, but now Shane could also hear something else in his speech. Flat Boston vowels tinged his accent.

The guards either knew what he was saying or had been through this so many times before that they knew what was required of them, because they rushed to Shane, pulled him up, and began clipping the wires.

"Gently, gently," Santander said. "We're civilized men; let's try to behave that way." He smiled at Shane as wire cutters snipped the restraints on his wrists.

"Perhaps the armchair," the white-haired man instructed.

The guards led Shane to the chair and motioned for

him to sit, then backed off a short distance, their eyes like those of starving men staring at a steaming meal.

"What happened to Jody and Tremaine?" Shane said. The Hispanic man's smile widened, but he didn't answer. A grandfather clock tick-tocked from the corner of the room, its brass pendulum rhythmically slicing up the minutes.

"They are doing just fine," the white-haired man finally responded. "As will you. But first we must get to know one another . . . chat for a spell. I look forward to my all-too-infrequent civilized visitors."

"I'd like to believe that, Colonel."

"You should." He smiled. "You see, living out here in the desert, I don't have much opportunity to talk to men who have opinions formed by Western culture or world literature. These men are uneducated." He motioned to the four armed *celadores*. "They can endlessly discuss sex or the Old Testament, but as a steady diet, even those worthwhile subjects can become pretty stale."

"So you are a colonel, then." Shane's words seemed to surprise him.

"I beg your pardon?"

"I called you Colonel, you didn't correct me."

He smiled slowly. "And what do you think that proves?"

"You're the White Angel?"

He began slowly turning a diamond ring on his index finger. "Since I'm a man who has, on occasion, targeted my enemies with extreme forms of death, I have been given many names: the 'White Angel,' the 'Crow,' and earlier, before my promotion to colonel, 'Captain Death.' Childishly colorful, but quite useful nonetheless, because these names strike fear into my enemies. Fear is a useful currency." He seemed to choose each word with great care, delighting in each syllable, like a man tasting a perfectly seasoned dish.

"You take yourself pretty seriously."

"Yes, as a matter of fact, I do—and for good reason. What I do affects the politics of nations. If you are a wise man worthy of my interest, you will take what I say seriously as well."

"So what is this little talk really about?"

"Weakness," Santa Cortez said softly, his voice now almost a whisper.

"Yours or mine?" Shane asked.

"It will be a shared experience." An evil shine came into his eyes, a penetrating madness that Shane didn't like at all.

"How so?"

"This is hard for a man such as myself to admit . . . but my weakness has defined me since adolescence. At first it frightened me, even sickened me, because I couldn't control or understand it. Later, I saw it for what it really was and began to take a measure of strength from it."

Shane was beginning to dread what he was about to hear.

"It started when I was a child. I would, on occasion, catch and set fire to a neighborhood pet—a cat or a small dog. I had an uncontrollable urge to administer pain . . . to watch an animal die painfully . . . to put my hands on it as it passed over the threshold, to feel it convulse . . . take its final breath. It was as close to a feeling of love as I have ever been able to experience.

"My father eventually caught me. He was an admiral in the Argentine navy, a man of strict discipline and rules. He took me to a doctor, who said I had a disassociative, psychotic disorder. So I was sent to Boston, to a clinic, where I lived until college. In America I learned about democratic principles. I learned to love freedom and a constitutional government. After I returned to Argentina, I chose to fight for democracy in my own country—to drive the Marxist dictators out of power. As an American, I'm sure you share my hatred of left-wing governments. I fought Marxist thieves in my country, but since my conviction for political murder, I have had to fight them from my neighbor state, Colombia. So you see, I am a freedom fighter much like your own Founding Fathers. I have deep-seated political beliefs, but underneath, I still have my deadly cravings. Pain and death seem to nourish me, so I have made this childhood weakness a political strength."

"You kill people—torture them."

"My violence is labeled madness. Fear is my Trojan horse. My enemies ingest it, absorbing it inside them, where it then spreads and weakens them."

"Why are we sitting in Aunt Bea's den, discussing this? I can't absolve you, and you can't change."

"I find my excitement is magnified when I take the time to interact with my targets."

"So, we're talking about my torture?"

"We are."

"Maybe you and I can make a deal," Shane said as fear suddenly swept through him.

The White Angel smiled, gently touching the longish hair at his temples, brushing it carefully behind his ear with his fingers. "You were saying?"

"I have a million dollars in a bank in Aruba. I'd be willing to arrange a wire transfer. You need funds to fight your war. I can help you."

"Ahh, I see. So you have money to negotiate for your safety?"

"A million U.S. dollars, in cash, to turn me and Tremaine loose."

"And how would this transaction be accomplished?"

"Because of the escrow instructions, it has to be done in person. You, and one or two of your *celadores,* come back to Aruba with me. We contact Sandy Mantoor, his bank releases the funds, then I turn them over to you. Once you take delivery, you can wire the money to any bank in the world."

"I see." He put a hand up to his delicate mouth. "I'm disappointed you didn't start with your best offer," he said softly. "I know you have much more than that. But you see, Sergeant, it really doesn't matter, because I have already made an acceptable arrangement with Mr. Dean."

"With Jody!"

"You thought he was dead, and he would have been—just like you and the Negro. But Mr. Dean had ten million in kidnap insurance. We concluded a transaction with his insurance company an hour ago. The funds were transferred when I turned him loose. You'll have to admit, it's much cleaner than trying to go to Aruba and deal with that criminal Mantoor family, take a chance on being captured on foreign soil, sold to my Marxist enemies for cash. I put nothing past the Mantoors. So . . . thank you, but I must decline your offer."

"Jody paid you?"

"Worse. He also contracted me to kill you and Mr. Lane." He smiled at Shane. "So, like the cat who has cornered his mouse, I can play with both of you for hours, bat you around, watch you try and get away, maybe put a paw on your tail, chew your head and ears, listen to you squeak. Then slowly you will become tired; shock will numb your nervous system. You will have no fight left, and like the cat, I will become angry with you for not playing. In retaliation, I will make your end . . . well . . . interesting." He smiled again, and Shane couldn't help noticing that this time the smile was warm, almost as if the White Angel had developed true affection for him.

Then Santander Cortez moved to the window and looked out at the lit compound. "The Negro didn't hold up as well as I would have thought. Sometimes men surprise me . . . strength of will is a unique and rare quality."

"Where is he?"

"I'll show you. . . ." He turned to the *celadores*. "*Afuera al Negro, ándele.*"

The guards quickly moved to Shane, yanked him to his feet, and led him out the back door of the house and across the compound.

They went through a locked gate and were soon off the base, moving across the desert. The cold night air lessened the stench of the surrounding town, but it was still there, lingering stubbornly.

Shane didn't know where they were heading or what horrors were in store for him.

Then he saw Tremaine, lit by the light of a portable generator.

He was tied to a chain-link fence, bleeding from a hundred cuts, his head down on his chest, vomit puddling at his feet. Enormous strips of his skin had been removed.

"You son of a bitch," Shane said softly, the spectacle taking his breath away.

"Not a pretty sight, I admit, but fun while it lasted." Santander paused to let the moment sink in. "And there are hidden benefits: these guards will tell the story—how I skinned the *pobre* Negro, cutting him in slices while he screamed, finding ecstasy in his agony. The story will grow with each telling. The Trojan horse of my legend of terror will be dragged into the depths of my Marxist enemies and fester in their imaginations: win-win."

Shane moved on rubbery legs toward Tremaine. He could barely believe the human wreckage in front of him. Then the destroyed man coughed, and blood ran out of Tremaine's mouth.

"Shit! He's still alive," Shane murmured.

"Go ahead. Get a good look," Cortez whispered. "Ask him how he liked it."

As Shane moved closer to Tremaine, he heard a gasp or a rattle, or maybe it was a whisper. He was close enough to see that Tremaine's right eye was wide open, staring at him, disembodied. Then he heard the rattling sound again, followed by a cough and a sigh. He thought Tremaine was trying to tell him something.

"What?" Shane asked, his own voice a croak. "What is it?"

Shane's left thigh throbbed, so he used his right knee to kneel. He got as close as he could until his ear was next to Tremaine's shattered mouth.

Then he heard the noise again . . . a weak stirring of sounds against a rush of exhaled air. "Werrrr . . . riigghh . . ." Tremaine breathed softly into his ear.

Shane watched as Tremaine's lips trembled.

"Sheee . . ." the black man said, and coughed up more blood.

"What?" Shane whispered. "She?"

"Ifffff . . ."

"If?" Shane asked.

Tremaine Lane let out what air was left inside him like a long pensive sigh of exasperation. Then his head dropped, and Shane knew he was gone.

Suddenly Shane knew what he had been trying to say.

She . . . if . . . Sheriff.

Tremaine Lane was working undercover.

THE SOLEMN PROMISE

46

SHANE WAS YANKED to his feet and pushed toward the floodlit fence, which had been securely anchored in concrete. He was held firmly by two *celadores* as Tremaine's dead body was unwired, then slumped to the ground at Shane's feet.

"Next," Santander said, smiling slightly.

Shane was turned and pushed up against the fence. One of the *celadores* began to wire his right wrist to the top rail as the other one grabbed his left and did the same. The White Angel unsnapped a leather box he had been carrying. When Cortez opened it, Shane could see surgical scalpels mounted on blue velvet. They glittered ominously in the generator's harsh light.

"I think, to start, perhaps the number-three handle with a four-four size-ten blade. It makes a nice, shallow three-millimeter cut." Santander picked a long, bent, chrome-handled instrument out of the case, reached in with his fingers, and selected a small curved blade, then snapped it onto the end, tightening it with the set screw. "I am sorry that I am forgoing normal surgical sterilization techniques. I used to scrub for the fun of it, but it was really just foreplay, because you'll be long gone before any infection could set in."

"Knock yourself out," Shane murmured as the White Angel moved forward, holding the scalpel delicately between his thumb and forefinger. "We'll need to get that shirt off." Santa turned and barked the order. "La camisa!" One of the *celadores* ripped Shane's shirt. Then the White Angel stepped forward and placed the tip of the scalpel under Shane's nipple. He pressed lightly, and Shane felt the blade pierce his skin.

"Is this not a feeling close to ecstasy?" Cortez said, his voice turning husky with sexual passion.

Shane spit in his face.

Out of nowhere, gunfire erupted on all sides of them. Shane spun his head in time to see half a dozen separate muzzle flashes in the desert. All four *celadores* standing near him went down quickly, riddled with bullets. Immediately, Santander Cortez fell, blood spurting out of a huge hole in his neck.

Shane heard orders shouted in Spanish and saw movement at the edge of his vision. Then twenty men dressed in faded khaki ran toward him while reloading and firing their automags.

He heard Alexa scream, "Not him! Don't shoot! Not him!"

He thought he saw Luis Rosario, in his porkpie hat, also yelling in Spanish.

Seconds later, hands were pulling at his wrists, untwisting the wire. He fell, with his wounded leg buckling under him. Then Shane was on his back, looking up into Alexa's blue eyes, her hand cradling his head as he lay in the sand. Jo-Jo Knight appeared over her shoulder, a smoking Uzi clutched in his fist.

"Ahh, damn . . . lookit you," Alexa said sadly, studying his beaten face. "I can't leave you alone for a minute."

He forced a weak smile just as more automatic weapons cut loose. Soldiers standing near him were now being cut down by a vicious barrage of machine-gun fire coming from the direction of the garrison. The troops around him dove into a shallow wash, proned out, then began returning fire. Jo-Jo Knight and Luis Rosario grabbed Shane.

"Let's get this gringo outta here," Rosario said. They lifted him quickly and began carrying him as best they could away from the firefight.

Alexa spun and emptied a 9-millimeter clip in the direction of the fort, trying to set up some cover fire but at the same time exposing herself dangerously. Miraculously, she wasn't hit. They began moving across the uneven desert terrain, stumbling in the dark, Rosario and Knight half-carrying, half-yanking Shane along, dragging him like a sack of vegetables.

"Will you guys put me down? I can walk!" he yelled as Rosario and Knight, each supporting a side, kept running until they were a safe distance away, then stopped to help Shane get his feet under him. Alexa pushed the eject button on her Astra, dropped the empty clip onto the sand at her feet, then slammed in a new one. They kept moving, but more slowly now, Shane struggling to keep his leg working under him until they finally came to an old English lorry with primered fenders parked by the road with several other army surplus trucks.

"Let's take this one," Rosario said. They helped Shane onto the back of the truck while Jo-Jo Knight got behind the wheel.

He turned a switch on the dash, which substituted for an ig-nition key on most military vehicles. The engine started.

Alexa and Luis jumped up on the back of the flatbed next to Shane.

"Roll it!" she yelled.

The lorry rumbled across the desert, past three or four other deserted military vehicles. They could hear the sounds of the firefight receding behind them.

"Who were those guys?" Shane asked.

"Marxist rebels," Alexa said. When Shane looked surprised, she added: "We take help wherever we find it."

Soon they were back on the dirt road, heading out of Mai-cao. The old English lorry creaked and groaned and bounced through potholes. A few miles farther they hit pavement. The heavy sand tires vibrated on the two-lane concrete road that announced the beginning of Maicao's unconventional airport.

Shane saw a small blue and white Citation jet with U.S. tail markings taxiing on the ground near them, already turning around, and readying itself for takeoff. The lorry swung under the starboard wing and stopped.

Somehow, they got Shane out of the back, carrying and dragging him to the waiting plane.

"Will you guys let go of me?" he demanded. They ignored his request and pushed him roughly up the ladder into the jet.

"Okay, 'Darker Than Me,' let's do this dust off," Rosario said to Jo-Jo Knight, who was pulling the Citation's cabin door closed behind them.

Almost before the door was latched, the jet was rolling. They hurtled down the poorly lit runway, engines screaming to ro-tation speed, and then the small executive jet lifted off the tarmac. The strange, six-lane runway fell away beneath them as the government pilot banked right, heading north toward the Caribbean Sea fifteen miles away.

"Thank God you found me," Shane said.

Alexa grinned. "I told you that pill would locate you within a meter." Shane smiled and took her hand.

"We found out from a CIA internal briefing in Washington that this garrison was being used to billet a right-wing Colombian death squad, commanded by an ex–Argentine colonel named Raphael Aziz," Alexa continued.

"Aziz?" he said. "Is he the White Angel?"

She nodded. "We knew from the satellite tracking that you were on that base. Rosario has some very interesting contacts. He got us hooked up with that band of Marxist guerrillas through a drug source he has in Medellín. So we made a deal with Aziz's guerrilla enemies, who were already near here. They agreed to give us some backup in return for finding out where Colonel Aziz was. We surrounded the place, but before we could move, out you came."

"He skinned Tremaine Lane alive," Shane said softly.

She didn't answer but squeezed his hand. "You need a hospital."

"I'll settle for a kiss."

So that's what they did until Luis Rosario and Jo-Jo Knight dropped into the two seats facing them.

"Is this what white people do after a gunfight?" Rosario asked. "Cubans just drink and sing."

"I thought Cubans drank and made love to sheep." Knight grinned.

"Okay, okay." Alexa grinned. "Knock it off, you guys."

Jo-Jo said, "Unless you want this bird to circle over the water, we need to figure out where we want to go. Here's what me and this little freeway dancer figured out: your buddy Jody tried to cash in the escrow account in Aruba, but Sandro and Papa Joe beat him to it. By the time he showed up, they already cleaned it out. I think Papa Joe also set up the Vikings to be killed by the San Andresitos in Maicao after you delivered the product up there. You guys were just donkeys; he was never gonna share that money with you."

"After Jody went to Aruba and discovered the money was gone, he disappeared on a charter flight to Florida," Rosario said. "We lost the trail in Miami. Can't figure why he'd be going to Florida, anyway."

"Jody's not going there," Shane said. "He might have filed his flight plan for Miami, but trust me, he's going wherever Papa Joe and Sandy Mantoor are. Jody's gonna kill those two for setting him up and taking his money." Shane ran it over in his mind for a minute. "Papa Joe's got a house in Palm Springs. Maybe there."

Alexa shook her head. "After we broke the code book and found José Mondragon's name, we hit that desert house looking for clues to where you might be. I'm afraid that site got burned. José won't be going back to the Springs."

Shane gave it some more thought. "L.A.," he finally said.

"Why L.A.?" Alexa frowned. "That's the hardest place for him to hide. Three thousand cops there know he's alive and what he looks like."

"Because that's where Lisa told me she was going, and Lisa's his only contact to Papa Joe. I know this guy. It's personal. . . . Jody is gonna get his money back, or die trying."

Alexa went forward to tell the pilot while Shane put his head back on the seat and closed his eyes. He was bone-tired. Sleep came in seconds.

■ ■ ■

They were at Ryder Field . . . back in the sixth grade. Jody in his Pirates uniform, smiling at Shane . . . slamming a ball into his pitcher's mitt, pulling it out, throwing it back again. "Good game, Hot Sauce . . . Way t'call the hitters."

"You threw the Ks," Shane answered, his own voice bright and happy.

"We're a team. Nothing can ever change that." Jody grinned.

Shane suddenly felt the need to tell Jody how he really felt: how much his friendship meant . . . what it was like to have been left at a hospital . . . to have never known his own parents . . . to be raised by strangers. How he never knew his mother. How he would lie in bed wondering why she had left him. Who was she? Why didn't she care enough to keep him? "You're all I have," Shane finally said. "You're the only one who ever cared about me."

Little Jody grinned and dropped the ball, throwing his arm around his ten-year-old buddy. "Don't you forget it, Hot Sauce."

"I'll never forget," Shane said, with all his heart. "You have my solemn promise."

CITY OF ANGELS 47

THEY MADE A fuel stop at Love Field in Dallas. Alexa had radioed ahead and arranged for a medical team to take a look at Shane's leg. The bullet had passed through the lastus laterus muscle, barely missing the abductor canal.

So much for karma.

The slug had threaded its way through a complex maze of potential disasters while doing very little damage. They stitched and bandaged him up, gave him a shot of antibiotics, then told him to check with a doctor in L.A.

They took off from Love Field an hour later.

Los Angeles was in the middle of a horrible inversion layer that trapped the city's smoggy pollutants like smoke under a blanket.

The Citation landed at Van Nuys airport at three-thirty in

the afternoon, taxied up to the small Customs shack at the end of Runway 2-6, and shut down.

Tony Filosiani was waiting for them beside the grandfather of the Crown Vics. The old beige and brown Ford fit the funky L.A. day.

"I'm sorry about the way this went down, Sergeant," the chief said as they deplaned. "I know we mind-fucked ya, but I didn't know what else t'do."

"It saved my life," Shane admitted as he limped over to the car and stood leaning against it. "It fooled me, so I fooled Jody."

"We been trying t'get a fix on this Lisa St. Marie person you radioed me about," Filosiani said, getting right to business. "We finally got an address from the whadda-ya-callit . . . from the taxes."

"The State Real Estate Tax Board?" Alexa corrected.

"Yeah. She bought a condo in Century City two years ago. The address just came in. I got a five-man jump-out squad stationed over there. They say, according to the doorman, she's upstairs. They got the place covered till we get there."

"Let's go. I'll fill you in on the way," Shane said through punched and swollen lips. Then he turned to Jo-Jo and Luis. "Thanks for the backup, guys." He shook hands with Knight.

When the fed pulled his hand back, he found that he had the STD transmitter in his palm.

"I found that floating in the airplane toilet," Shane said. "Guess it's yours."

"Damn . . . I hope ya washed it off," Knight said, glowering at the little white pill.

Shane shook hands with Rosario. "Stay in touch, *amigo*,"

he said, then turned and opened the rear door of the plainwrap. As he slid into the chief's musty car, Shane could see that true to form, the Day-Glo Dago had cut himself no slack when it came to the perks of office. The backseat was torn, and the car smelled of stale tobacco.

Alexa paused to say good-bye to Jo-Jo and Luis, kissing both of them lightly on the cheek. "You guys are the best," she told them.

"Hear that, you little Cuban faggot?" Jo-Jo said, grinning. "I'm the best."

"Ain't what she told me," Luis said, winking at Alexa. "She told me she thinks you're the biggest, slowest sack a'shit this side a'the post office."

"At least I don't roast no live chickens in motel bathtubs, you greasy Santeria."

Chief Filosiani shook his head in mock distress, but he was grinning as he settled behind the wheel. Alexa followed, and Chief Filosiani pulled away from the Customs building.

"Them two . . . Jesus," he said, shaking his head. "They never stop with that shit."

Filosiani turned onto the 101 Freeway, took it to the 405, then over the hill into West L.A.

In less than twenty minutes they were in Century City, pulling up to a twenty-story high-rise with a huge marble monument sign out front that announced the building: CENTURY PARK WEST.

The tall steel-and-glass tower poked up through the afternoon sky, its top-floor mirrored windows disappearing into the brown L.A. muck.

They were met by Lieutenant Lincoln Heart, who was leading the team of jump-outs. Heart was ebony black, and his short-sleeved Class C uniform barely concealed a physique of rippling muscles.

There were two blue-uniformed officers waiting in the lobby. They learned that two more were already up on Lisa's floor, watching her apartment.

"You got a floor plan?" Filosiani asked.

"Yep, got it from the building manager. Ms. St. Marie's got an east view, two-bedroom," Lieutenant Heart said as he opened a folded Xerox of the plan. They studied it while Heart continued: "According to the doorman, she came home last night 'bout midnight. Her car's still in the underground garage. Far as he knows, she hasn't left and nobody's been up to see her." Lieutenant Heart reached into his pocket and produced a key. "Here's the master to that floor."

"How you wanna do this, Lieutenant Hamilton?" Filosiani quizzed Alexa. It was his management style to be a coach to his officers but let them run the operations.

Shane smiled when he called her "Lieutenant," realizing that in his absence, her promotion had come through.

"We need to get Ms. St. Marie to cooperate, and I think Shane has the best chance of turning her. We may need to use her as bait to lure Jody. If she knows where Papa Joe is, we'll need to get that, too." Alexa looked over at Shane. "For all those reasons, Shane should be on point," Alexa said.

"Good analysis," Filosiani noted. "I agree."

"How's the leg feel?" Alexa asked.

"Okay," Shane said, and surprisingly, aside from some occasional throbbing and muscle weakness, he had very little pain. "Lemme give it a try. But I have to do it alone. If we do a SWAT-type entry, she'll clam up."

Filosiani nodded.

"Anybody got a piece I could borrow?" Shane asked.

"Here," Alexa said, "I have a backup." She handed him another Astra 9.

"What is it with you and these little Spanish Astras?" He grinned.

She smiled. "Great little purse gun, eight-shot clip, no hammer, doesn't snag coming out. Stop complaining . . . you still owe me four hundred for the last one."

He chambered the Astra and stuck it into his belt, zippering his light windbreaker over it. Then the four of them stepped onto the elevator.

They rode in silence, listening to the innocuous elevator music and light chimes that announced each passing floor. As the elevator stopped, Lieutenant Heart gave Shane the master key.

They exited on sixteen—Lisa's floor. As they got out of the elevator, they saw two more of Lieutenant Heart's blue shirts watching Lisa's door from the stairwell up the hall.

"You're up," Filosiani said. "Number sixteen-twelve."

Shane limped on his bad leg across the plush carpet to Lisa's apartment while Filosiani motioned to the men in the stairwell to stay back.

He rang the bell next to a pair of massive oak double doors. He could hear the chimes inside, waited, then tried again.

Nothing.

He knocked on the door and, when nobody answered, took out the master key and silently fitted it into the lock. He pulled Alexa's Astra, jacked a round into the pipe, then quietly pushed the door open.

The hallway was mirrored on both sides to give the narrow corridor a wider feel.

An old fear hit him.

Shane hated going through mirrored entries when he was shaking a house; too easy to get spotted. He took a deep breath before quickly slipping into the white-on-white condo. He stopped just before entering the living room, keeping his back flat to the mirrored wall on the right, using the mirrors opposite him to search the living room. His ears were straining for any sound of movement. Nothing.

Out of the corner of his vision, he saw Alexa appear in the front doorway with yet another Astra in her right hand. She had more of those little automatics than the Spanish Mafia. He put a finger to his lips and motioned for her to stay outside.

She nodded and held her position as Shane moved carefully into the empty living room. He slid past the wall-to-ceiling plate-glass window and checked the kitchen.

Nothing.

He worked his way down the apartment's center hall, pausing at the guest bedroom door, pushing it slowly open, checking inside.

Empty.

He continued on to the master suite. He had a premonition of death, almost as if he could see around the corner into the future. A cold fear was beginning to ice the edges of his stomach. He cracked the bedroom door and looked in. The bed was mussed, but empty. He entered cautiously, checking the perimeter of the room first. The suite was spacious, dominated by a king-size bed and a plate-glass window that took in the smog-drenched Hillcrest Country Club sixteen stories below.

The bedroom was deserted. The bathroom wasn't.

He found her there, naked.

It wasn't pretty.

What human beings were capable of doing to one another sometimes horrified him.

She was lying in her tub brutally shot in five places. Both kneecaps were shattered, as well as both elbows. The kill shot had opened a gaping hole in the center of her chest. Lisa had been blond and pale in life, but lying in her tub, naked and bloodless, she looked like a broken doll in its white porcelain container. Papery skin wrapped her lifeless body like thin, transparent tissue. Her blond hair was tipped in dried blood, turning the feathered ends red.

Sex goddess in repose.

"Shit!" Shane heard himself say, then called out in a loud voice, "I've got her! It's clear, master bath!"

In seconds, Alexa and Filosiani entered with Lieutenant Heart and the two jump-outs from the stairwell.

"Okay," Filosiani said as soon as he saw the body. "Everybody out. This here's a crime scene. Let's not foul it for Forensics with our own prints and fibers."

They all backed out of the bathroom and stood in the hall.

"Jody's our doer," Shane said softly.

"Then he's turning into a monster," Alexa said softly.

"No," Shane answered, "he's just decided not to hide it anymore."

Filosiani said, "I'll get Homicide out here. My guess is, if she knew where Sandro Mantoor and José Mondragon are, then Jody musta found out before he killed her."

"She was pretty tough," Alexa said, with a tinge of admiration as she looked toward the bedroom door. "She must have taken all four joint shots before she talked. After he got what he wanted, he put the fifth round through her heart."

"Sure is the way it looks." Shane shuddered.

"So how do we find Papa Joe?" Alexa said. "If Jody gets to him first, he'll get the money, kill Sandy and José, and run. Once he gets out of the country, we'll lose jurisdiction and probably never find him."

"There's a guy, an ex-Air Unit pilot named David VanKirk," Shane said. "IAD terminated him for making night flights, smuggling dope in from Mexico with his police helicopter. If you've still got an address, I'd send somebody out to his place to sit on him. Jody may try and use that chopper to get outta California."

"Good idea," Filosiani said. Because his cell phone wasn't working in this steel-and-glass building, he ran toward the elevator on his way outside to call Homicide and gather up a surveillance detail on David VanKirk.

"This is a dead end, of course," Alexa said softly. "Without Lisa, we've got nothing . . . nobody . . . no place to start. My guess is Jody won't take a chance on VanKirk."

Shane nodded.

However, there was one other possibility that began tickling Shane's thoughts. It was a huge long shot, but he had been on such a cold streak, he figured he was due. He hoped it was time for him to finally cash a winner.

48

MESSENGER

"TREMAINE LANE WAS an L.A. County Sheriff." Shane was standing outside of Century Park East with Lisa and Filosiani. The Homicide team had just arrived, and the Forensics techs were unpacking their blue windowless van.

"Tremaine wasn't in Shephard's file. We don't have any background on him," Alexa answered.

"He was working undercover. The whole Viking thing started at the Sheriff's Department. I always wondered if maybe the culture had somehow migrated to us, through one of these joint-ops task forces we're always running. Tremaine and Hector Rodriquez were tight. Is there any way to pull Sergeant Rodriquez's assignment jacket to see if he ever worked a joint-op with Tremaine Lane?"

"Easy enough," Filosiani said, then picked up the radio on

the nearest squad car and got a patch through to the Records Division. He identified himself, told them what he wanted, and asked for a rush.

"Roger that, sir," the female Records Division clerk said. In less than a minute, she was back on the air. "In July of '99, Sergeant Hector Rodriquez of SWAT was assigned to the Cobra Unit in the Valley. Cobra was working with L.A. Impact, which included half a dozen county sheriffs. They worked a big arms deal in the Sunland. Ten Class A felony arrests came down."

"Do you have the names of the other sheriffs who were in on that bust?" Filosiani asked.

"No, sir. You have to get that from Sheriff Messenger's office."

"Call over there and tell Bill Messenger I need a meeting. Tell him it can't wait. I'll be there in ten minutes."

■ ■ ■

At five-foot-seven and 135 pounds, Bill Messenger barely made the Sheriff's Department height and weight regs. He was a dark-complexioned, second-generation Egyptian American with close-cropped, silver-gray hair and a penchant for perfectly tailored, double-breasted suits. The jacket he was wearing had brass buttons on it, giving him a distinct Napoleonic tilt. Titanium-framed glasses, as spartan as his waistline, rested atop a Roman nose.

"What's the emergency, Tony?" Messenger said, negotiating his way across his cream and tan office, threading past two form-over-function Danish modern chairs that squatted on delicate tapered legs like futuristic spiders. He shook hands with Tony, Shane, and Alexa. The two L.A. law-enforcement heads were exactly the same height, but that's where the similarities ended. Standing nose to nose, they were the yin and yang of law enforcement. The Day-Glo Dago radiated warmth of personality, while William "Bill" Messenger had the emotional temperature of a garden snake.

"We got a problem," Tony said, looking at the door. "Mind if I close that?"

"My secretary doesn't leak," Messenger said testily.

"Yeah, but her husband might." Tony kicked the door shut, and by mistake it closed too hard, slamming loudly.

Bill Messenger winced.

"Who are these people?" the sheriff asked, looking at Shane and Alexa.

"This is Lieutenant Alexa Hamilton," Tony began.

"The Medal of Valor winner who died a week ago?" Messenger said, and cocked a bushy eyebrow.

"I'll get to that. And this is Sergeant Shane Scully," Tony added.

"The man who killed her. You run a strange shop, Tony." Messenger was glaring at both of them.

"The staged killing of Lieutenant Hamilton was part of an undercover op," Filosiani said. "This pertains to the problem you had a few years back with that rogue group of sheriffs who called themselves Vikings."

"Not to quibble, but that didn't happen on my watch. Sheriff Bloch hosted that disaster. However, I ended up with the mop and pail after he died."

"The culture has spread to us," Tony said bluntly.

"Too bad. The Vikings were racists . . . minority-hating sheriffs who took their suspects down into county aqueducts and beat them. I had my hands full, and was never sure I rooted them all out. I fielded three civil-liberties lawsuits when I tried to arrange a lineup to check my men for that silly tattoo they all had on their ankles. 'Illegal body search.' The courts called it. 'Unconstitutional' . . . 'Lack of probable cause.' " He shook his head sadly. "They want a perfect department, but they won't let me do what it takes to weed out the bad apples."

"The LAPD Vikings aren't racists," Shane said. "But they are killers."

"What makes you say they're not racists?" Messenger challenged. " 'Cause my Vikings did everything but burn crosses and hang people from trees."

"I know they aren't, because I've been undercover with them for the past week."

"That's why you staged the phony shooting?" Messenger said, looking at Tony. "To set his cover?"

"Yeah, but it's a long story, and I don't really have time for it now," Filosiani said. "The reason we're here is that we found out one of your deputies, Sergeant Tremaine Lane, was working inside that LAPD deep-cover unit without my knowledge. We now believe he was a Sheriff's Department plant reporting back to you, Bill."

"I think not," Messenger said, but his bearing had suddenly turned rigid.

"Your undercover is dead," Shane said. "Cut to pieces. Skinned alive by a death-squad maniac, then left to die hanging on a fence in Colombia. I was there when it happened."

"I see." Messenger didn't move.

"I understand you have a responsibility to protect the identity of your UCs," Tony said. " 'Specially since you've been infiltrating a sister law-enforcement agency without notifying its chief in advance," he added sharply. "But the fact is, we're running short on time and I'd really appreciate it if I could cut through the fuckin' cow shit and get a straight answer here before more people die."

Sheriff Messenger finally moved. He crossed the room and actually threw the lock on the door, which moments before he had insisted they leave open. Then he turned and walked back to the center of the room, using the little journey around his spacious office to compose his thoughts.

"Okay," he finally said. "Let's say, for the sake of argument, that Sergeant Lane *was* working a special assignment for me . . . and now you say he's dead?"

"Yes, sir," Shane said. "He had joined an off-the-books LAPD squad who also called themselves Vikings, complete with the same ankle tattoos as your sheriffs. I think Tremaine got duked into the unit by one of our SWAT sergeants, Hector Rodriquez, who worked a joint-ops with him in the Valley two years ago."

"How do I know my guy's really dead?" Messenger said.

" 'Cause I'm telling you. I was there! I saw him die!"

"Excuse me for doubting your word, Sergeant, but I watch the news. I understand your own department ran a psychological profile on you just last year. You could be delusional, a disenfranchised troublemaker. Owing to the sensitivity of all this, you're going to have to tell me something more to convince me."

"Tremaine and I got captured in Colombia, in a town just across the Venezuelan border, called Maicao. His skin was peeled off in strips. Jesus . . . what the hell else you want from me?" Shane was starting to get hot, glowering at the emotionless little man.

"Calm down, Sergeant," Tony said softly. "Bill's gonna help out . . . 'cause if he don't, I'm gonna run a stick through his nuts and roast 'em over a slow fire in the governor's office."

"Yeah, and just how you think you're gonna do that, Tony?"

"You put a guy in my department without clearing it with me first. I'll get the district attorney to subpoena your Command Directive, then I'll roll it up and jam it so far up your ass, you'll be able to start breathing through it."

The county sheriff took off his titanium glasses, pulled a silk handkerchief out of his pocket, and went to work giving the lenses a thorough cleaning . . . then he slipped them carefully back onto his nose.

"Okay, let's also say, just for the hell of it, that I might acknowledge that Sergeant Lane was working in an undercover capacity inside your department." Messenger was speaking slower now, as if his words had solemn weight. "And let's say he stumbled into your rogue Viking unit. Since your man here says he's dead and can't report in, that would seem to end it. How am I supposed to help you?"

"He'd been undercover for two months. . . . I don't know how you guys supervise UCs, Bill, but over in my 'strange' shop, we set up phone drops, get interim reports. So unless you're running this place like a Carnival Cruise, you got his re-back file. We need those reports. We need to know everything Sergeant Lane found out, 'cause this thing is coming unglued. Most of that unit is already dead, and the ones who ain't are running for the airport. Like I said, we don't have a lotta time."

Bill Messenger pushed his titanium rims higher up on his nose. He went to his desk, opened a bottom drawer, then took out a metal lockbox. He opened it, pulled out a file, and threw it on the desk between them.

"You keep the ops reports in your desk drawer?" Tony said, smiling.

"For obvious reasons, I was supervising the Viking mop-up myself," Messenger said in a hard, clipped voice. "What do you need to know?"

"We're trying to get a line on an Argentine national named José Mondragon," Tony said. "We need to know where he lives when he's in L.A. We think one of our Viking cops is about to kill him. We need José alive, to make a money-laundering case we're settin' up."

"I can already tell you his L.A. residence's not in there. He stayed in hotels," Messenger said, motioning toward the manila folder. "But help yourself."

Shane picked up the file, opened it, and found the section on José Mondragon. "House in Palm Springs," he read. "We already know about that."

"No kidding," Messenger complained. "You hit that place harder than a Mexican piñata. That was the one good contact point we had."

"Maybe if we'd known you guys were in on our case, we coulda worked something else out," Tony fired back.

Shane scanned Tremaine's report quickly: "José is married to a diplomat's daughter. Didn't know that. Lives half the year in Argentina." He looked up. "Anything in here about an Argentine colonel named Raphael Aziz?" Shane asked.

Messenger shook his head sharply, so Shane kept scanning Tremaine's UC report. "Polo . . . Says here José's a member of the L.A. Polo Club. Plays polo at Will Rogers Park in Santa Monica." Shane looked up at Messenger.

"We checked that out. José stopped playing there two years ago, then shipped his polo pony back to Argentina. It's a dead end."

Shane kept reading. "His license plate number for his Jag is in here. Did you run it?"

"Yep," Messenger said stiffly. "Car is registered to one of Blackstone's companies in Switzerland, no local address."

"Dead end," Alexa said.

The sheriff nodded.

"Known associates, Lisa St. Marie," Shane read.

"She'd be a good place to start," Messenger said quickly. "Go find her. José Mondragon used her as a sexual spy, so if you roll her, she probably has some good stuff on him."

"Lisa ain't gonna be much help," Tony said.

"Why not?"

"She just ain't."

"I thought we were cooperating," Messenger snapped.

"She was tortured and shot five times in her condo a few hours ago. She's at the morgue."

The diminutive sheriff didn't react.

Shane kept reading: "He once kept a single-engine plane at the Santa Monica Airport, but sold it two years ago." Shane looked up. "If he played polo in Santa Monica and flew his plane out there, I wonder if he had a house out there, too."

"Don't know. Sounds like a good place to start." Messenger glanced at his watch, anxious to be rid of them. "Why don't you check it out?"

Shane closed the file and looked up at the sheriff. "Can we get a copy of this?" he asked. "I'd like to look it over more carefully."

"If my man is dead, then you can have it. But you'll have to take a poly first. I want to know you're telling the truth about all this."

"Good going, Bill. Good cooperation," Filosiani snapped.

"Tony, Tony, Tony," Messenger sighed. "You never cooperated with anybody. Not once in your whole career. I can't take any more bad press on this Viking thing. This all started here at the Sheriff's Department, so if you kick it up again, I'm gonna have to suffer through a bunch of newspaper and TV recaps. We looked like a buncha Klansmen when the *Los Angeles Times* broke that piece three years ago. I'm finally getting past it. If it's spread to your department, I'm sorry, but my responsibility is to see it's not back here. That's what Sergeant Lane was trying to determine."

"I'll take the polygraph," Shane said suddenly.

"All you gotta do is convince my poly operator that Sergeant Lane is really dead. If that's the case, then I can't protect him anymore, and you can have his files."

Shane took the polygraph and passed.

Half an hour later they left the sheriff's office with a copy of the classified folder.

When they reached the parking lot, they looked up and saw Bill Messenger staring down at them from his office window on the fourth floor of the big, boxy Sheriff's Building. He looked even tinier standing behind the huge expanse of glass.

"First time I actually liked that prick," Tony said as they got into the Crown Vic and pulled away.

49

RULES

THEY READ THE file in Chief Filosiani's sparsely furnished office. There was nothing in the Sheriff's Department folder that gave them any clue to José Mondragon's whereabouts. After going over it several times, they began to lose hope.

Shane used the phone in the chief's office to call Chooch at Filosiani's house.

"Thank God, you're safe, man," his son said, relief in his voice.

"Get your stuff ready; Alexa and I will be over to get you in an hour."

They checked the Santa Monica Polo Club and talked to the club manager, who confirmed that José Mondragon had not been a member for years. The club had no address on file for him, or anybody else for that matter; they didn't even have a membership list because all you needed to play was a horse and enough friends to make up a team. The team captains rounded up their players and scheduled the matches. The manager did remember José's horse, though, because he said it was a world-class polo pony, a coal-black Arabian named Sir Anthony of Aquitaine. He confirmed what Bill Messenger had told them. The horse had been shipped to Argentina two years ago.

The polo club was a dead end.

So was the airport where José had kept the plane. The Cessna he flew didn't even belong to him. It was leased from an FBO and, true to José's practice, the Blackstone Corporation was the only name on the lease. Nobody at the airfield even remembered him.

"I'm out of ideas," Shane said as he limped out of the chief's office with Tony and Alexa. They walked across the seafoam-green carpet, past the blond-wood paneling, and finally got into the large elevator. "Jody's so far ahead of us that if he knows where José is, he's already working on him like he did on Lisa," Shane continued. "José will be dead. Jody will have the money and be gone."

"But nobody knows where José is," Alexa countered. "Maybe Jody can't find him, either."

"Maybe," Shane said, but he didn't have much hope.

They climbed back into the chief's Crown Vic, Tony behind the wheel, Alexa in the front, Shane in the back. His leg was now throbbing horribly, but he clenched his jaw and tried to ignore the pain.

Twenty minutes later they pulled up in front of a very modest two-story Tudor with a small lawn and, judging from the depth of the lot, almost no backyard.

Chooch was waiting out front with his overnight bag at his feet. If the chief looked like a butcher, then Mary Filosiani was equally well cast as the butcher's wife. A pleasant, dark-haired woman in a print dress, she was standing beside Chooch. She kissed him good-bye, and Chooch walked up to the car.

Shane got out and gave his son a hug. "Boy, am I glad to see you," he said in Chooch's ear.

Chooch just hung on, his arms unabashedly around Shane. When he finally pulled back, he had tears in his eyes. "Man, I was so worried about you," Chooch said, looking at the damage to Shane's face.

"How was quarterback camp?"

"Get the fuck outta here," Chooch smiled. "I was only up there for ten hours before you got your big dumb ass kidnapped. So I came right back."

"Oh, yeah," Shane grinned. "I forgot. And watch your mouth."

The chief let them borrow the Crown Vic to drive back to Venice. "I been thinkin' I'd trade it in for a fresher model anyway," he smiled. "It's one thing tryin' to set a good example for the troops; it's another to ride around in a garbage can with wheels."

Shane threw Chooch's luggage into the back and got behind the wheel.

■ ■ ■

They were silent for most of the drive back to Venice. Several times Shane looked over and saw Chooch or Alexa smiling at him.

"What?" he said, and suddenly they all started laughing.

They pulled into the garage at the canal house and parked next to Shane's dusty Acura, then walked into the small kitchen, where Shane opened the freezer and pulled out a package of four frozen New York steaks. He set them on the counter to defrost.

"Let's get the barbecue going, Bud," he said to Chooch, who grinned and pulled a bag of charcoal briquettes from the cupboard. The boy took it outside and filled the orange Weber barbecue that was sitting on a small patch of poured concrete in the backyard.

It was just about dusk. Shane put his arm around Alexa as they looked out the sliding glass door at his son, starting the fire in the backyard. It was wonderful to be home, but bubbling under that relief was a strange, unsettled feeling.

"I know what you're thinking," Alexa said softly.

"Now you and Jody both can do it, huh? Walk right inside my head, without knocking."

"You feel like it's not over, but it is. Sometimes things just don't wrap up perfectly."

"Yeah, I know . . . it's just . . ."

"We're alive and we're together, babe," she said. "You and me and Chooch. What more can we ask for?"

"You're right, as usual." He snapped his fingers. "Just a minute. I forgot something." He turned and limped down the hall into the bedroom, where he opened the top dresser drawer and pulled out the engagement ring in Murray Steinberg's slightly crushed black-leather box.

Shane walked back outside, where he found Alexa and Chooch poking at the briquettes with long-handled tongs, spreading them out.

Shane turned and faced Alexa, took her hand, then slipped the two-carat engagement ring onto her finger. "There," he said, "now it's official."

"It's about time, is what it is," Chooch said, smiling. "But aren't you supposed to ask her first?"

"She said yes two days ago," Shane told him, taking her in his arms as Chooch smiled his approval.

As the setting sun lit the edges of the rippling canal, Shane cooked the steaks, Alexa made a salad, and Chooch set the table.

They sat in the backyard and ate quietly, counting their blessings, grinning like children.

Later that night, Shane and Alexa made love in his bed while Chooch watched TV in the living room.

Shane felt as if he had completed an impossible journey. He had been looking for something that didn't exist, but in its place he had found something even more valuable.

If only he hadn't lost Jody. If only Jody hadn't confessed that he'd never cared . . . that he hadn't loved Shane the way Shane had once loved him. That realization caused a sadness that he suspected was produced by betrayal as much as by loss. It touched on old issues of abandonment that he had lugged around his entire life. Shane's parents had dumped him at a hospital's back door like human trash. He had been infant number 732. City Services finally named him Shane. He had picked the name Scully, after his favorite baseball announcer, Vince Scully. But that first betrayal by his parents had caused an ache inside of him that had never left.

Why did my mother leave me like that? Didn't she care?

He had asked himself these same two questions over and over again, day after day, year after year, until they had almost lost their meaning.

The Deans had filled in some of the emptiness, until Jody

had snatched it away again, coming back into his life two weeks ago.

Alexa had fallen asleep beside him, but he lay awake, thinking and listening to the TV in the other room.

He fell asleep some time during Leno.

• • •

Jody had his back to a field where beautiful horses ran, galloping around the edges of the wooden perimeter fence. The horses came to an abrupt halt each time they reached the rail, sticking their magnificent heads over, snorting angry air from flared nostrils, looking across the fence line at the distant city, before turning and galloping back across the field to the other side. But Jody didn't turn to watch them. His eyes were only on Shane.

"You don't get to play unless you sign up," Jody said. "You have to register first."

"I know," Shane answered. "But it sure would be fun to play."

"They have rules about that," Jody said seriously.

"I know," Shane said. "Rules."

"It's not like Little League, where everybody can play," Jody continued. "Here, you have to register. They have to know who you are."

"I know," Shane said. "Rules—you have to register."

Riders were now magically up on the horses, galloping across the open field in their team shirts, swinging their polo mallets at the little white ball that flew energetically with each whack. As it came close to where they were standing, Shane was surprised to see that it was a baseball they were hitting.

"I have to go," Jody said. "You can stay and watch, but don't get too close. They have rules about that, too."

"I know . . ." Shane said.

Then Jody turned and walked out of the dream.

The horses were now galloping near the fence. The baseball flew by the spot where Shane was standing, and the horses raced to catch it. He could feel the slipstreaming air against his face as they thundered past.

"Rules," Shane said softly in the darkened bedroom, the word still on his lips as he opened his eyes.

When he spoke, he woke Alexa, and she turned over and looked at him. "What?" she asked.

Shane wasn't sure. He just knew that he was terribly troubled by the innocuous dream, as if something was lying there on the bottom of his subconscious, something important that he'd forgotten to pursue, but he didn't know what it was. "Rules in polo," he said. "Everybody has to register, or they can't play."

"What?" Alexa looked at the digital clock. "God, it's twelve-thirty," she said, turning on the bedside lamp.

"Maybe we should make sure Chooch got to bed and isn't sleeping on the couch out there." She got up, put on her robe, and left the bedroom.

"Rules," Shane repeated, trying to figure out what his subconscious was trying to tell him. "Everybody has rules." He sat up in bed, his heart pounding because he knew this was important but didn't, for the life of him, know why.

He had spoken for ten minutes on the phone to the polo club guy. They *didn't* have rules; that was the point. The man had stated that all you needed was a horse and a team to play on. "Rules," he said again, as Alexa returned to the room.

"What?"

"Everybody has rules. You can't play without registering first."

She turned off the light. "Chooch is in his bedroom, conked."

"Good."

"What on earth are you talking about?"

"A dream," he said. "I was with Jody, watching a bunch of men playing polo, only they were hitting a baseball, and in my dream he said, 'You don't get to play unless you register,' that you can't play because there are rules. . . ."

She looked at him. "Okay, there are rules. How does that apply?"

"I don't know. . . ." He looked at her and shook his head ruefully. "Polo . . . rules in polo. Of course, there're rules in polo. Shit."

She smiled and kissed him then got back into bed. Shane hugged her, feeling her breath on his neck, the slow beating of her heart, and then, wrapped in her safe cocoon, he was quickly asleep.

He was back on the polo field. Only now he was petting a huge Arabian horse that poked his nose over the fence where Shane was standing. He knew, without asking, that the horse was Sir Anthony of Aquitaine. He was coal-black and eating a cube of sugar out of Shane's hand.

"I've never seen a horse as beautiful as you," he said in the dream.

The stallion snorted. His black coat was shining. "I'd sure love to have a horse like you," Shane said in wonder. "If you ever have a colt . . ."

Shane suddenly woke up again, this time with a start. His heart was pounding, slamming in his chest. *Shit,* he thought as he lay in bed. *What is this?*

He got out of bed and quietly limped out of the room. Wearing only his Jockey shorts, he went down the hall, then out into the backyard, where he sat in one of the metal chairs and watched the quarter-moon ripple on the still water. His thigh had been bandaged with white medical wrap, but some of the stitches must have broken loose, because a dried bloodstain the size of a grapefruit had leaked through the gauze. He was going to have to get his wounded thigh redressed.

"Rules," he said again softly, returning to his dream. "Horses . . . polo . . ." *You can't ride. . . . Why can't you ride? You can't own an Arabian horse without . . . without what? Shit.* He sat there turning it over in his mind. *You have to register to ride . . . to play? Why do I want a damn horse, a colt? Why? I'd have to register. I'd . . .*

He lunged out of the chair, headed into the house, turned on the lights in the bedroom, and put a hand on Alexa's shoulder.

She rolled over and glared at him. "What are you doing?" she asked. "Are you ever going to sleep?"

"Listen, if you owned an Arabian horse, wouldn't you have to list him with some kind of Thoroughbred registry?"

"I guess . . ."

"You do, you have to. There're rules about it. I think I read somewhere with all Thoroughbreds, you have to register them to protect the bloodlines and stud fees. Thoroughbred horses are registered at birth . . . when they're colts. There's some kinda Arabian horse registry."

"So?"

"It'll have the address of the owner."

"Unless his horse is registered to Blackstone Corporation in Switzerland, like everything else this guy owns."

"Sir Anthony of Aquitaine?" Shane smiled. "No fucking way. That horse is his status symbol. He might register his car or a house to the company, but this animal's a champion. . . . It's in Papa Joe's name. Count on it. José is in the fucking horse registry, I'll bet you anything. It'll be somewhere on the Internet."

She rolled out of bed and put on her robe. "Let's get Chooch out of the sack. He's our best computer jock."

It was so easy, it was almost ridiculous. The registry was called exactly what Shane had guessed: the Arabian Horse Registry. Sir Anthony of Aquitaine was in the stallion listings. Below that was a lot of stuff about his bloodline: out of this sire and that mare, going back six generations, but at the bottom was the owner's name and address, right there on the screen:

> José Luis Mondragon
> 2457 Malibu Canyon Road
> Malibu, California

50

COWBOYS AND INDIANS

THEY CALLED TONY Filosiani from the Pacific Coast Highway, waking him up.

"Malibu?" he said after Alexa filled him in over her cell phone. "You guys go in the county without Sheriff's Department jurisdiction and Messenger will throw one a'his Egyptian conniptions."

"Then call him and get us some backup," Alexa said.

"I'll try."

Shane slowed down the Acura to make the turnoff from PCH onto Malibu Canyon Road. That two-lane highway climbed up into the coastal mountains, becoming a dark, treacherous, winding two-lane that widened periodically to include a center passing lane. The road snaked along a ridge above a deep river gorge, and they flashed by a sign that said they were leaving Ventura and passing back into L.A. County. Shane was slowing, looking for the address. There were very few intersecting roads on the two-lane highway and even fewer driveways. Shane had to be careful not to overdrive his headlights and shoot past 2457 Malibu Canyon Road.

Then he saw it.

The address was painted on a mailbox on the left-hand canyon side of the road. Shane braked hard, snapping his headlights off as he made the turn, heading slowly down the dirt drive into the canyon below. The driveway was rutted from a recent rain. It headed down, switching back and forth, into the narrow valley.

"Wait a minute," Alexa said. "Stop."

Shane put on the brakes. "What?"

"We can't go down there without Sheriff's backup," she said.

"If Jody's down there, I want him."

"You aren't thinking straight."

"Is that any way to talk to your future husband?" he scowled theatrically. "Gimme my ring back."

"You're not man enough to take it, buster." She hit him playfully on the shoulder with the back of her hand. "If we wait, we get two things—we get backup, and we get jurisdiction."

"I haven't had a shred of jurisdiction since I choppered outta that fuckin' hangar two weeks ago. And as far as backup goes, guess what?" She stared at him apprehensively. "You're it."

"Okay, but at least don't drive all the way down there. Let's find a hole in the bushes and park it."

"Good suggestion. I've got enough Bondo in this sled already."

They rolled slowly down the road, keeping the headlights off and the engine on, with Shane riding the brake.

Finally, they could see the roofs of some ranch buildings below, so Shane started looking for a place to stash the Acura. He found a good spot about a quarter mile from the end of the dirt driveway: a trash area with two large Dumpsters. Shane rolled the car in between the two metal bins and shut off the engine, then reached up and pulled the bulb out of the dome light on the headliner. He had long before removed the plastic cover for easy access. He stuck the bulb in the ashtray, then both of them quietly opened the doors and slipped out of the car.

"Okay," he whispered, "I'm taking point."

"Will you cut it out with the John Wayne bullshit? Let's just move on this together."

"No," he said sharply. "I want you back twenty yards at least."

"Why? Because you're afraid I might stop one?"

"Yeah," Shane said.

"Or is it because, if you find Jody, you're gonna take him out and you don't want a witness?"

Shane gave her such a withering scowl that she shrugged. "Just asking."

They headed down the drive with Shane out front, limping badly but keeping about twenty yards of separation. When he came to the end of the road, he kneeled down to check the surroundings. Pain shot up his leg.

There were two horse barns, some stables, and three houses in a cluster next to a training corral that contained a center turnstile. Long metal bridle poles used for breaking horses carouseled out from the turnstile. There were lights on in the main house and a couple of spots on light poles over by the corral that threw a dim glow over the entire front yard. Two empty cars were parked by the main house.

Then Shane saw the big blue and white motor home. It was under some shade trees, about thirty yards to his left.

"Jody's here," Shane whispered to Alexa, who had moved up and was just kneeling down beside him.

"How do you know?"

He pointed at the thirty-seven-foot, double-axle rig. "That's his. We used it to go to Palm Springs, dropped it in the Valley before we left for Aruba."

"How did he get that monster down this narrow, winding road?" she asked.

"You're right. There must be another way in and out of here."

"What're you gonna do?"

"There used to be an auto-mag in that rig before we left town. It was Victory Smith's. Maybe it's still there. I'd like to get my hands on it. Not that I don't love these little Spanish Astras," he said, smiling.

"Shane," she said softly. "I think . . ."

"I know, wait for the sheriff. Tell you what, why don't you go back up the road and flag him down when he gets here."

"Right. Great idea, dick-brain."

Shane didn't respond but moved off, heading toward the motor home.

He was thankful for the quarter moon that gave a little light but didn't flood the yard. He crept along the perimeter, out of range of the corral lights, hugging the moon shadows until he was at the back of the motor home. He paused to listen, heard nothing and snuck up the side, pulled Alexa's Astra, thumbed off the safety, and tried the door handle.

Unlocked.

Shane pulled open the metal door and looked back. Alexa had moved up behind him to take a cover position at the rear of the vehicle. She had her gun in both hands, held slightly up in a range-ready firing stance. From there, she was in a good position to protect his back. He nodded at her, then carefully climbed up the three steps into the motor home.

Sandro Mantoor was inside . . .

He had been hacked to death, then dismembered. His head was sitting in the sink, staring with lifeless eyes at a spot about a foot over Shane's head.

"Fuck," he whispered, afraid to inhale, swallowing hard to keep his stomach bile down. The carnage was almost impossible to absorb. Blood squished in the carpeting under his feet. He found Sandy's arms on the double bed; his torso in the stall shower. Then he heard movement behind him. He spun and aimed the Astra at the door.

Alexa's face poked through the opening, looking in at him. Shane hurried to keep her from coming inside. He met her at the threshold, blocking her view of the mutilation, quickly pushing her outside and closing the door behind him.

She saw his pale expression. "What is it?" she asked. "What's in there?"

"He . . . he . . ." Shane stopped, took a deep breath. "It's a mess in there. You don't wanna see it. He butchered a guy—Sandro Mantoor. He's in pieces all over the place. Head's in the fucking sink."

"God, no . . ."

Shane was shaking now; his wounded leg felt weak and was beginning to go numb.

"When you're on backup you're supposed to cover the exit line, not come inside," he said, anger replacing shock.

"I think I saw somebody coming out of the house a minute ago. He went into the barn carrying a valise."

"Was it Jody?"

"I don't know. I couldn't tell. Too far away."

"I'm gonna get closer. This time, back me up, okay? Don't move in unless something goes down."

He took off toward the house, his heart pounding. It took him almost five minutes to reach the west wall because he was favoring his left leg and because he had to stay wide to keep out of the light coming from the two poles by the corral. He hugged the perimeter of the yard before finally reaching the side of the house. He stood and peeked through the living-room window.

Papa Joe Mondragon was sitting in a chair, facing a wall. His head was slumped over, and he looked as though he was sleeping. Other than José, the room appeared empty. Shane made a slow circuit around the house to get to the east-side window, which would allow him a better view.

When he got there, he wished he hadn't. José's face had been beaten to a red pulp. He looked as if he was still breathing, but blood was running down his chin, dripping and staining his collar and crotch.

Shane wondered how Jody could have gone so far out of control.

Suddenly, cars were coming down the road. He turned around in time to see two Sheriff Department black-and-whites barreling into the yard. They weren't using sirens, but drove in with their gumballs flashing, throwing colored light all over the place.

Before Shane could plan his next move, two shots rang out—flat, barking sounds that came from the direction of the barn. One of the sheriffs who had just gotten out of his car went down immediately and started screaming in pain.

The sheriff's cars' bar lights strobed red and blue patterns across the front of the barn. Then Shane saw Alexa moving toward them, holding up her badge.

"Stop, throw down your weapon!" the second sheriff's deputy yelled at her, leveling a riot gun at her over his door.

"LAPD," she shouted, but kept coming.

"Throw down your gun. Get facedown on the ground!" the sheriff yelled back.

Now Shane heard a horse galloping. He turned and faced the sound but couldn't see anything, so he made his way around the side of the barn just in time to see a fleeing dark shape. The rider's head was low on the horse's neck, behind the mane. He spurred the animal on, galloping fast down the narrow trail, into a riverbed that was framed by narrow canyon walls.

Shane made a limping run across the open space toward the barn door.

Two more shots rang out. Then he heard Alexa scream, "No! He's a police officer." But the sheriff opened up on Shane anyway. Bullets whizzed all around, pinging and ricocheting off nearby farm equipment and thunking into the soft wood of the barn walls.

Shane dove inside the barn and slammed the door shut. The building was huge, with stalls on both sides. Shane had never been much of a horseback rider, limiting his saddle time to a couple of weekends at a dude ranch in Arizona, where he'd been more interested in his date than in any of the swayback nags stabled there. He grabbed a halter off a nearby hook, then opened the nearest stall containing a horse. It was a large chestnut bay with a black mane and tail. He wrapped the halter around the horse's neck and tied it to a corner post, found a bridle hanging in the stall, grabbed it, and tried to push it into the horse's mouth. The animal reared up and spit the bit back at him.

"Nice horsey," Shane said, sounding like a seven-year-old.

He finally wrestled the bridle on but decided he'd have to forgo the saddle. He'd wasted too much time already.

Shane pulled the stubborn bay out of the stall and led it out the back of the barn, where he tried to mount it. With his blown left leg, he was having no luck, so he pulled the horse over to a nearby stable rail and managed to get on by climbing up, then swinging aboard. He suddenly heard more sirens as additional sheriff's cars arrived.

He kicked the horse in the withers and it bolted out of the open corral with Shane barely aboard.

He was flying down the road behind the barn, desperately holding handfuls of the horse's coarse mane, almost dropping the reins and the Astra 9—all of them tangled in his white-knuckled grip.

The horse was galloping down the trail full tilt when Shane saw dark shapes coming at him fast. At the last second, he ducked and avoided being knocked senseless by a low branch. Soon he was away from the farm, galloping along the wet, sandy wash, the horse's metal shoes splashing water and ringing on stones. Shane's eyes were straining for any shape that resembled a man on horseback up ahead.

He was bouncing painfully on the horse's bony back, his nuts slamming mercilessly up between his legs.

Fuck this, he thought, reining in the horse and slowing him. The horse's footing was unsure in the rocky wash. He didn't want the animal to stumble and go down.

The wash narrowed, and Shane was forced to ride slowly down the center of the rocky stream. He was leaning down close to the horse's neck to avoid another low limb when a shot rang out and clipped a branch not three feet from him.

Shane lost his grip, fell off the horse, and splashed loudly into the stream. He lay still, the icy water flowing over him. The eight-shot Astra 9-millimeter was still in his hand. He'd managed to hold it high, keeping it dry.

He wasn't sure how long he waited there, but it seemed an eternity. He was freezing now; his whole body feeling as numb as his left leg.

"Who you think you're kidding, Hot Sauce? How long you gonna try and play dead?" his old friend called out to him from somewhere in the dark. Shane didn't answer. He tried to pinpoint the direction the sound was coming from.

"You were always a better catcher than an Indian." Jody's voice came down to him from about forty or fifty yards away, up high and on the right. Shane didn't think Jody could see him, or he would have fired again. He was trying to lure Shane into a conversation so he could find him and end it.

When another shot rang out, Shane's suspicions were confirmed. The bullet thunked into a rock forty or fifty feet to his right.

"So, Hot Sauce, who woulda ever figured it would come to this, huh?" Jody called out. "You an' me crawlin' around in the dirt. Cowboys and Indians."

Shane began to move slowly away from the voice, being careful to not splash any water. He thought he might have a slight advantage because he now had a rough fix on where Jody was, while Jody was obviously still trying to locate him. Jody had always won these games of hide-and-seek when they were kids. It was uncanny the way he could tell what Shane was thinking, where he would try to hide next.

Then, true to that memory, Jody echoed that very thought. "I could always find ya, Hot Sauce . . . and this won't be any different. Course, it doesn't have to end that way. We could make a deal."

Shane slipped out of the water, up onto the bank on the east side of the wash. He managed to squirm up the slight incline in front of him, finally reaching a spot behind some scrub brush. Once he was there, he used the foliage for a screen and sat up slowly.

"So, Shane . . . think it over. It doesn't have to end with you dead. Maybe we can still find some flex in the deal."

Shane thought he could see Jody about twenty yards off to the left behind some rocks, lit by the faint quarter moon. His old friend was looking down and to his right, searching the stream. Shane started to travel in a counterclockwise circle, staying out of Jody's vision, being careful not to crack a twig or kick a pebble.

"Throw out your gun and stand up," Jody called out. "We'll work something out. There's plenty here for both of us."

Shane kept inching slowly up the hill and around to his right. He finally worked his way to the flat ground behind Jody. He could now see the back of Jody's head and a piece of his right shoulder as his childhood friend huddled down behind a rocky outcropping. Shane edged closer, not sure if he could muster the courage to actually do what he now knew he had to.

And then, without any warning, Jody sensed him and spun around.

Something, God knows what, kept Shane from pulling the trigger and killing him in that instant when he had the chance. Immediately his advantage was lost, and now they were about ten feet apart, both holding handguns aimed at each other, the barrels glinting in the moonlight.

Shane could see the madness in Jody's eyes.

"Put the gun down, Jody." Shane's voice was shaking.

"You can't win, Hot Sauce. I'll know a split second before you do, and I'll beat ya."

"Put it down . . ."

"I'm sorry about what I told ya in Joe's desert house. That was a mistake. I never shoulda told ya I didn't care. I could see it in your eyes. . . . I broke it between us when I told ya that." He smiled weirdly. "But when I said I never felt love, well . . . that's not exactly right, Salsa. There were a few times I felt it, but I was always inside your head. I felt it through you."

"Put the gun down." Shane's voice was weak.

"I'll give ya a piece a'my end." Jody kicked the bag at his feet. "José transferred the cash. Hundred-thousand-dollar bearer bonds. The whole fifty mil is in this gym bag. I'm not talking a fifty-fifty split or anything screwy like that, 'cause I been through too much . . . been too far. But how 'bout ten percent? That's a good payday. Five mil. Then you and I go our separate ways. Least we don't end it this way . . . with you dead."

"Why did you butcher Sandro Mantoor like that?" Shane asked, his voice still shaking.

"Felt like it," Jody said without emotion. "Matter of fact,

there's something kinda sweet about it when ya do it slow like that."

Shane knew he had to end this. He had to pull the trigger. He couldn't trust Jody to the courts. He was smart and handsome. He might find a way to O.J. his way out, just like he always had before.

"Don't do it, Hot Sauce," Jody warned sharply. "Don't even think about it."

In that moment, Shane lost his resolve. Even though he knew Jody was a sociopath, a monster, he couldn't pull the trigger. Jody must have sensed that, too, because he went on talking.

"I may not have loved you, man," he said softly. "But that was only because I couldn't. That piece wasn't in me . . . just wasn't there. But, Shane, I respected you more than anybody I ever knew. That's why I'll cut this deal. I want us both alive. What's love anyway? It's just a buncha horseshit and a four-letter word."

And then, as if a long-hidden door had opened, Shane was suddenly inside Jody's head, just as Jody must have always been inside his.

What Shane saw was indescribable and horrible—black, poisonous, and beyond all reason.

They fired simultaneously.

51 HUNTINGTON HOUSE

A LL THE CHILDREN have their own beds and foot lockers," she said. "We have set morning bathroom times, and of course, we all eat together in Spring Hall. He'll be one of the youngest, but I think he'll be fine."

Shane was looking up at her. She was pleasant-looking with a round face, but she had acne. She smiled at him, so he smiled back.

"Will he go to school here, at Huntington House?" a woman he couldn't see asked.

He was holding her hand, but she was out of sight above him. Shane felt very tiny, forced to crane his neck up to see the pleasant woman with the acne.

"Yes, school will be here at Huntington House until the sixth grade and then, depending on how Shane does, we'll arrange *for him to attend either St. Augustus Elementary School, which is just a few blocks away, or he can go across town to Havenhurst."*

"Well, then, it's all settled," the invisible woman said.

"Fifty over ninety and falling," a man's voice said, piercing Shane's consciousness. A siren was somewhere behind him.

"Hit him with another A-shot, fifty cc's," a voice commanded.

"Come on, Shane," the pleasant woman with acne said. "We'll show you around." He held her hand, but he had never felt so alone. He was becoming agitated, even frightened. He could feel his heart begin to beat hard in his chest. What would happen to him? Who were these people?

"Heart rate and BP up again, but he's leaking inside. We're gonna need to get him typed, stat."

"Here's the playroom," the pleasant woman said. "Look at all the nice toys."

Shane tried to move toward the toys, but a hand pulled him back. "No, not now. It's not a play period yet."

He looked up at her but could no longer see her, either. He could now only hear her voice: "Play period's at three in the afternoon."

"Stand by with a crash unit. We've got a Code Blue coming in. ETA four minutes."

They were walking along a corridor where the walls were getting narrower and higher, until Shane felt overwhelmed and dwarfed by the place. It was getting dark, too. The lights suddenly dimmed.

"We'll show you where you're going to sleep," the pleasant woman said, but she now seemed far away. . . . Suddenly Shane was wandering alone in the dark and narrowing hallway. He

was getting smaller and smaller with each step. But a bright light, beautiful and pure, was coming from a crack under a doorway down the hall. Then he heard Jody.

"A fireman? Really? You wanna climb through a window with a hose? What kind of bullshit job is that?"

"But Jody, wouldn't it be neat to save somebody's life?"

"A fireman? Shit, I don't wanna be a fireman."

"What do you wanna be?"

"I don't know. I never know."

"This guy's in de-fib! Hit the paddles! Clear!"

He felt a sharp pain in his chest.

They were at Ryder Field in their Little League uniforms. Shane was rubbing the sore place on his chest.

"Jody, when I give you the curve sign, don't throw the fast-ball. You hit me in the chest. I wasn't ready," *Shane said. It was almost dark, and the park ranger hadn't turned on the field lights yet.*

"Just the heater." *Jody grinned.* "I'm gonna stick with the heater."

"Outta the way; hit him again! Clear!"

Something buzzed. A jolt hit his chest.

They were in Jody's bedroom with the lights out. Night music.

"A cop?" *Jody sneered.* "I thought you were gonna be a damn fireman."

"If you're a cop, you stand between right and wrong. You'd really get a chance to count."

"You believe that?"

"Hit it again!"

Sharp pain. A buckling explosion in his chest that for a moment brought the lights back on in Jody's bedroom.

He was looking at Jody in the other bed, propped up on an elbow, staring at him speculatively.

"We'll be friends forever," Shane told him, glad the lights were back on.

"No, we won't, Hot Sauce. It's not in the plan!"

"But that can't be, Jody. I'm like your brother," Shane pleaded.

"I'll give you something 'fore you go—something so you won't forget me."

"What is it?" Shane asked. "When do I get it?"

"When it's time. It's a secret," Jody grinned. "A special gift."

"I'm losing him," the man's voice said.

The towering walls disappeared, and Shane was bathed in a light so white and pure that he marveled at it. Then, almost as if he were being lifted by an invisible hand, he was flying fast and low, but rising quickly. Up . . . up . . . he went.

"My God, what fun," he laughed, banking into the light, streaking toward it until he almost reached its center. But then, without warning, he pulled up and hovered there, bathed in its radiant beauty. He glanced over and saw the Dean family floating somewhere beyond the light. Fred and Marge waved at him. . . . "Shane, we're so glad you're here," they told him.

He looked down and saw Alexa and Chooch below him.

Jody was there, too, standing on the pitcher's mound, frowning down at the rosin bag in his hand.

Suddenly, a woman he didn't know was floating toward him, smiling. She was beautiful, with rich, chestnut hair and his same blue eyes. She reached out to him.

"Come with me, son. We're together now." Her voice was soft, like music. "I never meant to leave you, but I couldn't help it. It was an accident."

*"Are you my mother?" he said, thinking this was perfect.
He wouldn't have to stay at Huntington House with strangers.
Now he could finally have a real home with a real family.*

*"Yes, I'm your mother," she said. "You have to believe I
always loved you. I wanted to keep you, darling. I had to leave,
but I was always here waiting, and now you've finally come to
me. Now you're finally—"*

Without warning, everything ended.

52

JODY'S GIFT

WHEN SHANE CAME to, he was in ICU and it was two weeks later. They told him he'd been in a coma produced by a gunshot wound to the head. Jody's bullet had entered his scalp just above the hairline at the parietal bone and had traveled a scary, improbable path, hugging the subcutaneous connective tissue between his scalp and scull. It cracked the bone over the cerebellum in three places, then exited the back of his head at the base of his neck at something called the lamdoidal suture, without ever entering his brain cavity. Shane had suffered multiple concussions, and his head had to be opened to release the pressure of built-up cerebrospinal fluid inside his skull.

They had kept him sedated for two weeks so he wouldn't

thrash around and possibly cause more discharge inside his cranium.

When he finally regained consciousness, nurses and doctors swarmed over him. Shots were given, blood pressure taken, and strict orders posted: NO VISITORS.

The wall opposite his bed in ICU was all glass; he looked up and saw Alexa and Chooch with their noses pressed against the window, like children watching a glassed-off exhibit. He stuck his tongue out at them weakly, and they both waved and laughed.

Later that day, when he woke up again, Alexa was holding his hand.

"Alexa," he whispered. "I . . . I . . ."

"Shhh," she said. "I had to raise hell to get in here. If you set off that heart monitor you're hooked to, I'll never get back in again."

"What happened?" Shane asked. The last thing he remembered was sitting in the backyard, telling Chooch he was going to ask Alexa to marry him.

"Jody's dead," Alexa said. "You hit him right between the eyes. Pretty nice shooting for a cop who can barely get weapons-qualified each June."

"No . . ." Shane said. "Jody . . . Jody committed suicide two years ago, in the Rampart Division parking lot."

"Jeez, you lost a big piece," she said, looking worried.

"I what?"

She leaned down and kissed him, brushing her lips gently across his. "Maybe it's for the best," she told him.

■ ■ ■

Eventually, it all returned. Little bits floated back like ugly puzzle pieces drifting in on a brown memory tide.

There were still a few holes in his calendar, but they gradually began to fill, creeping back like ghastly visitors, wandering in the ballroom of his memory until they finally found their correct chairs.

He left the hospital two weeks later, rolled out into the parking lot by a nurse pushing a folding wheelchair. When he stood, he felt twenty feet tall and two inches wide. He teetered precariously before lowering himself into Alexa's car. His scalp had been stitched and bandaged. His neck was already healing. There was an ugly puckered welt there from the gunfight in Maicao. The hole in his thigh was now a pink divot the size of a quarter. All in all, he was damn lucky to be alive.

Chooch was in the backseat and never took his hand off Shane's shoulder, as if letting go, even for a second, might cause some kind of permanent separation.

"We need to set the wedding date." Alexa smiled. "You keep saying you remember asking me, but I think I'd better close the deal while you're still lucid."

"How 'bout this weekend," Shane said. "By this weekend, I'll be kickin' ass." But despite this bravado, he felt lightheaded and was forced to lean back against the headrest.

■ ■ ■

Actually, the date they set was two months later. It was a June fifteenth wedding that took place at the Police Academy Chapel.

The service was small, but importantly attended. There were a dozen cops from his old homicide table, along with their wives, as well as some old partners from Patrol. Of course, Buddy made the trip. No way to freeze him out. Buddy slapped backs and talked retailing.

Chooch was the best man, and Buddy gave the bride away.

Because he didn't have anyone else, and because something told him it would mean a lot, Shane asked Tony Filosiani to stand up for him, to be his one and only usher.

They were married at four in the afternoon. The ceremony was short and simple, but the emotions were not. Alexa cried when they exchanged rings. The reception was behind the chapel. After it was over and the guests had left, they lingered outside, smiling as Tony and his wife, Mary, traded guarded looks with Buddy. Shane, Chooch, and Alexa stood on the steps looking out at the San Gabriel Mountains, majestic, almost purple in the bright, smog-free California afternoon.

"Some weddin'. Glad t'be part of it," Tony enthused. "You guys should know, when I'm in a wedding, I make marriages that last. You two got an obligation not to screw up my perfect record, not countin' my sister."

Shane smiled and nodded. "Yes, sir. That order is accepted."

"Good. And now, I got another little weddin' gift, Shane. I put you in for the MOV and the Police Board approved it. Gonna get the medal at this December's ceremony."

"His-and-her medals." Alexa smiled.

"Once Papa Joe gets outta the hospital, he'll testify." Tony went on: "We're gonna kill this billion-dollar parallel-market scam for good. The Justice Department has already opened their investigation. Without laundries, these drug cartels can't function. We hit 'em where they live—in the pocketbook. The CEOs of the companies laundering this shit are gonna be toast. We brought it to 'em, Shane. You made the difference."

Finally Buddy went back to the hotel to pack. Shane, Alexa, and Chooch slipped away to Venice.

They were glad to be safe at home. They changed out of their wedding costumes and met in the backyard ten minutes later. Shane was in shorts, a T-shirt, and flip-flops. Chooch was in his baggies and saggies, Alexa in a sweatshirt and leggings.

Shane poured them all flutes of cold champagne. They toasted the wedding and stood on their patch of grass, watching the sunset over the blue Pacific a block away.

"Where's the honeymoon?" Chooch asked, grinning.

"How about Aruba?" Alexa said, smiling. "I still have my room key." She dug in her purse and threw it on the glass-top table.

"How about anyplace on earth but there?" Shane said.

"I'll miss you guys while you're gone," Chooch said.

"No, you won't," Shane grinned.

"How come?"

" 'Cause we're gonna wait till Christmas and you're going with us," Alexa finished.

"Really? Is that allowed, taking your kid on the honeymoon?"

"From now on, this family stays together," Shane said.

■ ■ ■

That night Shane lay awake in bed, listening to Alexa sleep beside him . . . the slow breathing, the warmth of her next to him. They hadn't made love. It was strange not to consummate their marriage on the wedding night, but Alexa had been told by the doctors not to do it for a month, because they wanted to keep his heart rate and blood pressure down until they were sure everything had stopped leaking inside his head. There was one week left on that ridiculous sentence. Shane had argued, but Alexa stood firm. He probably wasn't going to win many arguments with her, or as the Day-Glo Dago would say, "Fugedaboutit."

So instead of sex, he lay on his back, looking at the ceiling, turning his new wedding band around on his finger, reflecting, trying to make sense of all that had happened.

He'd been very close to death. The docs told him that his heart had stopped twice. He'd flown down that heavenly corridor, chasing a column of pure white light. He'd seen all of the people in his life that had mattered: the Deans, Jody, Chooch, and Alexa.

Then he thought of the beautiful chestnut-haired woman whom he had known on sight was his mother.

"I'm sorry," she had said. "It was an accident. I didn't want to leave you."

What kind of accident would take you away from your child, make you leave him at the back door of a hospital? Then suddenly he realized that she had *not* put him there; she'd died and somebody else had. She'd come to him in a near-death experience and told him that she always loved him . . . always wanted him. Shane didn't think that when you had a near-death vision, it included lies.

Whatever caused her disappearance, he now knew it hadn't been her fault. His mother *had* loved him, and with that realization, a piece of the darkness that had always haunted him finally slipped away.

He closed his eyes and tried to see her again. He could almost create the vision, but not quite. Yet in its place there was a memory of her love . . . gentle and pure and full of warmth.

"So what is love, anyway?" Jody had scoffed. *"Just a lotta horseshit and a four-letter word."*

Boy, Shane thought, *poor Jody. Jody had missed out on everything.* Suddenly, Shane felt sorry for him—sorry he couldn't have found a way to fix that.

Jody might not have been able to love Shane, but Shane had loved Jody, and in his memory he still did.

He closed his eyes and wondered if the gift Jody promised to him had been the bullet that took him to the edge but gave him a chance to meet his mother, to feel her warmth, to finally experience her love, if only for a few precious seconds. Seconds that had changed him and taken away his painful darkness.

Before he fell asleep, he decided that was it. That was Jody's gift.

From the very beginning, that must have been God's plan.

POSTSCRIPT

All-American Tobacco is a fictitious company, but some of the underlying events of this story were inspired by national headlines. There is currently a billion-dollar civil case pending against Phillip Morris, filed by the Colombian government, over alleged lost cigarette taxes. In 1998 a Reynolds Tobacco subsidiary settled a case involving taxes on cigarettes transported from Canada and paid fifteen million dollars in fines and penalties. A former executive of that company went to jail. Hundreds of other Fortune 500 companies were investigated by the U.S. government. Finally, Bonnie Tishler, Assistant Commissioner of U.S. Customs Service, in a statement before the Congress of the United States, on June 19, 1999, stated that the Treasury Department had elected not to pursue prosecution. "It is very difficult, with a large Corporate structure, to get your hands around exactly who may or may not be facilitating the business of money laundering. . . . By punishing the U.S. Corporations, we may in turn be punishing . . . their ability to sell their products to countries such as Colombia. It could hurt our ability to export and cost us jobs, while at the same time not really making any progress against the drug cartels. . . . The object of our investigation is not to put U.S. companies in jail."

Instead of prosecuting corporate officers, the federal government elected to mail out warnings to hundreds of U.S. companies that helped launder billions in Colombian drug dollars.

To date, no further action has been taken.

ACKNOWLEDGMENTS

Again, there are many people who have helped me get this book into print. Grace Curcio, my loyal coworker (she makes me call her that), has been a friend and adviser for twenty-five years and typed the rough drafts on all seven of my novels. Since I work seven day weeks, she gets very little rest. She is my secret weapon and my treasure.

Kathy Ezso inputs everything into the computer, does countless rewrites, offering helpful notes and suggestions. Without her, I would be lost.

Christine Trepczyk has read this draft, checked it for logic, and pitched in when we needed an extra hand doing cleanup.

Thanks to Jo Swerling, who read and encouraged me through the writing, and to Roy Huggins, who has been a wonderful "last eye" on all of my manuscripts.

Wayne Williams, my friend and editor, has done his usual great job of criticizing, nitpicking, and reorganizing sentences, always making the book stronger and tighter.

I want to thank Charles Spicer, my editor at St. Martin's Press, for his friendship and editorial help. He has worked tirelessly to push me further and higher, always with a gentle style that bespeaks his nature.

A huge note of gratitude to Sally Richardson, my publisher, who has been a believer from the beginning and helped keep me on the road with excellent advice.

ACKNOWLEDGMENTS

Thanks to Dorsey Mills for her assistance and to John Murphy for great publicity.

To my wife, Marcia, and my three children, Tawnia, Chelsea, and Cody. Your love makes me strong, and at the end of the day, I'm really only showing off on paper, trying to look worthy in your eyes.